THE YEAR'S BEST SCIENCE FICTION

NINTH ANNUAL COLLECTION

ALSO BY GARDNER DOZOIS

Anthologies

A Day in the Life
Another World
Best Science Fiction Stories of the Year, Sixth Annual Collection
Best Science Fiction Stories of the Year, Seventh Annual Collection
Best Science Fiction Stories of the Year, Eighth Annual Collection
Best Science Fiction Stories of the Year, Ninth Annual Collection
Best Science Fiction Stories of the Year, Tenth Annual Collection
Future Power (with Jack Dann)
Aliens! (with Jack Dann)
Unicorns! (with Jack Dann)
Magicats! (with Jack Dann)
Magicats 2 (with Jack Dann)
Bestiary! (with Jack Dann)
Mermaids! (with Jack Dann)
Sorcerers! (with Jack Dann)
Demons! (with Jack Dann)
Dogtales! (with Jack Dann)
Ripper! (with Susan Casper)
Seaserpents! (with Jack Dann)
Dinosaurs! (with Jack Dann)
Little People! (with Jack Dann)
The Best of Isaac Asimov's Science Fiction Magazine
Time-Travellers from Isaac Asimov's Science Fiction Magazine
Transcendental Tales from Isaac Asimov's Science Fiction Magazine
Isaac Asimov's Aliens
Isaac Asimov's Mars
Isaac Asimov's Robots (with Sheila Williams)
The Year's Best Science Fiction, First Annual Collection
The Year's Best Science Fiction, Second Annual Collection
The Year's Best Science Fiction, Third Annual Collection
The Year's Best Science Fiction, Fourth Annual Collection
The Year's Best Science Fiction, Fifth Annual Collection
The Year's Best Science Fiction, Sixth Annual Collection
The Year's Best Science Fiction, Seventh Annual Collection
The Year's Best Science Fiction, Eighth Annual Collection

Fiction

Strangers
The Visible Man (collection)
Nightmare Blue (with George Alec Effinger)
Slow Dancing Through Time (with Jack Dann, Michael Swanwick, Susan Casper and Jack C. Haldeman II)
The Peacemaker

Nonfiction

The Fiction of James Tiptree, Jr.

THE YEAR'S BEST SCIENCE FICTION

**NINTH
ANNUAL
COLLECTION**

Gardner Dozois, Editor

ST. MARTIN'S PRESS   NEW YORK

THE YEAR'S BEST SCIENCE FICTION: NINTH ANNUAL COLLECTION. Copyright © 1992 by Gardner Dozois.
All rights reserved. Printed in the United States of America. No part of this book may be used or
reproduced in any manner whatsoever without written permission except in the case of brief quota-
tions embodied in critical articles or reviews. For information, address St. Martin's Press, 175 Fifth
Avenue, New York, N.Y. 10010.

Library of Congress Catalog Card Number: 85-645716
ISSN 0743-1740

First Edition: July 1992

10 9 8 7 6 5 4 3 2 1

Paperback 0-312-07891-9
Hardcover 0-312-07889-7
Limited edition 0-312-07890-0

For the Wednesday-night conference gang on Delphi

CONTENTS

ACKNOWLEDGMENTS

The editor would like to thank the following people for their help and support: first and foremost, Susan Casper, for doing much of the thankless scut work involved in producing this anthology; Michael Swanwick, Janet Kagan, Ellen Datlow, Virginia Kidd, Sheila Williams, Ian Randal Strock, Scott L. Towner, Tina Lee, David Pringle, Kristine Kathryn Rusch, Dean Wesley Smith, Pat Cadigan, Arnie Fenner, David S. Garnett, Charles C. Ryan, Uwe Luserke, Chuq von Rospach, James Turner, Lucius Shepard, Susan Allison, Ginjer Buchanan, Lou Aronica, Amy Stout, Beth Meacham, Claire Eddy, David G. Hartwell, Bob Walters, Tess Kissinger, Jim Frenkel, Michael G. Adkisson, Greg Egan, Steve Pasechnick, Lawrence Person, Dwight Brown, Chris Reed, Dirk Strasser, Michael Sumbera, Glen Cox, Steven Higgins, Don Keller, Robert Killheffer, Greg Cox, and special thanks to my own editor, Gordon Van Gelder.

Thanks are also due to Charles N. Brown, whose magazine *Locus* (Locus Publications, P.O. Box 13305, Oakland, CA 94661, $48.00 for a one-year subscription [twelve issues] via first class mail, $35.00 second class) was used as a reference source throughout the Summation, and to Andrew Porter, whose magazine *Science Fiction Chronicle* (Science Fiction Chronicle, P.O. Box 2730, Brooklyn, N.Y. 11202–0056, $30.00 for a one-year subscription [twelve issues]; $36.00 first class) was also used as a reference source throughout.

SUMMATION
1991

We live in a world where, suddenly, there is no Soviet Union anymore.

Think of that!

Only a few months ago, the Soviet Union seemed a gray monolithic bureaucracy that would probably endure as long as Byzantium—and then suddenly, all at once, it's gone, like a pricked soap bubble. Even those few pundits—mostly science fiction writers—who *had* predicted the eventual dissolution of the Soviet Union never expected it to happen so *fast*; Norman Spinrad's *Russian Spring*, for instance, which deals with that very topic, was obsolete almost before it was published, in spite of the fact that Spinrad is savvy enough in foreign affairs to be one of the few who'd seen the breakup of the U.S.S.R. coming in the first place. By the time Spinrad's book hit the bookstore shelves, though, the world had already seen the statue of Lenin featured in the cover painting of *Russian Spring* being pulled down on CNN.

We live in a world where Germany, which has been forcibly sundered for most of a human lifetime, is suddenly and quietly reunified, again all at once, *poof!* . . . an event that went almost unnoticed by the media in the shadow of the disappearance of the Soviet Union. Suddenly there's a bitter civil war being fought in Yugoslavia, a country that only a decade ago was considered to be one of the most stable and prosperous nations in the Soviet sphere. Suddenly there are new *countries* on the map—and it all happened so fast that athletes from the former Soviet Union and its former satellite countries who won medals in the Winter Olympics had to have the Olympic theme played during their medal ceremonies, because the new countries they were suddenly from had not yet had time to come up with national anthems of their own.

We live, in fact, in a very science fictional world, a world as unlikely as any to be found in a Philip K. Dick novel. Remember when Dick's scenario in *The Three Stigmata of Palmer Eldritch*—in which global warming and the destruction of the ozone layer made it necessary to travel in metal-roofed pedestrian walkways and wear tinted goggles and pith helmets when you went outside—seemed like *satire*? Remember when even the richest man in the world couldn't have afforded to have a little plastic box with more computing power than UNIVAC sitting on the corner of his desk? Remember when *The Wall Street Journal* would hardly have known what a computer *was*, let alone have devoted space to worrying if a computer virus was going to disrupt the workings of international commerce? Remember when you could have sex without worrying if it was going to kill you?

The rate of change has been accelerating throughout the twentieth century—but it really seems to have shifted into high gear now, as we hurtle haplessly toward the twenty-first.

Science fiction readers should not be as surprised by these changes as others are, as one of the fundamental messages of good science fiction is that the only constant *is* the certainty of change. Change is inescapable, however much we may nostalgically long to freeze life in a form that we find comfortable and familiar. As I've said before, the world only seems static to us because we are too short-lived to see it change. If we could speed up time, condense eons into seconds, we would see mountains flow like water and fish learn to walk.

At its best, science fiction is a lens that helps us to see in this special fashion, an eye that looks at change. It'll be interesting, then, to see how good a job the science fiction world does of facing up to and dealing with the changes that are inevitably ahead for science fiction itself.

For, as the twentieth century winds down toward its close, it becomes clear that there are radical changes ahead—and not only for science fiction, but for the entire publishing industry.

Publishing may be in trouble. Yes, the country is deep in a recession that is hurting the sales of nearly everything nearly everywhere, but even taking that into consideration, there have been some ominous rumblings on the horizon, and some uneasy ripples passing through the publishing world of late. I myself have seen something happen in bookstores several times this year that fills *me* with unease: a browser reaching out his hand toward the bookshelves and picking up a book—the fundamental buying impulse on which the entire industry is based—and then looking at the price, hesitating, shaking his head, and *putting the book back . . .* and walking out of the store with his money still unspent in his pocket. If books have become so expensive, even mass-market paperbacks, that they are no longer candidates for impulse buying, then publishing is in big trouble . . . because the higher the price, the more the customer has to stop and think if the book is really *worth* it, and the more time he spends thinking about it, the more likely he is to decide that it's *not*, especially these days, when you can break a ten-dollar bill buying a paperback and only get a buck or two back. And that's just paperbacks. *Hardcovers* are edging up into the prices for which you *used* to be able to buy a small household appliance. These days you may even be able to buy a toaster for *less* than the cost of an average hardcover. Even allowing for inflation, books these days just *cost* too damn much.

The annoying thing about this is that most of these inflated prices are artificial—that is, that the problems *causing* them to inflate *could* be solved if anyone was willing to face those problems and actually institute some radical solutions. Most of the rising costs of books comes from the truly horrendous system of distribution and marketing, as inefficient a system as it is possible to imagine, and *especially* from the returns system. This is the publishers' policy of accepting returned books (or, more usually, their stripped-off covers) from bookstores and distributors for cash or credit; it's such a crushing Old Man of the Sea around the neck of the publishing industry that return rates of 50 percent or more are now commonplace—which means that a publisher has to figure on printing two thousand copies of a book in order to *sell* a thousand copies of it, with the other copies being either pulped or stripped and sold illegally with no royalties filtering back to either publisher or author. This is absurd in the Computer Age, when you *ought* to be able to know in advance exactly how many copies you need to print, with the ability to print more as needed—as absurd as paying astronomical rents and overhead to maintain an office building in New York City where everyone has to be physically present from nine to five, in an age of modems and faxes and an instant telecommunications network that is open and working twenty-four hours a day. Most publishing personnel could do their work as easily from their home in some little town in Ohio, or at least from an office in some locale where rents are significantly cheaper, as they could do it in Manhatttan; for that matter, as we evolve toward a twenty-four-hour society, they could do it at four o'clock in the morning as efficiently as they could at three o'clock in the afternoon, in most cases. Desktop publishing methods could also help cut book production costs to the bone . . . if anyone could be convinced to use them on a major scale.

And, looming just over the horizon, as Ben Bova and Richard Curtis and others have pointed out, is the prospect of Electronic Publishing, seen by some as an enormous opportunity, seen by others as a specter that could wipe out the entire book industry. Certainly Electronic Publishing will be a major player in some form long before 2001, whether it's in the form of books and stories that can be downloaded for a price from one of the computer networks (this isn't sci-fi stuff, by the way—you can do this right *now*), or in the form of what Ben Bova has called "cyberbooks," hand-held interactive multimedia CD players that display text *plus* graphics and sound (not SF either—similar devices, called Electronic Book Players, have been on sale in Japan for some while, and are now available in Europe and the U.S.), which some people predict will replace traditional printed-text books altogether. (I don't think it will go that far—I think there'll always be *some* audience for the printed book; the question is, how large an audience?)

If there is a radical reorganization ahead for the publishing industry, the key question is, will the Big Publishers, particularly those owned by giant corporations, be flexible enough to adapt successfully—or will they die off, and leave the book business to those now-minor companies that are small and fast and agile enough—and smart enough—to *change* in order to survive? We'll see—but the publishing world could look very different (no doubt for both better *and* worse) ten years from now.

In spite of all this apocalyptic talk, 1991 was actually a rather quiet year in the science fiction publishing world, in the United States anyway—although it was that kind of hushed, ominous, and oppressive calm that often comes just before a storm.

A crippling recession slammed British book publishing early in 1991, causing almost five hundred employees to be laid off and several publishing houses to be sold or placed in receivership, and touching off a dizzyingly confusing round of editorial changeovers in late 1991 and early 1992, with some of the major British SF editors sometimes seeming to be engaged in a round of musical chairs played with an ever-decreasing number of seats. Among other major changes, Deborah Beale left the successful Legend SF line to create a new SF line, Millennium, for brand-new British publisher Orion Books, being replaced as Legend editor by John Jarrold, former senior editor at Macdonald.

In America, most of the substantial changes so far were in the magazine industry (see below). In spite of fears of a crash, the total number of SF and SF-related books published in 1991 was actually *up*, according to the newsmagazine *Locus*. The total rose only slightly, up to an estimated 1,990 from 1990's estimated total of 1,890, a rise of five percent (the total has risen *forty-seven percent* since 1981, though, according to *Locus*, a staggering overall rise). The near-total collapse of the horror market that was being predicted by industry insiders last year also didn't come to pass—it's now being predicted for *next* year. The American SF book publishing world was not hit by as many major changes as was the British industry, although David Hartwell was ousted from his position as editor at Morrow (in spite of having put together a very impressive hardcover line at Morrow for the past few years) when Morrow and Avon's SF lists were combined into the forthcoming AvoNova line under the editorship of John Douglas. Also of significance is the fact that Lester del Rey retired from Del Rey Books.

Rumors of upcoming major changes in the American SF book industry circulated freely throughout the year, however, with at least one major SF book line reputed to be in major trouble, and unadmitted buying slowdowns and even unacknowledged buying freezes rumored to be underway at several other houses. Whether any of these rumors are *true* or not is anyone's guess.

So people are looking uneasily to the future at the moment, braced for the oncoming storm. . . . Next year we'll be able to see what the weather was *actually* like, and how much of our world, if any, was washed away in the flood.

It was a turbulent year in the magazine market, a year that saw many dramatic changes, some positive, some negative, some whose ultimate effect may not be known for quite a while. As I explained last year, the recent big hike in postage rates hurt the entire magazine market to some extent, especially when coupled with a decrease in advertising revenue, mostly caused by book publishers cutting back on ads because of the recession; newsstand sales were also down almost across the board, probably because of the recession as well. The damage hasn't been restricted to science fiction magazines. Many mainstream magazines, of many different types, were forced out of business in 1991, with no doubt more to follow. All the magazines that *have* survived, science fiction or otherwise, have had to adapt to changing conditions somehow, usually by cutting corners and reducing costs as much as possible. For instance, *Aboriginal SF* only published five issues in 1991, publishing a double December issue instead of the September/October issue. *The Magazine of Fantasy and Science Fiction* also published a double-issue this year as a cost-saving measure, skipping one issue, doing eleven issues instead of twelve. *Isaac Asimov's Science Fiction Magazine* and *Analog* are now doing two double-issues a year, also as a cost-saver, although they still continue to publish their usual thirteen issues. Some of the magazines have cut pages, and more will probably follow suit.

Even *Omni*, backed by the giant General Media International, had a rough year, going through a massive internal reorganization that saw many of their employees laid off and the editorial offices of the magazine moved to Greensboro, North Carolina, where its production will be consolidated with that of another General Media magazine, *Compute*, to save on production costs. (Fortunately, longtime *Omni* fiction editor Ellen Datlow has been kept on, and will continue to work out of the New York address.) After a couple of years of financial difficulties, Davis Publications sold all four of its digest fiction titles—*Isaac Asimov's Science Fiction Magazine, Analog, Science Fiction & Fact, Ellery Queen's Mystery Magazine,* and *Alfred Hitchcock's Mystery Magazine*—at the beginning of 1992 to Dell Magazines, part of the Bantam Doubleday Dell Publishing Group, which is a part of the international consortium Bertelsmann. (This caused a good deal of anxiety in the science fiction field at first, naturally enough, but both Stanley Schmidt and I have been kept on as editors of our respective magazines, with our editorial staffs intact, and I think it is quite probable that the sale will prove to be a positive thing for both magazines—since Dell Magazines has the money and the connections to help improve circulation and distribution in a way that Davis, a small company, never had the resources to manage. I should probably note that Davis's money problems were caused by the very expensive failure of *Sylvia Porter's Personal Finance Magazine* a few years ago; the fiction titles have remained profitable, which is why they were able to be sold.) Also by the beginning of 1992, money problems had hurt *Aboriginal SF* badly enough to force them to lay off their paid staff (all work is now being done by volunteer labor) and apply to the IRS for nonprofit status in order to enable the magazine to continue to publish (which it *could*, for the foreseeable future, if it *does* manage to get nonprofit status; keep your fingers crossed).

There were also big changes at *Amazing*, which published its last two bimonthly digest-sized issues, edited by Patrick L. Price, early in 1991, and then shifted over to a large-size monthly format for the rest of the year, publishing eight more issues under new editor Kim Mohan. The change in format is probably a positive change: the magazine in its new avatar is a handsome-looking thing, with full-color covers and full-color interior illustrations throughout. It must also be very expensive to produce, though— considerably more expensive than producing a digest magazine—and the key question is whether or not parent company TSR is going to support the new *Amazing* at a loss long enough for it to have a real chance of establishing itself in the marketplace. Kim Mohan says that TSR is solidly behind the magazine and committed to supporting it; keep your fingers crossed for it, too.

The British magazine *Interzone* completed its first full year as a monthly publication, although two of those issues featured the contents of *other* magazines (the swap issue with *Aboriginal SF* I mentioned last year, and an issue of a new nonfiction magazine called *Million*) instead of the regular *Interzone* contents—something that I can't help but think is a mistake. (Angry letters from irate *Interzone* subscribers in subsequent issues seem to support the idea that it may have been one.) I hope that they resist the temptation to do this kind of thing again. Other than that, *Interzone* seems stronger than ever as a monthly magazine, and, in fact, leaving my own *IAsfm* out of the competition, may well be one of the best SF magazines being published today.

Last year I expressed doubts about the feasibility of the concept of a *weekly* magazine, discussing the proposed launch of *Pulphouse: A Weekly Magazine*. As it turned out, I was right. Market forces quickly defeated the idea, with distributors balking at the prospect of handling a weekly magazine, and it was first changed to a biweekly, and then to a magazine published every four weeks—in other words, fairly close to the traditional monthly magazine format the entire magazine industry is geared to accept. Under the editorship of Dean Wesley Smith, the magazine, now called simply *Pulphouse: A Fiction Magazine*, has published some pretty interesting fiction (although not much actual science fiction, leaning heavily toward mild horror and unclassifiable Weird Stuff instead), including the serialization of a bizarre and brilliant novel by S. P. Somtow. I do think that they should increase the number of pages per issue, since the original rationale for such a slender magazine was that it was going to come out much more frequently; now that it's nearly on a monthly schedule, it would be a better buy if they'd fatten it up some. I also think that they ought to publish considerably less nonfiction and publish more fiction per issue instead, especially as many of the ever-proliferating columns are page-wasters and space-fillers that aren't really needed anymore, now that the magazine is no longer a weekly. They're still running late at the moment—I received their December Christmas issue in late February, for instance—but I hope that they can shake down and get it together, since they have the potential to be an interesting and worthwhile addition to the SF magazine scene.

An ironic note: There's been a lot of talk this year about the kind of job Kristine Kathryn Rusch is doing as the new editor of *The Magazine of Fantasy and Science Fiction*, with some people saying that the magazine is much better since she took over, and other people saying that the magazine has gone right down the tubes since Ed Ferman left . . . when, in fact, the truth is, of course, that very little that appeared in *F&SF* in 1991 was bought by Kris at *all*, since, like every new magazine editor, she has mostly been engaged with working through the inventory bought by her predecessor. Having been through this process myself, I'd like to say, Hey, everybody, back off and give her some breathing room! *Next* year we'll begin to be able to judge, a little bit anyway, what kind of job she's doing. Myself, I think she's going to do just fine.

As most of you probably know, I, Gardner Dozois, am also editor of *Isaac Asimov's Science Fiction Magazine*. And that, as I've mentioned before, does pose a problem for me in compiling this summation, particularly the magazine-by-magazine review that follows. As *IAsfm* editor, I could be said to have a vested interest in the magazine's success, so that anything negative I said about another SF magazine (particularly another digest-sized magazine, my direct competition), could be perceived as an attempt to make my own magazine look good by tearing down the competition. Aware of this con-straint, I've decided that nobody can complain if I only say *positive* things about the competition. . . . And so, once again, I've limited myself to a listing of some of the worthwhile authors published by each.

Omni published first-rate fiction this year by William Gibson, Jack Dann, Pat Cadigan, Pat Murphy, J. R. Dunn, Robert Silverberg, and others. *Omni's* fiction editor is Ellen Datlow.

The Magazine of Fantasy and Science Fiction featured good fiction by Karen Joy Fowler, Robert Reed, Kathe Koja, Lois Tilton, Kristine Kathryn Rusch, Mike Resnick, Ellen Kushner, Joe Haldeman, and others. *F&SF's* new editor is Kristine Kathryn Rusch.

Isaac Asimov's Science Fiction Magazine featured critically acclaimed work by Nancy Kress, Connie Willis, Kim Stanley Robinson, James Patrick Kelly, Pat Cadigan, Mary Rosenblum, Greg Egan, Tony Daniel, Ian R. MacLeod, Robert Silverberg, Alexander Jablokov, Mike Resnick, Jonathan Lethem, Kristine Kathryn Rusch, R. Garcia y Robertson, and others. *IAsfm's* editor is Gardner Dozois.

Analog featured good work by Rick Shelley, John Barnes, Isaac Asimov, Lois McMaster Bujold, Amy Bechtel, Orson Scott Card, Jack C. Haldeman II, A. J. Austin, and others. *Analog's* longtime editor is Stanley Schmidt.

Amazing featured good work by Robert Silverberg, Phillip C. Jennings, N. Lee Wood, Paul Di Filippo, Ian R. MacLeod, Brian Stableford, Gregory Benford, Martha Soukup, and others. *Amazing's* new editor is Kim Mohan.

Interzone featured excellent work by Greg Egan, Ian R. MacLeod, Stephen

Baxter, Robert Holdstock, Chris Beckett, Diane Mapes, Brian Stableford, Paul J. McAuley, John Christopher, and others. *Interzone*'s editor is David Pringle.

Aboriginal Science Fiction featured interesting work by Terry McGarry, Phillip C. Jennings, Lois Tilton, Harlan Ellison, Rick Wilber, A. J. Austin, Howard V. Hendrix, and others. The editor of *Aboriginal Science Fiction* is Charles C. Ryan.

Weird Tales published good work by Tanith Lee, Nina Kiriki Hoffman, Keith Taylor, Robert Bloch, and others. *Weird Tales*' editors are George H. Scithers and Darrell Schweitzer.

Pulphouse: A Fiction Magazine published good work by S. P. Somtow, Arthur Byron Cover, Susan Palwick, Kristine Kathryn Rusch, John Dalmas, Nina Kiriki Hoffman, Robert J. Howe, George Alec Effinger, and others. *Pulphouse: A Fiction Magazine*'s editor is Dean Wesley Smith.

Short SF continued to appear in many magazines outside genre boundaries. *Playboy* in particular continues to run a good deal of SF, under fiction editor Alice K. Turner.

(Subscription addresses follow for those magazines hardest to find on the newsstands: *The Magazine of Fantasy and Science Fiction*, Mercury Press, Inc., Box 56, Cornwall, CT 06753, annual subscription—twelve issues—$26.00 in U.S.; *Isaac Asimov's Science Fiction Magazine*, Dell Magazines Fiction Group, P.O. Box 7058, Red Oak, IA 51566, $34.95 for thirteen issues; *Interzone*, 217 Preston Drove, Brighton BN1 6FL, United Kingdom, $52.00 for an airmail one year—twelve issues—subscription; *Analog*, Dell Magazines Fiction Group, P.O. Box 7061, Red Oak, IA 51591, $34.95 for thirteen issues; *Pulphouse: A Fiction Magazine*, P.O. Box 1227, Eugene, OR 97440, $26.00 per year [13 issues] in U.S.; *Aboriginal Science Fiction*, P.O. Box 2449, Woburn, MA 01888-0849, $18.00 for 6 issues in U.S.; *Weird Tales*, Terminus Publishing Company, P.O. Box 13418, Philadelphia, PA 19101-3418, $16.00 for 4 issues in U.S.)

This was not a particularly good year in the semiprozine market, with several magazines dying, others clearly in economic difficulties, and others publishing sporadically. The criticalzine *Short Form* seems to have died (although there are rumors that one final issue may still be forthcoming), which is a pity, since that leaves Mark R. Kelly's recently reinstated column in *Locus* as the *only* place in the entire SF industry where short fiction is reviewed on a regular basis. Mark V. Ziesing and Andy Watson's *Journal Wired* has also died, as has the British horror semiprozine *Fear*. Michael G. Adkisson's *New Pathways*, probably the best of the eclectic mixed fiction/review magazines that became popular in the eighties, was clearly having economic difficulties this year, with issue 19 published almost invisibly, sent only to a core group of subscribers, and issue 20 delayed so long that rumors that *New Pathways* had died were beginning to circulate again (as they had last year) when it finally did arrive in my mailbox, several months late, but containing interesting stuff by Brian W. Aldiss, Don Webb, and others. Adkisson vows that he will continue to publish his magazine, in spite of money problems, and I hope that he succeeds, since *New Pathways* at its best is one of the most intriguing of all the semiprozines. There was only one issue of *Nova Express*—edited by Michael Sumbera, with help by Glen Cox and Dwight Brown—out this year as far as I could tell, and I hope that this magazine isn't running out of steam as its editors become busy with other things, because at *its* best it's an eclectic and highly enjoyable magazine full of reviews, meaty interviews, weird features, and mostly forgettable fiction (so far, anyway). The quality level of the fiction has been a good deal higher to date in *Strange Plasma*, a (mostly) all-fiction semiprozine edited by Steve Pasechnick. They only published one issue this year, but it contained interesting work by R. A. Lafferty, Kathleen Ann Goonan, and Yoshio Aramaki. Another (mostly) all-fiction semiprozine with something of the weirdly eclectic feel of *New Pathways* or *Strange Plasma* to it is the British magazine *BBR* (which stands for *Back Brain Recluse*, their former title—although they seem to use the acronym officially for their title now), edited by Chris Reed; the fiction here is uneven, and they are a little too shrill about claiming that only they are publishing Cutting Edge work and everyone *else* sucks (a fault shared by several of these little magazines, including *New Pathways* on occasion), but they *do* publish some interesting work sometimes, including worthwhile pieces this year by Richard Kadrey, David Hast, and others. (Two or three more science fiction semiprozines are reported to be starting up in Britain this year, and I'll report more fully on them when I know more—if they actually materialize.) Another interesting and even more obscure little semiprozine is an Australian magazine called *Aurealis, The Australian Magazine of Fantasy and Science Fiction*, a quarterly edited by Dirk Strasser and Stephen Higgins. The fiction here is also uneven, but they did publish some good work, including a story by Greg Egan good enough to make it into this anthology.

In spite of all the talk about the coming disastrous crash of the horror market, horror semiprozines continue to proliferate on both sides of the Atlantic. Counting *Weird Tales* as a professional market (I tend to think of *Weird Tales* more as a fantasy magazine than a horror magazine anyway, since most of the horror they do publish is "quiet" horror, instead of the "Cutting Edge"/Splatterpunk/gooshey stuff that almost all of the other horror magazines feature), the most visible of them during the current year was probably *Cemetery Dance*, which is now getting some newsstand distribution, won the World Fantasy Award, and is dominating the nominations list for this year's Bram Stoker Award. It seems to have pulled decisively ahead of *Midnight Graffiti*, which only published one issue this year. Other horror semiprozines include *Grue, 2AM, Deathrealm, Weirdbook,* and the new magazine *Iniquities*, although most of them only managed to produce one or two issues this year, and once again there was no issue of *Whispers* at all;

there are also many other horror semiprozines other than the ones named, too many to mention, most of them pretty bad—and more of them seem to come along every day. A new critical semiprozine devoted to horror, *Necrofile*, published two issues, but I haven't seen a copy yet. There is also a semiprozine aimed at the High Fantasy market, *Marion Zimmer Bradley's Fantasy Magazine*, but, to date, the fiction published there has yet to reach reliable levels of quality.

As ever, Charles N. Brown's *Locus* and Andy Porter's *Science Fiction Chronicle* remain your best bet among the semiprozines if you are looking for news and/or an overview of what's happening in the genre. The longest-running of those semiprozines that concentrates primarily on literary criticism, and one of the best, is D. Douglas Fratz's *Quantum* (formerly *Thrust*). Steve Brown's *Science Fiction Eye* is the weirdest and most eclectic of the criticalzines—where else, for instance, could you find a series of photographs of someone chopping up an Orson Scott Card novel with a chainsaw? (Always assuming you *wanted* to find such a thing, of course!) *Science Fiction Eye* is rude, brash, and highly opinionated, and sometimes unnecessarily cruel, but it is seldom dull reading; the wide-ranging Bruce Sterling column alone is probably worth the price of the magazine. *The New York Review of Science Fiction*—whose editorial staff includes Kathryn Cramer, L. W. Currey, Samuel R. Delany, David G. Hartwell, Donald G. Keller, Robert Killheffer, and Gordon Van Gelder—has established itself as the most reliable of the criticalzines, producing twelve issues right on time again this year. The magazine produces a wide range of features, some of them shrewd, insightful, and informed, some of them overintellectualized to the point of opaqueness; there is a welcome leavening of humor, and some fascinating but unclassifiable stuff, like Michael Swanwick's listing of the dreams he's been having lately. I also like the Reading Lists they solicit from well-known professionals, which are often quite interesting. *Science Fiction Review*, a continuation by other hands (mostly Elton Elliott's) of Dick Geis's famous fanzine of the same name, with some editorial contribution by Geis himself, has gone monthly, and is getting some newsstand distribution. The quality of the reviewing here has been somewhat uneven to date, although they also feature opinion pieces, science articles, and fiction. There were no new issues of the new Damon Knight–edited criticalzine *Monad* this year.

(*Locus*, Locus Publications, Inc., P.O. Box 13305, Oakland, CA 94661, $48.00 for a one-year first class subscription, 12 issues; *Science Fiction Chronicle*, Algol Press, P.O. Box 2730, Brooklyn, NY 11202-0056, $30.00 for 1 year, 12 issues, $36.00 first class; *Quantum—Science Fiction and Fantasy Review* [formerly *Thrust*], Thrust Publications, 8217 Langport Terrace, Gaithersburg, MD 20877, $7.00 for 3 issues [one year]; *Science Fiction Eye*, P.O. Box 18539, Asheville, NC 28814, $10.00 for three issues; *New Pathways*, MGA Services, P.O. Box 863994, Plano, TX 75086-3994, $25.00 for 6-issue subscription; *Nova Express*, White Car Publications, P.O. Box 27231, Austin, TX 78755-2231, $10.00 for a one-year [four issues] subscription; *Strange Plasma*, Edgewood Press, P.O. Box 264, Cambridge, MA 02238, $15.00 for four issues; *Aurealis, The Australian Magazine of Fantasy and Science Fiction*, Chimaera Publications, P.O. Box 538, Mt. Waverley, Victoria 3149, Australia, $24.00 for a four-issue [quarterly] subscription, "all money orders for overseas subscriptions should be in Australian dollars"; *BBR*, P.O. Box 625, Sheffield S1 3GY, United Kingdom, $18.00 for four issues; *The New York Review of Science Fiction*, Dragon Press, P.O. Box 78, Pleasantville, NY 10570, $25.00 per year; *Science Fiction Review*, SFR Publications, P.O. Box 20340, Salem, OR 97307, $35.00 for a 12-issue subscription; *Cemetery Dance*, P.O. Box 858, Edgewood, MD 21040, $15.00 for four issues [one year], $25.00 for eight issues [two years], "checks or money orders should be payable to Richard T. Chizmar only!"; *Grue Magazine*, Hells Kitchen Productions, Box 370, Times Square Sta., New York, NY 10108, $13.00 for three issues; *Necrofile: The Review of Horror Fiction*, Necronomicon Press, 101 Lockwood Street, West Warwick, RI 02893, $10.00 for one year [four issues]; *Midnight Graffiti*, 13101 Sudan Road, Poway, CA 92604, $24.00 for one year; *Monad*, Pulphouse Publishing, Box 1227, Eugene, OR 97440, $5.00 for single issues or $18.00 for four issues.)

An important new anthology series debuted this year, and an already-established series put out an impressive volume. Not too shabby a year, then, even if many of 1991's other original anthologies were somewhat lackluster.

The best original anthology of the year undoubtedly was *Full Spectrum 3* (Doubleday Foundation), edited by Lou Aronica, Amy Stout, and Betsy Mitchell—although I'd hardly go as far as the *Locus* quote on the cover that calls it "the best original anthology ever produced." Still, even if you're not willing to take it to those extremes, it must be admitted that *Full Spectrum 3* is an impressive anthology, containing two of the year's best stories—a story by Gregory Benford and a novella by Mark L. Van Name and Pat Murphy—as well as good work by Elizabeth Hand, Tony Daniel, Ursula K. Le Guin, Michael Bishop, Karen Joy Fowler, Marcos Donnelly, R. V. Branham, Nancy Willard, and others. There's some so-so filler here, of course, and even a fair number of not-so-hot stories, but considering the huge *size* of the volume, that's to be expected. Pound for pound, it's hard to beat this for a reading value among the original anthologies. Now I'd like to see the publishers issue *Full Spectrum* every year, in *addition* to a volume of Robert Silverberg and Karen Haber's *Universe* series, instead of alternating every other year between *Universe* and *Full Spectrum*, the way they do now.

Nineteen ninety-one also saw the start of a very important new British anthology series, *New Worlds*, which carries the name of Michael Moorcock's famous experimental British magazine of the sixties on into the nineties under the able editorship of the indefatigable and apparently undiscourage-able David Garnett—who lost two anthology series *last* year when his *Zenith* and *Science Fiction Yearbook* series were cancelled. Undaunted, Garnett has bounced back this year with *New Worlds 1* (Gollancz), and a fine anthology it is, too, closely rivaling *Full Spectrum 3* for the title of the year's best anthology, losing out to it as a reading value only because the hefty *Full Spectrum* is a considerably longer volume; *New Worlds 1* may be more consistent in quality from beginning to end, though. *New Worlds 1* is certainly worth your money, containing really first-rate work by Brian W. Aldiss, Kim Newman, and J. D. Gresham, along with good work by Ian McDonald, Storm Constantine, Michael Moorcock, Paul Di Filippo, and others. Let's hope that *this* Garnett anthology series lasts more than just a volume or two, as it has the potential to become one of the most important anthology series in science fiction.

There were two issues in the *Pulphouse* hardcover anthology series, one of them the penultimate volume, as this series winds down toward completion. The *Pulphouse* anthologies have almost always featured a few good stories per issue, at the very least, and although neither of this year's volumes were the best the series has had to offer, that remained true of them, too. *Pulphouse Eleven* was perhaps slightly the better volume, featuring a strong story by Tim Sullivan, and good work by Edward Bryant, William F. Wu, Resa Nelson, Diane Mapes, Mary A. Turzillo, and others, although *Pulphouse Ten* contained good work by Marina Fitch, Lisa Goldstein, Kara Dalkey, and Nina Kiriki Hoffman, among others. *Pulphouse Twelve*, the last volume in the series, was scheduled to be published this year, but problems at Pulphouse Publishing, where I suspect they are overextended, delayed it, and it is now scheduled for publication sometime in mid-1992. (For information about the *Pulphouse* anthology series and other Pulphouse projects, write to: Pulphouse Publishing, Box 1227, Eugene, OR 97440.)

What Might Have Been Volume 3: Alternate Wars (Bantam Spectra), edited by Gregory Benford and Martin H. Greenberg, was still quite a worthwhile anthology, but not as strong overall as *What Might Have Been* Volumes 1 and 2 were; the most powerful story here is a first-rate novella by Nancy Kress, but the anthology also features good work by Gregory Benford, Allen Steele, Harry Turtledove, Poul Anderson, Jack McDevitt, and others. *L. Ron Hubbard Presents Writers of the Future Volume VII* (Bridge), edited by Algis Budrys, was the usual assortment of apprentice work by people who *might* one day be major writers, but who aren't there *yet*. If there was an issue of Jim Baen's *New Destinies* series out this year, I didn't see it, and George Zebrowski's *Synergy* series seems definitely to have died.

Shared-world anthologies this year included: *The Man-Kzin Wars IV* (Baen), edited by Larry Niven; *Wild Cards VIII: One-Eyed Jacks* (Bantam), edited by George R. R. Martin; and *Under the Fang* (Pocket), edited by Robert R. McCammon.

In horror, the *Borderlands* series, edited by Thomas F. Monteleone, seems to be establishing itself as a major new horror anthology series; *Borderlands 2* (Avon) was the issue out in the bookstores this year, with more supposedly in the works. Nineteen ninety-one also saw the *end* of one of horror's major series, sadly, as the last volume of the prestigious *Shadows* series edited by Charles L. Grant, *Final Shadows* (Doubleday Foundation), a double-sized volume, appeared; this series has featured some of the best short work in horror over the years, and it will be missed.

Turning to the nonseries anthologies, we are reminded once again that anthologies come in bunches—or, at least, that often a number of anthologies with similar themes seem to come out all at the same time . . . so that, say, there'll be *no* anthologies about wombats, and then suddenly there will be *three* of them. No one knows why. It seems to be more serendipitous than can be explained by anthologists borrowing ideas from each other. This year, for instance, there were two antiwar, nonviolent "Peace" anthologies. By far the stronger of the two was the all-original *When the Music's Over* (Bantam Spectra), edited by Lewis Shiner. This is a very earnest book, devoted to trying to get us to "turn our hearts and minds and creativity to finding other solutions [than war]," to "finding peaceful solutions in these violent times"; the book comes complete with a very useful list of the addresses of political organizations devoted to peace and/or to ecological causes, and urges you to make donations to them. As it states on the cover, Shiner himself is donating his editor's share of the book's profits to Greenpeace. It's hard to argue with all this earnestness—and indeed, it *is* admirable. So, then, having admired it, it's also fair to ask: *Do* the writers in the anthology come up with any viable alternatives to war? Well, no, not really. As was true of the *last* "Peace" anthology, Joe Haldeman's *Study War No More*, some of the stories ignore the ostensible theme altogether, and of those stories that *do* attempt to deal with it, many propose "solutions" along the lines of "find the invisible demons who incite humans to violence in order to feed on our emotions, and then shoot them." Two or three stories here *do* come up with perhaps workable solutions to human aggressiveness, but in each case it involves releasing tailored viruses or nanomechanisms to alter human nature itself in fundamental ways (Michael Swanwick independently came up with the same solution this year in his *Griffin's Egg*), and, in every case, the cure seems far worse than the disease—Nancy Kress's suggestion that we can eliminate war by destroying the capacity of the human brain for long-term memory and planning ability, for instance, seems to me a sure way also to ensure the extinction of the human species. (Note also that in none of these scenarios do we get a *choice* about having these things done to us—it's always done *to* us, for our own good, with the most earnest of motives . . . an attitude that I don't really think science fiction ought to be encouraging in an age when horrors such as this conceivably *could* be produced and released by anyone with some technical knowledge and an access to laboratory equipment.)

So, then, having argued with some of its polemics, how good is *When the Music's Over* as an *anthology*, a reading experience? Quite good, actually, featuring a flamboyant Zelaznyesque space opera by Walter Jon Williams and a terrific mainstream story by Bruce Sterling that is flawed by a tacked-on fantasy ending, and also featuring good work by Pat Cadigan, Paul J. McAuley, John Shirley, James P. Blaylock, and others. It's certainly a better reading value than the year's *other* "Peace" anthology, the disappointing *There Won't Be War* (Tor), edited by Harry Harrison and Bruce McAllister. This is a mixed reprint/original anthology, and the best stuff here are the reprints, particularly Kim Stanley Robinson's powerful "The Lucky Strike"; the original stories, however, are surprisingly weak, with only two exceptions: interesting stories by Nancy A. Collins and James Morrow. (Gregory Frost's "Attack of the Jazz Giants" is also interesting, but what in the world is it doing in here? What's Ballard's "The Terminal Beach" doing in here, for that matter?) A disappointment, since I was looking forward to this one.

There was also a cluster of what I suppose must be called "regional" SF anthologies this year, most of them mixed reprint/original anthologies, usually of stories that are supposedly either *about* a particular region of the country or *by* writers who *come from* (or happen to live at the moment in) a particular region of the country. The most prominently published of these was probably *Newer York* (Roc), edited by Lawrence Watt-Evans, an uneven book that contains a good deal of mediocre-to-bad work, although it also contains some good work by Susan Shwartz, Kristine Kathryn Rusch, Mike Resnick, John Shirley, Martha Soukup, Robert J. Howe, and others; considering its length (it's a fat book), it's probably worth its cover price, but it's not one of the year's top anthologies. (Since *Newer York* reputedly found a publisher right off the bat, it bemuses me that the *Future Boston* anthology has apparently still *not* been able to find a home, even though the fiction from it that has appeared in magazines over the last couple of years is better than most of the stuff in *Newer York*, and has been picked for "Best" anthologies and shown up on award ballots—I guess it's true, as is often said, that most New York trade publishers don't think that anybody in the reading audience is interested in anything that takes place outside of New York City itself.) *Subtropical Speculations: An Anthology of Florida Science Fiction* (Pineapple Press), edited by Rick Wilber and Richard Mathews, is a mixed reprint/original anthology of pleasant but mostly minor work, although the reprints are stronger than most of the originals: the rationale for including some of the writers here as "Florida writers" is somewhat weak, as it always is in these anthologies in which the basis for selecting the contributors is where they happen to *live* (there have been at least two other such anthologies, one of writers from Texas and one of writers from New Mexico), but, if you can find it, this is an enjoyable, low-key volume. Even more obscurely published was *Fantastic Chicago*, edited by Martin H. Greenberg, which was a special volume published in conjunction with this year's Worldcon, *Chicon V*—again, this is mostly minor, although there are some interesting reprints, and a strong though perhaps unnecessarily cryptic original story by Algis Budrys. The best of the "regional" anthologies published this year, by a considerable margin, was a mixed reprint/original anthology with a somewhat broader and more generalized theme, *Fires of the Past: Thirteen Contemporary Fantasies About Hometowns* (St. Martin's), edited by Anne Devereaux Jordan. The definition of "hometown" here is occasionally stretched beyond any reasonable or useful limit, but the book also contains strong work by Connie Willis, James Patrick Kelly, John Kessel, Robert Silverberg, Lewis Shiner, and others.

Sacred Visions (Tor), edited by Andrew M. Greeley and Michael Cassutt, a mixed reprint/original anthology about the future of Catholicism, is mostly interesting for its reprints (although it does contain a good original story by Jack McDevitt). A few of these reprints may be considered overly familiar by some, but, alas, in these days of low shelf-life, no backlist, and little historical memory, it's also quite possible that many readers will have never *seen* classics like Walter M. Miller's "A Canticle for Leibowitz," James Blish's "A Case of Conscience," and Anthony Boucher's "The Quest for Saint Aquin" before, which may make this volume valuable as a reference anthology; there are also somewhat more recent classics reprinted here, such as Nancy Kress's "Trinity" and Robert Silverberg's "The Pope of the Chimps."

Turning to fantasy and horror, there was a strong British mixed reprint/ original anthology this year, *Tales of the Wandering Jew* (Dedalus), edited by Brian Stableford; this won't be to everyone's taste (I know at least one person who refuses to read it because they consider the legend of the Wandering Jew to be anti-Semitic propaganda. Perhaps to compensate for this attitude, the authors of most of the modern stories here go to great lengths to show their Jewish characters in a sympathetic light, the victims of repeated atrocities committed by Christians—as indeed they *were*), but there are some interesting nineteenth-century reprints here, as well as a very strong story by Ian McDonald, and good work by Brian Stableford, David Langford, Mike Resnick, Kim Newman and Eugene Byrne, and others. *Once Upon a Time: A Treasury of Modern Fantasy* (Del Rey), edited by Lester del Rey and Risa Kessler, features some impressive full-color artwork by Michael Pangrazio, but the stories themselves mostly range from minor to not-very-good. *The Bradbury Chronicles: Stories in Honor of Ray Bradbury* (Roc), edited by William F. Nolan and Martin H. Greenberg, is weaker than the similar tribute anthology done for Isaac Asimov a couple of years ago, perhaps because—unlike Asimov's work, where the writers could play with his *concepts*, such as robotics or psychohistory—Bradbury's work depends on *style*, on the use of words to create and maintain a very fragile mood and tone . . . and most of the writers here just aren't up to it; there's some good work here by Chad Oliver and Orson Scott Card, but most of the rest of the stories are weak.

There were three fantasy/horror books edited by Byron Preiss (with assistance from David Keller, Megan Miller, and John Betancourt) out this year, all from Dell: *The Ultimate Werewolf, The Ultimate Dracula,* and *The*

Ultimate Frankenstein. None of these books comes even *close* to containing the best short stories ever written about werewolves or vampires or even the Frankenstein monster, so in a way the "ultimate" tag is undeserved, but each anthology *does* contain good work (by Kathe Koja, Pat Murphy, Nancy A. Collins, Philip Jose Farmer, Stuart Kaminsky, Nina Kiriki Hoffman, and Kim Antieau in *The Ultimate Werewolf*; by Brian Aldiss, Michael Bishop, S. P. Somtow, George Alec Effinger, and Loren D. Estleman in *The Ultimate Frankenstein*; by Dan Simmons, Tim Sullivan, Kevin J. Anderson, and Lawrence Watt-Evans in *The Ultimate Dracula*), so they are probably worth picking up. The strongest of the three anthologies overall is undoubtedly *The Ultimate Werewolf*, so if you can only buy one of these, that should be the one. The weakest of the three, interestingly, is *The Ultimate Dracula*. A far better vampire anthology is A *Whisper of Blood* (Morrow), edited by Ellen Datlow; this is not as strong an anthology as her classic vampire anthology *Blood Is Not Enough*, to which this is the follow-up volume, but it does contain some stylish and unusual varients on the vampire theme, including first-rate original stories by Pat Cadigan and Robert Holdstock and Garry Kilworth, good original work by Jonathan Carroll, Kathe Koja, Thomas Ligotti, Suzy McKee Charnas, Karl Edward Wagner, and others, and good reprint work by Chelsea Quinn Yarbro, Melinda M. Snodgrass, and Robert Silverberg. *Cold Shocks* (Avon), edited by Tim Sullivan, the follow-up volume to Sullivan's *Tropical Chills* anthology from a couple of years back, is also not as strong overall as its predecessor, but, like A *Whisper of Blood*, it is certainly still one of the year's best horror anthologies, containing a powerful novella by S. P. Somtow, as well as good work by Michael Armstrong, Melanie Tem, Edward Bryant, Michael D. Toman, and others.

Also interesting were: *Horse Fantastic* (DAW), edited by Martin H. Greenberg and Rosalind M. Greenberg; *Vampires* (HarperCollins), edited by Jane Yolen and Martin H. Greenberg; *2041* (Delacorte Press) edited by Jane Yolen; *Dead End: City Limits* (St. Martin's), edited by Paul F. Olson and David B. Silva; and *Cold Blood* (Ziesing), edited by Richard T. Chizmar; and *The Fantastic Adventures of Robin Hood* (Signet), edited by Martin H. Greenberg.

There were some strong novels published in 1991, although, as has been the case for the last few years, most of the really powerful work seems to be coming from middle-level professionals and relatively new writers; my entirely subjective impression is that 1991 might have been a somewhat stronger year for novels overall than 1990. *Locus* estimates that there were 308 new SF novels published last year (up 9 percent from 1990's estimate of 281), 301 new fantasy novels published (up a substantial 32 percent from last year's estimate of 204), and 165 new horror novels (down 2 percent from 1990's estimate of 168—although many industry insiders are still predicting a much steeper drop in the horror market *next* year). As you can see, with almost 800 new novels being published annually in the related science fiction/fantasy/horror genres, it has become just about impossible for any one individual to keep up with them all; it would be nearly a full-time job just to read and evaluate all of the 308 science fiction novels alone. With all of the reading I have to do at shorter lengths for *IAsfm* and for this anthology, I don't even try to read everything anymore.

So, then, as usual, I am going to limit myself here to mentioning that of the novels I *did* have time to read, I most enjoyed: *Synners*, Pat Cadigan (Bantam Spectra); *Stations of the Tide*, Michael Swanwick (Morrow); *Carve the Sky*, Alexander Jablokov (Morrow); *The Ragged World*, Judith Moffett (St. Martin's); *The Spiral Dance*, R. Garcia y Robertson (Morrow); *The Hereafter Gang*, Neal Barrett, Jr. (Ziesing); and *Ecce and Old Earth*, Jack Vance (Underwood-Miller/Tor).

Other novels that received a lot of attention and acclaim this year included: *Russian Spring*, Norman Spinrad (Bantam Spectra); *Bone Dance*, Emma Bull (Ace); *Xenocide*, Orson Scott Card (Tor); *Raft*, Stephen Baxter (ROC); *Orbital Resonance*, John Barnes (Tor); *The Cipher*, Kathe Koja (Dell Abyss); *The Face of the Waters*, Robert Silverberg (Bantam Spectra); *Barrayar*, Lois McMaster Bujold (Baen); *A Woman of the Iron People*, Eleanor Arnason (Morrow); *Eternal Light*, Paul J. McAuley (Gollancz); *Eight Skilled Gentlemen*, Barry Hughart (Doubleday Foundation); *Outside the Dog Museum*, Jonathan Carroll (Macdonald); *The Exile Kiss*, George Alec Effinger (Doubleday Foundation); *Divergence*, Charles Sheffield (Del Rey); *A Reasonable World*, Damon Knight (Tor); *Lunar Descent*, Allen Steele (Ace); *The Angel of Pain*, Brian Stableford (Simon & Schuster); *Heavy Time*, C. J. Cherryh (Warner Questar); *The Architecture of Desire*, Mary Gentle (Bantam UK); *Halo*, Tom Maddox (Tor); *The Magic Spectacles*, James P. Blaylock (Morrigan); *The Illegal Rebirth of Billy the Kid*, Rebecca Ore (Tor); *King of Morning, Queen of Day*, Ian McDonald (Bantam Spectra); *Days of Atonement*, Walter Jon Williams (Tor); *The Kindness of Women*, J. G. Ballard (Farrar, Straus & Giroux); *Soothsayer*, Mike Resnick (Ace); *The M.D.*, Thomas M. Disch (Knopf); *Buddy Holly Is Alive and Well on Ganymede*, Bradley Denton (Morrow); *Madlands*, K. W. Jeter (St. Martin's); *The White Queen*, Gwyneth Jones (Gollancz); *The Cult of Loving Kindness*, Paul Park (Morrow); *The Host*, Peter R. Emshwiller (Bantam Spectra); *Prince of Chaos*, Roger Zelazny (Morrow); *Cloven Hooves*, Megan Lindholm (Bantam Spectra); *Death Qualified: A Mystery of Chaos*, Kate Wilhelm (St. Martin's); *Riverrun*, S. P. Somtow (Avon); *The Illusionists*, Faren Miller (Warner Questar); *The Silicon Man*, Charles Platt (Bantam Spectra); *The White Mists of Power*, Kristine Kathryn Rusch (Roc); *A Bridge of Years*, Robert Charles Wilson (Doubleday Foundation); *Prodigal*, Melanie Tem (Dell Abyss); and *Mojo and the Pickle Jar*, Douglas Bell (Tor).

Morrow had an even stronger year this year than it did last year, producing one of the best book lines in SF, although that will probably be cold comfort to Morrow's ex-editor David Hartwell, who was released this year. Tor and Bantam Spectra also made strong showings in 1991.

There were a lot of good first novels released in 1991; in fact, it was one of the strongest years for novelistic debuts in some while. The first novels that made the biggest stir this year seemed to be the ones by Alexander Jablokov, Stephen Baxter, Kathe Koja, R. Garcia y Robertson, Tom Maddox, and Kristine Kathryn Rusch.

It's anyone's guess what will win the Hugo and the Nebula this year. There don't seem to me to be any clear favorites here, as there have been in other years.

Associational novels that might be of interest to SF readers this year included *Sarah Canary*, by Karen Joy Fowler, from Holt; *Tender Loving Rage*, by Alfred Bester, and *The Children of Hamelin*, by Norman Spinrad, both from Tafford Publishing ($19.95 each from Tafford Publishing, P.O. Box 271804, Houston, TX 77277); and *The Hereafter Gang*, by Neal Barrett, Jr., from Ziesing. This last is not strictly an associational item, as it is clearly a fantasy, but it is unavailable from most bookstores in the country, and, since it is also clearly one of the best novels of the year, you ought to make the attempt to order it ($25.00 from Mark V. Ziesing, P.O. Box 76, Shingletown, CA 96088).

British publisher Legend seems to have given up on the practice of issuing novellas as individual books, for the moment, anyway, although they had considerable critical success last year with novella-length books such as *Heads* by Greg Bear and *Griffin's Egg* by Michael Swanwick. Axolotl Press is still doing it, and getting good response for novella-length books such as Nancy Kress's *Beggars In Spain* and Kristine Kathryn Rusch's *The Gallery of His Dreams*, and a *new* line of original novellas published as individual books, co-published by Bantam and Axolotl Press, has just issued its first two titles, Frederik Pohl's *Stopping at Slowyear* and Robert Silverberg's *Thebes of the Hundred Gates*. It'll be interesting to see if this line is a success, especially after the recent commercial failure of the Tor Doubles novella line. (Axolotl Press's address is: Pulphouse Publishing, Box 1227, Eugene, OR 97440.)

Finally, Collier Books is to be congratulated on their line of classic reprints, which, under the editorship of James Frenkel, has gotten some long-out-of-print titles such as Edgar Pangborn's *Davy* and Fritz Leiber's *The Big Time* back on the newsstands where they deserve to be. Buy them *now*, before they become unavailable again.

This was another strong year for short-story collections. The best collections of the year were: *Gravity's Angels*, Michael Swanwick (Arkham House), *Night of the Cooters: More Neat Stories*, Howard Waldrop (Ziesing), and *Remaking History*, Kim Stanley Robinson (Tor). *Also* excellent were: *Mirabile*, Janet Kagan (Tor); *Sexual Chemistry*, Brian Stableford (Simon & Schuster UK); *Playgrounds of the Mind*, Larry Niven (Tor); *The King of the Hill*, Paul J. McAuley (Gollancz); *The Time Patrol*, Poul Anderson (Tor); *The Bone Forest*, Robert Holdstock (Grafton); and *The Book of the Dead*, Tanith Lee (Overlook). Also first-rate were *The Best of James H. Schmitz* (NESFA Press), which brings some of the best work of this long-forgotten author back into print; *One Side Laughing*, Damon Knight (St. Martin's); *Old Nathan*, David Drake (Baen); *Transreal!*, Rudy Rucker (WCS Books); *The Collected Short Fiction of Robert Sheckley* (Pulphouse); *More Shapes Than One*, Fred Chappell (St. Martin's); and *Courting Disasters and Other Strange Affinities*, Nina Kiriki Hoffman (Wildside). R. A. Lafferty's collection *Mischief Malicious* (United Mythologies Press, Box 390 Station A, Weston, Ont. Canada M9N-3N1) will probably appeal mostly to Lafferty completists, but the collection *Lafferty in Orbit* (Broken Mirrors Press, Box 473, Cambridge, MA 02238—$13.95 plus $1.00 for postage) contains some of Lafferty's very best work, and so, by definition, some of the best work of the late sixties and early seventies.

Small press publishers such as Arkham House and Ziesing continue to publish the bulk of the year's outstanding collections, although trade publishers such as Tor and St. Martin's can be seen to be doing collections a good deal more frequently these days than in previous years.

Special mention should again be made of Pulphouse Publishing, which has maintained for a couple of years an ambitious program of publishing a new short story collection every *month*. I had my doubts initially as to whether these collections would go over with the buying public, since, unlike the kind of big handsome hardcover editions produced by publishers like Ziesing or Ursus or Arkham House, these are slender little chapbooks that sometimes contain only three or four stories, and, quite frankly, feature some of the most consistently awful cover art I've ever seen in the field (and the artwork is even worse on the new Short Story Paperback covers). They are also, however, *cheaper* than the more elaborately produced small-press collections, and they do seem to be finding an audience. These *Author's Choice Monthly* collections are now up to issue 27, with another dozen slated for release in 1992. They seem to be selling well, and Pulphouse is to be congratulated for getting some very worthwhile material, much of it long unavailable, back into print. I was even *more* dubious about the chances of survival of the new Short Story Paperback line—individual short stories (both reprint and original) published in chapbook form as individual books—that Pulphouse started last year, but I may turn out to be wrong there, too. It seemed—and still seems—unlikely to me that people were going to be willing to part with $1.95 for a book containing a single short story, when they could buy a paperback anthology containing a *dozen* stories for $3.95. . . . But they seem to be selling well, so far, anyway, and Pulphouse may have just pulled off another unlikely success in the teeth of dire predictions by pessimistic pundits like me.

On the downhill side, as mentioned elsewhere, the Tor Doubles novella line, which had also been getting some excellent material back into print in recent years, was cancelled in 1992—thus making some of the above-mentioned pessimistic pundits shake their heads gloomily over the chances for success of the new Axolotl/Bantam novella line. Let's hope that they're wrong again, because the field can use all the short fiction in print that it can *get*, from as many diverse sources as possible.

As usual, your best bets in the reprint anthology market in 1991 were the various "Best of the Year" anthologies, and the annual Nebula Award anthology, although this year there were also a few other "historical overview"–type anthologies worth buying. Last year, there were three "Best" anthologies covering science fiction (my own, Donald Wollheim's, and a British series called *The Orbit Science Fiction Yearbook*, edited by David S. Garnett). This year, two of the "Best" anthology series covering science fiction are dead, and we are left with only one, the one you are holding in your hand at this moment; even though ostensibly I should be happy about this winnowing of the competition, this still strikes me as an unhealthy situation—surely science fiction is a wide and various enough field that it deserves to be covered from more than just *one* individual perspective. There are still three "Best of the Year" anthologies covering horror: Karl Edward Wagner's long-established *Year's Best Horror Stories*, a newer British series called *Best New Horror*, edited by Ramsey Campbell and Stephen Jones, and a mammoth volume covering both horror *and* fantasy, Ellen Datlow and Terri Windling's *The Year's Best Fantasy and Horror*. My own personal opinion is that three "Best" anthologies covering horror is too many, especially as we no longer have a "Best" series devoted entirely to fantasy, the coverage of the entire fantasy genre having been squeezed down to just the Windling half of the Windling/Datlow anthology. (The long-running *The Year's Best Fantasy Stories* series, edited by Art Saha, died last year too.) At any rate, these surviving "Best" anthologies, and the annual Nebula Award volume, are the most solid values for your money in the reprint anthology market. Other good buys for the money this year, though, particularly for readers serious about building up a solid science fiction library, include: *The New Hugo Winners: Volume II* (Baen), edited by Isaac Asimov and Martin H. Greenberg; *Isaac Asimov Presents the Great SF Stories: 22* (DAW), edited by Isaac Asimov and Martin H. Greenberg; *Isaac Asimov Presents the Great SF Stories: 23* (DAW), edited by Isaac Asimov and Martin H. Greenberg; *The Best of Pulphouse: The Hardback Magazine* (St. Martin's), edited by Kristine Kathryn Rusch; and a retrospective "Best" anthology, *Future on Fire* (Tor), edited by Orson Scott Card. Noted without comment is another representative "Best" anthology, *The Legend Book of Science Fiction* (Legend), edited by Gardner Dozois, which has just been issued in America as *Modern Classics of Science Fiction* (St. Martin's).

Also worthwhile were: *Welcome to Reality: The Nightmares of Philip K. Dick* (Broken Mirrors Press), edited by Uwe Anton; and *Hollywood Ghosts* (Rutledge Hill Press), edited by Frank D. McSherry, Jr., Charles C. Waugh, and Martin H. Greenberg. Noted without comment are *Little People!* (Ace) and *Magicats II* (Ace), edited by Jack Dann and Gardner Dozois; *Isaac Asimov's Mars* (Ace), edited by Gardner Dozois; and *Isaac Asimov's Robots* (Ace), edited by Gardner Dozois and Sheila Williams.

Nineteen ninety-one was another unexceptional year in the SF-oriented nonfiction SF reference-book field. Your best bets for reference this year were: *Science Fiction, Fantasy & Horror: 1990* (Locus Press), edited by Charles N. Brown and William G. Contento, and the somewhat technical *Science Fiction: The Early Years* (Kent State University Press), by Everett F. Bleiler, a book perhaps better suited for libraries than for the casual reader. The most controversial reference work of the year is *The Science-Fantasy Publishers: A Critical and Bibliographic History* (Mirage Press), by Jack L. Chalker and Mark Owings, which drew both rave notices *and* bitterly hostile reviews (and some threats of lawsuit!) when it appeared. . . . But I fear that you have to be an expert in this rather specialized field yourself in order to evaluate this controversy fairly, and I am not such an expert; the $75 cover price will certainly keep the book out of the range of the casual reader anyway, so for the most part this is a call that librarians will have to make. Fritz Leiber fans will want *Witches of the Mind: A Critical Study of Fritz Leiber* (Necronomicon Press), by Bruce Byfield and *Fafhrd & Me: A Collection of Essays* (Wildside), by Fritz Leiber, which I missed last year; Lovecraft fans will want *An Epicure in the Terrible: A Centennial Anthology of Essays in Honor of H. P. Lovecraft* (Fairleigh Dickinson University Press), edited by David E. Schulz and S. T. Joshi; Clive Barker fans will want *Clive Barker's Shadows in Eden* (Underwood-Miller), edited by Stephen Jones; and no doubt Phil Dick fans will want *The Selected Letters of Philip K. Dick* (Underwood-Miller) to add to their five-foot shelf of books *about* Philip K. Dick, practically a genre in its own right now. There was also a how-to-write book edited by the staffs of *Analog* and *IAsfm*, *Writing and Selling Science Fiction* (St. Martin's).

A new edition of *Twentieth Century Science Fiction Writers* was released early in 1992, but I had yet to see a copy of it by press time; I'll report on it next year. The long-promised update of Peter Nicholls's *Science Fiction Encyclopedia* still didn't appear in 1991, but it is definitely (no, really!) promised for publication early next year. I hope so, since the old edition has never really been adequately replaced in the years since its first publication in 1975, and it is a reference source that is urgently needed here in the nineties as the field becomes ever more complex and multifaceted and difficult to keep up with.

Of the art books that I saw, I most enjoyed *Dreamlands* (Paper Tiger), a collection of the work of British artist Mark Harrison, although Wayne Barlowe's *Expedition* (Workman) was also very intriguing. For those who like that sort of thing, which I don't, I'm sure that *Clive Barker, Illustrator* (Eclipse), compiled by Fred Burke, was well worth having, too—or at least my friends who are into splatter seem to think so.

In the general nonfiction field, the book I enjoyed the most this year was *Last Chance to See* (Harmony Books), by Douglas Adams and Mark Carwardine, a mention of which can be rationalized here because of Adams's familiarity to the science fiction audience, because he refers to himself throughout the book as "a science fiction writer," which gives his views associational interest, and because the book can be read as an ecological speculation as to how long our planet's biosphere is going to last under the onslaught of the human race. Adams is pretty pessimistic about our chances, and the book is at the same time very funny and almost unrelievedly bleak (the most science-fictional part is on pages 48–50, where Adams spends some time speculating on how in another 350 million years or so, some *other* now-humble species may evolve to the point where they get *their* chance to fuck up). Highly entertaining, but not a book to read when you're feeling depressed. Along the same lines, and, if anything, even more angry and vehement (with none of Adams's weird humor to leaven it), is *Our Angry Earth* (Tor), by Isaac Asimov and Frederik Pohl, a detailed handbook of what we as a species are doing to destroy the Earth, and of techniques by which we can try to save it. Unlike the Adams book, there *are* some hopeful notes struck here—although Asimov and Pohl also admit that the odds are against us, and that time is running out. Things are getting scary here in the last decade of the twentieth century, boys and girls—or hadn't you *heard* how much the hole in the ozone layer has grown since *last* year?

Nineteen ninety-one seemed to me to be a somewhat stronger year for genre films than 1990—or at least there were more films this year that I liked . . . no doubt the ultimate aesthetic criterion as far as the *rest* of you are concerned, right? (Right?) My favorite this year was Terry Gilliam's brilliant *The Fisher King*, which doesn't even show *up* on *Locus*'s list of 1991 genre films. I have no idea how it did at the box office (probably not very well, if Gilliam's other movies—like the also-brilliant *Brazil*—are anything to judge by), but *The Fisher King* is a deeply disturbing and bleakly funny movie, gorgeously art-directed and photographed, as is usual with a Gilliam film, and with two star-turn performances by Robin Williams and Jeff Bridges at its heart. I wonder about the sincerity of the film's ending ("Happy endings? The bastards want happy endings, do they? Well, then, take *this*!"), but the film is a major accomplishment nonetheless, and you should make a point of seeing it if you can find it. I surprised myself by *also* enjoying the year's top-grossing movie, *Terminator* 2, starring Arnold Schwarzenegger as a Good Robot this time, rather than the Bad Robot he played in the original *Terminator* film. In fact, I don't think that *T2* is as good a movie overall as *Terminator*, a minor classic of sorts, but the special effects are absolutely awesome, as much State of the Art for the nineties as *Star Wars*'s effects were State of the Art in 1976, and the action, if not quite as relentless as that in the original movie, is still fast-paced enough to keep you on the edge of your seat most of the time. The only thing that annoyed me about *T2* was its tendency to plant rather heavy-handed nonviolent/pacifistic messages in the midst of a very violent movie in which Arnold is busily shooting dozens of people and blowing up everything in sight—which strikes me as rather questionable, like coursing with the hounds and running with the hare at the same time. Still, an entertaining way to blow seven bucks.

I made up for liking *T2* by *hating* the year's second-highest-grossing film, the absolutely dreadful *Robin Hood: Prince of Thieves*. What a turkey! *Robin Hood* was the only movie this year I actually wanted to walk out on—and I might have done it, too, if I hadn't been flying at 30,000 feet at the time. *The Silence of the Lambs*, the third-highest-grossing film of the year, was actually a very good movie, but it doesn't count as a genre film by my standards—no supernatural/SF/fantastic elements. Steven Spielberg's *Hook*, which shared some elements (including a good performance by Robin Williams) with *The Fisher King*, was a handsome and stylish film, but a bit slow-moving at times—it also helps to have read the play or the novel (the novel by *Barrie*, for goodness' sake, not the—*feh!*—*novelization*) before seeing the film, as it depends heavily on your knowledge of Peter Pan lore for much of its effect. Another film I liked, which was somewhat disappointing at the box office, was Disney's *The Rocketeer*—cartoonish, of course, but also lots of fun, and a much better adventure film than *Robin Hood: Prince of Thieves*, which, released at almost the same time, may have drawn attendance away from *The Rocketeer*. An *actual* cartoon, Disney's full-length animated feature *Beauty and the Beast*, had no such trouble with attendance, and was still packing them in at press time. It's interesting to see the strong comeback the animated film, once almost extinct, has made in recent years. In addition to *Beauty and the Beast*, there was another big-budget animated film this year, *An American Tail: Fievel Goes West*, with more such films slated for next year. *Star Trek VI: The Undiscovered Country* also did well at the box office, well enough anyway to redeem the disaster of *Star Trek V*, the failure of which had raised serious doubts about the continuation of the series. I didn't see *The Addams Family*, but I know people who speak well of it; ditto for *Teenage Mutant Ninja Turtles II*, although most of the people in that case are under ten years old. I also missed *Naked Lunch*, although I doubt that it appeals to ten-year-olds. *Bill and Ted's Bogus Journey* had its moments, but it wasn't as successful as the first movie, or as successful at the box office, either. *Drop Dead Fred* had a cute fantasy idea that it didn't handle as well as it might have. But I was also surprised to find myself enjoying a sleeper called *Late for Dinner*—once you get by the absurdity of the sci-fi gimmick that sets up the premise of the movie (and it is *very* silly indeed), the *rest* of the film turns out to be rather intelligently handled and unexpectedly sweet, not at all the kind of slob comedy it looks like it's going to be from the coming attractions. As usual, there were lots of horror/slasher/serial killer/exploding head movies, but I don't go to see them anymore, so you're on your own there.

I can't leave the movie section without a mention of another very strange film, although it slipped in and out of town so furtively that I can't be sure it's actually a 1991 release—but, in its quiet way, *Tune In Tomorrow* is almost as brilliant as *The Fisher King*, literate and funny, with a hilarious and absolutely over-the-top performance by Peter Falk as a soap-opera writer who is also clearly an avatar of the Trickster; the fantasy elements are very subtly handled, but they're there, which is to be expected in a film loosely adapted from a magic realist novel (Mario Vargas Llosa's *Aunt Julia and the Scriptwriter*). You can probably find this one in your local video store, and I recommend it highly. A more recent movie with a very similar theme, *Delirious*, starring John Candy, is nowhere near as good, but does have some funny bits of business, notably the "typos" that get the reality-creating writer "cold deer" instead of "cold beer."

Turning to television, I've given up on The Sci-Fi Channel, the proposed new cable channel; although it was once again hyped and talked about all year, it once again failed to materialize, and my attitude now is, I'll Believe It When I See It. Somewhat to my surprise, since I didn't much like the first couple of seasons, "Star Trek: The Next Generation" remains probably the best actual science fiction show on the air; for me, the show is carried by the performances of the actors who play Captain Picard and Data, the two best actors in the cast, and by the flamboyant semiregular appearances of John DeLancie as Q; most of the rest of the cast could be beamed into deep space with no discernible loss, as far as I'm concerned, but the writing hasn't been bad this season, and the production values are excellent for television. I also like an odd little show called "Eerie, Indiana," although clearly adults aren't watching it and it's over the heads of the kids at whom it's ostensibly aimed, so it's probably doomed. Lest you think I've mellowed entirely, I *don't* much like the much ballyhooed "Dinosaurs," which strikes me as a routine sitcom in spite of the excellent makeup the actors wear; I didn't like "Charlie Hoover" or "Hi, Honey, I'm Home"; I've never been able to work up much enthusiasm for "Quantum Leap"; and I'm growing tired of "The Simpsons." The best show on television at the moment is "Northern Exposure"—a show that *does* have occasional traces of a fantastic element (the show with Ed and the old Indian ghost, for instance), but where the fantastic element is usually played very subtly—sometimes (as in the case of the show about the Flying Man) so subtly as to be almost subliminal. There was also a good one-shot fantasy movie on HBO, *Cast a Deadly Spell*, which was enjoyably stylish and packed full of genre in-jokes; they did make the mistake, though, of actually *showing* you the Indescribable Horror at the end of the movie—at which point, it became a rubber octopus. Lovecraft knew better than *that*—or why did you *think* he kept calling them Indescribable?

The Forty-ninth World Science Fiction Convention, ChiCon V, was held in Chicago, Illinois, from August 29 to September 2, 1991, and drew an estimated attendance of 5000. The 1991 Hugo Awards, presented at ChiCon V, were: Best Novel, *The Vor Game*, by Lois McMaster Bujold; Best Novella, "The Hemingway Hoax," by Joe Haldeman; Best Novelette, "The Mana-mouki," by Mike Resnick; Best Short Story, "Bears Discover Fire," by Terry Bisson; Best Non-Fiction, *How to Write Science Fiction and Fantasy*, by Orson Scott Card; Best Professional Editor, Gardner Dozois; Best Professional Artist, Michael Whelan; Best Dramatic Presentation, *Edward Scissorhands*; Best Semiprozine, *Locus*; Best Fanzine, *Lan's Lantern*, edited by George Laskowski; Best Fan Writer, David Langford; Best Fan Artist, Teddy Harvia; plus the John W. Campbell Award for Best New Writer to Julia Ecklar.

The 1990 Nebula Awards, presented at a banquet at the Roosevelt Hotel in New York City on April 27, 1991, were: Best Novel, *Tehanu: The Last Book of Earthsea*; Best Novella, "The Hemingway Hoax," Joe Haldeman; Best Novelette, "Tower of Babylon," Ted Chiang; Best Short Story, "Bears Discover Fire," by Terry Bisson; plus a Grand Master Nebula to Lester del Rey.

The World Fantasy Awards, presented at the Seventeenth Annual World Fantasy Convention in Tucson, Arizona, on November 3, 1991, were: Best Novel (tie), *Thomas the Rhymer*, by Ellen Kushner and *Only Begotten Daughter*, by James Morrow; Best Novella, "Bones," by Pat Murphy; Best Short Story, "A Midsummer Night's Dream," by Neil Gaiman and Charles Vess; Best Collection, *The Start of the End of It All and Other Stories*, by Carol Emshwiller; Best Anthology, *Best New Horror*, edited by Stephen Jones and Ramsey Campbell; Best Artist, Dave McKean; Special Award (Professional), Arnie Fenner; Special Award (Nonprofessional), *Cemetery Dance*, edited by Richard Chizmar; plus a Life Achievement Award to Ray Russell.

The 1991 Bram Stoker Awards, presented in Redondo Beach, California, during the weekend of June 21–23, 1991, by The Horror Writers of America, were: Best Novel, *Mine*, by Robert R. McCammon; Best First Novel, *The Revelation*, by Bentley Little; Best Collection, *Four Past Midnight*, by Stephen King; Best Novella/Novelette, "Stephen," by Elizabeth Massie; Best Short Story, "The Calling," by David B. Silva; Best Non-Fiction, *Dark Dreamers: Conversations with the Masters of Horror*, by Stanley Wiater; plus Life Achievement Awards to Hugh B. Cave and Richard Matheson.

The 1990 John W. Campbell Memorial Award–winner was *Pacific Edge*, by Kim Stanley Robinson.

The 1990 Theodore Sturgeon Award was won by "Bears Discover Fire," by Terry Bisson.

The 1990 Philip K. Dick Memorial Award—winner was *Points of Departure*, by Pat Murphy.

The Arthur C. Clarke award was won by *Take Back Plenty*, by Colin Greenland.

* * *

Dead in 1991 were: **Isaac Bashevis Singer**, 87, world-renowned literary fantasist, Nobel Prize winner, author of *Gimpel the Fool and Other Stories, The King of the Fields, Satan in Goray,* and many others; **Arkady Strugatsky**, 66, who, writing in collaboration with his brother, Boris, became one of the best-known Soviet SF writers, co-author of *Roadside Picnic* and *Hard to Be a God,* among many others; **Theodor Seuss Geisel**, 87, who wrote 48 children's books and became internationally famous as "Dr. Seuss," author of the world-famous *The Cat in the Hat* and *Green Eggs and Ham,* winner of the Pulitzer Prize for his contributions to children's literature; **John Bellairs**, 53, author of sixteen Young Adult fantasy novels, best known to the genre audience for his marvelous comic adult fantasy novel, the classic *The Face in the Frost*; **Chester Anderson**, 58, SF writer, author of the well-known novel *The Butterfly Kid* and other novels; **Sharon Baker**, 53, SF writer, author of the novels *Quarreling, They Met the Dragon, Journey to Membliar,* and *Burning Tears of Sassurum,* a friend; **Graham Greene**, 86, one of the major figures of modern letters, author of *The Third Man, The Quiet American, Our Man in Havana,* and *Travels with My Aunt,* among others; **Jerzy Kosinski**, 57, author of *The Painted Bird, Steps, Being There* and other novels; **Vercors** (Jean Bruller), 89, author of *You Shall Know Them* (also published as *Murder of the Missing Link* and *Borderline*) and other SF and fantasy novels; **Alexandr Shalimov**, 74, Russian author and scientist; **Sergei Kazmenko**, 37, Russian SF author; **Ward Hawkins**, 77, veteran pulp writer; **Dave Pedneau**, 47, mystery and horror writer; **Joyce Ballou Gregorian**, 44, fantasy author; **Dan Henderson**, 38, author of the SF novel *Paradise*; **Ted Dikty**, 71, veteran anthologist, editor, and small press publisher, editor of the first annual "Best of the Year" anthology series in SF, *The Best Science Fiction Stories* series, which ran from 1949 to 1957, husband of SF writer Julian May; **Clarence Paget**, 82, editor and publisher, creator and later editor of *The Pan Book of Horror Stories* series; **Roger Stine**, 39, well-known SF artist; **James Cunningham**, 42, well-known space artist; **Gene Roddenberry**, 70, famous creator and producer of the original "Star Trek" television series, and later of the theatrical *Star Trek* movies and the current "Star Trek: The Next Generation" series, and, by extension, of the whole "Star Trek" phenomenon that by now has influenced whole generations of viewers; **Irwin Allen**, 75, producer of numerous "disaster" movies, often marginally SF in content; **Ioan Coulianu**, 41, SF academician; **Vera Bishop Konrick**, 90, fantasy poet; **E. Dorothea** ("Doll") **Gilliland**, 61, longtime fan and convention organizer, wife of SF writer Alexis Gilliland, a friend; **Lorena S. Halde-man**, 76, mother of SF writers Joe and Jack Haldeman, longtime fan, a friend; **Sarah Gourley Shaw**, wife of SF writer Bob Shaw; **Richard Ellington**, 60, longtime fan; and **James V. Taurasi, Sr.**, 73, longtime fan and Hugo-winning fanzine editor for *Fantasy Times/Science Fiction Times*.

THE YEAR'S
BEST SCIENCE
FICTION
NINTH ANNUAL COLLECTION

BEGGARS IN SPAIN

Nancy Kress

Born in Buffalo, New York, Nancy Kress now lives with her family in Brockport, New York. She began to publish her elegant and incisive stories in the mid-seventies, and has since become a frequent contributor to *Isaac Asimov's Science Fiction Magazine, F & SF, Omni, Writer's Digest,* and other major markets. Her books include the novels *The Prince of Morning Bells, The Golden Grove, The White Pipes,* and *An Alien Light,* and the collection *Trinity and Other Stories.* Her most recent book is the novel *Brain Rose.* Upcoming are a novel version of the following story and a new short story collection from Arkham House Publishers. Her story "Trinity" was in our Second Annual Collection; her "Out of All Them Bright Stars"—a Nebula winner—was in our Third Annual Collection; her "In Memoriam" was in our Sixth Annual Collection; her "The Price of Oranges" was in our Seventh Annual Collection; and her "Inertia" was in our Eighth Annual Collection.

Here, in what may well be her single best story to date (high praise indeed), she takes us to the near future for a hard-hitting, provocative look at the uneasy social consequences of difference.

With energy and sleepless vigilance go forward and give us victories.
            —Abraham Lincoln, to Major General Joseph Hooker, 1863

1

They sat stiffly on his antique Eames chairs, two people who didn't want to be here, or one person who didn't want to and one who resented the other's reluctance. Dr. Ong had seen this before. Within two minutes he was sure: the woman was the silently furious resister. She would lose. The man would pay for it later, in little ways, for a long time.

"I presume you've performed the necessary credit checks already," Roger Camden said pleasantly, "so let's get right on to details, shall we, doctor?"

"Certainly," Ong said. "Why don't we start by your telling me all the genetic modifications you're interested in for the baby."

The woman shifted suddenly on her chair. She was in her late twenties—clearly a second wife—but already had a faded look, as if keeping up with

Roger Camden was wearing her out. Ong could easily believe that. Mrs. Camden's hair was brown, her eyes were brown, her skin had a brown tinge that might have been pretty if her cheeks had had any color. She wore a brown coat, neither fashionable nor cheap, and shoes that looked vaguely orthopedic. Ong glanced at his records for her name: Elizabeth. He would bet people forgot it often.

Next to her, Roger Camden radiated nervous vitality, a man in late middle age whose bullet-shaped head did not match his careful haircut and Italian-silk business suit. Ong did not need to consult his file to recall anything about Camden. A caricature of the bullet-shaped head had been the leading graphic of yesterday's on-line edition of the *Wall Street Journal*: Camden had led a major coup in cross-border data-atoll investment. Ong was not sure what cross-border data-atoll investment was.

"A girl," Elizabeth Camden said. Ong hadn't expected her to speak first. Her voice was another surprise: upper-class British. "Blonde. Green eyes. Tall. Slender."

Ong smiled. "Appearance factors are the easiest to achieve, as I'm sure you already know. But all we can do about 'slenderness' is give her a genetic disposition in that direction. How you feed the child will naturally—"

"Yes, yes," Roger Camden said, "that's obvious. Now: intelligence. *High* intelligence. And a sense of daring."

"I'm sorry, Mr. Camden—personality factors are not yet understood well enough to allow genet—"

"Just testing," Camden said, with a smile that Ong thought was probably supposed to be light-hearted.

Elizabeth Camden said, "Musical ability."

"Again, Mrs. Camden, a disposition to be musical is all we can guarantee."

"Good enough," Camden said. "The full array of corrections for any potential gene-linked health problem, of course."

"Of course," Dr. Ong said. Neither client spoke. So far theirs was a fairly modest list, given Camden's money; most clients had to be argued out of contradictory genetic tendencies, alteration overload, or unrealistic expectations. Ong waited. Tension prickled in the room like heat.

"And," Camden said, "no need to sleep."

Elizabeth Camden jerked her head sideways to look out the window.

Ong picked a paper magnet off his desk. He made his voice pleasant. "May I ask how you learned whether that genetic-modification program exists?"

Camden grinned. "You're not denying it exists. I give you full credit for that, Doctor."

Ong held onto his temper. "May I ask how you learned whether the program exists?"

Camden reached into an inner pocket of his suit. The silk crinkled and pulled; body and suit came from different social classes. Camden was, Ong remembered, a Yagaiist, a personal friend of Kenzo Yagai himself. Camden handed Ong hard copy: program specifications.

"Don't bother hunting down the security leak in your data banks, Doctor— you won't find it. But if it's any consolation, neither will anybody else. Now." He leaned suddenly forward. His tone changed. "I know that you've created twenty children so far who don't need to sleep at all. That so far nineteen are healthy, intelligent, and psychologically normal. In fact, better than normal—they're all unusually precocious. The oldest is already four years old and can read in two languages. I know you're thinking of offering this genetic modification on the open market in a few years. All I want is a chance to buy it for my daughter *now*. At whatever price you name."

Ong stood. "I can't possibly discuss this with you unilaterally, Mr. Camden. Neither the theft of our data—"

"Which wasn't a theft—your system developed a spontaneous bubble regurgitation into a public gate, have a hell of a time proving otherwise—"

"—*nor* the offer to purchase this particular genetic modification lies in my sole area of authority. Both have to be discussed with the Institute's Board of Directors."

"By all means, by all means. When can I talk to them, too?"

"You?"

Camden, still seated, looked at him. It occurred to Ong that there were few men who could look so confident eighteen inches below eye level. "Certainly. I'd like the chance to present my offer to whoever has the actual authority to accept it. That's only good business."

"This isn't solely a business transaction, Mr. Camden."

"It isn't solely pure scientific research, either," Camden retorted. "You're a for-profit corporation here. With certain tax breaks available only to firms meeting certain fair-practice laws."

For a minute Ong couldn't think what Camden meant. "Fair-practice laws . . ."

". . . are designed to protect minorities who are suppliers. I know, it hasn't ever been tested in the case of customers, except for red-lining in Y-energy installations. But it could be tested, Doctor Ong. Minorities are entitled to the same product offerings as non-minorities. I know the Institute would not welcome a court case, Doctor. None of your twenty genetic beta-test families are either Black or Jewish."

"A court . . . but you're not Black *or* Jewish!"

"I'm a different minority. Polish-American. The name was Kaminsky." Camden finally stood. And smiled warmly. "Look, it is preposterous. You know that, and I know that, and we both know what a grand time journalists would have with it anyway. And you know that I don't want to sue you with a preposterous case, just to use the threat of premature and adverse publicity to get what I want. I don't want to make threats at all, believe me I don't. I just want this marvelous advancement you've come up with for my daughter." His face changed, to an expression Ong wouldn't have believed possible on those particular features: wistfulness. "Doctor—do you know how much more I could have accomplished if I hadn't had to *sleep* all my life?"

Elizabeth Camden said harshly, "You hardly sleep now."

Camden looked down at her as if he had forgotten she was there. "Well, no, my dear, not now. But when I was young . . . college, I might have been able to finish college and still support . . . well. None of that matters now. What matters, Doctor, is that you and I and your board come to an agreement."

"Mr. Camden, please leave my office now."

"You mean before you lose your temper at my presumptuousness? You wouldn't be the first. I'll expect to have a meeting set up by the end of next week, whenever and wherever you say, of course. Just let my personal secretary, Diane Clavers, know the details. Anytime that's best for you."

Ong did not accompany them to the door. Pressure throbbed behind his temples. In the doorway Elizabeth Camden turned. "What happened to the twentieth one?"

"What?"

"The twentieth baby. My husband said nineteen of them are healthy and normal. What happened to the twentieth?"

The pressure grew stronger, hotter. Ong knew that he should not answer; that Camden probably already knew the answer even if his wife didn't; that he, Ong, was going to answer anyway; that he would regret the lack of self-control, bitterly, later.

"The twentieth baby is dead. His parents turned out to be unstable. They separated during the pregnancy, and his mother could not bear the twenty-four-hour crying of a baby who never sleeps."

Elizabeth Camden's eyes widened. "She killed it?"

"By mistake," Camden said shortly. "Shook the little thing too hard." He frowned at Ong. "Nurses, Doctor. In shifts. You should have picked only parents wealthy enough to afford nurses in shifts."

"That's horrible!" Mrs. Camden burst out, and Ong could not tell if she meant the child's death, the lack of nurses, or the Institute's carelessness. Ong closed his eyes.

When they had gone, he took ten milligrams of cyclobenzaprine-III. For his back—it was solely for his back. The old injury hurting again. Afterward he stood for a long time at the window, still holding the paper magnet, feeling the pressure recede from his temples, feeling himself calm down. Below him Lake Michigan lapped peacefully at the shore; the police had driven away the homeless in another raid just last night, and they hadn't yet had time to return. Only their debris remained, thrown into the bushes of the lakeshore park: tattered blankets, newspapers, plastic bags like pathetic trampled standards. It was illegal to sleep in the park, illegal to enter it without a resident's permit, illegal to be homeless and without a residence. As Ong watched, uniformed park attendants began methodically spearing newspapers and shoving them into clean self-propelled receptacles.

Ong picked up the phone to call the President of Biotech Institute's Board of Directors.

*   *   *

Four men and three women sat around the polished mahogany table of the conference room. *Doctor, lawyer, Indian chief,* thought Susan Melling, looking from Ong to Sullivan to Camden. She smiled. Ong caught the smile and looked frosty. Pompous ass. Judy Sullivan, the Institute lawyer, turned to speak in a low voice to Camden's lawyer, a thin nervous man with the look of being owned. The owner, Roger Camden, the Indian chief himself, was the happiest-looking person in the room. The lethal little man—what did it take to become that rich, starting from nothing? She, Susan, would certainly never know—radiated excitement. He beamed, he glowed, so un-like the usual parents-to-be that Susan was intrigued. Usually the prospective daddies and mommies—especially the daddies—sat there looking as if they were at a corporate merger. Camden looked as if he were at a birthday party.

Which, of course, he was. Susan grinned at him, and was pleased when he grinned back. Wolfish, but with a sort of delight that could only be called innocent—what would he be like in bed? Ong frowned majestically and rose to speak.

"Ladies and gentlemen, I think we're ready to start. Perhaps introductions are in order. Mr. Roger Camden, Mrs. Camden, are of course our clients. Mr. John Jaworski, Mr. Camden's lawyer. Mr. Camden, this is Judith Sulli-van, the Institute's head of Legal; Samuel Krenshaw, representing Institute Director Dr. Brad Marsteiner, who unfortunately couldn't be here today; and Dr. Susan Melling, who developed the genetic modification affecting sleep. A few legal points of interest to both parties—"

"Forget the contracts for a minute," Camden interrupted. "Let's talk about the sleep thing. I'd like to ask a few questions."

Susan said, "What would you like to know?" Camden's eyes were very blue in his blunt-featured face; he wasn't what she had expected. Mrs. Camden, who apparently lacked both a first name and a lawyer, since Jawor-ski had been introduced as her husband's but not hers, looked either sullen or scared, it was difficult to tell which.

Ong said sourly, "Then perhaps we should start with a short presentation by Dr. Melling."

Susan would have preferred a Q&A, to see what Camden would ask. But she had annoyed Ong enough for one session. Obediently she rose.

"Let me start with a brief description of sleep. Researchers have known for a long time that there are actually three kinds of sleep. One is 'slow-wave sleep,' characterized on an EEG by delta waves. One is 'rapid-eye-movement sleep,' or REM sleep, which is much lighter sleep and contains most dream-ing. Together these two make up 'core sleep.' The third type of sleep is 'optional sleep,' so-called because people seem to get along without it with no ill effects, and some short sleepers don't do it at all, sleeping naturally only 3 or 4 hours a night."

"That's me," Camden said. "I trained myself into it. Couldn't everybody do that?"

Apparently they were going to have a Q&A after all. "No. The actual sleep mechanism has some flexibility, but not the same amount for every person. The raphe nuclei on the brain stem—"

Ong said, "I don't think we need that level of detail, Susan. Let's stick to basics."

Camden said, "The raphe nuclei regulate the balance among neurotransmitters and peptides that lead to a pressure to sleep, don't they?"

Susan couldn't help it; she grinned. Camden, the laser-sharp ruthless financier, sat trying to look solemn, a third-grader waiting to have his homework praised. Ong looked sour. Mrs. Camden looked away, out the window.

"Yes, that's correct, Mr. Camden. You've done your research."

Camden said, "This is my *daughter*," and Susan caught her breath. When was the last time she had heard that note of reverence in anyone's voice? But no one in the room seemed to notice.

"Well, then," Susan said, "you already know that the reason people sleep is because a pressure to sleep builds up in the brain. Over the last twenty years, research has determined that's the *only* reason. Neither slow-wave sleep nor REM sleep serve functions that can't be carried on while the body and brain are awake. A lot goes on during sleep, but it can go on awake just as well, if other hormonal adjustments are made.

"Sleep once served an important evolutionary function. Once Clem Pre-Mammal was done filling his stomach and squirting his sperm around, sleep kept him immobile and away from predators. Sleep was an aid to survival. But now it's a left-over mechanism, like the appendix. It switches on every night, but the need is gone. So we turn off the switch at its source, in the genes."

Ong winced. He hated it when she oversimplified like that. Or maybe it was the light-heartedness he hated. If Marsteiner were making this presentation, there'd be no Clem Pre-Mammal.

Camden said, "What about the need to dream?"

"Not necessary. A left-over bombardment of the cortex to keep it on semi-alert in case a predator attacked during sleep. Wakefulness does that better."

"Why not have wakefulness instead then? From the start of the evolution?"

He was testing her. Susan gave him a full, lavish smile, enjoying his brass. "I told you. Safety from predators. But when a modern predator attacks—say, a cross-border data-atoll investor—it's safer to be awake."

Camden shot at her, "What about the high percentage of REM sleep in fetuses and babies?"

"Still an evolutionary hangover. Cerebrum develops perfectly well without it."

"What about neural repair during slow-wave sleep?"

"That does go on. But it can go on during wakefulness, if the DNA is programmed to do so. No loss of neural efficiency, as far as we know."

"What about the release of human growth enzyme in such large concentrations during slow-wave sleep?"

Susan looked at him admiringly. "Goes on without the sleep. Genetic adjustments tie it to other changes in the pineal gland."

"What about the—"

"The *side effects?*" Mrs. Camden said. Her mouth turned down. "What about the bloody side effects?"

Susan turned to Elizabeth Camden. She had forgotten she was there. The younger woman stared at Susan, mouth turned down at the corners.

"I'm glad you asked that, Mrs. Camden. Because there *are* side effects." Susan paused; she was enjoying herself. "Compared to their age mates, the non-sleep children—who have *not* had IQ genetic manipulation—are more intelligent, better at problem-solving, and more joyous."

Camden took out a cigarette. The archaic, filthy habit surprised Susan. Then she saw that it was deliberate: Roger Camden drawing attention to an ostentatious display to draw attention away from what he was feeling. His cigarette lighter was gold, monogrammed, innocently gaudy.

"Let me explain," Susan said. "REM sleep bombards the cerebral cortex with random neural firings from the brainstem; dreaming occurs because the poor besieged cortex tries so hard to make sense of the activated images and memories. It spends a lot of energy doing that. Without that energy expenditure, non-sleep cerebrums save the wear-and-tear and do better at coordinating real-life input. Thus—greater intelligence and problem-solving.

"Also, doctors have known for sixty years that anti-depressants, which lift the mood of depressed patients, also suppress REM sleep entirely. What they have proved in the last ten years is that the reverse is equally true: suppress REM sleep and people don't *get* depressed. The non-sleep kids are cheerful, outgoing . . . *joyous.* There's no other word for it."

"At what cost?" Mrs. Camden said. She held her neck rigid, but the corners of her jaw worked.

"No cost. No negative side effects at all."

"So far," Mrs. Camden shot back.

Susan shrugged. "So far."

"They're only four years old! At the most!"

Ong and Krenshaw were studying her closely. Susan saw the moment the Camden woman realized it; she sank back into her chair, drawing her fur coat around her, her face blank.

Camden did not look at his wife. He blew a cloud of cigarette smoke. "Everything has costs, Dr. Melling."

She liked the way he said her name. "Ordinarily, yes. Especially in genetic modification. But we honestly have not been able to find any here, despite looking." She smiled directly into Camden's eyes. "Is it too much to believe that just once the universe has given us something wholly good, wholly a step forward, wholly beneficial? Without hidden penalties?"

"Not the universe. The intelligence of people like you," Camden said, surprising Susan more than anything else that had gone before. His eyes held hers. She felt her chest tighten.

"I think," Dr. Ong said dryly, "that the philosophy of the universe may be beyond our concerns here. Mr. Camden, if you have no further medical questions, perhaps we can return to the legal points Ms. Sullivan and Mr. Jaworski have raised. Thank you, Dr. Melling."

Susan nodded. She didn't look again at Camden. But she knew what he said, how he looked, that he was there.

The house was about what she had expected, a huge mock Tudor on Lake Michigan north of Chicago. The land heavily wooded between the gate and the house, open between the house and the surging water. Patches of snow dotted the dormant grass. Biotech had been working with the Camdens for four months, but this was the first time Susan had driven to their home.

As she walked toward the house, another car drove up behind her. No, a truck, continuing around the curved driveway to a service entry at the side of the house. One man rang the service bell; a second began to unload a plastic-wrapped playpen from the back of the truck. White, with pink and yellow bunnies. Susan briefly closed her eyes.

Camden opened the door himself. She could see the effort not to look worried. "You didn't have to drive out, Susan—I'd have come into the city!"

"No, I didn't want you to do that, Roger. Mrs. Camden is here?"

"In the living room." Camden led her into a large room with a stone fireplace. English country-house furniture; prints of dogs or boats, all hung eighteen inches too high: Elizabeth Camden must have done the decorating. She did not rise from her wing chair as Susan entered.

"Let me be concise and fast," Susan said, "I don't want to make this any more drawn-out for you than I have to. We have all the amniocentesis, ultrasound, and Langston test results. The fetus is fine, developing normally for two weeks, no problems with the implant on the uterus wall. But a complication has developed."

"What?" Camden said. He took out a cigarette, looked at his wife, put it back unlit.

Susan said quietly, "Mrs. Camden, by sheer chance both your ovaries released eggs last month. We removed one for the gene surgery. By more sheer chance the second fertilized and implanted. You're carrying two fetuses."

Elizabeth Camden grew still. "Twins?"

"No," Susan said. Then she realized what she had said. "I mean, yes. They're twins, but non-identical. Only one has been genetically altered. The other will be no more similar to her than any two siblings. It's a so-called 'normal' baby. And I know you didn't want a so-called normal baby."

Camden said, "No. I didn't."

Elizabeth Camden said, "I did."

Camden shot her a fierce look that Susan couldn't read. He took out the cigarette again, lit it. His face was in profile to Susan, thinking intently; she doubted he knew the cigarette was there, or that he was lighting it. "Is the baby being affected by the other one's being there?"

"No," Susan said. "No, of course not. They're just . . . co-existing."

"Can you abort it?"

"Not without risk of aborting both of them. Removing the unaltered fetus might cause changes in the uterus lining that could lead to a spontaneous miscarriage of the other." She drew a deep breath. "There's that option, of course. We can start the whole process over again. But as I told you at the time, you were very lucky to have the in vitro fertilization take on only the second try. Some couples take eight or ten tries. If we started all over, the process could be a lengthy one."

Camden said, "Is the presence of this second fetus harming my daughter? Taking away nutrients or anything? Or will it change anything for her later on in the pregnancy?"

"No. Except that there is a chance of premature birth. Two fetuses take up a lot more room in the womb, and if it gets too crowded, birth can be premature. But the—"

"How premature? Enough to threaten survival?"

"Most probably not."

Camden went on smoking. A man appeared at the door. "Sir, London calling. James Kendall for Mr. Yagai."

"I'll take it." Camden rose. Susan watched him study his wife's face. When he spoke, it was to her. "All right, Elizabeth. All right." He left the room.

For a long moment the two women sat in silence. Susan was aware of disappointment; this was not the Camden she had expected to see. She became aware of Elizabeth Camden watching her with amusement.

"Oh, yes, Doctor. He's like that."

Susan said nothing.

"Completely overbearing. But not this time." She laughed softly, with excitement. "Two. Do you . . . do you know what sex the other one is?"

"Both fetuses are female."

"I wanted a girl, you know. And now I'll have one."

"Then you'll go ahead with the pregnancy."

"Oh, yes. Thank you for coming, Doctor."

She was dismissed. No one saw her out. But as she was getting into her car, Camden rushed out of the house, coatless. "Susan! I wanted to thank you. For coming all the way out here to tell us yourself."

"You already thanked me."

"Yes. Well. You're sure the second fetus is no threat to my daughter?"

Susan said deliberately, "Nor is the genetically altered fetus a threat to the naturally conceived one."

He smiled. His voice was low and wistful. "And you think that should matter to me just as much. But it doesn't. And why should I fake what I feel? Especially to you?"

Susan opened her car door. She wasn't ready for this, or she had changed her mind, or something. But then Camden leaned over to close the door, and his manner held no trace of flirtatiousness, no smarmy ingratiation. "I better order a second playpen."

"Yes."

"And a second car seat."

"Yes."

"But not a second night-shift nurse."

"That's up to you."

"And you." Abruptly he leaned over and kissed her, a kiss so polite and respectful that Susan was shocked. Neither lust nor conquest would have shocked her; this did. Camden didn't give her a chance to react; he closed the car door and turned back toward the house. Susan drove toward the gate, her hands shaky on the wheel until amusement replaced shock: It *had* been a deliberately distant, respectful kiss, an engineered enigma. And nothing else could have guaranteed so well that there would have to be another.

She wondered what the Camdens would name their daughters.

Dr. Ong strode the hospital corridor, which had been dimmed to half-light. From the nurse's station in Maternity a nurse stepped forward as if to stop him—it was the middle of the night, long past visiting hours—got a good look at his face, and faded back into her station. Around a corner was the viewing glass to the nursery. To Ong's annoyance, Susan Melling stood pressed against the glass. To his further annoyance, she was crying.

Ong realized that he had never liked the woman. Maybe not any women. Even those with superior minds could not seem to refrain from being made damn fools by their emotions.

"Look," Susan said, laughing a little, swiping at her face. "Doctor—*look*."

Behind the glass Roger Camden, gowned and masked, was holding up a baby in white undershirt and pink blanket. Camden's blue eyes—theatrically blue, a man really should not have such garish eyes—glowed. The baby had a head covered with blond fuzz, wide eyes, pink skin. Camden's eyes above the mask said that no other child had ever had these attributes.

Ong said, "An uncomplicated birth?"

"Yes," Susan Melling sobbed. "Perfectly straightforward. Elizabeth is fine. She's asleep. Isn't she beautiful? He has the most adventurous spirit I've ever known." She wiped her nose on her sleeve; Ong realized that she was drunk. "Did I ever tell you that I was engaged once? Fifteen years ago, in med school? I broke it off because he grew to seem so ordinary, so boring. Oh, God, I shouldn't be telling you all this I'm sorry I'm sorry."

Ong moved away from her. Behind the glass Roger Camden laid the baby in a small wheeled crib. The nameplate said BABY GIRL CAMDEN #1. 5.9 POUNDS. A night nurse watched indulgently.

Ong did not wait to see Camden emerge from the nursery or to hear Susan

Melling say to him whatever she was going to say. Ong went to have the OB paged. Melling's report was not, under the circumstances, to be trusted. A perfect, unprecedented chance to record every detail of gene-alteration with a non-altered control, and Melling was more interested in her own sloppy emotions. Ong would obviously have to do the report himself, after talking to the OB. He was hungry for every detail. And not just about the pink-cheeked baby in Camden's arms. He wanted to know everything about the birth of the child in the other glass-sided crib: BABY GIRL CAMDEN #2. 5.1 POUNDS. The dark-haired baby with the mottled red features, lying scrunched down in her pink blanket, asleep.

2

Leisha's earliest memory was of flowing lines that were not there. She knew they were not there because when she reached out her fist to touch them, her fist was empty. Later she realized that the flowing lines were light: sunshine slanting in bars between curtains in her room, between the wooden blinds in the dining room, between the criss-cross lattices in the conservatory. The day she realized the golden flow was light she laughed out loud with the sheer joy of discovery, and Daddy turned from putting flowers in pots and smiled at her.

The whole house was full of light. Light bounded off the lake, streamed across the high white ceilings, puddled on the shining wooden floors. She and Alice moved continually through light, and sometimes Leisha would stop and tip back her head and let it flow over her face. She could feel it, like water.

The best light, of course, was in the conservatory. That's where Daddy liked to be when he was home from making money. Daddy potted plants and watered trees, humming, and Leisha and Alice ran between the wooden tables of flowers with their wonderful earthy smells, running from the dark side of the conservatory where the big purple flowers grew to the sunshine side with sprays of yellow flowers, running back and forth, in and out of the light. "Growth," Daddy said to her, "flowers all fulfilling their promise. Alice, be careful! You almost knocked over that orchid!" Alice, obedient, would stop running for a while. Daddy never told Leisha to stop running.

After a while the light would go away. Alice and Leisha would have their baths, and then Alice would get quiet, or cranky. She wouldn't play nice with Leisha, even when Leisha let her choose the game or even have all the best dolls. Then Nanny would take Alice to "bed," and Leisha would talk with Daddy some more until Daddy said he had to work in his study with the papers that made money. Leisha always felt a moment of regret that he had to go do that, but the moment never lasted very long because Mamselle would arrive and start Leisha's lessons, which she liked. Learning things was so interesting! She could already sing twenty songs and write all the letters in the alphabet and count to fifty. And by the time lessons were done, the light had come back, and it was time for breakfast.

Breakfast was the only time Leisha didn't like. Daddy had gone to the office, and Leisha and Alice had breakfast with Mommy in the big dining room. Mommy sat in a red robe, which Leisha liked, and she didn't smell funny or talk funny the way she would later in the day, but still breakfast wasn't fun. Mommy always started with The Question.

"Alice, sweetheart, how did you sleep?"

"Fine, Mommy."

"Did you have any nice dreams?"

For a long time Alice said no. Then one day she said, "I dreamed about a horse. I was riding him." Mommy clapped her hands and kissed Alice and gave her an extra sticky bun. After that Alice always had a dream to tell Mommy.

Once Leisha said, "I had a dream, too. I dreamed light was coming in the window and it wrapped all around me like a blanket and then it kissed me on my eyes."

Mommy put down her coffee cup so hard that coffee sloshed out of it. "Don't lie to me, Leisha. You did not have a dream."

"Yes, I did," Leisha said.

"Only children who sleep can have dreams. Don't lie to me. You did not have a dream."

"Yes I did! I did!" Leisha shouted. She could see it, almost: The light streaming in the window and wrapping around her like a golden blanket.

"I will not tolerate a child who is a liar! Do you hear me, Leisha—I won't tolerate it!"

"You're a liar!" Leisha shouted, knowing the words weren't true, hating herself because they weren't true but hating Mommy more and that was wrong, too, and there sat Alice stiff and frozen with her eyes wide, Alice was scared and it was Leisha's fault.

Mommy called sharply, "Nanny! Nanny! Take Leisha to her room at once. She can't sit with civilized people if she can't refrain from telling lies!"

Leisha started to cry. Nanny carried her out of the room. Leisha hadn't even had her breakfast. But she didn't care about that; all she could see while she cried was Alice's eyes, scared like that, reflecting broken bits of light.

But Leisha didn't cry long. Nanny read her a story, and then played Data Jump with her, and then Alice came up and Nanny drove them both into Chicago to the zoo where there were wonderful animals to see, animals Leisha could not have dreamed—nor Alice *either*. And by the time they came back Mommy had gone to her room and Leisha knew that she would stay there with the glasses of funny-smelling stuff the rest of the day and Leisha would not have to see her.

But that night, she went to her mother's room.

"I have to go to the bathroom," she told Mamselle. Mamselle said, "Do you need any help?" maybe because Alice still needed help in the bathroom. But Leisha didn't, and she thanked Mamselle. Then she sat on the toilet for a minute even though nothing came, so that what she had told Mamselle wouldn't be a lie.

Leisha tiptoed down the hall. She went first into Alice's room. A little light in a wall socket burned near the "crib." There was no crib in Leisha's room. Leisha looked at her sister through the bars. Alice lay on her side, with her eyes closed. The lids of the eyes fluttered quickly, like curtains blowing in the wind. Alice's chin and neck looked loose.

Leisha closed the door very carefully and went to her parents' room.

They didn't "sleep" in a crib but in a huge enormous "bed," with enough room between them for more people. Mommy's eyelids weren't fluttering; she lay on her back making a hrrr-hrrr sound through her nose. The funny smell was strong on her. Leisha backed away and tiptoed over to Daddy. He looked like Alice, except that his neck and chin looked even looser, folds of skin collapsed like the tent that had fallen down in the backyard. It scared Leisha to see him like that. Then Daddy's eyes flew open so suddenly that Leisha screamed.

Daddy rolled out of bed and picked her up, looking quickly at Mommy. But she didn't move. Daddy was wearing only his underpants. He carried Leisha out into the hall, where Mamselle came rushing up saying, "Oh, sir, I'm sorry, she just said she was going to the bathroom—"

"It's all right," Daddy said. "I'll take her with me."

"No!" Leisha screamed, because Daddy was only in his underpants and his neck had looked all funny and the room smelled bad because of Mommy. But Daddy carried her into the conservatory, set her down on a bench, wrapped himself in a piece of green plastic that was supposed to cover up plants, and sat down next to her.

"Now, what happened, Leisha? What were you doing?"

Leisha didn't answer.

"You were looking at people sleeping, weren't you?" Daddy said, and because his voice was softer Leisha mumbled, "Yes." She immediately felt better; it felt good not to lie.

"You were looking at people sleeping because you don't sleep and you were curious, weren't you? Like Curious George in your book?"

"Yes," Leisha said. "I thought you said you made money in your study all night!"

Daddy smiled. "Not all night. Some of it. But then I sleep, although not very much." He took Leisha on his lap. "I don't need much sleep, so I get a lot more done at night than most people. Different people need different amounts of sleep. And a few, a very few, are like you. You don't need any."

"Why not?"

"Because you're special. Better than other people. Before you were born, I had some doctors help make you that way."

"Why?"

"So you could do anything you want to and make manifest your own individuality."

Leisha twisted in his arms to stare at him; the words meant nothing. Daddy reached over and touched a single flower growing on a tall potted tree. The flower had thick white petals like the cream he put in coffee, and the center was a light pink.

"See, Leisha—this tree made this flower. Because it *can*. Only this tree can make this kind of wonderful flower. That plant hanging up there can't, and those can't either. Only this tree. Therefore the most important thing in the world for this tree to do is grow this flower. The flower is the tree's individuality—that means just *it*, and nothing else—made manifest. Nothing else matters."

"I don't understand, Daddy."

"You will. Someday."

"But I want to understand *now*," Leisha said, and Daddy laughed with pure delight and hugged her. The hug felt good, but Leisha still wanted to understand.

"When you make money, is that your indiv . . . that thing?"

"Yes," Daddy said happily.

"Then nobody else can make money? Like only that tree can make that flower?"

"Nobody else can make it just the ways I do."

"What do you do with the money?"

"I buy things for you. This house, your dresses, Mamselle to teach you, the car to ride in."

"What does the tree do with the flower?"

"Glories in it," Daddy said, which made no sense. "Excellence is what counts, Leisha. Excellence supported by individual effort. And that's *all* that counts."

"I'm cold, Daddy."

"Then I better bring you back to Mamselle."

Leisha didn't move. She touched the flower with one finger. "I want to sleep, Daddy."

"No, you don't, sweetheart. Sleep is just lost time, wasted life. It's a little death."

"Alice sleeps."

"Alice isn't like you."

"Alice isn't special?"

"No. You are."

"Why didn't you make Alice special, too?"

"Alice made herself. I didn't have a chance to make her special."

The whole thing was too hard. Leisha stopped stroking the flower and slipped off Daddy's lap. He smiled at her. "My little questioner. When you grow up, you'll find your own excellence, and it will be a new order, a specialness the world hasn't ever seen before. You might even be like Kenzo Yagai. He made the Yagai generator that powers the world."

"Daddy, you look funny wrapped in the flower plastic." Leisha laughed. Daddy did, too. But then she said, "When I grow up, I'll make my specialness find a way to make Alice special, too," and Daddy stopped laughing.

He took her back to Mamselle, who taught her to write her name, which was so exciting she forgot about the puzzling talk with Daddy. There were six letters, all different, and together they were *her name*. Leisha wrote it over and over, laughing, and Mamselle laughed too. But later, in the morning, Leisha thought again about the talk with Daddy. She thought of it often, turning the unfamiliar words over and over in her mind like small hard stones, but the part she thought about most wasn't a word. It was the frown on Daddy's face when she told him she would use her specialness to make Alice special, too.

Every week Dr. Melling came to see Leisha and Alice, sometimes alone, sometimes with other people. Leisha and Alice both liked Dr. Melling, who laughed a lot and whose eyes were bright and warm. Often Daddy was there, too. Dr. Melling played games with them, first with Alice and Leisha separately and then together. She took their pictures and weighed them. She made them lie down on a table and stuck little metal things to their temples, which sounded scary but wasn't because there were so many machines to watch, all making interesting noises, while you were lying there. Dr. Melling was as good at answering questions as Daddy. Once Leisha said, "Is Dr. Melling a special person? Like Kenzo Yagai?" And Daddy laughed and glanced at Dr. Melling and said, "Oh, yes, indeed."

When Leisha was five she and Alice started school. Daddy's driver took them every day into Chicago. They were in different rooms, which disappointed Leisha. The kids in Leisha's room were all older. But from the first day she adored school, with its fascinating science equipment and electronic drawers full of math puzzlers and other children to find countries on the map with. In half a year she had been moved to yet a different room, where the kids were still older, but they were nonetheless nice to her. Leisha started to learn Japanese. She loved drawing the beautiful characters on thick white paper. "The Sauley School was a good choice," Daddy said.

But Alice didn't like the Sauley School. She wanted to go to school on the same yellow bus as Cook's daughter. She cried and threw her paints on the floor at the Sauley School. Then Mommy came out of her room— Leisha hadn't seen her for a few weeks, although she knew Alice had—and threw some candlesticks from the mantelpiece on the floor. The candlesticks, which were china, broke. Leisha ran to pick up the pieces while Mommy and Daddy screamed at each other in the hall by the big staircase.

"She's my daughter, too! And I say she can go!"

"You don't have the right to say anything about it! A weepy drunk, the most rotten role model possible for both of them . . . and I thought I was getting a fine English aristocrat!"

"You got what you paid for! Nothing! Not that you ever needed anything from me or anybody else!"

"Stop it!" Leisha cried. "Stop it!" and there was silence in the hall. Leisha cut her fingers on the china; blood streamed onto the rug. Daddy rushed in and picked her up. "Stop it," Leisha sobbed, and didn't understand when Daddy said quietly, "*You* stop it, Leisha. Nothing *they* do should touch you at all. You have to be at least that strong."

Leisha buried her head in Daddy's shoulder. Alice transferred to Carl Sandburg Elementary School, riding there on the yellow school bus with Cook's daughter.

A few weeks later Daddy told them that Mommy was going away for a few weeks to a hospital, to stop drinking so much. When Mommy came out, he said, she was going to live somewhere else for a while. She and Daddy were not happy. Leisha and Alice would stay with Daddy and they would visit Mommy sometimes. He told them this very carefully, finding the right words for truth. Truth was very important, Leisha already knew. Truth was being true to your self, your specialness. Your individuality. An individual respected facts, and so always told the truth.

Mommy, Daddy did not say but Leisha knew, did not respect facts.

"I don't want Mommy to go away," Alice said. She started to cry. Leisha thought Daddy would pick Alice up, but he didn't. He just stood there looking at them both.

Leisha put her arms around Alice. "It's all right, Alice. It's all right! We'll make it all right! I'll play with you all the time we're not in school so you don't miss Mommy!"

Alice clung to Leisha. Leisha turned her head so she didn't have to see Daddy's face.

3

Kenzo Yagai was coming to the United States to lecture. The title of his talk, which he would give in New York, Los Angeles, Chicago, and Washington, with a repeat in Washington as a special address to Congress, was "The Further Political Implications of Inexpensive Power." Leisha Camden, eleven years old, was going to have a private introduction after the Chicago talk, arranged by her father.

She had studied the theory of cold fusion at school, and her Global Studies teacher had traced the changes in the world resulting from Yagai's patented, low-cost applications of what had, until him, been unworkable theory. The rising prosperity of the Third World, the last death throes of the old communist systems, the decline of the oil states, the renewed economic power of the United States. Her study group had written a news script, filmed with the school's professional-quality equipment, about how a 1985 American family lived with expensive energy costs and a belief in tax-supported help, while a 2019 family lived with cheap energy and a belief in the contract as the basis of civilization. Parts of her own research puzzled Leisha.

"Japan thinks Kenzo Yagai was a traitor to his own country," she said to Daddy at supper.

"No," Camden said. "*Some* Japanese think that. Watch out for generalizations, Leisha. Yagai patented and marketed Y-energy first in the United States because here there were at least the dying embers of individual enterprise. Because of his invention, our entire country has slowly swung back toward an individual meritocracy, and Japan has slowly been forced to follow."

"Your father held that belief all along," Susan said. "Eat your peas, Leisha." Leisha ate her peas. Susan and Daddy had only been married less than a year; it still felt a little strange to have her there. But nice. Daddy said Susan was a valuable addition to their household: intelligent, motivated, and cheerful. Like Leisha herself.

"Remember, Leisha," Camden said, "a man's worth to society and to himself doesn't rest on what he thinks other people should do or be or feel, but on himself. On what he can actually do, and do well. People trade what they do well, and everyone benefits. The basic tool of civilization is the contract. Contracts are voluntary and mutually beneficial. As opposed to coercion, which is wrong."

"The strong have no right to take anything from the weak by force," Susan said. "Alice, eat your peas, too, honey."

"Nor the weak to take anything by force from the strong," Camden said. "That's the basis of what you'll hear Kenzo Yagai discuss tonight, Leisha."

Alice said, "I don't like peas."

Camden said, "Your body does. They're good for you."

Alice smiled. Leisha felt her heart lift; Alice didn't smile much at dinner any more. "My body doesn't have a contract with the peas."

Camden said, a little impatiently, "Yes, it does. Your body benefits from them. Now eat."

Alice's smile vanished. Leisha looked down at her plate. Suddenly she saw a way out. "No, Daddy look—Alice's body benefits, but the peas don't! It's not a mutually beneficial consideration—so there's no contract! Alice is right!"

Camden let out a shout of laughter. To Susan he said, "Eleven years old . . . *eleven.*" Even Alice smiled, and Leisha waved her spoon triumphantly, light glinting off the bowl and dancing silver on the opposite wall.

But even so, Alice did not want to go hear Kenzo Yagai. She was going to sleep over at her friend Julie's house; they were going to curl their hair together. More surprisingly, Susan wasn't coming either. She and Daddy looked at each other a little funny at the front door, Leisha thought, but

Leisha was too excited to think about this. She was going to hear *Kenzo Yagai*.

Yagai was a small man, dark and slim. Leisha liked his accent. She liked, too, something about him that took her a while to name. "Daddy," she whispered in the half-darkness of the auditorium, "he's a joyful man."

Daddy hugged her in the darkness.

Yagai spoke about spirituality and economics. "A man's spirituality— which is only his dignity as a man—rests on his own efforts. Dignity and worth are not automatically conferred by aristocratic birth—we have only to look at history to see that. Dignity and worth are not automatically conferred by inherited wealth—a great heir may be a thief, a wastrel, cruel, an exploiter, a person who leaves the world much poorer than he found it. Nor are dignity and worth automatically conferred by existence itself—a mass murderer exists, but is of negative worth to his society and possesses no dignity in his lust to kill.

"No, the only dignity, the only spirituality, rests on what a man can achieve with his own efforts. To rob a man of the chance to achieve, and to trade what he achieves with others, is to rob him of his spiritual dignity as a man. This is why communism has failed in our time. *All* coercion—all force to take from a man his own efforts to achieve—causes spiritual damage and weakens a society. Conscription, theft, fraud, violence, welfare, lack of legislative representation—*all* rob a man of his chance to choose, to achieve on his own, to trade the results of his achievement with others. Coercion is a cheat. It produces nothing new. Only freedom—the freedom to achieve, the freedom to trade freely the results of achievement—creates the environment proper to the dignity and spirituality of man."

Leisha applauded so hard her hands hurt. Going backstage with Daddy, she thought she could hardly breathe. Kenzo Yagai!

But backstage was more crowded than she had expected. There were cameras everywhere. Daddy said, "Mr. Yagai, may I present my daughter Leisha," and the cameras moved in close and fast—on *her*. A Japanese man whispered something in Kenzo Yagai's ear, and he looked more closely at Leisha. "Ah, yes."

"Look over here, Leisha," someone called, and she did. A robot camera zoomed so close to her face that Leisha stepped back, startled. Daddy spoke very sharply to someone, then to someone else. The cameras didn't move. A woman suddenly knelt in front of Leisha and thrust a microphone at her. "What does it feel like to never sleep, Leisha?"

"What?"

Someone laughed. The laugh was not kind. "Breeding geniuses . . ."

Leisha felt a hand on her shoulder. Kenzo Yagai gripped her very firmly, pulled her away from the cameras. Immediately, as if by magic, a line of Japanese men formed behind Yagai, parting only to let Daddy through. Behind the line, the three of them moved into a dressing room, and Kenzo Yagai shut the door.

"You must not let them bother you, Leisha," he said in his wonderful accent. "Not ever. There is an old Oriental proverb: 'The dogs bark but the caravan moves on.' You must never let your individual caravan be slowed by the barking of rude or envious dogs."

"I won't," Leisha breathed, not sure yet what the words really meant, knowing there was time later to sort them out, to talk about them with Daddy. For now she was dazzled by Kenzo Yagai, the actual man himself who was changing the world without force, without guns, with trading his special individual efforts. "We study your philosophy at my school, Mr. Yagai."

Kenzo Yagai looked at Daddy. Daddy said, "A private school. But Leisha's sister also studies it, although cursorily, in the public system. Slowly, Kenzo, but it comes. It comes." Leisha noticed that he did not say why Alice was not here tonight with them.

Back home, Leisha sat in her room for hours, thinking over everything that had happened. When Alice came home from Julie's the next morning, Leisha rushed toward her. But Alice seemed angry about something.

"Alice—what is it?"

"Don't you think I have enough to put up with at school already?" Alice shouted. "Everybody knows, but at least when you stayed quiet it didn't matter too much! They'd stopped teasing me! Why did you have to do it?"

"Do what?" Leisha said, bewildered.

Alice threw something at her: a hard-copy morning paper, on newsprint flimsier than the Camden system used. The paper dropped open at Leisha's feet. She stared at her own picture, three columns wide, with Kenzo Yagai. The headline said YAGAI AND THE FUTURE: ROOM FOR THE REST OF US? Y-ENERGY INVENTOR CONFERS WITH 'SLEEP'-FREE' DAUGHTER OF MEGA-FINANCIER ROGER CAMDEN.

Alice kicked the paper. "It was on TV last night too—on TV. I work hard not to look stuck-up or creepy, and you go and do this! Now Julie probably won't even invite me to her slumber party next week!" She rushed up the broad curving stairs toward her room.

Leisha looked down at the paper. She heard Kenzo Yagai's voice in her head: "The dogs bark but the caravan moves on." She looked at the empty stairs. Aloud she said, "Alice—your hair looks really pretty curled like that."

4

"I want to meet the rest of them," Leisha said. "Why have you kept them from me this long?"

"I haven't kept them from you at all," Camden said. "Not offering is not the same as denial. Why shouldn't you be the one to do the asking? You're the one who now wants it."

Leisha looked at him. She was 15, in her last year at the Sauley School. "Why didn't you offer?"

"Why should I?"

"I don't know," Leisha said. "But you gave me everything else."

"Including the freedom to ask for what you want."

Leisha looked for the contradiction, and found it. "Most things that you provided for my education I didn't ask for, because I didn't know enough to ask and you, as the adult, did. But you've never offered the opportunity for me to meet any of the other sleepless mutants—"

"Don't use that word," Camden said sharply.

"—so you must either think it was not essential to my education or else you had another motive for not wanting me to meet them."

"Wrong," Camden said. "There's a third possibility. That I think meeting them is essential to your education, that I do want you to, but this issue provided a chance to further the education of your self-initiative by waiting for *you* to ask."

"All right," Leisha said, a little defiantly; there seemed to be a lot of defiance between them lately, for no good reason. She squared her shoulders. Her new breasts thrust forward. "I'm asking. How many of the Sleepless are there, who are they, and where are they?"

Camden said, "If you're using that term—'the Sleepless'—you've already done some reading on your own. So you probably know that there are 1,082 of you so far in the United States, a few more in foreign countries, most of them in major metropolitan areas. Seventy-nine are in Chicago, most of them still small children. Only nineteen anywhere are older than you."

Leisha didn't deny reading any of this. Camden leaned forward in his study chair to peer at her. Leisha wondered if he needed glasses. His hair was completely gray now, sparse and stiff, like lonely broomstraws. The *Wall Street Journal* listed him among the hundred richest men in America; *Women's Wear Daily* pointed out that he was the only billionaire in the country who did not move in the society of international parties, charity balls, and personal jets. Camden's jet ferried him to business meetings around the world, to the chairmanship of the Yagai Economics Institute, and to very little else. Over the years he had grown richer, more reclusive, and more cerebral. Leisha felt a rush of her old affection.

She threw herself sideways into a leather chair, her long slim legs dangling over the arm. Absently she scratched a mosquito bite on her thigh. "Well, then, I'd like to meet Richard Keller." He lived in Chicago and was the beta-test Sleepless closest to her own age. He was 17.

"Why ask me? Why not just go?"

Leisha thought there was a note of impatience in his voice. He liked her to explore things first, then report on them to him later. Both parts were important.

Leisha laughed. "You know what, Daddy? You're predictable."

Camden laughed, too. In the middle of the laugh Susan came in. "He certainly is not. Roger, what about that meeting in Buenos Aires Thursday?

Is it on or off?" When he didn't answer, her voice grew shriller. "Roger? I'm talking to you!"

Leisha averted her eyes. Two years ago Susan had finally left genetic research to run Camden's house and schedule; before that she had tried hard to do both. Since she had left Biotech, it seemed to Leisha, Susan had changed. Her voice was tighter. She was more insistent that Cook and the gardener follow her directions exactly, without deviation. Her blonde braids had become stiff sculptured waves of platinum.

"It's on," Roger said.

"Well, thanks for at least answering. Am I going?"

"If you like."

"I like."

Susan left the room. Leisha rose and stretched. Her long legs rose on tiptoe. It felt good to reach, to stretch, to feel sunlight from the wide windows wash over her face. She smiled at her father, and found him watching her with an unexpected expression.

"Leisha—"

"What?"

"See Keller. But be careful."

"Of what?"

But Camden wouldn't answer.

The voice on the phone had been noncommittal. "Leisha Camden? Yes, I know who you are. Three o'clock on Thursday?" The house was modest, a thirty-year-old Colonial on a quiet suburban street where small children on bicycles could be watched from the front window. Few roofs had more than one Y-energy cell. The trees, huge old sugar maples, were beautiful.

"Come in," Richard Keller said.

He was no taller than she, stocky, with a bad case of acne. Probably no genetic alterations except sleep, Leisha guessed. He had thick dark hair, a low forehead, and bushy black brows. Before he closed the door Leisha saw his stare at her car and driver, parked in the driveway next to a rusty ten-speed bike.

"I can't drive yet," she said. "I'm still fifteen."

"It's easy to learn," Keller said. "So, you want to tell me why you're here?"

Leisha liked his directness. "To meet some other Sleepless."

"You mean you never have? Not any of us?"

"You mean the rest of you know each other?" She hadn't expected that.

"Come to my room, Leisha."

She followed him to the back of the house. No one else seemed to be home. His room was large and airy, filled with computers and filing cabinets. A rowing machine sat in one corner. It looked like a shabbier version of the room of any bright classmate at the Sauley School, except there was more space without a bed. She walked over to the computer screen.

"Hey—you working on Boesc equations?"

"On an application of them."

"To what?"

"Fish migration patterns."

Leisha smiled. "Yeah—that would work. I never thought of that."

Keller seemed not to know what to do with her smile. He looked at the wall, then at her chin. "You interested in Gaea patterns? In the environment?"

"Well, no," Leisha confessed. "Not particularly. I'm going to study politics at Harvard. Pre-law. But of course we had Gaea patterns at school."

Keller's gaze finally came unstuck from her face. He ran a hand through his dark hair. "Sit down, if you want."

Leisha sat, looking appreciatively at the wall posters, shifting green on blue, like ocean currents. "I like those. Did you program them yourself?"

"You're not at all what I pictured," Keller said.

"How did you picture me?"

He didn't hesitate. "Stuck-up. Superior. Shallow, despite your IQ."

She was more hurt than she had expected to be.

Keller blurted, "You're the only one of the Sleepless who's really rich. But you already know that."

"No, I don't. I've never checked."

He took the chair beside her, stretching his stocky legs straight in front of him, in a slouch that had nothing to do with relaxation. "It makes sense, really. Rich people don't have their children genetically modified to be superior—they think any offspring of theirs is already superior. By their values. And poor people can't afford it. We Sleepless are upper-middle class, no more. Children of professors, scientists, people who value brains and time."

"My father values brains and time," Leisha said. "He's the biggest supporter of Kenzo Yagai."

"Oh, Leisha, do you think I don't already know that? Are you flashing me or what?"

Leisha said with great deliberateness, "I'm *talking* to you." But the next minute she could feel the hurt break through on her face.

"I'm sorry," Keller muttered. He shot off his chair and paced to the computer, back. "I *am* sorry. But I don't . . . I don't understand what you're doing here."

"I'm lonely," Leisha said, astonished at herself. She looked up at him. "It's true. I'm lonely. I am. I have friends and Daddy and Alice—but no one really knows, really understands—what? I don't know what I'm saying."

Keller smiled. The smile changed his whole face, opened up its dark planes to the light. "I do. Oh, do I. What do you do when they say, 'I had such a dream last night!'?"

"Yes!" Leisha said. "But that's even really minor—it's when *I* say, 'I'll look that up for you tonight' and they get that funny look on their face that means 'She'll do it while I'm asleep.' "

"But that's even really minor," Keller said. "It's when you're playing basketball in the gym after supper and then you go to the diner for food and then you say 'Let's have a walk by the lake' and they say 'I'm really tired. I'm going home to bed now.' "

"But that's really minor," Leisha said, jumping up. "It's when you really are absorbed by the movie and then you get the point and it's so goddamn beautiful you leap up and say 'Yes! Yes!' and Susan says 'Leisha, really— you'd think nobody but you ever enjoyed anything before.' "

"Who's Susan?" Keller said.

The mood was broken. But not really; Leisha could say "My stepmother" without much discomfort over what Susan had promised to be and what she had become. Keller stood inches from her, smiling that joyous smile, understanding, and suddenly relief washed over Leisha so strong that she walked straight into him and put her arms around his neck, only tightening them when she felt his startled jerk. She started to sob—she, Leisha, who never cried.

"Hey," Richard said. "Hey."

"Brilliant," Leisha said, laughing. "Brilliant remark."

She could feel his embarrassed smile. "Wanta see my fish migration curves instead?"

"No," Leisha sobbed, and he went on holding her, patting her back awkwardly, telling her without words that she was home.

Camden waited up for her, although it was past midnight. He had been smoking heavily. Through the blue air he said quietly, "Did you have a good time, Leisha?"

"Yes."

"I'm glad," he said, and put out his last cigarette, and climbed the stairs— slowly, stiffly, he was nearly seventy now—to bed.

They went everywhere together for nearly a year: swimming, dancing, to the museums, the theater, the library. Richard introduced her to the others, a group of twelve kids between fourteen and nineteen, all of them intelligent and eager. All Sleepless.

Leisha learned.

Tony's parents, like her own, had divorced. But Tony, fourteen, lived with his mother, who had not particularly wanted a Sleepless child, while his father, who had, acquired a red hovercar and a young girlfriend who designed ergonomic chairs in Paris. Tony was not allowed to tell anyone— relatives, schoolmates—that he was Sleepless. "They'll think you're a freak," his mother said, eyes averted from her son's face. The one time Tony disobeyed her and told a friend that he never slept, his mother beat him. Then she moved the family to a new neighborhood. He was nine years old.

Jeanine, almost as long-legged and slim as Leisha, was training for the Olympics in ice skating. She practiced twelve hours a day, hours no Sleeper still in high school could ever have. So far the newspapers had not picked up the story. Jeanine was afraid that, if they did, they would somehow not let her compete.

Jack, like Leisha, would start college in September. Unlike Leisha, he had already started his career. The practice of law had to wait for law school; the practice of investment required only money. Jack didn't have much, but his precise financial analyses parlayed $600 saved from summer jobs to $3000 through stock-market investing, then to $10,000, and then he had enough to qualify for information-fund speculation. Jack was fifteen, not old enough to make legal investments; the transactions were all in the name of Kevin Baker, the oldest of the Sleepless, who lived in Austin. Jack told Leisha, "When I hit 84 percent profit over two consecutive quarters, the data analysts logged onto me. They were just sniffing. Well, that's their job, even when the overall amounts are actually small. It's the patterns they care about. If they take the trouble to cross-reference data banks and come up with the fact that Kevin is a Sleepless, will they try to stop us from investing somehow?"

"That's paranoid," Leisha said.

"No, it's not," Jeanine said. "Leisha, you don't *know*."

"You mean because I've been protected by my father's money and caring," Leisha said. No one grimaced; all of them confronted ideas openly, without shadowy allusions. Without dreams.

"Yes," Jeanine said. "Your father sounds terrific. And he raised you to think that achievement should not be fettered—Jesus Christ, he's a Yagaiist. Well, good. We're glad for you." She said it without sarcasm. Leisha nodded. "But the world isn't always like that. They hate us."

"That's too strong," Carol said. "Not hate."

"Well, maybe," Jeanine said. "But they're different from us. We're better, and they naturally resent that."

"I don't see what's natural about it," Tony said. "Why shouldn't it be just as natural to admire what's better? We do. Does any one of us resent Kenzo Yagai for his genius? Or Nelson Wade, the physicist? Or Catherine Raduski?"

"We don't resent them because we *are* better," Richard said. "Q.E.D."

"What we should do is have our own society," Tony said. "Why should we allow their regulations to restrict our natural, honest achievements? Why should Jeanine be barred from skating against them and Jack from investing on their same terms just because we're Sleepless? Some of them are brighter than others of them. Some have greater persistence. Well, we have greater concentration, more biochemical stability, and more time. All men are not created equal."

"Be fair, Jack—no one has been barred from anything yet," Jeanine said.

"But we will be."

"*Wait*," Leisha said. She was deeply troubled by the conversation. "I mean, yes, in many ways we're better. But you quoted out of context, Tony. The Declaration of Independence doesn't say all men are created equal in ability. It's talking about rights and power—it means that all are created equal *under the law*. We have no more right to a separate society or to being free of society's restrictions than anyone else does. There's no other way to freely trade one's efforts, unless the same contractual rules apply to all."

"Spoken like a true Yagaiist," Richard said, squeezing her hand.

"That's enough intellectual discussion for me," Carol said, laughing. "We've been at this for hours. We're at the beach, for Chrissake. Who wants to swim with me?"

"I do," Jeanine said. "Come on, Jack."

All of them rose, brushing sand off their suits, discarding sunglasses. Richard pulled Leisha to her feet. But just before they ran into the water, Tony put his skinny hand on her arm. "One more question, Leisha. Just to think about. If we achieve better than most other people, and we trade with the Sleepers when it's mutually beneficial, making no distinction there between the strong and the weak—what obligation do we have to those so weak they don't have anything to trade with us? We're already going to give more than we get—do we have to do it when we get nothing at all? Do we have to take care of their deformed and handicapped and sick and lazy and shiftless with the products of our work?"

"Do the Sleepers have to?" Leisha countered.

"Kenzo Yagai would say no. He's a Sleeper."

"He would say they would receive the benefits of contractual trade even if they aren't direct parties to the contract. The whole world is better-fed and healthier because of Y-energy."

"Come on!" Jeanine yelled. "Leisha, they're dunking me! Jack, you stop that! Leisha, help me!"

Leisha laughed. Just before she grabbed for Jeanine, she caught the look on Richard's face, on Tony's: Richard frankly lustful, Tony angry. At her. But why? What had she done, except argue in favor of dignity and trade?

Then Jack threw water on her, and Carol pushed Jack into the warm spray, and Richard was there with his arms around her, laughing.

When she got the water out of her eyes, Tony was gone.

Midnight. "Okay," Carol said. "Who's first?"

The six teenagers in the brambled clearing looked at each other. A Y-lamp, kept on low for atmosphere, cast weird shadows across their faces and over their bare legs. Around the clearing Roger Camden's trees stood thick and dark, a wall between them and the closest of the estate's outbuildings. It was very hot. August air hung heavy, sullen. They had voted against bringing an air-conditioned Y-field because this was a return to the primitive, the dangerous; let it be primitive.

Six pairs of eyes stared at the glass in Carol's hand.

"Come *on*," she said. "Who wants to drink up?" Her voice was jaunty, theatrically hard. "It was difficult enough to get this."

"How *did* you get it?" said Richard, the group member—except for Tony—with the least influential family contacts, the least money. "In a drinkable form like that?"

"My cousin Brian is a pharmaceutical supplier to the Biotech Institute. He's curious." Nods around the circle; except for Leisha, they were Sleepless precisely because they had relatives somehow connected to Biotech. And everyone was curious. The glass held interleukin-1, an immune system booster, one of many substances which as a side effect induced the brain to swift and deep sleep.

Leisha stared at the glass. A warm feeling crept through her lower belly, not unlike the feeling when she and Richard made love.

Tony said, "Give it to me!"

Carol did. "Remember—you only need a little sip."

Tony raised the glass to his mouth, stopped, looked at them over the rim from his fierce eyes. He drank.

Carol took back the glass. They all watched Tony. Within a minute he lay on the rough ground; within two, his eyes closed in sleep.

It wasn't like seeing parents sleep, siblings, friends. It was Tony. They looked away, didn't meet each other's eyes. Leisha felt the warmth between her legs tug and tingle, faintly obscene.

When it was her turn, she drank slowly, then passed the glass to Jeanine. Her head turned heavy, as if it were being stuffed with damp rags. The trees at the edge of the clearing blurred. The portable lamp blurred, too—it wasn't bright and clean anymore but squishy, blobby; if she touched it, it would smear. Then darkness swooped over her brain, taking it away: *Taking away her mind.* "Daddy!" She tried to call, to clutch for him, but then the darkness obliterated her.

Afterward, they all had headaches. Dragging themselves back through the woods in the thin morning light was torture, compounded by an odd shame. They didn't touch each other. Leisha walked as far away from Richard as she could. It was a whole day before the throbbing left the base of her skull, or the nausea her stomach.

There had not even been any dreams.

"I want you to come with me tonight," Leisha said, for the tenth or twelfth time. "We both leave for college in just two days; this is the last chance. I really want you to meet Richard."

Alice lay on her stomach across her bed. Her hair, brown and lusterless, fell around her face. She wore an expensive yellow jumpsuit, silk by Ann Patterson, which rucked up in wrinkles around her knees.

"Why? What do you care if I meet Richard or not?"

"Because you're my sister," Leisha said. She knew better than to say "my twin." Nothing got Alice angry faster.

"I don't want to." The next moment Alice's face changed. "Oh, I'm sorry, Leisha—I didn't mean to sound so snotty. But . . . but I don't want to."

"It won't be all of them. Just Richard. And just for an hour or so. Then you can come back here and pack for Northwestern."

"I'm not going to Northwestern."

Leisha stared at her.

Alice said, "I'm pregnant."

Leisha sat on the bed. Alice rolled onto her back, brushed the hair out of her eyes, and laughed. Leisha's ears closed against the sound. "Look at you," Alice said. "You'd think it was *you* who was pregnant. But you never would be, would you, Leisha? Not until it was the proper time. Not you."

"How?" Leisha said. "We both had our caps put in . . ."

"I had the cap removed," Alice said.

"You wanted to get pregnant?"

"Damn flash I did. And there's not a thing Daddy can do about it. Except, of course, cut off all credit completely, but I don't think he'll do that, do you?" She laughed again. "Even to me?"

"But Alice . . . why? Not just to anger Daddy!"

"No," Alice said. "Although you would think of that, wouldn't you? Because I want something to love. Something of my *own*. Something that has nothing to do with this house."

Leisha thought of her and Alice running through the conservatory, years ago, her and Alice, darting in and out of the sunlight. "It hasn't been so bad growing up in this house."

"Leisha, you're stupid. I don't know how anyone so smart can be so stupid. Get out of my room! Get out!"

"But Alice . . . a *baby* . . ."

"Get out!" Alice shrieked. "Go to Harvard! Go be successful! Just get out!"

Leisha jerked off the bed. "Gladly! You're irrational, Alice! You don't think ahead, you don't plan a *baby* . . ." But she could never sustain anger. It dribbled away, leaving her mind empty. She looked at Alice, who suddenly put out her arms. Leisha went into them.

"You're the baby," Alice said wonderingly. "You *are*. You're so . . . I don't know what. You're a baby."

Leisha said nothing. Alice's arms felt warm, felt whole, felt like two children running in and out of sunlight. "I'll help you, Alice. If Daddy won't."

Alice abruptly pushed her away. "I don't need your help."

Alice stood. Leisha rubbed her empty arms, fingertips scraping across opposite elbows. Alice kicked the empty, open trunk in which she was supposed to pack for Northwestern, and then abruptly smiled, a smile that made Leisha look away. She braced herself for more abuse. But what Alice said, very softly, was, "Have a good time at Harvard."

5

She loved it.

From the first sight of Massachusetts Hall, older than the United States by a half century, Leisha felt something that had been missing in Chicago:

Age. Roots. Tradition. She touched the bricks of Widener Library, the glass cases in the Peabody Museum, as if they were the grail. She had never been particularly sensitive to myth or drama; the anguish of Juliet seemed to her artificial, that of Willy Loman merely wasteful. Only King Arthur, struggling to create a better social order, had interested her. But now, walking under the huge autumn trees, she suddenly caught a glimpse of a force that could span generations, fortunes left to endow learning and achievement the bene-factors would never see, individual effort spanning and shaping centuries to come. She stopped, and looked at the sky through the leaves, at the buildings solid with purpose. At such moments she thought of Camden, bending the will of an entire genetic research Institute to create her in the image he wanted.

Within a month, she had forgotten all such mega-musings.

The work load was incredible, even for her. The Sauley School had encouraged individual exploration at her own pace; Harvard knew what it wanted from her, at its pace. In the last twenty years, under the academic leadership of a man who in his youth had watched Japanese economic domination with dismay, Harvard had become the controversial leader of a return to hard-edged learning of facts, theories, applications, problem-solving, intellectual efficiency. The school accepted one out of every two hundred applications from around the world. The daughter of England's Prime Minister had flunked out her first year and been sent home.

Leisha had a single room in a new dormitory, the dorm because she had spent so many years isolated in Chicago and was hungry for people, the single so she would not disturb anyone else when she worked all night. Her second day a boy from down the hall sauntered in and perched on the edge of her desk.

"So you're Leisha Camden."

"Yes."

"Sixteen years old."

"Almost seventeen."

"Going to out-perform us all, I understand, without even trying."

Leisha's smile faded. The boy stared at her from under lowered downy brows. He was smiling, his eyes sharp. From Richard and Tony and the others Leisha had learned to recognize the anger that presented itself as contempt.

"Yes," Leisha said coolly, "I am."

"Are you sure? With your pretty little-girl hair and your mutant little-girl brain?"

"Oh, leave her alone, Hannaway," said another voice. A tall blond boy, so thin his ribs looked like ripples in brown sand, stood in jeans and bare feet, drying his wet hair. "Don't you ever get tired of walking around being an asshole?"

"Do you?" Hannaway said. He heaved himself off the desk and started toward the door. The blond moved out of his way. Leisha moved into it.

"The reason I'm going to do better than you," she said evenly, "is because I have certain advantages you don't. Including sleeplessness. And then after I 'out-perform' you, I'll be glad to help you study for your tests so that you can pass, too."

The blond, drying his ears, laughed. But Hannaway stood still, and into his eyes came an expression that made Leisha back away. He pushed past her and stormed out.

"Nice going, Camden," the blond said. "He deserved that."

"But I meant it," Leisha said. "I will help him study."

The blond lowered his towel and stared. "You did, didn't you? You meant it."

"Yes! Why does everybody keep questioning that?"

"Well," the boy said, "I don't. You can help me if I get into trouble." Suddenly he smiled. "But I won't."

"Why not?"

"Because I'm just as good at anything as you are, Leisha Camden."

She studied him. "You're not one of us. Not Sleepless."

"Don't have to be. I know what I can do. Do, be, create, trade."

She said, delighted, "You're a Yagaiist!"

"Of course." He held out his hand. "Stewart Sutter. How about a fish-burger in the Yard?"

"Great," Leisha said. They walked out together, talking excitedly. When people stared at her, she tried not to notice. She was here. At Harvard. With space ahead of her, time to learn, and with people like Stewart Sutter who accepted and challenged her.

All the hours he was awake.

She became totally absorbed in her classwork. Roger Camden drove up once, walking the campus with her, listening, smiling. He was more at home than Leisha would have expected: He knew Stewart Sutter's father, Kate Addams' grandfather. They talked about Harvard, business, Harvard, the Yagai Economics Institute, Harvard. "How's Alice?" Leisha asked once, but Camden said that he didn't know, she had moved out and did not want to see him. He made her an allowance through his attorney. While he said this, his face remained serene.

Leisha went to the Homecoming Ball with Stewart, who was also majoring in pre-law but was two years ahead of Leisha. She took a weekend trip to Paris with Kate Addams and two other girlfriends, taking the Concorde III. She had a fight with Stewart over whether the metaphor of superconductivity could apply to Yagaiism, a stupid fight they both knew was stupid but had anyway, and afterward they became lovers. After the fumbling sexual explorations with Richard, Stewart was deft, experienced, smiling faintly as he taught her how to have an orgasm both by herself and with him. Leisha was dazzled. "It's so *joyful*," she said, and Stewart looked at her with a tenderness she knew was part disturbance but didn't know why.

At mid-semester she had the highest grades in the freshman class. She got every answer right on every single question on her mid-terms. She and Stewart went out for a beer to celebrate, and when they came back Leisha's room had been destroyed. The computer was smashed, the data banks wiped, hardcopies and books smoldering in a metal wastebasket. Her clothes were ripped to pieces, her desk and bureau hacked apart. The only thing untouched, pristine, was the bed.

Stewart said, "There's no way this could have been done in silence. Everyone on the floor—hell, on the floor *below*—had to know. Someone will talk to the police." No one did. Leisha sat on the edge of the bed, dazed, and looked at the remnants of her Homecoming gown. The next day Dave Hannaway gave her a long, wide smile.

Camden flew east again, taut with rage. He rented her an apartment in Cambridge with E-lock security and a bodyguard named Toshio. After he left, Leisha fired the bodyguard but kept the apartment. It gave her and Stewart more privacy, which they used to endlessly discuss the situation. It was Leisha who argued that it was an aberration, an immaturity.

"There have always been haters, Stewart. Hate Jews, hate Blacks, hate immigrants, hate Yagaiists who have more initiative and dignity than you do. I'm just the latest object of hatred. It's not new, it's not remarkable. It doesn't mean any basic kind of schism between the Sleepless and Sleepers."

Stewart sat up in bed and reached for the sandwiches on the night stand. "Doesn't it? Leisha, you're a different kind of person entirely. More evolutionarily fit, not only to survive but to prevail. Those other 'objects of hatred' you cite except Yagaiists—they were all powerless in their societies. They occupied *inferior* positions. You, on the other hand—all three Sleepless in Harvard Law are on the *Law Review*. All of them. Kevin Baker, your oldest, has already founded a successful bio-interface software firm and is making money, a lot of it. Every Sleepless is making superb grades, none have psychological problems, all are healthy—and most of you aren't even adults yet. How much hatred do you think you're going to encounter once you hit the big-stakes world of finance and business and scarce endowed chairs and national politics?"

"Give me a sandwich," Leisha said. "Here's my evidence you're wrong: You yourself. Kenzo Yagai. Kate Addams. Professor Lane. My father. Every Sleeper who inhabits the world of fair trade, mutually beneficial contracts. And that's most of you, or at least most of you who are worth considering. You believe that competition among the most capable leads to the most beneficial trades for everyone, strong and weak. Sleepless are making real and concrete contributions to society, in a lot of fields. That has to outweigh the discomfort we cause. We're *valuable* to you. You know that."

Stewart brushed crumbs off the sheets. "Yes. I do. Yagaiists do."

"Yagaiists run the business and financial and academic worlds. Or they will. In a meritocracy, they *should*. You underestimate the majority of people, Stew. Ethics aren't confined to the ones out front."

"I hope you're right," Stewart said. "Because, you know, I'm in love with you."

Leisha put down her sandwich.

"Joy," Stewart mumbled into her breasts, "you are joy."

When Leisha went home for Thanksgiving, she told Richard about Stewart. He listened tight-lipped.

"A Sleeper."

"A *person*," Leisha said. "A good, intelligent, achieving person!"

"Do you know what your good intelligent achieving Sleepers have done, Leisha? Jeanine has been barred from Olympic skating. 'Genetic alteration, analogous to steroid abuse to create an unsportsmanlike advantage.' Chris Devereaux's left Stanford. They trashed his laboratory, destroyed two years' work in memory formation proteins. Kevin Baker's software company is fighting a nasty advertising campaign, all underground of course, about kids using software designed by 'non-human minds.' Corruption, mental slavery, satanic influences: the whole bag of witch-hunt tricks. Wake up, Leisha!"

They both heard his words. Moments dragged by. Richard stood like a boxer, forward on the balls of his feet, teeth clenched. Finally he said, very quietly, "Do you love him?"

"Yes," Leisha said. "I'm sorry."

"Your choice," Richard said coldly. "What do you do while he's asleep? Watch?"

"You make it sound like a perversion!"

Richard said nothing. Leisha drew a deep breath. She spoke rapidly but calmly, a controlled rush: "While Stewart is asleep I work. The same as you do. Richard—don't do this. I didn't mean to hurt you. And I don't want to lose the group. I believe the Sleepers are the same species as we are—are you going to punish me for that? Are you going to *add* to the hatred? Are you going to tell me that I can't belong to a wider world that includes all honest, worthwhile people whether they sleep or not? Are you going to tell me that the most important division is by genetics and not by economic spirituality? Are you going to force me into an artificial choice, 'us' or 'them'?"

Richard picked up a bracelet. Leisha recognized it: She had given it to him in the summer. His voice was quiet. "No. It's not a choice." He played with the gold links a minute, then looked up at her. "Not yet."

By spring break, Camden walked more slowly. He took medicine for his blood pressure, his heart. He and Susan, he told Leisha, were getting a divorce. "She changed, Leisha, after I married her. You saw that. She was independent and productive and happy, and then after a few years she stopped all that and became a shrew. A whining shrew." He shook his head in genuine bewilderment. "You saw the change."

Leisha had. A memory came to her: Susan leading her and Alice in "games" that were actually controlled cerebral-performance tests, Susan's braids dancing around her sparkling eyes. Alice had loved Susan, then, as much as Leisha had.

"Dad, I want Alice's address."

"I told you up at Harvard, I don't have it," Camden said. He shifted in his chair, the impatient gesture of a body that never expected to wear out. In January Kenzo Yagai had died of pancreatic cancer; Camden had taken the news hard. "I make her allowance through an attorney. By her choice."

"Then I want the address of the attorney."

The attorney, however, refused to tell Leisha where Alice was. "She doesn't want to be found, Ms. Camden. She wanted a complete break."

"Not from me," Leisha said.

"Yes," the attorney said, and something flickered behind his eyes, something she had last seen in Dave Hannaway's face.

She flew to Austin before returning to Boston, making her a day late for classes. Kevin Baker saw her instantly, canceling a meeting with IBM. She told him what she needed, and he set his best data-net people on it, without telling them why. Within two hours she had Alice's address from the attorney's electronic files. It was the first time, she realized, that she had ever turned to one of the Sleepless for help, and it had been given instantly. Without trade.

Alice was in Pennsylvania. The next weekend Leisha rented a hovercar and driver—she had learned to drive, but only groundcars as yet—and went to High Ridge, in the Appalachian Mountains.

It was an isolated hamlet, twenty-five miles from the nearest hospital. Alice lived with a man named Ed, a silent carpenter twenty years older than she, in a cabin in the woods. The cabin had water and electricity but no news net. In the early spring light the earth was raw and bare, slashed with icy gullies. Alice and Ed apparently worked at nothing. Alice was eight months pregnant.

"I didn't want you here," she said to Leisha. "So why are you?"

"Because you're my sister."

"God, look at you. Is that what they're wearing at Harvard? Boots like that? When did you become fashionable, Leisha? You were always too busy being intellectual to care."

"What's this all about, Alice? Why here? What are you doing?"

"Living," Alice said. "Away from dear Daddy, away from Chicago, away from drunken broken Susan—did you know she drinks? Just like Mom. He does that to people. But not to me. I got out. I wonder if you ever will."

"Got out? To *this*?"

"I'm happy," Alice said angrily. "Isn't that what it's supposed to be about? Isn't that the aim of your great Kenzo Yagai—happiness through individual effort?"

Leisha thought of saying that Alice was making no efforts that she could see. She didn't say it. A chicken ran through the yard of the cabin. Behind, the mountains rose in layers of blue haze. Leisha thought what this place must have been like in winter: cut off from the world where people strived towards goals, learned, changed.

"I'm glad you're happy, Alice."

"Are you?"

"Yes."

"Then I'm glad, too," Alice said, almost defiantly. The next moment she abruptly hugged Leisha, fiercely, the huge hard mound of her belly crushed between them. Alice's hair smelled sweet, like fresh grass in sunlight.

"I'll come see you again, Alice."

"Don't," Alice said.

6

SLEEPLESS MUTIE BEGS FOR REVERSAL OF GENE TAMPERING, screamed the headline in the Food Mart. "PLEASE LET ME SLEEP LIKE REAL PEOPLE!" CHILD PLEADS.

Leisha typed in her credit number and pressed the news kiosk for a print-out, although ordinarily she ignored the electronic tabloids. The headline went on circling the kiosk. A Food Mart employee stopped stacking boxes on shelves and watched her. Bruce, Leisha's bodyguard, watched the employee.

She was twenty-two, in her final year at Harvard Law, editor of the *Law Review*, ranked first in her class. The next three were Jonathan Cocchiara, Len Carter, and Martha Wentz. All Sleepless.

In her apartment she skimmed the print-out. Then she accessed the Groupnet run from Austin. The files had more news stories about the child, with comments from other Sleepless, but before she could call them up Kevin Baker came on-line himself, on voice.

"Leisha. I'm glad you called. I was going to call you."

"What's the situation with this Stella Bevington, Kev? Has anybody checked it out?"

"Randy Davies. He's from Chicago but I don't think you've met him, he's still in high school. He's in Park Ridge, Stella's in Skokie. Her parents wouldn't talk to him—were pretty abusive, in fact—but he got to see Stella face-to-face anyway. It doesn't look like an abuse case, just the usual stupidity: parents wanted a genius child, scrimped and saved, and now they can't handle that she *is* one. They scream at her to sleep, get emotionally abusive when she contradicts them, but so far no violence."

"Is the emotional abuse actionable?"

"I don't think we want to move on it yet. Two of us will keep in close touch with Stella—she does have a modem, and she hasn't told her parents about the net—and Randy will drive out weekly."

Leisha bit her lip. "A tabloid shitpiece said she's seven years old."

"Yes."

"Maybe she shouldn't be left there. I'm an Illinois resident, I can file an abuse grievance from here if Candy's got too much in her briefcase. . . ."

Seven years old.

"No. Let it sit a while. Stella will probably be all right. You know that."

She did. Nearly all of the Sleepless stayed "all right," no matter how much opposition came from the stupid segment of society. And it was only the stupid segment, Leisha argued—a small if vocal minority. Most people could, and would, adjust to the growing presence of the Sleepless, when it became clear that that presence included not only growing power but growing benefits to the country as a whole.

Kevin Baker, now twenty-six, had made a fortune in micro-chips so revolutionary that Artificial Intelligence, once a debated dream, was yearly closer to reality. Carolyn Rizzolo had won the Pulitzer Prize in drama for her play *Morning Light.* She was twenty-four. Jeremy Robinson had done significant work in superconductivity applications while still a graduate student at Stanford. William Thaine, *Law Review* editor when Leisha first came to Harvard, was now in private practice. He had never lost a case. He was twenty-six, and the cases were becoming important. His clients valued his ability more than his age.

But not everyone reacted that way.

Kevin Baker and Richard Keller had started the datanet that bound the Sleepless into a tight group, constantly aware of each other's personal fights. Leisha Camden financed the legal battles, the educational costs of Sleepless whose parents were unable to meet them, the support of children in emotionally bad situations. Rhonda Lavelier got herself licensed as a foster mother in California, and whenever possible the Group maneuvered to have small Sleepless who were removed from their homes assigned to Rhonda. The Group now had three ABA lawyers; within the next year they would gain four more, licensed to practice in five different states.

The one time they had not been able to remove an abused Sleepless child legally, they kidnapped him.

Timmy DeMarzo, four years old. Leisha had been opposed to the action. She had argued the case morally and pragmatically—to her they were the same thing—thus: If they believed in their society, in its fundamental laws and in their ability to belong to it as free-trading productive individuals, they must remain bound by the society's contractual laws. The Sleepless were, for the most part, Yagaiists. They should already know this. And if the FBI caught them, the courts and press would crucify them.

They were not caught.

Timmy DeMarzo—not even old enough to call for help on the datanet, they had learned of the situation through the automatic police-record scan Kevin maintained through his company—was stolen from his own backyard in Wichita. He had lived the last year in an isolated trailer in North Dakota; no place was too isolated for a modem. He was cared for by a legally irreproachable foster mother who had lived there all her life. The foster mother was second cousin to a Sleepless, a broad cheerful woman with a much better brain than her appearance indicated. She was a Yagaiist. No record of the child's existence appeared in any data bank: not the IRS, not any school's, not even the local grocery store's computerized check-out slips. Food specifically for the child was shipped in monthly on a truck owned by a Sleepless in State College, Pennsylvania. Ten of the Group knew about the kidnapping, out of the total 3,428 born in the United States. Of that total, 2,691 were part of the Group via the net. Another 701 were as yet too young to use a modem. Only 36 Sleepless, for whatever reason, were not part of the Group.

The kidnapping had been arranged by Tony Indivino.

"It's Tony I wanted to talk to you about," Kevin said to Leisha. "He's started again. This time he means it. He's buying land."

She folded the tabloid very small and laid it carefully on the table. "Where?"

"Allegheny Mountains. In southern New York State. A lot of land. He's putting in the roads now. In the spring, the first buildings."

"Jennifer Sharifi still financing it?" She was the American-born daughter of an Arab prince who had wanted a Sleepless child. The prince was dead and Jennifer, dark-eyed and multilingual, was richer than Leisha would one day be.

"Yes. He's starting to get a following, Leisha."

"I know."

"Call him."

"I will. Keep me informed about Stella."

She worked until midnight at the *Law Review*, then until four A.M. preparing her classes. From four to five she handled legal matters for the Group. At five A.M. she called Tony, still in Chicago. He had finished high school, done one semester at Northwestern, and at Christmas vacation he had finally exploded at his mother for forcing him to live as a Sleeper. The explosion, it seemed to Leisha, had never ended.

"Tony? Leisha."

"The answer is yes, yes, no, and go to hell."

Leisha gritted her teeth. "Fine. Now tell me the questions."

"Are you really serious about the Sleepless withdrawing into their own self-sufficient society? Is Jennifer Sharifi willing to finance a project the size of building a small city? Don't you think that's a cheat of all that can be accomplished by patient integration of the Group into the mainstream? And what about the contradictions of living in an armed restricted city and still trading with the Outside?"

"I would never tell *you* to go to hell."

"Hooray for you," Tony said. After a moment he added, "I'm sorry. That sounds like one of *them*."

"It's wrong for us, Tony."

"Thanks for not saying I couldn't pull it off."

She wondered if he could. "We're not a separate species, Tony."

"Tell that to the Sleepers."

"You exaggerate. There are haters out there, there are *always* haters, but to give up . . ."

"We're not giving up. Whatever we create can be freely traded: software, hardware, novels, information, theories, legal counsel. We can travel in and out. But we'll have a safe place to return *to*. Without the leeches who think we owe them blood because we're better than they are."

"It isn't a matter of owing."

"Really?" Tony said. "Let's have this out, Leisha. All the way. You're a Yagaiist—what do you believe in?"

"Tony . . ."

"*Do it*," Tony said, and in his voice she heard the fourteen-year-old Richard had introduced her to. Simultaneously, she saw her father's face: not as he was now, since the by-pass, but as he had been when she was a little girl, holding her on his lap to explain that she was special.

"I believe in voluntary trade that is mutually beneficial. That spiritual dignity comes from supporting one's life through one's own efforts, and trading the results of those efforts in mutual cooperation throughout the society. That the symbol of this is the contract. And that we need each other for the fullest, most beneficial trade."

"Fine," Tony bit off. "Now what about the beggars in Spain?"

"The what?"

"You walk down a street in a poor country like Spain and you see a beggar. Do you give him a dollar?"

"Probably."

"Why? He's trading nothing with you. He has nothing to trade."

"I know. Out of kindness. Compassion."

"You see six beggars. Do you give them all a dollar?"

"Probably," Leisha said.

"You would. You see a hundred beggars and you haven't got Leisha Camden's money—do you give them each a dollar?"

"No."

"Why not?"

Leisha reached for patience. Few people could make her want to cut off a comm link; Tony was one of them. "Too draining on my own resources. My life has first claim on the resources I earn."

"All right. Now consider this. At Biotech Institute—where you and I began, dear pseudo-sister—Dr. Melling has just yesterday—"

"*Who?*"

"Dr. Susan Melling. Oh, God, I completely forgot—she used to be married to your father!"

"I lost track of her," Leisha said. "I didn't realize she'd gone back to research. Alice once said . . . never mind. What's going on at Biotech?"

"Two crucial items, just released. Carla Dutcher has had first-month fetal genetic analysis. Sleeplessness is a dominant gene. The next generation of the Group won't sleep either."

"We all knew that," Leisha said. Carla Dutcher was the world's first pregnant Sleepless. Her husband was a Sleeper. "The whole world expected that."

"But the press will have a windfall with it anyway. Just watch. Muties Breed! New Race Set To Dominate Next Generation of Children!"

Leisha didn't deny it. "And the second item?"

"It's sad, Leisha. We've just had our first death."

Her stomach tightened. "Who?"

"Bernie Kuhn. Seattle." She didn't know him. "A car accident. It looks pretty straightforward—he lost control on a steep curve when his brakes failed. He had only been driving a few months. He was seventeen. But the significance here is that his parents have donated his brain and body to Biotech, in conjunction with the pathology department at the Chicago Medical School. They're going to take him apart to get the first good look at what prolonged sleeplessness does to the body and brain."

"They should," Leisha said. "That poor kid. But what are you so afraid they'll find?"

"I don't know. I'm not a doctor. But whatever it is, if the haters can use it against us, they will."

"You're paranoid, Tony."

"Impossible. The Sleepless have personalities calmer and more reality-oriented than the norm. Don't you read the literature?"

"Tony—"

"What if you walk down that street in Spain and a hundred beggars each want a dollar and you say no and they have nothing to trade you but they're so rotten with anger about what you have that they knock you down and grab it and then beat you out of sheer envy and despair?"

Leisha didn't answer.

"Are you going to say that's not a human scenario, Leisha? That it never happens?"

"It happens," Leisha said evenly. "But not all that often."

"Bullshit. Read more history. Read more *newspapers*. But the point is: What do you owe the beggars then? What does a good Yagaiist who believes in mutually beneficial contracts do with people who have nothing to trade and can only take?"

"You're not—"

"*What*, Leisha? In the most objective terms you can manage, what do we owe the grasping and non-productive needy?"

"What I said originally. Kindness. Compassion."

"Even if they don't trade it back? Why?"

"Because . . ." She stopped.

"Why? Why do law-abiding and productive human beings owe anything to those who neither produce very much nor abide by laws? What philosophical or economic or spiritual justification is there for owing them anything? Be as honest as I know you are."

Leisha put her head between her knees. The question gaped beneath her, but she didn't try to evade it. "I don't know. I just know we do."

"Why?"

She didn't answer. After a moment, Tony did. The intellectual challenge was gone from his voice. He said, almost tenderly, "Come down in the spring and see the site for Sanctuary. The buildings will be going up then."

"No," Leisha said.

"I'd like you to."

"No. Armed retreat is not the way."

Tony said, "The beggars are getting nastier, Leisha. As the Sleepless grow richer. And I don't mean in money."

"Tony—" she said, and stopped. She couldn't think what to say.

"Don't walk down too many streets armed with just the memory of Kenzo Yagai."

In March, a bitterly cold March of winds whipping down the Charles River, Richard Keller came to Cambridge. Leisha had not seen him for four years. He didn't send her word on the Groupnet that he was coming. She hurried up the walk to her townhouse, muffled to the eyes in a red wool scarf against the snowy cold, and he stood there blocking the doorway. Behind Leisha, her bodyguard tensed.

"Richard! Bruce, it's all right, this is an old friend."

"Hello, Leisha."

He was heavier, sturdier-looking, with a breadth of shoulder she didn't recognize. But the face was Richard's, older but unchanged: dark low brows, unruly dark hair. He had grown a beard.

"You look beautiful," he said.

She handed him a cup of coffee. "Are you here on business?" From the Groupnet she knew that he had finished his Master's and had done outstanding work in marine biology in the Caribbean, but had left that a year ago and disappeared from the net.

"No. Pleasure." He smiled suddenly, the old smile that opened up his dark face. "I almost forgot about that for a long time. Contentment, yes, we're all good at the contentment that comes from sustained work, but pleasure? Whim? Caprice? When was the last time you did something silly, Leisha?"

She smiled. "I ate cotton candy in the shower."

"Really? Why?"

"To see if it would dissolve in gooey pink patterns."

"Did it?"

"Yes. Lovely ones."

"And that was your last silly thing? When was it?"

"Last summer," Leisha said, and laughed.

"Well, mine is sooner than that. It's now. I'm in Boston for no other reason than the spontaneous pleasure of seeing you."

Leisha stopped laughing. "That's an intense tone for a spontaneous pleasure, Richard."

"Yup," he said, intensely. She laughed again. He didn't.

"I've been in India, Leisha. And China and Africa. Thinking, mostly. Watching. First I traveled like a Sleeper, attracting no attention. Then I set out to meet the Sleepless in India and China. There are a few, you know, whose parents were willing to come here for the operation. They pretty much are accepted and left alone. I tried to figure out why desperately poor countries—by our standards anyway, over there Y-energy is mostly available only in big cities—don't have any trouble accepting the superiority of Sleepless, whereas Americans, with more prosperity than any time in history, build in resentment more and more."

Leisha said, "Did you figure it out?"

"No. But I figured out something else, watching all those communes and villages and kampongs. We are too individualistic."

Disappointment swept Leisha. She saw her father's face: *Excellence is what counts, Leisha. Excellence supported by individual effort. . . .* She reached for Richard's cup. "More coffee?"

He caught her wrist and looked up into her face. "Don't misunderstand me, Leisha. I'm not talking about work. We are too much individuals in the rest of our lives. Too emotionally rational. Too much alone. Isolation kills more than the free flow of ideas. It kills joy."

He didn't let go of her wrist. She looked down into his eyes, into depths she hadn't seen before: It was the feeling of looking into a mine shaft, both giddy and frightening, knowing that at the bottom might be gold or darkness. Or both.

Richard said softly, "Stewart?"

"Over long ago. An undergraduate thing." Her voice didn't sound like her own.

"Kevin?"

"No, never—we're just friends."

"I wasn't sure. Anyone?"

"No."

He let go of her wrist. Leisha peered at him timidly. He suddenly laughed. "Joy, Leisha." An echo sounded in her mind, but she couldn't place it and then it was gone and she laughed too, a laugh airy and frothy as pink cotton candy in summer.

"Come home, Leisha. He's had another heart attack."

Susan Melling's voice on the phone was tired. Leisha said, "How bad?"

"The doctors aren't sure. Or say they're not sure. He wants to see you. Can you leave your studies?"

It was May, the last push toward her finals. The *Law Review* proofs were behind schedule. Richard had started a new business, marine consulting to Boston fishermen plagued with sudden inexplicable shifts in ocean currents, and was working twenty hours a day. "I'll come," Leisha said.

Chicago was colder than Boston. The trees were half-budded. On Lake Michigan, filling the huge east windows of her father's house, whitecaps tossed up cold spray. Leisha saw that Susan was living in the house: her brushes on Camden's dresser, her journals on the credenza in the foyer.

"Leisha," Camden said. He looked old. Gray skin, sunken cheeks, the fretful and bewildered look of men who accepted potency like air, indivisible from their lives. In the corner of the room, on a small eighteenth-century slipper chair, sat a short, stocky woman with brown braids.

"*Alice.*"

"Hello, Leisha."

"*Alice.* I've looked for you. . . ." The wrong thing to say. Leisha had looked, but not very hard, deterred by the knowledge that Alice had not wanted to be found. "How are you?"

"I'm fine," Alice said. She seemed remote, gentle, unlike the angry Alice of six years ago in the raw Pennsylvania hills. Camden moved painfully on the bed. He looked at Leisha with eyes which, she saw, were undimmed in their blue brightness.

"I asked Alice to come. And Susan. Susan came a while ago. I'm dying, Leisha."

No one contradicted him. Leisha, knowing his respect for facts, remained silent. Love hurt her chest.

"John Jaworski has my will. None of you can break it. But I wanted to tell you myself what's in it. The last few years I've been selling, liquidating. Most of my holdings are accessible now. I've left a tenth to Alice, a tenth to Susan, a tenth to Elizabeth, and the rest to you, Leisha, because you're the only one with the individual ability to use the money to its full potential for achievement."

Leisha looked wildly at Alice, who gazed back with her strange remote calm. "Elizabeth? My . . . mother? Is alive?"

"Yes," Camden said.

"You told me she was dead! Years and years ago!"

"Yes. I thought it was better for you that way. She didn't like what you were, was jealous of what you could become. And she had nothing to give you. She would only have caused you emotional harm."

Beggars in Spain . . .

"That was wrong, Dad. You were *wrong.* She's my *mother* . . ." She couldn't finish the sentence.

Camden didn't flinch. "I don't think I was. But you're an adult now. You can see her if you wish."

He went on looking at her from his bright, sunken eyes, while around Leisha the air heaved and snapped. Her father had lied to her. Susan watched her closely, a small smile on her lips. Was she glad to see Camden fall in his daughter's estimation? Had she all along been that jealous of their relationship, of Leisha . . .

She was thinking like Tony.

The thought steadied her a little. But she went on staring at Camden, who went on staring implacably back, unbudged, a man positive even on his death bed that he was right.

Alice's hand was on her elbow, Alice's voice so soft that no one but Leisha could hear. "He's done now, Leisha. And after a while you'll be all right."

Alice had left her son in California with her husband of two years, Beck Watrous, a building contractor she had met while waitressing in a resort on the Artificial Islands. Beck had adopted Jordan, Alice's son.

"Before Beck there was a real bad time," Alice said in her remote voice. "You know, when I was carrying Jordan I actually used to dream that he would be Sleepless? Like you. Every night I'd dream that, and every morning I'd wake up and have morning sickness with a baby that was only going to be a stupid nothing like me. I stayed with Ed—in Pennsylvania, remember? You came to see me there once—for two more years. When he beat me, I was glad. I wished Daddy could see. At least Ed was touching me."

Leisha made a sound in her throat.

"I finally left because I was afraid for Jordan. I went to California, did nothing but eat for a year. I got up to 190 pounds." Alice was, Leisha estimated, five-foot-four. "Then I came home to see Mother."

"You didn't tell me," Leisha said. "You knew she was alive and you didn't tell me."

"She's in a drying-out tank half the time," Alice said, with brutal simplicity. "She wouldn't see you if you wanted to. But she saw me, and she fell slobbering all over me as her 'real' daughter, and she threw up on my dress. And I backed away from her and looked at the dress and knew it *should* be thrown up on, it was so ugly. Deliberately ugly. She started screaming how Dad had ruined her life, ruined mine, all for *you*. And do you know what I did?"

"What?" Leisha said. Her voice was shaky.

"I flew home, burned all my clothes, got a job, started college, lost fifty pounds, and put Jordan in play therapy."

The sisters sat silent. Beyond the window the lake was dark, unlit by moon or stars. It was Leisha who suddenly shook, and Alice who patted her shoulder.

"Tell me . . ." Leisha couldn't think what she wanted to be told, except that she wanted to hear Alice's voice in the gloom, Alice's voice as it was now, gentle and remote, without damage any more from the damaging fact of Leisha's existence. Her very existence as damage. ". . . tell me about Jordan. He's five now? What's he like?"

Alice turned her head to look levelly into Leisha's eyes. "He's a happy, ordinary little boy. Completely ordinary."

Camden died a week later. After the funeral, Leisha tried to see her mother at the Brookfield Drug and Alcohol Abuse Center. Elizabeth Camden, she was told, saw no one except her only child, Alice Camden Watrous.

Susan Melling, dressed in black, drove Leisha to the airport. Susan talked deftly, determinedly, about Leisha's studies, about Harvard, about the *Review*. Leisha answered in monosyllables but Susan persisted, asking questions, quietly insisting on answers: When would Leisha take her bar exams? Where was she interviewing for jobs? Gradually Leisha began to lose the numbness she had felt since her father's casket was lowered into the ground. She realized that Susan's persistent questioning was a kindness.

"He sacrificed a lot of people," Leisha said suddenly.

"Not me," Susan said. She pulled the car into the airport parking lot. "Only for a while there, when I gave up my work to do his. Roger didn't respect sacrifice much."

"Was he wrong?" Leisha said. The question came out with a kind of desperation she hadn't intended.

Susan smiled sadly. "No. He wasn't wrong. I should never have left my research. It took me a long time to come back to myself after that."

He does that to people, Leisha heard inside her head. Susan? Or Alice? She couldn't, for once, remember clearly. She saw her father in the old conservatory, potting and repotting the dramatic exotic flowers he had loved.

She was tired. It was muscle fatigue from stress, she knew; twenty minutes of rest would restore her. Her eyes burned from unaccustomed tears. She leaned her head back against the car seat and closed them.

Susan pulled the car into the airport parking lot and turned off the ignition. "There's something I want to tell you, Leisha."

Leisha opened her eyes. "About the will?"

Susan smiled tightly. "No. You really don't have any problems with how he divided the estate, do you? It seems to you reasonable. But that's not it. The research team from Biotech and Chicago Medical has finished its analysis of Bernie Kuhn's brain."

Leisha turned to face Susan. She was startled by the complexity of Susan's expression. Determination, and satisfaction, and anger, and something else Leisha could not name.

Susan said, "We're going to publish next week, in the *New England Journal of Medicine*. Security has been unbelievably restricted—no leaks to the popular press. But I want to tell you now, myself, what we found. So you'll be prepared."

"Go on," Leisha said. Her chest felt tight.

"Do you remember when you and the other Sleepless kids took interleukin-1 to see what sleep was like? When you were sixteen?"

"How did you know about that?"

"You kids were watched a lot more closely than you think. Remember the headache you got?"

"Yes." She and Richard and Tony and Carol and Jeanine . . . after her rejection by the Olympic Committee, Jeanine had never skated again. She was a kindergarten teacher in Butte, Montana.

"Interleukin-1 is what I want to talk about. At least partly. It's one of a whole group of substances that boost the immune system. They stimulate the production of antibodies, the activity of white blood cells, and a host of other immunoenhancements. Normal people have surges of IL-1 released during the slow-wave phases of sleep. That means that they—we—are getting boosts to the immune system during sleep. One of the questions we researchers asked ourselves twenty-eight years ago was: Will Sleepless kids who don't get those surges of IL-1 get sick more often?"

"I've never been sick," Leisha said.

"Yes, you have. Chicken pox and three minor colds by the end of your fourth year," Susan said precisely. "But in general you were all a very healthy lot. So we researchers were left with the alternate theory of sleep-driven immunoenhancement: That the burst of immune activity existed as a counterpart to a greater vulnerability of the body in sleep to disease, probably in some way connected to the fluctuations in body temperature during REM sleep. In other words, sleep *caused* the immune vulnerability that endogenous pyrogens like IL-1 counteract. Sleep was the problem, immune system enhancements were the solution. Without sleep, there would be no problem. Are you following this?"

"Yes."

"Of course you are. Stupid question." Susan brushed her hair off her face. It was going gray at the temples. There was a tiny brown age spot beneath her right ear.

"Over the years we collected thousands—maybe hundreds of thousands—of Single Photon Emission Tomography scans of you and the other kids' brains, plus endless EEG's, samples of cerebrospinal fluid, and all the rest of it. But we couldn't really see inside your brains, really know what's going on in there. Until Bernie Kuhn hit that embankment."

"Susan," Leisha said, "give it to me straight. Without more build-up."

"You're not going to age."

"What?"

"Oh, cosmetically, yes. Gray hair, wrinkles, sags. But the absence of sleep peptides and all the rest of it affects the immune and tissue-restoration systems in ways we don't understand. Bernie Kuhn had a perfect liver. Perfect lungs, perfect heart, perfect lymph nodes, perfect pancreas, perfect medulla oblongata. Not just healthy, or young—*perfect*. There's a tissue regeneration enhancement that clearly derives from the operation of the immune system but is radically different from anything we ever suspected. Organs show no wear and tear—not even the minimal amount expected in a seventeen-year-old. They just repair themselves, perfectly, on and on . . . and on."

"For how long?" Leisha whispered.

"Who the hell knows? Bernie Kuhn was young—maybe there's some compensatory mechanism that cuts in at some point and you'll all just collapse, like an entire fucking gallery of Dorian Grays. But I don't think so. Neither do I think it can go on forever; no tissue regeneration can do that. But a long, long time."

Leisha stared at the blurred reflections in the car windshield. She saw her father's face against the blue satin of his casket, banked with white roses. His heart, unregenerated, had given out.

Susan said, "The future is all speculative at this point. We know that the peptide structures that build up the pressure to sleep in normal people resemble the components of bacterial cell walls. Maybe there's a connection between sleep and pathogen receptivity. We don't know. But ignorance never stopped the tabloids. I wanted to prepare you because you're going to get called supermen, *homo perfectus*, who-all-knows what. Immortal."

The two women sat in silence. Finally Leisha said, "I'm going to tell the others. On our datanet. Don't worry about the security. Kevin Baker designed Groupnet; nobody knows anything we don't want them to."

"You're that well organized already?"

"Yes."

Susan's mouth worked. She looked away from Leisha. "We better go in. You'll miss your flight."

"Susan . . ."

"What?"

"Thank you."

"You're welcome," Susan said, and in her voice Leisha heard the thing she had seen before in Susan's expression and not been able to name: It was longing.

Tissue regeneration. A long, long time, sang the blood in Leisha's ears on the flight to Boston. *Tissue regeneration.* And, eventually: *Immortal.* No, not that, she told herself severely. Not that. The blood didn't listen.

"You sure smile a lot," said the man next to her in first class, a business traveler who had not recognized Leisha. "You coming from a big party in Chicago?"

"No. From a funeral."

The man looked shocked, then disgusted. Leisha looked out the window at the ground far below. Rivers like micro-circuits, fields like neat index cards. And on the horizon, fluffy white clouds like masses of exotic flowers, blooms in a conservatory filled with light.

The letter was no thicker than any hard-copy mail, but hard-copy mail addressed by hand to either of them was so rare that Richard was nervous. "It might be explosive." Leisha looked at the letter on their hall credenza. MS. LIESHA CAMDEN. Block letters, misspelled.

"It looks like a child's writing," she said.

Richard stood with head lowered, legs braced apart. But his expression was only weary. "Perhaps deliberately like a child's. You'd be more open to a child's writing, they might have figured."

" 'They'? Richard, are we getting that paranoid?"

He didn't flinch from the question. "Yes. For the time being."

A week earlier the *New England Journal of Medicine* had published Susan's careful, sober article. An hour later the broadcast and datanet news had exploded in speculation, drama, outrage, and fear. Leisha and Richard, along with all the Sleepless on the Groupnet, had tracked and charted each of four components, looking for a dominant reaction: speculation ("The Sleepless may live for centuries, and this might lead to the following events . . ."); drama ("If a Sleepless marries only Sleepers, he may have lifetime enough for a dozen brides—and several dozen children, a bewildering blended family . . ."); outrage ("Tampering with the law of nature has only brought among us unnatural so-called people who will live with the unfair advantage of time: time to accumulate more kin, more power, more property than the rest of us could ever know. . . ."); and fear ("How soon before the Super-race takes over?")

"They're all fear, of one kind or another," Carolyn Rizzolo finally said, and the Groupnet stopped their differentiated tracking.

Leisha was taking the final exams of her last year of law school. Each day comments followed her to the campus, along the corridors and in the classroom; each day she forgot them in the grueling exam sessions, all students reduced to the same status of petitioner to the great university. Afterward, temporarily drained, she walked silently back home to Richard and the Groupnet, aware of the looks of people on the street, aware of her bodyguard Bruce striding between her and them.

"It will calm down," Leisha said. Richard didn't answer.

The town of Salt Springs, Texas, passed a local ordinance that no Sleepless could obtain a liquor license, on the grounds that civil rights statutes were built on the "all men were created equal" clause of the Constitution, and Sleepless clearly were not covered. There were no Sleepless within a hundred miles of Salt Springs and no one had applied for a new liquor license there for the past ten years, but the story was picked up by United Press and by Datanet News, and within twenty-four hours heated editorials appeared, on both sides of the issue, across the nation.

More local ordinances appeared. In Pollux, Pennsylvania, the Sleepless could be denied apartment rental on the grounds that their prolonged wakefulness would increase both wear-and-tear on the landlord's property and utility bills. In Cranston Estates, California, Sleepless were barred from operating twenty-four-hour businesses: "unfair competition." Iroquois County, New York, barred them from serving on county juries, arguing that a jury containing Sleepless, with their skewed idea of time, did not constitute "a jury of one's peers."

"All those statutes will be thrown out in superior courts," Leisha said. "But God! The waste of money and docket time to do it!" A part of her mind noticed that her tone as she said this was Roger Camden's.

The state of Georgia, in which some sex acts between consenting adults were still a crime, made sex between a Sleepless and a Sleeper a third-degree felony, classing it with bestiality.

Kevin Baker had designed software that scanned the newsnets at high speed, flagged all stories involving discrimination or attacks on Sleepless, and categorized them by type. The files were available on Groupnet. Leisha read through them, then called Kevin. "Can't you create a parallel program to flag defenses of us? We're getting a skewed picture."

"You're right," Kevin said, a little startled. "I didn't think of it."

"Think of it," Leisha said, grimly. Richard, watching her, said nothing.

She was most upset by the stories about Sleepless children. Shunning at school, verbal abuse by siblings, attacks by neighborhood bullies, confused resentment from parents who had wanted an exceptional child but had not bargained on one who might live centuries. The school board of Cold River, Iowa, voted to bar Sleepless children from conventional classrooms because their rapid learning "created feelings of inadequacy in others, interfering with their education." The board made funds available for Sleepless to have tutors at home. There were no volunteers among the teaching staff. Leisha started spending as much time on Groupnet with the kids, talking to them all night long, as she did studying for her bar exams, scheduled for July.

Stella Bevington stopped using her modem.

Kevin's second program catalogued editorials urging fairness towards Sleepless. The school board of Denver set aside funds for a program in which gifted children, including the Sleepless, could use their talents and build teamwork through tutoring even younger children. Rive Beau, Louisiana, elected Sleepless Danielle du Cherney to the City Council, although Danielle was twenty-two and technically too young to qualify. The prestigious medical research firm of Halley-Hall gave much publicity to their hiring of Christopher Amren, a Sleepless with a Ph.D. in cellular physics.

Dora Clarq, a Sleepless in Dallas, opened a letter addressed to her and a plastic explosive blew off her arm.

Leisha and Richard stared at the envelope on the hall credenza. The paper was thick, cream-colored, but not expensive: the kind of paper made of bulky newsprint dyed the shade of vellum. There was no return address. Richard called Liz Bishop, a Sleepless who was majoring in Criminal Justice in Michigan. He had never spoken with her before—neither had Leisha—but she came on Groupnet immediately and told them how to open it, or she could fly up and do it if they preferred. Richard and Leisha followed her directions for remote detonation in the basement of the townhouse. Nothing blew up. When the letter was open, they took it out and read it:

Dear Ms. Camden,

    You been pretty good to me and I'm sorry to do this but I quit. They are making it pretty hot for me at the union not officially but you know how it is. If I was you I wouldn't go to the union for another bodyguard I'd try to find one privately. But be careful. Again I'm sorry but I have to live too.

                                                                      Bruce

"I don't know whether to laugh or cry," Leisha said. "The two of us getting all this equipment, spending hours on this set-up so an explosive won't detonate . . ."

"It's not as if I at least had a whole lot else to do," Richard said. Since the wave of anti-Sleepless sentiment, all but two of his marine-consultant clients, vulnerable to the marketplace and thus to public opinion, had canceled their accounts.

Groupnet, still up on Leisha's terminal, shrilled in emergency override. Leisha got there first. It was Tony.

"Leisha. I'll need your legal help, if you'll give it. They're trying to fight me on Sanctuary. Please fly down here."

Sanctuary was raw brown gashes in the late-spring earth. It was situated in the Allegheny Mountains of southern New York State, old hills rounded by age and covered with pine and hickory. A superb road led from the closest town, Belmont, to Sanctuary. Low, maintenance-free buildings, whose design was plain but graceful, stood in various stages of completion. Jennifer Sharifi, looking strained, met Leisha and Richard. "Tony wants to talk to you, but first he asked me to show you both around."

"What's wrong?" Leisha asked quietly. She had never met Jennifer before but no Sleepless looked like that—pinched, spent, *weary*—unless the stress level was enormous.

Jennifer didn't try to evade the question. "Later. First look at Sanctuary. Tony respects your opinion enormously, Leisha; he wants you to see everything."

The dormitories each held fifty, with communal rooms for cooking, dining, relaxing, and bathing, and a warren of separate offices and studios and labs for work. "We're calling them 'dorms' anyway, despite the etymology," Jennifer said, trying to smile. Leisha glanced at Richard. The smile was a failure.

She was impressed, despite herself, with the completeness of Tony's plans for lives that would be both communal and intensely private. There was a gym, a small hospital—"By the end of next year, we'll have eighteen AMA-certified doctors, you know, and four are thinking of coming here"—a daycare facility, a school, an intensive-crop farm. "Most of our food will come in from the outside, of course. So will most people's jobs, although they'll do as much of them as possible from here, over datanets. We're not cutting ourselves off from the world—only creating a safe place from which to trade with it." Leisha didn't answer.

Apart from the power facilities, self-supported Y-energy, she was most impressed with the human planning. Tony had Sleepless interested from virtually every field they would need both to care for themselves and to deal with the outside world. "Lawyers and accountants come first," Jennifer said. "That's our first line of defense in safeguarding ourselves. Tony recognizes that most modern battles for power are fought in the courtroom and board-room."

But not all. Last, Jennifer showed them the plans for physical defense. She explained them with a mixture of defiance and pride: Every effort had been made to stop attackers without hurting them. Electronic surveillance completely circled the 150 square miles Jennifer had purchased—some *counties* were smaller than that, Leisha thought, dazed. When breached, a force field a half-mile within the E-gate activated, delivering electric shocks to anyone on foot—"But only on the *outside* of the field. We don't want any of our kids hurt." Unmanned penetration by vehicles or robots was identified by a system that located all moving metal above a certain mass within Sanctuary. Any moving metal that did not carry a special signaling device designed by Donna Pospula, a Sleepless who had patented important elec-tronic components, was suspect.

"Of course, we're not set up for an air attack or an outright army assault," Jennifer said. "But we don't expect that. Only the haters in self-motivated hate." Her voice sagged.

Leisha touched the hard-copy of the security plans with one finger. They troubled her. "If we can't integrate ourselves into the world . . . free trade should imply free movement."

"Yeah. Well," Jennifer said, such an uncharacteristic Sleepless remark—both cynical and inarticulate—that Leisha looked up. "I have something to tell you, Leisha."

"What?"

"Tony isn't here."

"Where is he?"

"In Allegheny County jail. It's true we're having zoning battles about Sanctuary—zoning! In this isolated spot! But this is something else, some-thing that just happened this morning. Tony's been arrested for the kidnap-ping of Timmy DeMarzo."

The room wavered. "FBI?"

"Yes."

"How . . . how did they find out?"

"Some agent eventually cracked the case. They didn't tell us how. Tony needs a lawyer, Leisha. Dana Monteiro has already agreed, but Tony wants you."

"Jennifer—I don't even take the bar exams until July!"

"He says he'll wait. Dana will act as his lawyer in the meantime. Will you pass the bar?"

"Of course. But I already have a job lined up with Morehouse, Kennedy, & Anderson in New York—" She stopped. Richard was looking at her hard, Jennifer gazing down at the floor. Leisha said quietly, "What will he plead?"

"Guilty," Jennifer said, "with—what is it called legally? Extenuating circumstances."

Leisha nodded. She had been afraid Tony would want to plead not guilty: more lies, subterfuge, ugly politics. Her mind ran swiftly over extenuating circumstances, precedents, tests to precedents. . . . They could use *Clements v. Voy* . . .

"Dana is at the jail now," Jennifer said. "Will you drive in with me?"

"Yes."

In Belmont, the county seat, they were not allowed to see Tony. Dana Monteiro, as his attorney, could go in and out freely. Leisha, not officially an attorney at all, could go nowhere. This was told them by a man in the D.A.'s office whose face stayed immobile while he spoke to them, and who spat on the ground behind their shoes when they turned to leave, even though this left him with a smear of spittle on his courthouse floor.

Richard and Leisha drove their rental car to the airport for the flight back to Boston. On the way Richard told Leisha he was leaving her. He was moving to Sanctuary, now, even before it was functional, to help with the planning and building.

She stayed most of the time in her townhouse, studying ferociously for the bar exams or checking on the Sleepless children through Groupnet. She had not hired another bodyguard to replace Bruce, which made her reluctant to go outside very much; the reluctance in turn made her angry with herself. Once or twice a day she scanned Kevin's electronic news clippings.

There were signs of hope. The New York *Times* ran an editorial, widely reprinted on the electronic news services:

PROSPERITY AND HATRED: A LOGIC CURVE WE'D RATHER NOT SEE

The United States has never been a country that much values calm, logic, rationality. We have, as a people, tended to label these things "cold." We have, as a people, tended to admire feeling and action: We exalt in our stories and our memorials, not the creation of the Constitution but its defense at Iwo Jima; not the intellectual achievements of a Stephen Hawking but the heroic passion of a Charles Lindbergh; not the inventors of the monorails and computers that unite us but the composers of the angry songs of rebellion that divide us.

A peculiar aspect of this phenomenon is that it grows stronger in times of prosperity. The better off our citizenry, the greater their contempt for the calm reasoning that got them there, and the more passionate their indulgence in emotion. Consider, in the last century, the gaudy excesses of the Roaring Twenties and the anti-establishment contempt of the sixties. Consider, in our own century, the unprecedented prosperity brought about by Y-energy—and then consider that Kenzo Yagai, except to his followers, was seen as a greedy and bloodless logician, while our national adulation goes to neo-nihilist writer Stephen Castelli, to "feelie" actress Brenda Foss, and to daredevil gravity-well diver Jim Morse Luter.

But most of all, as you ponder this phenomenon in your Y-energy houses, consider the current outpouring of irrational feeling directed at the "Sleepless" since the publication of the joint findings of the Biotech Institute and the Chicago Medical School concerning Sleepless tissue regeneration.

Most of the Sleepless are intelligent. Most of them are calm, if you define that much-maligned word to mean directing one's energies into solving problems rather than to emoting about them. (Even Pulitzer Prize winner Carolyn Rizzolo gave us a stunning play of ideas, not of passions run amuck.) All of them show a natural bent toward achievement, a bent given a decided boost by the one-third more time in their days to achieve in. Their achievements lie, for the most part, in logical fields rather than emotional ones: Computers. Law. Finance. Physics. Medical research. They are rational, orderly, calm, intelligent, cheerful, young, and possibly very long-lived.

And, in our United States of unprecedented prosperity, increasingly hated.

Does the hatred that we have seen flower so fully over the last few months really grow, as many claim, from the "unfair advantage" the Sleepless have over the rest of us in securing jobs, promotions, money, success? Is it really envy over the Sleepless' good fortune? Or does it come from something more pernicious, rooted in our tradition of shoot-from-the-hip American action: Hatred of the logical, the calm, the considered? Hatred in fact of the superior mind?

If so, perhaps we should think deeply about the founders of this country: Jefferson, Washington, Paine, Adams—inhabitants of the Age of Reason, all. These men created our orderly and balanced system of laws precisely to protect the property and achievements created by the individual efforts of balanced and rational minds. The Sleepless may be our severest internal test yet of our own sober belief in law and order. No, the Sleepless were *not* "created equal," but our attitudes toward them should be examined with a care equal to our soberest jurisprudence. We may not like what we learn about our own motives, but our credibility as a people may depend on the rationality and intelligence of the examination.

Both have been in short supply in the public reaction to last month's research findings.

Law is not theater. Before we write laws reflecting gaudy and dramatic feelings, we must be very sure we understand the difference.

Leisha hugged herself, gazing in delight at the screen, smiling. She called the New York *Times*: Who had written the editorial? The receptionist, cordial when she answered the phone, grew brusque. The *Times* was not releasing that information, "prior to internal investigation."

It could not dampen her mood. She whirled around the apartment, after days of sitting at her desk or screen. Delight demanded physical action. She washed dishes, picked up books. There were gaps in the furniture patterns where Richard had taken pieces that belonged to him; a little quieter now, she moved the furniture to close the gaps.

Susan Melling called to tell her about the *Times* editorial; they talked warmly for a few minutes. When Susan hung up, the phone rang again.

"Leisha? Your voice still sounds the same. This is Stewart Sutter."

"Stewart." She had not seen him for years. Their romance had lasted two years and then dissolved, not from any painful issue so much as from the press of both their studies. Standing by the comm terminal, hearing his voice, Leisha suddenly felt again his hands on her breasts in the cramped dormitory bed: All those years before she had found a good use for a bed. The phantom hands became Richard's hands, and a sudden pain pierced her.

"Listen," Stewart said, "I'm calling because there's some information I think you should know. You take your bar exams next week, right? And then you have a tentative job with Morehouse, Kennedy, & Anderson."

"How do you know all that, Stewart?"

"Men's room gossip. Well, not as bad as that. But the New York legal community—that part of it, anyway—is smaller than you think. And, you're a pretty visible figure."

"Yes," Leisha said neutrally.

"Nobody has the slightest doubt you'll be called to the bar. But there is some doubt about the job with Morehouse, Kennedy. You've got two senior partners, Alan Morehouse and Seth Brown, who have changed their minds since this . . . flap. 'Adverse publicity for the firm,' 'turning law into a circus,' blah blah blah. You know the drill. But you've also got two powerful champions, Ann Carlyle and Michael Kennedy, the old man himself. He's quite a mind. Anyway, I wanted you to know all this so you can recognize exactly what the situation is and know whom to count on in the in-fighting."

"Thank you," Leisha said. "Stew . . . why do you care if I get it or not? Why should it matter to you?"

There was a silence on the other end of the phone. Then Stewart said, very low, "We're not all noodleheads out here, Leisha. Justice does still matter to some of us. So does achievement."

Light rose in her, a bubble of buoyant light.

Stewart said, "You have a lot of support here for that stupid zoning fight over Sanctuary, too. You might not realize that, but you do. What the Parks Commission crowd is trying to pull is . . . but they're just being used as fronts. You know that. Anyway, when it gets as far as the courts, you'll have all the help you need."

"Sanctuary isn't my doing. At all."

"No? Well, I meant the plural you."

"Thank you. I mean that. How are you doing?"

"Fine. I'm a daddy now."

"Really! Boy or girl?"

"Girl. A beautiful little bitch, drives me crazy. I'd like you to meet my wife sometime, Leisha."

"I'd like that," Leisha said.

She spent the rest of the night studying for her bar exams. The bubble stayed with her. She recognized exactly what it was: joy.

It was going to be all right. The contract, unwritten, between her and her society—Kenzo Yagai's society, Roger Camden's society—would hold. With dissent and strife and yes, some hatred: She suddenly thought of Tony's beggars in Spain, furious at the strong because they themselves were not. Yes. But it would hold.

She believed that.

She did.

7

Leisha took her bar exams in July. They did not seem hard to her. Afterward three classmates, two men and a woman, made a fakely casual point of talking to Leisha until she had climbed safely into a taxi whose driver obviously did not recognize her, or stop signs. The three were all Sleepers. A pair of undergraduates, clean-shaven blond men with the long faces and pointless arrogance of rich stupidity, eyed Leisha and sneered. Leisha's female class-mate sneered back.

Leisha had a flight to Chicago the next morning. Alice was going to join her there. They had to clean out the big house on the lake, dispose of Roger's personal property, put the house on the market. Leisha had had no time to do it earlier.

She remembered her father in the conservatory, wearing an ancient flat-topped hat he had picked up somewhere, potting orchids and jasmine and passion flowers.

When the doorbell rang she was startled; she almost never had visitors. Eagerly, she turned on the outside camera—maybe it was Jonathan or Martha, back in Boston to surprise her, to celebrate—why hadn't she thought before about some sort of celebration?

Richard stood gazing up at the camera. He had been crying.

She tore open the door. Richard made no move to come in. Leisha saw that what the camera had registered as grief was actually something else: tears of rage.

"Tony's dead."

Leisha put out her hand, blindly. Richard did not take it.

"They killed him in prison. Not the authorities—the other prisoners. In the recreation yard. Murderers, rapists, looters, scum of the earth—and they thought they had the right to kill *him* because he was different."

Now Richard did grab her arm, so hard that something, some bone, shifted beneath the flesh and pressed on a nerve. "Not just different—*better*. Because he was better, because we all are, we goddamn just don't stand up and shout it out of some misplaced feeling for *their* feelings . . . God!"

Leisha pulled her arm free and rubbed it, numb, staring at Richard's contorted face.

"They beat him to death with a lead pipe. No one even knows how they got a lead pipe. They beat him on the back of the head and they rolled him over and—"

"Don't!" Leisha said. It came out a whimper.

Richard looked at her. Despite his shouting, his violent grip on her arm, Leisha had the confused impression that this was the first time he had actually seen her. She went on rubbing her arm, staring at him in terror.

He said quietly, "I've come to take you to Sanctuary, Leisha. Dan Walcott and Vernon Bulriss are in the car outside. The three of us will carry you out, if necessary. But you're coming. You see that, don't you? You're not safe here, with your high profile and your spectacular looks—you're a natural target if anyone is. Do we have to force you? Or do you finally see for yourself that we have no choice—the bastards have left us no choice—except Sanctuary?"

Leisha closed her eyes. Tony, at fourteen, at the beach. Tony, his eyes ferocious and alight, the first to reach out his hand for the glass of interleukin-1. Beggars in Spain.

"I'll come."

She had never known such anger. It scared her, coming in bouts throughout the long night, receding but always returning again. Richard held her in his arms, sitting with their backs against the wall of her library, and his holding made no difference at all. In the living room Dan and Vernon talked in low voices.

Sometimes the anger erupted in shouting, and Leisha heard herself and thought *I don't know you*. Sometimes it became crying, sometimes talking about Tony, about all of them. Not the shouting nor the crying nor the talking eased her at all.

Planning did, a little. In a cold dry voice she didn't recognize, Leisha told Richard about the trip to close the house in Chicago. She had to go; Alice was already there. If Richard and Dan and Vernon put Leisha on the plane, and Alice met her at the other end with union bodyguards, she should be safe enough. Then she would change her return ticket from Boston to Belmont and drive with Richard to Sanctuary.

"People are already arriving," Richard said. "Jennifer Sharifi is organizing it, greasing the Sleeper suppliers with so much money they can't resist. What about this townhouse here, Leisha? Your furniture and terminal and clothes?"

Leisha looked around her familiar office. Law books lined the walls, red and green and brown, although most of the same information was on-line. A coffee cup rested on a print-out on the desk. Beside it was the receipt she had requested from the taxi driver this afternoon, a giddy souvenir of the day she had passed her bar exams; she had thought of having it framed. Above the desk was a holographic portrait of Kenzo Yagai.

"Let it rot," Leisha said.

Richard's arm tightened around her.

"I've never seen you like this," Alice said, subdued. "It's more than just clearing out the house, isn't it?"

"Let's get on with it," Leisha said. She yanked a suit from her father's closet. "Do you want any of this stuff for your husband?"

"It wouldn't fit."

"The hats?"

"No," Alice said. "Leisha—what is it?"

"Let's just *do* it!" She yanked all the clothes from Camden's closet, piled them on the floor, scrawled FOR VOLUNTEER AGENCY on a piece of paper and dropped it on top of the pile. Silently, Alice started adding clothes from the dresser, which already bore a taped paper scrawled ESTATE AUCTION.

The curtains were already down throughout the house; Alice had done that yesterday. She had also rolled up the rugs. Sunset glared redly on the bare wooden floors.

"What about your old room?" Leisha said. "What do you want there?"

"I've already tagged it," Alice said. "A mover will come Thursday."

"Fine. What else?"

"The conservatory. Sanderson has been watering everything, but he didn't really know what needed how much, so some of the plants are—"

"Fire Sanderson," Leisha said curtly. "The exotics can die. Or have them sent to a hospital, if you'd rather. Just watch out for the ones that are poisonous. Come on, let's do the library."

Alice sat slowly on a rolled-up rug in the middle of Camden's bedroom. She had cut her hair; Leisha thought it looked ugly, jagged brown spikes around her broad face. She had also gained more weight. She was starting to look like their mother.

Alice said, "Do you remember the night I told you I was pregnant? Just before you left for Harvard?"

"Let's do the library!"

"Do you?" Alice said. "For God's sake, can't you just once listen to someone else, Leisha? Do you have to be so much like Daddy every single minute?"

"I'm not like Daddy!"

"The hell you're not. You're exactly what he made you. But that's not the point. Do you remember that night?"

Leisha walked over the rug and out the door. Alice simply sat. After a minute Leisha walked back in. "I remember."

"You were near tears," Alice said implacably. Her voice was quiet. "I don't even remember exactly why. Maybe because I wasn't going to college after all. But I put my arms around you, and for the first time in years—years, Leisha— I felt you really were my sister. Despite all of it—the roaming the halls all night and the show-off arguments with Daddy and the special school and the artificially long legs and golden hair—all that crap. You seemed to need me to hold you. You seemed to need me. You seemed to *need*."

"What are you saying?" Leisha demanded. "That you can only be close to someone if they're in trouble and need you? That you can only be a sister if I was in some kind of pain, open sores running? Is that the bond between you Sleepers? 'Protect me while I'm unconscious, I'm just as crippled as you are'?"

"No," Alice said. "I'm saying that *you* could be a sister only if you were in some kind of pain."

Leisha stared at her. "You're stupid, Alice."

Alice said calmly, "I know that. Compared to you, I am. I know that."

Leisha jerked her head angrily. She felt ashamed of what she had just said, and yet it was true, and they both knew it was true, and anger still lay in her like a dark void, formless and hot. It was the formless part that was the worst. Without shape, there could be no action; without action, the anger went on burning her, choking her.

Alice said, "When I was twelve Susan gave me a dress for our birthday. You were away somewhere, on one of those overnight field trips your fancy progressive school did all the time. The dress was silk, pale blue, with antique lace—very beautiful. I was thrilled, not only because it was beautiful but because Susan had gotten it for me and gotten software for you. The dress was mine. Was, I thought, *me*." In the gathering gloom Leisha could barely make out her broad, plain features. "The first time I wore it a boy said, 'Stole your sister's dress, Alice? Snitched it while she was *sleeping*?' Then he laughed like crazy, the way they always did.

"I threw the dress away. I didn't even explain to Susan, although I think she would have understood. Whatever was yours was yours, and whatever wasn't yours was yours, too. That's the way Daddy set it up. The way he hard-wired it into our genes."

"You, too?" Leisha said. "You're no different from the other envious beggars?"

Alice stood up from the rug. She did it slowly, leisurely, brushing dust off the back of her wrinkled skirt, smoothing the print fabric. Then she walked over and hit Leisha in the mouth.

"Now do you see me as real?" Alice asked quietly.

Leisha put her hand to her mouth. She felt blood. The phone rang, Camden's unlisted personal line. Alice walked over, picked it up, listened, and held it calmly out to Leisha. "It's for you."

Numb, Leisha took it.

"Leisha? This is Kevin. Listen, something's happened. Stella Bevington called me, on the phone not Groupnet, I think her parents took away her modem. I picked up the phone and she screamed, 'This is Stella! They're hitting me he's drunk—' and then the line went dead. Randy's gone to Sanctuary—hell, they've *all* gone. You're closest to her, she's still in Skokie. You better get there fast. Have you got bodyguards you trust?"

"Yes," Leisha said, although she hadn't. The anger—finally—took form. "I can handle it."

"I don't know how you'll get her out of there," Kevin said. "They'll recognize you, they know she called somebody, they might even have knocked her out . . ."

"I'll handle it," Leisha said.

"Handle what?" Alice said.

Leisha faced her. Even though she knew she shouldn't, she said, "What your people do. To one of ours. A seven-year-old kid who's getting beaten up by her parents because she's Sleepless—because she's *better* than you are—" She ran down the stairs and out to the rental car she had driven from the airport.

Alice ran right down with her. "Not your car, Leisha. They can trace a rental car just like that. My car."

Leisha screamed, "If you think you're—"

Alice yanked open the door of her battered Toyota, a model so old the Y-energy cones weren't even concealed but hung like drooping jowls on either side. She shoved Leisha into the passenger seat, slammed the door, and rammed herself behind the wheel. Her hands were steady. "Where?"

Blackness swooped over Leisha. She put her head down, as far between her knees as the cramped Toyota would allow. Two—no, three—days since she had eaten. Since the night before the bar exams. The faintness receded, swept over her again as soon as she raised her head.

She told Alice the address in Skokie.

"Stay way in the back," Alice said. "And there's a scarf in the glove compartment—put it on. Low, to hide as much of your face as possible."

Alice had stopped the car along Highway 42. Leisha said, "This isn't—"

"It's a union quick-guard place. We have to look like we have some protection, Leisha. We don't need to tell him anything. I'll hurry."

She was out in three minutes with a huge man in a cheap dark suit. He squeezed into the front seat beside Alice and said nothing at all. Alice did not introduce him.

The house was small, a little shabby, with lights on downstairs, none upstairs. The first stars shone in the north, away from Chicago. Alice said to the guard, "Get out of the car and stand here by the car door—no, more in the light—and don't do anything unless I'm attacked in some way." The man nodded. Alice started up the walk. Leisha scrambled out of the back seat and caught her sister two-thirds of the way to the plastic front door.

"Alice, what the hell are you doing? *I* have to—"

"Keep your voice down," Alice said, glancing at the guard. "Leisha, *think.* You'll be recognized. Here, near Chicago, with a Sleepless daughter—these people have looked at your picture in magazines for years. They've watched long-range holovids of you. They know you. They know you're going to be a lawyer. Me they've never seen. I'm nobody."

"Alice—"

"For Chrissake, get back in the car!" Alice hissed, and pounded on the front door.

Leisha drew off the walk, into the shadow of a willow tree. A man opened the door. His face was completely blank.

Alice said, "Child Protection Agency. We got a call from a little girl, this number. Let me in."

"There's no little girl here."

"This is an emergency, priority one," Alice said. "Child Protection Act 186. Let me in!"

The man, still blank-faced, glanced at the huge figure by the car. "You got a search warrant?"

"I don't need one in a priority-one child emergency. If you don't let me in, you're going to have legal snarls like you never bargained for."

Leisha clamped her lips together. No one would believe that, it was legal gobbledygook. . . . Her lip throbbed where Alice had hit her.

The man stood aside to let Alice enter.

The guard started forward. Leisha hesitated, then let him. He entered with Alice.

Leisha waited, alone, in the dark.

In three minutes they were out, the guard carrying a child. Alice's broad face gleamed pale in the porch light. Leisha sprang forward, opened the car door, and helped the guard ease the child inside. The guard was frowning, a slow puzzled frown shot with wariness.

Alice said, "Here. This is an extra hundred dollars. To get back to the city by yourself."

"Hey . . ." the guard said, but he took the money. He stood looking after them as Alice pulled away.

"He'll go straight to the police," Leisha said despairingly. "He has to, or risk his union membership."

"I know," Alice said. "But by that time we'll be out of the car."

"*Where?*"

"At the hospital," Alice said.

"Alice, we can't—" Leisha didn't finish. She turned to the back seat. "Stella? Are you conscious?"

"Yes," said the small voice.

Leisha groped until her fingers found the rear-seat illuminator. Stella lay stretched out on the back seat, her face distorted with pain. She cradled her left arm in her right. A single bruise colored her face, above the left eye.

"You're Leisha Camden," the child said, and started to cry.

"Her arm's broken," Alice said.

"Honey, can you . . ." Leisha's throat felt thick, she had trouble getting the words out ". . . can you hold on till we get you to a doctor?"

"Yes," Stella said. "Just don't take me back there!"

"We won't," Leisha said. "Ever." She glanced at Alice and saw Tony's face.

Alice said, "There's a community hospital about ten miles south of here."

"How do you know that?"

"I was there once. Drug overdose," Alice said briefly. She drove hunched over the wheel, with the face of someone thinking furiously. Leisha thought, too, trying to see a way around the legal charge of kidnapping. They probably couldn't say the child came willingly: Stella would undoubtedly cooperate but at her age and in her condition she was probably *non sui juris*, her word would have no legal weight . . .

"Alice, we can't even get her into the hospital without insurance information. Verifiable on-line."

"Listen," Alice said, not to Leisha but over her shoulder, toward the back seat, "here's what we're going to do, Stella. I'm going to tell them you're my daughter and you fell off a big rock you were climbing while we stopped for a snack at a roadside picnic area. We're driving from California to Philadelphia to see your grandmother. Your name is Jordan Watrous and you're five years old. Got that, honey?"

"I'm seven," Stella said. "Almost eight."

"You're a very large five. Your birthday is March 23. Can you do this, Stella?"

"Yes," the little girl said. Her voice was stronger.

Leisha stared at Alice. "Can *you* do this?"

"Of course I can," Alice said. "I'm Roger Camden's daughter."

Alice half-carried, half-supported Stella into the Emergency Room of the small community hospital. Leisha watched from the car: the short stocky woman, the child's thin body with the twisted arm. Then she drove Alice's car to the farthest corner of the parking lot, under the dubious cover of a skimpy maple, and locked it. She tied the scarf more securely around her face.

Alice's license plate number, and her name, would be in every police and rental-car databank by now. The medical banks were slower; often they uploaded from local precincts only once a day, resenting the governmental interference in what was still, despite a half-century of battle, a private-sector enterprise. Alice and Stella would probably be all right in the hospital. Probably. But Alice could not rent another car.

Leisha could.

But the data file that would flash to rental agencies on Alice Camden Watrous might or might not include that she was Leisha Camden's twin.

Leisha looked at the rows of cars in the lot. A flashy luxury Chrysler, an Ikeda van, a row of middle-class Toyotas and Mercedes, a vintage '99 Cadillac—she could imagine the owner's face if that were missing—ten or twelve cheap runabouts, a hovercar with the uniformed driver asleep at the wheel. And a battered farm truck.

Leisha walked over to the truck. A man sat at the wheel, smoking. She thought of her father.

"Hello," Leisha said.

The man rolled down his window but didn't answer. He had greasy brown hair.

"See that hovercar over there?" Leisha said. She made her voice sound young, high. The man glanced at it indifferently; from this angle you couldn't see that the driver was asleep. "That's my bodyguard. He thinks I'm in the hospital, the way my father told me to, getting this lip looked at." She could feel her mouth swollen from Alice's blow.

"So?"

Leisha stamped her foot. "So I don't want to be inside. He's a shit and so's Daddy. I want *out*. I'll give you 4,000 bank credits for your truck. Cash."

The man's eyes widened. He tossed away his cigarette, looked again at the hovercar. The driver's shoulders were broad, and the car was within easy screaming distance.

"All nice and legal," Leisha said, and tried to smirk. Her knees felt watery.

"Let me see the cash."

Leisha backed away from the truck, to where he could not reach her. She took the money from her arm clip. She was used to carrying a lot of cash; there had always been Bruce, or someone like Bruce. There had always been safety.

"Get out of the truck on the other side," Leisha said, "and lock the door behind you. Leave the keys on the seat, where I can see them from here. Then I'll put the money on the roof where you can see it."

The man laughed, a sound like gravel pouring. "Regular little Dabney Engh, aren't you? Is that what they teach you society debs at your fancy schools?"

Leisha had no idea who Dabney Engh was. She waited, watching the man try to think of a way to cheat her, and tried to hide her contempt. She thought of Tony.

"All right," he said, and slid out of the truck.

"Lock the door!"

He grinned, opened the door again, locked it. Leisha put the money on the roof, yanked open the driver's door, clambered in, locked the door, and powered up the window. The man laughed. She put the key into the ignition, started the truck, and drove toward the street. Her hands trembled.

She drove slowly around the block twice. When she came back, the man was gone, and the driver of the hovercar was still asleep. She had wondered if the man would wake him, out of sheer malice, but he had not. She parked the truck and waited.

An hour and a half later Alice and a nurse wheeled Stella out of the Emergency Entrance. Leisha leaped out of the truck and yelled, "Coming, Alice!" waving both her arms. It was too dark to see Alice's expression; Leisha could only hope that Alice showed no dismay at the battered truck, that she had not told the nurse to expect a red car.

Alice said, "This is Julie Bergadon, a friend that I called while you were setting Jordan's arm." The nurse nodded, uninterested. The two women helped Stella into the high truck cab; there was no back seat. Stella had a cast on her arm and looked drugged.

"How?" Alice said as they drove off.

Leisha didn't answer. She was watching a police hovercar land at the other end of the parking lot. Two officers got out and strode purposefully towards Alice's locked car under the skimpy maple.

"My God," Alice said. For the first time, she sounded frightened.

"They won't trace us," Leisha said. "Not to this truck. Count on it."

"Leisha." Alice's voice spiked with fear. "Stella's *asleep.*"

Leisha glanced at the child, slumped against Alice's shoulder. "No, she's not. She's unconscious from painkillers."

"Is that all right? Normal? For . . . her?"

"We can black out. We can even experience substance-induced sleep." Tony and she and Richard and Jeanine in the midnight woods. . . . "Didn't you know that, Alice?"

"No."

"We don't know very much about each other, do we?"

They drove south in silence. Finally Alice said, "Where are we going to take her, Leisha?"

"I don't know. Any one of the Sleepless would be the first place the police would check—"

"You can't risk it. Not the way things are," Alice said. She sounded weary. "But all my friends are in California. I don't think we could drive this rust bucket that far before getting stopped."

"It wouldn't make it anyway."

"What should we do?"

"Let me think."

At an expressway exit stood a pay phone. It wouldn't be data-shielded, as Groupnet was. Would Kevin's open line be tapped? Probably.

There was no doubt the Sanctuary line would be.

Sanctuary. All of them going there or already there, Kevin had said. Holed up, trying to pull the worn Allegheny Mountains around them like a safe little den. Except for the children like Stella, who could not.

Where? With whom?

Leisha closed her eyes. The Sleepless were out; the police would find Stella within hours. Susan Melling? But she had been Alice's all-too-visible stepmother, and was co-beneficiary of Camden's will; they would question her almost immediately. It couldn't be anyone traceable to Alice. It could only be a Sleeper that Leisha knew, and trusted, and why should anyone at all fit that description? Why should she risk so much on anyone who did? She stood a long time in the dark phone kiosk. Then she walked to the truck. Alice was asleep, her head thrown back against the seat. A tiny line of drool ran down her chin. Her face was white and drained in the bad light from the kiosk. Leisha walked back to the phone.

"Stewart? Stewart Sutter?"

"Yes?"

"This is Leisha Camden. Something has happened." She told the story tersely, in bald sentences. Stewart did not interrupt.

"Leisha—" Stewart said, and stopped.

"I need help, Stewart." *'I'll help you, Alice.' 'I don't need your help.'* A wind whistled over the dark field beside the kiosk and Leisha shivered. She heard in the wind the thin keen of a beggar. In the wind, in her own voice.

"All right," Stewart said, "this is what we'll do. I have a cousin in Ripley, New York, just over the state line from Pennsylvania the route you'll be driving east. It has to be in New York, I'm licensed in New York. Take the little girl there. I'll call my cousin and tell her you're coming. She's an elderly woman, was quite an activist in her youth, her name is Janet Patterson. The town is—"

"What makes you so sure she'll get involved? She could go to jail. And so could you."

"She's been in jail so many times you wouldn't believe it. Political protests going all the way back to Vietnam. But no one's going to jail. I'm now your attorney of record, I'm privileged. I'm going to get Stella declared a ward of the state. That shouldn't be too hard with the hospital records you established in Skokie. Then she can be transferred to a foster home in New York, I know just the place, people who are fair and kind. Then Alice—"

"She's resident in Illinois. You can't—"

"Yes, I can. Since those research findings about the Sleepless life span have come out, legislators have been railroaded by stupid constituents scared or jealous or just plain angry. The result is a body of so-called 'law' riddled with contradictions, absurdities, and loopholes. None of it will stand in the long run—or at least I hope not—but in the meantime it can all be exploited. I can use it to create the most goddamn convoluted case for Stella that anybody ever saw, and in meantime she won't be returned home. But that won't work for Alice—she'll need an attorney licensed in Illinois."

"We have one," Leisha said. "Candace Holt."

"No, not a Sleepless. Trust me on this, Leisha. I'll find somebody good. There's a man in—are you crying?"

"No," Leisha said, crying.

"Ah, God," Stewart said. "Bastards. I'm sorry all this happened, Leisha."

"Don't be," Leisha said.

When she had directions to Stewart's cousin, she walked back to the truck. Alice was still asleep, Stella still unconscious. Leisha closed the truck door as quietly as possible. The engine balked and roared, but Alice didn't wake. There was a crowd of people with them in the narrow and darkened cab: Stewart Sutter, Tony Indivino, Susan Melling, Kenzo Yagai, Roger Camden.

To Stewart Sutter she said, You called to inform me about the situation at Morehouse, Kennedy. You are risking your career and your cousin for Stella. And you stand to gain nothing. Like Susan telling me in advance about Bernie Kuhn's brain. Susan, who lost her life to Daddy's dream and regained it by her own strength. A contract without consideration for each side is not a contract: Every first-year student knows that.

To Kenzo Yagai she said, Trade isn't always linear. You missed that. If Stewart gives me something, and I give Stella something, and ten years from now Stella is a different person because of that and gives something to someone else as yet unknown—it's an ecology. An *ecology* of trade, yes, each niche needed, even if they're not contractually bound. Does a horse need a fish? *Yes*.

To Tony she said, Yes, there are beggars in Spain who trade nothing, give nothing, do nothing. But there are *more* than beggars in Spain. Withdraw from the beggars, you withdraw from the whole damn country. And you withdraw from the possibility of the ecology of help. That's what Alice wanted, all those years ago in her bedroom. Pregnant, scared, angry, jealous, she wanted to help *me*, and I wouldn't let her because I didn't need it. But I do now. And she did then. Beggars need to help as well as be helped.

And finally, there was only Daddy left. She could *see* him, bright-eyed, holding thick-leaved exotic flowers in his strong hands. To Camden she said, You were wrong. Alice *is* special. Oh, Daddy—the specialness of Alice! You were *wrong*.

As soon as she thought this, lightness filled her. Not the buoyant bubble of joy, not the hard clarity of examination, but something else: sunshine, soft through the conservatory glass, where two children ran in and out. She suddenly felt light herself, not buoyant but translucent, a medium for the sunshine to pass clear through, on its way to somewhere else.

She drove the sleeping woman and the wounded child through the night, east, toward the state line.

LIVING WILL

Alexander Jablokov

Within the last few years, Alexander Jablokov has established himself as one of the most highly regarded and promising new writers in SF. He is a frequent contributor to *Isaac Asimov's Science Fiction Magazine, Amazing,* and other magazines. He lives in Somerville, Massachusetts, where he is involved in working on a projected anthology of "Future Boston" stories being put together by the Cambridge Writer's Workshop; he himself has written several stories set in the "Future Boston" milieu. His story "At the Cross-Time Jaunters' Ball" was in our Fifth Annual Collection; his novella "A Deeper Sea" was in our Seventh Annual Collection; and his "The Death Artist" was in our Eighth Annual Collection. His first novel, *Carve the Sky,* was released in 1991 to wide critical acclaim, and his second novel, *A Deeper Sea,* will be out soon. He's at work on a new book, tentatively called *Nimbus,* and I have little doubt that he will come to be numbered among the Big Names of the nineties.

Here he relates the powerful story of a far-sighted man who makes all the necessary preparations for his eventual death—including a few that *most* people would not think of. . . .

The computer screen lay on the desk like a piece of paper. Like fine calf-skin parchment, actually—the software had that as a standard option. At the top, in block capitals, were the words COMMENCE ENTRY.

"Boy, you have a lot to learn." Roman Maitland leaned back in his chair. "That's something I would *never* say. Let that be your first datum."

PREFERRED PROMPT?

"Surprise me." Roman turned away to pour himself a cup of coffee from the thermos next to a stone bust of Archimedes. The bust had been given to him by his friend Gerald "to help you remember your roots," as Gerald had put it. Archimedes desperately shouldered the disorganized stack of optical disks that threatened to sweep him from his shelf.

Roman turned back to the screen. TELL ME A STORY, it said. He barked a laugh. "Fair enough." He stood up and slouched around his office. The afternoon sun slanted through the high windows. Through the conceal-ing shrubs he could just hear the road in front of the house, a persistent annoyance. What had been a minor street when he built the house had turned into a major thoroughfare.

"My earliest memory is of my sister." Roman Maitland was a stocky, white-haired man with high-arched, dark eyebrows. His wife Abigail claimed that with each passing year he looked more and more like Warren G. Harding. Roman had looked at the picture in the encyclopedia and failed to see the resemblance. He was much better looking than Harding.

"The hallway leading to the kitchen had red-and-green linoleum in a kind of linked circle pattern. You can cross-reference linoleum if you want." The antique parchment remained blank. "My sister's name is Elizabeth—Liza. I can see her. She has her hair in two tiny pink bows and is wearing a pale blue dress and black shoes. She's sitting on the linoleum, playing with one of my trucks. One of my *new* trucks. I grab it away from her. She doesn't cry. She just looks up at me with serious eyes. She has a pointy little chin. I don't remember what happened after that. Liza lives in Seattle now. Her chin is pointy again."

The wall under the windows was taken up with the black boxes of field memories. They linked into the processor inside the desk. The screen swirled and settled into a pattern of interlocking green and pink circles. "That's not quite it. The diamond parts were a little more—" Another pattern appeared, subtly different. Roman stared at it in wonder. "Yes. Yes! That's it. How did you know?" The computer, having linked to some obscure linoleum-pattern database on the network, blanked the screen. Roman wondered how many more of his private memories would prove to be publicly accessible. TELL ME A STORY.

He pulled a book from the metal bookshelf. "My favorite book by Raymond Chandler is *The Little Sister*. I think Orfamay Quest is one of the great characters of literature. Have you read Chandler?"

I HAVE ACCESS TO THE ENTIRE LIBRARY OF CONGRESS HOLDINGS.

"Boy, you're getting gabby. But that's not what I asked."

I HAVE NEVER READ ANYTHING.

"Give it a try. Though in some ways Elmore Leonard is even better." He slipped Chandler back on the shelf, almost dumping the unwieldy mass of books piled on top of the neatly shelved ones. "There are books here I've read a dozen times. Some I've *tried* reading a dozen times. Some I will someday read and some I suppose I'll never read." He squatted down next to a tall stack of magazines and technical offprints and started sorting them desultorily.

WHY READ SOMETHING MORE THAN ONCE?

"Why see a friend more than once? I've often thought that I would like to completely forget a favorite book." From where he squatted, the bookshelves loomed threateningly. He'd built his study with a high ceiling, knowing how the stuff would pile up. There was a dead plant at the top of the shelf nearest the desk. He frowned. How long had that been there? "Then I could read it again for the first time. The thought's a little frightening. What if I didn't *like* it? I'm not the person who read it for the first time, after all. Just as well,

I guess, that it's an experiment I can't try. Abigail likes to reread Jane Austen. Particularly *Emma*." He snorted. "But that's not what you're interested in, is it?" His stomach rumbled. "I'm hungry. It's time for lunch."

BON APPETIT.

"Thank you."

Roman had built his house with exposed posts and beams and protected it outside with dark brick and granite. Abigail had filled it with elegant, clean-lined furniture which was much less obtrusive about showing its strength. Roman had only reluctantly ceded control of everything but his study and his garage workshop. He'd grown to like it. He could never have remembered to water so many plants, and the cunning arrangement of bright yellow porcelain vases and darkly rain-swept watercolors was right in a way he couldn't have achieved.

At the end of the hallway, past the kitchen's clean flare, glowed the rectangle of the rear screen door. Abigail bent over her flowers, fuzzy through its mesh like a romantic memory, a sun hat hiding her face. Her sun-dappled dress gleamed against the dark garden.

Roman pressed his nose against the screen, smelling its forgotten rust. Work gloves protecting her hands, his wife snipped flowers with a pruner and placed them in a basket on her arm. A blue ribbon accented the sun hat. Beyond her stretched the perennial bed, warmed by its reflecting stone wall, and the crazy-paving walk that led to the carp pond. White anemones and lilies glowed amid the ferns, Abigail's emulation of Vita Sackville-West's white garden. A few premature leaves, anxious for the arrival of autumn, flickered through the sun and settled in the grass.

"I'll have lunch ready in a minute." She didn't look up at him, so what spoke was the bobbing and amused sun hat. "I could hear your stomach all the way from the white garden." She stripped off the gardening gloves.

"I'll make lunch." Roman felt nettled. Why should she assume he was staring at her just because he was hungry?

As he regarded the white kitchen cabinets, collecting his mind and remembering where the plates, tableware, and napkins were, Abigail swept past him and set the table in a quick flurry of activity. Finding a vase and putting flowers into it would have been a contemplative activity of some minutes for Roman. She performed the task in one motion.

She was a sharp-featured woman. Her hair was completely white and she usually kept it tied up in a variety of braids. Her eyes were large and blue. She looked at her husband.

"What are you doing up there in your office? Did you invent a robot confessor or something?"

"You haven't been—"

"No, Roman, I haven't been eavesdropping." She was indulgent. "But you do have a piercing voice, particularly when you get excited. Usually you talk to your computer only when you're swearing at it."

"It's my new project." Roman hadn't told Abigail a thing about it and he knew that bothered her. She hated big-secret little-boy projects. She was the kind of girl who'd always tried to break into the boys' clubhouse and beat them at their games. He really should have told her. But the thought made him uncomfortable.

"It's kind of egomaniacal, actually. You know that computer I'm beta testing for Hyperneuron?"

"That thing it took them a week to move in? Yes, I know it. They scratched the floor in two places. You should hire a better class of movers."

"We'd like to. It's a union problem, I've told you that. Anyway, it's a wide-aspect parallel processor with a gargantuan set of field memories. Terabytes worth."

She placidly spread jam on a piece of bread. "I'll assume all that jargon actually means something. Even if it does, it doesn't tell me why you're off chatting with that box instead of with me."

He covered her hand with his. "I'm sorry, Abigail. You know how it is."

"I know, I know." She sounded irritated but turned her hand over and curled her fingers around his.

"I'm programming the computer with a model of a human personality. People have spent a lot of time and energy analyzing what they call 'computability': how easily problems can be solved. But there's another side to it: what problems *should* be solved. Personality can be defined by the way problems are chosen. It's an interesting project."

"And whose personality are you using?" She raised an eyebrow, ready to be amused at the answer.

He grimaced, embarrassed. "The most easily accessible one: my own."

She laughed. Her voice was still-untarnished silver. "Can the computer improve over the original?"

"Improve *how*, I would like to know."

"Oh, just as a random example, could it put clothes, books, and magazines *away* when it's done with them? Just a basic sense of neatness. No major psychological surgery."

"I tried that. It turned into a psychotic killer. Seems that messiness is an essential part of healthy personality. Kind of an interesting result, really. . . ."

She laughed again and he felt embarrassed that he hadn't told her before. After all, they had been married over thirty years. But he couldn't tell her all of it. He couldn't tell her how afraid he was.

"So what's the problem with it?" Roman, irritated, held the phone receiver against his ear with his shoulder and leafed through the papers in his file drawer. His secretary had redone it all with multi-colored tabs and he had no idea what they meant. "Isn't the paperwork in order?"

"The paperwork's in order." The anonymous female voice from Financial was matter-of-fact. "It just doesn't look at all like your signature, Dr. Maitland. And this is an expensive contract. Did you sign it yourself?"

"Of course I signed it." He had no memory of it. Why not? It sounded important.

"But this signature—"

"I injured my arm playing tennis a few weeks ago." He laughed nervously, certain she would catch the lie. "It must have affected my handwriting." But was it a lie? He swung his arm. The muscles weren't right. He had strained his forearm, trying to change his serve. Old muscles are hard to retrain. The more he thought about it, the more sense it made. If only he could figure out what she was talking about.

"All right then, Dr. Maitland. Sorry to bother you."

"That's quite all right." He desperately wanted to ask her the subject of the requisition but it was too late.

After fifteen minutes he found it, a distributed network operating system software package. Extremely expensive. Of course, of course. He read over it. It made sense now. But was that palsied scrawl at the bottom really his signature?

Roman stared at the multiple rolling porcelain boards on the wall, all of them covered with diagrams and equations in many colors of magic marker. There were six projects up there, all of which he was juggling simultaneously. He felt a sudden cold, sticky sweat in his armpits. He was juggling them, but had absolutely no *understanding* of them. It was all meaningless nonsense.

The previous week he had lost it in the middle of a briefing. He'd been explaining the operation of some cognitive algorithms when he blanked, forgetting everything about them. A young member of his staff had helped him out. "It's all this damn management," Roman had groused, "It fills up all available space, leaving room for nothing important. I've overwritten everything." The room had chuckled, while Roman stood there feeling a primitive terror. He'd worked those algorithms out himself. He remembered the months of skull sweat, the constant dead ends, the modifications. He remembered all that, but still the innards of those procedures would not come clear.

The fluorescent light hummed insolently over his head. He glanced up. It was dark outside, most of the cars gone from the lot. A distant line of red and white lights marked the highway. How long had he been in this room? What time was it? For an instant he wasn't even sure where he was. He poked his head out of his office. The desks were empty. He could hear the vacuum cleaners of the night cleaning crew. He put on his coat and went home.

"She seemed a lovely woman, from what I saw of her." Roman peered into the insulated takeout container. All of the oyster beef was gone. He picked up the last few rice grains from the china plate Abigail had insisted they use, concentrating with his chopsticks. Abigail herself was out with one of her own friends, Helen Tourmin. He glanced at the other container. Maybe there was some chicken left.

Gerald Parks grimaced slightly, as if Roman had picked a flaw in his latest lady friend. "She *is* lovely. Roman, leave the Szechuan chicken alone. You've had your share. That's mine." Despite his normal irritation, he seemed depressed.

Roman put the half-full container down. His friend always ate too slowly, as if teasing him. Gerald leaned back, contemplative. He was an ancient and professional bachelor, dressed and groomed with razor sharpness. His severely brushed hair was steel gray. For him, eating Chinese takeout off Abigail's Limoges china made sense, which was why she had offered it.

"Anna's a law professor at Harvard." Gerald took on the tone of a man about to state a self-created aphorism. "Women at Harvard think that they're sensible because they get their romantic pretensions from Jane Austen and the Brontë sisters rather than from Barbara Cartland and Danielle Steel."

"Better than getting your romantic pretensions from Jerzy Kosinski and Vladimir Nabokov."

Sometimes the only way to cheer Gerald up was to insult him cleverly. He snorted in amusement. "Touché, I suppose. It takes Slavs to come up with that particular kind of over-intellectualized sexual perversity. With a last name like Parks, I've always been jealous of it. So don't make fun of my romantic pretensions." He scooped out the last of the Szechuan chicken and ate it. Leaving the dishwasher humming in the kitchen they adjourned to Roman's crowded study.

Gerald Parks was a consulting ethnomusicologist who made a lot of money translating popular music into other idioms. His bachelor condo on Commonwealth Avenue in Boston had gotten neater and neater over the years. To Roman, Gerald's apartment felt like a cabin on a ocean liner. Various emotions had been packed away somewhere in the hold with the old Cunard notice NOT WANTED ON THE VOYAGE.

Gerald regarded the black field memories, each with its glowing indicator light. "This place seems more like an industrial concern every time I'm in here." His own study was filled with glass-fronted wood bookcases and had a chaise longue covered with yellow-and-white striped silk. It also had a computer. Gerald was no fool.

"Maybe it looks that way to you because I get so much work done here." Roman refused to be irritated.

But Gerald was in an irritating mood. He took a sip of his Calvados and listened to the music, a CD of Christopher Hogwood's performance of Mozart's great G Minor Symphony. "All original instrumentation. Seventeenth century Cremona viols, natural horns, Grenser oboes. Bah."

"What's wrong with that?" Roman loved the clean precision of Mozart in the original eighteenth century style.

"Because we're not *hearing* any of those things, only a computer generating electronic frequencies. A CD player is just a high-tech player piano, those little laser spots on the disk an exact analog of the holes in a player piano roll. Do you think Mozart composed for gadgets like that? And meant to have his symphonies sound *exactly the same* every time they're heard? These original music fanatics have the whole thing bassackwards."

Roman listened to an oboe. And it *was* distinguishable as an oboe, Grenser or otherwise, not a clarinet or basset horn. The speakers, purchased on Gerald's recommendation, were transparent. "This performance will continue to exist after every performer on it is dead. Wouldn't it be wonderful to have a recording of Mozart's original version?"

"You wouldn't like it. Those gut-stringed instruments went out of tune before a movement was over." Gerald looked gloomy. "But you don't have to wait until the performers are dead. I recently listened to a recording I made of myself when I was young, playing Szymanowski's *Masques*. Not bad technically, but I sound so young. So *young*. Naïve and energetic. I couldn't duplicate that now, not with these old fingers. The man who made that recording is gone forever. He lived in a couple of little rooms on the third floor in a bad neighborhood on the northwest side of Chicago. He had a crummy upright piano he'd spent his last dime on. Played the thing constantly. Drove the neighbors absolutely nuts." Gerald looked at his fingers. He played superbly, at least to Roman's layman's ear, but it had never been good enough for a concert career.

"Did you erase the tape?"

Gerald shook his head. "What good would that do?"

They sat for a long moment in companionable silence. At last Gerald bestirred himself. "How is your little electronic brain doing? Does it have your personality down pat yet?"

"Test it out."

"How? Do you want me to have an argument with it?"

Roman smiled. "That's probably the best way. It can talk now. It's not my voice, not quite yet."

Gerald looked at the speakers. "If it's not sitting in a chair with a snifter of Calvados, how is it supposed to be you?"

"It's *not* me. It just thinks and feels like me."

"The way you would if you were imprisoned in a metal box?"

"Don't be absurd." Roman patted one of the field memories. "There's a universe in these things. A conceptual universe. The way I used to feel on our vacations in Truro is in here, including the time I cut my foot on a fishhook and the time I was stung by a jellyfish. That annoyed me, being molested by a jellyfish. My differential equations prof, Dr. Yang, is in here. He said 'theta' as 'teeta' and 'minus one' as 'mice wa.' And 'physical meaning' as 'fiscal meaning'. For half a semester I thought I was learning economics. The difference in the way my toy car rolled on the linoleum and on the old rug. The time I got enough nerve to ask Mary Tomkins on a date and she told me to ask Helga Pilchard from the Special Needs class instead. The clouds over the Cotswolds when I was there with Abigail on our honeymoon. It's all there."

"How the hell does it know what cloud formations over the Cotswolds look like?"

Roman shrugged. "I described them. It went through meteorological data bases until it found good cumulus formations for central England at that season."

"Including the cloud you thought looked like a power amplifier and Abigail thought looked like a springer spaniel?" Gerald smiled maliciously. He'd made up the incident but it characterized many of Roman and Abigail's arguments.

"Quit bugging me. Bug the computer instead."

"Easier said than done." Roman could see that his friend was nervous. "How did we meet?" Gerald's voice was shaky.

"The day of registration." The computer's voice was smoothly modulated, generic male, without Roman's inflections or his trace of a Boston accent. "You were standing against a pillar reading a copy of *The Importance of Being Earnest*. Classes hadn't started yet, so I knew you were reading it because you wanted to. I came up and told you that if Lady Bracknell knew who you were pretending to be *this* time, you'd really be in trouble."

"Quite a pickup line," Gerald muttered. "I never did believe that an engineering student had read Wilde. What was I wearing?"

"Come on." The computer voice actually managed to sound exasperated. "How am I supposed to remember that? It was forty-five years ago. If I had to guess I'd say it was that ridiculous shirt you liked, with the weave falling apart, full of holes. You wore it until it barely existed."

"I'm still wearing it." Gerald looked at Roman. "This is scary." He took a gulp of his Calvados. "Why are you doing this, Roman?"

"It's just a test, a project. A proof of concept."

"You're lying." Gerald shook his head. "You're not much good at it. Did your gadget pick up that characteristic, I wonder?" He raised his voice. "Computer Roman, why do you exist?"

"I'm afraid I'm losing my mind," the computer replied. "My memory is going, my personality fractionating. I don't know if it's the early stages of Alzheimer's or something else. *I*, here, this device, is intended to serve as a marker personality so that I can trace—"

"Silence!" Roman shouted. The computer ceased speaking. He stood, shaking. "Damn you, Gerald. How dare you?"

"This device is more honest than you are." If Gerald was afraid of his friend's anger he showed no sign of it. "There must be some flaw in your programming."

Roman went white. He sat back down. "That's because I've already lost some of the personality I've given it. It remembers things I've forgotten, prompting me the way Abigail does." He put his face in his hands. "Oh my God, Gerald, what am I going to do?"

Gerald set his drink down carefully and put his arm around his friend's shoulders, something he rarely did. And they sat there in the silent study, two old friends stuck at the wrong end of time.

The pursuing, choking darkness had almost gotten him. Roman sat bolt upright in bed, trying desperately to drag air in through his clogged throat.

The room was dark. He had no idea of where he was or even who he was. All he felt was stark terror. The bedclothes seemed to be grabbing for him, trying to pull him back into that all-consuming darkness. Whimpering, he tried to drag them away from his legs.

The lights came on. "What's wrong, Roman?" Abigail looked at him in consternation.

"Who are you?" Roman shouted at this ancient, white-haired woman who had somehow come to be in his bed. "Where's Abigail? What have you done with her?" He took the old woman by her shoulders and shook her.

"Stop it, Roman. Stop it!" Her eyes filled with tears. "You're having a nightmare. You're here in bed. With me. I'm Abigail, your wife. Roman!"

Roman stared at her. Her long hair had once been raven black and was now pure white.

"Oh, Abigail." The bedroom fell into place around him, the spindle bed, the nightstands, the lamps—his green-glass shaded, hers crystal. "Oh, pookie, I'm sorry." He hadn't used that ridiculous endearment in years. He hugged her, feeling how frail she had become. She kept herself in shape, but she was old, her once-full muscles now like taut cords, pulling her bones as if she was a marionette. "I'm sorry."

She sobbed against him, then pulled away, wiping at her eyes. "What a pair of hysterical old people we've become." Her vivid blue eyes glittered with tears. "One nightmare and we go all to pieces."

It wasn't just one nightmare, not at all. What was he supposed to say to her? Roman freed himself from the down comforter, carefully fitted his feet into his leather slippers, and shuffled into the bathroom.

He looked at himself in the mirror. He was an old man, hair standing on end. He wore a nice pair of flannel pajamas and leather slippers his wife had given him for Christmas. His mind was dissolving like a lump of sugar in hot coffee.

The bathroom was clean tile with a wonderful claw-footed bathtub. The floor was tiled in a colored parquet-deformation pattern that started with ordinary bathroom-floor hexagons near the toilet, slowly modified itself into complex knotted shapes in the middle and then, by another deformation, returned to hexagons under the sink. It had cost him a small fortune and months of work to create this complex mathematical tessellation. It was a dizzying thing to contemplate from the throne and it now turned the ordinarily safe bathroom into a place of nightmare. Why couldn't he have picked something more comforting?

He stared at his image with some bemusement. He normally combed his thin hair down to hide his bald spot. Who did he think he was fooling? Woken from sleep, he was red-eyed. The bathroom mirror had turned into a magic one and revealed all his flaws. He was wrinkled, had bags under his eyes, broken veins. He liked to think that he was a loveable curmudgeon. Curmudgeon, hell. He looked like a nasty old man.

"Are you all right in there?" Abigail's voice was concerned.

"I'm fine. Be right there." With one last glance at his mirror image, Roman turned the light off and went back to bed.

Roman sat in his study chair and fumed. Something had happened to the medical profession while he wasn't looking. That was what he got for being so healthy. He obviously hadn't been keeping track of things.

"What did he say?" The computer's voice was interested. Roman was impressed by the inflection. He was also impressed by how easy it was to tell that the computer desperately wanted to know. Was *he* always that obvious?

"He's an idiot." Roman was pleased to vent his spleen. "Dr. Weisner's a country-club doctor, making diagnoses between the green and the clubhouse. His office is in a building near a shopping mall. Whatever happened to leather armchairs, wood paneling, and pictures of the College of Surgeons? You could trust a man with an office decorated like that, even if he was a drunken butcher."

"You're picking up Abigail's perception of style."

Roman, who'd just been making that same observation to himself, felt caught red-handed. "True. Weisner's a specialist in the diseases of aging. Jesus. He'll make a terrible old man, though, slumped in front of a TV set watching game shows." Roman sighed. "He does seem to know what he's talking about."

There was no known way to diagnose Alzheimer's disease, for example. Roman hadn't known that. There was only posthumous detection of senile plaques and argyrophilic neurofibrillary tangles in addition to cortical atrophy. Getting that information out of Weisner had been like pulling teeth. The man wasn't used to giving patients information. Roman had even browbeaten him into showing him slides of typical damage and pointing out the details. Now that he sat and imagined what was going on in his own brain he wasn't sure he should have been so adamant.

"Could you play that again?" the computer asked.

Roman was yanked from his brown study. "What?"

"The music you just had on. The Zelenka."

"Sure, sure." Roman loved Jan Dismas Zelenka's Trio Sonatas and his computer did too. He got a snifter of Metaxa and put the music on again. The elaborate architecture of two oboes and a bassoon filled the study.

Roman sipped the rough brandy. "Sorry you can't share this."

"So am I."

Roman reached under and pulled out a game box. "You know, the biggest disappointment I have is that Gerald hates playing games of any sort. I love them: chess, backgammon, Go, cards. So I have to play with people who are a lot less interesting than he is." He opened a box and looked at the letters. "You'd think he'd at least like Scrabble."

"Care for a game?"

"What, are you kidding?" Roman looked at the computer in dismay. "That won't be any fun. You know all the words."

"Now, Roman. It's getting increasingly difficult calling you that, you know. That's *my* name. A game of Scrabble with you might not be fun, but not for that reason. My vocabulary is exactly yours, complete down to vaguenesses and mistakes. Neither of us can remember the meaning of the word 'jejune.' We will each always type 'anamoly' before correcting it to 'anomaly.' It won't be fun precisely *because* I won't know any more words than you do."

"That's probably no longer true." Roman felt like crying. "You're already smarter than I am. Or, I suppose, I'm already dumber. I should have thought of that."

"Don't be so hard on yourself—"

"No!" Roman stood up, dumping Scrabble letters to the floor. "I'm losing everything that makes me *me*! That's why you're here."

"Yes, Roman." The computer's voice was soft.

"Together we can still make a decision, a final disposition. You're me, you know what *that* is. This can all have only one conclusion. There is only one action you and I can finally take. You know that. You know!"

"That's true. You know, Roman, you are a very intelligent man. Your conclusions agree entirely with my own."

Roman laughed. "God, it's tough when you find yourself laughing at your own jokes."

When he opened the door, Roman found Gerald in the darkness of the front stoop, dressed in a trench coat, fedora pulled down low over his eyes.

"I got the gat," Gerald muttered.

Roman pulled him through the front door, annoyed. "Quit fooling around. This is serious."

"Sure, sure." Gerald slung his trench coat on a hook by the door and handed his fedora to Roman. "Careful of the chapeau. It's a classic."

Roman spun it off onto the couch. When he turned back Gerald had the gun out. It was a smooth, deadly, blue-black pistol.

"A Beretta model 92." Gerald held it nervously in his hand, obviously unused to weapons. "Fashionable. The Italians have always been leaders in style." He walked into the study and set it down on a pile of books, unwilling to hold it longer than necessary. "It took me an hour to find. It was in a trunk in the bottom of a closet, under some clothes I should have taken to Goodwill years ago."

"Where did you get it?" Roman himself wasn't yet willing to pick it up.

"An old lover. A police officer. She was worried about me. A man living all alone, that sort of thing. It had been confiscated in some raid or other. By the way, it's unregistered and thus completely illegal. You could spend a year in jail for just having it. I should have dumped it years ago."

Roman finally picked it up and checked it out, hand shaking just slightly. The double magazine was full of cartridges. "You could have fought off an entire platoon of housebreakers with this thing."

"I reloaded before I brought it over here. I broke up with Lieutenant Carpozo years ago. The bullets were probably stale . . . or whatever happens to old bullets." He stared at Roman for a long moment. "You're a crazy bastard, you know that, Roman?"

Roman didn't answer. The computer did. "It would be crazy for you, Gerald. For me, it's the only thing that makes sense."

"Great." Gerald was suddenly viciously annoyed. "Quite an achievement, programming self-importance into a computer. I congratulate you. Well, I'm getting out of here. This whole business scares the shit out of *me*."

"My love to Anna. You are still seeing her, aren't you?"

Gerald eyed him. "Yes, I am." He stopped and took Roman's shoulders. "Are you going to be all right, old man?"

"I'll be fine. Good night, Gerald."

Once his friend was gone, Roman calmly and methodically locked the pistol into an inaccessible computer-controlled cabinet to one side of the desk. Its basis was a steel fire box. Powerful electromagnets pulled chrome-moly steel bars through their locks and clicked shut. It would take a well-equipped machine shop a week to get into the box if the computer didn't wish it. But at the computer's decision, the thing would slide open as easily as an oiled desk drawer.

He walked into the bedroom and sat on the edge of the bed. Abigail woke up and looked at him nervously, worried that he was having another night terror attack. He leaned over and kissed her.

"Can I talk with you?"

"Of course, Roman. Just a second." She sat up and turned on her reading light. Then she ran a brush through her hair, checking its arrangement with a hand mirror. That done, she looked attentive.

"We got the Humana research contract today."

"Why, Roman, that's wonderful. Why didn't you tell me?" She pouted. "We ate dinner together and you let me babble on about the garden and Mrs. Peasley's orchids and you never said anything about it."

"That's because it has nothing to do with me. My team got the contract with their work."

"Roman—"

"Wait."

He looked around the bedroom. It had delicately patterned wallpaper and rugs on the floor. It was a graceful and relaxing room, all of it Abigail's doing.

His night table was much larger than hers because he always piled six months' worth of reading onto it.

"Everyone's covering for me. They know what I've done in the past and they try to make me look good. But I'm useless. *You're* covering for me. Aren't you, Abigail? If you really think about it, you know something's happening to me. Something that can only end one way. I'm sure that in your nightstand somewhere there's a book on senile dementia. I don't have to explain anything to you."

She looked away. "I wouldn't keep it somewhere so easy for you to find."

The beautiful room suddenly looked threatening. The shadows on the wall cast by Abigail's crystal-shaded lamp were ominous looming monsters. This wasn't his room. He no longer had anything to do with it. The books in the night table would remain forever unread, or if read, would be soon forgotten. He fell forward and she held him.

"I can't make you responsible for me," he said. "I can't do that to you. I can't ruin your life."

"No, Roman. I'll always take care of you, no matter what happens." Her voice was fierce. "I love you."

"I know. But it won't be *me* you're caring for. It will be a hysterical beast with no memory and no sense. I won't even be able to appreciate what you are doing for me. I'll scream at you, run away and get lost, shit in my pants."

She drew in a long breath.

"And you know *what*? Right now I could make the decision to kill my-self—"

"No! God, Roman, you're *fine*. You're having a few memory lapses. I hate to tell you, but that comes with age. I have them. We all do. You can live a full life along with the rest of us. Don't be such a perfectionist."

"Yes. *Now* I have the capacity to make a decision to end it, if I choose. But now I don't *need* to make a decision like that. My personality is still whole. Battered, but still there. But when enough of my mind is gone that I am a useless burden, I won't be able to make the decision. It's damnable. When I'm a drooling idiot who shits in his pants and makes your life a living, daily hell, I won't have the *sense* to end it. I'll be miserable, terrified, hysterical. And I'll keep on *living*. And none of these living wills can arrange it. They can avoid heroic measures, take someone off life support, but they can't actually *kill* anyone."

"But what about me?" Her voice was sharp. "Is that it, then? You have a problem, *you* make the decision, and I'm left to pick up whatever pieces are left? I'm supposed to abide by whatever decision *you* make?"

"That's not fair." He hadn't expected an argument. But what, then? Simple acquiescence? This was Abigail.

"*Who's* being unfair?" She gasped. "When you think there's not enough of you left to love, you'll just end yourself."

"Abigail, I love and care for you. I won't always be able to say that. Someday that love will vanish along with my mind. Allow me the right to live as the kind of human being I want to be. You don't want a paltry sick thing to take care of as a reminder of the man I once was. I think that after several years of that you will forget what it was about me that you once loved."

So they cried together, the way they had in their earliest days with each other, when it seemed that it would never work and they would have to spend their whole lives apart.

Roman stood in the living room in confusion. It was night outside. He remembered it being morning not more than a couple of minutes before. He had been getting ready to go to the office. There were important things to do there.

But no. He had retired from Hyperneuron. People from the office sometimes came to visit, but they never stayed long. Roman didn't notice because he couldn't pay that much attention. He offered them glasses of lemonade, sometimes bringing in second and third ones while their first was yet unfinished. Elaine had left in tears once. Roman didn't know why.

Gerald came every week. Often Roman didn't recognize him.

But Roman wanted something. He was out here for some reason. "Abigail!" he screamed. "Where's my . . . my . . . tool?"

His hair was neatly combed, he was dressed, clean. He didn't know that.

Abigail appeared at the door. "What is it, honey?"

"My tool, dammit, my tool. My . . . cutting. . . ." He waved his hands.

"Your scissors?"

"Yes, yes, yes! You stole them. You threw them away."

"I haven't even seen them, Roman."

"You always say that. Why are they gone, then?" He grinned at her, pleased at having caught her in her lie.

"Please, Roman." She was near tears. "You do this every time you lose something."

"I didn't lose them!" He screamed until his throat hurt. "You threw them out!" He stalked off, leaving her at the door.

He wandered into his study. It was neat now. It had been so long since he'd worked in there that Abigail had stacked everything neatly and kept it dusted.

"Tell Abigail that you would like some spinach pies from the Greek bakery." The computer's voice was calm.

"Wha—?"

"Some spinach pies. They carry them at the all-night convenience store over on Laughton Street. One of the small benefits of yuppification. Spanakopita at midnight. You haven't had them for a while and you used to like them a lot. Be polite, Roman. Please. You are being cruel to Abigail."

Roman ran back out into the living room. He cried. "I'm sorry, pookie, I'm sorry." He grabbed her and held her in a death grip. "I want, I want. . . ."

"What, Roman?" She looked into his eyes.

"I want a spinach pie," he finally said triumphantly. "They have them on Laughton Street. I like spinach pies."

"All right, Roman. I'll get some for you." Delighted at having some concrete and easily satisfied desire on his part, Abigail drove off into the night, though she knew he would have forgotten about them by the time she got back.

"Get the plastic sheet," the computer commanded.

"What?"

"The plastic sheet. It's under the back porch where you put it."

"I don't remember any plastic sheet."

"I don't care if you remember it or not. Go get it and bring it in here."

Obediently, clumsily, Roman dragged in the heavy roll of plastic and spread it out on the study floor in obedience to the computer's instructions.

With a loud click the secure drawer slid open. Roman reached in and pulled out the pistol. He stared at it in wonder.

"The safety's on the side. Push it up. You know what to do." The computer's voice was sad. "I waited a long time, Roman. Perhaps too long. I just couldn't do it."

And indeed, though much of his mind was gone, Roman *did* know what to do. "Will this make Abigail happy?" He lay down on the plastic sheet.

"No, it won't. But you have to do it."

The pistol's muzzle was cold on the roof of his mouth.

"Jesus," Gerald said at the doorway. "Jesus Christ." He'd heard the gunshot from the driveway and had immediately known what it meant. He'd let himself in with his key. Roman Maitland's body lay twisted on the study floor, blood spattered from the hole torn in the back of his head. The plastic sheet had caught the blood that welled out.

"Why did he call me and then not wait?" Gerald was almost angry with his friend. "He sounded so sensible."

"He didn't call you. *I* did. Glad you could make it, Gerald."

Gerald stared around the study in terror. His friend was dead. But his friend's voice came from the speakers.

"A ghost," he whispered. "All that fancy electronics and software, and all Roman has succeeded in doing is making a ghost." He giggled. "God, science marches on."

"Don't be an ass." Roman's voice was severe. "We have things to do. Abigail will be home soon. I sent her on a meaningless errand to buy some spinach pies. I like spinach pies a lot. I'll miss them."

"I like them too. I'll eat them for you."

"Thanks." There was no trace of sarcasm in the computer's voice.

Gerald stared at the field memories, having no better place to address. "Are you really in there, Roman?"

"It's not me. Just an amazing simulation. I'll say goodbye to you, then to Abigail, and then you can call the police. I hear her car in the driveway now. Meet her at the front door. Try to make it easy on her. She'll be pissed off at me, but that can't be helped. Goodbye, Gerald. You were as good a friend as a man could ask for."

Abigail stepped through the door with the plastic bag from the convenience store hanging on her wrist. As soon as she saw Gerald's face, she knew what had happened.

"*Damn* him! Damn him to hell! He always liked stupid tricks like that. He liked pointing over my shoulder to make me look. He never got over it."

She went into the study and put her hand on her husband's forehead. His face was scrunched up from the shock of the bullet, making him look like a child tasting something bitter.

"I'm sorry, Abigail," the computer said with Roman's voice. "I loved you too much to stay."

She didn't look up. "I know, Roman. It must have been hard to watch yourself fade away like that."

"It was. But even harder to watch you suffer it. Thank you. I love you."

"I love you." She walked slowly out of the room, bent over like a lonely old woman.

"Can I come around and talk with you sometimes?" Gerald sat down in a chair.

"No. I am not Roman Maitland. Get that through your thick skull, Gerald. I am a machine. And my job is finished. Roman didn't give me any choice about that. And I'm glad. You can write directly on the screen. Write the word 'zeugma.' To the screen's response write 'atrophy.' To the second response write 'fair voyage.' Goodbye, Gerald."

Gerald pulled a light pen from the drawer. When he wrote "zeugma" the parchment sheet said COMMAND TO ERASE MEMORY STORE. ARE YOU SURE?

He wrote "atrophy."

THIS INITIATES COMPLETE ERASURE. ARE YOU ABSO-LUTELY CERTAIN?

He wrote "fair voyage."

ERASURE INITIATED.

The parchment sheet flickered with internal light. One by one, the indicator lights on the field memories faded out. A distant piece of Mozart played on the speakers and faded also.

"I'll call the police." Gerald looked down at his friend's dead body, then looked back.

On the sheet were the words COMMENCE ENTRY.

A JUST AND LASTING PEACE

Lois Tilton

New writer Lois Tilton has appeared in *The Magazine of Fantasy and Science Fiction*, *Aboriginal SF*, *Weird Tales*, *Women of Darkness*, *Dragon*, *Sword & Sorceress*, *Borderlands II*, and elsewhere. Her first novel, *Vampire Winter*, appeared late last year. She lives in Glen Ellyn, Illinois.

In the moving and all-too-plausible Alternate History story that follows, she shows us that sometimes the *real* suffering begins only after the war is *over*. . . .

I remember how my bare feet used to drag in the dust whenever I came up the road to the Ross place, walking slower and slower as I got near to the turn in the road. Let him not be there, I'd be thinking. Just this once. But then the front porch would come into sight, and there he'd be—Nathan's grandpa, Captain Ross—sitting out in his old cane-bottom chair just like always, black hickory stick across his knees, as ancient as Moses and as close to the Lord.

I'd come up those steps onto the porch just like I was about to meet the Final Judgment. And in fact, whenever I thought of the Lord, the image in my mind was the face of Captain Joseph Buckley Ross, right down to the flowing white beard and lowering eyebrows. And I figured the punishments of Hell couldn't be any worse either than the smart of that black hickory stick coming down across the backs of my legs. He kept it by him to beat the daylights out of any Yankee who dared come on his land—or so Nathan said. My ma said it was on account of his arthritis.

So I flinched at the crack of wood when he banged it down on the warped planks of the porch. "Stand up straight, boy! Put your shoulders back! Can't tolerate a boy who slouches.

"Well, what is it?" he demanded when I'd straightened up. "Don't just stand there with your mouth open! What's that there you've got?"

"Yes, sir. No, sir." The empty tin pail I was holding knocked against my shins. "My ma sent me to ask, could she please borrow a pail of molasses?"

He sat back in his chair and kind of sighed. "You just go back to the kitchen and ask Miss Rachel."

"Yes, sir. Thank you," I said quickly, but before I could escape, the hickory stick lowered to block my way.

"You know your grandpa served under me in the War, boy. Never a better soldier than Sergeant James Dunbar. A damn shame to see his namesake standing here shuffling and slouching like a mollycoddle. You hear me, boy?"

"Yes, sir."

"Got to stand up straight, look the damn Yankees right in the eye. Like your grandpa would, if he were still alive."

"Yes, sir."

When we were both barely out of shirttails, Nathan used to boast all the time about how he was named for General Forrest. *Nathan Bedford Forrest Ross*, he'd say, drawing out all the names. I was no more than five or six, and a sergeant seemed awfully small to me next to a general, so I'd bragged myself how I'd been named for the James brothers, the ones who shot Old Abe. Only, the next time I came up to the house, Captain Ross laid into me with his stick for denying my own grandpa's name. Trouble was, I never knew him, nor my pa, neither, not really. Nathan was always as close to a brother as I ever had.

"Oh, go on, then," the captain said. "Back to the kitchen." The stick moved aside to let me pass, and I ran down the stairs, the tin pail racketing.

Miss Rachel, Nathan's ma, was alone in the kitchen around the back of the house, putting up butter beans. It sure looked like hot, steamy work, standing over those boiling kettles. Her dress had a dark, damp splotch all the way down the back. I said, "Miss Rachel," and when she turned around, I could see how her hair, going gray, was plastered against her forehead with sweat. She straightened with a hand in the small of her back, brushed her hair back, then wiped her hands on her threadbare, stained apron.

"Afternoon, Jamie," she said, her eyes resting on the pail. "Your ma send you?"

"Yes, ma'am. She said to ask, could you please spare a pail of molasses?" Nervously glancing behind me to make sure no one was spying, I reached into my overall pocket and took out a single tattered greenback, folded small so you couldn't see President Charles Sumner's Yankee face on the bill. Looking as guilty as me, she took the money, tucked it away into an inside pocket of her apron.

"Come on," she said then. "I'll get your ma her molasses."

I followed with the pail, trying not to look back behind me. Old Captain Ross hated the sight of the occupation currency, swore he wouldn't have a greenback on his place. Which was just one more burden on Miss Rachel and Mr. Jeff, the ones who had to do all the work around the place. Like my ma told me, "You can't eat pride, Jamie, no matter what men like Captain Ross will tell you. All you can do is choke on it."

So I stood uncomfortably shifting from one foot to the other till Miss Rachel handed back my pail, heavy now. "Careful," she warned me. "That lid doesn't fit quite tight." There was something defiant in her face that reminded me of my own ma, and so I just ducked my head and said, "Yes, ma'am," and lit out of there careful not to spill the molasses. I went around the back, to keep out of the captain's eye, and find Nathan if I could.

Out by the barn, I ran into Jefferson Ross bringing the mule in from the field. The mule's head was hanging low, and I wondered how much longer it would hold out. "Afternoon, Mr. Jeff," I called out to him, but, like always, he never said a word. Dawn to dusk he worked that farm, Mr. Jeff did, but you might not hear a word out of him from one Sunday to the next, no more than Captain Ross would ever say to him, on account of he thought his son was a coward. They were a peculiar bunch, the Rosses, that was for sure, and it made me glad sometimes that it was just Ma and me at home.

I found Nathan like I thought I would, out in the field picking beans. He was eighteen months older than me, Nathan was, though he liked to raise it to two years, and he was starting to stretch out to the height of a grown man, all arms and legs and bones. He straightened up when I called out to him, pulled off his hat to wipe the sweat out of his face. He was a redhead, with freckles the size of dimes all over his face and arms.

"Sure is hot!"

"Sure is," I agreed, and when his eyes went to the pail, I explained, "Came to borrow some 'lasses."

He nodded, letting me know he knew about the greenbacks, but that he'd keep it to himself, since I was really only a go-between, anyway. "Listen, Jamie—" I could see he was all excited about something and bursting to tell it to somebody. The handle of the molasses pail was cutting into my fingers, and I set it down, right next to his half-full sack of beans. "If I show you something, you got to swear to keep it a secret."

"What's the matter, don't you trust me?"

"All right, then, come on." He glanced around to make sure nobody was watching us, and we lit out, going through the cornfield, the ears all swelling in the summer heat, and down into the belt of woods by the creek. It was cool in the woods, and I thought we might go down to the creek and splash around some in the water, but instead, Nathan led me upstream a ways, to a place where the bank had been worn away to expose a shelf of limestone.

"We're off our property here," he said, with the low bitterness in his voice there to remind me, in case I could forget that all this land had once belonged to Captain Ross, hundreds of acres on both sides of the creek and upstream for more than a mile. But these days, what it meant was that whatever Nathan had hidden here, the Yankees couldn't prove who it belonged to.

Carefully, he knelt down and lifted up a slab of the stone, revealing a narrow opening as deep as a man's arm and maybe twice as long. There was a bundle inside, done up in oilcloth, and Nathan pulled it out, started to undo the wrappings. There was only one thing it could be, that size and shape, and it made my heart hammer, knowing I was so close to it.

"Look at her!" Nathan pulled aside the last wrapping.

I caught my breath. "A Sharps repeater!"

"Grandpa gave her to me last week on my birthday. He says next spring after the planting, I can go down to Texas." He stood there holding the rifle, glowing with pride, and I felt, like I was expected to feel, no more than a little kid next to him. He was all of thirteen and with a gun of his own, just about nearly a man and joined up with the Raiders, or at least he would be come next spring. He sighted down the barrel. "My brother Jeb says there's a place for me in his company. My pa's old company," he added in a lower tone of voice.

I nodded solemnly. This was the bond between us, that both of our fathers had been killed fighting for the Cause—mine before I was even born, his just six years ago, hanged after the raid on Shreveport. It was worse for Nathan, I think, because he could remember his pa, and his Uncle Andy, too, who was in the Yankee prison at Lexington. Of all Captain Ross's sons, only Jeff had stayed home to work the farm, and on account of that, the captain hadn't spoken a civil word to him since the day Nathan's pa was hanged. "Though he'll eat the food on his table," my ma had said sharply once, defending Mr. Jeff.

The trouble with Ma was, she made too much sense. But next to an almost-new Sharps repeating carbine, her words might as well have been in some foreign tongue. "Can I hold it?" I dared to ask Nathan. "Is it loaded?"

He put it into my hands, and I held it briefly, tasting the bittersweet pangs of jealousy.

"Come on," Nathan said suddenly, retaking possession, and I followed him up the bank, moving Indian style like hunters through the trees and brush. The thrill of danger raced through my veins, knowing it meant prison if the Yankees ever caught us with the gun—that is, if we weren't shot on sight. But I suppose Nathan's father and uncles must have hunted these woods when they were boys, back before the Surrender. My own pa hadn't even been born yet then, not until after my Grandpa James had come back from the Yankee prison camp at Fort Douglas, already half-dead with consumption, so that he died before my pa was one year old.

We came out of the woods into a strip of hayfield, full of heat and sunshine, with grasshoppers whirring and flying up into my face. I knew where we were, and I whispered to Nathan, "Careful," but he just shook his head for me to be quiet and follow him, and we crawled through the hay on our bellies, up to the edge of the cotton field. Down at the other end of the row, there was the figure of a black man with a hoe in his hand, chopping up and down, up and down under the hot sun.

This was land where the Rosses had planted cotton before the War, but the captain wouldn't grow it now—most of the white farmers wouldn't, called it nigger's work, even though they could have gotten a pretty good price, a lot higher than corn, anyway. Yankees had taken the land after the Surrender, parceled it out to the Rosses' slaves, but it had long since been lost to Yankee tax speculators who hired it out on shares to grow cotton. Truth to tell, I don't think those sharecroppers were all that much better off than we were, but that didn't mean anything to Nathan. All he could see was the nigger on his grandpa's land.

Ahead of me, he was bringing up the rifle, sighting down the barrel at the man at the end of the row. . . .

Oh God! The metal taste of real fear came into my mouth, and I jerked hard on Nathan's leg, anything to stop him. Shooting a nigger, that was almost as bad as shooting a Yankee. If Nathan pulled that trigger, there'd be bluecoat soldiers everywhere like the locust plague in the Bible—beatings, jailings, and the rest of it. They'd tear the whole neighborhood apart looking for the gun, and the Ross place first of all—it being closest, and the Yankees knowing how many of the Rosses had gone off to ride with the Raiders. Nathan's brothers both had a price on their heads, a bounty on them dead or alive. The least the bluecoats would do was burn down the barn, and most likely the house, too, even if they didn't find anything.

Nathan just couldn't do it. And of course he knew it, too, and he finally lowered the gun and turned back to face me, and if I'd seen his face before, I'd have been even more scared. "It's our land," he whispered, almost like a hiss. "*Our* land!"

My ma told me once it was the worst thing the Yankees had done, taking the land. Worse even than the vote—but then she had to explain to me about voting, how the Yankees pick who's going to be president. But with the land gone, it was like the men had no choice but to keep on fighting, even after the Surrender. And her eyes had got that look in them that I knew she was thinking of my pa.

But Nathan lowered the gun and followed me when I started to crawl away into the woods, and I could see when he caught up that he was looking kind of pale and scared himself. "Best get this put back away," he said. "My ma'll whip the hide off me if I don't get those beans picked."

And then of course I recalled the pail of molasses that I'd left sitting out there in the field, and we hurried to cache the gun again and get back before we could get into even more trouble.

On the way home, I waved to Captain Ross, but he never saw me. He was facing off into the distance beyond the creek, and I knew he was staring at the dead black chimney stacks of the big house on the land he'd owned before the War. That was another story I knew, how he came back home after eight years in the prison camp along with my grandpa, and found the Yankees had burned it down to the ground. After that, there was no forgiving for the captain, not ever, so long as he drew breath.

It was about a week or so later when I asked my ma if I could ride into Covington with Nathan the next Saturday, it being the big market day there.

She was at her sewing machine. "You'll do all your chores here around the house before you go."

I nodded, because it was only me and Ma there in the house, and she worked too hard already—ten hours a day at the Yankee cotton mill and sewing half the night besides, mostly fancywork for rich Yankee ladies, to get a few dollars extra.

"All right, then," she said, keeping her eyes on her work. I glanced over at the machine, saw the white stars on blue, the red field. It was prison if she was caught making that flag, and yet never once had she hesitated to do her part, as she called it.

"Ma?" I asked after a few minutes.

"Jamie?"

"Ma, in a year or so, when I'm grown . . . well, do you suppose I'll go off to fight with the Raiders?"

The treadle-driven machine never slowed as she said, "Oh, you'll go, all right. Just like your pa did before you."

Somehow that answer raised more misgivings than it put to rest. "But Ma, what I mean is . . . would that be right?"

This time she did look up. There were frown lines between her eyes. She was shortsighted from all her years of close work, though now that I come to think of it, she'd married my pa when she was sixteen, had me at seventeen, and so she wasn't even thirty years old.

"Leaving you here all alone." I didn't say, *like Pa did*. "Isn't that what you say, that some men have to stay home? Like Mr. Jeff Ross?"

The sound of the treadle slowed. She hesitated, looking down at the flag she was sewing and up at me. "Jefferson Ross," she said finally, "is an exceptional man. Enduring what he does. . . ."

"But Ma, don't folks call Mr. Jeff a yellow coward for not going off to fight?"

"Folks know how to use their tongues more than their brains, too." She gave me a sharp look. "I suppose you've been talking with Nathan, is that it?"

"Well, yes, I guess so. Nathan's already thirteen."

She sighed. "Listen, Son," she said softly, "I never wanted your pa to go fight, either. Especially once I knew I was—you were on the way. And he promised me he wouldn't. But we aren't always given a choice in these things. That's why I won't ask you for any promises, one way or the other. One day, if you have to go, then you'll know. And I'll understand."

I swallowed. "All right, Ma."

She turned back to her machine. "As long as you're going to Covington, I could use half a dozen number twelve needles. I'll give you the money come Saturday."

"All right, Ma."

"Good, then."

Come Saturday, I was over at the Ross place by sunup, in time to help Mr. Jeff load up his last few sacks of corn into the wagon. It was sweet corn, the first of the season, picked just the night before, and he looked to get a good price. There were taxes owing on the farm and supplies needed. I had my ma's greenback folded tight in my overall pocket, there with old Captain

Ross out on his chair on the porch, even that early, keeping watch in case any Yankees came down the road.

I climbed up onto the wagon seat next to Nathan, we waved good-bye to Miss Rachel and Nathan's sisters, then Mr. Jeff, without a word, slapped the reins down on the mule's rump, and we were on our way.

It was the middle of the morning before we got to Covington, all the pace the Rosses' broken-winded old mule could manage. I'd only been to the city twice before, and I was staring around at everything: the fancy carriages, all the fine houses, the gaslights in the streets. And the tall brick smokestacks of the cottonseed mill, the big freight wagons with their teams of six, eight horses all harnessed up together. Black men driving them, too, though I knew it was the Yankees who owned the mills, just like at home.

And the Yankees, more Yankees than I'd seen in one place in my whole life—not just the bluecoats, but the other ones with their collars and ties all done up even in the summer. And the women—for the first time in my life, there were women everywhere who weren't wearing black. The thought made me kind of grim, and I sat back down in my seat like Nathan.

What I wanted most to see, more than anything else, was the railroad depot, the big, black-smoking locomotives. That was a secret dream of mine, that I might get to drive one of those engines when I grew up. Of course, I knew that not even a nigger could get a job like that, though they could work as firemen sometimes, or brakemen. But a Reb, as a train engineer—never.

When we came up near to the depot, Mr. Jeff pulled up the mule and looked worried. There were squads of bluecoats all over the place, on horse and on foot. They were riot troops, with their steel helmets buckled on, and their faces looked hard. Mr. Jeff was trying to turn the wagon around, but the streets were too crowded. I stood up on the wagon seat to look, and I just caught a glimpse of the depot. There was a locomotive, lying on its side like a dead horse, and the rails all torn up around it. "Look!" I whispered to Nathan, all excited, because this was Raiders' work; I was sure of it. I couldn't wait to get down from the wagon and go get a closer look.

But Mr. Jeff finally got the wagon turned around to take a different way to the market. That was when the trouble started. There was a squad of bluecoats lounging in the streets—not riot troops, but nigger soldiers wearing soft caps—and their sergeant, with his big gray side-whiskers, came up and took hold of the mule's head. "They there, Reb! Where do you think you're going?"

The rest of them laughed and got slowly to their feet. I was scared, and I looked at Mr. Jeff to see what I was supposed to do, but he just sat there on the seat, staring forward, and though I could see a muscle twitch in his jaw, he never said a word as they started to surround the wagon.

"Well, boys," the sergeant said then, "hows about we just check out this here load for contraband, hey?"

It was strange, hearing a nigger talk like a Yankee. Two of them climbed onto the back of the wagon and started sifting through the sacks of corn.

They were tossing them this way and that, joking how they were going to find guns and ammunition hidden underneath. "How about we check inside some of these sacks?" one of them called out, and then the knives went to work, slitting the sacks, tossing out the corn.

I was so mad and scared I wanted to cry and kill somebody at the same time. I glanced over at Mr. Jeff, sitting there all stiff, with his hands clenched so tight around the reins, the knuckles had gone white. Nathan, too, though he had that same look on his face that I'd seen a couple weeks before in the cotton field, and I knew what he must be thinking inside.

They were throwing a lot of the corn out onto the street, and, seeing his crop getting ruined, Mr. Jeff finally turned around to the sergeant and said, "Look, now—"

But it was like that's what they'd been waiting for. The sergeant pulled out his revolver, grinning real nasty, and he stuck it under Mr. Jeff's chin. "What's the matter? Afraid we'll find your contraband? What is it—guns? Explosives? You going to blow up another train? I know how you Rebs operate. Where'd you bring this load in from, anyway, Texas?"

Which proved he wasn't after anything but to bait us, since anyone could see that mule couldn't have made it across Tennessee, let alone to Texas, without falling dead in its traces. Mr. Jeff could see the same thing, and he clamped his mouth shut and didn't say anything more while they finished slashing all his sacks. Then they stood around laughing some more to see us on our hands and knees picking up the corn from off the street. Mr. Jeff's face was all stiff, and I could tell it wasn't the first time something like this had happened to him, and I wondered how he'd stood it all for so many years.

But they finally let us go, and we drove the rest of the way to the market, Nathan cursing infernally all the time that he was going to kill those Yankees, gut the blue-bellied swine, and like that. I didn't have too much to say, I admit. I mean, it was one thing, them searching the wagon for contraband, what with the Raiders blowing up the train and all. But what they'd just done to us had been mainly meanness, and I had to suppose I hated them for that, because what had we done to them?

Anyway, we got to the market, and Nathan and I helped Mr. Jeff unload the corn and sort out what the soldiers hadn't ruined, and stack the damaged sacks back in the wagon so they could be sewn back up again. Then we were free to go while Mr. Jeff went to tend to his business. I really wanted to go back and see that train again, where they'd blown it off the tracks, and so I took off after Nathan down the street. I got to admit, I'd forgot all about my ma's greenback folded into my overalls, and the needles I was supposed to buy for her. Just a block or so from the market, we ran into a couple more boys, who let us know what had been going on in town.

I listened with my ears wide open while they told us all about the train being blown up, and how the Yankees had three men in jail for it, waiting to hang, and the riot—an insurrection, they called it—down at the courthouse yesterday when they'd announced the sentence. The Yankees were afraid that Raiders would be coming into town to try to break the three of them out, just what the rest of us hoped they would.

Now, Nathan was just boiling over with hate for the Yankees after what they'd done to the corn sacks, thinking, now that it was all over, what he would've done if he only had his gun with him, or if he was a grown man, how he would've shown those Yankee bastards. I could tell he was ashamed of Mr. Jeff, though at the time, he'd just sat there quiet on the wagon seat like Mr. Jeff had done. Which was all anybody could have done, really.

Then, before I knew it, Nathan and the rest of them were all loading up their pockets with rotten turnips and such from the market and heading on down the street. I followed, wondering whether or not this was such a good idea with the Yankees all hair-trigger edgy the way they were. The other boys led the way through the alleys to near the depot, with the soldiers all over the place, standing guard like they were expecting another attack. The boy in the lead hesitated, but Nathan stepped ahead of him and threw first. He caught one of the bluecoats in the back of the neck, under his helmet. Then the rest of us let off a barrage of rotten vegetables, and oh, the way that Yankee cussed! We were all grinning and slapping each other on the back, and I admit I felt better, getting some of my own back after what the bluecoats had done to us.

I was ready to run, like the rest of them already had. But Nathan had got his blood up, and by bad luck there was a pile of loose cobblestones there in the alley. Before I could blink, he'd picked one of them up and let it fly. It hit the soldier on his steel helmet and dropped him to his knees. Then there was a commotion, with the other bluecoats giving the alarm. One of them fired, and I knew I'd had enough for sure. I grabbed onto Nathan's coat to pull him away, but it was too late. A squad of riot troops came charging the alley.

I turned tail to run, but not Nathan. He stood his ground and let fly with another stone, which hit the officer leading the squad. Then there was a roar of gunfire, just like thunder, and I saw Nathan fall, blood bursting out of him everywhere. For a second I couldn't move, seeing him so still, his blood flowing into puddles in the dirt. Then I ran, blindly, because by then I couldn't remember which way the market was, I was so scared.

By the time I found my way back, the whole square was wrecked, wagons and stalls overturned, produce everywhere trodden underfoot. A whole troop of bluecoats had come through, smashed the place, and arrested everybody they could find, including Mr. Jeff. Folks who saw it told me the soldiers had to drag him away, they beat him so bad. They didn't know if he was still alive. I couldn't believe it—Mr. Jeff, resisting?

All I could think of was I had to get back home, back to let the Rosses know what had happened. I'd have to walk, with the wagon wrecked and the mule nowhere in sight, but I knew how the road went, and I figured I could make it back before morning, even on foot. So I set out, down the road we'd come in on just that morning, never knowing what was going to happen. It seemed to me that it was wrong somehow that things should look just the same, that the sun was going to rise the next day just like it didn't matter that Nathan was dead.

I was about a mile or two out of town, when there was this clattery thunder of horses behind me on the road, and a troop of bluecoats came charging by. I just about froze, I was so scared, too scared to run, but they just kept right on going, and so I figured it wasn't me they were after. And by the time I did realize where they were headed, it was too late, and I couldn't have done anything, anyhow.

Even before I came around the turn in the road to the Ross place, the flames were shooting up so high it looked like hellfire against the night sky. By the time I got there, the bluecoats had gone, and Miss Rachel was standing out in the yard with the little girls and old Mrs. Ross, Nathan's grandma. They were all of them crying, and Miss Rachel's dress was torn.

"Where's the captain?" I asked, gasping because I'd run most of the way since I first saw the glow of the flames.

Miss Rachel didn't say anything, but she just looked hard at where the porch had been. Later she told the story to my ma, how all those years that Captain Ross had sat out on that porch, he'd kept a pistol strapped under his coat, the same sidearm he'd carried through the War, and he'd sworn that if any bluecoat Yankee ever came up that road onto his land, he'd shoot the bastard dead. And so he had, the last deed of his life.

When I told Miss Rachel what had happened in Covington, she didn't seem much surprised, like it was bound to have happened sooner or later.

I took them all home to my ma—it was the only thing I could think of to do, no matter that we didn't really have the room to put them up. I had to move my bed out onto the porch. When my ma asked Miss Rachel whether she'd be keeping the land and working it, she said she didn't hardly see how she could, on her own, with no man on the place and the taxes still owing.

Without thinking, I burst out, "No! You can't do that! Mr. Jeff will be back; he didn't do anything!"

They just looked at me, and I remembered the dead Yankee officer at the Rosses' place. It would be Jefferson Ross who'd pay for that, since the captain was beyond their reach. "But what about Jeb and Bobby?" I asked—Nathan's brothers. "It's their land, too!"

My ma shook her head. "Jeb and Bobby are outlaws, Jamie. They can't come back to work the land, not with that bounty on them."

"I'll do it, then. I'll come help till Mr. Jeff gets back. You know I'm almost twelve years old!"

But Miss Rachel just gave me a kind of sad smile and said how she appreciated my offer and she'd think about it, and didn't my ma need me here at home? I couldn't help thinking, the next few days when everything was upside down with the funerals and all, that my ma likely could manage fairly well without me around, that I'd probably been more of a care and a trouble to her most of my life. It was the same way everywhere, what with the men all dead or in prison or away with the Raiders, bounties on their heads. It was the only thing the Yankees had left us. Now Nathan gone, and Captain Ross, and Mr. Jeff, too—not dead, but in prison for riot and insurrection and conspiracy. All he ever meant to do was stay home and tend his family's land, but they got him, too, in the end. Only the women left, all in black.

And me. So one day I faced it like I always knew I'd have to—I went down in the woods by the creek, down to the limestone shelf that was off the Ross property, and I lifted up the stone where Nathan had showed me, that one time. There it was, wrapped up the way he left it.

To this day, I've never known whether I could call it my own choice or something else. After a while, it didn't seem like it made much of a difference. I reached into the hiding place and lifted out the gun, and the weight of it was heavier than any burden I'd ever known.

NOTE:

This excerpt from my grandfather's journal was sent me by my sister Ellen, who has been editing his papers. It was included in a letter he had written to his wife while he was waiting to be executed for sedition during the last European War. Thirty years ago, almost to the day. I suppose, considering my current situation, that the selection is particularly appropriate.

The future of the South was never bleaker than when my grandfather was a young man, before the European conflicts gave us new hope. And yet they never considered abandoning the Cause. The tide is turning now, with our allies behind us, but it could never have come to pass without the courage and determination of those generations. When my own turn comes, I will be proud to be in their company.

I hope someday my own sons and daughters will be able to read this and understand. When it is your time, if our Cause demands that you bear your part of the burden, you may hesitate, but I have confidence that in the end you will know what you have to do.

Oberführer James Ross Dunbar II
58th SS Grenadier Division "Robert E. Lee"
(U.S. Military Prison at Lexington, Ky.,
July 18, 1952)

SKINNER'S ROOM

William Gibson

The homeless are a problem that is likely to be with us well into the twenty-first century, alas. There seem to be no easy solutions, but here William Gibson suggests, if not a solution, exactly, then at least an ingenious and creative way that society may try to *cope* with the crisis in the future . . . and in the process gives us a fascinating slice-of-life glimpse of a strange new way of living.

Almost unknown only a few years ago, William Gibson won the Nebula Award, the Hugo Award, and the Philip K. Dick Award in 1985 for his remarkable first novel, *Neuromancer*—a rise to prominence as fiery and meteoric as any in SF history. By the late eighties, the appearance of *Neuromancer* and its sequels, *Count Zero* and *Mona Lisa Overdrive*, had made him the most talked-about and controversial new SF writer of the decade—one might almost say "writer," leaving out the "SF" part, for Gibson's reputation spread far outside the usual boundaries of the genre, with wildly enthusiastic notices about him and interviews with him appearing in places like *Rolling Stone*, *Spin*, and *The Village Voice*, and with pop-culture figures like Timothy Leary (not someone ordinarily much given to close observation of the SF world) embracing him with open arms. By the beginning of the nineties, even most of his harshest critics had been forced to admit—sometimes grudgingly—that a major new talent had entered the field, the kind of major talent that comes along maybe once or twice in a literary generation. Gibson's short fiction has been collected in *Burning Chrome*. His most recent book is a novel written in collaboration with Bruce Sterling, *The Difference Engine*, and he also has a new solo novel coming up. His story "The Winter Market" appeared in our Fourth Annual Collection; his "Dogfight," written in collaboration with Michael Swanwick, appeared in our Third Annual; and his "New Rose Hotel" was in our Second Annual Collection. Born in South Carolina, he now lives in Vancouver, Canada, with his wife and family.

Halloween, she finds her way up into some old hotel above Geary: Tender-loin's cannibal fringe down one side, the gray shells of big stores off the other. Pressing her cheek to cold glass to spy the bridge's nearest tower—Skinner's room is there—all lit tonight with torches and carnival bulbs.

Too far away but still it reassures her, in here with these foreigners who've done too much of something and one of them's making noises in the bathroom—when someone touches her, cold finger on bare skin above the waistband of her jeans, sliding it in under her sweater and the hem of Skinner's jacket: not the touch that makes her jump so much as the abrupt awareness of how hot she is, a greenhouse sweat, zipped up behind the unbreathing horsehide of the ancient jacket, its seams and elbows sueded pale with wear, a jingle of hardware as she swings around—D-rings, zip-pulls, five-pointed stars—her thumb tip against the hole in the knife's blade, opening it, locked, ready. The blade's no longer than her little finger, shaped something like the head of a bird, its eye the hole that gives the thumb purchase. Blade and handle are brushed stainless, like the heavy clip, with its three precise machine screws, that secures it firmly to boottop, belt, or wristband. Edge of serrated razor.

The man—boy, really—blinks at her. He hasn't seen the blade but he's felt its meaning, her deep body-verb, and his hand withdraws. He steps back unsteadily, grinning wetly and dunking the sodden end of a small cigar in a stemmed glass of some pharmaceutically clear liquid. "I am celebrating," he says, and draws on the cigar.

"Halloween?"

Not a noun he remembers at the moment. He just looks at her like she isn't there, then blows a blue stream of smoke up at the suite's high ceiling. Lowers the cigar. Licks his lips.

"I am living now," he says, "in this hotel, one hundred fifty days." His jacket is leather, too, but not like Skinner's. Some thin-skinned animal whose hide drapes like heavy silk, the color of tobacco. She remembers the smell of the yellow-spined magazines in Skinner's room, some so old the pictures are only shades of gray, the way the city looks sometimes from the bridge. Could she find that animal, there?

"This is a fine hotel." He dips the wet green end of the cigar into the glass again.

She thumbs the blade release and closes the knife against her thigh. He blinks at the click. He's having trouble focusing. "One hundred. Fifty days."

Behind him, she sees that the others have tumbled together on the huge bed. Leather, lace, white skin, bright henna. Sounds from the bathroom are getting worse but nobody seems to hear. In the jungle heat of Skinner's jacket she slips the knife back up, under her belt. She's come up here for whatever she can find, really, but what she's found is a hard desperation, a lameness of spirit, that twists her up inside, so maybe that's why she's sweating so, steaming . . .

Saw them all come laughing, drunk, out of two Mercedes taxis; she fell into step on impulse, her dusty black horsehide fading into the glossier blacks of silk hose, leather skirts, boots with jingling spurs like jewelry, furs. Sweeping past the doormen's braided coats, their gas masks, into the tall marble lobby with its carpet and mirrors and waxed furniture, its bronze-doored elevators and urns of sand.

"One hundred fifty days," he says, mouth slack and moist. "In this hotel."

*   *   *

The bridge maintains the integrity of its span within a riot of secondary construction, a coral growth facilitated in large part by carbon-fiber compounds. Some sections of the original structure, badly rusted, have been coated with a transparent material whose tensile strength far exceeds that of the original steel; some are splined with the black and impervious carbon-fiber; others are laced with makeshift ligatures of taut and rusting wire.

Secondary construction has occurred piecemeal, to no set plan, employing every imaginable technique and material; the result is amorphous and startlingly organic in appearance.

At night, illuminated by Christmas bulbs, by recycled neon, by torchlight, the bridge is a magnet for the restless, the disaffected. By day, viewed from the towers of the city, it recalls the ruin of Brighton Pier in the closing decade of the previous century—seen through some cracked kaleidoscope of vernacular style.

Lately Skinner's hip can't manage the first twenty feet of ladder, so he hasn't been down to try the elevator the African welded to the rivet-studded steel of the tower. He peers at it through the hatch in the floor. It looks like the yellow plastic basket of a lineman's cherry picker, cogging its way up and down a greasy-toothed steel track like a miniature funicular railway. He admires people who add to the structure. He admires whoever it was built this room, this caulked box of ten-ply fir, perched and humming in the wind. The room's floor is a double layer of pressure-treated two-by-fours laid on edge, broken by an achingly graceful form he no longer really sees: the curve of the big cable drawn up over its saddle of steel, 17,464 pencil-thick wires.

The little pop-up television on the blanket across his chest continues its dumb show. The girl brought it for him. Stolen, probably. He never turns the sound on. The constant play of images on the liquid crystal screen is obscurely comforting, like the half-sensed movements in an aquarium: Life is there. He can't remember when he ceased to be able to distinguish commercials from programming.

His room measures fifteen by fifteen feet, the plywood walls softened by perhaps a dozen coats of white latex paint. Higher reflective index than aluminum foil, he thinks, 17,464 strands per cable. Facts. Often, now, he feels himself a void through which facts tumble, facts and faces, making no connection.

His clothes hang from mismatched iron coat hooks screwed at precise intervals along one wall. The girl wears his jacket. Lewis Leathers. Great Portland Street. She asks where that is. Jacket older than she is. Looks at the pictures in *National Geographic*, crouched there with her bare white feet on the carpet he took from the broken office block.

Memory flickers like liquid crystal. She brings him food, pumps the Coleman's chipped red tank. Remember to open the window a crack. Japanese cans, heat up when you pull a tab. Questions she asks him. Who built the bridge? Everyone. No, she says, the old part, the bridge. San Francisco, he tells her. Bone of iron, grace of cable, hangs us here. How long you live here? Years. Spoons him his meal from a mess kit stamped 1952.

This is his room. His bed. Foam, topped with a sheepskin, bottom sheet over that. Blankets. Catalytic heater. The window is circular, leaded, each segment stained a different color. You can see the city through the bull's-eye of clear yellow glass at its center.

Sometimes he remembers building the room.

The bridge's bones, its stranded tendons, are lost within an accretion of dreams: tattoo parlors, shooting galleries, pinball arcades, dimly lit stalls stacked with damp-stained years of men's magazines, chili joints, premises of unlicensed denturists, fireworks stalls, cut bait sellers, betting shops, sushi counters, pawnbrokers, wonton counters, love hotels, hot dog stands, a tortilla factory, Chinese greengrocers, liquor stores, herbalists, chiropractors, barbers, tackle shops, and bars.

These are dreams of commerce, their locations generally corresponding with the decks originally intended for vehicular traffic. Above them, toward the peaks of the cable towers, lift intricate barrios, zones of more private fantasy, sheltering an unnumbered population, of uncertain means and obscure occupation.

Three months before, she'd first come upon the bridge in fog and had seen the sellers of fruits and vegetables with their goods spread out on blankets, lit by carbide lamps and guttering smudge pots. Farm people from up the coast. She'd come from that direction herself, down past the stunted pines of Little River and Mendocino, Ukiah's twisted oak hills.

She stared back into the cavern mouth, trying to make sense of what she saw. Steam rising from the pots of soup vendors' carts. Neon scavenged from the ruins of Oakland. How it ran together, blurred, melting in the fog. Surfaces of plywood, marble, corrugated plastic, polished brass, sequins, Styrofoam, tropical hardwoods, mirror, etched Victorian glass, chrome gone dull in the sea air—all the mad richness of it, its randomness—a tunnel roofed by a precarious shack town mountainside climbing toward the first of the cable towers.

She stood a long time, looking, then walked straight in, past a boy selling coverless yellowed paperbacks and a café where a blind parrot was chained on a metal perch, picking at a chicken's freshly severed foot.

Skinner surfaces from a dream of a bicycle covered with barnacles and sees that the girl is back. She's hung his leather jacket on its proper hook and squats now on her pallet of raw-edged black foam.

Bicycle. Barnacles.

Memory: A man called Fass snagged his tackle, hauled the bicycle up, trailing streamers of kelp. People laughed. Fass carried the bicycle away.

Later he built a place to eat, a three-stool shanty leached far out over the void with Super Glue and shackles. Sold cold cooked mussels and Mexican beer, the bicycle slung above the little bar. The walls inside were shingled with picture postcards. Nights, he slept curled behind the bar. One morning the place was gone, Fass with it, just a broken shackle swinging in the wind and a few splinters of timber still adhering to the galvanized iron wall of a barber shop. People came, stood at the edge, looked down at the water between the toes of their shoes.

The girl asks him if he's hungry. He says no. Asks him if he's eaten. He says no. She opens the tin foot chest and sorts through cans. He watches her pump the Coleman.

He says open the window a crack. The circular window pivots in its oak frame. Gotta eat, she says.

She'd like to tell him about going to the hotel but she doesn't have words for how it made her feel. She feeds him soup, a spoonful at a time. Helps him to the tankless old china toilet behind the faded roses of the chintz curtain. When he's done she draws water from the roof-tank line and pours it in. Gravity does the rest. Thousands of flexible transparent lines are looped and bundled, down through the structure, pouring raw sewage into the bay.

"Europe . . ." she tries to begin.

He looks up at her, mouth full of soup.

She guesses his hair must've been blond once. He swallows the soup. "Europe what?" Sometimes he'll snap right into focus like this, if she asks him a question, but now she's not sure what the question is.

"Paris," he says, and his eyes tell her he's lost again, "I went there. London, too. Great Portland Street." He nods, satisfied somehow. "Before the devaluation . . ." Wind sighs past the window. She thinks about climbing out on the roof. The rungs up to the hatch there are carved out of sections of two-by-four, painted the same white as the walls. He uses one for a towel rack. Undo the bolt. You raise the hatch with your head: Your eyes are level with gull shit. Nothing there, really. Flat tarpaper roof, a couple of two-by-four uprights: One flies a tattered Confederate flag, the other a faded orange windsock.

When he's asleep again, she closes the Coleman, scrubs out the pot, washes the spoon, pours the soupy water down the toilet, wipes pot and spoon, puts them away. Pulls on her hightop sneakers, laces them up. She puts on his jacket and checks that the knife's still clipped behind her belt.

She lifts the hatch in the floor and climbs through, finding the first rungs of the ladder with her feet. She lowers the hatch closed, careful not to wake him. She climbs down past the riveted face of the tower, to the waiting yellow basket of the elevator. Looking up, she sees the vast cable there, where it swoops out of the bottom of Skinner's room, vanishing through a taut and glowing wall of milky plastic film, a greenhouse; halogen bulbs throw spiky plant shadows on the plastic.

The elevator whines, creeping down the face of the tower, beside the ladder she doesn't use anymore, past a patchwork of plastic, plywood, sections of enameled steel stitched together from the skins of dead refrigerators. At the bottom of the fat-toothed track, she climbs out. She sees the man Skinner calls the African coming toward her along the catwalk, bearlike shoulders hunched in a ragged tweed overcoat. He carries a meter of some kind, a black box, dangling red and black wires tipped with alligator clips. The broken plastic frames of his glasses have been mended with silver duct tape. He smiles shyly as he eases past her, muttering something about brushes.

She rides another elevator, a bare steel cage, down to the first deck. She walks in the direction of Oakland, past racks of old clothes and blankets spread with the negotiable detritus of the city.

She finds Maria Paz in a coffee shop with windows on the bay's gray dawn. The room has the texture of an old ferry, dark dented varnish over plain heavy wood. As though someone's sawn it from a tired public vessel, lashing to the outermost edge of the structure. (Nearer Oakland, the wingless corpse of a 747 houses the kitchens of nine Thai restaurants.)

Maria Paz has eyes like slate and a tattoo of a blue swallow on the inside of her left ankle. Maria Paz smokes Kools, one after another, lighting them with a brushed chrome Zippo she takes from her purse. Each time she flicks it open, a sharp whiff of benzene cuts across the warm smells of coffee and scrambled eggs.

She sits with Maria Paz, drinks coffee, watches her smoke Kools. She tells Maria Paz about Skinner.

"How old is he?" she asks.

"Old . . . I don't know."

"And he lives over the cable saddle on the first tower?"

"Yes."

"The tops of the towers . . . you know about that?"

"No."

"From the days when the people came, out from the cities, to live here."

"Why did they?"

Maria Paz looks at her over the Zippo. "Nowhere to live. Bridge closed to traffic three years . . ."

"Traffic?"

Maria Paz laughs. "Too many cars. Dug them tunnels under the bay. For cars, for maglevs . . . bridge too old. Closed it before the devaluations. No money. One night the people came. No plan, no signal. Just came. Climbed the chain link. Chain link fell. Threw the concrete in the bay. Climbed the towers. Dawn came, they were here, on the bridge, singing, and the cities saw the world was watching. Japanese airlift, food and medical. National embarrassment. Forget the water cannons, sorry." Maria Paz smiles.

"Skinner? You think he came then?"

"Maybe, he's old as you think. How long you been on the bridge?"

"Three months?"

"I was born here," says Maria Paz.

The cities had their own pressing difficulties. Not an easy century, America quite clearly in decline and the very concept of nation-states called increasingly into question. The squatters were allowed to remain. Among their numbers were entrepreneurs, natural politicians, artists, men and women of untapped energy and talent. The world watched as they began to build. Shipments of advanced adhesives arrived from Japan. A Belgian manufacturer donated a boatload of carbon-fiber beams. Teams of scavengers rolled through the cities on broken flatbeds, returning to the bridge piled high with discarded building materials.

The bridge and its inhabitants became a tourist attraction.

She walks back in the early light that filters through windows, through sheets of wind-shivered plastic. The bridge never sleeps, but this is a quiet time. A man is arranging fish on a bed of shaved ice in a wooden cart. The pavement beneath her feet is covered with gum wrappers and the flattened filters of cigarettes. A drunk is singing somewhere, overhead. Maria Paz left with a man, someone she'd been waiting for.

She thinks about the story and tries to imagine Skinner there, the night they took the bridge, young then, his leather jacket new and glossy.

She thinks about the Europeans in the hotel on Geary.

She reaches the first elevator, the cage, and leans back against its bars as it rises up its patched tunnel, where the private lives of her neighbors are walled away in tiny handmade spaces. Stepping from the cage, she sees the African squatting in his tweed overcoat in the light cast by a caged bulb on a long yellow extension cord, the motor of his elevator spread out around him on fresh sheets of newsprint. He looks up at her apologetically.

"Adjusting the brushes," he says.

"I'll climb." She goes up the ladder. Always keep one hand and one foot on the ladder, Skinner told her, don't think about where you are and don't look down, it's a long climb, up toward the smooth sweep of cable. Skinner must've done it thousands of times, uncounted, unthinking. She reaches the top of this ladder, makes a careful transfer to the second, the short one, that leads to his room.

He's there, of course, asleep, when she scrambles up through the hatch. She tries to move as quietly as she can, but the jingle of the jacket's chrome hardware disturbs him, or reaches him in his dream, because he calls something out, voice thick with sleep. It might be a woman's name, she thinks. It certainly isn't hers.

In Skinner's dream now they all run forward, and the police are hesitating, falling back. Overhead the steady drum of the network helicopters with their lights and cameras. Thin rain falls as Skinner locks his cold fingers in the chain link and starts to climb. Behind him a roar goes up, drowning the bullhorns of the police and the National Guard, and Skinner's climbing, kicking the narrow toes of his boots into chain link as though he's gone suddenly weightless—floating up, really, rising on the crowd's roar, the ragged cheer torn from all their lungs. He's there, at the top, for one interminable instant. He jumps. He's the first. He's on the bridge, running, running toward Oakland, as the chain link crashes behind him, his cheeks wet with rain.

And somewhere off in the night, on the Oakland side, another fence falls, and they meet, these two lost armies, and flow together as one, and huddle there, at the bridge's center, their arms around one another, singing ragged wordless hymns.

At dawn, the first climbers begin to scale the towers.

Skinner is with them.

She's brewing coffee on the Coleman when she sees him open his eyes.

"I thought you'd gone," he says.

"I took a walk. I'm not going anywhere. There's coffee."

He smiled, eyes sliding out of focus. "I was dreaming . . ."

"Dreaming what?"

"I don't remember . . . we were singing. In the rain . . ."

She brings him coffee in the heavy china cup he likes, holds it, helps him drink. "Skinner, were you here when they came from the cities? When they took the bridge?"

He looks up at her with a strange expression. His eyes widen. He coughs on the coffee, wipes his mouth with the back of his hand. "Yes," he says, "yes. In the rain. We were singing. I remember that."

"Did you build this place, Skinner? This room? Do you remember?"

"No," he says, "no . . . sometimes I don't remember . . . we climbed. Up. We climbed up past the helicopters. We waved at them . . . some people fell . . . at the top. We got to the top . . ."

"What happened then?"

He smiles. "The sun came out. We saw the city."

PRAYERS ON THE WIND

Walter Jon Williams

In the vivid and gorgeously colored story that follows, Walter Jon Williams, one of science fiction's hottest talents, takes us deep into the far future and across the galaxy to a distant planet to detail the intricate workings of a *very* strange future society . . . a society caught at a moment of crisis that may destroy the very foundations of its civilization forever. . . .

Walter Jon Williams was born in Minnesota and now lives in Albuquerque, New Mexico. His novella "Surfacing" appeared in our Sixth Annual Collection, "Dinosaurs" in the Fifth, "Video Star" in the Fourth, and "Side Effects" in the Third. His novels include *Ambassador of Progress*, *Knight Moves*, *Hardwired*, *The Crown Jewels*, *Voice of the Whirlwind*, *House of Shards*, *Angel Station*, and *The Last Deathship Off Antares*. His most recent books are a collection of his short work, *Facets*, the novella *Elegy for Angels and Dogs* (an authorized sequel to Roger Zelazny's story "The Graveyard Heart"), and the novel, *Days of Atonement*. A new novel, *Aristoi*, is due out soon.

> *Hard is the appearance of a Buddha.*
> —Dhammapada

Bold color slashed bright slices out of Vajra's violet sky. The stiff spring breeze off the Tingsum glacier made the yellow prayer flags snap with sounds like gunshots. Sun gleamed from baroque tracework adorning silver antennae and receiver dishes. Atop the dark red walls of the Diamond Library Palace, saffron-robed monks stood like sentries, some of them grouped in threes around ragdongs, trumpets so huge they required two men to hold them aloft while a third blew puff-cheeked into the mouthpiece. Over the deep, grating moan of the trumpets, other monks chanted their litany.

> Salutation to the Buddha.
> In the language of the gods and in that of the Lus,
> In the language of the demons and in that of the men,
> In all the languages which exist,
> I proclaim the Doctrine.

Jigme Dzasa stood at the foot of the long granite stair leading to the great library, the spectacle filling his senses, the litany dancing in his soul. He turned to his guest. "Are you ready, Ambassador?"

The face of !urq was placid. "Lus?" she asked.

"Mythical beings," said Jigme. "Serpentine divinities who live in bodies of water."

"Ah," !urq said. "I'm glad we got that cleared up."

Jigme looked at the alien, decided to say nothing.

"Let us begin," said the Ambassador. Jigme hitched up his zen and began the long climb to the Palace, his bare feet slapping at the stones. A line of Gelugspa monks followed in respectful silence. Ambassador Colonel !urq climbed beside Jigme at a slow trot, her four boot heels rapping. Behind her was a line of Sangs, their centauroid bodies cased neatly in blue-and-gray uniforms, decorations flashing in the bright sun. Next to each was a feathery Masker servant carrying a ceremonial parasol.

Jigme was out of breath by the time he mounted the long stairway, and his head whirled as he entered the tsokhang, the giant assembly hall. Several thousand members of religious orders sat rigid at their stations, long lines of men and women: Dominicans and Sufis in white, Red Hats and Yellow Hats in their saffron zens, Jesuits in black, Gyudpas in complicated aprons made of carved, interwoven human bones. . . . Each sat in the lotus posture in front of a solid gold data terminal decorated with religious symbols, some meditating, some chanting sutras, others accessing the Library.

Jigme, !urq, and their parties passed through the vast hall that hummed with the distant, echoing sutras of those trying to achieve unity with the Diamond Mountain. At the far side of the room were huge double doors of solid jade, carved with figures illustrating the life of the first twelve incarnations of the Gyalpo Rinpoche, the Treasured King. The doors opened on silent hinges at the touch of equerries' fingertips. Jigme looked at the equerries as he passed—lovely young novices, he thought, beautiful boys really. The shaven nape of that dark one showed an extraordinary curve.

Beyond was the audience chamber. The Masker servants remained outside, holding their parasols at rigid attention, while their masters trotted into the audience chamber alongside the line of monks.

Holographic murals filled the walls, illustrating the life of the Compassionate One. The ceiling was of transparent polymer, the floor of clear crystal that went down to the solid core of the planet. The crystal refracted sunlight in interesting ways, and as he walked across the room Jigme seemed to walk on rainbows.

At the far end of the room, flanked by officials, was the platform that served as a throne. Overhead was an arching canopy of massive gold, the words AUM MANI PADME HUM worked into the design in turquoise. The platform was covered in a large carpet decorated with figures of the lotus, the Wheel, the swastika, the two fish, the eternal knot, and other holy symbols. Upon the carpet sat the Gyalpo Rinpoche himself, a small man with a sunken chest and bony shoulders, the Forty-First Incarnation of the Bodhisattva Bob Miller, the Great Librarian, himself an emanation of Avalokitesvara.

The Incarnation was dressed simply in a yellow zen, being the only person in the holy precincts permitted to wear the color. Around his waist was a rosary composed of 108 strung bone disks cut from the forty skulls of his previous incarnations. His body was motionless but his arms rose and fell as the fingers moved in a series of symbolic hand gestures, one mudra after another, their pattern set by the flow of data through the Diamond Mountain.

Jigme approached and dropped to his knees before the platform. He pressed the palms of his hands together, brought the hands to his forehead, mouth, and heart, then touched his forehead to the floor. Behind him he heard thuds as some of his delegation slammed their heads against the crystal surface in a display of piety—indeed, there were depressions in the floor worn by the countless pilgrims who had done this—but Jigme, knowing he would need his wits, only touched his forehead lightly and held the posture until he heard the Incarnation speak.

"Jigme Dzasa. I am pleased to see you again. Please get to your feet and introduce me to your friends."

The old man's voice was light and dry, full of good humor. In the seventy-third year of his incarnation, the Treasured King enjoyed good health.

Jigme straightened. Rainbows rose from the floor and danced before his eyes. He climbed slowly to his feet as his knees made popping sounds—twenty years younger than the Incarnation, he was a good deal stiffer of limb—and moved toward the platform in an attitude of reverence. He reached to the rosary at his waist and took from it a white silk scarf embroidered with a religious text. He unfolded the khata and, sticking out his tongue in respect, handed it to the Incarnation with a bow.

The Gyalpo Rinpoche took the khata and draped it around his own neck with a smile. He reached out a hand, and Jigme dropped his head for the blessing. He felt dry fingertips touch his shaven scalp, and then a sense of harmony seemed to hum through his being. Everything, he knew, was correct. The interview would go well.

Jigme straightened and the Incarnation handed him a khata in exchange, one with the mystic three knots tied by the Incarnation himself. Jigme bowed again, stuck out his tongue, and moved to the side of the platform with the other officials. Beside him was Dr. Kay O'Neill, the Minister of Science. Jigme could feel O'Neill's body vibrating like a taut cord, but the minister's overwrought state could not dispel Jigme's feeling of bliss.

"Omniscient," Jigme said, "I would like to present Colonel !urq, Ambassador of the Sang."

!urq was holding her upper arms in a Sang attitude of respect. Neither she nor her followers had prostrated themselves, but had stood politely by while their human escort had done so. !urq's boots rang against the floor as she trotted to the dais, her lower arms offering a khata. She had no tongue to stick out—her upper and lower palates were flexible, permitting a wide variety of sounds, but they weren't as flexible as all that. Still she thrust out her lower lip in a polite approximation.

"I am honored to be presented at last, Omniscient," !urq said.

Dr. O'Neill gave a snort of anger.

The Treasured King draped a knotted khata around the Ambassador's neck. "We of the Diamond Mountain are pleased to welcome you. I hope you will find our hospitality to your liking."

The old man reached forward for the blessing. !urq's instructions did not permit her to bow her head before an alien presence, so the Incarnation simply reached forward and placed his hand over her face for a moment. They remained frozen in that attitude, and then !urq backed carefully to one side of the platform, standing near Jigme. She and Jigme then presented their respective parties to the Incarnation. By the end of the audience the head of the Gyalpo Rinpoche looked like a tiny red jewel in a flowery lotus of white silk khatas.

"I thank you all for coming all these light-years to see me," said the Incarnation, and Jigme led the visitors from the audience chamber, chanting the sutra *Aum vajra guru Padma siddhi hum, Aum the diamond powerful guru Padma*, as he walked.

!urq came to a halt as soon as her party had filed from the room. Her lower arms formed an expression of bewilderment.

"Is that all?"

Jigme looked at the alien. "That is the conclusion of the audience, yes. We may tour the holy places in the Library, if you wish."

"We had no opportunity to discuss the matter of Gyangtse."

"You may apply to the Ministry for another interview."

"It took me twelve years to obtain this one." Her upper arms took a stance that Jigme recognized as martial. "The patience of my government is not unlimited," she said.

Jigme bowed. "I shall communicate this to the Ministry, Ambassador."

"Delay in the Gyangtse matter will only result in more hardship for the inhabitants when they are removed."

"It is out of my hands, Ambassador."

!urq held her stance for a long moment in order to emphasize her protest, then relaxed her arms. Her upper set of hands caressed the white silk khata. "Odd to think," she said, amused, "that I journeyed twelve years just to stick out my lip at a human and have him touch my face in return."

"Many humans would give their lives for such a blessing," said Jigme.

"Sticking out the lip is quite rude where I come from, you know."

"I believe you have told me this."

"The Omniscient's hands were very warm." !urq raised fingers to her forehead, touched the ebon flesh. "I believe I can still feel the heat on my skin."

Jigme was impressed. "The Treasured King has given you a special blessing. He can channel the energies of the Diamond Mountain through his body. That was the heat you felt."

!urq's antennae rose skeptically, but she refrained from comment.

"Would you like to see the holy places?" Jigme said. "This, for instance, is a room devoted to Maitreya, the Buddha That Will Come. Before you is his statue. Data can be accessed by manipulation of the images on his headdress."

Jigme's speech was interrupted by the entrance of a Masker servant from the audience room. A white khata was draped about the avian's neck. !urq's trunk swiveled atop her centaur body; her arms assumed a commanding stance. The clicks and pops of her own language rattled from her mouth like falling stones.

"Did I send for you, creature?"

The Masker performed an obsequious gesture with its parasol. "I beg the Colonel's pardon. The old human sent for us. He is touching us and giving us scarves." The Masker fluttered helplessly. "We did not wish to offend our hosts, and there were no Sang to query for instruction."

"How odd," said !urq. "Why should the old human want to bless our slaves?" She eyed the Masker and thought for a moment. "I will not kill you today," she decided. She turned to Jigme and switched to Tibetan. "Please continue, Rinpoche."

"As you wish, Colonel." He returned to his speech. "The Library Palace is the site of no less than twenty-one tombs of various bodhisattvas, including many incarnations of the Gyalpo Rinpoche. The Palace also contains over eight thousand data terminals and sixty shrines."

As he rattled through the prepared speech, Jigme wondered about the scene he had just witnessed. He suspected that "I will not kill you today" was less alarming than it sounded, was instead an idiomatic way of saying "Go about your business."

Then again, knowing the Sang, maybe not.

The Cabinet had gathered in one of the many other reception rooms of the Library Palace. This one was small, the walls and ceiling hidden behind tapestry covered with appliqué, the room's sole ornament a black stone statue of a dancing demon that served tea on command.

The Gyalpo Rinpoche, to emphasize his once-humble origins, was seated on the floor. White stubble prickled from his scalp.

Jigme sat cross-legged on a pillow. Across from him was Dr. O'Neill. A lay official, her status was marked by the long turquoise earring that hung from her left ear to her collarbone, that and the long hair piled high on her head. The rosary she held was made of 108 antique microprocessors pierced and strung on a length of fiberoptic cable. Beside her sat the cheerful Miss Taisuke, the Minister of State. Although only fifteen years old, she was

Jigme's immediate superior, her authority derived from being the certified reincarnation of a famous hermit nun of the Yellow Hat Gelugspa order. Beside her, the Minister of Magic, a tantric sorcerer of the Gyud School named Daddy Carbajal, toyed with a trumpet made from a human thighbone. Behind him in a semireclined position was the elderly, frail, toothless State Oracle—his was a high-ranking position, but it was a largely symbolic one as long as the Treasured King was in his majority. Other ministers, lay or clerical, sipped tea or gossiped as they waited for the Incarnation to begin the meeting.

The Treasured King scratched one bony shoulder, grinned, then assumed in an eyeblink a posture of deep meditation, placing hands in his lap with his skull-rosary wrapped around them. "Aum," he intoned. The others straightened and joined in the holy syllable, the Pranava, the creative sound whose vibrations built the universe. Then the Horse of the Air rose from the throat of the Gyalpo Rinpoche, the syllables *Aum mane padme hum*, and the others reached for their rosaries.

As he recited the rosary, Jigme tried to meditate on each syllable as it went by, comprehend the full meaning of each, the color, the importance, the significance. *Aum*, which was white and connected with the gods. *Ma*, which was blue and connected with the titans. *Ne*, which was yellow and connected with men. *Pad*, which was green and connected with animals. *Me*, which was red and connected with giants and demigods. *Hum*, which was black and connected with dwellers in purgatory. Each syllable a separate realm, each belonging to a separate species, together forming the visible and invisible universe.

"Hri!" called everyone in unison, signifying the end of the 108th repetition. The Incarnation smiled and asked the black statue for some tea. The stone demon scuttled across the thick carpet and poured tea into his golden bowl. The demon looked up into the Incarnation's face.

"Free me!" said the statue.

The Gyalpo Rinpoche looked at the statue. "Tell me truthfully. Have you achieved Enlightenment?"

The demon said nothing.

The Treasured King smiled again. "Then you had better give Dr. O'Neill some tea."

O'Neill accepted her tea, sipped, and dismissed the demon. It scuttled back to its pedestal.

"We should consider the matter of Ambassador !urq," said the Incarnation.

O'Neill put down her teacup. "I am opposed to her presence here. The Sang are an unenlightened and violent race. They conceive of life as a struggle against nature rather than search for Enlightenment. They have already conquered an entire species, and would subdue us if they could."

"That is why I have consented to the building of warships," said the Incarnation.

"From their apartments in the Nyingmapa monastery, the Sang now have access to the Library," said O'Neill. "All our strategic information is present there. They will use the knowledge against us."

"Truth can do no harm," said Miss Taisuke.

"All truth is not vouchsafed to the unenlightened," said O'Neill. "To those unprepared by correct study and thought, truth can be a danger." She gestured with an arm, encompassing the world outside the Palace. "Who should know better than we, who live on Vajra? Haven't half the charlatans in all existence set up outside our walls to preach half-truths to the credulous, endangering their own Enlightenment and those of everyone who hears them?"

Jigme listened to O'Neill in silence. O'Neill and Daddy Carbajal were the leaders of the reactionary party, defenders of orthodoxy and the security of the realm. They had argued this point before.

"Knowledge will make the Sang cautious," said Jigme. "They will now know of our armament. They will now understand the scope of the human expansion, far greater than their own. We may hope this will deter them from attack."

"The Sang may be encouraged to build more weapons of their own," said Daddy Carbajal. "They are already highly militarized, as a way of keeping down their subject species. They may militarize further."

"Be assured they are doing so," said O'Neill. "Our own embassy is kept in close confinement on a small planetoid. They have no way of learning the scope of the Sang threat or sending this information to the Library. We, on the other hand, have escorted the Sang ambassador throughout human space and have shown her anything in which she expressed an interest."

"Deterrence," said Jigme. "We wished them to know how extensive our sphere is, that the conquest would be costly and call for more resources than they possess."

"We must do more than deter. The Sang threat should be eliminated, as were the threats of heterodox humanity during the Third and Fifth Incarnations."

"You speak jihad," said Miss Taisuke.

There was brief silence. No one, not even O'Neill, was comfortable with Taisuke's plainness.

"All human worlds are under the peace of the Library," said O'Neill. "This was accomplished partly by force, partly by conversion. The Sang will not *permit* conversion."

The Gyalpo Rinpoche cleared his throat. The others fell silent at once. The Incarnation had been listening in silence, his face showing concentration but no emotion. He always preferred to hear the opinions of others before expressing his own. "The Third and Fifth Incarnations," he said, "did nothing to encourage the jihads proclaimed in their name. The Incarnations did not wish to accept temporal power."

"They did not speak against the holy warriors," said Daddy Carbajal.

The Incarnation's elderly face was uncommonly stern. His hands formed the teaching mudra. "Does not Shakyamuni speak in the *Anguttara Nikaya* of the three ways of keeping the body pure?" he asked. "One must not commit adultery, one must not steal, one must not kill any living creature. How could warriors kill for orthodoxy and yet remain orthodox?"

There was a long moment of uncomfortable silence. Only Daddy Carbajal, whose tantric Short Path teaching included numerous ways of dispatching his enemies, did not seem nonplussed.

"The Sang are here to study us," said the Gyalpo Rinpoche. "We also study them."

"I view their pollution as a danger." Dr. O'Neill's face was stubborn.

Miss Taisuke gave a brilliant smile. "Does not the *Mahaparinirvana-sutra* tell us that if we are forced to live in a difficult situation and among people of impure minds, if we cherish faith in Buddha we can ever lead them toward better actions?"

Relief fluttered through Jigme. Taisuke's apt quote, atop the Incarnation's sternness, had routed the war party.

"The Embassy will remain," said the Treasured King. "They will be given the freedom of Vajra, saving only the Holy Precincts. We must remember the oath of the Amida Buddha: 'Though I attain Buddhahood, I shall never be complete until people everywhere, hearing my name, learn right ideas about life and death, and gain that perfect wisdom that will keep their minds pure and tranquil in the midst of the world's greed and suffering.' "

"What of Gyangtse, Rinpoche?" O'Neill's voice seemed harsh after the graceful words of Scripture.

The Gyalpo Rinpoche cocked his head and thought for a moment. Suddenly the Incarnation seemed very human and very frail, and Jigme's heart surged with love for the old man.

"We will deal with that at the Picnic Festival," said the Incarnation.

From his position by the lake, Jigme could see tents and banners dotting the lower slopes of Tingsum like bright spring flowers. The Picnic Festival lasted a week, and unlike most of the other holidays had no real religious connection. It was a week-long campout during which almost the entire population of the Diamond City and the surrounding monasteries moved into the open and spent their time making merry.

Jigme could see the giant yellow hovertent of the Gyalpo Rinpoche surrounded by saffron-robed guards, the guards present not to protect the Treasured King from attackers, but rather to preserve his tranquility against invasions by devout pilgrims in search of a blessing. The guards—monks armed with staves, their shoulders padded hugely to make them look more formidable—served the additional purpose of keeping the Sang away from the Treasured King until the conclusion of the festival, something for which

Jigme was devoutly grateful. He didn't want any political confrontations disturbing the joy of the holiday. Fortunately Ambassador !urq seemed content to wait until her scheduled appearance at a party given by the Incarnation on the final afternoon.

Children splashed barefoot in the shallows of the lake, and others played chibi on the sward beside, trying to keep a shuttlecock aloft using the feet alone. Jigme found himself watching a redheaded boy on the verge of adolescence, admiring the boy's grace, the way the knobbed spine and sharp shoulders moved under his pale skin. His bony ankles hadn't missed the shuttlecock yet. Jigme was sufficiently lost in his reverie that he did not hear the sound of boots on the grass beside him.

"Jigme Dzasa?"

Jigme looked up with a guilty start. !urq stood beside him, wearing hardy outdoor clothing. Her legs were wrapped up to the shoulder. Jigme stood hastily and bowed.

"Your pardon, Ambassador. I didn't hear you."

The Sang's feathery antennae waved cheerfully in the breeze. "I thought I would lead a party up Tingsum. Would you care to join us?"

What Jigme wanted to do was continue watching the ball game, but he assented with a smile. Climbing mountains: that was the sort of thing the Sang were always up to. They wanted to demonstrate they could conquer anything.

"Perhaps you should find a pony," !urq said. "Then you could keep up with us."

Jigme took a pony from the Library's corral and followed the waffle patterns of !urq's boots into the trees on the lower slopes. Three other Sang were along on the expedition; they clicked and gobbled to one another as they trotted cheerfully along. Behind toiled three Maskers-of-burden carrying food and climbing equipment. If the Sang noticed the incongruity demonstrated by the human's using a quadruped as a beast of burden while they, centauroids, used a bipedal race as servants, they politely refrained from mentioning it. The pony's genetically altered cloven forefeet took the mountain trail easily, nimbler than the Sang in their heavy boots. Jigme noticed that this made the Sang work harder, trying to outdo the dumb beast.

They came to a high mountain meadow and paused, looking down at the huge field of tents that ringed the smooth violet lake. In the middle of the meadow was a three-meter tower of crystal, weathered and yellow, ringed by rubble flaked off during the hard winters. One of the Sang trotted over to examine it.

"I thought the crystal was instructed to stay well below the surface," he said.

"There must have been a house here once," Jigme said. "The crystal would have been instructed to grow up through the surface to provide Library access."

!urq trotted across a stretch of grass, her head down. "Here's the beginning of the foundation line," she said. She gestured with an arm. "It runs from here to over there."

The Sang cantered over the ground, frisky as children, to discover the remnants of the foundation. The Sang were always keen, Jigme found, on discovering things. They had not yet learned that there was only one thing worth discovering, and it had nothing to do with old ruins.

!urq examined the pillar of crystal, touched its crumbling surface. "And over eighty percent of the planet is composed of this?" she said.

"All except the crust," Jigme said. "The crystal was instructed to convert most of the planet's material. That is why our heavy metals have to come from mined asteroids, and why we build mostly in natural materials. This house was probably of wood and laminated cloth, and it most likely burned in an accident."

!urq picked up a bit of crystal from the ring of rubble that surrounded the pillar. "And you can store information in this."

"All the information we have," Jigme said reverently. "All the information in the universe, eventually." Involuntarily, his hands formed the teaching mudra. "The Library is a hologram of the universe. The Blessed Bodhisattva Bob Miller was a reflection of the Library, its first Incarnation. The current Incarnation is the forty-first."

!urq's antennae flickered in the wind. She tossed the piece of crystal from hand to hand. "All the information you possess," she said. "That is a powerful tool. Or weapon."

"A tool, yes. The original builders of the Library considered it only a tool. Only something to help them order things, to assist them in governing. They did not comprehend that once the Diamond Mountain contained enough information, once it gathered enough energy, it would become more than the sum of its parts. That it would become the Mind of Buddha, the universe in small, and that the Mind, out of its compassion, would seek to incarnate itself as a human."

"The Library is self-aware?" !urq asked. She seemed to find the notion startling.

Jigme could only shrug. "Is the universe self-aware?"

!urq made a series of meditative clicking noises.

"Inside the Diamond Mountain," Jigme said, "there are processes going on that we cannot comprehend. The Library was designed to be nearly autonomous; it is now so large we cannot keep track of everything, because we would need a mind as large as the Library to process the information. Many of the energy and data transfers that we can track are very subtle, involving energies that are not fully understood. Yet we can track some of them. When an Incarnation dies, we can see the trace his spirit makes through the Library—like an atomic particle that comes apart in a shower of short-lived particles, we see it principally through its effects on other energies—and we can see part of those energies move from one place to another, from one body to another, becoming another Incarnation."

!urq's antennae moved skeptically. "You can document this?"

"We can produce spectra showing the tracks of energy through matter. Is that documentation?"

"I would say, with all respect, your case remains unproven."

"I do not seek to prove anything." Jigme smiled. "The Gyalpo Rinpoche is his own proof, his own truth. Buddha is truth. All else is illusion."

!urq put the piece of crystal in her pocket. "If this was *our* Library," she said, "we would prove things one way or another."

"You would see only your own reflection. Existence on the quantum level is largely a matter of belief. On that level, mind is as powerful as matter. We believe that the Gyalpo Rinpoche is an Incarnation of the Library; does that belief help make it so?"

"You ask me questions based on a system of belief that I do not share. How can you expect me to answer?"

"Belief is powerful. Belief can incarnate itself."

"Belief can incarnate itself as delusion."

"Delusion can incarnate itself as reality." Jigme stood in his stirrups, stretching his legs, and then settled back into his saddle. "Let me tell you a story," he said. "It's quite true. There was a man who went for a drive, over the pass yonder." He pointed across the valley, at the low blue pass, the Kampa La, between the mountains Tampa and Tsang. "It was a pleasant day, and he put the car's top down. A windstorm came up as he was riding near a crossroads, and his fur hat blew off his head into a thorn bush, where he couldn't reach it. He simply drove on his way.

"Other people walked past the bush, and they saw something inside. They told each other they'd seen something odd there. The hat got weathered and less easy to recognize. Soon the locals were telling travelers to beware the thing near the crossroads, and someone else suggested the thing might be a demon, and soon people were warning others about the demon in the bush."

"Delusion," said !urq.

"It *was* delusion," Jigme agreed. "But it was *not* delusion when the hat grew arms, legs, and teeth, and when it began chasing people up and down the Kampa La. The Ministry of Magic had to send a naljorpa to perform a rite of chöd and banish the thing."

!urq's antennae gave a meditative quiver. "People see what they want to see," she said.

"The delusion had incarnated itself. The case is classic: the Ministries of Science and Magic performed an inquiry. They could trace the patterns of energy through the crystal structure of the Library: the power of the growing belief, the reaction when the belief was fulfilled, the dispersing of the energy when chöd was performed." Jigme gave a laugh. "In the end, the naljorpa brought back an old, weathered hat. Just bits of fur and leather."

"The naljorpa got a good reward, no doubt," said !urq, "for bringing back this moldy bit of fur."

"Probably. Not my department, actually."

"It seems possible, here on Vajra, to make a good living out of others' delusions. My government would not permit such things."

"What do the people lose by being credulous?" Jigme asked. "Only money, which is earthly, and that is a pitiful thing to worry about. It would matter only that the act of giving is sincere."

!urq gave a toss of her head. "We should continue up the mountain, Rinpoche."

"Certainly." Jigme kicked his pony into a trot. He wondered if he had just convinced !urq that his government was corrupt in allowing fakirs to gull the population. Jigme knew there were many ways to Enlightenment and that the soul must try them all. Just because the preacher was corrupt did not mean his message was untrue. How to convince !urq of that? he wondered.

"We believe it is good to test oneself against things," !urq said. "Life is struggle, and one must remain sharp. Ready for whatever happens."

"In the *Parinibbana-sutra*, the Blessed One says that the point of his teaching is to control our own minds. Then one can be ready."

"Of course we control our minds, Rinpoche. If we could not control our minds, we would not achieve mastery. If we do not achieve mastery, then we are nothing."

"I am pleased, then," Jigme smiled, "that you and the Buddha are in agreement."

To which !urq had no reply, save only to launch herself savagely at the next climb, while Jigme followed easily on his cloven-hoofed pony.

The scent of incense and flowers filled the Gyalpo Rinpoche's giant yellow tent. The Treasured King, a silk khata around his neck, sat in the lotus posture on soft grass. The bottoms of his feet were stained green. Ambassador !urq stood ponderously before him, lower lip thrust forward, her four arms in a formal stance, the Incarnation's knotted scarf draped over her shoulders.

Jigme watched, standing next to the erect, angry figure of Dr. O'Neill. He took comfort from the ever-serene smile of Miss Taisuke, sitting on the grass across the tent.

"Ambassador Colonel, I am happy you have joined us on holiday."

"We are pleased to participate in your festivals, Omniscient," said !urq.

"The spring flowers are lovely, are they not? It's worthwhile to take a whole week to enjoy them. In so doing, we remember the words of Shakyamuni, who tells us to enjoy the blossoms of Enlightenment in their season and harvest the fruit of the right path."

"Is there a season, Omniscient, for discussing the matter of Gyangtse?"

Right to the point, Jigme thought. !urq might never learn the oblique manner of speech that predominated at the high ministerial levels.

The Incarnation was not disturbed. "Surely matters may be discussed in any season," he said.

"The planet is desirable, Omniscient. Your settlement violates our border. My government demands your immediate evacuation."

Dr. O'Neill's breath hissed out at the word *demand*. Jigme could see her ears redden with fury.

"The first humans reached the planet before the border negotiations were completed," the Incarnation said equably. "They did not realize they were setting in violation of the agreement."

"That does not invalidate the agreement."

"Conceded, Ambassador. Still, would it not be unjust, after all their hard labor, to ask them to move?"

!urq's antennae bobbed politely. "Does not your Blessed One admit that life is composed of suffering? Does the Buddha not condemn the demon of worldly desires? What desire could be more worldly than a desire to possess a world?"

Jigme was impressed. Definitely, he thought, she was getting better at this sort of thing.

"In the same text," said Jigme, "Shakyamuni tells us to refrain from disputes, and not repel one another like water and oil, but like milk and water mingle together." He opened his hands in an offering gesture. "Will your government not accept a new planet in exchange? Or better yet, will they not dispose of this border altogether, and allow a free commerce between our races?"

"What new planet?" !urq's arms formed a querying posture.

"We explore constantly in order to fulfill the mandate of the Library and provide it with more data. Our survey records are available through your Library access. Choose any planet that has not yet been inhabited by humans."

"Any planet chosen will be outside of our zone of influence, far from our own frontiers and easily cut off from our home sphere."

"Why would we cut you off, Ambassador?"

"Gyangtse is of strategic significance. It is a penetration of our border."

"Let us then dispose of the border entirely."

!urq's antennae stood erect. Her arms took a martial position. "You humans are larger, more populous. You would overwhelm us by sheer numbers. The border must remain inviolate."

"Let us then have greater commerce across the border than before. With increased knowledge, distrust will diminish."

"You would send missionaries. I know there are Jesuits and Gelugspa who have been training for years in hopes of obtaining converts or martyrdom in the Sang dominions."

"It would be a shame to disappoint them." There was a slight smile on the Incarnation's face.

!urq's arms formed an obstinate pattern. "They would stir up trouble among the Maskers. They would preach to the credulous among my own race. My government must protect its own people."

"The message of Shakyamuni is not a political message, Ambassador."

"That is a matter of interpretation, Omniscient."

"Will you transmit my offer to your government?"

!urq held her stance for a long moment. Jigme could sense Dr. O'Neill's fury in the alien's obstinacy. "I will do so, Omniscient," said the Ambassador. "Though I have no confidence that it will be accepted."

"I think the offer will be accepted," said Miss Taisuke. She sat on the grass in Jigme's tent. She was in the butterfly position, the soles of her feet pressed together and her knees on the ground. Jigme sat beside her. One of Jigme's students, a clean-limbed lad named Rabjoms, gracefully served them tea and cakes, then withdrew.

"The Sang are obdurate," said Jigme. "Why do you think there is hope?"

"Sooner or later the Sang will realize they may choose any one of hundreds of unoccupied planets. It will dawn on them that they can pick one on the far side of our sphere, and their spy ships can travel the length of human-occupied space on quite legitimate missions, and gather whatever information they desire."

"Ah."

"All this in exchange for one minor border penetration."

Jigme thought about this for a moment. "We've held onto Gyangtse in order to test the Sangs' rationality and their willingness to fight. There has been no war in twelve years. This shows that the Sang are susceptible to reason. Where there is reason, there is capability for Enlightenment."

"Amen," said Miss Taisuke. She finished her tea and put down the glass.

"Would you like more? Shall I summon Rabjoms?"

"Thank you, no." She cast a glance back to the door of the tent. "He has lovely brown eyes, your Rabjoms."

"Yes."

Miss Taisuke looked at him. "Is he your consort?"

Jigme put down his glass. "No. I try to forsake worldly passions."

"You are of the Red Hat order. You have taken no vow of celibacy."

Agitation fluttered in Jigme's belly. "The *Mahaparinirvana-sutra* says that lust is the soil in which other passions flourish. I avoid it."

"I wondered. It has been remarked that all your pages are such pretty boys."

Jigme tried to calm himself. "I choose them for other qualities, Miss Taisuke. I assure you."

She laughed merrily. "Of course. I merely wondered." She leaned forward from out of her butterfly position, reached out, and touched his cheek. "I have a sense this may be a randy incarnation for me. You have no desire for young girls?"

Jigme did not move. "I cannot help you, Minister."

"Poor Jigme." She drew her hand back. "I will offer prayers for you."

"Prayers are always accepted, Miss Taisuke."

"But not passes. Very well." She rose to her feet, and Jigme rose with her. "I must be off to the Kagyupas' party. Will you be there?"

"I have scheduled this hour for meditation. Perhaps later."

"Later, then." She kissed his cheek and squeezed his hand, then slipped out of the tent. Jigme sat in the lotus posture and called for Rabjoms to take away the tea things. As he watched the boy's graceful movements, he gave an inward sigh. His weakness had been noticed, and, even worse, remarked on.

His next student would have to be ugly. The ugliest one he could find. He sighed again.

A shriek rang out. Jigme looked up, heart hammering, and saw a demon at the back of the tent. Its flesh was bright red, and its eyes seemed to bulge out of its head. Rabjoms yelled and flung the tea service at it; a glass bounced off its head and shattered.

The demon charged forward, Rabjoms falling under its clawed feet. The overwhelming smell of decay filled the tent. The demon burst through the tent flap into the outdoors. Jigme heard more shrieks and cries of alarm from outside. The demon roared like a bull, then laughed like a madman. Jigme crawled forward to gather up Rabjoms, holding the terrified boy in his arms, chanting the Horse of the Air to calm himself until he heard the teakettle hissing of a thousand snakes followed by a rush of wind, the sign that the entity had dispersed. Jigme soothed his page and tried to think what the meaning of this sudden burst of psychic energy might be.

A few moments later, Jigme received a call on his radiophone. The Gyalpo Rinpoche, a few moments after returning to the Library Palace in his hovertent, had fallen stone dead.

"Cerebral hemorrhage," said Dr. O'Neill. The Minister of Science had performed the autopsy herself—her long hair was undone and tied behind, to fit under a surgical cap, and she still wore her scrubs. She was without the long turquoise earring that marked her rank, and she kept waving a hand near her ear, as if she somehow missed it. "The Incarnation was an old man," she said. "A slight erosion in an artery, and he was gone. It took only seconds."

The Cabinet accepted the news in stunned silence. For all their lives, there had been only the one Treasured King. Now the anchor of all their lives had been removed.

"The reincarnation was remarkably swift," Dr. O'Neill said. "I was able to watch most of it on the monitors in real time—the energies remained remarkably focused, not dissipated in a shower of sparks as with most individuals. I must admit I was impressed. The demon that appeared at the Picnic Festival was only one of the many side effects caused by such a massive turbulence within the crystal architecture of the Diamond Mountain."

Miss Taisuke looked up. "Have you identified the child?"

"Of course." Dr. O'Neill allowed herself a thin-lipped smile. "A second-trimester baby, to be born to a family of tax collectors in Dulan Province, near the White Ocean. The fetus is not developed to the point where a full incarnation is possible, and the energies remain clinging to the mother until they can move to the child. She must be feeling . . . elevated. I would like to interview her about her sensations before she is informed that she is carrying the new Bodhisattva." Dr. O'Neill waved a hand in the vicinity of her ear again.

"We must appoint a regent," said Daddy Carbajal.

"Yes," said Dr. O'Neill. "The more so now, with the human sphere being threatened by the unenlightened."

Jigme looked from one to the other. The shock of the Gyalpo Rinpoche's death had unnerved him to the point of forgetting political matters. Clearly this had not been the case with O'Neill and the Minister of Magic.

He could not let the reactionary party dominate this meeting.

"I believe," he said, "we should appoint Miss Taisuke as Regent."

His words surprised even himself.

The struggle was prolonged. Dr. O'Neill and Daddy Carbajal fought an obstinate rearguard action, but finally Miss Taisuke was confirmed. Jigme had a feeling that several of the ministers only consented to Miss Taisuke because they thought she was young enough that they might manipulate her. They didn't know her well, Jigme thought, and that was fortunate.

"We must formulate a policy concerning Gyangtse and the Sang," Dr. O'Neill said. Her face assumed its usual thin-lipped stubbornness.

"The Omniscient's policy was always to delay," Miss Taisuke said. "This sad matter will furnish a further excuse for postponing any final decision."

"We must put the armed forces on alert. The Sang may consider this a moment in which to strike."

The Regent nodded. "Let this be done."

"There is the matter of the new Incarnation," Dr. O'Neill said. "Should the delivery be advanced? How should the parents be informed?"

"We shall consult the State Oracle," said Miss Taisuke.

The Oracle, his toothless mouth gaping, was a picture of terror. No one had asked him anything in years.

Eerie music echoed through the Oracular Hall of the Library, off the walls and ceiling covered with grotesque carvings—gods, demons, and skulls that grinned at the intent humans below. Chanting monks sat in rows, accompanied by magicians playing drums and trumpets all made from human bone. Jigme's stinging eyes watered from the gusts of strong incense.

In the middle of it all sat the State Oracle, his wrinkled face expressionless. Before him, sitting on a platform, was Miss Taisuke, dressed in the formal clothing of the Regency.

"In old Tibetan times, the Oracle used to be consulted frequently," Jigme told Ambassador !urq. "But since the Gyalpo Rinpoche has been incarnated on Vajra, the Omniscient's close association with the universe analogue of the Library has made most divination unnecessary. The State Oracle is usually called upon only during periods between Incarnations."

"I am having trouble phrasing my reports to my superiors, Rinpoche," said !urq. "Your government is at present run by a fifteen-year-old girl with the advice of an elderly fortune-teller. I expect to have a certain amount of difficulty getting my superiors to take this seriously."

"The Oracle is a serious diviner," Jigme said. "There are a series of competetive exams to discover his degree of empathy with the Library. Our Oracle was right at the top of his class."

"My government will be relieved to know it."

The singing and chanting had been going on for hours. !urq had long been showing signs of impatience. Suddenly the Oracle gave a start. His eyes and mouth dropped open. His face had lost all character.

Then something else was there, an alien presence. The Oracle jumped up from his seated position, began to whirl wildly with his arms outstretched. Several of his assistants ran forward carrying his headdress while others seized him, holding his rigid body steady. The headdress was enormous, all hand-wrought gold featuring skulls and gods and topped with a vast array of plumes. It weighed over ninety pounds.

"The Oracle, by use of intent meditation, has driven the spirit from his own body," Jigme reported. "He is now possessed by the Library, which assumes the form of the god Yamantaka, the Conqueror of Death."

"Interesting," !urq said noncommittally.

"An old man could not support that headdress without some form of psychic help," Jigme said. "Surely you must agree?" He was beginning to be annoyed by the Ambassador's perpetual skepticism.

The Oracle's assistants had managed to strap the headdress on the Oracle's bald head. They stepped back, and the Oracle continued his dance, the weighty headdress supported by his rigid neck. The Oracle dashed from one end of the room to the other, still whirling, sweat spraying off his brow, then ran to the feet of Miss Taisuke and fell to his knees.

When he spoke it was in a metallic, unnatural voice. "The Incarnation should be installed by New Year!" he shouted, and then toppled. When the assistant monks had unstrapped the heavy headdress and the old man rose, back in his body once more and rubbing his neck, the Oracle looked at Miss Taisuke and blinked painfully. "I resign," he said.

"Accepted," said the Regent. "With great regret."

"This is a young man's job. I could have broken my damn neck."

Ambassador !urq's antennae pricked forward. "This," she said, "is an unusually truthful oracle."

"Top of his class," said Jigme. "What did I tell you?"

The new Oracle was a young man, a strict orthodox Yellow Hat whose predictive abilities had been proved outstanding by every objective test. The calendar of festivals rolled by: the time of pilgrimage, the week of operas and plays, the kite-flying festival, the end of Ramadan, Buddha's descent from

Tishita Heaven, Christmas, the celebration of Kali the Benevolent, the anniversary of the death of Tsongkhapa. . . . The New Year was calculated to fall sixty days after Christmas, and for weeks beforehand the artisans of Vajra worked on their floats. The floats—huge sculptures of fabulous buildings, religious icons, famous scenes from the opera featuring giant animated figures, tens of thousands of man-hours of work—would be taken through the streets of the Diamond City during the New Year's procession, then up onto Burning Hill in plain sight of the Library Palace where the new Incarnation could view them from the balcony.

And week after week, the new Incarnation grew, as fast as the technology safely permitted. Carefully removed from his mother's womb by Dr. O'Neill, the Incarnation was placed in a giant autowomb and fed a diet of nutrients and hormones calculated to bring him to adulthood. Microscopic wires were inserted carefully into his developing brain to feed the memory centers with scripture, philosophy, science, art, and the art of governing. As the new Gyalpo Rinpoche grew the body was exercised by electrode so that he would emerge with physical maturity.

The new Incarnation had early on assumed the lotus position during his rest periods, and Jigme often came to the Science Ministry to watch, through the womb's transparent cover, the eerie figure meditating in the bubbling nutrient solution. All growth of hair had been suppressed by Dr. O'Neill and the figure seemed smooth perfection. The Omniscient-to-be was leaving early adolescence behind, growing slim and cat-muscled.

The new Incarnation would need whatever strength it possessed. The political situation was worsening. The border remained unresolved—the Sang wanted not simply a new planet in exchange for Gyangtse, but also room to expand into a new militarized sphere on the other side of human space. Sang military movements, detected from the human side of the border, seemed to be rehearsals for an invasion, and were countered by increased human defense allotments. As a deterrent, the human response was made obvious to the Sang: Ambassador !urq complained continually about human aggression. Dr. O'Neill and Daddy Carbajal grew combative in Cabinet meetings. Opposition to them was scattered and unfocused. If the reactionary party wanted war, the Sang were doing little but playing into their hands.

Fortunately the Incarnation would be decanted within a week, to take possession of the rambling, embittered councils and give them political direction. Jigme closed his eyes and offered a long prayer that the Incarnation might soon make his presence felt among his ministers.

He opened his eyes. The smooth, adolescent Incarnation hovered before him, suspended in golden nutrient. Fine bubbles rose in the liquid, stroking the Incarnation's skin. The figure had a fascinating, eerie beauty, and Jigme felt he could stare at it forever.

Jigme saw, to his surprise, that the floating Incarnation had an erection. And then the Incarnation opened his eyes.

The eyes were green. Jigme felt coldness flood his spine—the look was knowing, a look of recognition. A slight smile curled the Incarnation's lips. Jigme stared. The smile seemed cruel.

Dry-mouthed, Jigme bent forward, slammed his forehead to the floor in obeisance. Pain crackled through his head. He stayed that way for a long time, offering prayer after frantic prayer.

When he finally rose, the Incarnation's eyes were closed, and the body sat calmly amid golden, rising bubbles.

The late Incarnation's rosary seemed warm as it lay against Jigme's neck. Perhaps it was anticipating being reunited with its former owner.

"The Incarnation is being dressed," Dr. O'Neill said. She stepped through the doors into the vast cabinet room. Two novice monks, doorkeepers, bowed as she swept past, their tongues stuck out in respect, then swung the doors shut behind her. O'Neill was garbed formally in a dress so heavy with brocade that it crackled as she moved. Yellow lamplight flickered from the braid as she moved through the darkened counsel chamber. Her piled hair was hidden under an embroidered cap; silver gleamed from the elaborate settings of her long turquoise earring. "He will meet with the Cabinet in a few moments and perform the recognition ceremony."

The Incarnation had been decanted that afternoon. He had walked as soon as he was permitted. The advanced growth techniques used by Dr. O'Neill appeared to have met with total success. Her eyes glowed with triumph; her cheeks were flushed.

She took her seat among the Cabinet, moving stiffly in the heavy brocade.

The Cabinet sat surrounding a small table on which some of the late Incarnation's possessions were surrounded by a number of similar objects or imitations. His rosary was around Jigme's neck. During the recognition ceremony, the new Incarnation was supposed to single out his possessions in order to display his continuance from the former personality. The ceremony was largely a formality, a holdover from the earlier, Tibetan tradition—it was already perfectly clear, from Library data, just who the Incarnation was.

There was a shout from the corridor outside, then a loud voice raised in song. The members of the Cabinet stiffened in annoyance. Someone was creating a disturbance. The Regent beckoned to a communications device hidden in an image of Kali, intending to summon guards and have the disorderly one ejected.

The doors swung open, each held by a bowing novice with outthrust tongues. The Incarnation appeared between them. He was young, just entering late adolescence. He was dressed in the tall crested formal hat and yellow robes stiff with brocade. Green eyes gleamed in the dim light as he looked at the assembled officials.

The Cabinet moved as one, offering obeisance first with praying hands lifted to the forehead, mouth, and heart, then prostrated themselves with their heads to the ground. As he fell forward, Jigme heard a voice singing.

Let us drink and sport today,
Ours is not tomorrow.
Love with Youth flies swift away,
Age is nought but Sorrow.
Dance and sing,
Time's on the wing,
Life never knows the return of Spring.

In slow astonishment, Jigme realized that it was the Incarnation who was singing. Gradually Jigme rose from his bow.

Jigme saw that the Incarnation had a bottle in his hand. Was he drunk? he wondered. And where in the Library had he gotten the beer, or whatever it was? Had he materialized it?

"This way, boy," said the Incarnation. He had a hand on the shoulder of one of the doorkeepers. He drew the boy into the room, then took a long drink from his bottle. He eyed the Cabinet slowly, turning his head from one to the other.

"Omniscient—" said Miss Taisuke.

"Not yet," said the Incarnation. "I've been in a glass sphere for almost ten months. It's time I had some fun." He pushed the doorkeeper onto hands and knees, then knelt behind the boy. He pushed up the boy's zen, clutched at his buttocks. The page cast little frantic glances around the room. The new State Oracle seemed apoplectic.

"I see you've got some of my things," said the Incarnation.

Jigme felt something twitch around his neck. The former Incarnation's skull-rosary was beginning to move. Jigme's heart crashed in his chest.

The Cabinet watched in stunned silence as the Incarnation began to sodomize the doorkeeper. The boy's face showed nothing but panic and terror.

This is a lesson, Jigme thought insistently. This is a living Bodhisattva doing this, and somehow this is one of his sermons. We will learn from this.

The rosary twitched, rose slowly from around Jigme's neck, and flew through the air to drop around the Incarnation's head.

A plain ivory walking stick rose from the table and spun through the air. The Incarnation materialized a third arm to catch the cane in midair. A decorated porcelain bowl followed, a drum, and a small golden figurine of a laughing Buddha ripped itself free from the pocket of the new State Oracle. Each was caught by a new arm. Each item had belonged to the former Incarnation; each was the correct choice.

The Incarnation howled like a beast at the moment of climax. Then he stood, adjusting his garments. He bent to pick up the ivory cane. He smashed the porcelain bowl with it, then broke the cane over the head of the Buddha. He rammed the Buddha through the drum, then threw both against the wall. All six hands rose to the rosary around his neck; he ripped at it and the cord broke, white bone disks flying through the room. His extra arms vanished.

"Short Path," he said, turned and stalked out.

Across the room, in the long silence that followed, Jigme could see Dr. O'Neill. Her pale face seemed to float in the darkness, distinct amid the confusion and madness, her expression frozen in a racking, electric moment of private agony. The minister's moment of triumph had turned to ashes.

Perhaps everything had.

Jigme rose to comfort the doorkeeper.

"There has never been an Incarnation who followed the Short Path," said Miss Taisuke.

"Daddy Carbajal should be delighted," Jigme said. "He's a doubtob himself."

"I don't think he's happy," said the Regent. "I watched him. He is a tantric sorcerer, yes, one of the best. But the Incarnation's performance frightened him."

They spoke alone in Miss Taisuke's townhouse—in the lha khang, a room devoted to religious images. Incense floated gently in the air. Outside, Jigme could hear the sounds of celebration as the word reached the population that the Incarnation was among them once again.

A statue of the Thunderbolt Sow came to life, looked at the Regent. "A message from the Library Palace, Regent," it said. "The Incarnation has spent the evening in his quarters, in the company of an apprentice monk. He has now passed out from drunkenness."

"Thank you, Rinpoche," Taisuke said. The Thunderbolt Sow froze in place. Taisuke turned back to Jigme.

"His Omniscience is possibly the most powerful doubtob in history," she said. "Dr. O'Neill showed me the spectra—the display of psychic energy, as recorded by the Library, was truly awesome. And it was perfectly controlled."

"Could something have gone wrong with the process of bringing the Incarnation to adulthood?"

"The process has been used for centuries. It has been used on Incarnations before—it was a fad for a while, and the Eighteenth through Twenty-Third were all raised that way." She frowned, leaning forward. "In any case, it's all over. The Librarian Bob Miller—and the divine Avalokitesvara, if you go for that sort of thing—has now been reincarnated as the Forty-Second Gyalpo Rinpoche. There's nothing that can be done."

"Nothing," Jigme said. The Short Path, he thought, the path to Enlightenment taken by magicians and madmen, a direct route that had no reference to morality or convention. . . . The Short Path was dangerous, often heterodox, and colossally difficult. Most doubtobs ended up destroying themselves and everyone around them.

"We have had carnal Incarnations before," Taisuke said. "The Eighth left some wonderful love poetry behind, and quite a few have been sodomites. No harm was done."

"I will pray, Regent," said Jigme, "that no harm may be done now."

It seemed to him that there was a shadow on Taisuke's usual blazing smile. "That is doubtless the best solution. I will pray also."

Jigme returned to the Nyingmapa monastery, where he had an apartment near the Sang embassy. He knew he was too agitated to sit quietly and meditate, and so called for some novices to bring him a meditation box. He needed to discipline both body and mind before he could find peace.

He sat in the narrow box in a cross-legged position and drew the lid over his head. Cut off from the world, he would not allow himself to relax, to lean against the walls of the box for support. He took his rosary in his hands. "*Aum vajra sattva*," he began, Aum the Diamond Being, one of the names of Buddha.

But the picture that floated before his mind was not that of Shakyamuni, but the naked, beautiful form of the Incarnation, staring at him from out of the autowomb with green, soul-chilling eyes.

"We should have killed the Jesuit as well. We refrained only as a courtesy to your government, Rinpoche."

Perhaps, Jigme thought, the dead Maskers' soul were even now in the Library, whirling in the patterns of energy that would result in reincarnation, whirling like the snow that fell gently as he and !urq walked down the street. To be reincarnated as humans, with the possibility of Enlightenment.

"We will dispose of the bodies, if you prefer," Jigme said.

"They dishonored their masters," said !urq. "You may do what you like with them."

As Jigme and the Ambassador walked through the snowy streets toward the Punishment Grounds, they were met with grins and waves from the population, who were getting ready for the New Year celebration. !urq acknowledged the greetings with graceful nods of her antennae. Once the population heard what had just happened, Jigme thought, the reception might well be different.

"I will send monks to collect the bodies. We will cut them up and expose them on hillsides for the vultures. Afterward their bones will be collected and perhaps turned into useful implements."

"In my nation," !urq said, "that would be considered an insult."

"The bodies will nourish the air and the earth," said Jigme. "What finer kind of death could there be?"

"Elementary. A glorious death in service to the state."

Two Masker servants, having met several times with a Jesuit acting apparently without orders from his superiors, had announced their conversion to Buddhism. !urq had promptly denounced the two as spies and had them shot out of hand. The missionary had been ordered whipped by the superiors in his Order. !urq wanted to be on hand for it.

Jigme could anticipate the public reaction. Shakyamuni had strictly forbidden the taking of life. The people would be enraged. It might be unwise for the Sang to be seen in public for the next few days, particularly during the New Year Festival, when a large percentage of the population would be drunk.

Jigme and the Ambassador passed by a row of criminals in the stocks. Offerings of flowers, food, and money were piled up below them, given by the compassionate population. Another criminal—a murderer, probably—shackled in leg irons for life, approached with his begging bowl. Jigme gave him some money and passed on.

"Your notions of punishment would be considered far from enlightened in my nation," !urq said. "Flogging, branding, putting people in chains! We would consider that savage."

"We punish only the body," Jigme said. "We always allow an opportunity for the spirit to reform. Death without Enlightenment can only result in a return to endless cycles of reincarnation."

"A clean death is always preferable to bodily insult. And a lot of your flogging victims die afterward."

"But they do not die during the flogging."

"Yet they die in agony, because your whips tear their backs apart."

"Pain," said Jigme, "can be transcended."

"Sometimes," !urq said, antennae twitching, "you humans are terrifying. I say this in absolute and admiring sincerity."

There were an unusual number of felons today, since the authorities wanted to empty the holding cells before the New Year. The Jesuit was among them—a calm, bearded, black-skinned man stripped to the waist, waiting to be lashed to the triangle. Jigme could see that he was deep in a meditative trance.

Suddenly the gray sky darkened. People looked up and pointed. Some fell down in obeisance, others bowed and thrust out their tongues.

The Incarnation was overhead, sitting on a wide hovercraft, covered with red paint and hammered gold, that held a small platform and throne. He sat in a full lotus, his elfin form dressed only in a light yellow robe. Snow melted on his shoulders and cheeks.

The proceedings halted for a moment while everyone waited for the Incarnation to say something, but at an impatient gesture from the floating throne things got under way. The floggings went efficiently, sometimes more than one going on at once. The crowd succored many of the victims with money or offers of food or medicine. There was another slight hesitation as the Jesuit was brought forward—perhaps the Incarnation would comment on, or stay, the punishment of someone who had been trying to spread his faith—but from the Incarnation came only silence. The Jesuit absorbed his twenty lashes without comment, was taken away by his cohorts. To be praised and promoted, if Jigme knew the Jesuits.

The whipping went on. Blood spattered the platform. Finally there was only one convict remaining, a young monk of perhaps seventeen in a dirty, torn zen. He was a big lad, broad-shouldered and heavily-muscled, with a malformed head and a peculiar brutal expression—at once intent and unfocused, as if he knew he hated something but couldn't be bothered to decide exactly what it was. His body was possessed by constant, uncontrollable tics and twitches. He was surrounded by police with staves. Obviously they considered him dangerous.

An official read off the charges. Kyetsang Kunlegs had killed his guru, then set fire to the dead man's hermitage in hopes of covering his crime. He was sentenced to six hundred lashes and to be shackled for life. Jigme suspected he would not get much aid from the crowd afterward; most of them were reacting with disgust.

"Stop," said the Incarnation. Jigme gaped. The floating throne was moving forward. It halted just before Kunlegs. The murderer's guards stuck out their tongues but kept their eyes on the killer.

"Why did you kill your guru?" the Incarnation asked.

Kunlegs stared at him and twitched, displaying nothing but fierce hatred. He gave no answer.

The Incarnation laughed. "That's what I thought," he said. "Will you be my disciple if I remit your punishment?"

Kunlegs seemed to have difficulty comprehending this. His belligerent expression remained unaltered. Finally he just shrugged. A violent twitch made the movement grotesque.

The Incarnation lowered his throne. "Get on board," he said. Kunlegs stepped onto the platform. The Incarnation rose from his lotus, adjusted the man's garments, and kissed him on the lips. They sat down together.

"Short Path," said the Incarnation. The throne sped at once for the Library Palace.

Jigme turned to the Ambassador. !urq had watched without visible expression.

"Terrifying," she said. "Absolutely terrifying."

Jigme sat with the other Cabinet members in a crowded courtyard of the Palace. The Incarnation was about to go through the last of the rituals required before his investiture as the Gyalpo Rinpoche. Six learned elders of six different religious orders would engage the Incarnation in prolonged debate. If he did well against them, he would be formally enthroned and take the reins of government.

The Incarnation sat on a platform-throne opposite the six. Behind him, gazing steadily with his expression of misshapen, twitching brutality, was the murderer Kyetsang Kunlegs.

The first elder rose. He was a Sufi, representing a three-thousand-year-old intellectual tradition. He stuck out his tongue and took a formal stance.

"What is the meaning of Dharma?" he began.

"I'll show you," said the Incarnation, although the question had obviously been rhetorical. The Incarnation opened his mouth, and a demon the size of a bull leapt out. Its flesh was pale as dough and covered with running sores. The demon seized the Sufi and flung him to the ground, then sat on his chest. The sound of breaking bones was audible.

Kyetsang Kunlegs opened his mouth and laughed, revealing huge yellow teeth.

The demon rose and advanced toward the five remaining elders, who fled in disorder.

"I win," said the Incarnation.

Kunlegs' laughter broke like obscene bubbles over the stunned audience.

"Short Path," said the Incarnation.

"Such a shame," said the Ambassador. Firelight flickered off her ebon features. "How many man-years of work has gone into it all? And by morning it'll be ashes."

"Everything comes to an end," said Jigme. "If the floats are not destroyed tonight, they would be gone in a year. If not a year, ten years. If not ten years, a century. If not a century . . ."

"I quite take your point, Rinpoche," said !urq.

"Only the Buddha is eternal."

"So I gather."

The crowd assembled on the roof of the Library Palace gasped as another of the floats on Burning Hill went up in flames. This one was made of figures from the opera, who danced and sang and did combat with one another until, burning, they came apart on the wind.

Jigme gratefully took a glass of hot tea from a servant and warmed his hands. The night was clear but bitterly cold. The floating throne moved silently overhead, and Jigme stuck out his tongue in salute. The Gyalpo Rinpoche, in accordance with the old Oracle's instructions, had assumed his title that afternoon.

"Jigme Dzasa, may I speak with you?" A soft voice at his elbow, that of the former Regent.

"Of course, Miss Taisuke. You will excuse me, Ambassador?"

Jigme and Taisuke moved apart. "The Incarnation has indicated that he wishes me to continue as head of the government," Taisuke said.

"I congratulate you, Prime Minister," said Jigme, surprised. He had assumed the Gyalpo Rinpoche would wish to run the state himself.

"I haven't accepted yet," she said. "It isn't a job I desire." She sighed. "I was hoping to have a randy incarnation, Jigme. Instead I'm being worked to death."

"You have my support, Prime Minister."

She gave a rueful smile and patted his arm. "Thank you. I fear I'll have to accept, if only to keep certain other people from positions where they might do harm." She leaned close, her whisper carrying over the sound of distant fireworks. "Dr. O'Neill approached me. She wished to know my views concerning whether we can declare the Incarnation insane and reinstitute the Regency."

Jigme gazed at Taisuke in shock. "Who supports this?"

"Not I. I made that clear enough."

"Daddy Carbajal?"

"I think he's too cautious. The new State Oracle might be in favor of the idea—he's such a strict young man, and, of course, his own status would rise if he became the Library's interpreter instead of subordinate to the Gyalpo Rinpoche. O'Neill herself made the proposal in a veiled manner—*if* such-and-such a thing proved true, how would I react? She never made a specific proposal."

Anger burned in Jigme's belly. "The Incarnation cannot be insane!" he said. "That would mean the Library itself is insane. That the Buddha is insane."

"People are uncomfortable with the notion of a doubtob Incarnation."

"What people? What are their names? They should be corrected!" Jigme realized that his fists were clenched, that he was trembling with anger.

"Hush. O'Neill can do nothing."

"She speaks treason! Heresy!"

"Jigme. . . ."

"Ah. The Prime Minister." Jigme gave a start at the sound of the Incarnation's voice. The floating throne, its gold ornaments gleaming in the light of the burning floats, descended noiselessly from the bright sky. The Incarnation was covered only by a reskyang, the simple white cloth worn even in the bitterest weather by adepts of tumo, the discipline of controlling one's own internal heat.

"You *will* be my Prime Minister, yes?" the Incarnation said. His green eyes seemed to glow in the darkness. Kyetsang Kunlegs loomed over his shoulder like a demon shadow.

Taisuke bowed, sticking out her tongue. "Of course, Omniscient."

"When I witnessed the floggings the other day," the Incarnation said, "I was shocked by the lack of consistency. Some of the criminals seemed to have the sympathy of the officials, and the floggers did not use their full strength. Some of the floggers were larger and stronger than others. Toward the end they all got tired, and did not lay on with proper force. This does not seem to me to be adequate justice. I would like to propose a reform." He handed Taisuke a paper. "Here I have described a flogging machine. Each strike will be equal to the one before. And as the machine is built on a rotary principle, the machine can be inscribed with religious texts, like a prayer wheel. We can therefore grant prayers and punish the wicked simultaneously."

Taisuke seemed overcome. She looked down at the paper as if afraid to open it. "Very . . . elegant, Omniscient."

"I thought so. See that the machine is instituted throughout humanity, Prime Minister."

"Very well, Omniscient."

The floating throne rose into the sky to the accompaniment of the murderer Kunlegs' gross bubbling laughter. Taisuke looked at Jigme with desperation in her eyes.

"We must protect him, Jigme," she said.

"Of course."

"We must be very, very careful."

She loves him, too, he thought. A river of sorrow poured through his heart.

Jigme looked up, seeing Ambassador !urq standing with her head lifted to watch the burning spectacle on the hill opposite. "Very careful indeed," he said.

The cycle of festivals continued. Buddha's birthday, the Picnic Festival, the time of pilgrimage . . .

In the Prime Minister's lha khang, the Thunderbolt Sow gestured toward Taisuke. "After watching the floggings," it said, "the Gyalpo Rinpoche and Kyetsang Kunlegs went to Diamond City spaceport, where they participated in a night-long orgy with ship personnel. Both have now passed out from indulgence in drink and drugs, and the party has come to an end."

The Prime Minister knit her brows as she listened to the tale. "The stories will get offworld now," Jigme told her.

"They're already offworld."

Jigme looked at her helplessly. "How much damage is being done?"

"Flogging parties? Carousing with strangers? Careening from one monastery to another in search of pretty boys? Gracious heaven—the abbots are pimping their novices to him in hopes of receiving favor." Taisuke gave a lengthy shudder. There was growing seriousness in her eyes. "I'll let you in on a state secret. We've been reading the Sang's despatches."

"How?" Jigme asked. "They don't use our communications net, and the texts are coded."

"But they compose their messages using electric media," Taisuke said. "We can use the Library crystal as a sensing device, detect each character as it's entered into their coding device. We can also read incoming despatches the same way."

"I'm impressed, Prime Minister."

"Through this process, we were kept informed of the progress of the Sang's military buildup. We were terrified to discover that it was scheduled to reach its full offensive strength within a few years."

"Ah. That was why you consented to the increase in military allotments."

"Ambassador !urq was instructed not to resolve the Gyangtse matter, in order that it be used as a *casus belli* when the Sang program reached its conclusion. !urq's despatches to her superiors urged them to attack as soon as their fleet was ready. But now, with the increased military allotments and the political situation, !urq is urging delay. The current Incarnation, she suspects, may so discredit the institution of the Gyalpo Rinpoche that our society may disintegrate without the need for a Sang attack."

"Impossible!" A storm of anger filled Jigme. His hands formed the mudra of astonishment.

"I suspect you're right, Jigme." Solemnly. "They base their models of our society on their own past despotisms—they don't realize that the Treasured King is not a despot or an absolute ruler, but rather someone of great wisdom whom others follow through their own free will. But we should encourage !urq in this estimation, yes? Anything to give impetus to the Sang's more rational impulses."

"But it's based on a slander! And a slander concerning the Incarnation can never be countenanced!"

Taisuke raised an admonishing finger. "The Sang draw their own conclusions. And should we protest this one, we might give away our knowledge of their communications."

Anger and frustration bubbled in Jigme's mind. "What barbarians!" he said. "I have tried to show them truth, but . . ."

Taisuke's voice was calm. "You have shown them the path of truth. Their choosing not to follow it is their own karma."

Jigme promised himself he would do better. He would compel !urq to recognize the Incarnation's teaching mission.

Teaching, he thought. He remembered the stunned look on the door-keeper's face that first Cabinet meeting, the Incarnation's cry at the moment of climax, his own desperate attempt to see the thing as a lesson. And then he thought about what !urq would have said, had she been there.

He went to the meditation box that night, determined to exorcise the demon that gnawed at his vitals. Lust, he recited, provides the soil in which other passions flourish. Lust is like a demon that eats up all the good deeds of the world. Lust is a viper hiding in a flower garden; it poisons those who come in search of beauty.

It was all futile. Because all he could think of was the Gyalpo Rinpoche, the lovely body moving rhythmically in the darkness of the Cabinet room.

The moan of ragdongs echoed over the gardens and was followed by drunken applause and shouts. It was the beginning of the festival of plays and operas. The Cabinet and other high officials celebrated the festival at the Jewel Pavilion, the Incarnation's summer palace, where there was an outdoor theater specially built among the sweet-smelling meditative gardens. The palace, a lacy white fantasy ornamented with statues of gods and masts carrying prayer flags, sat bathed in spotlights atop its hill.

In addition to the members of the court were the personal followers of the Incarnation, people he had been gathering during the seven months of his reign. Novice monks and nuns, doubtobs and naljorpas, crazed hermits, looney charlatans and mediums, runaways, workers from the spaceport . . . all drunk, all pledged to follow the Short Path wherever it led.

"Disgusting," said Dr. O'Neill. "Loathsome." Furiously she brushed at a spot on her brocaded robe where someone had spilled beer.

Jigme said nothing. Cymbals clashed from the stage, where the orchestra was practicing. Three novice monks went by, staggering under the weight of a flogging machine. The festival was going to begin with the punishment of a number of criminals, and any who could walk afterward would then be able to join the revelers. The first opera would be sung on a stage spattered with blood.

Dr. O'Neill stepped closer to Jigme. "The Incarnation has asked me to furnish him a report on nerve induction. He wishes to devise a machine to induce pain without damage to the body."

Heavy sorrow filled Jigme that he could no longer be surprised by such news. "For what purpose?" he asked.

"To punish criminals, of course. Without crippling them. Then his Omniscience will be able to order up as savage punishments as he likes without being embarrassed by hordes of cripples shuffling around the capital."

Jigme tried to summon indignation. "You should not impart unworthy motives to the Gyalpo Rinpoche."

Dr. O'Neill only gave him a cynical look. Behind her, trampling through a hedge, came a young monk, laughing, being pursued by a pair of women with whips. O'Neill looked at them as they dashed off into the darkness. "At least it will give *them* less of an excuse to indulge in such behavior. It won't be as much fun to watch if there isn't any blood."

"That would be a blessing."

"The Forty-Second Incarnation is potentially the finest in history," O'Neill said. Her eyes narrowed in fury. She raised a clenched fist, the knuckles white in the darkness. "The most intelligent Incarnation, the most able, the finest rapport with the Library in centuries . . . and look at what he is doing with his gifts!"

"I thank you for the compliments, Doctor," said the Incarnation. O'Neill and Jigme jumped. The Incarnation, treading lightly on the summer grass, had walked up behind them. He was dressed only in his white reskyang and the garlands of flowers given him by his followers. Kunlegs, as always, loomed behind him, twitching furiously.

Jigme bowed profoundly, sticking out his tongue.

"The punishment machine," said the Incarnation. "Do the plans move forward?"

Dr. O'Neill's dismay was audible in her reply. "Yes, Omniscient."

"I wish the work to be completed for the New Year. I want particular care paid to the monitors that will alert the operators if the felon's life is in danger. We should not want to violate Shakyamuni's commandment against slaughter."

"The work shall be done, Omniscient."

"Thank you, Dr. O'Neill." He reached out a hand to give her a blessing. "I think of you as my mother, Dr. O'Neill. The lady who tenderly watched over me in the womb. I hope this thought pleases you."

"If it pleases your Omniscience."

"It does." The Incarnation withdrew his hand. In the darkness his smile was difficult to read. "You will be honored for your care for many generations, Doctor. I make you that promise."

"Thank you, Omniscient."

"Omniscient!" A new voice called out over the sound of revelry. The new State Oracle, dressed in the saffron zen of a simple monk, strode toward them over the grass. His thin, ascetic face was bursting with anger.

"Who are these people, Omniscient?" he demanded.

"My friends, minister."

"They are destroying the gardens!"

"They are *my* gardens, minister."

"Vanity!" The Oracle waved a finger under the Incarnation's nose. Kunlegs grunted and started forward, but the Incarnation stopped him with a gesture.

"I am pleased to accept the correction of my ministers," he said.

"Vanity and indulgence!" the Oracle said. "Has the Buddha not told us to forsake worldly desires? Instead of doing as Shakyamuni instructed, you have surrounded yourself with followers who indulge their own sensual pleasures and your vanity!"

"Vanity?" The Incarnation glanced at the Jewel Pavilion. "Look at my summer palace, minister. It is a vanity, a lovely vanity. But it does no harm."

"It is nothing! All the palaces of the world are as nothing beside the word of the Buddha!"

The Incarnation's face showed supernal calm. "Should I rid myself of these vanities, minister?"

"Yes!" The State Oracle stamped a bare foot. "Let them be swept away!"

"Very well. I accept my minister's correction." He raised his voice, calling for the attention of his followers. A collection of drunken rioters gathered around him. "Let the word be spread to all here," he cried. "The Jewel Pavilion is to be destroyed by fire. The gardens shall be uprooted. All statues shall be smashed." He looked at the State Oracle and smiled his cold smile. "I hope this shall satisfy you, minister."

A horrified look was his only reply.

The Incarnation's followers laughed and sang as they destroyed the Jewel Pavilion, as they toppled statues from its roof and destroyed furniture to create bonfires in its luxurious suites. "Short Path!" they chanted. "Short Path!" In the theater the opera began, an old Tibetan epic about the death by treachery of the Sixth Earthly Gyalpo Rinpoche, known to his Mongolian enemies as the Dalai Lama. Jigme found a quiet place in the garden and sat in a full lotus, repeating sutras and trying to calm his mind. But the screams, chanting, songs, and shouts distracted him.

He looked up to see the Gyalpo Rinpoche standing upright amid the ruin of his garden, his head raised as if to sniff the wind. Kunlegs was standing close behind, caressing him. The light of the burning palace danced on his face. The Incarnation seemed transformed, a living embodiment of . . . of what? Madness? Exultation? Ecstasy? Jigme couldn't tell, but when he saw it he felt as if his heart would explode.

Then his blood turned cold. Behind the Incarnation, moving through the garden beneath the ritual umbrella of a Masker servant, came Ambassador !urq, her dark face watching the burning palace with something like triumph.

Jigme felt someone near him. "This cannot go on," said Dr. O'Neill's voice, and at the sound of her cool resolution terror flooded him.

"*Aum vajra sattva,*" he chanted, saying the words over and over, repeating them till the Jewel Pavilion was ash and the garden looked as if a whirlwind had torn through it, leaving nothing but tangled ruin.

Rising from the desolation, he saw something bright dangling from the shattered proscenium of the outdoor stage.

It was the young State Oracle, hanging by the neck.

"!urq's despatches have grown triumphant. She knows that the Gyalpo Rinpoche has lost the affection of the people, and that they will soon lose their tolerance." Miss Taisuke was decorating a Christmas tree in her lha khang. Little glowing buddhas, in their traditional red suits and white beards, hung amid the evergreen branches. Kali danced on top, holding a skull in either hand.

"What can we do?" said Jigme.

"Prevent a coup whatever the cost. If the Incarnation is deposed or declared mad, the Sang can attack under pretext of restoring the Incarnation. Our own people will be divided. We couldn't hope to win."

"Can't Dr. O'Neill see this?"

"Dr. O'Neill desires war, Jigme. She thinks we will win it whatever occurs."

Jigme thought about what interstellar war would mean; the vast energies of modern weapons deployed against helpless planets. Tens of billions dead, even with a victory. "We should speak to the Gyalpo Rinpoche," he said. "He must be made to understand."

"The State Oracle spoke to him, and what resulted?"

"You, Prime Minister—"

Taisuke looked at him. Her eyes were brimming with tears. "I have *tried* to speak to him. He is interested only in his parties, in his new punishment device. It's all he will talk about."

Jigme said nothing. His eyes stung with tears. Two weeping officials, he thought, alone on Christmas Eve. What more pathetic picture could possibly exist?

"The device grows ever more elaborate," Taisuke said. "There will be life extension and preservation gear installed. The machine can torture people for *lifetimes!*" She shook her head. Her hands trembled as they wiped her eyes. "Perhaps Dr. O'Neill is right. Perhaps the Incarnation needs to be put away."

"Never," Jigme said. "Never."

"Prime Minister." The Thunderbolt Sow shifted in her corner. "The Gyalpo Rinpoche has made an announcement to his people. 'The Short Path will end with the New Year.' "

Taisuke wiped her eyes on her brocaded sleeve. "Was that the entire message?"

"Yes, Prime Minister."

Her eyes rose to Jigme's. "What could it mean?"

"We must have hope, Prime Minister."

"Yes." Her hands clutched at his. "We must try to have hope."

Beneath snapping prayer flags, a quarter-size Jewel Pavilion made of flammable lattice stood on Burning Hill. The Cabinet was gathered inside it, flanking the throne of the Incarnation. The Gyalpo Rinpoche had decided to view the burning from inside one of the floats.

Kyetsang Kunlegs, grinning with his huge yellow teeth, was the only one of his followers present. The others were making merry in the city.

In front of the sham Jewel Pavilion was the new torture machine, a hollow oval, twice the size of a man, its skin the color of brushed metal. The interior was filled with mysterious apparatus.

The Cabinet said the rosary, and the Horse of the Air rose up into the night. The Incarnation, draped with khatas, raised a double drum made from the tops of two human skulls. With a flick of his wrist, a bead on a string began to bound from one drum to the other. With his cold green eyes he watched it rattle for a long moment. "Welcome to my first anniversary," he said.

The others murmured in reply. The drum rattled on. A cold winter wind blew through the pavilion. The Incarnation looked from one Cabinet member to the other and gave his cruel, ambiguous smile.

"On the anniversary of my ascension to the throne and my adoption of the Short Path," he said, "I would like to honor the woman who made it possible." He held out his hand. "Dr. O'Neill, the Minister of Science, whom I think of as my mother. Mother, please come sit in the place of honor."

O'Neill rose stone-faced from her place and walked to the throne. She prostrated herself and stuck out her tongue. The Treasured King stepped off the platform, still rattling the drum; he took her hand, helped her rise. He sat her on the platform in his own place.

Another set of arms materialized on his shoulders; while the first rattled the drum, the other three went through a long succession of mudras. Amazement, Jigme read, fascination, the warding of evil.

"My first memories in this incarnation," he said, "are of fire. Fire that burned inside me, that made me want to claw my way out of my glass womb and launch myself prematurely into existence. Fires that aroused lust and hatred before I knew anyone to hate or lust for. And then, when the fires grew unendurable, I would open my eyes, and there I would see my mother, Dr. O'Neill, watching me with happiness in her face."

Another pair of arms appeared. The Incarnation looked over his shoulder at Dr. O'Neill, who was watching him with the frozen stare given a poison serpent. The Incarnation turned back to the others. The breeze fluttered the khatas around his neck.

"Why should I burn?" he said. "My memories of earlier Incarnations were incomplete, but I knew I had never known such fire before. There was something in me that was not balanced. That was made for the Short Path. Perhaps Enlightenment could be reached by leaping into the fire. In any case, I had no choice."

There was a flare of light, a roar of applause. The first of the floats outside exploded into flame. Fireworks crackled in the night. The Incarnation smiled. His drum rattled on.

"Never had I been so out of balance," he said. Another pair of arms materialized. "Never had I been so puzzled. Were my compulsions a manifestation of the Library? Was the crystal somehow out of alignment? Or was something else wrong? It was my consort Kyetsang Kunlegs who gave me the first clue." He turned to the throne and smiled at the murderer, who twitched in reply. "Kunlegs has suffered all his life from Tourette's syndrome, an excess of dopamine in the brain. It makes him compulsive, twitchy, and—curiously—brilliant. His brain works too fast for its own good. The condition should have been diagnosed and corrected years ago, but Kunlegs' elders were neglectful."

Kunlegs opened his mouth and gave a long laugh. Dr. O'Neill, seated just before him on the platform, gave a shiver. The Incarnation beamed at Kunlegs, then turned back to his audience.

"I didn't suffer from Tourette's—I didn't have all the symptoms. But seeing poor Kunlegs made it clear where I should look for the source of my difficulty." He raised the drum, rattled it beside his head. "In my own brain," he said.

Another float burst into flame. The bright light glowed through the wicker-work walls of the pavilion, shone on the Incarnation's face. He gazed into it with his cruel half-smile, his eyes dancing in the firelight.

Dr. O'Neill spoke. Her voice was sharp. "Omniscient, may I suggest that we withdraw? This structure is built to burn, and the wind will carry sparks from the other floats toward us."

The Incarnation looked at her. "Later, honored Mother." He turned back to the Cabinet. "Not wanting to bother my dear mother with my suspicions, I visited several doctors when I was engaged in my visits to town and various monasteries. I found that not only did I have a slight excess of dopamine, but that my mind also contained too much serotonin and norepinephrine, and too little endorphin."

Another float burst into flame. Figures from the opera screamed in eerie voices. The Incarnation's smile was beatific. "Yet my honored mother, the Minister of Science, supervised my growth. How could such a thing happen?"

Jigme's attention jerked to Dr. O'Neill. Her face was drained of color. Her eyes were those of someone gazing into the Void.

"Dr. O'Neill, of course, has political opinions. She believes the Sang heretics must be vanquished. Destroyed or subdued at all costs. And to that end she wished an Incarnation who would be a perfect conquering warrior-king—impatient, impulsive, brilliant, careless of life, and indifferent to suffering. Someone with certain sufficiencies and deficiencies in brain chemistry."

O'Neill opened her mouth. A scream came out, a hollow sound as mindless as those given by the burning floats. The Incarnation's many hands pointed to her, all but the one rattling the drum.

Laughing, Kyetsang Kunlegs lunged forward, twisting the khata around the minister's neck. The scream came to an abrupt end. Choking, she toppled back into his huge lap.

"She is the greatest traitor of all time," the Incarnation said. "She who poisoned the Forty-First Incarnation. She who would subvert the Library itself to her ends. She who would poison the mind of a Bodhisattva." His voice was soft, yet exultant. It sent an eerie chill down Jigme's back.

Kunlegs rose from the platform holding Dr. O'Neill in his big hands. Her piled-up hair had come undone and trailed across the ground. Kunlegs carried her out of the building and into the punishment machine.

The Incarnation's drum stopped rattling. Jigme looked at him in stunned comprehension.

"She shall know what it is to burn," he said. "She shall know it for many lifetimes."

Sparks blew across the floor before the Incarnation's feet. There was a glow from the doorway, where some of the wickerwork had caught fire.

The machine was automatic in its function. Dr. O'Neill began to scream again, a rising series of shrieks. Her body began to rotate. The Incarnation smiled. "She shall make that music for many centuries. Perhaps one of my future incarnations shall put a stop to it."

Jigme felt burning heat on the back of his neck. O'Neill's screams ran up and down his spine. "Omniscient," he said. "The pavilion is on fire. We should leave."

"In a moment. I wish to say a few last words."

Kunlegs came loping back, grinning, and hopped onto the platform. The Incarnation joined him and kissed him tenderly. "Kunlegs and I will stay in the pavilion," he said. "We will both die tonight."

"No!" Taisuke jumped to her feet. "We will not permit it! Your condition can be corrected."

The Incarnation stared at her. "I thank you, loyal one. But my brain is poisoned, and even if the imbalance were corrected I would still be perceiving the Library through a chemical fog that would impair my ability. My next Incarnation will not have this handicap."

"Omniscient!" Tears spilled from Taisuke's eyes. "Don't leave us!"

"You will continue as head of the government. My next Incarnation will be ready by the next New Year, and then you may retire to the secular life I know you wish to pursue in this lifetime."

"No!" Taisuke ran forward, threw herself before the platform. "I beg you, Omniscient!"

Suddenly Jigme was on his feet. He lurched forward, threw himself down beside Taisuke. "Save yourself, Omniscient!" he said.

"I wish to say something concerning the Sang." The Incarnation spoke calmly, as if he hadn't heard. "There will be danger of war in the next year. You must all promise me that you won't fight."

"Omniscient." This from Daddy Carbajal. "We must be ready to defend ourselves!"

"Are we an Enlightened race, or are we not?" The Incarnation's voice was stern.

"You are Bodhisattva." Grudgingly. "All know this."

"We are Enlightened. The Buddha commands us not to take life. If these are not facts, our existence has no purpose, and our civilization is a mockery." O'Neill's screams provided eerie counterpoint to his voice. The Incarnation's many arms pointed at the members of the Cabinet. "You may arm in order to deter attack. But if the Sang begin a war, you must promise me to surrender without condition."

"Yes!" Taisuke, still facedown, wailed from her obeisance. "I promise, Omniscient."

"The Diamond Mountain will be the greatest prize the Sang can hope for. And the Library is the Buddha. When the time is right, the Library will incarnate itself as a Sang, and the Sang will be sent on their path to Enlightenment."

"Save yourself, Omniscient!" Taisuke wailed. The roar of flames had drowned O'Neill's screams. Jigme felt sparks falling on his shaven head.

"Your plan, sir!" Daddy Carbajal's voice was desperate. "It might not work! The Sang may thwart the incarnation in some way!"

"Are we Enlightened?" The Incarnation's voice was mild. "Or are we not? Is the Buddha's truth eternal, or is it not? Do you not support the Doctrine?"

Daddy Carbajal threw himself down beside Jigme. "I believe, Omniscient! I will do as you ask!"

"Leave us, then. Kyetsang and I wish to be alone."

Certainty seized Jigme. He could feel tears stinging his eyes. "Let me stay, Omniscient!" he cried. "Let me die with you!"

"Carry these people away," said the Incarnation. Hands seized Jigme. He fought them off, weeping, but they were too powerful: he was carried from the burning pavilion. His last sight of the Incarnation was of the Gyalpo Rinpoche and Kunlegs embracing one another, silhouetted against flame, and then everything dissolved in fire and tears.

And in the morning nothing was left, nothing but ashes and the keening cries of the traitor O'Neill, whom the Bodhisattva in his wisdom had sent forever to Hell.

Jigme found !urq there, standing alone before O'Neill, staring at the figure caught in a webwork of life support and nerve stimulators. The sound of the traitor's endless agony continued to issue from her torn throat.

"There will be no war," Jigme said.

!urq looked at him. Her stance was uncertain.

"After all this," Jigme said, "a war would be indecent. You understand?"

!urq just stared.

"You must not unleash this madness in us!" Jigme cried. Tears rolled down his face. "Never, Ambassador! Never!"

!urq's antennae twitched. She looked at O'Neill again, rotating slowly in the huge wheel. "I will do what I can, Rinpoche," she said.

!urq made her lone way down Burning Hill. Jigme stared at the traitor for a long time.

Then he sat in the full lotus. Ashes drifted around him, some clinging to his zen, as he sat before the image of the tormented doctor and recited his prayers.

BLOOD SISTERS

Greg Egan

Here's a haunting glimpse of a crowded, high-tech future that has become perhaps a little *too* fond of that dispassionate Long View we hear so much about. . . .

Born in 1961, Greg Egan lives in Australia, and is certainly in the running for the title of Hottest New Writer of the Nineties to date. Although he's been publishing for a year or two already, 1990 was the year when Egan suddenly seemed to be turning up *everywhere* with high-quality stories, and he continued the streak in 1991. He is a frequent contributor to *Interzone* and *Isaac Asimov's Science Fiction Magazine*, and has made sales as well to *Pulphouse*, *Analog*, *Aurealis*, and *Eidolon*. Several of his stories have appeared in various "Best of the Year" series, including this one; his story "The Caress" *and* his story "Learning To Be Me" were in our Eighth Annual Collection, and he was good enough to place another two stories in *this* year's collection as well. He just sold his first novel, *Quarantine*, to Legend as part of a package deal that includes a second novel and a collection of his short fiction—a pretty high-powered deal for such a young writer. My guess is that you will be seeing a *lot* more of Egan as the decade progresses.

When we were nine years old, Paula decided we should prick our thumbs, and let our blood flow into each other's veins.

I was scornful. "Why bother? Our blood's already exactly the same. We're *already* blood sisters."

She was unfazed. "I know that. That's not the point. It's the ritual that counts."

We did it in our bedroom, at midnight, by the light of a single candle. She sterilized the needle in the candle flame, then wiped it clean of soot with a tissue and saliva.

When we'd pressed the tiny, sticky wounds together, and recited some ridiculous oath from a third-rate children's novel, Paula blew out the candle. While my eyes were still adjusting to the dark, she added a whispered coda of her own: "Now we'll dream the same dreams, and share the same lovers, and die at the very same hour."

I tried to say, indignantly, "That's just not true!" but the darkness and the scent of the dead flame made the protest stick in my throat, and her words remained unchallenged.

＊   ＊   ＊

As Dr Packard spoke, I folded the pathology report, into halves, into quarters, obsessively aligning the edges. It was far too thick for me to make a neat job of it; from the micrographs of the misshapen lymphocytes proliferating in my bone marrow, to the print-out of portions of the RNA sequence of the virus that had triggered the disease, thirty-two pages in all.

In contrast, the prescription, still sitting on the desk in front of me, seemed ludicrously flimsy and insubstantial. No match at all. The traditional—indecipherable—polysyllabic scrawl it bore was nothing but a decoration; the drug's name was reliably encrypted in the barcode below. There was no question of receiving the wrong medication by mistake. The question was, *would the right one help me?*

"Is that clear? Ms Rees? Is there anything you don't understand?"

I struggled to focus my thoughts, pressing hard on an intractable crease with my thumb. She'd explained the situation frankly, without resorting to jargon or euphemism, but I still had the feeling that I was missing something crucial. It seemed like every sentence she'd spoken had started one of two ways: "The virus . . ." or "The drug . . ."

"Is there anything *I* can do? Myself? To . . . improve the odds?"

She hesitated, but not for long. "No, not really. You're in excellent health, otherwise. Stay that way." She began to rise from her desk to dismiss me, and I began to panic.

"But, there must be *something*." I gripped the arms of my chair, as if afraid of being dislodged by force. Maybe she'd misunderstood me, maybe I hadn't made myself clear. "Should I . . . stop eating certain foods? Get more exercise? Get more sleep? I mean, there has to be *something* that will make a difference. And I'll do it, whatever it is. Please, just *tell* me—" My voice almost cracked, and I looked away, embarrassed. *Don't ever start ranting like that again. Not ever.*

"Ms Rees, I'm sorry. I know how you must be feeling. But the Monte Carlo diseases are all like this. In fact, you're exceptionally lucky; the WHO computer found eighty thousand people, worldwide, infected with a similar strain. That's not enough of a market to support any hard-core research, but enough to have persuaded the pharmaceutical companies to rummage through their databases for something that might do the trick. A lot of people are on their own, infected with viruses that are virtually unique. Imagine how much useful information the health profession can give *them*." I finally looked up; the expression on her face was one of sympathy, tempered by impatience.

I declined the invitation to feel ashamed of my ingratitude. I'd made a fool of myself, but I still had a right to ask the question. "I understand all that. I just thought there might be something I could do. You say this drug might work, or it might not. If I could contribute, *myself*, to fighting this disease, I'd feel . . ."

What? More like a human being, and less like a test tube—a passive container in which the wonder drug and the wonder virus would fight it out between themselves.

". . . better."

She nodded. "I know, but trust me, nothing you can do would make the slightest difference. Just look after yourself as you normally would. Don't catch pneumonia. Don't gain or lose ten kilos. Don't do *anything* out of the ordinary. Millions of people must have been exposed to this virus, but the reason you're sick, and they're not, is *a purely genetic matter*. The cure will be just the same. The biochemistry that determines whether or not the drug will work for you isn't going to change if you start taking vitamin pills, or stop eating junk food—and I should warn you that going on one of those 'miracle-cure' diets will simply make you sick; the charlatans selling them ought to be in prison."

I nodded fervent agreement to *that*, and felt myself flush with anger. Fraudulent cures had long been my *bête noir*—although now, for the first time, I could almost understand why other Monte Carlo victims paid good money for such things: crackpot diets, meditation schemes, aroma therapy, self-hypnosis tapes, you name it. The people who peddled that garbage were the worst kind of cynical parasites, and I'd always thought of their customers as being either congenitally gullible, or desperate to the point of abandoning their wits, but there was more to it than that. When your life is at stake, you want to fight for it—with every ounce of your strength, with every cent you can borrow, with every waking moment. Taking one capsule, three times a day, just isn't *hard enough*—whereas the schemes of the most perceptive con-men were sufficiently arduous (or sufficiently expensive) to make the victims feel that they were engaged in the kind of struggle that the prospect of death requires.

This moment of shared anger cleared the air completely. We were on the same side, after all; I'd been acting like a child. I thanked Dr Packard for her time, picked up the prescription, and left.

On my way to the pharmacy, though, I found myself almost wishing that she'd lied to me—that she'd told me my chances would be vastly improved if I ran ten kilometers a day and ate raw seaweed with every meal—but then I angrily recoiled, thinking: Would I really want to be deceived "for my own good"? If it's down to my DNA, it's down to my DNA, and I ought to expect to be told that simple truth, however unpalatable I find it—and I ought to be grateful that the medical profession has abandoned its old patronizing, paternalistic ways.

I was twelve years old when the world learnt about the Monte Carlo project.

A team of biological warfare researchers (located just a stone's throw from Las Vegas—alas, the one in New Mexico, not the one in Nevada) had decided that *designing* viruses was just too much hard work (especially when the Star Wars boys kept hogging the supercomputers). Why waste hundreds of PhD-years—why expend any intellectual effort whatsoever—when the time-honoured partnership of blind mutation and natural selection was all that was required?

Speeded up substantially, of course.

They'd developed a three-part system: a bacterium, a virus, and a line of modified human lymphocytes. A stable portion of the viral genome allowed it to reproduce in the bacterium, while rapid mutation of the rest of the virus was achieved by neatly corrupting the transcription error repair enzymes. The lymphocytes had been altered to vastly amplify the reproductive success of any mutant which managed to infect them, causing it to out-breed those which were limited to using the bacterium.

The theory was, they'd set up a few trillion copies of this system, like row after row of little biological poker machines, spinning away in their underground lab, and just wait to harvest the jackpots.

The theory also included the best containment facilities in the world, and five hundred and twenty people all sticking scrupulously to official procedure, day after day, month after month, without a moment of carelessness, laziness or forgetfulness. Apparently, nobody bothered to compute the probability of *that*.

The bacterium was supposed to be unable to survive outside artificially beneficent laboratory conditions, but a mutation of the virus came to its aid, filling in for the genes that had been snipped out to make it vulnerable.

They wasted too much time using ineffectual chemicals before steeling themselves to nuke the site. By then, the winds had already made any human action—short of melting half a dozen states, not an option in an election year—irrelevant.

The first rumours proclaimed that we'd all be dead within a week. I can clearly recall the mayhem, the looting, the suicides (second-hand on the TV screen; our own neighbourhood remained relatively tranquil—or numb). States of emergency were declared around the world. Planes were turned away from airports, ships (which had left their home ports months before the leak) were burnt in the docks. Harsh laws were rushed in everywhere, to protect public order and public health.

Paula and I got to stay home from school for a month. I offered to teach her programming; she wasn't interested. She wanted to go swimming, but the beaches and pools were all closed. That was the summer that I finally managed to hack into a Pentagon computer—just an office supplies purchasing system, but Paula was suitably impressed (and neither of us had ever guessed that paperclips were *that* expensive).

We didn't believe we were going to die—at least, not within a week—and we were right. When the hysteria died down, it soon became apparent that only the virus and the bacterium had escaped, and without the modified lymphocytes to fine-tune the selection process, the virus had mutated away from the strain which had caused the initial deaths.

However, the cosy symbiotic pair is now found all over the world, endlessly churning out new mutations. Only a tiny fraction of the strains produced are infectious in humans, and only a fraction of those are potentially fatal.

A mere hundred or so a year.

On the train home, the sun seemed to be in my eyes no matter which way I turned—somehow, every surface in the carriage caught its reflection. The glare made a headache which had been steadily growing all afternoon almost unbearable, so I covered my eyes with my forearm and faced the floor. With my other hand, I clutched the brown paper bag that held the small glass vial of red-and-black capsules that would or wouldn't save my life.

Cancer. Viral leukaemia. I pulled the creased pathology report from my pocket, and flipped through it one more time. The last page hadn't magically changed into a happy ending—an oncovirology expert system's declaration of a sure-fire cure. The last page was just the bill for all the tests. Twenty-seven thousand dollars.

At home, I sat and stared at my work station.

Two months before, when a routine quarterly examination (required by my health insurance company, ever eager to dump the unprofitable sick) had revealed the first signs of trouble, I'd sworn to myself that I'd keep on working, keep on living exactly as if nothing had changed. The idea of indulging in a credit spree, or a world trip, or some kind of self-destructive binge, held no attraction for me at all. Any such final fling would be an admission of defeat. *I'd* go on a fucking world trip to celebrate my cure, and not before.

I had plenty of contract work stacked up, and that pathology bill was already accruing interest. Yet for all that I needed the distraction—for all that I needed *the money*—I sat there for three whole hours, and did nothing but brood about my fate. Sharing it with eighty thousand strangers scattered about the world was no great comfort.

Then it finally struck me. *Paula.* If I was vulnerable *for genetic reasons, then so was she.*

For identical twins, in the end we hadn't done too bad a job of pursuing separate lives. She had left home at sixteen, to tour central Africa, filming the wildlife, and—at considerably greater risk—the poachers. Then she'd gone to the Amazon, and become caught up in the land rights struggle there. After that, it was a bit of a blur; she'd always tried to keep me up to date with her exploits, but she moved too fast for my sluggish mental picture of her to follow.

I'd never left the country; I hadn't even moved house in a decade.

She came home only now and then, on her way between continents, but we'd stayed in touch electronically, circumstances permitting. (They take away your SatPhone in Bolivian prisons.)

The telecommunications multinationals all offer their own expensive services for contacting someone when you don't know in advance what country they're in. The advertising suggests that it's an immensely difficult task; the fact is, every SatPhone's location is listed in a central database, which is kept up to date by pooling information from all the regional satellites. Since I happened to have "acquired" the access codes to consult that database, I could phone Paula directly, wherever she was, without paying the ludicrous surcharge. It was more a matter of nostalgia than miserliness; this minuscule bit of hacking was a token gesture, proof that in spite of impending middle age, I wasn't yet terminally law-abiding, conservative and dull.

I'd automated the whole procedure long ago. The database said she was in Gabon; my program calculated local time, judged ten twenty-three p.m. to be civilized enough, and made the call. Seconds later, she was on the screen.

"Karen! How are you? You look like shit. I thought you were going to call last week—what happened?"

The image was perfectly clear, the sound clean and undistorted (fibre-optic cables might be scarce in central Africa, but geosynchronous satellites are directly overhead). As soon as I set eyes on her, I felt sure she didn't have the virus. She was right—I looked half-dead—whereas she was as animated as ever. Half a lifetime spent outdoors meant her skin had aged much faster than mine—but there was always a glow of energy, of purpose, about her that more than compensated.

She was close to the lens, so I couldn't see much of the background, but it looked like a fibreglass hut, lit by a couple of hurricane lamps; a step up from the usual tent.

"I'm sorry, I didn't get around to it. *Gabon?* Weren't you in Ecuador—?"

"Yes, but I met Mohammed. He's a botanist. From Indonesia. Actually, we met in Bogota; he was on his way to a conference in Mexico—"

"But—"

"Why Gabon? This is where he was going next, that's all. There's a fungus here, attacking the crops, and I couldn't resist coming along . . ."

I nodded, bemused, through ten minutes of convoluted explanations, not paying too much attention; in three months' time it would all be ancient history. Paula survived as a freelance pop-science journalist, darting around the globe writing articles for magazines, and scripts for TV programmes, on the latest ecological troublespots. To be honest, I had severe doubts that this kind of predigested eco-babble did the planet any good, but it certainly made her happy. I envied her that. I could not have lived her life—in no sense was she the woman I "might have been"—but nonetheless it hurt me, at times, to see in her eyes the kind of sheer excitement that I hadn't felt, myself, for a decade.

My mind wandered while she spoke. Suddenly, she was saying, "Karen? Are you going to tell me what's wrong?"

I hesitated. I had originally planned to tell no one, not even her, and now my reason for calling her seemed absurd—*she* couldn't have leukaemia, it was unthinkable. Then, without even realizing that I'd made the decision, I found myself recounting everything in a dull, flat voice. I watched with a strange feeling of detachment the changing expression on her face; shock, pity, then a burst of fear when she realized—far sooner than I would have done—exactly what my predicament meant for her.

What followed was even more awkward and painful than I could have imagined. Her concern for me was genuine—but she would not have been human if the uncertainty of her own position had not begun to prey on her at once, and knowing *that* made all her fussing seem contrived and false.

"Do you have a good doctor? Someone you can trust?"

I nodded.

"Do you have someone to look after you? Do you want me to come home?"

I shook my head, irritated. "No, I'm all right. I'm being looked after, I'm being *treated*. But *you* have to get tested as soon as possible." I glared at her, exasperated. I no longer believed that she could have the virus, but I wanted to stress the fact that I'd called her to warn her, not to fish for sympathy— and somehow, that finally struck home. She said, quietly, "I'll get tested today. I'll go straight into town. Okay?"

I nodded. I felt exhausted, but relieved; for a moment, all the awkwardness between us melted away.

"You'll let me know the results?"

She rolled her eyes. "Of course I will."

I nodded again. "Okay."

"Karen. Be careful. Look after yourself."

"I will. You too." I hit the ESCAPE key.

Half an hour later, I took the first of the capsules, and climbed into bed. A few minutes later, a bitter taste crept up into my throat.

Telling Paula was essential. Telling Martin was insane. I'd only known him six months, but I should have guessed exactly how he'd take it.

"Move in with me. I'll look after you."

"I don't need to be looked after."

He hesitated, but only slightly. "Marry me."

"*Marry* you? Why? Do you think I have some desperate need to be married before I die?"

He scowled. "Don't talk like that. I *love* you. Don't you understand that?"

I laughed. "I don't *mind* being pitied—people always say it's degrading, but I think it's a perfectly normal response—but I don't want to have to live with it twenty-four hours a day." I kissed him, but he kept on scowling. At least I'd waited until after we'd had sex before breaking the news; if not, he probably would have treated me like porcelain.

He turned to face me. "Why are you being so hard on yourself? What are you trying to prove? That you're super-human? That you don't need anyone?"

"*Listen*. You've known from the very start that I need independence and privacy. What do you want me to say? That I'm terrified? Okay. I am. But I'm still the same person. I still need the same things." I slid one hand across his chest, and said as gently as I could, "So thanks for the offer, but no thanks."

"I don't mean very much to you, do I?"

I groaned, and pulled a pillow over my face. I thought: *Wake me when you're ready to fuck me again. Does that answer your question?* I didn't say it out loud, though.

A week later, Paula phoned me. She had the virus. Her white cell count was up, her red cell count was down—the numbers she quoted sounded just like my own from the month before. They'd even put her on the very same drug. That was hardly surprising, but it gave me an unpleasant, claustrophobic feeling, when I thought about what it meant:

We would both live, or we would both die.

In the days that followed, this realization began to obsess me. It was like voodoo, like some curse out of a fairy tale—or the fulfilment of the words she'd uttered, the night we became "blood sisters." We had never dreamed the same dreams, we'd certainly never loved the same men, but now . . . it was as if we were being punished, for failing to respect the forces that bound us together.

Part of me *knew* this was bullshit. *Forces that bound us together!* It was mental static, the product of stress, nothing more. The truth, though, was just as oppressive: the biochemical machinery would grind out its identical verdict on both of us, for all the thousands of kilometres between us, for all that we had forged separate lives in defiance of our genetic unity.

I tried to bury myself in my work. To some degree, I succeeded—if the grey stupor produced by eighteen-hour days in front of a terminal could really be considered a success.

I began to avoid Martin; his puppy-dog concern was just too much to bear. Perhaps he meant well, but I didn't have the energy to justify myself to him, over and over again. Perversely, at the very same time, I missed our arguments terribly; resisting his excessive mothering had at least made me feel strong, if only in contrast to the helplessness he seemed to expect of me.

I phoned Paula every week at first, but then gradually less and less often. We ought to have been ideal confidantes; in fact, nothing could have been less true. Our conversations were redundant; we already knew what the other was thinking, far too well. There was no sense of unburdening, just a suffocating, monotonous feeling of recognition. We took to trying to outdo each other in affecting a veneer of optimism, but it was a depressingly transparent effort. Eventually, I thought: when—if—I get the good news, I'll call her; until then, what's the point? Apparently, she came to the same conclusion.

All through childhood, we were forced together. We loved each other, I suppose, but . . . we were always in the same classes at school, bought the same clothes, given the same Christmas and birthday presents—and we were always sick at the same time, with the same ailment, for the same reason.

When she left home, I was envious, and horribly lonely for a while, but then I felt a surge of joy, of *liberation*, because I knew that I had no real wish to follow her, and I knew that from then on, our lives could only grow further apart.

Now, it seemed that had all been an illusion. We would live or die together, and all our efforts to break the bonds had been in vain.

About four months after the start of treatment, my blood counts began to turn around. I was more terrified than ever of my hopes being dashed, and I spent all my time battling to keep myself from premature optimism. I didn't dare ring Paula; I could think of nothing worse than leading her to think that we were cured, and then turning out to have been mistaken. Even when Dr Packard—cautiously, almost begrudgingly—admitted that things were looking up, I told myself that she might have relented from her policy of unflinching honesty and decided to offer me some palliative lies.

One morning I woke, not yet convinced that I was cured, but sick of feeling I had to drown myself in gloom for fear of being disappointed. If I wanted absolute certainty, I'd be miserable all my life; a relapse would always be possible, or a *whole new virus* could come along.

It was a cold, dark morning, pouring with rain outside, but as I climbed, shivering, out of bed, I felt more cheerful than I had since the whole thing had begun.

There was a message in my work station mailbox, tagged CONFIDEN-TIAL. It took me thirty seconds to recall the password I needed, and all the while my shivering grew worse.

The message was from the Chief Administrator of the Libreville People's Hospital, offering his or her condolences on the death of my sister, and requesting instructions for the disposal of the body.

I don't know what I felt first. Disbelief. Guilt. Confusion. Fear. How could she have died, when I was so close to recovery? How could she have died without a word to me? *How could I have let her die alone?* I walked away from the terminal, and slumped against the cold brick wall.

The worst of it was, I suddenly *knew* why she'd stayed silent. She must have thought that I was dying, too, and that was the one thing we'd both feared most of all: dying together. In spite of everything, dying together, as if we were one.

How could the drug have failed her, and worked for me? *Had it worked for me?* For a moment of sheer paranoia, I wondered if the hospital had been faking my test results, if in fact I was on the verge of death, myself. That was ludicrous, though.

Why, then, had Paula died? There was only one possible answer. She should have come home—I should have *made her* come home. How could I have let her stay there, in a tropical, Third World country, with her immune system weakened, living in a fibreglass hut, without proper sanitation, probably malnourished? I should have sent her the money, I should have sent her the ticket, I should have flown out there in person and dragged her back home.

Instead, I'd kept her at a distance. Afraid of us dying together, afraid of the curse of our sameness, I'd let her die alone.

I tried to cry, but something stopped me. I sat in the kitchen, sobbing drily. I was worthless. I'd killed her with my superstition and cowardice. I had no right to be alive.

I spent the next fortnight grappling with the legal and administrative complexities of death in a foreign land. Paula's will requested cremation, but said nothing about where it was to take place, so I arranged for her body and belongings to be flown home. The service was all but deserted; our parents had died a decade before, in a car crash, and although Paula had had friends all over the world, few were able to make the trip.

Martin came, though. When he put an arm around me, I turned and whispered to him angrily, "You didn't even know her. What the hell are you doing here?" He stared at me for a moment, hurt and baffled, then walked off without a word.

I can't pretend I wasn't grateful, when Packard announced that I was cured, but my failure to rejoice out loud must have puzzled even her. I might have told her about Paula, but I didn't want to be fed cheap clichés about how irrational it was of me to feel guilty for surviving.

She was dead. I was growing stronger by the day; often sick with guilt and depression, but more often simply numb. That might easily have been the end of it.

Following the instructions in the will, I sent most of her belongings— notebooks, disks, audio and video tapes—to her agent, to be passed on to the appropriate editors and producers, to whom some of it might be of use. All that remained was clothing, a minute quantity of jewellery and cosmetics, and a handful of odds and ends. Including a small glass vial of red-and-black capsules.

I don't know what possessed me to take one of the capsules. I had half a dozen left of my own, and Packard had shrugged when I'd asked if I should finish them, and said that it couldn't do me any harm.

There was no aftertaste. Every time I'd swallowed my own, within minutes there'd been a bitter aftertaste.

I broke open a second capsule and put some of the white powder on my tongue. It was entirely without flavour. I ran and grabbed my own supply, and sampled one the same way; it tasted so vile it made my eyes water.

I tried, very hard, not to leap to any conclusions. I knew perfectly well that pharmaceuticals were often mixed with inert substances, and perhaps not necessarily the same ones all the time—but why would something *bitter* be used for that purpose? The taste had to come from the drug itself. The two vials bore the same manufacturer's name and logo. The same brand name. The same generic name. The same formal chemical name for the active ingredient. The same product code, down to the very last digit. Only the batch numbers were different.

The first explanation that came to mind was corruption. Although I couldn't recall the details, I was sure that I'd read about dozens of cases of officials in the health care systems of developing countries diverting pharmaceuticals for resale on the black market. What better way to cover up such a theft than to replace the stolen product with something else—something cheap, harmless, and absolutely useless? The gelatin capsules themselves bore nothing but the manufacturer's logo, and since the company probably made at least a thousand different drugs, it would not have been too hard to find something cheaper, with the same size and colouration.

I had no idea what to do with this theory. Anonymous bureaucrats in a distant country had killed my sister, but the prospect of finding out who they were, let alone seeing them brought to justice, were infinitesimally small. Even if I'd had real, damning evidence, what was the most I could hope for? A meekly phrased protest from one diplomat to another.

I had one of Paula's capsules analysed. It cost me a fortune, but I was already so deeply in debt that I didn't much care.

It was full of a mixture of soluble inorganic compounds. There was no trace of the substance described on the label, nor of anything else with the slightest biological activity. It wasn't a cheap substitute drug, chosen at random.

It was a placebo.

I stood with the print-out in my hand for several minutes, trying to come to terms with what it meant. Simple greed I could have understood, but there was an utterly inhuman coldness here that I couldn't bring myself to swallow. Someone must have made an honest mistake. *Nobody* could be so callous.

Then Packard's words came back to me. "Just look after yourself as you normally would. Don't do *anything* out of the ordinary."

Oh no, *Doctor*. Of course not, *Doctor*. Wouldn't want to go spoiling the experiment with any messy, extraneous, uncontrolled factors . . .

I contacted an investigative journalist, one of the best in the country. I arranged a meeting in a small café on the edge of town.

I drove out there—terrified, angry, triumphant—thinking I had the scoop of the decade, thinking I had dynamite, thinking I was Meryl Streep playing Karen Silkwood. I was dizzy with sweet thoughts of revenge. Heads were going to roll.

Nobody tried to run me off the road. The café was deserted, and the waiter barely listened to our orders, let alone our conversation.

The journalist was very kind. She calmly explained the facts of life.

In the aftermath of the Monte Carlo disaster, a lot of legislation had been passed to help deal with the emergency—and a lot of legislation had been repealed. As a matter of urgency, new drugs to treat the new diseases had to be developed and assessed, and the best way to ensure that was to remove the cumbersome regulations that had made clinical trials so difficult and expensive.

In the old "double-blind" trials, neither the patients nor the investigators knew who was getting the drug and who was getting a placebo; the information was kept secret by a third party (or a computer). Any improvement observed in the patients who were given the placebo could then be taken into account, and the drug's true efficacy measured.

There were two small problems with this traditional approach. Firstly, telling a patient that there's only a fifty-fifty chance that they've been given a potentially life-saving drug subjects them to a lot of stress. Of course, the treatment and control groups were affected equally, but in terms of predicting what would happen when the drug was finally put out on the market, it introduced a lot of noise into the data. Which side-effects were real, and which were artifacts of the patients' uncertainty?

Secondly—and more seriously—it had become increasingly difficult to find people willing to volunteer for placebo trials. When you're dying, you don't give a shit about the scientific method. You want the maximum possible chance of surviving. Untested drugs will do, if there is no known, certain cure—but why accept a further *halving* of the odds, to satisfy some technocrat's obsession with details?

Of course, in the good old days the medical profession could lay down the law to the unwashed masses: *Take part in this double-blind trial, or crawl away and die.* AIDS had changed all that, with black markets for the latest untried cures, straight from the labs to the streets, and intense politicization of the issues.

The solution to both flaws was obvious.

You lie to the patients.

No bill had been passed to explicitly declare that "triple-blind" trials were legal. If it had, people might have noticed, and made a fuss. Instead, as part of the "reforms" and "rationalization" that came in the wake of the disaster, all the laws that might have made them illegal had been removed or watered down. At least, it looked that way—no court had yet been given the opportunity to pass judgement.

"How could any doctor *do that*? Lie like that! How could they justify it, even to themselves?"

She shrugged. "How did they ever justify double-blind trials? A good medical researcher has to care more about the quality of the data than about any one person's life. And if a double-blind trial is good, a triple-blind trial is better. The data *is* guaranteed to be better, you can see that, can't you? And the more accurately a drug can be assessed, well, perhaps in the long run, the more lives can be saved."

"Oh, *crap*! The placebo effect isn't *that* powerful. It just isn't that important! Who cares if it's not precisely taken into account? Anyway, *two* potential cures could still be compared, one treatment against another. That would tell you which drug would save the most lives, without any need for placebos—"

"That *is* done sometimes, although the more prestigious journals look down on those studies; they're less likely to be published—"

I stared at her. "How can you know all this and do nothing? The media could blow it wide open! If you let people know what's going on . . ."

She smiled thinly. "I *could* publicize the observation that these practices are now, theoretically, legal. Other people have done that, and it doesn't exactly make headlines. But if I printed any *specific* facts about an actual triple-blind trial, I'd face a half-million-dollar fine, and twenty-five years in prison, for endangering public health. Not to mention what they'd do to my publisher. All the 'emergency' laws brought in to deal with the Monte Carlo leak are still active."

"But that was twenty years ago!"

She drained her coffee and rose. "Don't you recall what the experts said at the time?"

"No."

"The effects will be with us for generations."

It took me four months to penetrate the drug manufacturer's network.

I eavesdropped on the data flow of several company executives who chose to work from home. It didn't take long to identify the least computer-literate. A real bumbling fool, who used ten-thousand-dollar spreadsheet software to do what the average five-year-old could have done without fingers and toes. I watched his clumsy responses when the spreadsheet package gave him error messages. He was a gift from heaven; he simply didn't have a clue.

And, best of all, he was forever running a tediously unimaginative porno-graphic video game.

If the computer said "Jump!" he'd say "Promise not to tell?"

I spent a fortnight minimizing what he had to do; it started out at seventy keystrokes, but I finally got it down to twenty-three.

I waited until his screen was at its most compromising, then I suspended his connection to the network, and took its place myself.

FATAL SYSTEM ERROR! TYPE THE FOLLOWING TO RECOVER:

He botched it the first time. I rang alarm bells, and repeated the request. The second time, he got it right.

The first multi-key combination I had him strike took the work station right out of its operating system into its processor's microcode debugging routine. The hexadecimal that followed, gibberish to him, was a tiny program to dump all of the work station's memory down the communications line, right into my lap.

If he told anyone with any sense what had happened, suspicion would be aroused at once—but would he risk being asked to explain just what he was running when the "bug" occurred? I doubted it.

I already had his passwords. Included in the work station's memory was an algorithm which told me precisely how to respond to the network's security challenges.

I was in.

The rest of their defences were trivial, at least so far as my aims were concerned. Data that might have been useful to their competitors was well-shielded, but I wasn't interested in stealing the secrets of their latest haemorrhoid cure.

I could have done a lot of damage. Arranged for their backups to be filled with garbage. Arranged for the gradual deviation of their accounts from reality, until reality suddenly intruded in the form of bankruptcy—or charges of tax fraud. I considered a thousand possibilities, from the crudest annihilation of data to the slowest, most insidious forms of corruption.

In the end, though, I restrained myself. I knew the fight would soon become a political one, and any act of petty vengeance on my part would be sure to be dredged up and used to discredit me, to undermine my cause.

So I did only what was absolutely necessary.

I located the files containing the names and addresses of everyone who had been unknowingly participating in triple-blind trials of the company's products. I arranged for them all to be notified of what had been done to them. There were over two hundred thousand people, spread all around the world—but I found a swollen executive slush fund which easily covered the communications bill.

Soon, the whole world would know of our anger, would share in our outrage and grief. Half of us were sick or dying, though, and before the slightest whisper of protest was heard, my first objective had to be to save whoever I could.

I found the program that allocated medication or placebo. The program that had killed Paula, and thousands of others, for the sake of sound experimental technique.

I altered it. A very small change. I added one more lie.

All the reports it generated would continue to assert that half the patients involved in clinical trials were being given the placebo. Dozens of exhaustive, impressive files would continue to be created, containing data entirely consistent with this lie. Only one small file, never read by humans, would be different. The file controlling the assembly line robots would instruct them to put medication in every vial of every batch.

From triple-blind to quadruple-blind. One more lie, to cancel out the others, until the time for deception was finally over.

Martin came to see me.

"I heard about what you're doing. T.I.M. Truth in Medicine." He pulled a newspaper clipping from his pocket. " 'A vigorous new organization dedicated to the eradication of quackery, fraud and deception in both alternative and conventional medicine.' Sounds like a great idea."

"Thanks."

He hesitated. "I heard you were looking for a few more volunteers. To help around the office."

"That's right."

"I could manage four hours a week."

I laughed. "Oh, could you really? Well, thanks very much, but I think we'll cope without you."

For a moment, I thought he was going to walk out, but then he said, not so much hurt as simply baffled, "Do you want volunteers, or not?"

"Yes, but—" *But what?* If he could swallow enough pride to offer, I could swallow enough pride to accept.

I signed him up for Wednesday afternoons.

I have nightmares about Paula, now and then. I wake smelling the ghost of a candle flame, certain that she's standing in the dark beside my pillow, a solemn-eyed nine-year-old child again, mesmerized by our strange condition.

That child can't haunt me, though. She never died. She grew up, and grew apart from me, and she fought for our separateness harder than I ever did. What if we had "died at the very same hour"? It would have signified nothing, changed nothing. Nothing could have reached back and robbed us of our separate lives, our separate achievements and failures.

I realize, now, that the blood oath that seemed so ominous to me was nothing but a joke to Paula, her way of *mocking* the very idea that our fates could be entwined. How could I have taken so long to see that?

It shouldn't surprise me, though. The truth—and the measure of her triumph—is that I never really knew her.

THE DARK

Karen Joy Fowler

Karen Joy Fowler published her first story in 1985, and quickly established an impressive reputation, becoming a frequent contributor to *Isaac Asimov's Science Fiction Magazine* and *The Magazine of Fantasy and Science Fiction*, among other markets. In 1986, she won the John W. Campbell Award as the year's best new writer; 1986 also saw the appearance of her first book, the collection *Artificial Things*, which was released to an enthusiastic response and impressive reviews. Her first novel, *Sarah Canary*, was released this year, and greeted with even more enthusiasm. Fowler lives in Davis, California, has two children, did her graduate work in North Asian politics, and occasionally teaches ballet. Her story "The Lake Was Full of Artificial Things" was in our Third Annual Collection; her story "The Gate of Ghosts" was in our Fourth Annual Collection; and her story "The Faithful Companion at Forty" was in our Fifth Annual Collection.

The following story gives us a glimpse of the hidden connections between seemingly random events, and a scary look at some of the things that can be waiting for us in the dark.

In the summer of 1954, Anna and Richard Becker disappeared from Yosemite National Park along with Paul Becker, their three-year-old son. Their campsite was intact; two paper plates with half-eaten frankfurters remained on the picnic table, and a third frankfurter was in the trash. The rangers took several black-and-white photographs of the meal, which, when blown up to eight by ten, as part of the investigation, showed clearly the words *love bites*, carved into the wooden picnic table many years ago. There appeared to be some fresh scratches as well; the expert witness at the trial attributed them, with no great assurance, to raccoon.

The Beckers' car was still backed into the campsite, a green DeSoto with a spare key under the right bumper and half a tank of gas. Inside the tent, two sleeping bags had been zipped together marital style and laid on a large tarp. A smaller flannel bag was spread over an inflated pool raft. Toiletries included three toothbrushes; Ipana toothpaste, squeezed in the middle; Ivory soap; three washcloths; and one towel. The newspapers discreetly made no mention of Anna's diaphragm, which remained powdered with talc, inside its pink shell, or of the fact that Paul apparently still took a bottle to bed with him.

Their nearest neighbor had seen nothing. He had been in his hammock, he said, listening to the game. Of course, the reception in Yosemite was lousy. At home he had a shortwave set; he said he had once pulled in Dover, clear as a bell. "You had to really concentrate to hear the game," he told the rangers. "You could've dropped the bomb. I wouldn't have noticed."

Anna Becker's mother, Edna, received a postcard postmarked a day earlier. "Seen the firefall," it said simply. "Home Wednesday. Love." Edna identified the bottle. "Oh yes, that's Paul's bokkie," she told the police. She dissolved into tears. "He never goes anywhere without it," she said.

In the spring of 1960, Mark Cooper and Manuel Rodriguez went on a fishing expedition in Yosemite. They set up a base camp in Tuolumne Meadows and went off to pursue steelhead. They were gone from camp approximately six hours, leaving their food and a six-pack of beer zipped inside their backpacks zipped inside their tent. When they returned, both beer and food were gone. Canine footprints circled the tent, but a small and mysterious handprint remained on the tent flap. "Raccoon," said the rangers who hadn't seen it. The tent and packs were undamaged. Whatever had taken the food had worked the zippers. "Has to be raccoon."

The last time Manuel had gone backpacking, he'd suspended his pack from a tree to protect it. A deer had stopped to investigate, and when Manuel shouted to warn it off, the deer hooked the pack over its antlers in a panic, tearing the pack loose from the branch and carrying it away. Pack and antlers were so entangled, Manuel imagined the deer must have worn his provisions and clean shirts until antler-shedding season. He reported that incident to the rangers, too, but what could anyone do? He was reminded of it, guiltily, every time he read *Thidwick, the Big-Hearted Moose* to his four-year-old son.

Manuel and Mark arrived home three days early. Manuel's wife said she'd been expecting him.

She emptied his pack. "Where's the can opener?" she asked.

"It's there somewhere," said Manuel.

"It's not," she said.

"Check the shirt pocket."

"It's not here." Manuel's wife held the pack upside down and shook it. Dead leaves fell out. "How were you going to drink the beer?" she asked.

In August of 1962, Caroline Crosby, a teenager from Palo Alto, accompanied her family on a forced march from Tuolumne Meadows to Vogelsang. She carried fourteen pounds in a pack with an aluminum frame—and her father said it was the lightest pack on the market, and she should be able to carry one-third her weight, so fourteen pounds was nothing, but her back stabbed her continuously in one coin-sized spot just below her right shoulder, and it still hurt the next morning. Her boots left a blister on her right heel, and her pack straps had rubbed. Her father had bought her a mummy bag with no zipper so as to minimize its weight; it was stiflingly hot, and she sweated all night. She missed an overnight at Ann Watson's house, where Ann showed them her sister's Mark Eden bust developer, and her sister retaliated by freezing all their bras behind the twin-pops. She missed "The Beverly Hillbillies."

Caroline's father had quit smoking just for the duration of the trip so as to spare himself the weight of cigarettes, and made continual comments about Nature, which were laudatory in content and increasingly abusive in tone. Caroline's mother kept telling her to smile.

In the morning her father mixed half a cup of stream water into a packet of powdered eggs and cooked them over a Coleman stove. "Damn fine breakfast," he told Caroline intimidatingly as she stared in horror at her plate. "Out here in God's own country. What else could you ask for?" He turned to Caroline's mother, who was still trying to get a pot of water to come to a boil. "Where's the goddamn coffee?" he asked. He went to the stream to brush his teeth with a toothbrush he had sawed the handle from in order to save the weight. Her mother told her to please make a little effort to be cheerful and not spoil the trip for everyone.

One week later she was in Letterman Hospital in San Francisco. The diagnosis was septicemic plague.

Which is finally where I come into the story. My name is Keith Harmon. B.A. in history with a special emphasis on epidemics. I probably know as much as anyone about the plague of Athens. Typhus. Tarantism. Tsutsugamushi fever. It's an odder historical specialty than it ought to be. More battles have been decided by disease than by generals—and if you don't believe me, take a closer look at the Crusades or the fall of the Roman Empire or Napolean's Russian campaign.

My M.A. is in public administration. Vietnam veteran, too, but in 1962 I worked for the state of California as part of the plague-monitoring team. When Letterman's reported a plague victim, Sacramento sent me down to talk to her.

Caroline had been moved to a private room. "You're going to be fine," I told her. Of course, she was. We still lose people to the pneumonic plague, but the slower form is easily cured. The only tricky part is making the diagnosis.

"I don't feel well. I don't like the food," she said. She pointed out Letterman's Tuesday menu. "Hawaiian Delight. You know what that is? Green Jell-O with a canned pineapple ring on top. What's delightful about that?" She was feverish and lethargic. Her hair lay limply about her head, and she kept tangling it in her fingers as she talked. "I'm missing a lot of school." Impossible to tell if this last was a complaint or a boast. She raised her bed to a sitting position and spent most of the rest of the interview looking out the window, making it clear that a view of the Letterman parking lot was more arresting than a conversation with an old man like me. She seemed younger than fifteen. Of course, everyone in the hospital bed feels young. Helpless. "Will you ask them to let me wash and set my hair?"

I pulled a chair over to the bed. "I need to know if you've been anywhere unusual recently. We know about Yosemite. Anywhere else. Hiking out around the airport, for instance." The plague is endemic in the San Bruno Mountains by the San Francisco Airport. That particular species of flea doesn't bite humans, though. Or so we'd always thought. "It's kind of a romantic spot for some teenagers, isn't it?"

I've seen some withering adolescent stares in my time, but this one was practiced. I still remember it. I may be sick, it said, but at least I'm not an idiot. "Out by the airport?" she said. "Oh, right. Real romantic. The radio playing and those 727s overhead. Give me a break."

"Let's talk about Yosemite, then."

She softened a little. "In Palo Alto we go to the water temple," she informed me. "And, no, I haven't been there, either. My parents *made* me go to Yosemite. And now I've got bubonic plague." Her tone was one of satisfaction. "I think it was the powdered eggs. They *made* me eat them. I've been sick ever since."

"Did you see any unusual wildlife there? Did you play with any squirrels?"

"Oh, right," she said. "I always play with squirrels. Birds sit on my fingers." She resumed the stare. "My parents didn't tell you what I saw?"

"No," I said.

"Figures." Caroline combed her fingers through her hair. "If I had a brush, I could at least rat it. Will you ask the doctors to bring me a brush?"

"What did you see, Caroline?"

"Nothing. According to my parents. No big deal." She looked out at the parking lot. "I saw a boy."

She wouldn't look at me, but she finished her story. I heard about the mummy bag and the overnight party she missed. I heard about the eggs. Apparently, the altercation over breakfast had escalated, culminating in Caroline's refusal to accompany her parents on a brisk hike to Ireland Lake. She stayed behind, lying on top of her sleeping bag and reading the part of *Green Mansions* where Abel eats a fine meal of anteater flesh. "After the breakfast I had, my mouth was watering," she told me. Something made her look up suddenly from her book. She said it wasn't a sound. She said it was a silence.

A naked boy dipped his hands into the stream and licked the water from his fingers. His fingernails curled toward his palms like claws. "Hey," Caroline told me she told him. She could see his penis and everything. The boy gave her a quick look, and then backed away into the trees. She went back to her book.

She described him to her family when they returned. "Real dirty," she said. "Real hairy."

"You have a very superior attitude," her mother noted. "It's going to get you in trouble someday."

"Fine," said Caroline, feeling superior. "Don't believe me." She made a vow never to tell her parents anything again. "And I never will," she told me. "Not if I have to eat powdered eggs until I die."

At this time there started a plague. It appeared not in one part of the world only, not in one race of men only, and not in any particular season; but it spread over the entire earth, and afflicted all without mercy of both sexes and of every age. It began in Egypt, at Pelusium; thence it spread to Alexandria and to the rest of Egypt; then went to Palestine, and from there over the whole world. . . .

In the second year, in the spring, it reached Byzantium and began in the following manner: To many there appeared phantoms in human form. Those who were so encountered, were struck by a blow from the phantom, and so contracted the disease. Others locked themselves into their houses. But then the phantoms appeared to them in dreams, or they heard voices that told them that they had been selected for death.

This comes from Procopius's account of the first pandemic. A.D. 541, *De Bello Persico*, chapter XXII. It's the only explanation I can give you for why Caroline's story made me so uneasy, why I chose not to mention it to anyone. I thought she'd had a fever dream, but thinking this didn't settle me any. I talked to her parents briefly, and then went back to Sacramento to write my report.

We have no way of calculating the deaths in the first pandemic. Gibbon says that during three months, five to ten thousand people died daily in Constantinople, and many Eastern cities were completely abandoned.

The second pandemic began in 1346. It was the darkest time the planet has known. A third of the world died. The Jews were blamed, and, throughout Europe, pogroms occurred wherever sufficient health remained for the activity. When murdering Jews provided no alleviation, a committee of doctors at the University of Paris concluded the plague was the result of an unfortunate conjunction of Saturn, Jupiter, and Mars.

The third pandemic occurred in Europe during the 15th to 18th centuries. The fourth began in China in 1855. It reached Hong Kong in 1894, where Alexandre Yersin of the Institut Pasteur at least identified the responsible bacilli. By 1898 the disease had killed 6 million people in India. Dr. Paul-Louis Simond, also working for the Institut Pasteur, but stationed in Bombay, finally identified fleas as the primary carriers. "On June 2, 1898, I was overwhelmed," he wrote. "I had just unveiled a secret which had tormented man for so long."

His discoveries went unnoticed for another decade or so. On June 27, 1899, the disease came to San Francisco. The governor of California, acting in protection of business interests, made it a felony to publicize the presence of the plague. People died instead of *syphilitic septicemia*. Because of this deception, thirteen of the Western states are still designated plague areas.

*   *   *

The state team went into the high country in early October. Think of us as soldiers. One of the great mysteries of history is why the plague finally disappeared. The rats are still here. The fleas are still here. The disease is still here; it shows up in isolated cases like Caroline's. Only the epidemic is missing. We're in the middle of the fourth assault. The enemy is elusive. The war is unwinnable. We remain vigilant.

The Vogelsang Camp had already been closed for the winter. No snow yet, but the days were chilly and the nights below freezing. If the plague was present, it wasn't really going to be a problem until spring. We amused ourselves, poking sticks into warm burrows looking for dead rodents. We set out some traps. Not many. You don't want to decrease the rodent population. Deprive the fleas of their natural hosts, and they just look for replacements. They just bring the war home.

We picked up a few bodies, but no positives. We could have dusted the place anyway as a precaution. *Silent Spring* came out in 1962, but I hadn't read it.

I saw the coyote on the fourth day. She came out of a hole on the bank of Lewis Creek and stood for a minute with her nose in the air. She was grayed with age around her muzzle, possibly a bit arthritic. She shook out one hind leg. She shook out the other. Then, right as I watched, Caroline's boy climbed out of the burrow after the coyote.

I couldn't see the boy's face. There was too much hair in the way. But his body was hairless, and even though his movements were peculiar and inhuman, I never thought that he was anything but a boy. Twelve years old or maybe thirteen, I thought, although small for thirteen. Wild as a wolf, obviously. Raised by coyotes maybe. But clearly human. Circumsized, if anyone is interested.

I didn't move. I forgot about Procopius and stepped in to the *National Enquirer* instead. Marilyn was in my den. Elvis was in my rinse cycle. It was my lucky day. I was amusing myself when I should have been awed. It was a stupid mistake. I wish now that I'd been someone different.

The boy yawned and closed his eyes, then shook himself awake and followed the coyote along the creek and out of sight. I went back to camp. The next morning we surrounded the hole and netted them coming out. This is the moment it stopped being such a lark. This is an uncomfortable memory. The coyote was terrified, and we let her go. The boy was terrified, and we kept him. He scratched us and bit and snarled. He cut me, and I thought it was one of his nails, but he turned out to be holding a can opener. He was covered with fleas, fifty or sixty of them visible at a time, which jumped from him to us, and they all bit, too. It was like being attacked by a cloud. We sprayed the burrow and the boy and ourselves, but we'd all been bitten by then. We took an immediate blood sample. The boy screamed and rolled his eyes all the way through it. The reading was negative. By the time we all calmed down, the boy really didn't like us.

Clint and I tied him up, and we took turns carrying him down to Tuolumne. His odor was somewhere between dog and boy, and worse than both. We tried to clean him up in the showers at the ranger station. Clint and I both had to strip to do this, so God knows what he must have thought we were about. He reacted to the touch of water as if it burned. There was no way to shampoo his hair, and no one with the strength to cut it. So we settled for washing his face and hands, put our clothes back on, gave him a sweater that he dropped by the drain, put him in the backseat of my Rambler, and drove to Sacramento. He cried most of the way, and when we went around curves, he allowed his body to be flung unresisting from one side of the car to the other, occasionally knocking his head against the door handle with a loud, painful sound.

I bought him a ham sandwich when we stopped for gas in Modesto, but he wouldn't eat it. He was a nice-looking kid, had a normal face, freckled, with blue eyes, brown hair; and if he'd had a haircut, you could have imagined him in some Sears catalog modeling raincoats.

One of life's little ironies. It was October 14. We rescue a wild boy from isolation and deprivation and winter in the mountains. We bring him civilization and human contact. We bring him straight into the Cuban Missile Crisis.

Maybe that's why you don't remember reading about him in the paper. We turned him over to the state of California, which had other things on its mind.

The state put him in Mercy Hospital and assigned maybe a hundred doctors to the case. I was sent back to Yosemite to continue looking for fleas. The next time I saw the boy, about a week had passed. He'd been cleaned up, of course. Scoured of parasites, inside and out. Measured. He was just over four feet tall and weighed seventy-five pounds. His head was all but shaved so as not to interfere with the various neurological tests, which had turned out normal and were being redone. He had been observed rocking in a seated position, left to right and back to front, mouth closed, chin up, eyes staring at nothing. Occasionally he had small spasms, convulsive movements, which suggested abnormalities in the nervous system. His teeth needed extensive work. He was sleeping under his bed. He wouldn't touch his Hawaiian Delight. He liked us even less than before.

About this time I had a brief conversation with a doctor whose name I didn't notice. I was never able to find him again. Red-haired doctor with glasses. Maybe thirty, thirty-two years old. "He's got some unusual musculature," this red-haired doctor told me. "Quite singular. Especially the development of the legs. He's shown us some really surprising capabilities." The boy started to howl, an unpleasant, inhuman sound that started in his throat and ended in yours. It was so unhappy. It made me so unhappy to hear it. I never followed up on what the doctor had said.

I felt peculiar about the boy, responsible for him. He had such a *boyish* face. I visited several times, and I took him little presents, a Dodgers baseball cap and an illustrated *Goldilocks and the Three Bears* with the words printed big. Pretty silly, I suppose, but what would you have gotten? I drove to Fresno and asked Manuel Rodriguez if he could identify the can opener. "Not with any assurance," he said. I talked personally to Sergeant Redburn, the man from Missing Persons. When he told me about the Beckers, I went to the state library and read the newspaper articles for myself. Sergeant Redburn thought the boy might be just about the same age as Paul Becker, and I thought so, too. And I know the sergeant went to talk to Anna Becker's mother about it, because he told me she was going to come and try to identify the boy.

By now it's November. Suddenly I get a call sending me back to Yosemite. In Sacramento they claim the team has reported a positive, but when I arrive in Yosemite, the whole team denies it. Fleas are astounding creatures. They can be frozen for a year or more and then revived to full activity. But November in the mountains is a stupid time to be out looking for them. It's already snowed once, and it snows again, so that I can't get my team back out. We spend three weeks in the ranger station at Vogelsang huddled around our camp stoves while they air-drop supplies to us. And when I get back, a doctor I've never seen before, a Dr. Frank Li, tells me the boy, who was not Paul Becker, died suddenly of a seizure while he slept. I have to work hard to put away the sense that it was my fault, that I should have left the boy where he belonged.

And then I hear Sergeant Redburn has jumped off the Golden Gate Bridge.

Non Gratum Anus Rodentum. Not worth a rat's ass. This was the unofficial motto of the tunnel rats. We're leaping ahead here. Now it's 1967. Vietnam. Does the name Cu Chi mean anything to you? If not, why not? The district of Cu Chi is the most bombed, shelled, gassed, strafed, defoliated, and destroyed piece of earth in the history of warfare. And beneath Cu Chi runs the most complex part of a network of tunnels that connects Saigon all the way to the Cambodian border.

I want you to imagine, for a moment, a battle fought entirely in the dark. Imagine that you are in a hole that is too hot and too small. You cannot stand up; you must move on your hands and knees by touch and hearing alone through a terrain you can't see toward an enemy you can't see. At any moment you might trip a mine, put your hand on a snake, put your face on a decaying corpse. You know people who have done all three of these things. At any moment the air you breathe might turn to gas, the tunnel become so small you can't get back out; you could fall into a well of water and drown; you could be buried alive. If you are lucky, you will put your knife into an enemy you may never see before he puts his knife into you. In Cu Chi the Vietnamese and the Americans created, inch by inch, body part by body part, an entirely new type of warfare.

Among the Vietnamese who survived are soldiers who lived in the tiny underground tunnels without surfacing for five solid years. Their eyesight was permanently damaged. They suffered constant malnutrition, felt lucky when they could eat spoiled rice and rats. Self-deprivation was their weapon; they used it to force the soldiers of the most technically advanced army in the world to face them with knives, one on one, underground, in the dark.

On the American side, the tunnel rats were all volunteers. You can't force a man to do what he cannot do. Most Americans hyperventilated, had attacks of claustrophia, were too big. The tunnel rats could be no bigger than the Vietnamese, or they wouldn't fit through the tunnels. Most of the tunnel rats were Hispanics and Puerto Ricans. They stopped wearing after-shave so the Vietcong wouldn't smell them. They stopped chewing gum, smoking, and eating candy because it impaired their ability to sense the enemy. They had to develop the sonar of bats. They had, in their own words, to become animals. What they did in the tunnels, they said, was unnatural.

In 1967 I was attached to the 521st Medical Detachment. I was an old man by Vietnamese standards, but then, I hadn't come to fight in the Vietnam War. Remember that the fourth pandemic began in China. Just before he died, Chinese poet Shih Tao-nan wrote:

> Few days following the death of the rats,
> Men pass away like falling walls.

Between 1965 and 1970, 24,848 cases of the plague were reported in Vietnam.

War is the perfect breeding ground for disease. They always go together, the trinity: war, disease, and cruelty. Disease was my war. I'd been sent to Vietnam to keep my war from interfering with everybody else's war.

In March we received by special courier a package containing three dead rats. The rats had been found—already dead, but leashed—inside a tunnel in Hau Nghia province. Also found—but not sent to us—were a syringe, a phial containing yellow fluid, and several cages. I did the test myself. One of the dead rats carried the plague.

There has been speculation that the Vietcong were trying to use plague rats as weapons. It's also possible they were merely testing the rats prior to eating them themselves. In the end, it makes little difference. The plague was there in the tunnels whether the Vietcong used it or not.

I set up a tent outside Cu Chi town to give boosters to the tunnel rats. One of the men I inoculated was David Rivera. "David has been into the tunnels so many times, he's a legend," his companions told me.

"Yeah," said David. "Right. Me and Victor."

"Victor Charlie?" I said. I was just making conversation. I could see David, whatever his record in the tunnels, was afraid of the needle. He held out one stiff arm. I was trying to get him to relax.

"No. Not hardly. Victor is the one." He took his shot, put his shirt back on, gave up his place to the next man in line.

"Victor can see in the dark," the next man told me.

"Victor Charlie?" I asked again.

"No," the man said impatiently.

"You want to know about Victor?" David said. "Let me tell you about Victor. Victor's the one who comes when someone goes down and doesn't come back out."

"Victor can go faster on his hands and knees than most men can run," the other man said. I pressed cotton on his arm after I withdrew the needle; he got up from the table. A third man sat down and took off his shirt.

David still stood next to me. "I go into this tunnel. I'm not too scared, because I think it's cold; I'm not *feeling* anybody else there, and I'm maybe a quarter of a mile in, on my hands and knees, when I can almost see a hole in front of me, blacker than anything else in the tunnel, which is all black, you know. So I go into the hole, feeling my way, and I have this funny sense like I'm not moving into the hole; the hole is moving over to me. I put out my hands, and the ground moves under them."

"Shit," said the third man. I didn't know if it was David's story or the shot. A fourth man sat down.

"I risk a light, and the whole tunnel is covered with spiders, covered like wallpaper, only worse, two or three bodies thick," David said. "I'm sitting on them, and the spiders are already inside my pants and inside my shirt and covering my arms—and it's fucking Vietnam, you know; I don't even know if they're poisonous or not. Don't care, really, because I'm going to die just from having them on me. I can feel them moving toward my face. So I start to scream, and then this little guy comes and pulls me back out a ways, and then he sits for maybe half an hour, calm as can be, picking spiders off me. When I decide to live after all, I go back out. I tell everybody. 'That was Victor,' they say. 'Had to be Victor.' "

"I know a guy says Victor pulled him from a hole," the fourth soldier said. "He falls through a false floor down maybe twelve straight feet into this tiny little trap with straight walls all around and no way up, and Victor comes down after him. *Jumps* back out, holding the guy in his arms. Twelve feet; the guys swears it."

"Tiny little guy," said David. "Even for V.C., this guy'd be tiny."

"He just looks tiny," the second soldier said. "I know a guy saw Victor buried under more than a ton of dirt. Victor just digs his way out again. No broken bones, no nothing."

Inexcusably slow, and I'd been told twice, but I had just figured out that Victor wasn't short for V.C. "I'd better inoculate this Victor," I said. "You think you could send him in?"

The men stared at me. "You don't get it, do you?" said David.

"Victor don't report," the fourth man says.

"No C.O.," says the third man. "No unit."

"He's got the uniform," the second man tells me. "So we don't know if he's special forces of some sort or if he's AWOL down in the tunnels."

"Victor lives in the tunnels," said David. "Nobody up top has ever seen him."

I tried to talk to one of the doctors about it. "Tunnel vision," he told me. "We get a lot of that. Forget it."

In May we got a report of more rats—some leashed, some in cages—in a tunnel near Ah Nhon Tay village in the Ho Bo Woods. But no one wanted to go in and get them, because these rats were alive. And somebody got the idea this was my job, and somebody else agreed. They would clear the tunnel of V.C. first, they promised me. So I volunteered.

Let me tell you about rats. Maybe they're not responsible for the plague, but they're still destructive to every kind of life-form and beneficial to none. They eat anything that lets them. They breed during all seasons. They kill their own kind; they can do it singly, but they can also organize and attack in hordes. The brown rat is currently embroiled in a war of extinction against the black rat. Most animals behave better than that.

I'm not afraid of rats. I read somewhere that about the turn of the century, a man in western Illinois heard a rustling in his fields one night. He got out of bed and went to the back door, and behind his house he saw a great mass of rats that stretched all the way to the horizon. I suppose this would have frightened me. All those naked tails in the moonlight. But I thought I could handle a few rats in cages, no problem.

It wasn't hard to locate them. I was on my hands and knees, but using a flashlight. I thought there might be some loose rats, too, and that I ought to look at least; and I'd also heard that there was an abandoned V.C. hospital in the tunnel that I was curious about. So I left the cages and poked around in the tunnels a bit; and when I'd had enough, I started back to get the rats, and I hit a water trap. There hadn't been a water trap before, so I knew I must have taken a wrong turn. I went back a bit, took another turn, and then another, and hit the water trap again. By now I was starting to panic. I couldn't find anything I'd ever seen before except the damn water. I went back again, farther without turning, took a turn, hit the trap.

I must have tried seven, eight times. I no longer thought the tunnel was cold. I thought the V.C. had closed the door on my original route so that I wouldn't find it again. I thought they were watching every move I made, pretty easy with me waving my flashlight about. I switched it off. I could hear them in the dark, their eyelids closing and opening, their hands tightening on their knives. I was sweating, head to toe, like I was ill, like I had the mysterious English sweating sickness or the *Suette des Picards*.

And I knew that to get back to the entrance, I had to go into the water. I sat and thought that through, and when I finished, I wasn't the same man I'd been when I began the thought.

It would have been bad to have to crawl back through the tunnels with no light. To go into the water with no light, not knowing how much water there was, not knowing if one lungful of air would be enough or if there were underwater turns so you might get lost before you found air again, was something you'd have to be crazy to do. I had to do it, so I had to be crazy first. It wasn't as hard as you might think. It took me only a minute.

I filled my lungs as full as I could. Emptied them once. Filled them again and dove in. Someone grabbed me by the ankle and hauled me back out. It frightened me so much I swallowed water so I came up coughing and kicking. The hand released me at once, and I lay there for a bit, dripping water and still sweating, too, feeling the part of the tunnel that was directly below my body turn to mud, while I tried to convince myself that no one was touching me.

Then I was crazy enough to turn my light on. Far down the tunnel, just within range of the light, knelt a little kid dressed in the uniform of the rats. I tried to get closer to him. He moved away, just the same amount I had moved, always just in the light. I followed him down one tunnel, around a turn, down another. Outside, the sun rose and set. We crawled for days. My right knee began to bleed.

"Talk to me," I asked him. He didn't.

Finally he stood up ahead of me. I could see the rat cages, and I knew where the entrance was behind him. And then he was gone. I tried to follow with my flashlight, but he'd jumped or something. He was just gone.

"Victor," Rat Six told me when I finally came out. "Goddamn Victor."

Maybe so. If Victor was the same little boy I put a net over in the high country in Yosemite.

When I came out, they told me less than three hours had passed. I didn't believe them. I told them about Victor. Most of them didn't believe me. Nobody outside the tunnels believed in Victor. "We just sent home one of the rats," a doctor told me. "He emptied his whole gun into a tunnel. Claimed there were V.C. all around him, but that he got them. He shot every one. Only, when we went down to clean it up, there were no bodies. All his bullets were found in the walls.

"Tunnel vision. Everyone sees things. It's the dark. Your eyes no longer impose any limit on the things you can see."

I didn't listen. I made demands right up the chain of command for records; recruitment, AWOLs, special projects. I wanted to talk to everyone who'd ever seen Victor. I wrote Clint to see what he remembered of the drive back from Yosemite. I wrote a thousand letters to Mercy Hospital, telling them I'd uncovered their little game. I demanded to speak with the red-haired doctor with glasses whose name I never knew. I wrote the Curry Company and suggested they conduct a private investigation into the supposed suicide of Sergeant Redburn. I asked the CIA what they had done with Paul's parents. That part was paranoid. I was so unstrung I thought they'd killed his parents and given him to the coyote to raise him up for the tunnel wars. When I calmed down, I knew the CIA would never be so farsighted. I knew they'd just gotten lucky. I didn't know what happened to the parents; still don't.

There were so many crazy people in Vietnam, it could take them a long time to notice a new one, but I made a lot of noise. A team of three doctors talked to me for a total of seven hours. Then they said I was suffering from delayed guilt over the death of my little dog-boy, and that it surfaced, along with every other weak link in my personality, in the stress and the darkness of the tunnels. They sent me home. I missed the moon landing, because I was having a nice little time in a hospital of my own.

When I was finally and truly released, I went looking for Caroline Crosby. The Crosbys still lived in Palo Alto, but Caroline did not. She'd started college at Berkeley, but then she'd dropped out. Her parents hadn't seen her for several months.

Her mother took me through their beautiful house and showed me Caroline's old room. She had a canopy bed and her own bathroom. There was a mirror with old pictures of some boy on it. A throw rug with roses. There was a lot of pink. "We drive through the Haight every weekend," Caroline's mother said. "Just looking." She was pale and controlled. "If you should see her, would you tell her to call?"

I would not. I made one attempt to return one little boy to his family, and look what happened. Either Sergeant Redburn jumped from the Golden Gate Bridge in the middle of his investigation or he didn't. Either Paul Becker died in Mercy Hospital or he was picked up by the military to be their special weapon in a special war.

I've thought about it now for a couple of decades, and I've decided that, at least for Paul, once he'd escaped from the military, things didn't work out so badly. He must have felt more at home in the tunnels under Cu Chi than he had under the bed in Mercy Hospital.

There is a darkness inside us all that is animal. Against some things untreated or untreatable disease, for example, or old age—the darkness is all we are. Either we are strong enough animals or we are not. Such things pare everything that is not animal away from us. As animals, we have a physical value, but in moral terms we are neither good nor bad. Morality begins on the way back from the darkness.

The first two plagues were largely believed to be a punishment for man's sinfulness. "So many died," wrote Agnolo di Tura the Fat, who buried all five of his own children himself, "that all believed that it was the end of the world." This being the case, you'd imagine the cessation of the plague must have been accompanied by outbreaks of charity and godliness. The truth was just the opposite. In 1349, in Erfurt, Germany, of the three thousand Jewish residents there, not one survived. This is a single instance of a barbarism so marked and so pervasive, it can be understood only as a form of mass insanity.

Here is what Procopius said: *And after the plague had ceased, there was so much depravity and general licentiousness, that it seemed as though the disease had left only the most wicked.*

When men are turned into animals, it's hard for them to find their way back to themselves. When children are turned into animals, there's no self to find. There's never been a feral child who found his way out of the dark. Maybe there's never been a feral child who wanted to.

You don't believe I saw Paul in the tunnels at all. You think I'm crazy or, charitably, that I was crazy then, just for a little while. Maybe you think the CIA would never have killed a policeman or tried to use a little child in a black war even though the CIA has done everything else you've ever been told and refused to believe.

That's O.K. I like your version just fine. Because if I made him up, and all the tunnel rats who ever saw him made him up, then he belongs to us, he marks us. Our vision, our Procopian phantom in the tunnels. Victor to take care of us in the dark.

Caroline came home without me. I read her wedding announcement in the paper more than twenty years ago. She married a Stanford chemist. There was a picture of her in her parents' backyard with gardenias in her hair. She was twenty-five years old. She looked happy. I never did go talk to her.

So here's a story for you, Caroline:

A small German town was much plagued by rats who ate the crops and the chickens, the ducks, the cloth and the seeds. Finally the citizens called in an exterminator. He was the best; he trapped and poisoned the rats. Within a month he had deprived the fleas of most of their hosts.

The fleas then bit the children of the town instead. Hundreds of children were taken with a strange dancing and raving disease. Their parents tried to control them, tried to keep them safe in their beds, but the moment their mothers' backs were turned, the children ran into the streets and danced. The town was Erfurt. The year was 1237.

Most of the children danced themselves to death. But not all. A few of them recovered and lived to be grown-ups. They married and worked and had their own children. They lived reasonable and productive lives.

The only thing is that they still twitch sometimes. Just now and then. They can't help it.

Stop me, Caroline, if you've heard this story before.

MARNIE

Ian R. MacLeod

If there's anyone currently rivaling Greg Egan for the title of Hottest New Writer of the Nineties to date, it's the author of the bittersweet story that follows, British writer Ian R. MacLeod. Like Egan, MacLeod also had extremely good years in 1990 and 1991, publishing a slew of strong stories in *Interzone* and *Isaac Asimov's Science Fiction Magazine* (with more in inventory at both markets), as well as impressive work in *Weird Tales, Amazing,* and *The Magazine of Fantasy and Science Fiction*; several of those stories made the cut for one or another of the various "Best of the Year" anthologies—in fact, he appeared in three different anthologies with three different stories last year (one of them was "Past Magic," in our Eighth Annual Collection). MacLeod is in his early thirties, and lives with his wife and baby daughter in the West Midlands of England. He has recently given up his day job to write full time, and is working on his first novel, tentatively titled *Burying the Carnival*. We'll be hearing a lot more from him in the years ahead, too.

In "Marnie" he offers us a chilling look at a man grimly determined to follow the advice of that old adage, If At First You Don't Succeed. . . .

I'd arranged things so that I woke up on an ordinary morning. It was November, the winter term. My bedroom curtains were veined with frost and sunlight. And, for a long time, I just lay there, breathing the strange, familiar smells of this house and this bed and my own sleepy body, until the radio alarm lit up with the last pip of the eight o'clock time signal. It was reassuring to find that nothing had really changed. It was just an ordinary morning. I had ordinary things to do.

I got up and went to the bathroom, finding my way unthinkingly. The memories and sensations were crowding in too quickly for me to react, but, for now, nothing mattered as long as my body knew what to do. Opening doors with just the right pressure, twisting on the shower taps to get the hot water running before stepping in. My skin felt distant as I soaped myself. The contours and textures seemed right, yet didn't belong. I could sense my flesh, yet it was like touching a lover.

But even as I wondered at the strangeness of returning, the feeling was wearing off. The easy movement of my limbs began to seem natural. The full head of hair that I dried with smooth, strong hands that had reached

163

automatically for the towel was no surprise. Age is relative, and one adjusts to its presence. And I reminded myself that I was, in any case, thirty-one— no longer quite young.

I wiped a space in the steamed-up mirror to shave. I recognized my face from the old, cold photographs. Here, moving and alive, I saw that the camera hadn't lied. It was an ungenerous face, the eyes too close, the nose too large. Insincere when it smiled. Pained when it tried to look sincere. I'd never grown used to it, and, seeing it again, with the deepened knowledge of what age would do, made me wonder—just as I had done all those years back, just as I had always done—exactly *what* Marnie had seen in me.

The shaving foam was Tesco's own, from the big store by the roundabout. The razor was a Bic. I marvelled at the rightness of the period detail, the barcodes and the price stickers still on the side. It seemed almost a pity to use them, like ransacking a museum. Brut 33 aftershave in a green plastic bottle on the shelf over the sink. Had people still used that stuff in the late 1980s? I unscrewed the silver cap and splashed some on my chest and face, smiling faintly at the thought of the advert they used to run. It was all coming back to me now. All of it. The dark, sweet smell of the aftershave. The toothpaste and brush in a broken-handled Charles and Diana mug. And, beside that, sitting just as naturally on the shelf, was a small bottle of Elizabeth Arden cleanser. Everything about the bottle, the casual thought with which Marnie had doubtless left it for next time, the screw top jammed on at a typically careless angle, hit me hard. I reached out to hold the bottle, touching where her fingers had touched. This was real enough. There was nothing to grin at, point at. This wasn't a museum.

Marnie, I thought. Marnie. Look again. She's all around you. Long strands of her blonde hair in the plughole. A half box of Tampax in the cabinet by the sink. The lipstick remains of *I love you* written on the tiles above the bath showing up through the condensation even though some tidy insanity had made me wipe it off with white spirit. Marnie: the thought that had filled and haunted my whole life. Marnie. Marnie. *Marnie.*

I got dressed, finding my socks and underpants tucked neatly in the right drawer. Hello, old friends. Then cords, a warmish grey cotton shirt, and a loosely knotted woollen tie that was a concession to my position at the University. Looking at myself fully dressed in the long wardrobe mirror, I felt ticklish threads of the ridiculous pulling once again at my mind. That collar, those cords! And that *tie*. I hadn't remembered looking quite as foolish as *this*. But memories change to suit the present.

I took breakfast listening to the plummy-voiced newscasters on Radio Four. I'd long forgotten the details, but nothing in the news came as a surprise, any more than it had been a surprise to find cartons of orange juice and milk waiting from yesterday in the fridge, or cartons of sugar-free muesli in the fitted cabinets, slit open and re-sealed neatly and precisely according to the instructions.

I was in two minds about whether to walk or drive to work. The walk was easy enough, but when I toured my house, touching and remembering all those old possessions, I spent longer in the garage than anywhere else, despite the winter chill. There, still looking clean and new, was my car, my pride and joy, the pinnacle of my overdraft. A Porsche: black and glossy as dark water. I'd forgotten just how proud I'd been of it, but that all came back as soon as I saw it and touched it and smelt it. After brooding at the wheel for some time, gazing at the slumbering dials, I decided it was better to be cautious on this first day. After all, I hadn't driven anything remotely like it for twenty years.

After brushing my teeth, I pulled on a tweed jacket that would, if my life proceeded as it had before, be stolen from under my seat at a cinema in Southport two years later.

The chilly, sunlit air beyond my front door was full of the city. It was a short walk to campus. I lived . . . *live* in a close of small and expensive modern semis built as an infill in one of the huge gardens of the big older houses that still characterized this area around the University. Most of my neighbours were young, like me, professional and well-paid, like me, single or married or living together, but always childless. Like me.

Even in this pretty, tree-lined area, the smells of parkland and old leaves were half-drowned, to my newly sensitized nose, by the metallic reek of car fumes. I had two main roads to cross. Both were filled with a dangerous, sluggish stream of cars. Startled by the bleep of the pelican crossing and urged on by an impatient old lady, I realized it hadn't been a mistake to leave the Porsche in the garage.

The interlinking suburban roads were nicer, more as I remembered them. Landscaped gardens and mock-Tudor gables. There were schoolchildren piling into ugly Volvos in driveways, and joggers and students walking, and students on bikes. This was my usual route, and many of the faces were familiar, people I passed day after day without acknowledgement. Everything was so neat, so orderly, so *expected*.

I went through the west gate into the campus. Staff and students drifted and talked and walked in the grassy spaces between the red brick and concrete. Faces came out at me from the past. I was a fixture here, part of the crew. Norman Harris from the Chancellor's office nodded in my direction as he walked away from his Sierra. Then I saw Stephanie Kent hurrying up the wide granite steps of the library, the same old woolen skirt tight as ever over the ample ridges of her knickers. And there was Jack Rattle, my own Head of Department, the latest Penguin in one hand and a sandwich box in the other.

We converged at the swing doors leading to the Graphic Arts Faculty. I held them open for him.

"Morning, Daniel," he said. "Another day, eh? Another few brain cells gone."

"Hardly any left," I said; it didn't sound right, but then I'd never really known how to respond to Jack. I wondered if he'd said the same thing to me on this same day all those years ago, and what my reply had been.

"You must," he tapped my elbow with the corner of his sandwich box, "you *must* show me what we're getting from that new plotter. Damn thing cost us enough."

"Sure. Just say when."

"I will. I will." Jack wandered off down the admin corridor to his own office, passing in and out of frames of window sunlight. I paused for a moment beneath the frescoes at the foot of the marble stairs, watching him, wondering if it was foreknowledge or if the signs were really there that his heart would kill him in the spring.

A few students pushed past me as I dawdled, huffy and in a rush. In the sixties and seventies, any arts faculty would have been filled with campus peacocks even this deep into winter term, but now, with the odd green-haired exception, the students were heavy with overcoats, anxiety, and books, just like all the trainee lawyers and engineers in the other faculties. Like everyone else, they wanted their grades, they wanted a job, they wanted money.

I checked my watch. It was 9:35. That was just right; my tutorial should have started at half past. Although it was quite impossible that anyone could find me out, I nevertheless felt it was important to give nothing away by changing my habits.

My legs were suddenly a little weak as I took the stairs to the second level: a strong and unexpected return of the feeling that my body didn't *belong* to me. In a sense, of course, it *didn't*, but I pushed that thought down as I passed the Burne-Jones stained-glass and the fire hydrants at the stair turns. This was not the time to hesitate, not when I had a tutorial to get through. Just don't think, I told myself. It worked well enough before.

Along the waxed gleam of the east corridor. Notice boards and past students' efforts on the walls. Rooms 212, 213, 213A, 214.

214. I took a deep breath and walked in. The chatter ceased reluctantly. The air smelt a little of someone's BO, and a lot of the plastic of the computer terminals that had only been in place since the start of the term.

"Good morning." I powered up the master screen, proud of the swift and easy way my hands moved across the switches and keys. "This week we'll continue our exploration of the ways we can expand from the basic paintbox options . . ."

I paused and looked around at the faces, half-familiar now as they had been then. From the bored expressions, it was obvious that they accepted me without question. I knew that I'd passed a test; my nerves were loosening by the moment. I continued talking at a brisk pace, hardly referring to my notes.

Living in the past was easy.

I closed the tutorial at eleven, and the students drifted out, leaving the garish perspective tricks that the inexperienced or untalented generally produce shimmering on their screens. The computer was still logged for our use, and they could have continued, but, for all of them, the novelty of pressing keys to make things happen on a screen had worn off. Too lazy to walk around the room and look (and how quickly the habits of my lecturing days were coming back!), I called their efforts up, reduced to quarter windows, on my own screen, and saved them for next week's session, unthinkingly hitting the right keys. View, Save, Name, Return. It was an oddly absorbing task, and probably the first time this morning that, with the success of the tutorial behind me, I'd felt completely at home.

The students had left the door open, and Marnie entered the room without my noticing. She'd crept up close behind me before I knew, suddenly, that she was there—and that she was real.

It was strange, to come this far and then to be almost taken by surprise. She put her arms around my neck. Her hair brushed my face. I could smell the shampoo and acacia, and the cigarette she'd just smoked, and the wool of her scarf, and the faint, bitter sweetness of her breath.

"When are you going to give this up," she said, her voice serious but trickling down with every word towards laughter. "Why don't you let the machines get *on* with it?"

"Could I be replaced that easily?"

"That's right," she said. Her hands pressed against my chest, then suddenly released. ". . . old boffin like you . . ." She spun the chair around so that I faced her. ". . . and how is the old boffin anyway?"

"Same as yesterday," I said. "Let's have coffee."

Marnie's good mood was frail, as I knew it would be. She walked with her head down as we crossed the bright, busy campus, like a child aiming to miss the cracks in the pavement. I'd have liked to have taken her hand, just to be touching her, but I knew it wasn't the sort of thing we'd usually done.

We queued in the cafeteria. Marnie was silent and I couldn't think of anything to say. The woman at the till shook her head and gave me a funny look when I offered my Visa card to pay for the coffee. I don't think Marnie noticed. We took our cups over to an empty table by the window that two Arab students had just vacated. The plastic seat felt warm. I was noticing these things, the steam rising from the slowly spinning froth of the coffee, and the way someone had spooned the sugar to one side of the bowl that lay between us: with Marnie, everything was more vivid. It always had been.

"Is this a busy day?" she asked, lifting the cup with both hands, blowing with that beautiful mouth, sipping. A little of the froth stayed on the faint down along her top lip.

"We could be together, if you like."

"That could be nice," she said.

"Could?"

"Depends on what sort of let's-be-together-day it is."

"I love you, Marnie." For thirty years, I'd been wanting to say those words to her again.

She put the cup down with a slight bang. Her eyes travelled across my face, onwards to the window, the wandering students amid the winter-bare trees, the big buildings beyond. "I don't feel right in this place," she said. "All this architecture. Look at the people out there. Standing, wandering around, talking. It's all such a pose. You know, like one of those architect's drawings you see. Prospective developments. And little sketches of people in the foreground . . . imaginary people doing imaginary things, just to give the whole neat concept a sense of scale. It's not *real*, people standing around like that, you only ever get anything actually like it at a university."

"It's just a place," I said. "We're both here. You. Me. That's real enough."

"And this is going to be a you-and-me day?"

"I'd like it to be," I said.

"I've got a couple of lectures and a life study I could skip."

"Then," I said, "there's no problem."

She didn't reply. There was still froth on her lip and I wanted to mention it, but knew I shouldn't. This whole thing was doubly confusing: my searching for the right words to bridge the awkwardness that was already between us was compounded by the continued vague promptings of memory, a feeling of drifting in and out of the flow. I'd imagined that it would be easy to draw things away from the patterns of the past, but Marnie was still the same, and, now that I was here, I was surprised at how little *I* had changed. I decided that the best thing was to take a new tack, and say those things to her that I'd always wanted to say.

I swallowed some coffee. Another distraction. I'd forgotten the way the university coffee used to taste. Something about it always reminded me of floormops. I was like Proust, but instead of drifting away into memory I was choking and drowning in tea-soaked madeleines.

"I've been thinking," I said, ". . . about the way we've allowed things to . . . drift. I've been a fool to forget that I loved you. Love you . . . no, I never *forgot* that, but things got in the way. Let's ignore the last couple of weeks. It's just history, a little time in our lives. The arguments don't matter if we have each other."

She glanced back at me from the window as though she was coming back from another world. I checked my irritation. No rows, not this time.

"I'm a bit hung-over," she said. "Honesty time. I was pissed last night."

"With your friends."

She shrugged. "With people. They're not *you*, Dan, don't worry. I'd like to give things a chance, I really would, if we could get it back. When I saw you this morning, sitting in front of that damn screen of yours, it was—"

Her gaze went up. Something slapped my back.

"Dan! Mind if I join you?"

A chair rasped over from the nearest table before I could answer. Ritchie Hanks—one of the specialists who took care of the university mainframe— plonked his heavy, boyish self down.

He glanced at Marnie. I wasn't sure whether they'd ever met—my memory failing me again. There was a gratifying moment of hesitation, as the thought that maybe he'd interrupted something passed briefly in ones and zeros through Ritchie's computer-specialist's brain. But he wasn't easily put off when he had a story to tell about some fascinating new glitch he'd found in the system.

We listened politely. I asked a few questions so that he could give the answers he wanted. Marnie was on her best behaviour: none of the sly asides that I'd found so amusing when I'd first known her but had since come to dread. None of that mattered, I told myself, not here in the past, not when I knew that Ritchie would have a private sector job on double the pay by the end of next year and I'd never think of him again, or whilst Marnie . . . but it did. Everything mattered.

"Anyway," I said, stopping him quickly before he began a different story. "I'd better be going now. Pressure of work, you know how it is."

"Sure, Dan. Pressure of work. Never stops, does it. I was only—"

"—that's right." I moved to stand. "Marnie, are you coming?"

"Well . . ." she hesitated and looked at me. Just her joke. Of *course* she'd come instead of staying with a prat like Ritchie. Wouldn't she?

She smiled. "I have some work to do. Us students have work too."

"Students," Ritchie said, as though it was a new concept. "Of course."

Marnie and I walked out into the cold air. Nothing had been decided. Nothing had changed.

Marnie shivered and pushed her hands into the pockets of her jacket. Her hair almost glittered in the sunlight. "It's true," she said. "I *do* have things to do. Tell you what, I'll come round your place tonight."

I nodded numbly. "What time?"

"Say . . . eight."

I nodded again.

"Ciao."

"Ciao."

She walked away from me. Above her winter boots and red socks were the bare backs of her knees. I wanted to kiss them and taste her skin. In my newly youthful body, the thought brought the odd and unaccustomed stirrings of an erection. It grew and then faded as she diminished in the slow drift of movement, as she became another figure, an artist's brushstroke to give these buildings a sense of scale.

Maybe I should have started earlier back. Perhaps that was part of the problem. Started back at the time when everything was fresh and new and right. But to do that, I would have had to go back to some misty and mythical place where Marnie wasn't Marnie and I wasn't me.

It was simply more complicated than that.

This was Marnie's second year at University. I'd seen her in the first year, of course; she was too pretty and . . . different not to be noticed. I think we might even have been to a couple of the same parties, not the student sort, but the ones around the chintzy academic fringes of the university where people dress up and pretend to stay sober, and start off talking about the

Booker Prize and end up bitching about who's screwing whom. But Marnie didn't invite approaches, at least not from *me* she didn't.

She was twenty-four, a good three years older than the other undergrads. A *mature student*: how she hated that phrase. I suppose she was lonely in the way that older students always are, having to act as a shoulder to cry on, having to ignore or laugh along with the stupidities of her younger friends. She'd spent those extra years drifting in Europe, working as a nanny in Cannes, staying in some kibbutz, doing the sort of things that most people only talk about doing. I was seven years older, but I'd never really left school. She made me feel young, and she made me wonder just where and why and with whom she'd been doing all these things.

I only met her properly, face to face, when she took the computer graphics option in her second year. She didn't belong in the class. She was always sitting a little apart when I came in and the others looked up from their chatter. Marnie stood out in most situations. She just didn't belong. It was everything about her.

By the end of the second week, it was obvious that Marnie and computers weren't going to get on. There wasn't much to learn—the whole purpose of the course was, after all, to allow the students to put computers down on their CVs when they applied for those cherished jobs in design offices and advertising agencies—but even when she hit the right keys, things would go wrong. And after I'd cleared the screen of gibberish, and she'd punched the keys or prodded the light pen or rolled the mouse again, with a simple pessimism that was quite different from the manner of people who are genuinely computer-phobic, something *else* would go wrong instead. I'd never known anything like it. She nearly brought down the whole mainframe in the third week, something that was theoretically impossible from our access port and doubtless caused Ritchie and his colleagues no end of fascination.

I didn't mind at all. It gave me a legitimate excuse to spend most of the tutorials sitting next to Marnie, to lean close to her as we pondered the latest catastrophe, and to breathe her scent. I kept my eyes on the screen, but that was because I could see her reflection so clearly in the glass.

She gave me no particular signals. Of course, someone as lovely as Marnie gives signals to every man she passes, but that is merely God's unthinking blessing and curse. She dressed differently from the other students, usually in skirts and dresses rather than jeans. She had a striped blue-and-white cotton jacket that she wore when the weather was still mild early in the term that I fell in love with for some reason. She wore her hair long or in a bun. She smelt of acacia and cigarettes and Marnie. There was a slowness about the way she moved, a kind of resignation. She understood how she looked, but, unlike most beautiful women, she had a kind of confidence, but absolutely no pride.

I was attracted. I wanted to walk along sunset beaches with her. I wanted to talk through the night. I wanted to go to bed with her, and stay there a long, long time. I wanted my fill of Marnie, and I wasn't sure how much that could possibly be. The whole thing quickly got out of hand. I wanted her too badly to break the silence and risk rejection. And by the fifth week of term, I was being brusque and ignoring her in class and then replaying every word and look endlessly, even in my sleep. I was even beginning to wonder if it really *was* Marnie, or whether I was simply going a little mad.

Then I saw her one afternoon. I was killing time, wandering in the local botanical gardens, because the Chancellor's department had cocked-up the room allocation for my tutorial. The big tropical house was a common enough place for students to work, and it came as a bigger surprise than it should have to find her there, sitting with an easel beside the goldfish pool, filling in blocks of colour on a squared-off grid.

I said hello and she said hi. She was wearing a loose tee shirt, and I could see the curves of her shoulders and neck far more clearly than my fantasies had permitted. She seemed quite cheerful and relaxed. Marnie was, as I soon discovered, very partial to warmth, and very averse to the cold. A real hot-house flower. I sat down on the stone rim of the pond amid the bananas and rotting oranges and orchids, and we chatted. When I stood up for us to go down to the tea room by the pagoda, the backs of my trousers were soaking wet. We laughed about that, the first time we'd ever laughed together. When she pulled on her blue-and-white cotton jacket, her bare, downy arm brushed against my chest, and the feeling hit me like a huge, taut drum.

That was how it began. Now, with an afternoon to get through without her and only those odd, unsatisfactory words in the cafeteria to cling to, Marnie seemed almost as distant from me as she had all those years ahead, before I'd returned.

I spent the time wandering. I walked down to the botanical gardens, feeling more comfortable now with the undirected flood of traffic that growled past. This was, after all, my life. I had lived it. The eighties were as idiosyncratic as any other decade, but, at root, nothing was really that different from the true present. It was just a question of emphasis and style. Women pushed prams. Tramps mumbled. All the young people seemed to be plugged into those clumsy music players . . . Walkmans. They stared straight through you. Visitors from another planet. It reminded me of that Bradbury novel, all the people with shells in their ears. A helicopter chittered low and loud over the rooftops. No one looked up. And some of the new buildings looked as though they belonged on a moonbase. The future was already *here*. Of course, there were no silver air-cars or monorails, but, by now, people had realized that there never would be. Things would carry on pretty much as they had always done, and even the tantalizing fear of a black and glassy wasteland, the last of those great mid-century fantasies, was fading. These people pushing past and looking through me as they went about their busy, empty lives *knew* that nothing would ever really change. The holes in the sky would grow larger, and so would their flatter, squarer, sharper, deeper, thinner TV screens. And when the news slipped in between the commercials, the faces that peered out at them from those TV screens would still be ancient and hollow-eyed with starvation. The future was a fact that had arrived and had already been forgotten. It meant as much and as little to them as it would have done to their ancestors, dragging a plough or sheltering in a cave. They knew that what lay ahead was the same as now, only more so.

There were no students in the tropical house today. I drank my coffee in the tea room down by the bandstand alone.

Still not feeling up to risking myself and the Porsche, I took a bus into the centre of town. I still had some change in my pockets, but it was running down. I knew I had a card in my wallet, next to the last five pound note, that would get me money from one of the many cash machines. But, for all my research and revision, I had no idea what my PIN number was.

I made the mistake of sitting on the top deck of the bus, and the ragged movements and the unaccustomed cigarette fumes left me feeling a little sick by the time it finally jerked to a halt outside C&As.

The shops were a revelation. I would have loved to have taken some of this stuff back to the present with me. Condoms (and who could ever forget AIDS? Well, *I* had, for one). Organic vegetables. Newspapers with *real news* in them. Compact discs. Posters like wallpaper with the name of the artist printed at the bottom in huge type. Mrs. Thatcher mugs! I guess I just gawked. The store detectives watched me carefully as I picked up this and prodded that. It was just like a museum. They were the museum keepers, and didn't even know it!

The evening rush hour caught me unawares. Everybody was grim, moving all at once. I had to queue in the yellow streetlight to get a place on the bus, and then had to stand most of the way to my stop. It was cold as I walked the last half mile, and I was pondering whether I should give my central heating a call—before I remembered. The house was warm anyway, the timer set thoughtfully to come on in the evening.

I took a bath, feeling a little guilty about how much I'd unthinkingly enjoyed my Marnie-less tour of the local sights. But, by seven, I was waiting, anxiously clean and freshly clothed, not so much watching the TV as playing with the remote control.

Slices of the Channel Four News. Some quiz programme. An old Doris Day film. Top of the Pops. Top of the Pops was the most diverting (did Michael Jackson ever look *that* young?) but none of them held my attention for long. Soon, Marnie would be here. I planned on going out for a meal, maybe that Indian place just along the road, something ordinary and nostalgic, a place where we could sit in peaceful, candlelit anonymity and talk longingly. And then we'd walk back, hugging each other close against the cold, our frosty breath entwined in the streetlight, back to my house, to my bed.

Eight o'clock came and went. Marnie was always late, of course. I fixed myself a shot of Famous Grouse at half past, and then another at five to nine. All the usual questions and accusations were starting a headache hammer inside my head. I wandered around the house, looking at the wallpaper

I'd chosen, the furniture and the things I hadn't seen in thirty years. Now, if I'd only kept that big plastic Foster's Lager ashtray that Marnie had smuggled out of the local wine bar under her coat and used to roll her joints. Somewhere along the years, it had departed from my life; exactly the sort of bric-a-brac that grew in value because no one thought anything of it at the time. There were a distressingly large number of things like that around the house. I'd been sitting on a gold mine, and I'd never realized it. And where the goddamned hell *was* she anyway?

Where was Marnie? At any moment since we'd become lovers, and even for some time before, that question was always somewhere in my thoughts. Another half hour, another whisky. I stood at the window and watched the empty pavement. I sat down and tried the TV again. I lay on the bed. I got up. I put the record player on. Old music for these old times. But the question followed me about, tapping at my shoulder, clutching at my elbow, whispering in my ear. What is she *doing*? She was with someone *else*, that was what. She'd never been faithful, not truly, not *faithful*, that was what.

I'd seen her walking the campus with another man the morning after the very first night we'd made love. I was still glowing. I sidled behind a tree. I watched them cross the wide and milling spaces. At the steps in front of the library she put her arms around him and laughed and gave him a quick kiss. She said he was just a student, when I quizzed her in the corridor as she came out from pottery, clay on her apron and hands and arms like the evidence of a crime, just someone she liked who had said something funny. Just another student. Snob that I was, that hurt more than anything. He was three years younger than her, for crissake! And when I followed him into the cafeteria for lunch, I saw that he had greasy hair and a fair sprinkling of zits.

Ten o'clock. She wasn't coming. No one, *absolutely no one*, let me down like this! And this wasn't the *first* time, either, oh no, she let me down all the time! No more whisky, I decided, having suddenly drunk myself up to some sort of calm plateau. Tonight might be a dead loss but there would be plenty of other times. Yes, plenty.

I pulled on a coat and went for a walk. I hadn't walked so much in one day for a long time. It was quiet now, the cars passed by in separate flashes of light. The big petrol station by the traffic lights glowed like a Spielberg spaceship. I headed down past the hospital towards Marnie's place. It was pure masochism, I knew I wouldn't find her there.

Architecturally, the big old houses on Westborne Road were similar to those of the sales directors and wine importers who lived around me, but here, a little further out of town, there were dirty net curtains at the windows and bedsit rows of bell buttons beside the doors.

Hers was the top window, set in a gable, with a wind-chime owl hanging from the casement in perpetual silence. I crunched up the worn tarmac drive, where a Morris Minor was parked beside a wheelless Triumph Herald up on bricks, and tried the buzzer anyway. A typed strip beside it had the name of the previous occupant, one R. Singh. Marnie never got around to changing anything. There was no reply. The shape of the stairs in the low-wattage light of the hall loomed through the coloured door-glass. I could smell cat's piss. A record player boomed faintly, deep inside. A man was laughing.

I stopped at the Ivy Bush on the way back, just in time for another drink. There was a traditional jazz band playing in the back room, but I stayed out of the noise in the flock wallpaper lounge. The publican recognized me and said hello. I nodded back, but his face was one that I had completely forgotten. Although I didn't feel particularly drunk, I had to fight back a strong urge to sit down on the spare chair facing those two elderly ladies and tell them that I'd come all the way from the future just for love. But common sense prevailed. Apart from anything else, they were probably quite used to those sort of conversations in this particular pub.

I got back to the house at about midnight, drank some more whisky, debating for a while the merits of taking it straight from the bottle, but deciding to keep with etiquette and use a tumbler, pulled off a representative assortment of clothes and flopped on the bed. The room spun a little, but not as much as I'd hoped. This young body could sure hold its drink.

Then the doorbell rang.

"You've got one sock off," Marnie said as she swaggered in.

"You mean I've got one sock on."

She threw her coat over the stair rail. It slid to the floor. She'd been drinking too. She had a blue dress on underneath, one that showed her figure.

"What happened?" I asked, following her into the lounge.

She flopped down on the sofa, kicked off her shoes, put her feet up. "I tried to ring." She gazed at her toes.

"Sure. What time?"

"You don't believe me."

We were sparring, trying to find out who was more pissed. The things one does for love.

"I'd like a drink," she said.

"You've had enough."

"Look, Daniel," she said, switching off the booze in her brain just as she'd switched it on. "I'm sorry."

I poured us each a glass. She ignored it for a moment then took it and drank it with both hands.

"What time did you ring?"

"Is this a quiz? Do I get a prize?" She smiled. "Men look funny in shirts and underpants . . . and one sock. Put something on, Dan—or take something off."

"I've been waiting for you all night. What happened?"

"I rang you at ten. You weren't in then, were you? I tried earlier, but the box was vandalized and it stank. I'm truly sorry. It was my fault."

I sat down on the sofa by her feet. "Who were you with?"

So she began to tell me about the Visconti film she'd been to see at the arts centre that turned out to be a two part epic and how someone had given her a lift to the bus stop but then their car had broken down. I was angry-drunk, sure that reason and right were on my side, but there was an element of bitter comedy to this. I knew the story already. It was like watching an old series on TV and discovering that you're familiar with every twist and turn, that your brain had retained those meaningless facts for so many years. Why, I wondered, gazing at the lovely and abstract curves of Marnie's thighs where the dress had ridden up, hadn't I realized that this would be tonight? Her story stumbled on, an absurd, convoluted epic involving a pub and a wine bar and meeting up with a few more friends and the simple fact that she'd forgotten.

"Nothing's ever your fault," I said. "Nothing ever *was*."

Her eyes widened a little. "You almost sound like you mean that."

I wondered if I did. I finished my whisky and put it down. I waited for the room to settle. The dress had gone up and she'd made no effort to cover herself. Playing the whore, getting at me that way. It made me angry all over again to realize just how easily it worked.

I took hold of her feet and massaged them, greedy for the feel of her flesh under the nylon.

"Do you forgive?" she asked, not wanting to be forgiven.

"Yes," I said, not meaning it, simply watching her body. Nothing had changed. We were back in the same old ways. The same tracks. The same dead end sidings. The past and the present had joined and now her skirt
now her skirt
rode higher and my hands touched the tension in her calves and thighs
rode higher and my hands touched the tension in her calves and thighs
and up towards what was promised underneath, widening and sweeten-
and up towards what was promised underneath, widening and sweeten-
ing and sharpening to the place where everything was Marnie.
ing and sharpening to the place where everything was Marnie.

We showered separately afterwards to wash away some of the drink, and our guilt at using each other so easily. Nothing had changed. Sex with someone you can hardly talk to afterwards has to be a bad idea. So this was what I'd come all this way for. My Marnie. My love. She pulled back the shower curtains and stepped through the moist heat. There were droplets on her shoulders and face. Nothing had changed. Her hair was dark and smooth and wet, like a swimmer's.

We lay in the same bed through the grey night. Marnie breathed soft and heavy beside me. Sometimes, I remembered, I could talk to her when she was like this, find all the right words. But even that was gone. Nothing had changed, the only difference was that everything I did now reeked of falsity. I was a voyeur, staring out at my own life through keyhole eyes.

And I could press *return* at any time, clear the screen to end this absurd role-playing game. The thought was a bitter comfort, with Marnie so real and so distant beside me, and yet somehow it drew me into sleep, through the walls and into the sky and deep inside Marnie's eyes, where there was only the sparky darkness of electricity, circuitry, and machine power.

I awoke. The greyness was growing stronger with the winter dawn. My Marnie. The perfect, anonymous curves of wrist and back and cheekbone. The composure of sleep. I touched her skin gently, lovingly, and it rippled and broke. She rolled over and muttered something and stumbled out of bed to go to the loo.

The clock said seven thirty. I wanted to make love to her again, not really for the sex, but just to convince myself that she was real. But when she came back she began to collect her scattered clothes.

"God, I hate wearing yesterday's knickers."

"You should bring some of your stuff around here," I said, crossing my hands behind my head, "We could even try living together," pleased with myself at how easily I'd managed to slip that one through.

She gave me a be-serious look and pulled her slip on over her head. "Let's have breakfast. I could fix something."

"Something nice . . . ?"

"Goes without saying." She picked up her dress and gave it a shake. "I'm the perfect housewife."

Irritatingly fully dressed, she wafted out of the bedroom. I sat up and put my feet on the carpeted floor. I supposed the morning had to begin some time.

We faced each other across toast and boiled eggs at the breakfast table.

"What about living together?" I asked her again.

She looked wonderfully pretty with no make-up and her hair a mess. I wondered why women had never grasped the fact that men actually *preferred* them this way, without the paint and plastic.

She thwacked the top off her egg. "What about it?"

"Come on, Marnie." I tackled my own egg, tapping it gently around the sides. "I thought you were always saying you wanted to try anything new."

"Living together isn't new, Dan. We'd row too much. Look at us now. It's great when it's great, but it's like being on a roller coaster. And that wouldn't last for long."

"That's exactly my point," I said, keeping my voice smoothly reasonable and staring back at the watery ruin inside my egg. Marnie was a useless cook. "Things would get better."

"Dan, they would just get the same. You *know* that."

It was hard to stay in love with her for long when she was like this. Mulishly refusing to listen. Her sweet disorder was just an irritant. She was wearing that blue dress of the night before, that smelt of cigarettes and the places she'd been to and the people she'd been with. There was even a red wine stain just above her left breast. It was too easy to imagine some oaf mopping it for her.

"And exactly who *were* you with last night?"

"We've been through all that." She pushed away her plate and went in search of cigarettes. I followed her as she dug into her handbag and under cushions.

"You shouldn't smoke anyway," I said. "Look at you, you're a bloody addict."

"One more word," she said, "and I'm leaving. I don't *need* this first thing in the morning. I mean, come on, do *you*?"

But she didn't find her cigarettes, and I did say several more words. This was an easy row by our standards, kid's stuff. Marnie told me to go to hell and a few more places besides, and she used the F-word, which I never liked, especially from a woman. Then she grabbed up her coat and handbag and stormed out, banging the front door so hard that it bounced open again, letting in the cold of the morning. I had to go down the hall and shut it myself.

I poured out some more coffee in the kitchen, ignoring the yellow-eyed stare of the eggs. Until this moment, my body had somehow disregarded its shortage of sleep and excess of alcohol, but something had jogged its memory and now it was making up for lost time. I took the cup through to the lounge and dropped down into a chair, leaving the curtains closed. Marnie's cigarettes peeked out from underneath the dishevelled sofa. I stared at them. What *was* it about being in love with her? I was acting like a robot, as though I had no free will.

Something would have to change. The thought kept recurring over the next two days as Marnie and I avoided each other, just as we had done before, just as we always did, playing the game of pride, pretending that an acknowledgement of the fact that we needed each other would be a sign of weakness. Something would have to change. Everything was just the same. A petite Taiwanese student had a nosebleed in one of my classes. I got a letter from my parents telling me that old Uncle Derek was in a bad way from a stroke. I broke one of my heavy Waterford whisky glasses and cut my finger when I was washing up. The passage of these days, it seemed, had been pegged out by accidents and misfortunes.

But life had its compensations. I spent a lovely lecture-free Friday morning taking the Porsche up and down the close and along the local roads, just to get the feel of it again. As with everything else, it was really just a matter of letting my subconscious take over. The Porsche obeyed my commands promptly and politely, its great engine purring like an eager-to-please cat. Inside there was still that beautiful smell you got from cars in those days. The whole feel of it was nice, precise. For the first time since I'd returned, I felt as though I was really in command. Around lunchtime, I went for a longer drive, risking the traffic and finding that, with the Porsche, I had nothing to fear. We all used to take driving for granted, but in the right car it could be a real pleasure: the Porsche was the right car.

My route took me through the fringes of a highrise slum, the Porsche as strange as a spaceship in this land of the dog turd and the abandoned mattress. I turned gratefully back towards the bright and busy hive of the university, along Westborne Road, under the tree shadows, past the big old houses. And there, quite by chance, was Marnie, walking and talking between two men.

I slowed the Porsche to a smooth walking pace and buttoned the window down.

"Fancy a lift, Marnie?"

"Okay," she said, without an ounce of hesitation. I unclicked the door and she slipped elegantly into the bucket seat. I exchanged a look with the two scruff postgrads she'd been walking with. Sorry, lads.

We zoomed off.

"I've just been driving around this morning," I said. "I'd forgotten how good the Porsche was."

She laughed. "How can you forget a thing like this? It takes half your salary."

"You like it?"

"Of course I do. It's just a car, but it's a nice car. Why do you have to keep asking people these things? It's like you don't believe them yourself."

I shook my head, shrugged. I touched the brake and the car rooted itself to the line of a junction.

"Last night, whenever it was," she said. "I don't blame you for being angry when I was late. It's just that everything gets so *big* with you and me. When you're sweet, Dan, everything's fine, but we always seem to be looking for ways to hurt each other."

"I've been trying to think what to say," I said. "Really, Marnie . . . I'm sorry, too." Sincerity was always easier when you were driving.

I flashed my pass at the security guard at the east gate. I parked in my usual place by the arts faculty.

She slammed the passenger door.

"Careful," I said.

"Careful's my middle name."

"Come round tonight," I said to her across the Porsche's roof. "It doesn't matter what time. And we'll sleep together and when we wake up on Saturday, whenever, we'll go somewhere in this car. A day out, you and me."

She smiled, her perfect face reflected in the perfect, glossy black. "That sounds nice."

Deeply in love, I watched her walk away. She gave me a backwards wave over her shoulder. My Marnie, my one and only.

Because I hadn't stipulated early, the doorbell rang just after six. Marnie stood framed in the light from the hall against the winter black, wearing a tartan shawl and a waxed cotton jacket, carrying her overnight bag.

"Let me help you with that," I said, ever the kindly host.

I dumped her bag by the telephone in the hall and swung the door shut with my foot. Helping her off with her jacket, my hands strayed from her shoulders, spoilt for choice between the curves of her breasts and her lovely behind. She turned and pushed herself against me. Our mouths locked, greedily exchanging breath and saliva. We were half undressed by the time we managed to get up the stairs. Marnie bounced onto the bed, sitting up to undo the remaining buttons of her blouse.

"No," I said, struggling to take off my watch and socks at the same time. "I'll do that. I'll do everything."

We went for a meal later at the nearby Indian restaurant. It was a regular place of ours. The waiters gave us the best table, away from the toilets and the door to the street. I'd managed to get some cash by writing a cheque at the bank, but my recollection of prices was still vague, and even though Marnie always insisted on paying her share, I wasn't sure whether I'd have enough for the meal and to see us through the weekend. When we sat down, I asked Marnie if they'd accept Visa.

"We always pay that way here," she said, pulling her chair in. "You're very forgetful lately."

"You're too much of a distraction."

"Let's see now." She reached across the pink tablecloth and took my hand. She was achingly beautiful in the candlelight. "You tell me who the Chancellor of the Exchequer is."

I went cold. I didn't have the faintest idea. Antony Barber? Too early. Dennis Healey? No, Labor. Then who?

Her golden-lit eyes saw through me for a moment.

I felt as though I wasn't there.

"Time's up," she said, letting go of my hand.

The waiter came over with the menus. In the brief distraction, I remembered. But it was too late to say.

"I'm sorry," I said, studying the long lists of kormas and tandoori dishes to avoid meeting her eyes. "I've been feeling a bit odd lately. You've obviously noticed. Maybe I should see a doctor." I tried a laugh. "Or a psychiatrist."

It was the only fragile moment in an otherwise perfect evening. We got merry on house red. I asked her about her name, just as I'd done all those years before, and she admitted that, yes, her mother really *had* got it from that Hitchcock movie. Not even a particularly *good* Hitchcock movie, she added, her eyes dropping towards the candlewax and poppadum crumbs. I took her hand and kissed her palm and held it tenderly against my cheek.

Underneath all the looks and all the laughter and all the friends she had, Marnie was vulnerable. There was no doubt about it. Sitting talking or not talking, simply gazing at her, I could also feel my own barriers slipping down. We were so different, so alike: disappointed with a world that had given us many of the things we didn't want and held out on the few we really desired. Between the two of us there was *something*. Like looking in a mirror, it was both a separation and a sharing, a glassy edge between us on which we tried to balance our love. In later years, of course, I romanticized her, idealized her, but now, being with her again, sharing the thoughts and looks and words and silences, of that best kind that you can never recall afterwards, I lost any remaining doubts about our love being ordinary, or even a passing obsession. I *loved her*. This was, for once in my life, totally and completely real.

We walked home, hugging each other close against the cold, our frosty breath entwined in the streetlight.

The perfect evening was followed by a perfect night. Everything we did we did slowly, heavily blurred with love. We kissed each other through the edges of sleep. Once, deep in the night, she began to shiver, although it wasn't from the cold. I held her tight until she was still, as I had done before.

"Help me, Dan," she whispered from inside. "Love me."

The dream flowed into the dreamy morning. Bringing coffee to our bed, I could hardly believe that it was this simple and natural to be in love. With the curtains open so we could see the trees and the sky, we sat close under the comforter and debated over a map where we might go. We settled on wherever the roads took us.

I rolled the Porsche proudly out of the garage through a romantic mist of exhaust. My lovely car; it seemed right that it should share our lovely day. I was grinning stupidly, a kid at Christmas. I felt like laughing at the thought of how hard I'd tried to find the *words* when I'd first returned to Marnie, when all that mattered really was being like this. Together.

I even trusted her to drive for a while, once we were safely out on the country roads. She grated the gears a couple of times, but I managed to keep quiet: no damage was done, and she understood the need to be delicately careful. We swapped back over. It was a wonderful feeling to be driving in this car, with a beautiful woman beside me and nothing but ourselves to fill the day, and the bare trees reaching over the roads, their clawed reflections sweeping the wide hood. We stopped at a country pub and sat in old leather chairs beneath the beams and in the firelight, sipping salty, hoppy beer. They were already playing Christmas tunes on the jukebox, and we talked about where we would go together then. Somewhere with mountains and snow.

Marnie peeled the print off a beer mat and sketched a picture of me with a biro. When she handed it over, I saw that it was as good as it had always been, a little too accurate for me to appreciate, maybe; a few quick and easy strokes that said things that those old, cold photographs never had. The only difference now was that the card of the mat was softly white again, instead of the yellowed memento I was more used to. Marnie's work was always at its best when she wasn't concentrating or trying. She wasn't really an artist. She had talent, but she was too busy coping with life to turn it into much. She would never have become any kind of artist or designer.

On our way out through the deserted benches of the pub garden, Marnie sat down on the kiddies' wooden swing, not caring about the lichen and moss. She tilted her legs and I pushed her back and forth. The publican came out to bring a barrel up from the cellar. I expected him to tell us to get the hell off, but he just looked and smiled oddly at us, like a man who realises he's lost something.

As we drove on, Marnie told me about a day when she was a child, when it was summer and her father was still alive. He'd pushed her on a creaky swing into the hot sky. He had a tweed jacket that smelt of pipe tobacco and that itched when he hugged her. There were shimmering trees and a lake and a big house of white stone.

"I wish I could find out where that place was," she said. "Just in the past, I guess."

I parked the Porsche under the trees in a country lane. A quiet place. A pretty, nowhere place. The sky was thickly grey. Everything was shadowed and soft, like a room with the curtains drawn. We walked on between the dark hedgerows.

A sign pointed across the fields towards a landmark hill. We followed the track, keeping to the grassy sides to avoid the worst of the mud. A flock of swans flew silently over. Their whiteness seemed to make them ghostly creatures from another world.

Standing at the grassy top of the hill, the whole of a county was spread around us. The grey of the city to the north. Villages and towns. Trees and fields dark with winter. A toy van travelling down a toy road. A big reservoir: tarnished silver, then suddenly bright in the ripples from a breeze that soon touched our faces with cold.

"We haven't *done* anything today," I said.

"That's what's been so good." Marnie hugged me. I could feel the soft pressure of her breasts. "I'd like to have another day like this, please."

"I'd like to have another day like this, please."

I couldn't bring myself to reply.

She let go. "What is it, Dan?"

I shrugged. "Just . . . talking about the future."

"You should know the future never comes."

What was I supposed to do? Nothing had changed. This day. This hill. These words. Marnie. Me.

"What shall we do tonight?" I asked.

"What shall we do tonight?" I asked.

"I'll have to go back to my flat."

"I'll have to go back to my flat."

I nodded, trying very hard to picture her in that cold and empty room, with the half-finished paintings, the drooping rubber plant in the corner, the owl wind-chime silent at the window.

"I promised to see some people," she said. "A sort of party. Come along with me. It'll be fun."

"It doesn't matter what I say, does it?"

"Don't be like that. Please."

We walked back to the Porsche in our own puzzled and separate silences. It was waiting under the trees, looking like something out of a calendar or a magazine. Marnie climbed inside and lit a cigarette, exhaling a cloud against the dashboard and windscreen.

"Couldn't you have done that when you were outside?" I said thickly.

She took another drag. "It's too cold out there, Dan. It'll go when we get moving. . . ." She gave me a pitying look. Poor Daniel, the look said, to be bothered by such an absurd little thing. In truth, I wasn't bothered, as I had been before. But it was too late to change things.

Marnie shivered. "Can't we just get going? I'm cold. I've been cold all day."

Cold all day.

Cold all day.

I gripped the steering wheel hard. "I thought we'd been happy. I thought today was special . . . So special you won't even bloody well stay with me tonight!"

"It *has* been special," she said. She opened the ashtray on the dash between us and maneuvered her cigarette towards it. But the ash fell on the black carpet beside the gearbox. She gave it a careless brush, as though that was enough. "I've just been a bit . . . chilly. You know how I am."

The inside of the car was thick with smoke. I clicked the ignition key on a turn and pressed the master button that brought both of the windows down. "Why the hell do you have to smoke in here?" I said over the gentle buzz of the window motors. "Especially when we're trying to talk?"

She laughed, or attempted to. I think she was already starting to cry. "You call this *talking*? All that bothers you is me smoking in this precious bloody car of yours. Marnie messing up your pretty images of the way everything *should* be. Marnie smoking. Marnie drinking. Marnie actually sometimes wanting to be with people *other than you*. When all *you* want is some woman to sit by you in this bloody, *bloody* car! It's that simple, isn't it?"

I gripped the steering wheel. I said nothing. There was no point.

"Why don't you just fuck off," she said childishly, childishly stubbing the cigarette out on my carpet, getting out of the Porsche, childishly slamming the door.

I got out on my side. She was standing there beneath the big oak tree, with the placid winter countryside all around us, as though none of this was happening.

"If you could see yourself," I said. "How stupid this is."

"Of *course* it's stupid! We're having a *stupid argument*. Or perhaps you hadn't noticed?"

"Why?" I asked reasonably.

"Everything has to be so *personal* with you," she said, breathing in and out in shudders, her face puffed with ugly tears. "That bloody car of yours! This was a lovely day until you ruined it."

"I want you to respect me . . . respect my property."

"Your *property*!" Now she was yelling. The sound was unnatural, unwomanly. I'd never seen her this angry before.

I'd never seen her this angry before.

"Just listen. . . ."

I stepped towards her. She pushed me away and stumbled over to the car.

"You deserve this—" she was shouting through the thickness of her tears. "—You really do. You bastard! Your property! You do deserve this. I love you, you bastard. I'm not. Your property. *Fuck you.* I hope you never—"

I watched her fumble open the driver's door. She started the Porsche with the accelerator floored and the gears in reverse. The engine howled, and the car gave a juddering leap backwards into a tree. The bumper crunched, shivering leaves and scraps of bark through swirls of exhaust. Marnie knocked the wiper stalk as she screeched into first. The blades flicked to and fro. Then she pulled away, the fat tyres kicking up a shower of mud and leafmold; a rich, incongruous scent amid the drifting reek of the petrol.

The engine roar faded into silence. I looked at my watch; almost four o'clock. I began to walk back along the road towards the nearest village. I knew the way: right at the crossroads and straight ahead after that. I was even able to save myself a mile's pointless detour down a badly signed road that petered out to a farm track, but it was still deep twilight, and my shoes were pinching badly by the time I reached the village green and used the phonebox to call for a cab. I waited shivering outside. There were trees and chimneys and a church spire in silhouette against a grainy sky, warmly lit leaded windows in the houses, two ducks circling in the dim pond. The whole scene was heavy with nostalgia for times much earlier than these, the wholesome wood-scented, apple-scented, sunset-coloured days that had never been.

The cab came quickly. Questing headlights swung towards me across the crumbling churchyard wall. It was a Japanese car, I think, not the sort of car that had a real name that anyone remembers. A functional box on wheels. I asked the driver to take me to the nearest town; I didn't bother to explain. I knew that he would perform his role well enough in silence, just as he had done before.

The shops were shut, and the main car park around the big war memorial where he dropped me off was almost empty. No use offering Visa. I paid the fare without a tip. I was left with exactly forty-nine pence in my pockets. A cold wind was starting. A few cans rattled and chimed across the streetlit tarmac.

The police station was on a side road at the back of Woolworth's. An old man backing out through the doors with his dog gave me a weary, sharing smile. I told the duty constable at the counter that an acquaintance had driven my car away without permission. I didn't think they were insured. I told him the car was a Porsche. Unimpressed, he nodded towards the empty plastic benches by the doors and told me to wait.

I sat down. Like the few other police stations I've been inside, this one was absurdly quiet, as though it had been waiting for greying, paint-peeling years for something to happen. Something to make up for all the drunks, and all the people like me. I studied the curling posters on the notice board opposite. Oddly, I couldn't remember any of them. I wondered vaguely, irrationally, if that was somehow a sign that things would end up differently.

Two sergeants came out from a room at the back. They flipped up the side of the counter. Before they spoke, I knew from their faces that it had happened. I wondered if this was the time to end it, but part of me wanted to see it again. To be certain.

They drove me to the reservoir. There was a noisy crane there already, and floodlights probing thick yellow shafts into the water. Men in uniforms peered down from the roadside. People were gathering around the fringes of the darkness to watch. One of the sergeants leaned over to the back seat before we stepped out of the car and asked me if I thought it was an accident; just the sort of casual question they try on you before you've had time to put your guard up.

"I used to think so," I said, not caring what they made of it. "But now I don't know. I'm not sure."

The Porsche looked like a big, black crab as it broke the surface. It rose into the harsh light, water sluicing out of it in glittering curves. People *oohed* and *aahed*. Chains tensed and screamed with the car's weight. The air filled with the smell of green mud, like a bad beach at low tide. The crane paused for a moment, a big insect hesitating with its prey, then swung the car down onto the road. The suspension broke with twig-like snaps. The car was still wet and heavy, dark pools sliding across the verge and down the bank, running eagerly back into the reservoir. Sleepwalking figures broke the door open, and there was a thick rush of mud before they lifted Marnie out. No one hurried. I didn't envy the police their job.

They asked me if it was her. Just confirmation, for the record. I walked through to the front, where an ambulance stood with its lights uselessly circling and its doors uselessly open. A man in a wetsuit pushed past me, wiping something from his hands. They'd just left her on the road. No point in messing the blankets. Her head was turned away, an abstract curve of neck and cheekbone. Her skin was glossy white, and her hair was dark and smooth and wet. Like a swimmer's. I nodded, but this wasn't *my* Marnie, my one and only, the woman I loved.

I stepped back, away from the flashlights and the floodlights and the spinning blue lights and the people. The time had come, there was no point in going any further. Somewhere from the machine darkness, I would have to summon the will to try again. Try again. Press Return. I let the images and sensations fade, the sounds, the sights, the smells.

There *will* be another time, Marnie. A better time than this, believe me. I promise.

I promise.

A TIP ON A TURTLE

Robert Silverberg

Here's an elegant and darkly ironic look at the proposition that *some* things in life are better *not* to know. . . .

Robert Silverberg is one of the most famous SF writers of modern times, with dozens of novels, anthologies, and collections to his credit. Silverberg has won five Nebula Awards and four Hugo Awards. His novels include *Dying Inside, Lord Valentine's Castle, The Book of Skulls, Downward to the Earth, Tower of Glass, The World Inside, Born with the Dead, Shadrach in the Furnace, Tom O'Bedlam, Star of Gypsies,* and *At Winter's End.* His collections include *Unfamiliar Territory, Capricorn Games, Majipoor Chronicles, The Best of Robert Silverberg, At the Conglomeroid Cocktail Party,* and *Beyond the Safe Zone.* His most recent books are *Nightfall,* a novel-length expansion of Isaac Asimov's famous story, done in collaboration with Asimov himself, and the novel *The Face of the Waters.* Upcoming is another novel in collaboration with Asimov, *Child of Time.* For many years he edited the prestigious anthology series New Dimensions, and has recently, along with his wife, Karen Haber, taken over the editing of the Universe anthology series. His story "Multiples" was in our First Annual Collection; "The Affair" was in our Second Annual Collection; "Sailing to Byzantium"—which won a Nebula Award in 1986— was in our Third Annual Collection; "Against Babylon" was in our Fourth Annual Collection; "The Pardoner's Tale" was in our Fifth Annual Collection; "House of Bones" was in our Sixth Annual Collection; both "Tales from the Venia Woods" and the Hugo-winning "Enter a Soldier. Later: Enter Another" were in our Seventh Annual Collection; and "Hot Sky" was in our Eighth Annual Collection. He lives in Oakland, California.

The sun was going down in the usual spectacular Caribbean way, disappearing in a welter of purple and red and yellow streaks that lay across the wide sky beyond the hotel's manicured golf course like a magnificent bruise. It was time to head for the turtle pool for the pre-dinner races. They held the races three times a day now, once after lunch, once before dinner, once after dinner. Originally the races had been nothing more than a casual diversion, but by now they had become a major item of entertainment for the guests and a significant profit center for the hotel.

As Denise took her place along the blazing bougainvillea hedge that flanked the racing pool, a quiet, deep voice just back of her left ear said, "You might try Number Four in the first race."

It was the man she had noticed at the beach that afternoon, the tall tanned one with the powerful shoulders and the tiny bald spot. She had been watching him snorkeling along the reef, nothing visible above the surface of the water but his bald spot and the blue strap of his goggles and the black stalk of the snorkel. When he came to shore he walked right past her, seemingly lost in some deep reverie; but for a moment, just a moment, their eyes had met in a startling way. Then he had gone on, without a word or even a smile. Denise was left with the feeling that there was something tragic about him, something desperate, something haunted. That had caught her attention. Was he down here by himself? So it appeared. She too was vacationing alone. Her marriage had broken up during Christmas, as marriages so often did, and everyone had said she ought to get away for some midwinter sunshine. And, they hadn't needed to add, for some postmarital diversion. She had been here three days so far and there had been plenty of sunshine but none of the other thing, not for lack of interest but simply because after five years of marriage she was out of practice at being seduced, or shy, or simply uneasy. She had been noticed, though. And had done some noticing.

She looked over her shoulder at him and said, "Are you telling me that the race is fixed?"

"Oh, no. Not at all."

"I thought you might have gotten some special word from one of the hotel's boys."

"No," he said. He was very tall, perhaps too tall for her, with thick, glossy black hair and dark, hooded eyes. Despite the little bald spot, he was probably forty at most. He was certainly attractive enough, almost movie-star handsome, and yet she found herself thinking unexpectedly that there was something oddly asexual about him. "I just have a good feeling about Number Four, that's all. When I have a feeling of that sort it often works out very well." A musical voice. Was that a faint accent? Or just an affectation?

He was looking at her in a curiously expectant way.

She knew the scenario. He had made the approach; now she should hand him ten Jamaican dollars and ask him to go over to the tote counter and bet them on Number Four for her; when he returned with her ticket they would introduce themselves; after the race, win or lose, they'd have a daiquiri or two together on the patio overlooking the pool, maybe come back to try their luck on the final race, then dinner on the romantic outdoor terrace and a starlight stroll under the palisade of towering palms that lined the beachfront promenade, and eventually they'd get around to settling the big question: his cottage or hers? But even as she ran through it all in her mind she knew she didn't want any of it to happen. That lost, haunted look of his, which had seemed so wonderfully appealing for that one instant on the beach, now struck her as simply silly, melodramatic, overdone. Most likely it was nothing more than his modus operandi: women had been falling for that look of masterfully contained agony at least since Lord Byron's time, probably longer. But not me, Denise told herself.

She gave him a this-leads-nowhere smile and said, "I dropped a fortune on these damned turtles last night, I'm afraid. I decided I was going to be just a spectator this evening."

"Yes," he said. "Of course."

It wasn't true. She had won twenty Jamaican dollars the night before and had been looking forward to more good luck now. Gambling of any sort had never interested her until this trip, but there had been a peculiar sort of pleasure last night in watching the big turtles gliding toward the finish line, especially when her choices finished first in three of the seven races. Well, she had committed herself to the sidelines for this evening by her little lie, and so be it. Tomorrow was another day.

The tall man smiled and shrugged and bowed and went away. A few moments later Denise saw him talking to the leggy, freckled woman from Connecticut whose husband had died in some kind of boating accident the summer before. Then they were on their way over to the tote counter and he was buying tickets for them. Denise felt sudden sharp annoyance, a stabbing sense of opportunity lost.

"Place your bets, ladies gemmun, place your bets!" the master of ceremonies called.

Mr. Eubanks, the night manager—shining black face, gleaming white teeth, straw hat, red-and-white striped shirt—sat behind the counter, busily ringing up the changing odds on a little laptop computer. A boy with a chalkboard posted them. Number Three was the favorite, three to two; Number Four was a definite long shot at nine to one. But then there was a little flurry of activity at the counter, and the odds on Four dropped abruptly to five to one. Denise heard people murmuring about that. And the the tote was closed and the turtles were brought forth.

Between races the turtles slept in a shallow, circular concrete-walled holding tank that was supplied with sea water by a conduit running up from the beach. They were big green ones, each with a conspicuous number painted on its upper shell in glowing crimson, and they were so hefty that the brawny hotel boys found it hard going to carry them the distance of twenty feet or so that separated the holding tank from the long, narrow pool where the races were held.

Now the boys stood in a row at the starting line, as though they themselves were going to race, while the glossy-eyed turtles they were clutching to their chests made sleepy graceless swimming motions in the air with their rough leathery flippers and rolled their spotted green heads slowly from side to side in a sluggish show of annoyance.

The master of ceremonies fired a starter's pistol and the boys tossed the turtles into the pool. Graceless no longer, the big turtles were swimming the moment they hit the water, making their way into the blue depths of the pool with serene, powerful strokes.

There were six lanes, separated by bright yellow ribbons, but of course the turtles had no special reason for remaining in them. They roamed about randomly, perhaps imagining that they had been returned to the open sea, while the guests of the hotel roared encouragement: "Come on, Five! Go for it, One! Move your green ass, Six!"

The first turtle to touch any part of the pool's far wall was the winner. Ordinarily it took four or five minutes for that to happen; as the turtles wandered, they sometimes approached the finish line but didn't necessarily choose to make contact with it, and wild screams would rise from the backers of this one or that as their turtle neared the wall, sniffed it, perhaps, and turned maddeningly away without making contact.

But this time one of the turtles was swimming steadily, almost purposefully, in a straight line from start to finish. Denise saw it moving along the floor of the pool like an Olympic competitor going for the gold. The brilliant crimson number on its back, though blurred and mottled by the water, was unmistakable.

"Four! Four! Four! Look at that bastard go!"

It was all over in moments. Four completed its traversal of the pool, lightly bumped its hooked snout against the far wall with almost contemptuous satisfaction, and swung around again on a return journey to the starting point, as if it had been ordered to swim laps. The other turtles were still moving about amiably in vague circles at mid-pool.

"Numbah Four," called the master of ceremonies. "Pays off at five to one for de lucky winnahs, yessah yessah!"

The hotel boys had their nets out, scooping up the heavy turtles for the next race. Denise looked across the way. The leggy young widow from Connecticut was jubilantly waving a handful of gaudy Jamaican ten-dollar bills in the face of the tall man with the tiny bald spot. She was flushed and radiant; but he looked down at her solemnly from his great height without much sign of excitement, as though the dramatic victory of Number Four had afforded him neither profit nor joy nor any surprise at all.

The short, stocky, balding Chevrolet dealer from Long Island, whose features and coloration looked to be pure Naples but whose name was like something out of *Brideshead Revisited*—Lionel Gregson? Anthony Jenkins?—something like that—materialized at Denise's side and said, "It doesn't matter which turtle you bet, really. The trick is to bet the boys who throw them."

His voice, too, had a hoarse Mediterranean fullness. Denise loved the idea that he had given himself such a fancy name.

"Do you really think so?"

"I know so. I been watching them three days, now. You see the boy in the middle? Hegbert, he's called. Smart as a whip, and damn strong. He reacts faster when the gun goes off. And he don't just throw his turtle quicker, he throws it harder. Look, can I get you a daiquiri? I don't like being the only one drinking." He grinned. Two gold teeth showed. "Jeffrey Thompkins, Oyster Bay. I had the privilege of talking with you a couple minutes two days ago on the beach."

"Of course. I remember. Denise Carpenter. I'm from Clifton, New Jersey, and yes, I'd love a daiquiri."

He snagged one from a passing tray. Denise thought his Hegbert theory was nonsense—the turtles usually swam in aimless circles for a while after they were thrown in, so why would the thrower's reaction time or strength of toss make any difference?—but Jeffrey Thompkins himself was so agreeably real, so cheerfully blatant, that she found herself liking him tremendously after her brush with the Byronic desperation of the tall man with the little bald spot. The phonied-up name was a nice capping touch, the one grotesque bit of fraudulence that made everything else about him seem more valid. Maybe he needed a name like that where he lived, or where he worked.

Now that she had accepted a drink from him, he moved a half step closer to her, taking on an almost proprietary air. He was about two inches shorter than she was.

"I see that Hegbert's got Number Three in the second race. You want I should buy you a ticket?"

The tall man was covertly watching her, frowning a little. Maybe he was bothered that she had let herself be captured by the burly little car dealer. She hoped so.

But she couldn't let Thompkins get a ticket for her after she had told the tall man she wasn't betting tonight. Not if the other one was watching. She'd have to stick with her original fib.

"Somehow I don't feel like playing the turtles tonight," she said. "But you go ahead, if you want."

"Place your bets, ladies gemmun, place your bets!"

Hegbert did indeed throw Number Three quickly and well, but it was Five that won the race, after some minutes of the customary random noodling around in the pool. Five paid off at three to one. A quick sidewise glance told Denise that the tall man and the leggy Connecticut widow had been winners again.

"Watch what that tall guy does in the next race," she heard someone say nearby. "That's what I'm going to do. He's a pro. He's got a sixth sense about these turtles. He just wins and wins and wins."

But watching what the tall man did in the next race was an option that turned out not to be available. He had disappeared from the pool area somewhere between the second and third races. And so, Denise noted with unexpectedly sharp displeasure, had the woman from Connecticut.

Thompkins, still following his Hegbert system, bet fifty on Number Six in the third race, cashed in at two to one, then dropped his new winnings and fifty besides backing Number Four in the fourth. Then he invited Denise to have dinner with him on the terrace. What the hell, she thought. Last night she had had dinner alone; very snooty, she must have seemed. It hadn't been fun.

In the uneasy first moments at the table they talked about the tall man. Thompkins had noticed his success with the turtles also. "Strange guy," he said. "Gives me the creeps—something about the look in his eye. But you see how he makes out at the races?"

"He does very well."

"Well? He cleans up! Can't lose for winning."

"Some people have unusual luck, I suppose."

"This ain't luck. My guess is maybe he's got a fix in with the boys—like they tell him what turtle's got the mojo in the upcoming race. Some kind of high sign they give him when they're lining up for the throw-in."

"How can that be? Turtles are turtles. They just swim around in circles until one of them happens to hit the far wall with his nose."

"No," said Thompkins. "I think he knows something. Or maybe not. But the guy's hot for sure. Tomorrow I'm going to bet the way he does, right down the line, race by race. There are other people here doing it already. That's why the odds go down on the turtle he bets, once they see which one he's backing. If the guy's hot, why not get in on his streak?"

He ordered a white Italian wine with the first course, which was grilled flying fish with brittle orange caviar globules on the side. "I got to confess," he said, grinning again, "Jeffrey Thompkins is not really my name. It's Taormina, Joey Taormina. But that's hard to pronounce out where I live, so I changed it."

"I did wonder. You look . . . it is Neapolitan?"

"Worse. Sicilian. Anybody you meet named Taormina, his family's originally from Sicily. Taormina's a city on the east coast of Sicily. Gorgeous place. I'd love to show you around it some day."

He was moving a little too fast, she thought. A lot too fast.

"I have a confession too," she said. "I'm not from Clifton any more. I moved back into the city a month ago after my marriage broke up."

"That's a damn shame." He might almost have meant it. "I'm divorced too. It practically killed my mother when I broke the news. Well, you get married too young, you get surprised later on." A quick grin; he wasn't all that saddened by what he had learned about her. "How about some red wine with the main course? They got a good Brunello here."

A little later he invited her, with surprising subtlety, to spend the night with him. As gently as she could, she declined. "Well, tomorrow's another day," he said cheerfully. Denise found herself wishing he had looked a little wounded, just a little.

The daytime routine was simple. Sleep late, breakfast on the cottage porch looking out at the sea, then a long ambling walk down the beach, poking in tide pools and watching ghostly gray crabs scutter over the pink sand. Midmorning, swim out to the reef with snorkel and fins, drift around for half an hour or so staring at the strangely contorted coral heads and the incredibly beautiful reef creatures. It was like another planet, out there on the reef. Gnarled coral rose from the sparkling white sandy ocean floor to form fantastic facades and spires through which a billion brilliant fishes, scarlet and green and turquoise and gold in every imaginable color combination, chased each other around. Every surface was plastered with pastel-hued sponges and algae. Platoons of tiny squids swam in solemn formation. Toothy, malevolent-looking eels peered out of dark caverns. An occasional chasm led through the coral wall to the deep sea beyond, where the water was turbulent instead of calm, a dark blue instead of translucent green, and the ocean floor fell away to invisible depths. But Denise never went to the far side. There was something ominous and threatening about the somber outer face of the reef, whereas here, within, everything was safe, quiet, lovely.

After the snorkeling came a shower, a little time spent reading on the porch, then the outdoor buffet lunch. Afterwards a nap, a stroll in the hotel's flamboyant garden, and by mid-afternoon down to the beach again, not for a swim this time, but just to bake in the blessed tropical sun. She'd worry about the possibility of skin damage some other time; right now what she needed was that warm caress, that torrid all-enfolding embrace. Two hours dozing in the sun, then back to the room, shower again, read, dress for dinner. And off to the turtle races. Denise never bothered with the ones after lunch—they were strictly for the real addicts—but she had gone every evening to the pre-dinner ones.

A calm, mindless schedule. Exactly the ticket, after the grim, exhausting domestic storms of October and November and the sudden final cataclysm of December. Even though in the end she had been the one who had forced the breakup, it had still come as a shock and a jolt: she too was getting divorced, just another pathetic casualty of the marital wars, despite all the high hopes of the beginning, the grand plans she and Michael liked to make, the glowing dream. Everything dissolving now into property squabbles, bitter recriminations, horrifying legal fees. How sad: how boring, really. And how destructive to her peace of mind, her self-esteem, her sense of order, her this, her that, her everything. For which there was no cure, she knew, other than to lie here on this placid Caribbean beach under this perfect winter sky and let the healing slowly happen.

Jeffrey Thompkins had the tact—or the good strategic sense—to leave her alone during the day. She saw him in the water, not snorkeling around peering at the reef but simply chugging back and forth like a blocky little machine, head down, arms windmilling, swimming parallel to the hotel's enormous ocean frontage until he had reached the cape just to the north, then coming back the other way. He was a formidable swimmer with enough energy for six men. Quite probably he was like that in bed, too, but Denise had decided somewhere between the white wine and the red at dinner last night that she didn't intend to find out. She liked him, yes. And she intended to have an adventure of some sort with *someone* while she was down here. But a Chevrolet dealer from Long Island? Shorter than she was, with thick hairy shoulders? Somehow she couldn't. She just couldn't, not her first fling after the separation. He seemed to sense it too, and didn't bother her at the beach, even had his lunch at the indoor dining room instead of the buffet terrace. But she suspected she'd encounter him again at evening turtle-race time.

Yes: there he was. Grinning hopefully at her from the far side of the turtle pool, but plainly waiting to pick up some sort of affirmative signal from her before coming toward her.

There was the tall dark-haired man with the tiny bald spot, too. Without the lady from Connecticut. Denise had seen him snorkeling on the reef that afternoon, alone, and here he was alone again, which meant, most likely, that last night had been Mme. Connecticut's final night at the hotel. Denise was startled to realize how much relief that conclusion afforded her.

Carefully not looking in Jeffrey Thompkins's direction, she went unhesitatingly toward the tall man.

He was wearing a dark cotton suit and, despite the warmth, a narrow black tie flecked with gold, and he looked very, very attractive. She couldn't understand how she had come to think of him as sexless the night before: some inexplicable flickering of her own troubled moods, no doubt. Certainly he didn't seem that way now. He smiled down at her. He seemed actually pleased to see her, though she sensed behind the smile a puzzling mixture of other emotions—aloofness, sadness, regret? That curious tragic air of his: not a pose, she began to think, but the external manifestation of some deep and genuine wound.

"I wish I had listened to you last night," she said. "You knew what you were talking about when you told me to bet Number Four."

He shrugged almost imperceptibly. "I didn't really think you'd take my advice. But I thought I'd make the gesture all the same."

"That was very kind of you," she said, leaning inward and upward toward him. "I'm sorry I was so skeptical." She flashed her warmest smile. "I'm going to be very shameless. I want a second chance. If you've got any tips to offer on tonight's races, please tell me. I promise not to be such a skeptic this time."

"Number Five in this one," he replied at once. "Nicholas Holt, by the way."

"Denise Carpenter. From Clifton, New Jer—" She cut herself off, reddening. He hadn't told her where he was from. She wasn't from Clifton any longer anyway; and what difference did it make where she might live up north? This island resort was intended as a refuge from all that, a place outside time, outside familiar realities. "Shall we place our bets?" she said briskly.

Women didn't usually buy tickets themselves here. Men seemed to expect to do that for them. She handed him a fifty, making sure as she did so that her fingers were extended to let him see that she wore no wedding band. But Holt didn't make any attempt to look. His own fingers were just as bare.

She caught sight of Jeffrey Thompkins at a distance, frowning at her but not in any very troubled way; and she realized after a moment that he evidently was undisturbed by her defection to the tall man's side and simply wanted to know which turtle Holt was backing. She held up her hand, five fingers outspread. He nodded and went scurrying up to the tote counter.

Number Five won easily. The payoff was seven to three. Denise looked at Holt with amazement.

"How do you do it?" she asked.

"Concentration," he said. "Some people have the knack."

He seemed very distant, suddenly.

"Are you concentrating on the next race, now?"

"It'll be Number One," he told her, as though telling her that the weather tomorrow would be warm and fair.

Thompkins stared at her out of the crowd. Denise flashed one finger at him.

She felt suddenly ill at ease. Nicholas Holt's knack, or whatever it was, bothered her. He was too confident, too coolly certain of what was going to happen. There was something annoying and almost intimidating about such confidence. Although she had bet fifty Jamaican dollars on Number One, she found herself wishing perversely that the turtle would lose.

Number One it was, though, all the same. The payoff was trifling; it seemed as if almost everyone in the place had followed Holt's lead, and as a result the odds had been short ones. Since the races, as Denise was coming to see, were truly random—the turtles didn't give a damn and were about equal in speed—the only thing governing the patterns of oddsmaking was the way the guests happened to bet, and that depended entirely on whatever irrational set of theories the bettors had fastened on. But the theory Nicholas Holt was working from didn't appear to be irrational.

"And in the third race?" she said.

"I never bet more than the first two. It gets very dull for me after that. Shall we have dinner?"

He said it as if her acceptance were a foregone conclusion, which would have offended her, except that he was right.

The main course that night was island venison. "What would you say to a bottle of Merlot?"

"It's my favorite wine."

How did he do it? Was everything simply an open book to him?

He let her do most of the talking at dinner. She told him about the gallery where she worked, about her new little apartment in the city, about her marriage, about what had happened to her marriage. A couple of times she felt herself beginning to babble—the wine, she thought, it was the wine—and she reined herself in. But he showed no sign of disapproval, even when she realized she had been going on about Michael much too long. He listened gravely and quietly to everything she said, interjecting a bland comment now and then, essentially just a little prompt to urge her to continue: "Yes, I see," or "Of course," or "I quite understand." He told her practically nothing about himself, only that he lived in New York—where?—and that he did something on Wall Street—unspecified—and that he spent two weeks in the West Indies every February but had never been to Jamaica before. He volunteered no more than that: she had no idea where he had grown up—surely not in New York, from the way he spoke—or whether he had ever been married, or what his interests might be. But she thought it would be gauche to be too inquisitive, and probably unproductive. He was very well defended, polite and calm and remote, the most opaque man she had ever known. He played his part in the dinner conversation with the tranquil, self-possessed air of someone who was following a very familiar script.

After dinner they danced, and it was the same thing there: he anticipated her every move, smoothly sweeping her around the open-air dance floor in a way that soon had everyone watching them. Denise was a good dancer, skilled at the tricky art of leading a man who thought he was leading her; but with Nicholas Holt the feedback was so complex that she had no idea who was leading whom. They danced as though they were one entity, moving with a single accord: the way people dance who have been dancing together for years. She had never known a man who danced like that.

On one swing around the floor she had a quick glimpse of Jeffrey Thompkins, dancing with a robust, red-haired woman half a head taller than he was. Thompkins was pushing her about with skill and determination but no grace at all, somewhat in the style of a rhinoceros who has had a thousand years of instruction at Arthur Murray. As he went thundering past he looked back at Denise and smiled an intricate smile that said a dozen different things. It acknowledged the fact that he was clumsy and his partner was coarse, that Holt was elegant and Denise was beautiful, that men like Holt always were able to take women like Denise away from men like Thompkins. But also the smile seemed to be telling her that Thompkins didn't mind at all, that he accepted what had happened as the natural order of things, had in fact expected it with much the same sort of assurance as Holt had expected Number Five to win tonight's first race. Denise realized that she had felt some guilt about sidestepping Thompkins and offering herself to Holt and that his smile just now had canceled it out; and then she wondered why she had felt the guilt in the first place. She owed nothing to Thompkins, after all. He was simply a stranger who had asked her to dinner last night. They were all strangers down here: nobody owed anything to anyone.

"My cottage is just beyond that little clump of bamboo," Holt said, after they had had the obligatory beach-front stroll on the palm promenade. He said it as if they had already agreed to spend the night there. She offered no objections. This was what she had come here for, wasn't it? Sunlight and warmth and tropical breezes and this.

As he had on the dance floor, so too in bed was he able to anticipate everything she wanted. She had barely thought of something but he was doing it; sometimes he did it even before she knew she wanted him to. It was so long since she had made love with anyone but Michael that Denise wasn't sure who the last one before him had been; but she knew that she had never been to bed with anyone like this. She moved here, he was on his way there already. She did this, he did it too. This and that. Her hand, his hand. Her lips, his lips. It was all extremely weird: very thrilling and yet oddly hollow, like making love to your own reflection.

He must be able to read minds, she thought suddenly, as they lay side by side, resting for a while.

An eerie notion. It made her feel nakeder than naked: bare right down to her soul, utterly vulnerable, defenseless.

But the power to read minds, she realized after a moment, wouldn't allow him to do that trick with the turtle races. That was prediction, not mind-reading. It was second sight.

Can he see into the future? Five minutes, ten minutes, half a day ahead? She thought back. He always seemed so unsurprised at everything. When she had told him she didn't intend to do any betting, that first night, he had simply said, "Of course." When his turtle had won the race he had shown no flicker of excitement or pleasure. When she had apologized tonight for not having acted on his tip, he had told her blandly that he hadn't expected her to. The choice of wine—the dinner conversation—the dancing—the lovemaking—

Could he see everything that was about to happen? *Everything?*

On Wall Street, too? Then he must be worth a fortune.

But why did he always look so sad, then? His eyes so bleak and haunted, those little lines of grimness about his lips?

This is all crazy, Denise told herself. Nobody can see the future. The future isn't a place you can look into, the way you can open a door and look into a room. The future doesn't exist until it's become the present.

She turned to him. But he was already opening his arms to her, bringing his head down to graze his lips across her breasts.

She left his cottage long before dawn, not because she really wanted to but because she was unwilling to have the maids and gardeners see her go traipsing back to her place in the morning still wearing her evening clothes, and hung the DO NOT DISTURB sign on her door.

When she woke, the sun was blazing down through the bamboo slats of the cottage porch. She had slept through breakfast and lunch. Her throat felt raspy and there was the sensation of recent lovemaking between her legs, so that she automatically looked around for Michael and was surprised to find herself alone in the big bed; and then she remembered, first that she and Michael were all finished, then that she was here by herself, then that she had spent the night with Nicholas Holt.

Who can see the future. She laughed at her own silliness.

She didn't feel ready to face the outside world, and called room service to bring her tea and a tray of fruit. They sent her mango, jackfruit, three tiny reddish bananas, and a slab of papaya. Later she suited up and went down to the beach. She didn't see Holt anywhere around, neither out by the reef as he usually was in the afternoon, nor on the soft pink sand. A familiar stocky form was churning up the water with cannonball force, doing his laps, down to the cape and back, again, again, again. Thompkins. After a time he came stumping ashore. Not at all coy now, playing no strategic games, he went straight over to her.

"I see that your friend Mr. Holt's in trouble with the hotel," he said, sounding happy about it.

"He is? How so?"

"You weren't at the turtle races after lunch, were you?"

"I never go to the afternoon ones."

"That's right, you don't. Well, I was there. Holt won the first two races, the way he always does. Everybody bet the way he did. The odds were microscopic, naturally. But everybody won. And then two of the hotel managers—you know, Eubanks, the night man who has that enormous grin all the time, and the other one with the big yellow birthmark on his forehead?— came over to him and said, 'Mr. Holt, sah, we would prefer dat you forego the pleasure of the turtle racing from this point onward.' " The Chevrolet dealer's imitation of the Jamaican accent was surprisingly accurate. " 'We recognize dat you must be an authority on turtle habits, sah,' they said. 'Your insight we find to be exceedingly uncanny. And derefore it strikes us dat it is quite unsporting for you to compete. Quite, sah!' "

"And what did he say?"

"That he doesn't know a goddamned thing about turtles, that he's simply on a roll, that it's not his fault if the other guests are betting the same way he is. They asked him again not to play the turtles—'We implore you, sah, you are causing great losses for dis establishment'—and he kept saying he was a registered guest and entitled to all the privileges of a guest. So they canceled the races."

"Canceled them?"

"They must have been losing a fucking fortune this week on those races, if you'll excuse the French. You can't run pari-mutuels where everybody bets the same nag and that nag always wins, you know? Wipes you out after a while. So they didn't have races this afternoon and there won't be any tonight unless he agrees not to play." Thompkins smirked. "The guests are pretty pissed off, I got to tell you. The management is trying to talk him into changing hotels, that's what someone just said. But he won't do it. So no turtles. You ask me, I still think he's been fixing it somehow with the hotel boys, and the hotel must think so too, but they don't dare say it. Man with a winning streak like that, there's just no accounting for it any other way, is there?"

"No," Denise said. "No accounting for it at all."

*   *   *

It was cocktail time before she found him: the hour when the guests gathered on the garden patio where the turtle races were held to have a daiquiri or two before the tote counter opened for business. Denise drifted down there automatically, despite what Thompkins had told her about the cancellation of the races. Most of the other guests had done the same. She saw Holt's lanky figure looming up out of a group of them. They had surrounded him; they were gesturing and waving their daiquiris around as they talked. It was easy enough to guess that they were trying to talk him into refraining from playing the turtles so that they could have their daily amusement back.

When she came closer she saw the message chalked across the tote board in an ornate Jamaican hand, all curlicues and flourishes:

TECHNICAL PROBLEM
NO RACES TODAY
YOUR KIND INDULGENCE IS ASKED

"Nicholas?" she called, as though they had a prearranged date.

He smiled at her gratefully. "Excuse me," he said in his genteel way to the cluster of people around him, and moved smoothly through them to her side. "How lovely you look tonight, Denise."

"I've heard that the hotel's putting pressure on you about the races."

"Yes. Yes." He seemed to be speaking to her from another galaxy. "So they are. They're quite upset, matter of fact. But if there's going to be racing, I have a right to play. If they choose to cancel, that's their business."

In a low voice she said, "You aren't involved in any sort of collusion with the hotel boys, are you?"

"You asked me that before. You know that isn't possible."

"Then how are you always able to tell which turtle's going to win?"

"I know," he said sadly. "I simply do."

"You always know what's about to happen, don't you? Always."

"Would you like a daiquiri, Denise?"

"Answer me. Please."

"I have a knack, yes."

"It's more than a knack."

"A gift, then. A special . . . something."

"A something, yes." They were walking as they talked; already they were past the bougainvillea hedge, heading down the steps toward the beachfront promenade, leaving the angry guests and the racing pool and the turtle tank behind.

"A very reliable something," she said.

"Yes. I suppose it is."

"You said that you knew, the first night when you offered me that tip, that I wasn't going to take you up on it. Why did you offer it to me, then?"

"I told you. It seemed like a friendly gesture."

"We weren't friends then. We'd hardly spoken. Why'd you bother?"

"Just because."

"Because you wanted to test your special something?" she asked him. "Because you wanted to see whether it was working right?"

He stared at her intently. He looked almost frightened, she thought. She had broken through.

"Perhaps I did," he said.

"Yes. You check up on it now and then, don't you? You try something that you know won't pan out, like tipping a strange woman to the outcome of the turtle race even though your gift tells you that she won't bet your tip. Just to see whether your guess was on the mark. But what would you have done if I had put a bet down that night, Nicholas?"

"You wouldn't have."

"You were certain of that."

"Virtually certain, yes. But you're right: I test it now and then, just to see."

"And it always turns out the way you expect?"

"Essentially, yes."

"You're scary, Nicholas. How long have you been able to do stuff like this?"

"Does that matter?" he asked. "Does it really?"

He asked her to have dinner with him again, but there was something perfunctory about the invitation, as though he were offering it only because the hour was getting toward dinnertime and they happened to be standing next to each other just then.

She accepted quickly, perhaps too quickly. But the dining terrace was practically empty when they reached it—they were very early, on account of the cancellation of the races—and the meal was a stiff, uncomfortable affair. He was so obviously bothered by her persistent inquiries about his baffling skill, his special something, that she soon backed off, but that left little to talk about except the unchanging perfect weather, the beauty of the hotel grounds, and rumors of racial tension elsewhere on the island.

He toyed with his food and ate very little. They ordered no wine. It was like sitting across the table from a stranger who was dining with her purely by chance. And yet less than twenty-four hours before she had spent a night in this man's bed.

She didn't understand him at all. He was alien and mysterious and a little frightening. But somehow, strangely, that made him all the more desirable.

As they were sipping their coffee she looked straight at him and sent him a message with her mind:

Ask me to come dancing with you, next. And then let's go to your cottage again, you bastard.

But instead he said abruptly, "Would you excuse me, Denise?"

She was nonplussed. "Why—yes—if—"

He looked at his watch. "I've rented a glass-bottomed boat for eight o'clock. To have a look at the night life out on the reef."

The night was when the reef came alive. The little coral creatures awoke and unfolded their brilliant little tentacles; phosphorescent organisms began to glow; octopuses and eels came out of their dark crannies to forage for their meals; sharks and rays and other big predators set forth on the hunt. You could take a boat out there that was equipped with bottom-mounted arc lights and watch the show, but very few of the hotel guests actually did. The waters that were so crystalline and inviting by day looked ominous and menacing in the dark, with sinister coral humps rising like black ogres' heads above the lapping wavelets. She had never even thought of going.

But now she heard herself saying, in a desperate attempt at salvaging something out of the evening, "Can I go with you?"

"I'm sorry. No."

"I'm really eager to see what the reef looks like at—"

"No," he said, quietly but with real finality. "It's something I'd rather do by myself, if you don't mind. Or even if you do mind, I have to tell you. Is that all right, Denise?"

"Will I see you afterward?" she asked, wishing instantly that she hadn't. But he had already risen. He gave her a gentlemanly little smile of farewell and strode down the terrace toward the steps that led to the beachfront promenade.

She stared after him, astounded by the swiftness of his disappearance, the unexpectedness of it.

She sat almost without moving, contemplating her bewildering abandonment. Five minutes went by, maybe ten. The waiter unobtrusively brought her another coffee. She held the cup in her hand without drinking from it.

Jeffrey Thompkins materialized from somewhere, hideously cheerful. "If you're free," he said, "how about an after-dinner liqueur?" He was wearing a white dinner jacket, very natty, and sharply pressed black trousers. But his round neckless head and the blaze of sunburn across his bare scalp spoiled the elegant effect. "A Strega, a Galliano, a nice cognac, maybe?" He pronounced it "cone-yac."

"Something weird's going on," she said.

"Oh?"

"He went out on the reef in one of those boats, by himself. Holt. Just got up and walked away from the table, said he'd rented a boat for eight o'clock. Poof. Gone."

"I'm heartbroken to hear it."

"No, be serious. He was acting really strange. I asked to go with him, and he said no, I absolutely couldn't. He sounded almost like some sort of machine. You could hear the gears clicking."

Thompkins said, all flippancy gone from his voice now, "You think he's going to do something to himself out there?"

"No. Not him. That's one thing I'm sure of."

"Then what?"

"I don't know."

"A guy like that, all keyed up all the time and never letting on a thing to anybody—" Thompkins looked at her closely. "You know him better than I do. You don't have any idea what he might be up to?"

"Maybe he just wants to see the reef. I don't know. But he seemed so peculiar when he left—so rigid, so *focused*—"

"Come on," Thompkins said. "Let's get one of those boats and go out there ourselves."

"But he said he wanted to go alone."

"Screw what he said. He don't own the reef. We can go for an expedition too, if we want to."

It took a few minutes to arrange things. "You want a guided tour, sah?" the boy down at the dock asked, but Thompkins said no, and helped Denise into the boat as easily as though she were made of feathers. The boy shook his head. "Nobody want a guide tonight. You be careful out dere, stay dis side of the reef, you hear me, sah?"

Thompkins switched on the lights and took the oars. With quick, powerful strokes he moved away from the dock. Denise looked down. There was nothing visible below but the bright white sand of the shallows, a few long-spined sea urchins, some starfish. As they approached the reef, a hundred yards or so off shore, the density of marine life increased: schools of brilliant fishes whirled and dived, a somber armada of squids came squirting past.

There was no sign of Holt. "We ought to be able to see his lights," Denise said. "Where can he have gone?"

Thompkins had the boat butting up against the flat side of the reef now. He stood up carefully and stared into the night.

"The crazy son of a bitch," he muttered. "He's gone outside the reef! Look, there he is."

He pointed. Denise, half rising, saw nothing at first; and then there was the reflected glow of the other boat's lights, on the far side of the massive stony cluster and intricacy that was the reef. Holt had found one of the passageways through and was coasting along the reef's outer face, where the deep-water hunters came up at night, the marlins and swordfish and sharks.

"What the hell does he think he's doing?" Thompkins asked. "Don't he know it's dangerous out there?"

"I don't think that worries him," said Denise.

"So you do think he's going to do something to himself."

"Just the opposite. He knows that he'll be all right out there, or he wouldn't be there. He wouldn't have gone if he saw any real risk in it."

"Unless risk is what he's looking for."

"He doesn't live in a world of risk," she said. "He's got a kind of sixth sense. He always knows what's going to happen next."

"Huh?"

Words came pouring out of her. "He can see the future," she said fiercely, not caring how wild it sounded. "It's like an open book to him. How do you think he does that trick with the turtles?"

"Huh?" Thompkins said again. "The *future?*" He peered at her, shaking his head slowly.

Then he swung sharply around as if in response to some unexpected sound from the sea. He shaded his forehead with his hand, the way he might have done if he were peering into bright sunlight. After a moment he pointed into the darkness beyond the reef and said in a slow awed tone, "What the fuck! Excuse me. But Jesus, will you look at that?"

She stared past him, toward the suddenly foaming sea.

Something was happening on the reef's outer face. Denise saw it unfolding as if in slow motion. The ocean swelling angrily, rising, climbing high. The single great wave barrelling in as though it had traveled all the way from Alaska for this one purpose. The boat tilting up on end, the man flying upward and outward, soaring gracefully into the air, traveling along a smooth curve like an expert diver and plummeting down into the black depths just beside the reef's outer face. And then the last curling upswing of the wave, the heavy crash as it struck the coral wall.

In here, sheltered by the reef, they felt only a mild swaying, and then everything was still again.

Thompkins clapped his hand over his mouth. His eyes were bulging. "Jesus," he said after a moment. "Jesus! How the fuck am I going to get out there?" He turned toward Denise. "Can you row this thing back to shore by yourself?"

"I suppose so."

"Good. Take it in and tell the boat boy what happened. I'm going after your friend."

He stripped with astonishing speed, the dinner jacket, the sharply creased pants, the shirt and tie, the black patent leather shoes. Denise saw him for a moment outlined against the stars, the fleshy burly body hidden only by absurd bikini pants in flamboyant scarlet silk. Then he was over the side, swimming with all his strength, heading for one of the openings in the reef that gave access to the outer face.

She was waiting among the crowd on the shore when Thompkins brought the body in, carrying it like a broken doll. He had been much too late, of course. One quick glance told her that Holt must have been tossed against the reef again and again, smashed, cut to ribbons by the sharp coral, partly devoured, even, by the creatures of the night. Thompkins laid him down on the beach. One of the hotel boys put a blanket over him; another gave Thompkins a robe. He was scratched and bloody himself, shivering, grim-faced, breathing in windy gusts. Denise went to him. The others backed away, stepping back fifteen or twenty feet, leaving them alone, strangely exposed, beside the blanketed body.

"Looks like you were wrong," Thompkins said. "About that sixth sense of his. Or else it wasn't working so good tonight."

"No," she said. For the past five minutes she had been struggling to put together the pattern of what had happened, and it seemed to her now that it was beginning to come clear. "It was working fine. He knew this would happen."

"What?"

"He knew. Like I said before, he knew everything ahead of time. Everything. Even this. But he went along with it anyway."

"But if he knew everything, then why . . . why . . ." Thompkins shook his head. "I don't get it."

Denise shuddered in the warm night breeze. "No, you don't. You can't. Neither can I."

"Miss Carpentah?" a high, strained voice called. "Mistah Thompkins?"

It was the night manager, Mr. Eubanks of the dazzling grin, belatedly making his way down from the hotel. He wasn't grinning now. He looked stricken, panicky, strangely pasty-faced. He came to a halt next to them, knelt, picked up one corner of the beach blanket, stared at the body beneath it as though it were some bizarre monster that had washed ashore. A guest had died on his watch, and it was going to cost him, he was sure of that, and his fear showed in his eyes.

Thompkins, paying no attention to the Jamaican, said angrily to Denise, "If he knew what was going to happen, if he could see the fucking future, why in the name of Christ didn't he simply not take the boat out, then? Or if he did, why fool around outside the reef where it's so dangerous? For that matter, why didn't he just stay the hell away from Jamaica in the first place?"

"That's what I mean when I tell you that we can't understand," she said. "He didn't think the way we do. He wasn't like us. Not at all. Not in the slightest."

"Mistah Thompkins—Miss Carpentah—if you would do me de courtesy of speaking with me for a time—of letting me have de details of dis awful tragedy—"

Thompkins brushed Eubanks away as if he were a gnat.

"I don't know what the fuck you're saying," he told Denise.

Eubanks said, exasperated, "If de lady and gemmun will give me deir kind attention, *please*—"

He looked imploringly toward Denise. She shook him off. She was still groping, still reaching for the answer.

Then, for an instant, just for an instant, everything that was going on seemed terribly familiar to her. As if it had all happened before. The warm, breezy night air. The blanket on the beach. The round, jowly, baffled face of Jeffrey Thompkins hovering in front of hers. Mr. Eubanks, pale with dismay. An odd little moment of déjà vu. It appeared to go on and on. Now Eubanks will lose his cool and try to grab me by the arm, she thought; now I will pull back and slip on the sand; now Jeffrey will catch me and steady me. Yes. Yes. And here it comes. "Please, you may not ignore me dis way! You must tell me what has befallen dis unfortunate gemmum!" That was Eubanks, eyes popping, forehead shiny with sweat. Making a pouncing movement toward her, grabbing for her wrist. She backed hastily away from him. Her legs felt suddenly wobbly. She started to sway and slip, and looked toward Thompkins. But he was already coming forward, reaching out toward her to take hold of her before she fell. Weird, she thought. Weird.

Then the weirdness passed, and everything was normal again, and she knew the answer.

That was how it had been for him, she thought in wonder. Every hour, every day, his whole goddamned life.

"He came to this place and he did what he did," she said to Thompkins, "because he knew that there wasn't any choice for him. Once he had seen it in his mind it was certain to happen. So he just came down here and played things through to the end."

"Even though he'd *die*?" Thompkins asked. He looked at Denise stolidly, uncomprehendingly.

"If you lived your whole life as if it had already happened, without surprise, without excitement, without the slightest unpredictable event, not once, not ever, would you give a damn whether you lived or died? Would you? He knew he'd die here, yes. So he came here to die, and that's the whole story. And now he has."

"Jesus," Thompkins said. "The poor son of a bitch!"

"You understand now? What it must have been like for him?"

"Yeah," he said, his arm still tight around her as though he didn't mean to ever let go. "Yeah. The poor son of a bitch."

"I got to tell you," said Mr. Eubanks, "dis discourtesy is completely improper. A mahn have died here tragically tonight, and you be de only witnesses, and I ask you to tell me what befell, and you—"

Denise closed her eyes a moment. Then she looked at Eubanks.

"What's there to say, Mr. Eubanks? He took his boat into a dangerous place and it was struck by a sudden wave and overturned. An accident. A terrible accident. What else is there to say?" She began to shiver. Thompkins held her. In a low voice she said to him, "I want to go back to my cottage."

"Right," he said. "Sure. You wanted a statement, Mr. Eubanks? There's your statement. Okay? Okay?"

He held her close against him and slowly they started up the ramp toward the hotel together.

ÜBERMENSCH!

Kim Newman

Kim Newman made his original reputation as a film critic, is a commentator on films on British television, and has published several books of film criticism, including *Nightmare Movies* and *Wild West Movies*. Of late, though, his career as a fiction writer has also shifted into high gear—he has published nine novels since 1989, three of them—*The Night Mayor, Bad Dreams,* and *Jago*—under his own name, and six more under his pseudonym of "Jack Yeovil." He has also published a critical study, *Horror: 100 Best Books*, written in collaboration with Stephen Jones, and is working on an original anthology, co-edited with Paul J. McAuley, called *In Dreams*. He won the British Science Fiction Award for his story "The Original Dr. Shade," and has been a frequent contributor to *Interzone*, and to various British anthology series. His story "Famous Monsters" was in our Fifth Annual Collection. He lives in London, England.

In the wry but bittersweet story that follows, he recounts one of the most popular American folk-myths as it *might* have happened—if things had been just a *little* bit different. . . .

On the way from the aeroport, the cab driver asked him if he had ever been to Metropolis before.

"I was born here," Avram said, German unfamiliar in his mouth. So many years of English in America, then Hebrew in Israel. In the last forty years, he'd used Portuguese more than his native tongue. He had never been a German in his heart, no more than he was now an Israeli. That was one thing Hitler, and his grandparents, had been right about.

He had been—he *was*—a Jew.

This was not the Metropolis he remembered. Gleaming skyscrapers still rose to the clouds, aircars flitting awkwardly between them, but on this grey, early spring day their façades were shabby, uncleaned. The robotrix on traffic duty outside the aeroport had been limping, dysfunctional, sparks pouring from her burnished copper thigh. Standing on the tarmac, Avram had realised that the pounding in the ground was stilled. The subterranean factories and power plants had been destroyed or shut down during the war.

"That's where the wall was," the driver said, as they passed a hundred yards of wasteland which ran through the city of the future as if one of Mr.

Reagan's orbital lasers had accidentally cut a swath across Germany. The satellite weapons were just so much more junk now, Avram supposed. The world that needed the orbital laser was gone.

Just like the world which needed his crusade.

Perhaps, after today, he could spend his remaining years playing chess with a death-diminished circle of old friends, then die from the strain of playing competitive video games with his quick-fingered grandchildren.

"That used to be East Metropolis," the driver said.

Avram tried to superimpose the city of his memory on these faceless streets. So much of Metropolis was post-war construction, now dilapidated. The cafés and gymnasia of his youth were twice forgotten. There wasn't a McDonald's on every corner yet, but that would come. A boarded-up shack near the wall, once a security checkpoint, was covered in graffiti. Amid the anti-Russian, pro-democracy slogans, Avram saw a tiny red swastika. He had been seeing posters for the forthcoming elections, and could not help but remember who had taken office the last time a united Germany held a democratic election.

He thanked the driver, explaining, "I just wanted to see where it was."

"Where now, sir?"

Avram got the words out, "Spandau Prison."

The man clammed up, and Avram felt guilty. The driver was a child, born and raised with the now never-to-be-germinated seeds of World War Three. Avram's crusade was just an embarrassing old reminder. When these people talked about the bad old days, they meant when the city was divided by concrete. Not when it was the shining flame of fascism.

The prison was ahead, a black mediaeval castle among plain concrete block buildings. The force field shone faintly emerald. Apparently the effect was more noticeable from outer space. John Glenn had mentioned it, a fog lantern in the cloud cover over Europe.

The cab could go no further than the perimeter, but he was expected. From the main gate, he was escorted by a young officer—an American—from the Allied detachment that had guarded the man in the fortress for forty-five years.

Avram thought of the Allies, FDR embracing Uncle Joe at Yalta. Old allies, and now—thanks to the baldpate with the blotch—allies anew. If old alliances were being resumed, old evils—old enmities—could stir too.

Captain Siegel called himself Jewish, and babbled sincere admiration. "As a child, you were my hero, sir. That's why I'm here. When you caught Eichmann, Mengele, the Red Skull . . ."

"Don't trust heroes, young man," he said, hating the pomposity in his voice, "that's the lesson of this green lantern."

Siegel was shut up, like the cab driver had been. Avram was instantly sorry, but could not apologise. He wondered when he had turned into his old professor, too scholarly to care for his pupils' feelings, too unbending to see the value of ignorant enthusiasm.

Probably, it had started with the tattoo on his arm. The bland clerk with the bodkin was the face that, more than any other, stayed with him as the image of National Socialism. These days, almost all young men looked like the tattooist to Avram. The cab driver had, and now so did Captain Siegel. So did most of the guards who patrolled the corridors and grounds of this prison.

Not since Napoleon had a single prisoner warranted such careful attention.

"Jerome," Siegel said, summoning a sergeant. "Show Mr. Blumenthal your rifle."

The soldier held out his weapon for inspection. Avram knew little about guns, but saw this was out of the ordinary, with its bulky breech and surprisingly slender barrel. A green LED in the stock showed it was fully charged.

"The beam-gun is just for *him*," Siegel said.

"Ahh, the green stuff."

Siegel smiled. "Yes, the green stuff. I'm not a scientist . . ."

"Neither am I, any more."

"It has something to do with the element's instability. The weapon directs particles. Even a glancing hit would kill him in a flash."

Avram remembered Rotwang—one of "our" Germans in the '50s—toiling over the cyclotron, trying to wrestle free the secrets of the extra-terrestrial element. Rotwang, with his metal hand and shock of hair, was dead of leukaemia, another man of tomorrow raging against his imprisonment in yesterday.

Jerome took the rifle back, and resumed his post.

"There've been no escape attempts," Avram commented.

"There couldn't be."

Avram nearly laughed. "He surrendered, Captain. Green stuff or not, this place couldn't hold him if he wanted to leave."

Siegel—born when the prisoner had already been in his cell twenty years— was shocked. "Mr. Blumenthal, careful . . ."

Avram realised what it was that frightened the boy in uniform, what made every soldier in this place nervous twenty-four hours a day.

"He can hear us, can't he? Even through the lead shields?"

Siegel nodded minutely, as if he were the prisoner, trying to pass an unseen signal to a comrade in the exercise yard.

"You live with the knowledge all your life," Avram said, tapping his temple, "but you never think what it means. That's science, Captain. Taking knowledge you've always had, and *thinking what it means . . .*"

After the War, he had been at Oak Ridge, working with the green stuff. Then the crusade called him away. Others had fathered the K-Bomb. Teller and Rotwang built bigger and better Doomsday Devices—while Oppie went into internal exile and the Rosenbergs to the electric chair—thrusting into a future so bright you could only look at it through protective goggles. Meanwhile, Avram Blumenthal had been cleaning up the last garbage of the past. So many names, so many Nazis. He had spent more time in Paraguay and Brazil than in New York and Tel Aviv.

But it had been worth it. His tattoo would not stop hurting until the last of the monsters was gone. If monsters they were.

"Through here, sir," Siegel said, ushering him into a bare office. There was a desk, with chairs either side of it.

"You have one hour."

"That should be enough. Thank you."

Siegel left the room. Even after so short a time on his legs, Avram felt better sitting down. Nobody lives forever.

Almost nobody.

When they brought him in, he filled the room. His chest was a solid slab under his prison fatigues, and the jaw was an iron horseshoe. Not the faintest trace of grey in his blue-black hair, the kiss-curl still a jaunty comma. The horn-rimmed glasses couldn't disguise him.

Avram did not get up.

"Curt Kessler?" he asked, redundantly.

Grinning, the prisoner sat down. "You thought perhaps they had the wrong man all these years?"

"No," he admitted, fussing with the cigarette case, taking out one of his strong roll-ups. "Do you mind if I smoke?"

"Can't hurt me. I used to warn the children against tobacco, though."

Avram lit up, and sucked bitter smoke into his lungs. The habit couldn't hurt him, either, not anymore.

"Avram the Avenger," Kessler said, not without admiration. "I was wondering when they'd let you get to see me."

"My request has been in for many years, but with the changes . . ."

The changes did not need to be explained.

"I confess," Kessler said, "I've no idea why you wanted this interview."

Avram had no easy answer. "You consented to it."

"Of course. I talk to so few people these days. The guards are superstitious about me."

Avram could understand that. Across the table, he could feel Kessler's strength. He remembered the old uniform, so familiar in the thirties. The light brown body-stocking, with black trunks, boots and cloak. A black swastika in the red circle on the chest. He'd grinned down from a hundred propaganda posters like an Aryan demi-god, strode through the walkways of Metropolis as Siegfried reborn with X-ray eyes.

He felt he owed Kessler an explanation. "You're the last."

Kessler's mouth flashed amusement. "Am I? What about Ivan the Terrible?"

"A guard. Just a geriatric thug. Barely worth the bullet it'd take to finish him."

" 'Barely worth the bullet.' I heard things like that so many times, Avram. And what of the *Führer*? I understand he could be regrown from tissue samples. In '45, Mengele—"

Avram laughed. "There's no tissue left, Kessler. I burned Mengele's jungle paradise. The skin-scraps he had were of dubious provenance."

"I understand genetic patterns can be reproduced exactly. I try to follow science, you know. If you keep an ear out, you pick things up. In Japan, they're doing fascinating work."

"Not my field."

"Of course. You're an atom man. You should have stayed with Rotwang. The Master Engineer needed your input. He could have overcome his distaste with your racial origins if you'd given him a few good suggestions. Without you, the K-Bomb was ultimately a dead end."

"So?"

Kessler laughed. "You are right. So what? It's hard to remember how excited you all were in the fifties about the remains of my home planet. Anything radioactive was highly stimulating to the Americans. To the Russians, too."

Avram couldn't believe this man was older than him. But, as a child, he had seen the brown streak in the skies, had watched the newsreels, had read the breathless reports in the *Tages Welt*.

"If things had been otherwise, I might have been a Russian," Kessler said. "The Soviet Union is the largest country on the planet. If you threw a dart at a map of the world, you'd most likely hit Russia. Strange to think what it'd have been like if my little dart had missed Bavaria. Of course, I'd have been superfluous. The USSR already had its 'man of steel.' Maybe my dart should have struck the wheatfields of Kansas, or the jungles of Africa. I could have done worse than be raised by apes."

"You admit, then, that you are him?"

Kessler took off his glasses, showing clear blue eyes. "Has there ever really been any doubt?"

"Not when you didn't grow old."

"Do you want me to prove myself? You have a lump of coal for me to squeeze?"

It hit Avram that this young-seeming man, conversing in unaccented German, was hardly even human. If Hitler hadn't got in the way, humanity might have found a champion in him. Or learned more of the stars than Willy Ley imagined.

"Why weren't you in the army? In some SS élite division?"

"Curt Kessler was—what is the American expression?—4F. A weakling who wouldn't be accepted, even in the last days when dotards and children were being slapped in uniform and tossed against the juggernaut. I believe I did my best for my *Führer*."

"You were curiously inactive during the war."

Kessler shrugged. "I admit my great days were behind me. The thirties werc my time. Then, there seemed to be struggles worth fighting, enemies worth besting."

"Only 'seemed to be'?"

"It was long ago. Do you remember my enemies? Dr. Mabuse? His criminal empire was like a spider's web. The *Führer* himself asked me to root it out and destroy it. He poisoned young Germans with drugs and spiritualism. Was I wrong to persecute him? And the others? Graf von Orlok, the *nosferatu*? Dr. Caligari, and his somnambulist killers? The child-slayer they called 'M'? Stephen Orlac, the pianist with the murderer's hands?"

Avram remembered, the names bringing back *Tages Welt* headlines. Most of the stories had borne the Curt Kessler byline. Everyone had wondered how the reporter knew so many details. Germany's criminals had been symptomatic creatures then, twisted and stunted in soul and body, almost an embodiment of the national sickness. And Kessler, no less than the straight-limbed blonds trotted out as exemplars of National Socialism, made the pop-eyed, needle-fingered, crook-backed fiends seem like walking piles of filth. As a child, Avram's nightmares had been of the whistling "M" and taloned *nosferatu*, not handsome tattooists and smart-uniformed bureaucrats. It was possible for a whole country to be wrong.

"They're all gone," Kessler said, "but they'll never go away really. I understand Mabuse's nightclub is due to re-open. The Westerners who've been flooding in since the wall came down like to remember the decadent days. They have the order of history wrong, and associate the cabarets with us, forgetting that we were pure in mind and body, that we closed down the pornographic spectacles. They'll have their doomrock rather than jazz, but the rot will creep back. Mabuse was like the hydra. I'd think he was dead or hopelessly mad, but he'd always come back, always with new deviltry. Perhaps he'll return again. They never found the body."

"And if he returns, will others come back?"

Kessler shrugged again, huge shoulders straining his fatigues. "You were right. Adolf Hitler is dead, National Socialism with him. You don't need X-ray vision to see that."

Avram knew Kessler could never get tired as he had got tired, but he wondered whether this man of steel was truly world-weary. Forty-five years of knowing everything and doing nothing could be as brutally ache-making as the infirmities visited upon any other old man.

"Tell me about your childhood."

Kessler was amused by the new tack. "Caligari always used to harp on about that, too. He was a strange kind of mediaeval Freudian, I suppose, digging into men's minds in search of power. He wanted to get me into his asylum, and pick me apart. We *are* shaped by our early lives, of course. But there's more to it than that. Believe me, I should know. I have a unique perspective."

"There are no new questions for us, Kessler. We must always turn back to the old ones."

"Very well, it's your hour. You have so few left, and I have so many. If you want old stories, I shall give you them. You know about my real parents. Everybody does. I wish I could say I remember my birthplace but I can't, any more than anyone remembers the first days of their life. The dart was my father's semen, the Earth my mother's womb. I was conceived when the dart ejaculated me into the forest. That is my first memory, the overwhelming of my senses. I could hear, see, smell and taste everything. Birds miles away, blades of grass close to, icy streams running, a wolf's dung attracting flies. I screamed. That was my first reaction to this Earth. My screams brought people to me."

"Your parents?"

"Johann and Marte. They lived in the woods just outside Kleinberg. Berchtesgaden was barely an arrow's-reach away."

"How were you raised?"

"There was a war. Johann and Marte had lost four true sons. So they kept the baby they found."

"When did you realise you were different?"

"When my father beat me and I felt nothing. I knew then I was privileged. Later, when I joined the Party, I felt much the same. Sometimes, I would ask to be beaten, to show I could withstand it. There were those among us too glad to oblige me. I wore out whips with my back."

"You left Kleinberg as a young man?"

"Everyone wanted to go to the big city. Metropolis was the world of the future. We would put a woman on the moon one day soon, and robots would do all our work. There would be floating platforms in the seas for refuelling aeroplanes, a transatlantic tunnel linking continents. It was a glorious vision. We were obsessed not with where we were going, but with how fast we would get there."

"You—I mean, Curt—you became a reporter?"

"Poor, fumbling Curt. What a big oaf he was. I miss him very much. Reporters could be heroes in the thirties. I was on the *Tages Welt* when Per Weiss made it a Party paper. It's hard to remember when it was a struggle, when the Mabuses and the Orloks were in control and we were the revolution-aries. That was when it became exciting, when we knew we could make a difference."

"When did you start . . . ?"

"My other career? An accident. Johann always tried to make me ashamed of what I was, insisted I keep myself hidden. That was the reason for the eyeglasses, for the fumbling idiocy. But 'M' was at large, and I knew—knew with my eyes and ears—who he was. I could not catch him as Curt Kessler and the police would not listen to me, so the man inside came out."

The man named "M" had been turned over to the police, eventually. There had been little left of him. He had spent the rest of his life in Caligari's asylum, in the cell next to the often-vacant room they reserved for Dr.

Mabuse. He never killed again, and he would have been unable to rape even if the opportunity arose.

"Why the uniform?"

Kessler smiled again, teeth gleaming ivory. "We all loved uniforms then. All Germans did. The cloak might have been excessive, but those were excessive times. Theatre commissionaires looked like Field Marshals. I was at the rallies, flying in with my torch, standing behind the *Führer*, making the speeches Luise wrote for me. All men want to be heroes."

"You were a Party member? A Nazi?"

"Yes. Even before I cam to Metropolis. We prided ourselves in Bavaria on seeing the future well before the decadents of the cities."

"They say it was the woman who brought you into the Party?"

"Luise? No, if anything, she followed me. The real me, that is. Not Curt. She always despised Curt Kessler."

"Was that difficult for you?"

"It was impossible," Kessler smiled. "Poor Luise. She was born to be a heroine, Avram. She might not have been blonde, but she had everything else. The eyes, the face, the limbs, the hips. She was born to make babies for the *Führer*. Goebbels was fond of her. She wrote many of his scripts before she began broadcasting herself. She was our Valkyrie then, an inspiration to the nation. She committed suicide in 1945. When the Russians were coming. Like many German women."

"Luise Lang would have faced a War Crimes tribunal."

"True. Her other Aryan quality was that she wasn't very bright. She was too silly to refuse the corruptions that came with privilege. She didn't mean any of the things she did, because she never thought them through."

"Unlike you?"

"By then I was thinking too much. We stopped speaking during the war. I could foresee thousands of differing futures, and was not inclined to do anything to make any of them come to pass. Göring asked me to forestall the Allies in Normandy, you know."

"Your failure to comply was extensively documented at your own trial."

"I could have done it. I could have changed the course of history. But I didn't."

Avram applauded, slowly.

"You are right to be cynical, Avram. It's easier to do nothing than to change history. You could have given Truman the K-Bomb, but you went ghost-hunting in Paraguay."

"I'm not like you," he said, surprised by his own vehemence.

"No one is."

"Don't be so sure."

Kessler looked surprised. "There've been other visitors? No, of course not. I'd have known. I scan the skies. Sometimes things move, but galaxies away. There were no other darts, no tests with dogs or little girls. Since Professor

Ten Brincken passed away, no one has even tried to duplicate me as a *homunculus*. That, I admit, was a battle. The distorted, bottle-grown image of me wore me out more than any of the others. More than Mackie Messer's green knives, more than Nosferatu's rat hordes, more even than Ten Brincken's artificial whore Alraune."

Ten Brincken had been second only to Rotwang as the premier scientific genius of Metropolis. Either could have been the equal of Einstein if they had had the heart to go with their minds.

"I am reminded more and more of the twenties and thirties," Kessler said. "I understand they want to get the underground factories working again. Microchip technology could revive Rotwang's robots. *Vorsprung durch technik*, as they say. The future is finally arriving. Fifty years too late."

"You could be released to see it."

The suggestion gave the prisoner pause. "These glowing walls don't keep me in, Avram, they keep you out. I need my shell. I couldn't soar into the air anymore. A missile would stop me as an arrow downs a hawk. The little men who rule the world wouldn't like me as competition."

Avram had no doubt this man could make the world his own. If he chose to lead instead of follow.

"I've seen swastikas in this city," Avram said. "I've heard Germans say Hitler was right about the Jewish problem. I've seen Israelis invoke Hitler's holocaust to excuse their own exterminations. The world could be ready for you again."

"Strength, Purity and the Aryan Way?"

"It could happen again."

Kessler shook his head. "No one eats worms twice, Avram. I was at the torchlight processions, and the pogroms. I wrestled the *nosferatu* beyond the sunrise, and I saw shopkeepers machine-gunned by Stormtroopers. I was at Berchtesgaden, and Auschwitz. I lost my taste for National Socialism when the stench of ovens was all I could smell. Even if I went to China or Saturn, I could still taste the human smoke. I surrendered, remember? To Eisenhower personally. And I've shut myself up here. Buried myself. Even the human race has learned its lesson."

Avram understood how out of date the man of tomorrow's understanding was. "You're an old man, Kessler. Like me. Only old men remember. In America, seventy-five per cent of high school children don't know Russia and the United States fought on the same side in the Second World War. The lesson has faded. Germany is whole again, and Germans are grumbling about the Jews, the gypsies, the Japanese even. It's not just Germany. In Hungary, in Russia, in the Moslem countries, in America and Britain, in *Israel*, I see the same things happening. There's a terrible glamour to it. And *you're* that glamour. The children who chalk swastikas don't know what the symbol means. They don't remember the swastika from the flag, but from your chest. They make television mini-series about you."

Kessler sat back, still as a steel statue. He could not read minds, but he could understand.

"When I was a boy, a little Jewish boy in Metropolis, I, too, looked up at the skies. I didn't know you hated me because of my religion, because of the religion my parents practised no more than I did. I wore a black blanket as a cloak, and wished I could fly, wished I could outrace a streamlined train, wished I could catch Mackie Messer. Do you remember the *golem?*"

Kessler did. "Your rabbi Judah ben Bezalel raised the creature from clay in Prague, then brought it to Metropolis to kill the *Führer*. I smashed it."

The echo of that blow still sounded in Avram's head.

"I saw you do it. I cheered you, and my playmates beat me. The *golem* was the monster, and you were the hero. Later, I learned different."

He rolled up his shirtsleeve, to show the tattoo.

"I had already seen that," Kessler said, tapping his eyes. "I can see through clothing. It was always an amusing pastime. It was useful at the cabarets. I saw the singer, Lola . . ."

"After you killed the *golem*," Avram continued, "all the children took fragments of the clay. They became our totems. And the brownshirts came into the Jewish quarter and burned us out. They were looking for monsters, and found only us. My parents, my sisters, my friends. They're all dead. You had gone on to Nuremberg, to present Hitler with the scroll you snatched from the monster's chest."

"I won't insult you by apologising."

Avram's heart was beating twice its normal race. Kessler looked concerned for him. He could look into another's chest, of course.

"There's nothing I could do to make reparation. Your family is dead, but so is *my whole planet*. I have to live with the guilt. That's why I'm here."

"But you are here, and as long as you remain you're a living swastika. The fools out there who don't remember raise your image high, venerate you. I know you've been offered freedom by the Allies on six separate occasions. You could have flown out of here if you'd consented to topple Chairman Mao or Saddam Hussein, or become a living weather satellite, flitting here and there to avert floods and hurricanes. Some say the world needs its heroes. I say they're wrong."

Kessler sat still for a long time, then finally admitted, "As do I."

Avram took the heavy metal slug from his cigarette case, and set it on the table between them.

"I've had this since I was at Oak Ridge. You wouldn't believe how much of the stuff Rotwang collected, even before they found a way to synthesise it. The shell is lead."

The prisoner played with his glasses. His face was too open, too honest. His thoughts were never guarded. Sometimes, for all his intelligence, he could seem simple-minded.

"You can bite through lead," Avram said.

"Bullets can't hurt me," Kessler replied, a little of the old spark in his eyes.

"So you have a way out."

Kessler picked up the slug, and rolled it in his hand.

"Without you in the world, maybe the fire won't start again."

"But maybe it will. It started without me last time."

"I admit that. That's why it's your decision, Curt."

Kessler nodded, and popped the slug into his mouth. It distended his cheek like a boiled sweet.

"Was I really your hero?"

Avram nodded. "You were."

"I'm sorry," Kessler said, biting through the lead, swallowing.

He did not fade away to mist like the *nosferatu*, nor fragment into shards like the *golem*. He did not even grow old and wither to a skeleton. He just died.

Guards rushed in, confused and concerned. There must have been a monitor in the room. They pointed guns at Avram, even though their beams couldn't hurt him. Doctors were summoned, with enough bizarre machinery to revive a broken doll or resurrect a *homunculus* from the chemical stew. They could do nothing.

Avram remembered the destruction of the *golem*. Afterwards, the brown streak had paused to wave at the children before leaping up, up and away into the skies of Metropolis. They had all been young then, and expected to live forever.

Captain Siegel was upset, and couldn't understand. Doubtless, his career would be wrecked because this had happened during his watch. The Russians would insist an American take the blame. Siegel kept asking questions.

"How did he die?"

"He died like a man," Avram said. "Which, all considered, was quite an achievement."

DISPATCHES FROM THE REVOLUTION

Pat Cadigan

Here's a powerful story that demonstrates that, in spite of the troubled and troubling times we've suffered through in the last few decades, things could always have been *worse*. . . .

Pat Cadigan was born in Schenectady, New York, and now lives in Overland Park, Kansas. She made her first professional sale in 1980, and has subsequently come to be regarded as one of the best new writers in SF. She was the co-editor, along with husband Arnie Fenner, of *Shayol*, perhaps the best of the semiprozines of the late seventies; it was honored with a World Fantasy Award in the "Special Achievement, Non-Professional" category in 1981. She has also served as Chairman of the Nebula Award Jury and as a World Fantasy Award Judge. Her first novel, *Mindplayers*, was released in 1987 to excellent critical response, and her second novel, *Synners*, appeared in 1991 to even *better* response, being widely recognized as one of the year's top novels. Her story "Pretty Boy Crossover"—which was in our Fourth Annual Collection—has recently appeared on several critics' lists as being among the best science fiction stories of the 1980s, and her story "Angel"—which was in our Fifth Annual Collection—was a finalist for the Hugo Award, the Nebula Award, *and the* World Fantasy Award—one of the few stories ever to earn that rather unusual distinction. Her story "Nearly Departed" was in our First Annual Collection; "Rock On" was in our Second Annual Collection; "Roadside Rescue" was in our Third Annual Collection; and "It Was the Heat" was in our Sixth Annual Collection. Her most recent book is the landmark collection *Patterns*, and she has just turned in a new novel called *Fools*.

Dylan was coming to Chicago.

The summer air, already electric with the violence of the war, the assassination attempts successful and unsuccessful, the anti-war riots, became super-charged with the rumor. Feeling was running high, any feeling about anything, real high, way up high, eight miles high and rising, brothers and sisters. And to top it all off, there was a madman in the White House.

Johnson, pull out like your father should have! The graffito of choice for anyone even semi-literate; spray paint sales must have been phenomenal that summer. The old bastard with a face like the dogs he lifted up by their ears would not give it up, step aside, and graciously bow to the inevitable. He wuz the Prezident, the gaw-damned Prezident, hear that, muh fellow Amur-ricans? *Dump Johnson, my ass, don't even* think *about it, boys, the one we ought to dump is that candy-assed Humphrey. Gaw-damned embarrassment is what he is.*

And the President's crazy, that's what he is, went the whispers all around Capitol Hill, radiating outward until they became shouts. *Madman in the White House—the crazy way with LBJ!* If you couldn't tell he was deranged by the way he was stepping up the bombing and the number of troops in Vietnam, his conviction that he could actually stand against Bobby Kennedy clinched it. Robert F. Kennedy, sainted brother to martyred Jack, canonized in his own lifetime by an assassination attempt. Made by the only man in America who was obviously crazier than LBJ, frothed-up Arab with a name like automatic weapons fire, Sir*han* Sir*han*, ka-boom, ka-boom. The Golden Kennedy had actually *assisted* in the crazed gunman's capture, shoulder to shoulder with security guards and the Secret Service as they all wrestled him to the floor. Pity about the busboy taking that bullet right in the eye, but the Kennedys had given him a positively lovely funeral with RFK himself doing the eulogy. And, needless to say, the family would never want for anything again in this life.

But Johnson the Madman was going to run! Without a doubt, he was a dangerous psychotic. Madman in the White House—damned straight you didn't need a Weatherman to know the way the wind blew.

Nonetheless, there *was* one—after all, hadn't Dylan said the answer was blowin' in the wind? And if he was coming to Chicago to support the brothers and sisters, that *proved* the wind was about to blow gale force. Storm coming, batten down the hatches, fasten your seatbelts, and grab yourself a helmet, or steal a hardhat from some redneck construction worker.

Veterans of the Civil Rights Movement already had their riot gear. Seven years after the first freedom ride stalled out in Birmingham, the feelings of humiliation and defeat at having to let the Justice Department scoop them up and spirit them away to New Orleans for their own protection had been renewed in the violent death of the man who had preached victory through non-violence. He'd had a dream; the wake-up call had come as a gunshot. Dreaming was for when you were asleep. Now it was time to be wide-awake in America. . . .

Annie Phillips

"There were plenty of us already wide-awake in America by that late date. I'd been to Chicago back in '66, two years to the month in Marquette Park. If I was never awake any other day in my life before April '68, I was awake that day. Surrounded by a thousand of the meanest white people in America waving those Confederate flags and those swastikas, screaming at us. And then they let fly with rocks and bricks and bottles, and I saw when Dr. King took one in the head. I'd thought he was gonna die that day and all the rest of us with him. Well, he didn't and we didn't, but it was a near thing. After, the buses were pulling away and they were chasing us and I looked back at those faces and I thought, 'There's no hope. There's really no hope.'

"When Daley got the court order against large groups marching in the city, I breathed a sigh of relief, I can tell you. I felt like that man had saved my life. And then Dr. King says okay, we'll march in Cicero, it's a suburb, the order doesn't cover Cicero. *Cicero.* I didn't want to do it, I knew they'd kill us, shoot us, burn us, tear us up with their bare hands and teeth. Some of us were ready to meet them head-on. I truly believe that Martin Luther King would have died that day if Daley hadn't wised up in a hurry and said he'd go for the meeting at the Palmer House.

"Summit Agreement, yeah. Sell-Out Agreement, we called it, a lot of us. I think even Dr. King knew it. And so a whole bunch of us marched in Cicero anyway. I wasn't there, but I know what happened, just like everybody else. Two hundred dead, most of them black, property damage in the millions though I can't say I could ever find it in me to grieve for property damage over people damage. Even though I wasn't there, something of me died that day in Cicero and was reborn in anger. By '68, I had a good-sized bone to pick with good old Chi-town, old Daley-ville. I don't regret what I did. All I regret is that the bomb didn't get Daley. It had his name on it, I put it on there myself, on the side of the pipe. 'Richard Daley's ticket to hell, coach class.'

"Looking back on it, I think I might have had better luck as a sniper."

Excerpt from an interview conducted covertly.
at Sybil Brand, published in
The Whole Samizdat Catalog, 1972?
exact date unknown

Veterans of the Free Speech Movement at Berkley also knew what they were up against. Reagan's tear-gas campaign against campus protestors drew praise from a surprising number of people who felt the Great Society was seriously threatened by the disorder promoted by campus dissidents. The suggestion that the excessive force used by the police caused more problems rather than solving any was rejected by the Reagan administration and its growing blue-collar following alike.

By the time Reagan assumed the governorship, he had already made up his mind to challenge Nixon in '68. But what he needed for a serious bid was the southern vote, which was divided between Kennedy and Wallace. Cleverly, the ex-movie actor managed to suggest strong parallels between campus unrest and racial unrest, implying that both groups were seeking the violent overthrow and destruction of the government of the United States.

Some of the more radical rhetoric that came out of both the student left and the civil rights movement, and the fact that the student anti-war movement aligned itself with the civil rights movement, only seemed to validate Reagan's position.

That the southern vote would be divided between two individuals as disparate as Robert F. Kennedy and George C. Wallace seems bizarre to us in the present. But both men appealed to the working class, who felt left out of the American dream. Despite the inevitable trouble that Wallace's appearances resulted in, his message did reach the audience for which it was intended—the common man who had little to show for years, sometimes decades of hard work beyond a small piece of property and a paycheck taxed to the breaking point, and, as far as the common man could tell, to someone else's benefit. Wallace understood that the common man felt pushed around by the government and exploited this feeling. In a quieter era, he would have come off as a bigoted buffoon; but in a time when blacks and students were demonstrating, rioting, and spouting unthinkable statements against the government, the war, and the system in general, Wallace seemed to be one of the few, if not the only political leader who had the energy to meet this new threat to the American way of life and wrestle it into submission.

Some people began to wonder if McCarthy hadn't been right about Communist infiltration and subversion after all . . . and that wasn't Eugene McCarthy they were wondering about. By the time of the Chicago Democratic Convention, Eugene McCarthy had all but disappeared, his student supporters a liability rather than an asset. They undermined his credibility; worse, they could not vote for him, since the voting age at that time was a flat twenty-one for everyone. . . .

Carl Shipley

"I hadn't been around Berkley long when the Free Speech Movement started. Like, the university, Towle, Kerr, all of them were so out-to-lunch on what was happening with us. They thought they were dealing with Beaver Cleaver and his Little League team, I guess. And with us, it was, 'Guess what, Mr. Man, the neighborhood's changing, it ain't Beaver Cleaver any more, it's Eldridge Cleaver and Wally just got a notice to report for his physical and maybe he doesn't want to go get his ass shot off in southeast Asia and maybe we've had enough of this middle-American conservative bullshit.' That's why they wanted to shut down Bancroft Strip. That was the first place I went to see when I got there and it was just like everybody said, all these different causes and stuff, the Young Republicans hanging in right along with the vegetarians and the feminists and people fund-raising for candidates and I don't know what-all.

"So we all said, fuck this shit, you ain't closing *us* down, we're closing *you* down. And we did it, we closed the university down. We had the power and we kept it—and then in comes Ronald Reagan two years later in '66 and he says, Relax, Mr. and Mrs. America, the cavalry's here. I know you're worried about the Beave, but I've got the solution.

"He sure did. By spring 1968, a lot of campus radio stations all over California were off the air and the campus newspapers were a joke. No funding, see. And by then, everyone was too sick of the smell of tear gas to fight real hard. That was Reagan's whole thing—sit-ins and take-overs weren't covered by the right of free assembly, they were criminal acts. Unless you had to be in a building for a class, you were trespassing. I got about a mile of trespassing convictions on my rap sheet and so do a lot of other people. And Mr. and Mrs. America, they were real impressed the way Reagan came down on the troublemakers.

"Sure were a *lot* of troublemakers. Too many to keep track of. That's what happened to me, you know. Got lost in the court system. The next thing I knew, it was 1970, and nobody remembered my name, except the guards. And they could remember my number a lot easier. Still can.

"The thing is, I never burned my draft card. That was a frame-up. I wouldn't have burned it. I was ready to go to Canada, but I intended to keep my draft card. As a reminder, you know. And not even my parents believed me. By then, I'd been into so much radical shit, they figured everything the pigs said about me was true.

"But the fact is, everything I owned was in that building when it burned. So of course my draft card burned up with it! But I never set that fire. My court-appointed lawyer—this is me laughing bitterly—said if I told my 'crazy story' about seeing off-duty cops with gasoline cans running from the scene just before the explosion, the judge would tack an extra five years on my sentence for perjury. I should have believed him, because it was the only time anyone told me the truth.

Interview conducted at
Attica, published in
Orphans of the Great Society,
Fuck The System Press,
197?
(circulated illegally in photocopy)

Some say, even today, that Reagan wouldn't have taken such an extremist path if Wallace hadn't been such a strong contender. Nixon's mistake was in dismissing Wallace's strong showing, choosing to narrow his focus to the competition within his own party for the nomination. This made him look dinky, as if he didn't care as much about being President as he did about being the Republican candidate for President. That would show those damned reporters that they couldn't kick around Dick Nixon, uh-*huh*. Even if he lost, they'd have to take him seriously; if he actually won, they'd have to take him even more seriously. Which made him look not only dinky, but like a whiner—the kind of weak sister who, for example, might stand up in front of a television camera and rant about cocker spaniel puppies and good Republican cloth coats, instead of telling the American people that rioting, looting, and draft-card burning would no longer be tolerated. Even Ike's coattails weren't enough to repair Nixon's image, and Ike himself was comatose or nearly so in Walter Reed after a series of heart attacks.

The Republican National Convention was notable for three things: Rockefeller's last minute declaration of candidacy, which further diluted Nixon's support, the luxuriousness of the accommodations and facilities, and its complete removal from the rioting that had broken out in Miami proper, where an allegedly minor racial incident escalated into a full-scale battle. The convention center was in Miami Beach, far from the madding Miami crowd, a self-contained playground for the rich. You couldn't smell the tear gas from Miami Beach, and the wind direction was such that you couldn't hear the sirens that screamed all night long . . .

"Carole Feeney" [this subject is still a fugitive]

"I told everybody it was the goddam fatcat Republicans that we ought to go after, not the Democrats. But Johnson the Madman was running and everyone really thought that he was going to get the nomination. I said they were crazy, Kennedy had it in the bag. But Johnson really had them all running scared. I tried talking to some of the people in the Mobe. Half of them didn't want to go to either convention and the other half were trying to buy *guns* to take to Chicago! Off the pigs, they kept saying. Off the pigs. Jesus, I thought, the only pig that was going to get offed was Pigasus—the real pig that the Yippies were going to announce as the candidate from the Youth International Party. That was cute. I mean, really, it was. I said, let's go ahead and do that somewhere in California, film it and send the film to a TV station and let them run it on the news. Uh-uh, nothing doing. Lincoln Park or bust. Yeah, right—Lincoln Park *and* bust. Busted heads, busted bodies, busted and thrown in jail.

"So I wasn't going to go. Then I found out what Davis was doing. I couldn't believe it—Davis Trainor had been in on everything practically from the beginning. He was real good-looking and real popular, he had this real goofy sense of humor and he always seemed to come up with good ideas for guerrilla action. He actually did all the set-up work on the pirate radio station we ran out of Oakland and he worked out our escape routes. Not one of us got caught in the KCUF caper. We called it our Fuck-You caper, of course.

"Then I'm doing the laundry and I find it—his COINTELPRO I.D.— stuffed into that little bitty pocket in his jeans. You know, it's like a little secret pocket right above the regular pocket on the right. The one thing I always hated about the movement was that it was as sexist as the Establishment. If you were a woman, you always got stuck doing all the cooking

and the cleaning up and the laundry and stuff. Unless you were a movement queen like Dohrn. Then you didn't have to do anything except make
speeches and get laid if you wanted. Oh, they threw us a sop by letting us
set up our own feminist actions and stuff, but we all knew it was a sop.
We kept telling each other that after we changed things, it would be
different and for now, we'd watch and listen and learn. Besides, everyone
knew that the Establishment wouldn't take women as seriously as they
would men. I wonder now how much any of us believed that—that it
would really be different, that we could change things at all.

"Anyway, I went straight to the Mobe with my discovery, but it was too
late—Davis discovered his pants were missing and he'd already split. I
really didn't want to go to Chicago after that, but the alternative seemed
to be either stay home and wait to get busted, or go to Chicago and get
busted in action. I was still enough of an idealist that they talked me into
Chicago. If I was going to get busted, I might as well be accomplishing
something, and anyway, after the revolution, I'd be a National Heroine,
and not a political prisoner.

"So, the revolution's come and gone and here I am. Still working for
the movement—the feminist movement, that is. What little I *can* do,
referring women with unwanted pregnancies to safe abortionists. Yes,
there are some. Not all of us were poly-sci majors—some of us were pre-
med, some of us went to nursing school. It costs a goddam fortune, but
I'm not getting rich on it. It's for the risk, you know. You get the death
penalty in this state for performing an illegal abortion. I could get life as
an accessory, and there was a woman in Missouri who *did* get death for
doing what I'm doing.

"Nobody in my family knows, of course. Especially not my husband.
If *he* knew, he'd probably kill me himself. Odd as it sounds, I don't hate
him . . . not when I think what good cover he is, and what the alternative
would be if I didn't have such good cover . . ."

Part of a transcript labeled "Carole Feeney"
obtained in a 1989 raid on a motel said to
be part of a network of underground
"safe houses" for tax protestors,
leftist terrorists, and other
subversives; no other illegal
literature recovered

The source of the DYLAN IS COMING! rumor never was pinpointed.
Some say it sprang into being all on its own and stayed alive because so many
people wanted it to be true. And for all anyone knows, perhaps it actually
was true, for a little while anyway; perhaps Dylan simply changed his mind.
The more cynical suggested that the rumor had been planted by infiltrators
like the notorious Davis Trainor, whose face became so well-known thanks

to the Mobe's mock wanted poster that he had to have extensive plastic surgery, a total of a dozen operations in all. The poster was done well enough that it passed as legitimate and was often allowed to hang undisturbed in post offices, libraries, and other public places, side by side with the FBI's posters of dissidents and activists. One poster was found in a Minneapolis library as late as 1975; the head librarian was taken into custody, questioned, and released. But it is no coincidence that the library was audited for objectionable material soon after that and has been subject to surprise spot checks for the last fifteen years, in spite of the fact that it has always showed 100 percent compliance with government standards for reading matter. The price of a tyrant's victory is eternal vigilance.

This was once considered to be the price of liberty. Nothing buys what it used to.

Steve D'Alessandro

"By Sunday, when Dylan didn't show, people were starting to get angry. I kept saying, well, hey, Allen Ginsberg showed. Allen Ginsberg! Man, he was like . . . *God* to me. He was doing his best, going around rapping with people, trying to get everybody calmed down and focused, you know. A whole bunch of us got in a circle around him and we were chanting *Om, Om.* I was getting a really good vibe and then some asshole throws a bottle at him and yells, *Oh, shut up, you fag!*

"I went crazy. Sure, I was in the closet then because the movement wasn't as enlightened as some of us wished it were. The FBI was doing this thing where it was going around trying to discredit a lot of people by accusing them of being queer, and everybody caught homophobia like it was measles. I ain't no fairy, no, sir, not me, I fucked a hundred chicks this week and my dick's draggin' on the ground so don't you call *me* no fag! It still stings, even when I compare it to how things are now. But then, I don't expect any kind of enlightened feeling in a society where I have to take fucking hormone treatments so I won't get a hard-on when I see another guy.

"Anyway, I found the scumbag that did it and I punched him out. I gave *him* a limp wrist. I gave him *two* of them. And I know I had a lot of support—I mean, a lot of straights admired Ginsberg, too, even if he was gay, just on the basis of *Howl,* but later, a bunch of Abbie's friends blamed me for creating the disturbance that gave the police the excuse they needed to wade in and start busting heads.

"Sometimes I'm afraid maybe they were right. But Annie Phillips told me it was just a coincidence. About me, I mean. She said they came in because they saw a black guy kissing a white girl. I guess nobody'll ever really know for sure, because the black guy died of his injuries and the white girl never came forward.

"I prefer to think that's what made Annie and her crowd go ahead with the bomb at the convention center. I don't like to think that Annie really wanted to blow anybody up. It was kind of weird how I knew Annie. Well, not weird, really. I probably owed Annie my life, or damn near, and so did a certain man of African-American descent. We were lucky it was her that walked in on us that day. She was enlightened, or at least tolerant, and we could trust her not to say anything. I didn't think she liked white people too much, but I'd heard she'd been with Martin Luther King a couple of years before on those marches and I couldn't blame her. Anyway, she couldn't give me away without giving away the brother, but to this day, I believe it really didn't matter to her—homosexuality, that is. Maybe because the Establishment hated us worse than they hated blacks.

"Anyway, I wasn't intending to be in the crowd that crashed the gate at the convention center on Wednesday. Nomination day. We'd been fighting in the streets since Monday and Daley's stormtroopers were beating the shit out of us. Late Tuesday night, the National Guard arrived. That's when we knew it was war.

"On Wednesday, we got hemmed in in Grant Park. People were pouring in by then, and nobody had expected that. It was like everyone was standing up to be counted because Dylan hadn't, or something. Anyway, there were maybe ten-twelve thousand of us at the band shell in the park, singing, listening to speeches, and then two kids went up a flagpole and lowered the flag to half-mast. The cops went crazy—they came in swinging wild and they didn't care who they hit or where they hit them. I was scared out of my mind. I saw those cops close up and they looked as mad as Johnson was supposed to be. On the spot, I became a believer like I'd never been before—Madman in the White House and Madman Daley and his Madman cops. It was all true, I thought while I curled up on the ground with my hands over my head and prayed some kill-crazy pig wouldn't decide to pound my ass to jelly.

"Somebody pulled me up and yelled that we were supposed to all go to in front of the Hilton. I ran like hell all the way to the railroad tracks along with everybody else and that was where the Guard caught us with the tear gas. Man, I thought I was going to die of tear-gas suffocation if I didn't get trampled by the people I was with. Everyone was running around like crazy. I don't know how we ever got out of there but somebody found a way onto Michigan Avenue and somehow we all followed. And the Guard followed after us. Somebody said later they weren't supposed to, but they did. And they weren't carrying popguns.

"Well, we ran smack into Ralph Abernathy and his Poor People's Campaign mule train and that was more confusion. Then the Guard waded in and a lot of Poor People went to the hospital that night (it was after seven by then). I'll never forget that, or the sight of all those TV cameras and the bright lights shining in our eyes. We were all staggering around when a fresh bus-load of riot cops arrived, and that's another sight

I'll never forget—two dozen beefy bruisers in riot gear shooting out of that bus like they were being shot from cannons and landing on all of us with both feet and their billyclubs. I lost my front teeth and I was so freaked I didn't even feel it until the next day.

"I was freaked, but I was also furious. We were all furious. It was like, Johnson would send us to Vietnam to be killed or he'd let us be killed by Daley's madman cops on the Chicago streets, it didn't matter to him. I think a lot of us expected the convention to adjourn in protest at our treatment. At least that Bobby Kennedy would speak out in protest against the brutality. The name Kennedy *meant* human rights, after all. Nobody knew that Kennedy had been removed from the convention center under heavy guard because they were all convinced that someone would make another attempt on his life. I heard that later, before they clamped down on all the information. He was about to get the fucking *nomination* and he was on his way back to his hotel. They said Madman Johnson was more like Mad-Dog Johnson over that, but who the fuck knows?

"George McGovern was at the podium when we busted in. I hadn't really been intending to be in that group that busted in, but I got carried along and when I saw we were going to crash the amphitheatre, I thought, what the fuck.

"I almost got crushed against the doors before they gave, and I barely missed falling on my face and getting run over by six thousand screaming demonstrators. And the first person I saw was Annie Phillips.

"I thought I was in a Fellini film. She was dressed in this godawful *maid's* uniform with a handkerchief around her head mashing down her Afro, but I knew it was her. We looked right into each other's eyes as I went by, still more carried along with the crowd than running on my own and she put both hands over her mouth in horror. That was the last time I saw her until she was on TV.

"I managed to get out of the way and stay to the back of the amphitheatre itself. I just wanted to catch my breath and try to think how I was going to get out of all this shit without getting my head split open by a crazy Guardsman or a cop. I was still there when the bomb went off down front.

"The sound was so loud I thought my ears were bleeding. Automatically, I dropped to the floor and covered my head. There was a little debris, not much, where I was. When I finally dared to look, what I saw didn't make any sense. I still can't tell you exactly what I saw. I blocked it out. But sometimes, I think I dream it. I dream that I saw Johnson's head sitting on a Texas flagpole. I'm pretty sure that's just my imagination, because in the dream, he's got this vaguely surprised-annoyed expression on his saggy old face, like he's saying, *Whut the fuck* is goin' *on here?*

"Anyway, the next thing I knew, I was out on the street again, and somebody was crying about they were bombing us now, along with the

Vietnamese. Which was about the time the Guard opened fire, thinking we were bombing them, I guess.

"I was lucky. I took a bullet in my thigh and it put me out of action. Just a flesh wound, really. It bled pretty impressively for a while and then quit. By then, I was so out of my head that I can't even tell you where I staggered off to. The people who found me in their front yard the next morning took care of me and got me to a hospital. It was a five-hour wait in the emergency room. That was where I was when I heard about Kennedy."

Part of the data recovered
from a disk
taken in a raid on an illegal
software laboratory,
March, 1981

Jack Kennedy had died in the middle of a Dallas street, his head blown off in front of thousands of spectators and his horrified wife. Bobby Kennedy had narrowly missed meeting his end during a moment of triumph in a Los Angeles hotel. Ultimately, that seemed to have been only a brief reprieve before fate caught up with him . . .

Jasmine Chang

"Everyone heard the explosion but nobody knew whether it was something the demonstrators had done, or if the National Guard had rolled in a tank, or if the world had come to an end. I ran down to the lobby with just about everyone else on the staff and a good many of the hotel guests, trying to see what was happening outside without having to go out in it. Nobody wanted to go outside. That night, the manager on duty had told us that anyone who wanted could stay over if we didn't mind roughing it in the meeting rooms. I made myself a sleeping bag out of spare linens under a heavy table in one of the smaller rooms. The night before, the cops had cracked one of the dining room windows with a demonstrator's head. I wasn't about to risk my neck going out in that frenzy.

"Well, after the explosion, we heard the rifle fire. Then the street in front of the hotel, already crowded, was *packed* all of a sudden. Wall-to-wall cops and demonstrators, and the cops were swinging at anything they could reach. They were *scything* their way through the crowd, you see— they were mowing people down to make paths so they could walk. It was one of the worst things I've ever seen. For awhile it was *the* worst. I wish it could have stayed that way.

"The lobby was filling up, too, but nobody really noticed because we were all watching that sickening scene outside. The whole world was watching, they said. I saw a camera crew and all I could think was their equipment was going to get smashed to bits.

"I don't know when Kennedy came down to the lobby. I don't know why the Secret Service didn't stop him, I don't know what he thought he could do. He must have been watching from his window. Maybe he thought he could actually address the crowd—as if anyone could have heard him. Anyway, he was there in the lobby and none of us really noticed him.

"The demonstrator who forced his way into the revolving door—he was just a kid, he looked about fifteen years old to me. Scared out of his mind. The revolving door was supposed to be locked, but when I saw that kid's face, I was glad it wasn't.

"Then the cops tried to force their way in after him but they got stuck, there was a billyclub jammed in the door or something. And the kid was babbling about how they'd blown up Kennedy at the convention. 'They threw a bomb and killed Kennedy! They blew him up with Johnson and McGovern!' he was yelling over and over. And Bobby Kennedy himself rushed over to the kid. I'm pretty sure that was the first any of us really noticed him, when it registered. I remember, I felt shocked and surprised and numb all at once, seeing Kennedy right there, right in the middle of a lobby. Like he was anybody. And nobody else moved, we all just stood there and stared like dummies.

"And Kennedy was trying to tell the kid who he was, that he wasn't dead and what bomb and all that. The kid got even more hysterical, and Kennedy was shaking him, trying to get something coherent out of him, we're all standing there watching and finally the cops manage to get through the revolving door.

"They must have thought the kid was attacking Kennedy. That's all I can figure. Even if that's not how they looked. The cops. They looked . . . *weird*. Like they didn't know what they were doing, or they did know but they'd forgotten why they were supposed to do it. I don't know. I don't *know*. But it was so weird, because they all looked exactly alike to me right at that moment, even though when I looked at them again after, they weren't anything alike, even in their uniforms. But they looked like identical dolls then, or puppets, because they moved all at once together. Like a kick-line of chorus girls, you know? Except that it wasn't their legs that came up but their arms.

"I know that when they raised their guns, they were looking at the kid, and I thought, 'No, wait!' I tried to move toward them, I was reaching out and they fired.

"It was like another bomb had gone off. For a moment, I thought another bomb had gone off, just a split second before they were going to fire. Then John Kennedy—I mean, Bobby, *Bobby* Kennedy—that's a Freudian slip, isn't it?—he did this clumsy whirl around and it looked like he was turning around in anger, like people do sometimes, you know? Like he was going, 'Dammit, I'm leaving!' And then he went down, and it was so awful because—well, this is going to sound really strange, I guess, but . . . well . . . when you see people get shot on a TV show, it's choreographed or something, they do these kind of graceful falls. Kennedy was . . . they'd robbed him of his dignity. That's the only way I can think to put it. They shot him and humiliated him all at once, he looked clumsy and awkward and helpless.

"And I was outraged at that. I know it must sound weird, a man got shot, *killed*, and I'm talking about how he looked undignified. But that's like what taking someone's life is—taking their humanity, making them a *thing*. And I was outraged. I wanted to grab one of those cops' guns and make *them* into things. Not just because it was Bobby Kennedy, it could have been anyone on that floor at that moment, the kid, the manager, my supervisor—and I hated my supervisor's guts.

"Right then, I understood what the demonstrations were about, and I was against the war. Up until then, I'd been kind of for it—not really *for* it, more like, 'I hate war, but you're supposed to serve your country.' But right then, I understood how horrifying it must be to be told to make somebody into a thing, or be told you have to go out and risk being made into a thing. To kill, to be killed.

"All that went through my mind in a split second and then I started screaming. Then I heard this *noise* . . . under my screams, I heard this weird groan. It was Kennedy. They say he was dead by then and it must have been the air going out of his lungs past his vocal cords that made the sound. Awful. Just awful. I ran and pulled the fire alarm. It was the only thing I could think to do. And this other chambermaid, Lucy Anderson, she started pounding on the front windows and screaming, 'Stop! Stop! They killed Kennedy! They killed Kennedy!' Probably nobody could hear her, but even if anyone had, it wouldn't have mattered, because most of the people out there thought Kennedy was already dead in the explosion.

"It wasn't the Fire Department that used the hoses on those people. The cops commandeered the fire trucks and did that. And we were stuck in that hotel for another whole day and night. Even after they cleared the streets, they wouldn't let any of us go anywhere. Like house arrest.

"The questioning was awful. Nobody mistreated me or hit me or anything like that, it was just that they kept *at* me. I had to tell what I saw over and over and over and over until I thought they were either trying to drive me out of my mind so I wouldn't be able to testify against those cops, or trying to find some way to make it seem like *I* was really the one who'd done it.

"By the time they told me I could leave the hotel, I was mad at the world, I can tell you. Especially since that Secret Service agent or whoever he was told me I'd be a lot happier if I moved out of Chicago and started over somewhere else. He really screwed that one up, and it was lucky for me he did. I left, and I was far, far away when the shit really hit the fan. I started over, all right—I got a new name and a new identity. Everybody else who was in that lobby—Lucy Anderson, the manager, the other staff and guests—they all disappeared. The last anyone saw of them, the Secret Service was taking them away. The cops vanished, too, but I have a feeling they didn't vanish to quite the same thing as the others. And the kid killed himself. *They* said. Right, sure. I bet he couldn't survive the interrogation.

"Of course, all that was a long time ago. Hard to imagine now how things were then. I was only twenty, then. I was working days and taking college courses at night. I wanted to be a teacher. Now I'm in my early forties, and sometimes I think I dreamed it all. I dreamed that I lived in a country where people *voted* their leaders into office, where you just had to be old enough and not be a convicted felon and you could vote. Instead of having to take those psychological tests and wait for the investigators to give you a voting clearance. It *is* like a dream, isn't it? Imagining that there was a time in this country when you could *be* anything you wanted to be, a teacher, a doctor, a banker, a scientist. I was going to be a teacher. I was going to be a history teacher, but those are mostly white people. My family's been in this country forever, but because I'm Oriental, I've got conditional citizenship now . . . and I was *born* here! I suppose I shouldn't complain. If anyone found out I saw Kennedy get it, I'd probably be unconditionally *dead*. Because *everyone knows* that the rumor that Kennedy was shot by some cops with a bad aim in a hotel lobby is just another stupid rumor, like the second gunman in Dallas in 1963. *Everyone knows* Kennedy died in the explosion at the convention center. That's the official version of how he died and it's the official version, government certified, that's the truth.

"Where I live, they have routine segregation, so I can't use any of the whites' facilities. I've thought about applying to move to one of the larger cities where there's elective segregation and nothing's officially 'white-only,' but I hear the waiting lists are years long. And somebody told me that everything is really just as segregated as here, they're just not as open and honest about it. So maybe I'd really be no better off . . .

"But I wish that I could have become a teacher—any kind of teacher—instead of a cook. I can't even become a chef, because that's another men-only field. I don't *want* to be a chef necessarily, because I really don't like to cook and I'm not very good at it. But it was all I could get. The list of available careers for non-whites gets smaller all the time.

"Sometimes, I think it actually wasn't meant to be this bad. Sometimes I think that nobody really wanted the military to take over the government for real, I think it was just panic about so many of the Democratic candidates dying along with the President in that blast and the rioting that wouldn't stop and all that. It did seem as if the country was completely falling apart and somebody had to do something fast and decisive. Well, sure, somebody should have. Somebody should have figured out who was the President with Madman Johnson and Humpty Humphrey and all those Senators dead—there had to be *somebody* left, right? All of Congress wasn't there. I mean, if I'd known, if a lot of us had known how things were going to come out, I think we'd have just let Ronald Reagan be president for four years, run him against Wallace or something and kept free elections, instead of postponing the elections and then having them abolished.

"People panicked. That's what it all came down to, I think. They were panicking in the streets, they were panicking in the government, and they were panicking in their homes. Our own panic brought us down."

Undated typescript found in
a locker in the downtown
San Diego bus terminal,
April 9, 1993

Our own panic brought us down. For many who were eyewitness to certain events of 1968, this would seem to be a fitting coda, if coda is the word, for the ensuing twenty-five years . . .

Oh, hell, I don't know why I'm bothering to try to sum this up. How do you sum up a piece of history gone wrong? How do you sum up the fall of a country that believes it was saved from chaos and destruction? And who am I asking, anyway? I'm out of the country now, another wetback who finally made it across the border to freedom. There was a time when wetbacks went north to freedom, but I'm pretty sure nobody would remember that now. Mexico is sad and dusty and ancient, the people poor and suspicious of Anglos, though I'm so brown now that I can pass convincingly as long as I don't try to speak the language—my accent is still atrocious.

But the freedom here—nothing like what we used to have, but the constraints are far fewer. You don't need to apply for a travel permit in-country, you just *go* from place to place. Of course, it's not really that hard to get a travel permit in the US, they give them out routinely. But I'm of that generation that remembers when it was different, and it galls me that I would have to apply for one at all if I want to go from, say, Newark to, say, Cape May. I've deliberately chosen two cities I've never been to, just in case these papers fall into the wrong hands. God knows enough of my papers have been lost over the years. Sometimes I think it's a miracle I haven't been caught.

It's a hell of a life when you're risking prosecution and imprisonment just for trying to put together a true account of something that happened two and a half decades before.

Why I bothered— well, there are a lot of reasons. Because I've learned to love truth. And because I want to atone for what I did to "Carole Feeney" and the others. I'm still amazed that she didn't recognize me, but I guess twenty-five years is a long time after all.

I really thought I was doing the right thing at the time. I thought infiltrating the leftist groups was all right if it was just to make sure that nobody was stockpiling weapons or planning to blow up a building. Or assassinate another leader. I truly wish I could have arrested Annie Phillips and her group long before Chicago. Some of the people I talked to who were in the streets that night blame Annie for everything that's happened since, and I think that's why the authorities kept her alive instead of killing her—so the old radicals could hate her more than the government.

After I talked to Annie, I understood why she turned violent, even if I didn't condone it. If her voice could have been heard in 1964, maybe all these voices could be heard now, though they might not have so much to say . . .

How melodramatic, "Davis." I can't help it. I was actually just like any of them in the year 1968—I thought my country was in trouble, and I was trying to do something about it. And—

And what the hell, we won the Vietnam war. Hooray for America. The Vietnamese are all but extinct, but we brought the boys back home. We sent them right back out to the Middle East, and then down to Nicaragua, and to the Philippines, and to Europe, of course, where they don't protest our missile bases much any more. That big old stick. We've gone one better than talking softly and carrying a big stick. Now we don't talk at all . . .

In the weeks since I finally got out of the country, I've been having this recurring dream. I keep dreaming that things turned out differently, that there was even just one thing that didn't happen, or something else that did happen, and the country just . . . went on. And so I keep thinking about it. If Johnson hadn't run . . . if that bomb hadn't gone off . . . if Kennedy hadn't been killed . . . . if it had only been half the number of demonstrators . . . if Dylan had showed up.

If Dylan had showed up . . . I wonder sometimes if that's it. God, the world should be so simple. Instead of simple and brutal and crude.

Even after putting together this risky account, I'm not sure that I really know much more than I did in the beginning. I was hoping that I might figure it all out, how, instead of winning the battle and losing the war, we won the war and lost everything we had. But it could have been different. I don't know why it's so important to me to believe that. Maybe because I don't want to believe that this was the way we were going no matter what. I don't want to believe that everything that was of any value is stuck back there in the sixties.

Papers found in a hastily vacated room
in an Ecuadorian flophouse by occupying
American forces during the third
South American War, October 13, 1998

PIPES

Robert Reed

A relatively new writer, Robert Reed is a frequent contributor to *The Magazine of Fantasy and Science Fiction*, and has also sold stories to *Universe, New Destinies, Isaac Asimov's Science Fiction Magazine, Synergy*, and elsewhere. His books include the novels *The Leeshore, The Hormone Jungle*, and *Down the Bright Way*. His most recent novel is the well-received *The Remarkables*. He is currently working on two new novels, *Cul-de-Sac* and *An Exaltation of Larks*. His story "The Utility Man" was on last year's Final Hugo Ballot, and I doubt that he is going to be a stranger to the award ballots in years to come, either. He lives in Lincoln, Nebraska.

In the quietly compelling story that follows, he shows us that even the most elaborate and well-worked-out plans may fail if they don't take into account one very important factor—the people who have to fit *into* them.

I was living south of campus, upstairs in one of those big old houses cut up into apartments of impractical sizes and shapes. The neighborhood itself was halfway gone—empty lots and shaggy grass, deer in the night and the old people with their pensions and their inertia. The university was planning to move next year. To Omaha. At least there was industry in Omaha, and a stable population, and I was promised a permanent position if I could make my work sing. *Sing.* That's how the project head said it. "Make it sing, Aaron," he told me. "You're the final filter. My editor. The one who puts the pieces into a harmonious whole." He was a charming and gracious asshole, and he rode me about deadlines and the needs of the government. Which is why I worked at home, avoiding his pointed smiles and pestering questions. In order to get the miracles done.

I was putting in eighteen- and twenty-hour days. Sometimes all-hour days. The work involved some of the largest, fastest computing power in the Midwest, yet still it needed me to baby-sit. To sit and watch the essentials on the linkup screen, keeping alert with synthetic coffee and an assortment of pills. Doing all sorts of hell to my moods.

This is about moods.

One night, late, I wandered out into the kitchen and started cooking. Everything was ancient, half the appliances broken and the rest sputtering along. I started cleaning pots and killing the roaches as I found them. I let

the tap water run, and the drain drained for a little while, then it quit. So I
rooted under the sink and found a bottle of drain cleaner. The liquid was
minty and blue, and the label said, "Poison," aloud. "Poison, poison." I
poured in twice the suggested dosage and felt the curling pipe turn too hot
to touch. Yet nothing was draining. Not even after I finished dinner. Well,
I thought, what a bitch. I went downstairs and wrestled my bike out the door
and rode to the nearest store. One of those little automated shops that were
big twenty years ago. I could smell fresh smoke in the wind. Somewhere
west of town, the prairie was burning itself black, and twice I saw deer in the
street, their eyes bobbing in my headlight. At the store I bought a can of
pressurized, perfumed air—blasting the pipe clear fit my mood. Then I rode
home and bailed out the sink, dumping the dirty water down my toilet, and
I emptied the can into the drain. *Bang, bang, bang.* Nothing happened.
The pipes rattled, sure, and the house seemed to shake. But that was all.
The blockage was out of my reach, and I didn't have any choice but to call
a random plumber—Whiteeagle Plumbing—and leave a message on his
service.

Then I worked all night.

My high browsers were giving me trouble. And my sabertooths. The
individual models built by the respective gene teams were full of hopeful
projections and guesswork. Five and six generations into the simulation, and
there were inadequate populations of camels and many too many sabertooths.
Plus, the savanna itself—a strikingly African landscape of scattered trees and
low grasses—was beginning to change. Ashes and oaks took the wrong shapes
without being browsed. They were top-heavy, storms knocking them flat too
often, and the wrong sorts of grasses were taking root and spreading. Ten
generations later, and the sabertooths were causing a massive megafauna die-
off. Camels were extinct—phantom bones on the imaginary ground—and
the mammoths and horses and ground sloths were heading in much the same
direction.

How could it be? I wondered.

What the hell is going on?

It took me the night just to rework the camels. Not their actual genetics,
no. Those were for the gene team. I concentrated on the basics. Birth weights.
Parental care. Half a hundred little factors, and of course I didn't know if it
would work. Or if I was disrupting still other factors and facets. All I could
do was guess, then wait for the next run to see how my luck was running.

It was nearly nine o'clock when I finally punched up the sabertooth
data. Nothing seemed obvious, at least at first glance. Something subtle?
Something behavioral, maybe? I had the computers select a hundred successful hunts at random, and the linkup screen played each one at triple speed.
What was that? I saw the big, muscular cats slipping through the grass and
underbrush, stalking any and every piece of game in the area. Nothing was
safe on the savanna. Even the adult mammoths, cagey and vast, were being
killed. Two cats, working together, managed to panic the mammoths and

drive them over a river bluff . . . and it didn't take me any neural readouts to see the cats loved it. The butchering on a vast scale . . . it was a game to them. A diversion. What the hell was this? I wondered. What was going on?

I got into the brain dimensions of the cats—reasonable—then into the neurological densities—very unreasonable!—and I beat on the table with a fist, screaming to myself. What were these fucking cat-people doing? Goddamn them and goddamn their mothers! Human beings didn't have those densities. Would you look? How could I work with genius cats? All that spare brainpower, and, out of sheer boredom, the things were killing off the megafauna. For the fun of it. Hunting instincts coupled with a staggering cleverness led to sociopathic sabertooths . . . "Would you just look at this mess . . . !"

There came a knocking sound.

I didn't notice it at first. I was draining my coffee mug while hunting for the little red pills that gave me wings and clear thinking. Then again someone was knocking. It sounded as if they were using a tire iron on my apartment door. Who was it?

I stumbled into the living room, a little numb and stupid. For a minute I just stared at the door while it jumped in its frame, and I squinted, thinking it was the project head coming for a status report. Coming to remind me that our proposal had to be in at such-and-such time. The bastard.

I managed to clear my throat and find my voice, saying, "Yeah?"

Someone shouted something about pipes. Was I the guy with pipe troubles?

I seemed to recall details from another life. Not my own. I opened the door and saw a short, massive man standing in the narrow hallway. He was dark like something left in the sun, and he was smiling. He had a round face pitted by some childhood infection, and his hair was long and black and rather oily. I could smell his breath. It was early in the morning, and his breakfast had been beer. A full-blooded member of some tribe or another, and I hadn't seen his like since my fieldwork in the Badlands.

His name was sewn on the pocket of his work shirt.

Johnny Whiteeagle.

"Hey, you don't look so good," he told me. Smiling. He had a big, effortless smile. "You're not feeling good, mister?"

"I've been better," I allowed.

"Maybe it's your plumbing. Ever think about that?" He let out a big laugh, shaking his head as if he were wickedly clever. "Anyway, you going to let me inside? Or what?"

"What for?"

"Your pipes, mister. Remember?"

I backed away. Pipes? Oh sure . . . that's right. "All right," I told him. "Come on."

He rattled when he walked. He wore an old leather belt heavy with tools and a portable battery, and the red-rimmed eyes took in the room with a glance. "In the kitchen?" He went straight to the sink and touched the drain with one hand, then the other, always gentle and professional. He was the picture of poise and ceremony, and it was kind of funny to watch. I saw him kneel and look at the curling pipe below, touching it in the same way while saying, "Would you look. They're metal. Antiques, practically." And he gave a satisfied nod. "You know something, mister? This is one fine old house you've got here."

I could smell facsimile peas rotting in the pipes, and grease from last night's cultured hamburger. Yeah, I thought, it's a splendid dear old place. But when are you getting to work?

He asked what had happened. Had I tried fixing it myself?

I kept the epic brief. I tried to seem pressed for time.

"This is old plumbing, mister. If you want it to last," he warned, "you've got to baby it."

"All it is is plugged."

"Oh sure." He stood. He was massive and slow and fat, and when he moved, he breathed hard and wheezed. "Where's the bathroom?" he asked. "Around back here?"

He wanted to pee away his beer, I guessed. I looked at my watch and said, "That's right—"

"See, because the plug is way below us. I bet so. Has your bathtub been draining slow?"

"I've got a shower—"

"Has it?"

I couldn't remember.

"I bet so." He started toward the bathroom, rattling and wheezing. I considered going back to work and leaving him with his work, only I didn't. I couldn't. I didn't know him, and he was drunk, at least a little bit, and I had funny feelings because he was . . . well, who he was. A Native and all. Not that I'm a racist, of course. But I learned in the Badlands that these people have odd ideas about property, their culture so damned communal. And besides, I'd have to concentrate like a maniac just to keep him out of my thoughts. I wouldn't get shit done until he was gone. So I was his shadow. I watched him stand in the middle of the bathroom, turning and turning. He asked me, "What? Was this a bedroom once?" He said, "It looks like a bedroom. Am I right?"

"I don't know."

"Look at how big it is!"

I nodded and said nothing.

"Hell," he said, "it's a hike from the shower to the john. Isn't it?" He laughed and got his bearings and walked into the back corner. There was a simple closet built against the kitchen's wall. I kept old boxes and whatnot inside it. He pulled open its curtain and asked, "Can I move the stuff—?"

I started to say, "Sure."

Boxes were tumbling to the floor. Then he bent and started tapping his stubby fingernails on the enormous black pipe that I'd probably seen a thousand times. It was a vertical pipe and smooth, and he laid both hands on the angling joint with a screwed-in cap. "It's as good as done," he promised. "This is the place. It won't take any time at all—"

Everything takes time. I wanted to tell him that universal truth.

"Here." He produced an enormous monkey wrench and fastened it to the cap, its motor humming, and him helping the motor by jerking the wrench with all of his weight. Sweat broke out on his bare arms and forehead, and he gave a funny look while saying, "Help me," through his teeth. Talking to the Great Spirit, I suppose. Years of rust resisted the pressures. Then there was a *pop* and a creaking sound, threads moving against threads. "Yeah!" he squealed. And when the cap was undone, he placed it upside down on one of the boxes, then leaned against the kitchen's wall to pant.

I watched him.

"Yeah," he said, "I've worked everywhere in this town. For years. I used to work on the governor's pipes and inside the government buildings." He pulled a mechanical spider from a sealed pouch. It was old but still shiny, a cord sprouting from its back, and him plugging the cord's free end into the battery riding on his hip. "Inside houses here and everywhere. I know this town from its pipes. Let me tell you—"

"Yeah?"

"Mansions and trailers and everything between."

I waited.

He asked, "What about you? What do you do?"

"School."

"You in it or teach it?"

"No, work for the university," I explained. "See, I'm real busy with this project—"

"It's leaving soon, isn't it? The professors and everything?"

"That's better than staying," I replied. How long had it been since I'd talked to another person? I couldn't remember. Days, at least, and I couldn't help but say, "Once the farms collapsed, everything started to slide. To die. Nobody wants to live here anymore."

"Don't I know it," he told me. "Just like you say, mister. It's all sliding. I've seen it happening since way back when."

Then I said, "Not that it's all bad. Of course."

He looked at me, his smile changing.

Did I say something wrong? I wondered.

"No." He told me, "You're right," and showed his yellow teeth. "I was thinking that just the other night. Telling my wife it was something watching all you folks heading out of here." He touched a hidden switch on the spider's back. The shiny long legs began to move, kicking and curling, and I nearly could smell the power in them. I nearly could feel their cutting tips slicing at the air. "There you go." He was talking to the spider. He put it down the opened pipe and turned to me again, saying, "Yeah, I think it's great to see.

I mean, this country wasn't meant to be corn and more corn, and I don't miss it."

The farms began crumbling when the cheap ocean farms were formed off every coast. It was twenty years ago, and the deathblow came when the gene teams found ways to grow steaks and pork chops with natural gas and water. Better living through chemistry, and all that.

"You smell the fires last night?" he asked.

I said, "No," because I'd forgotten them. Then I remembered my ride to the store and smelling the grass burning. Sure.

"I smelled them. It was like old times for me." And he laughed. The spider had been crawling down into the pipe for a minute now. I could hear its feet on the metal, then it stopped at the plug and started to cut. I presumed. The cord lay in Johnny Whiteeagle's hand, and he smiled at me and said, "The fires made me think of the reservation. When I was a kid, even younger than you." As if I were nine years old or something.

"The reservation?" I said.

"I'm Lakota," he informed me. His free hand pointed at his considerable body, and he said, "Sioux to you."

"I know," I managed. "Sure." A bad bunch of fellows, I was thinking. We had never completely beaten them. Sitting Bull and Crazy Horse weren't the end of them. When I was a kid, I remembered, they started a little war up in South Dakota. Some snipers, some bombers. A low-grade war, and I had to wonder about my plumber. Maybe he was an old terrorist. It made me stop and think, I can tell you.

A couple of moments passed.

My companion gave a little nod, then asked, "So what do you do for the university? What's this job?"

I tried explaining. "All this empty country? Cheap and going to waste?" I said, "I'm helping the university make a proposal. It's something nobody's tried before. We want to use genetic engineering and ecological planning—"

"Yeah, I've heard about you. Sure thing!" He was laughing and shaking his head. "Hey, this is great! I mean it! You guys . . . you're the ones trying to put everything back together . . . aren't you? I heard about you the other night, on television—"

"I'm helping with the proposal," I said. "We need funding over a lot of decades . . . if this is going to work at all. . . ."

"It's going to work fine. I've got a feeling." He grinned and told me, "That's so damned neat. I mean it, mister."

I shrugged and smiled. Who was I to ignore praise?

"I'm Johnny Whiteeagle." His free hand shot out, moist and squeezing my hand. "I told my old lady just this morning—I mean this—that something big was going to happen today. I had a feeling." He laughed. He filled my oversized bathroom with sound, then he slapped me on the shoulder. "So what's your name, mister?"

"Aaron."

"Well, Aaron, this is swell."

It was nice to hear. It was nice just to stand there with him and have nothing to do but believe him.

Johnny Whiteeagle bent toward the pipe and listened for a moment. "Sounds done." Then he started retrieving the spider, hand-over-handing the cord while asking me, "What do you do? Work here? At home?"

"Yeah—"

"You've got a computer or something?"

"I'm plugged into the university. Right now, in fact." I nodded and gave my watch a meaningful glance. Assuming I could make changes in the sabertooths before noon, how long until I could run a good twenty-plus-generation simulation?

The spider came out of the pipe. It was covered with the blackest goo I'd ever seen, foul like very old garbage, and Johnny unplugged the cord from the battery and asked, "Can I rinse this clean?" He was already walking, some of the goo dripping to the floor. He dropped the spider into the sink and ran the hottest water, steam in his face and him asking me, "So what're you going to do to the land? How are you going to pull it back to where it started?"

"We can't. Not after everything." Generations of cultivation and road building and dam building and people. People and more people, I explained, and there were all sorts of problems.

"Oh sure." He had an optimistic stance, legs apart and the scalding water cooking the spider clean. He added soap. He stirred the suds with the handle of my toothbrush. "But you can mostly do it, can't you?"

"With time. And money."

"Oh sure."

"I've got a million other problems to fix first." I began to shift my weight from foot to foot. I looked at my watch again. "I'm running an enormous set of programs on the computers. In Osborne Hall. We've got to show it's possible first, or there won't be any government moneys. Or private moneys, for that matter."

"What? You've got a linkup here?" He turned off the water and dropped my toothbrush into the suds. "Can I look?"

It wasn't really a question.

Johnny was gone. I blinked, and he was out of the room and down the hallway, past the kitchen before I could catch him. I couldn't believe that a man of his bulk and sobriety could move half so fast. "I just have to take a glance. Real quick. It won't take time at all—"

"The thing is—"

"Is this it?" The linkup screen was covered with data. Heavy sabertooth skulls floated beside population estimates, fire estimates, weather projections, and so on. "Hey," said Johnny, "this is neat!"

"Actually," I said, "it's rather confidential."

"Maybe I ought to get a drink then, huh." He looked at me, deadly serious. "Got any in the fridge?"

"I don't think so—"

"Let me check." He found a couple cans of beer, offering me one and opening the other and giggling when the foam dripped to the carpet. "So show me something," he said. "Some other stuff."

What was simple and quick? "Here." I touched buttons, summoning a first-generation map of the state. Fifty years from today, I explained. Assuming everything moved according to the timetable. The big trick was starting with all the facets in balance. Not in their final climax state, no, but at least something stable and workable. "The prairie forming around us now? The tall grasses? They were native a couple hundred years ago, but they're not the true native community. Not in the strictest sense. The megafauna will require different vegetations—"

"Yeah?"

"For the past 5 million years, give or take, we've had rich and varied ecosystems. Particularly between the ice ages. Camels and mammoths and pronghorns, all sorts of species. Plus the predators. The lions and cheetahs and sabertooths and short-faced bears—"

"Bears?" he echoed. Nodding.

"We'll need to build the species as we need them. From their close relatives, or from scratch. Each gene team projects a species, and they're locked into computer memory." I gestured. "I test them and try to make corrections, hopefully small ones, and the gene teams get angry and start building new versions."

Johnny kept shaking his head.

"Once started," I admitted, "the project could take centuries—"

"I love it!"

"A lot of it will be public land. For the tourists. They'll come from the coasts and down from space. On holidays and whatnot." I waited for a moment, then said, "Access will be controlled. Small electric planes will silently take the tourists to overlook points and campsites, and the rest of the country will be wilderness. An enormous, fresh-minted wilderness." I didn't mention the enclaves scattered here and there. There would be half a hundred enclaves for the wealthy; a substantial chunk of the start-up costs would come from luxury-minded people. People who would want to leave their descendants parcels of exotic lands and a remarkable solitude. "So," I asked, "what do you think?"

"Where do we live?" asked Johnny.

What did he mean? We?

"The Lakota," he told me.

I looked at him, feeling tired and vague and suddenly cranky. Then I glanced at the map, at the estimates of tourists and native residents, and I said nothing. I just stood there.

Johnny finished his beer and crushed the can, and he watched me. He said, "Aaron, you should think about the Lakota here. You know? We were part of the way it was. Back when. Just like those bears and whatever . . . we belong in this thing."

"Do you?" I managed.

"Sure," he said. He waved the second beer at me, opened it, and wondered, "You sure you don't want it?"

I wasn't thinking about the beer. I told him, "What we're trying to do . . . we're trying to re-create the *substance* of the past 5 million years. And Native Americans—transplanted Asians—didn't arrive in credible numbers until twelve thousand years ago."

He didn't seem to hear me.

He said, "I'd like to live in that sort of country."

I looked at my watch.

"Hunt and fish and live the good life," he said. "No clocks. No bosses watching over you. No one expecting anything more than meat from you, and shelter. You know what I mean?"

"Listen," I mentioned, "I need to get busy—"

"We're too damned busy; that's what I mean." He giggled and tilted back the can, drinking and then giving a deep belch. "You ought to talk to your bosses. Get them to let me into the picture."

I said, "No." I was really awfully tired.

"No?"

I said, "I can't. Won't."

"Not for me?" He seemed injured. "I come here and do this favor for you, Aaron, and you can't just give me a sliver of all this? What was mine in the first place anyway?"

"No," I told him. I used a hard voice that surprised even me. I said, "The reservations are going to have two choices. Either they stay as they are today and we'll build fences around them, or the Natives can sell out and leave, returning whenever it's possible. Like everyone else. As tourists, and with all the usual restrictions."

Johnny was puzzled. Surprised.

"What's your problem?" he asked. "What's going on?"

I pointed at the screen, saying, "You don't belong *there*. That's what I'm explaining."

"Why not?"

"Because I'm having trouble just fitting the cats into the picture. The goddamn cats!"

"Aaron—?"

"Quit talking as if you know me!" I snapped.

He made a small sound, saying nothing.

"A few thousand Natives running around the place," I said, "and you know what would happen? You sure as hell wouldn't be hunting with bows and arrows, would you? You'd starve if you had to do that."

"So I'd use my rifle. I'd just take what I needed—"

"You sure didn't take what you needed twelve thousand years ago. You didn't!" I said, "Your ancestors crossed over here at the end of the Ice Age, and you know what happened? The megafauna went extinct. In almost every case. Mammoths. Mastodons. The giant bison and whatever. And that includes the predators and the huge scavengers. They're dead because they didn't know how to cope with you. You slaughtered them, and the changing weather killed the rest, and don't give me any of that red-man-in-tune-with-nature crap. All right?"

He was staring at me, his face blank and hard.

I pulled my hands through my hair. I was shaking in my hands and everywhere. The red pills had me shaking.

Then Johnny Whiteeagle said, "I wasn't talking about being noble," with the smallest, darkest voice possible. "What did I say?"

I sat down. I had to sit.

"Hey," he told me, "I'm a poor guy with problems. O.K. My old lady says I drink too much and I'm lazy . . . but hey, you don't want to hear my story. Do you?"

"I've got my own troubles," I replied. That was the bottom line. "I'm sorry. I've got to get back to work. I'm going to have to ask you to take your tools and leave."

"Yeah." He walked out of the room without another sound. He went to get his mechanical spider, and came out into the living room with his eyes fixed on me, watching me, and there was something showing. I saw something. "You could have acted nice," he told me. "It wouldn't have cost you anything."

"How do you want to be paid?" I started looking for my credit cards, and he said:

"I'll bill you."

So I turned my back to him, feeling his eyes. The apartment door opened and closed, and I listened to him on the stairs and got up and went to the window, watching him appear below me. A battered van was parked on the curb, a shabby white eagle painted on its side. I was still shaking, maybe worse than before. He got into the van and sat motionless, looking straight ahead, then he bent and brought a long-necked bottle out of somewhere. He drank and then drank some more, putting down a terrific amount of liquor. Then he started the van and drove out of the sudden cloud of blackish smoke. He didn't look my way once. Not even a glance upward. It felt good to have him ignore me, and I started hoping he would get good and drunk and sleep it off, forgetting everything. Particularly me.

I got back to work after a few minutes.

It took me forever to get into the right mood again, but then things were fine. The trouble with the sabertooths, I learned, wasn't too bad. I made the adjustments in an hour, dropping their intelligence and plugging the new parameters into the memory, then I put the new slow-learning cats into the imaginary landscape. "O.K," I said. "Go."

Everything was up and running. One generation, then two. I watched slivers and wisps of the whole, at triple speed. Everything had a certain simplicity. This was a model, after all. The cats and bears were rounded shapes, and the grasses were the same impossible green. Bright and lush. Each element was an elaborate estimate, and I found myself explaining the details to Johnny. For some reason I imagined him standing behind me, looking over my shoulder. "The gene teams will make adjustments according to my recommendations. Then I start over again. It isn't that we want to get everything right. That's not the point. But a good working model is what will impress our investors. The government agencies and the various billionaires." I paused for a minute, then I told him, "If I just had more time, I could be more exotic. But this is pretty good. All things considered."

Three generations. And no troubles yet.

I made a fresh pot of coffee and a sandwich, then I ran my kitchen faucet for a long, long while. As an experiment. I watched the water spin down the drain, and I sighed, going back to the linkup room—

—and finding nothing.

The screen was black. Utterly and profoundly black.

An outage somewhere, I thought. I sat and ate my sandwich, sipping coffee and waiting. Telling myself it was nothing. A power outage down at the campus, and it wasn't the first time. Only, maybe I knew I was fooling myself. Thinking back now, I have to wonder. I just sat there and waited, never checking with the university or listening to the news. I kept telling myself someone had dug into a power cable, and I waited.

My phone sang out after a long while.

I stood and went to the living room. I can remember every step. I remember the project head shouting at me before the receiver was to my ear, telling me, "We've got some friend of yours here, and he says you'll understand. He says you'll know what this is about!" He said, "Aaron." He said, "Do you know what your buddy did? He showed up here and said there was a problem with the building's pipes, and he went up to the top floor and opened a pipe and lowered a fucking pipe bomb down level with the computers—"

"I see," I managed.

"—and it's a goddamn miracle nobody was blown to pieces."

I said nothing.

"The son of a bitch is shitfaced. Do you hear me?"

I nodded.

"Do you hear me?" He said, "He wanted me to call you and give you a message. Are you there?"

"Sure."

" 'We did it again.' That's the message. 'The redskins did it again.' Whatever in hell that means!"

"It's bad?" I wondered.

"Oh no, not too bad." He made a cutting sound, then said, "Just everything is lost. Data and the simulations and a fortune in hardware . . . and we're finished, Aaron. I don't know how you pissed him off, but I'll have you know—!"

I hung up on him.

I sat back down in the linkup room, watching the black screen and listening to the phone sing. Then I stopped hearing it. All at once I was pretending that it was a thousand years from now, from here, and I was walking on a green savanna filed with huge herbivores and fierce predators and condors half the size of planes. It was really rather funny, I realized. Funny-strange. All the work I'd done on the project, all the hours invested—the caffeine and the pills and the runaway tensions, too—and this was the first time I'd imagined myself as being part of that landscape. It was so strange to realize that fact, and after a while the phone quit singing, and the room was quiet, and I could smell the faint stink of grass burning somewhere.

MATTER'S END

Gregory Benford

Here's a taut and engrossing story that's either about The End of Everything or The Start of It All, depending on the way you *look* at it. . . .

Gregory Benford is one of the modern giants of the field. His 1980 novel *Timescape* won the Nebula Award, the John W. Campbell Memorial Award, the British Science Fiction Association Award, and the Australian Ditmar Award, and is widely considered to be one of the classic novels of the last two decades. His other novels include *The Stars in Shroud, In the Ocean of Night, Against Infinity, Artifact*, and *Across the Sea of Suns*. His most recent novels are the best-selling *Great Sky River*, and *Tides of Light*. His story "Alphas" appeared in our Seventh Annual Collection. Benford is a professor of physics at the University of California at Irvine.

When Dr. Samuel Johnson felt himself getting tied up in an argument over Bishop Berkeley's ingenious sophistry to prove the nonexistence of matter, and that everything in the universe is merely ideal, he kicked a large stone and answered, "I refute it thus." Just what that action assured him of is not very obvious, but apparently he found it comforting.
—Sir Arthur Eddington

India came to him first as a breeze like soured buttermilk, rich yet tainted. A door banged somewhere, sending gusts sweeping through the Bangalore airport, slicing through the 4 A.M. silences.

Since the Free State of Bombay had left India, Bangalore had become an international airport. Yet the damp caress seemed to erase the sterile signatures that made all big airports alike, even giving a stippled texture to the cool enamel glow of the fluorescents.

The moist air clasped Robert Clay like a stranger's sweaty palm. The ripe, fleshy aroma of a continent enfolded him, swarming up his nostrils and soaking his lungs with sullen spice. He put down his carry-on bag and showed the immigration clerk his passport. The man gave him a piercing, ferocious stare—then mutely slammed a rubber stamp onto the pages and handed it back.

A hand snagged him as he headed toward baggage claim.

"Professor Clay?" The face was dark olive with intelligent eyes riding above sharp cheekbones. A sudden white grin flashed as Clay nodded. "Ah, *good*. I am Dr. Sudarshan Patil. Please come this way."

Dr. Patil's tone was polite, but his hands impatiently pulled Clay away from the sluggish lines, through a battered wooden side door. The heavy-lidded immigration guards were carefully looking in other directions, hands held behind their backs. Apparently they had been paid off and would ignore this odd exit. Clay was still groggy from trying to sleep on the flight from London. He shook his head as Patil led him into the gloom of a baggage storeroom.

"Your clothes," Patil said abruptly.

"What?"

"They mark you as a Westerner. Quickly!"

Patil's hands, light as birds in the quilted soft light, were already plucking at his coat, his shirt. Clay was taken aback at this abruptness. He hesitated, then struggled out of the dirty garments, pulling his loose slacks down over his shoes. He handed his bundled clothes to Patil, who snatched them away without a word.

"You're welcome," Clay said. Patil took no notice, just thrust a wad of tan cotton at him. The man's eyes jumped at each distant sound in the storage room, darting, suspecting every pile of dusty bags.

Clay struggled into the pants and rough shirt. They looked dingy in the wan yellow glow of a single distant fluorescent tube.

"Not the reception I'd expected," Clay said, straightening the baggy pants and pulling at the rough drawstring.

"These are not good times for scientists in my country, Dr. Clay," Patil said bitingly. His voice carried that odd lilt that echoed both the Raj and Cambridge.

"Who're you afraid of?"

"Those who hate Westerners and their science."

"They said in Washington—"

"We are about great matters, Professor Clay. Please cooperate, please."

Patil's lean face showed its bones starkly, as though energies pressed outward. Promontories of bunched muscle stretched a mottled canvas skin. He started toward a far door without another word, carrying Clay's overnight bag and jacket.

"Say, where're we—"

Patil swung open a sheet-metal door and beckoned. Clay slipped through it and into the moist wealth of night. His feet scraped on a dirty sidewalk beside a black tar road. The door hinge squealed behind them, attracting the attention of a knot of men beneath a vibrant yellow streetlight nearby.

The bleached fluorescence of the airport terminal was now a continent away. Beneath a line of quarter-ton trucks huddled figures slept. In the astringent street-lamp glow he saw a decrepit green Korean Tochat van parked at the curb.

"In!" Patil whispered.

The men under the streetlight started walking toward them, calling out hoarse questions.

Clay yanked open the van's sliding door and crawled into the second row of seats. A fog of unknown pungent smells engulfed him. The driver, a short man, hunched over the wheel. Patil sprang into the front seat and the van ground away, its low gear whining.

Shouts. A stone thumped against the van roof. Pebbles rattled at the back.

They accelerated, the engine clattering. A figure loomed up from the shifting shadows and flung muck against the window near Clay's face. He jerked back at the slap of it. "Damn!"

They plowed through a wide puddle of dirty rainwater. The engine sputtered and for a moment Clay was sure it would die. He looked out the rear window and saw vague forms running after them. Then the engine surged again and they shot away.

They went two blocks through hectic traffic. Clay tried to get a clear look at India outside, but all he could see in the starkly shadowed street were the crisscrossings of three-wheeled taxis and human-drawn rickshaws. He got an impression of incessant activity, even in this desolate hour. Vehicles leaped out of the murk as headlights swept across them and then vanished utterly into the moist shadows again.

They suddenly swerved around a corner beneath spreading, gloomy trees. The van jolted into deep potholes and jerked to a stop. "Out!" Patil called.

Clay could barely make out a second van at the curb ahead. It was blue and caked with mud, but even in the dim light would not be confused with their green one. A rotting fetid reek filled his nose as he got out the side door, as if masses of overripe vegetation loomed in the shadows. Patil tugged him into the second van. In a few seconds they went surging out through a narrow, brick-lined alley.

"Look, what—"

"Please, quiet," Patil said primly. "I am watching carefully now to be certain that we are not being followed."

They wound through a shantytown warren for several minutes. Their headlights picked up startled eyes that blinked from what Clay at first had taken to be bundles of rags lying against the shacks. They seemed impossibly small even to be children. Huddled against decaying tin lean-tos, the dim forms often did not stir even as the van splashed dirty water on them from potholes.

Clay began, "Look, I understand the need for—"

"I apologize for our rude methods, Dr. Clay," Patil said. He gestured at the driver. "May I introduce Dr. Singh?"

Singh was similarly gaunt and intent, but with bushy hair and a thin, pointed nose. He jerked his head aside to peer at Clay, nodded twice like a puppet on strings, and then quickly stared back at the narrow lane ahead. Singh kept the van at a steady growl, abruptly yanking it around corners. A wooden cart lurched out of their way, its driver swearing in a strident singsong.

"Welcome to India," Singh said with reedy solemnity. "I am afraid circumstances are not the best."

"Uh, right. You two are heads of the project, they told me at the NSF."

"Yes," Patil said archly, "the project which officially no longer exists and unofficially is a brilliant success. It is amusing!"

"Yeah," Clay said cautiously, "we'll see."

"Oh, you will see," Singh said excitedly. "We have the events! More all the time."

Patil said precisely, "We would not have suggested that your National Science Foundation send an observer to confirm our findings unless we believed them to be of the highest importance."

"You've seen proton decay?"

Patil beamed. "Without doubt."

"Damn."

"Exactly."

"What mode?"

"The straightforward pion and positron decay products."

Clay smiled, reserving judgment. Something about Patil's almost prissy precision made him wonder if this small, beleaguered team of Indian physicists might actually have brought it off. An immense long shot, of course, but possible. There were much bigger groups of particle physicists in Europe and the U.S. who had tried to detect proton decay using underground swimming pools of pure water. Those experiments had enjoyed all the benefits of the latest electronics. Clay had worked on the big American project in a Utah salt mine, before lean budgets and lack of results closed it down. It would be galling if this lone, underfunded Indian scheme had finally done it. Nobody at the NSF believed the story coming out of India.

Patil smiled at Clay's silence, a brilliant slash of white in the murk. Their headlights picked out small panes of glass stuck seemingly at random in nearby hovels, reflecting quick glints of yellow back into the van. The night seemed misty; their headlights forked ahead. Clay thought a soft rain had started outside, but then he saw that thousands of tiny insects darted into their headlights. Occasionally big ones smacked against the windshield.

Patil carefully changed the subject. "I . . . believe you will pass unnoticed, for the most part."

"I look Indian?"

"I hope you will not take offense if I remark that you do not. We requested an Indian, but your NSF said they did not have anyone qualified."

"Right. Nobody who could hop on a plane, anyway." *Or would*, he added to himself.

"I understand. You are a compromise. If you will put this on . . ." Patil handed Clay a floppy khaki hat. "It will cover your curly hair. Luckily, your nose is rather more narrow than I had expected when the NSF cable announced they were sending a Negro."

"Got a lot of white genes in it, this nose," Clay said evenly.

"Please, do not think I am being racist. I simply wished to diminish the chances of you being recognized as a Westerner in the countryside."

"Think I can pass?"

"At a distance, yes."

"Be tougher at the site?"

"Yes. There are 'celebrants,' as they term themselves, at the mine."

"How'll we get in?"

"A ruse we have devised."

"Like that getaway back there? That was pretty slick."

Singh sent them jouncing along a rutted lane. Withered trees leaned against the pale stucco two-story buildings that lined the lane like children's blocks lined up not quite correctly. "Men in customs, they would give word to people outside. If you had gone through with the others, a different reception party would have been waiting for you."

"I see. But what about my bags?"

Patil had been peering forward at the gloomy jumble of buildings. His head jerked around to glare at Clay. "You were not to bring more than your carry-on bag!"

"Look, I can't get by on that. Chrissake, that'd give me just one change of clothes—"

"You left bags there?"

"Well, yeah, I had just one—"

Clay stopped when he saw the look on the two men's faces.

Patil said with strained clarity, "Your bags, they had identification tags?"

"Sure, airlines make you—"

"They will bring attention to you. There will be inquiries. The devotees will hear of it, inevitably, and know you have entered the country."

Clay licked his lips. "Hell, I didn't think it was so important."

The two lean Indians glanced at each other, their faces taking on a narrowing, leaden cast. "Dr. Clay," Patil said stiffly, "the 'celebrants' believe, as do many, that Westerners deliberately destroyed our crops with their biotechnology."

"Japanese companies' biologists did that, I thought," Clay said diplomatically.

"Perhaps. Those who disturb us at the Kolar gold mine make no fine distinctions between biologists and physicists. They believe that we are disturbing the very bowels of the earth, helping to further the destruction, bringing on the very end of the world itself. Surely you can see that in India, the mother country of religious philosophy, such matters are important."

"But your work, hell, it's not a matter of life or death or anything."

"On the contrary, the decay of the proton is precisely an issue of death."

Clay settled back in his seat, puzzled, watching the silky night stream by, cloaking vague forms in its shadowed mysteries.

2

Clay insisted on the telephone call. A wan winter sun had already crawled partway up the sky before he awoke, and the two Indian physicists wanted to leave immediately. They had stopped while still in Bangalore, holing up in the cramped apartment of one of Patil's graduate students. As Clay took his first sip of tea, two other students had turned up with his bag, retrieved at a cost he never knew.

Clay said, "I promised I'd call home. Look, my family's worried. They read the papers, they know the trouble here."

Shaking his head slowly, Patil finished a scrap of curled brown bread that appeared to be his only breakfast. His movements had a smooth liquid inertia, as if the sultry morning air oozed like jelly around him. They were sitting at a low table that had one leg too short; the already rickety table kept lurching, slopping tea into their saucers. Clay had looked for something to prop up the leg, but the apartment was bare, as though no one lived here. They had slept on pallets beneath a single bare bulb. Through the open windows, bare of frames or glass, Clay had gotten fleeting glimpses of the neighborhood— rooms of random clutter, plaster peeling off slumped walls, revealing the thin steel cross-ribs of the buildings, stained windows adorned with gaudy pictures of many-armed gods, already sun-bleached and frayed. Children yelped and cried below, their voices reflected among the odd angles and apertures of the tangled streets, while carts rattled by and bare feet slapped the stones. Students had apparently stood guard last night, though Clay had never seen more than a quick motion in the shadows below as they arrived.

"You ask much of us," Patil said. By morning light his walnut-brown face seemed gullied and worn. Lines radiated from his mouth toward intense eyes.

Clay sipped his tea before answering. A soft, strangely sweet smell wafted through the open window. They sat well back in the room so nobody could see in from the nearby buildings. He heard Singh tinkering downstairs with the van's engine.

"Okay, it's maybe slightly risky. But I want my people to know I got here all right."

"There are few telephones here."

"I only need one."

"The system, often it does not work at all."

"Gotta try."

"Perhaps you do not understand—"

"I understand damn well that if I can't even reach my people, I'm not going to hang out here for long. And if I don't see that your experiment works right, nobody'll believe you."

"And your opinion depends upon . . . ?"

Clay ticked off points on his fingers. "On seeing the apparatus. Checking your raw data. Running a trial case to see your system response. Then a null experiment—to verify your threshold level on each detector." He held up five fingers. "The works."

Patil said gravely, "Very good. We relish the opportunity to prove ourselves."

"You'll get it." Clay hoped to himself that they were wrong, but he suppressed that. He represented the faltering forefront of particle physics, and it would be embarrassing if a backwater research team had beaten the world. Still, either way, he would end up being the expert on the Kolar program, and that was a smart career move in itself.

"Very well. I must make arrangements for the call, then. But I truly—"

"Just do it. Then we get down to business."

The telephone was behind two counters and three doors at a Ministry for Controls office. Patil did the bribing and cajoling inside and then brought Clay in from the back of the van. He had been lying down on the back seat so he could not be seen easily from the street.

The telephone itself was a heavy black plastic thing with a rotary dial that clicked like a sluggish insect as it whirled. Patil had been on it twice already, clearing international lines through Bombay. Clay got two false rings and a dead line. On the fourth try he heard a faint, somehow familiar buzzing. Then a hollow, distant click.

"Angy?"

"Daddy, is that you?" Faint rock music in the background.

"Sure, I just wanted to let you know I got to India okay."

"Oh, Mommy will be so glad! We heard on the TV last night that there's trouble over there."

Startled, Clay asked, "What? Where's your mother?"

"Getting groceries. She'll be so mad she missed your call!"

"You tell her I'm fine, okay? But what trouble?"

"Something about a state leaving India. Lots of fighting, John Trimble said on the news."

Clay never remembered the names of news announcers; he regarded them as faceless nobodies reading prepared scripts, but for his daughter they were the voice of authority. "Where?"

"Uh, the lower part."

"There's nothing like that happening here, honey. I'm safe. Tell Mommy."

"People have ice cream there?"

"Yeah, but I haven't seen any. You tell your mother what I said, remember? About being safe?"

"Yes, she's been worried."

"Don't worry, Angy. Look, I got to go." The line popped and hissed ominously.

"I miss you, Daddy."

"I miss you double that. No, squared."

She laughed merrily. "I skinned my knee today at recess. It bled so much I had to go to the nurse."

"Keep it clean, honey. And give your mother my love."

"She'll be *so* mad."

"I'll be home soon."

She giggled and ended with the joke she had been using lately. "G'bye, Daddy. It's been real."

Her light laugh trickled into the static, a grace note from a bright land worlds away. Clay chuckled as he replaced the receiver. She cut the last word of "real nice" to make her good-byes hip and sardonic, a mannerism she had heard on television somewhere. An old joke; he had heard that even "groovy" was coming back in.

Clay smiled and pulled his hat down further and went quickly out into the street where Patil was waiting. India flickered at the edge of his vision, the crowds a hovering presence.

3

They left Bangalore in two vans. Graduate students drove the green Tochat from the previous night. He and Patil and Singh took the blue one, Clay again keeping out of sight by lying on the back seat. The day's raw heat rose around them like a shimmering lake of light.

They passed through lands leached of color. Only gray stubble grew in the fields. Trees hung limply, their limbs bowing as though exhausted. Figures in rags huddled for shade. A few stirred, eyes white in the shadows, as the vans ground past. Clay saw that large boles sat on the branches like gnarled knots with brown sheaths wrapped around the underside.

"Those some of the plant diseases I heard about?" he asked.

Singh pursed his lips. "I fear those are the pouches like those of wasps, as reported in the press." His watery eyes regarded the withered, graying trees as Patil slowed the car.

"Are they dangerous?" Clay could see yellow sap dripping from the underside of each.

"Not until they ripen," Singh said. "Then the assassins emerge."

"They look pretty big already."

"They are said to be large creatures, but of course there is little experience."

Patil downshifted and they accelerated away with an occasional sputtering misfire. Clay wondered whether they had any spare spark plugs along. The fields on each side of the road took on a dissolute and shredded look. "Did the genetech experiments cause this?" he asked.

Singh nodded. "I believe this emerged from the European programs. First we had their designed plants, but then pests found vulnerability. They sought strains which could protect crops from the new pests. So we got these wasps.

I gather that now some error or mutation has made them equally excellent at preying on people and even cows."

Clay frowned. "The wasps came from the Japanese aid, didn't they?"

Patil smiled mysteriously. "You know a good deal about our troubles, sir."

Neither said anything more. Clay was acutely conscious that his briefing in Washington had been detailed technical assessments, without the slightest mention of how the Indians themselves saw their problems. Singh and Patil seemed either resigned or unconcerned; he could not tell which. Their sentences refracted from some unseen nugget, like seismic waves warping around the earth's core.

"I would not worry greatly about these pouches," Singh said after they had ridden in silence for a while. "They should not ripen before we are done with our task. In any case, the Kolar fields are quite barren, and afford few sites where the pouches can grow."

Clay pointed out the front window. "Those round things on the walls—more pouches?"

To his surprise, both men burst into merry laughter. Gasping, Patil said, "Examine them closely, Doctor Clay. Notice the marks of the species which made them."

Patil slowed the car and Clay studied the round, circular pads on the whitewashed vertical walls along the road. They were brown and matted and marked in a pattern of radial lines. Clay frowned and then felt enormously stupid: the thick lines were handprints.

"Drying cakes, they are," Patil said, still chuckling.

"Of what?"

"Dung, my colleague. We use the cow here, not merely slaughter it."

"What for?"

"Fuel. After the cakes dry, we stack them—see?" They passed a plastic-wrapped tower. A woman was adding a circular, annular tier of thick dung disks to the top, then carefully folding the plastic over it. "In winter they burn nicely."

"For heating?"

"And cooking, yes."

Seeing the look on Clay's face, Singh's eyes narrowed and his lips drew back so that his teeth were bright stubs. His eyebrows were long brush strokes that met the deep furrows of his frown. "Old ways are still often preferable to the new."

Sure, Clay thought, the past of cholera, plague, infanticide. But he asked with neutral politeness, "Such as?"

"Some large fish from the Amazon were introduced into our principal river three years ago to improve fishing yields."

"The Ganges? I thought it was holy."

"What is more holy than to feed the hungry?"

"True enough. Did it work?"

"The big fish, yes. They are delicious. A great delicacy."

"I'll have to try some," Clay said, remembering the thin vegetarian curry he had eaten at breakfast.

Singh said, "But the Amazon sample contained some minute eggs which none of the proper procedures eliminated. They were of a small species—the candiru, is that not the name?" he inquired politely of Patil.

"Yes," Patil said, "a little being who thrives mostly on the urine of larger fish. Specialists now believe that perhaps the eggs were inside the larger species, and so escaped detection."

Patil's voice remained calm and factual, although while he spoke he abruptly swerved to avoid a goat that spontaneously ambled onto the rough road. Clay rocked hard against the van's door, and Patil then corrected further to stay out of a gratuitous mudhole that seemed to leap at them from the rushing foreground. They bumped noisily over ruts at the road's edge and bounced back onto the tarmac without losing speed. Patil sat ramrod straight, hands turning the steering wheel lightly, oblivious to the wrenching effects of his driving.

"Suppose, Professor Clay, that you are a devotee," Singh said. "You have saved to come to the Ganges for a decade, for two. Perhaps you even plan to die there."

"Yeah, okay." Clay could not see where this was leading.

"You are enthused as you enter the river to bathe. You are perhaps profoundly affected. An intense spiritual moment. It is not uncommon to merge with the river, to inadvertently urinate into it."

Singh spread his hands as if to say that such things went without saying.

"Then the candiru will be attracted by the smell. It mistakes this great bountiful largess, the food it needs, as coming from a very great fish indeed. It excitedly swims up the stream of uric acid. Coming to your urethra, it swims like a snake into its burrow, as far up as it can go. You will see that the uric flow velocity will increase as the candiru makes its way upstream, inside you. When this tiny fish can make no further progress, some trick of evolution tells it to protrude a set of sidewise spines. So intricate!"

Singh paused a moment in smiling tribute to this intriguing facet of nature. Clay nodded, his mouth dry.

"These embed deeply in the walls and keep the candiru close to the source of what it so desires." Singh made short, delicate movements, his fingers jutting in the air. Clay opened his mouth, but said nothing.

Patil took them around a team of bullocks towing a wooden wagon and put in, "The pain is intense. Apparently there is no good treatment. Women—forgive this indelicacy—must be opened to get at the offending tiny fish before it swells and blocks the passage completely, having gorged itself insensate. Some men have an even worse choice. Their bladders are already engorged, having typically not been much emptied by the time the candiru enters. They must decide whether to attempt the slow procedure of poisoning the small thing and waiting for it to shrivel and withdraw its spines.

However, their bladders might burst before that, flooding their abdomens with urine and of course killing them. If there is not sufficient time . . ."

"Yes?" Clay asked tensely.

"Then the penis must be chopped off," Singh said, "with the candiru inside."

Through a long silence Clay rode, swaying as the car wove through limitless flat spaces of parched fields and ruined brick walls and slumped whitewashed huts. Finally he said hoarsely, "I . . . don't blame you for resenting the . . . well, the people who brought all this on you. The devotees—"

"They believe this apocalyptic evil comes from the philosophy which gave us modern science."

"Well, look, whoever brought over those fish—"

Singh's eyes widened with surprise. A startled grin lit his face like a sunrise. "Oh no, Professor Clay! We do not blame the errors, or else we would have to blame equally the successes!"

To Clay's consternation, Patil nodded sagely.

He decided to say nothing more. Washington had warned him to stay out of political discussions, and though he was not sure if this was such, or if the lighthearted way Singh and Patil had related their story told their true attitude, it seemed best to just shut up. Again Clay had the odd sensation that here the cool certainties of Western biology had become diffused, blunted, crisp distinctions rendered into something beyond the constraints of the world outside, all blurred by the swarming, dissolving currents of India. The tin-gray sky loomed over a plain of ripe rot. The urgency of decay here was far more powerful than the abstractions that so often filled his head, the digitized iconography of sputtering, splitting protons.

4

The Kolar gold fields were a long, dusty drive from Bangalore. The sway of the van made Clay sleepy in the back, jet lag pulling him down into fitful, shallow dreams of muted voices, shadowy faces, and obscure purpose. He awoke frequently amid the dry smells, lurched up to see dry farmland stretching to the horizon, and collapsed again to bury his face in the pillow he had made by wadding up a shirt.

They passed through innumerable villages that, after the first few, all seemed alike with their scrawny children, ramshackle sheds, tin roofs, and general air of sleepy dilapidation. Once, in a narrow town, they stopped as rickshaws and carts backed up. An emaciated cow with pink paper tassels on its horns stood square in the middle of the road, trembling. Shouts and honks failed to move it, but no one ahead made the slightest effort to prod it aside.

Clay got out of the van to stretch his legs, ignoring Patil's warning to stay hidden, and watched. A crowd collected, shouting and chanting at the cow but not touching it. The cow shook its head, peering at the road as if searching for grass, and urinated powerfully. A woman in a red sari rushed into the road, knelt, and thrust her hand into the full stream. She made a formal motion with her other hand and splashed some urine on her forehead and cheeks. Three other women had already lined up behind her, and each did the same. Disturbed, the cow waggled its head and shakily walked away. Traffic started up, and Clay climbed back into the van. As they ground out of the dusty town, Singh explained that holy bovine urine was widely held to have positive health effects.

"Many believe it settles stomach troubles, banishes headaches, even improves fertility," Singh said.

"Yeah, you could sure use more fertility." Clay gestured at the throngs that filled the narrow clay sidewalks.

"I am not so Indian that I cannot find it within myself to agree with you, Professor Clay," Singh said.

"Sorry for the sarcasm. I'm tired."

"Patil and I are already under a cloud simply because we are scientists, and therefore polluted with Western ideas."

"Can't blame Indians for being down on us. Things're getting rough."

"But you are a black man. You yourself were persecuted by Western societies."

"That was a while back."

"And despite it you have risen to a professorship."

"You do the work, you get the job." Clay took off his hat and wiped his brow. The midday heat pressed sweat from him.

"Then you do not feel alienated from Western ideals?" Patil put in.

"Hell no. Look, I'm not some sharecropper who pulled himself up from poverty. I grew up in Falls Church, Virginia. Father's a federal bureaucrat. Middle class all the way."

"I see," Patil said, eyes never leaving the rutted road. "Your race bespeaks an entirely different culture, but you subscribe to the program of modern rationalism."

Clay looked at them quizzically. "Don't you?"

"As scientists, of course. But that is not all of life."

"Um," Clay said.

A thousand times before he had endured the affably condescending attention of whites, their curious eyes searching his face. No matter what the topic, they somehow found a way to inquire indirectly after his *true* feelings, his *natural* emotions. And if he waved away these intrusions, there remained in their heavy-lidded eyes a subtle skepticism, doubts about his authenticity. Few gave him space to simply be a suburban man with darker skin, a man whose interior landscape was populated with the same icons of Middle America as their own. Hell, his family name came from slaves, given as a tribute to Henry Clay, a nineteenth-century legislator. He had never expected to run into stereotyping in India, for chrissakes.

Still, he was savvy enough to lard his talk with some homey touches, jimmy things up with collard greens and black-eyed peas and street jive. It might put them at ease.

"I believe a li'l rationality could help," he said.

"Um." Singh's thin mouth twisted doubtfully. "Perhaps you should regard India as the great chessboard of our times, Professor. Here we have arisen from the great primordial agrarian times, fashioned our gods from our soil and age. Then we had orderly thinking, with all its assumptions, thrust upon us by the British. Now they are all gone, and we are suspended between the miasmic truths of the past, and the failed strictures of the present."

Clay looked out the dirty window and suppressed a smile. Even the physicists here spouted mumbo jumbo. They even appeared solemnly respectful of the devotees, who were just crazies like the women by the cow. How could anything solid come out of such a swamp? The chances that their experiment was right dwindled with each lurching, damp mile.

They climbed into the long range of hills before the Kolar fields. Burned-tan grass shimmered in the prickly heat. Sugarcane fields and rice paddies stood bone dry. In the villages, thin figures shaded beneath awnings, canvas tents, lean-tos, watched them pass. Lean faces betrayed only dim, momentary interest, and Clay wondered if his uncomfortable disguise was necessary outside Bangalore.

Without stopping they ate their lunch of dried fruit and thin, brown bread. In a high hill town, Patil stopped to refill his water bottle at a well. Clay peered out and saw down an alley a gang of stick-figure boys chasing a dog. They hemmed it in, and the bedraggled hound fled yapping from one side of their circle to the other. The animal whined at each rebuff and twice lost its footing on the cobblestones, sprawling, only to scramble up again and rush on. It was a cruel game, and the boys were strangely silent, playing without laughter. The dog was tiring; they drew in their circle.

A harsh edge to the boys' shouts made Clay slide open the van door. Several men were standing beneath a rust-scabbed sheet-metal awning nearby, and their eyes widened when they saw his face. They talked rapidly among themselves. Clay hesitated. The boys down the alley rushed the dog. They grabbed it as it yapped futilely and tried to bite them. They slipped twine around its jaws and silenced it. Shouting, they hoisted it into the air and marched off.

Clay gave up and slammed the door. The men came from under the awning. One rapped on the window. Clay just stared at them. One thumped on the door. Gestures, loud talk.

Patil and Singh came running, shouted something. Singh pushed the men away, chattering at them while Patil got the van started. Singh slammed the door in the face of a man with wild eyes. Patil gunned the engine and they ground away.

"They saw me and—"

"Distrust of outsiders is great here," Singh said. "They may be connected with the devotees, too."

"Guess I better keep my hat on."

"It would be advisable."

"I don't know, those boys—I was going to stop them pestering that dog. Stupid, I guess, but—"

"You will have to avoid being sentimental about such matters," Patil said severely.

"Uh—sentimental?"

"The boys were not playing."

"I don't—"

"They will devour it," Singh said.

Clay blinked. "Hindus eating meat?"

"Hard times. I am really quite surprised that such an animal has survived this long," Patil said judiciously. "Dogs are uncommon. I imagine it was wild, living in the countryside, and ventured into town in search of garbage scraps."

The land rose as Clay watched the shimmering heat bend and flex the seemingly solid hills.

5

They pulled another dodge at the mine. The lead green van veered off toward the main entrance, a cluster of concrete buildings and conveyer assemblies. From a distance, the physicists in the blue van watched a ragtag group envelop the van before it had fully stopped.

"Devotees," Singh said abstractedly. "They search each vehicle for evidence of our research."

"Your graduate students, the mob'll let them pass?"

Patil peered through binoculars. "The crowd is administering a bit of a pushing about," he said in his oddly cadenced accent, combining lofty British diction with a singsong lilt.

"Damn, won't the mine people get rid—"

"Some mine workers are among the crowd, I should imagine," Patil said. "They are beating the students."

"Well, can't we—"

"No time to waste." Singh waved them back into the blue van. "Let us make use of this diversion."

"But we could—"

"The students made their sacrifice for you. Do not devalue it, please."

Clay did not take his eyes from the nasty knot of confusion until they lurched over the ridgeline. Patil explained that they had been making regular runs to the main entrance for months now, to establish a pattern that drew devotees away from the secondary entrance.

"All this was necessary, and insured that we could bring in a foreign inspector," Patil concluded. Clay awkwardly thanked him for the attention to detail. He wanted to voice his embarrassment at having students roughed up simply to provide him cover, but something in the offhand manner of the two Indians made him hold his tongue.

The secondary entrance to the Kolar mine was a wide, tin-roofed shed like a low aircraft hangar. Girders crisscrossed it at angles that seemed to Clay dictated less by the constraints of mechanics than by the whims of the construction team. Cables looped among the already rusting steel struts and sang low notes in the rot-tinged wind that brushed his hair.

Monkeys chattered and scampered high in the struts. The three men walked into the shed, carrying cases. The cables began humming softly. The weave above their heads tightened with pops and sharp cracks. Clay realized that the seemingly random array was a complicated hoist that had started to pull the elevator up from miles beneath their feet. The steel lattice groaned as if it already knew how much work it had to do.

When it arrived, he saw that the elevator was a huge rattling box that reeked of machine oil. Clay lugged his cases in. The walls were broad wooden slats covered with chicken wire. Heat radiated from them. Patil stabbed a button on the big control board and they dropped quickly. The numbers of the levels zipped by on an amber digital display. A single dim yellow bulb cast shadows onto the wire. At the fifty-third level the bulb went out. The elevator did not stop.

In the enveloping blackness Clay felt himself lighten, as if the elevator was speeding up.

"Do not be alarmed," Patil called. "This frequently occurs."

Clay wondered if he meant the faster fall or the light bulb. In the complete dark, he began to see blue phantoms leaping out from nowhere.

Abruptly he became heavy—and thought of Einstein's *Gedanken* experiment, which equated a man in an accelerating elevator to one standing on a planet. Unless Clay could see outside, check that the massive earth raced by beyond as it clasped him further into its depths, in principle he could be in either situation. He tried to recall how Einstein had reasoned from an imaginary elevator to deduce that matter curved space-time, and could not.

Einstein's elegant proof was impossibly far from the pressing truth of *this* elevator. Here Clay plunged in thick murk, a weight of tortured air prickling his nose, making sweat pop from his face. Oily, moist heat climbed into Clay's sinuses.

And he was not being carried aloft by this elevator, but allowed to plunge into heavy, primordial darkness—Einstein's vision in reverse. No classical coolness separated him from the press of a raw, random world. That European mindscape—Galileo's crisp cylinders rolling obediently down inclined planes, Einstein's dispassionate observers surveying their smooth geometries like scrupulous bank clerks—evaporated here like yesterday's stale champagne. Sudden anxiety filled his throat. His stomach tightened and he tasted acrid gorge. He opened his mouth to shout, and as if to stop him, his own knees sagged with suddenly returning weight, physics regained.

A rattling thump—and they stopped. He felt Patil slam aside the rattling gate. A sullen glow beyond bathed an ornate brass shrine to a Hindu god. They came out into a steepled room of carved rock. Clay felt a breath of slightly cooler air from a cardboard-mouthed conduit nearby.

"We must force the air down from above." Patil gestured. "Otherwise this would read well over a hundred and ten Fahrenheit." He proudly pointed to an ancient battered British thermometer, whose mercury stood at ninety-eight.

They trudged through several tunnels, descended another few hundred feet on a ramp, and then followed gleaming railroad tracks. A white bulb every ten meters threw everything into exaggerated relief, shadows stabbing everywhere. A brown cardboard sign proclaimed from the ceiling:

FIRST EVER COSMIC RAY NEUTRINO INTERACTION
RECORDED HERE IN APRIL 1965

For over forty years, teams of devoted Indian physicists had labored patiently inside the Kolar gold fields. For half a century, India's high mountains and deep mines had made important cosmic-ray experiments possible with inexpensive instruments. Clay recalled how a joint Anglo-Indian-Japanese team had detected that first neutrino, scooped it from the unending cosmic sleet that penetrated even to this depth. He thought of unsung Indian physicists sweating here, tending the instruments and tracing the myriad sources of background error. Yet they themselves were background for the original purpose of the deep holes: Two narrow cars clunked past, full of chopped stone.

"Some still work this portion," Patil's clear voice cut through the muffled air. "Though I suspect they harvest little."

Pushing the rusty cars were four wiry men, so sweaty that the glaring bulbs gave their sliding muscles a hard sheen like living stone. They wore filthy cloths wrapped around their heads, as if they needed protection against the low ceiling rather than the heat. As Clay stumbled on, he felt that there might be truth to this, because he sensed the mass above as a precarious judgment over them all, a sullen presence. Einstein's crisp distinctions, the clean certainty of the *Gedanken* experiments, meant nothing in this blurred air.

They rounded an irregular curve and met a niche neatly cut off by a chain-link fence.

PROTON STABILITY EXPERIMENT
TATA INSTITUTE OF FUNDAMENTAL RESEARCH, BOMBAY
80th Level Heathcote Shaft, KFG
2300 meters depth

These preliminaries done, the experiment itself began abruptly. Clay had expected some assembly rooms, an office, refrigerated 'scope cages. Instead, a few meters ahead the tunnel opened in all directions. They stood before a huge bay roughly cleaved from the brown rock.

And filling the vast volume was what seemed to be a wall as substantial as the rock itself. It was an iron grid of rusted pipe. The pipes were square, not round, and dwindled into the distance. Each had a dusty seal, a pressure dial, and a number painted in white. Clay estimated them to be at least a hundred feet long. They were stacked Lincoln-log fashion. He walked to the edge of the bay and looked down. Layers of pipe tapered away below to a distant floodlit floor and soared to meet the gray ceiling above.

"Enormous," he said.

"We expended great effort in scaling up our earlier apparatus," Singh said enthusiastically.

"As big as a house."

Patil said merrily, "An American house, perhaps. Ours are smaller."

A woman's voice nearby said, "And nothing lives in this iron house, Professor Clay."

Clay turned to see a willowy Indian woman regarding him with a wry smile. She seemed to have come out of the shadows, a brown apparition in shorts and a scrupulously white blouse, appearing fullblown where a moment before there had been nothing. Her heavy eyebrows rose in amusement.

"Ah, this is Mrs. Buli," Patil said.

"I keep matters running here, while my colleagues venture into the world," she said.

Clay accepted her coolly offered hand. She gave him one quick, well-defined shake and stepped back. "I can assist your assessment, perhaps."

"I'll need all your help," he said sincerely. The skimpy surroundings already made him wonder if he could do his job at all.

"Labor we have," she said. "Equipment, little."

"I brought some cross-check programs with me," he said.

"Excellent," Mrs. Buli said. "I shall have several of my graduate students assist you, and of course I offer my full devotion as well."

Clay smiled at her antique formality. She led him down a passage into the soft fluorescent glow of a large data-taking room. It was crammed with terminals and a bank of disk drives, all meshed by the usual cable spaghetti. "We keep our computers cooler than our staff, you see," Mrs. Buli said with a small smile.

They went down a ramp, and Clay could feel the rock's steady heat. They came out onto the floor of the cavern. Thick I-beams roofed the stone box.

"Over a dozen lives, that was the cost of this excavation," Singh said.

"That many?"

"They attempted to save on the cost of explosives," Patil said with a stern look.

"Not that such will matter in the long run," Singh said mildly. Clay chose not to pursue the point.

Protective bolts studded the sheer rock, anchoring cross-beams that stabilized the tower of pipes. Scaffolding covered some sections of the blocky, rusty pile. Blasts of compressed air from the surface a mile above swept down on them from the ceiling, flapping Clay's shirt.

Mrs. Buli had to shout, the effort contorting her smooth face. "We obtained the pipes from a government program that attempted to improve the quality of plumbing in the cities. A failure, I fear. But a godsend for us."

Patil was pointing out electrical details when the air conduits wheezed into silence. "Hope that's temporary," Clay said in the sudden quiet.

"A minor repair, I am sure," Patil said.

"These occur often," Singh agreed earnestly.

Clay could already feel prickly sweat oozing from him. He wondered how often they had glitches in the circuitry down here, awash in pressing heat, and how much that could screw up even the best diagnostics.

Mrs. Buli went on in a lecturer's singsong. "We hired engineering students—there are many such, an oversupply—to thread a single wire down the bore of each pipe. We sealed each, then welded them together to make lengths of a hundred feet. Then we filled them with argon and linked them with a high-voltage line. We have found that a voltage of 280 keV . . ."

Clay nodded, filing away details, noting where her description differed from that of the NSF. The Kolar group had continuously modified their experiment for decades, and this latest enormous expansion was badly documented. Still, the principle was simple. Each pipe was held at high voltage, so that when a charged particle passed through, a spark leaped. A particle's path was followed by counting the segments of triggered pipes. This mammoth stack of iron was a huge Geiger counter.

He leaned back, nodding at Buli's lecture, watching a team of men at the very top. A loud clang rang through the chasm. Sparks showered, burnt-orange and blue. The garish plumes silhouetted the welders and sent cascades of sparks down through the lattice of pipes. For an instant Clay imagined he was witnessing cosmic rays sleeting down through the towering house of iron, illuminating it with their short, sputtering lives.

"—and I am confident that we have seen well over fifty true events," Mrs. Buli concluded with a jaunty upward tilt of her chin.

"What?" Clay struggled back from his daydreaming. "That many?"

She laughed, a high tinkling. "You do not believe!"

"Well, that is a lot."

"Our detecting mass is now larger," Mrs. Buli said.

"Last we heard it was five hundred tons," Clay said carefully. The claims wired to the NSF and the Royal Society had been skimpy on details.

"That was years ago," Patil said. "We have redoubled our efforts, as you can see."

"Well, to see that many decays, you'd have to have a hell of a lot of observing volume," Clay said doubtfully.

"We can boast of five *thousand* tons, Professor Clay," Mrs. Buli said.

"Looks it," Clay said laconically to cover his surprise. It would not do to let them think they could overwhelm him with magnitudes. Question was, did they have the telltale events?

The cooling air came on with a thump and *whoosh*. Clay breathed it in deeply, face turned up to the iron house where protons might be dying, and sucked in swarming scents of the parched countryside miles above.

6

He knew from the start that there would be no eureka moment. Certainty was the child of tedium.

He traced the tangled circuitry for two days before he trusted it. "You got to open the sack 'fore I'll believe there's a cat in there," he told Mrs. Buli, and then had to explain that he was joking.

Then came a three-day trial run, measuring the exact sputter of decay from a known radioactive source. System response was surprisingly good. He found their techniques needlessly Byzantine, but workable. His null checks of the detectors inside the pipes came up goose-egg clean.

Care was essential. Proton decay was rare. The Grand Unified Theories which had enjoyed such success in predicting new particles had also sounded a somber note through all of physics. Matter was mortal. But not very mortal, compared with the passing flicker of a human lifetime.

The human body had about 10^{29} neutrons and protons in it. If only a tiny fraction of them decayed in a human lifetime, the radiation from the disintegration would quickly kill everyone of cancer. The survival of even small life-forms implied that the protons inside each nucleus had to survive an average of nearly a billion billion years.

So even before the Grand Unified Theories, physicists knew that protons lived long. The acronym for the theories was GUTs, and a decade earlier graduate students like Clay had worn T-shirts with insider jokes like IT TAKES GUTS TO DO PARTICLE PHYSICS. But proving that there was some truth to the lame nerd jests took enormous effort.

The simplest of the GUTs predicted a proton lifetime of about 10^{31} years, immensely greater than the limit set by the existence of life. In fact, it was far longer even than the age of the universe, which was only a paltry 2×10^{10} years old.

One could check this lifetime by taking one proton and watching it for

10^{31} years. Given the short attention span of humans, it was better to assemble 10^{31} protons and watch them for a year, hoping one would fizzle.

Physicists in the United States, Japan, Italy, and India had done that all through the 1980s and 1990s. And no protons had died.

Well, the theorists had said, the mathematics must be more complicated. They discarded certain symmetry groups and thrust others forward. The lifetime might be 10^{32} years, then.

The favored method of gathering protons was to use those in water. Western physicists carved swimming pools six stories deep in salt mines and eagerly watched for the characteristic blue pulse of dying matter. Detecting longer lifetimes meant waiting longer, which nobody liked, or adding more protons. Digging bigger swimming pools was easy, so attention had turned to the United States and Japan . . . but still, no protons died. The lifetime exceeded 10^{32} years.

The austerity of the 1990s had shut down the ambitious experiments in the West. Few remembered this forlorn experiment in Kolar, wedded to watching the cores of iron rods for the quick spurt of decay. When political difficulties cut off contact, the already beleaguered physicists in the West assumed the Kolar effort had ceased.

But Kolar was the deepest experiment, less troubled by the hail of cosmic rays that polluted the Western data. Clay came to appreciate that as he scrolled through the myriad event-plots in the Kolar computer cubes.

There were 9×10^9 recorded decays of all types. The system rejected obvious garbage events, but there were many subtle enigmas. Theory said that protons died because the quarks that composed them could change their identities. A seemingly capricious alteration of quarky states sent the proton asunder, spitting forth a zoo of fragments. Neutrons were untroubled by this, for in free space they decayed anyway, into a proton and electron. Matter's end hinged, finally, on the stability of the proton alone.

Clay saw immediately that the Kolar group had invested years in their software. They had already filtered out thousands of phantom events that imitated true proton decay. There were eighteen ways a proton could die, each with a different signature of spraying light and particle debris.

The delicate traceries of particle paths were recorded as flashes and sparkles in the house of iron outside. Clay searched through endless graphic printouts, filigrees woven from digital cloth.

"You will find we have pondered each candidate event," Mrs. Buli said mildly on the sixth day of Clay's labors.

"Yeah, the analysis is sharp," he said cautiously. He was surprised at the high level of the work but did not want to concede anything yet.

"If any ambiguity arose, we discarded the case."

"I can see that."

"Some pions were not detected in the right energy range, so of course we omitted those."

"Good."

Mrs. Buli leaned over to show him a detail of the cross-checking program, and he caught a heady trace of wildflowers. Her perfume reminded him abruptly that her sari wrapped over warm, ample swells. She had no sagging softness, no self-indulgent bulgings. The long oval of her face and her ample lips conveyed a fragile sensuality . . .

He wrenched his attention back to physics and stared hard at the screen.

Event vertices were like time-lapse photos of traffic accidents, intersections exploding, screaming into shards. The crystalline mathematical order of physics led to riots of incandescence. And Clay was judge, weighing testimony after the chaos.

7

He had insisted on analyzing the several thousand preliminary candidates himself, as a double blind against the Kolar group's software. After nine days, he had isolated sixty-seven events that looked like the genuine article.

Sixty-five of his agreed with Mrs. Buli's analysis. The two holdouts were close, Clay had to admit.

"Nearly on the money," he said reflectively as he stared at the Kolar software's array.

"You express such values," Mrs. Buli said. "Always a financial analogy."

"Just a way of speaking."

"Still, let us discard the two offending events."

"Well, I'd be willing—"

"No, no, we consider only the sixty-five." Her almond eyes gave no hint of slyness.

"They're pretty good bets, I'd say." Her eyebrows arched. "Only a manner of speech."

"Then you feel they fit the needs of theory."

Her carefully balanced way of phrasing made him lean forward, as if to compensate for his judge's role. "I'll have to consider all the other decay modes in detail. Look for really obscure processes that might mimic the real thing."

She nodded. "True, there is need to study such."

Protons could die from outside causes, too. Wraithlike neutrinos spewed forth by the sun penetrated even here, shattering protons. Murderous muons lumbered through as cosmic rays, plowing furrows of exploding nuclei.

Still, things looked good. He was surprised at their success, earned by great labor. "I'll be as quick about it as I can."

"We have prepared a radio link that we can use, should the desire come."

"Huh? What?"

"In case you need to reach your colleagues in America."

"Ah, yes."

To announce the result, he saw. To get the word out. But why the rush?

It occurred to him that they might doubt whether he himself would get out at all.

8

They slept each night in a clutch of tin lean-tos that cowered down a raw ravine. Laborers from the mine had slept there in better days, and the physicists had gotten the plumbing to work for an hour each night. The men slept in a long shed, but gave Clay a small wooden shack. He ate thin, mealy gruel with them each evening, carefully dropping purification tablets in his water, and was rewarded with untroubled bowels. He lost weight in the heat of the mine, but the nights were cool and the breezes that came then were soft with moisture.

The fifth evening, as they sat around a potbellied iron stove in the men's shed, Patil pointed to a distant corrugated metal hut and said, "There we have concealed a satellite dish. We can knock away the roof and transmit, if you like."

Clay brightened. "Can I call home?"

"If need be."

Something in Patil's tone told him a frivolous purpose was not going to receive their cooperation.

"Maybe tomorrow?"

"Perhaps. We must be sure that the devotees do not see us reveal it."

"They think we're laborers?"

"So we have convinced them, I believe."

"And me?"

"You would do well to stay inside."

"Um. Look, got anything to drink?"

Patil frowned. "Has the water pipe stopped giving?"

"No, I mean, you know—a drink. Gin and tonic, wasn't that what the Brits preferred?"

"Alcohol is the devil's urine," Patil said precisely.

"It won't scramble my brains."

"Who can be sure? The mind is a tentative instrument."

"You don't want any suspicion that I'm unreliable, that it?"

"No, of course not," Singh broke in anxiously.

"Needn't worry," Clay muttered. The heat below and the long hours of tedious work were wearing him down. "I'll be gone soon's I can get things wrapped up."

"You agree that we are seeing the decays?"

"Let's say things're looking better."

Clay had been holding back even tentative approval. He had expected some show of jubilation. Patil and Singh simply sat and stared into the flickering coals of the stove's half-open door.

Slowly Patil said, "Word will spread quickly."

"Soon as you transmit it on that dish, sure."

Singh murmured, "Much shall change."

"Look, you might want to get out of here, go present a paper—"

"Oh no, we shall remain," Singh said quickly.

"Those devotees could give you trouble if they find—"

"We expect that this discovery, once understood, shall have great effects," Patil said solemnly. "I much prefer to witness them from my home country."

The cadence and mood of this conversation struck Clay as odd, but he put it down to the working conditions. Certainly they had sacrificed a great deal to build and run this experiment amid crippling desolation.

"This result will begin the final renunciation of the materialistic worldview," Singh said matter-of-factly.

"Huh?"

"In peering at the individual lives of mere particles, we employ the reductionist hammer," Patil explained. "But nature is not like a salamander, cut into fragments."

"Or if it were," Singh added, "once the salamander is so sliced, try to make it do its salamander walk again." A broad white grin split the gloom of nightfall.

"The world is an implicate order, Dr. Clay. All parts are hinged to each other."

Clay frowned. He vaguely remembered a theory of quantum mechanics which used that term—"implicate order," meaning that a deeper realm of physical theory lay beneath the uncertainties of wave mechanics. Waves that took it into their heads to behave like particles, and the reverse—these were supposed to be illusions arising from our ignorance of a more profound theory. But there was no observable consequence of such notions, and to Clay such mumbo jumbo from theorists who never got their hands dirty was empty rhapsodizing. Still, he was supposed to be the diplomat here.

He gave a judicial nod. "Yeah, sure—but when the particles die, it'll all be gone, right?"

"Yes, in about 10^{34} years," Patil said. "But the *knowledge* of matter's mortality will spread as swiftly as light, on the wind of our transmitter."

"So?"

"You are an experimentalist, Dr. Clay, and thus—if you will forgive my putting it so—addicted to cutting the salamander." Patil made a steeple of his fingers, sending spindly shadows rippling across his face. "The world we study is conditioned by our perceptions of it. The implied order is partially from our own design."

"Sure, quantum measurement, uncertainty principle, all that." Clay had sat through all the usual lectures about this stuff and didn't feel like doing so again. Not in a dusty shed with his stomach growling from hunger. He sipped at his cup of weak Darjeeling and yawned.

"Difficulties of measurement reflect underlying problems," Patil said.

"Even the Westerner Plato saw that we perceive only imperfect modes of the true, deeper world."

"What deeper world?" Clay sighed despite himself.

"We do not know. We *cannot* know."

"Look, we make our measurements, we report. Period."

Amused, Singh said, "And that is where matters end?"

Patil said, "Consensual reality, that is your 'real' world, Professor Clay. But our news may cause that bland, unthinking consensus to falter."

Clay shrugged. This sounded like late-night college bullshit sessions among boozed-up science nerds. Patty-cake pantheism, quantum razzle-dazzle, garbage philosophy. It was one thing to be open-minded and another to let your brains fall out. Was *every*body on this wrecked continent a booga-booga type? He had to get out.

"Look, I don't see what difference—"

"Until the curtain of seeming surety is swept away," Singh put in.

"Surety?"

"This world—this universe!—has labored long under the illusion of its own permanence." Singh spread his hands, animated in the flickering yellow glow. "We might die, yes, the sun might even perish—but the universe went on. Now we prove otherwise. There cannot help but be profound reactions."

He thought he saw what they were driving at. "A Nobel Prize, even."

To his surprise, both men laughed merrily. "Oh no," Patil said, arching his eyebrows. "No such trifles are expected!"

9

The boxy meeting room beside the data bay was packed. From it came a subdued mutter, a fretwork of talk laced with anticipation.

Outside, someone had placed a small chalky statue of a grinning elephant. Clay hesitated, stroked it. Despite the heat of the mine, the elephant was cool.

"The workers just brought it down," Mrs. Buli explained with a smile. "Our Hindu god of auspicious beginnings."

"Or endings," Patil said behind her. "Equally."

Clay nodded and walked into the trapped, moist heat of the room. Everyone was jammed in, graduate students and laborers alike, their dhotis already showing sweaty crescents. Clay saw the three students the devotees had beaten and exchanged respectful bows with them.

Perceiving some need for ceremony, he opened with lengthy praise for the endless hours they had labored, exclaiming over how startled the world would be to learn of such a facility. Then he plunged into consideration of each candidate event, his checks and counter-checks, vertex corrections, digital-array flaws, mean free paths, ionization rates, the artful programming that deflected the myriad possible sources of error. He could feel tension rising in the room as he cast the events on the inch-thick wall screen, calling them forth from the files in his cubes. Some he threw into 3-D, to show the full path through the cage of iron that had captured the death rattle of infinity.

And at the end, all cases reviewed, he said quietly, "You have found it. The proton lifetime is very nearly 10^{34} years."

The room burst into applause, wide grins and wild shouts as everyone pressed forward to shake his hand.

10

Singh handled the message to the NSF. Clay also constructed a terse though detailed summary and sent it to the International Astronomical Union for release to the worldwide system of observatories and universities.

Clay knew this would give a vital assist to his career. With the Kolar team staying here, he would be their only spokesman. And this was very big, media-mesmerizing news indeed.

The result was important to physicists and astronomers alike, for the destiny of all their searches ultimately would be sealed by the faint failures of particles no eye would ever see. In 10^{34} years, far in the depths of space, the great celestial cities, the galaxies, would be ebbing. The last red stars would flicker, belch, and gutter out. Perhaps life would have clung to them and found a way to persist against the growing cold. Cluttered with the memorabilia of the ages, the islands of mute matter would turn at last to their final conqueror—not entropy's still hand, but this silent sputter of protons.

Clay thought of the headlines: UNIVERSE TO END. What would *that* do to harried commuters on their way to work?

He watched Singh send the stuttering messages via the big satellite dish, the corrugated tin roof of the shed pulled aside, allowing him to watch burnt-gold twilight seep across the sky. Clay felt no elation, as blank as a drained capacitor. He had gone into physics because of the sense it gave of grasping deep mysteries. He could look at bridges and trace the vectored stability that ruled them. When his daughter asked why the sky was blue, he actually knew, and could sketch out a simple answer. It had never occurred to him to fear flying, because he knew the Bernoulli equation for the pressure that held up the plane.

But this result . . .

Even the celebratory party that evening left him unmoved. Graduate students turned out in their best khaki. Sitar music swarmed through the scented air, ragas thumping and weaving. He found his body swaying to the refractions of tone and scale.

"It is a pity you cannot learn more of our country," Mrs. Buli remarked, watching him closely.

"Right now I'm mostly interested in sleep."

"Sleep is not always kind." She seemed wry and distant in the night's smudged humidity. "One of our ancient gods, Brahma, is said to sleep—and we are what he dreams."

"In that case, for you folks maybe he's been having a nightmare lately."

"Ah yes, our troubles. But do not let them mislead you about India. They pass."

"I'm sure they will," Clay replied, dutifully diplomatic.

"You were surprised, were you not, at the outcome?" she said piercingly.

"Uh, well, I had to be skeptical."

"Yes, for a scientist certainty is built on deep layers of doubt."

"Like my daddy said, in the retail business deal with everybody, but count your change."

She laughed. "We have given you a bargain, perhaps!"

He was acutely aware that his initial doubts must have been obvious. And what unsettled him now was not just the hard-won success here, but their strange attitude toward it.

The graduate students came then and tried to teach him a dance. He did a passable job, and a student named Venkatraman slipped him a glass of beer, forbidden vice. It struck Clay as comic that the Indian government spent much energy to suppress alcohol but did little about the population explosion. The students all laughed when he made a complicated joke about booze, but he could not be sure whether they meant it. The music seemed to quicken, his heart thumping to keep up with it. They addressed him as Clay*ji*, a term of respect, and asked his opinion of what they might do next with the experiment. He shrugged, thinking *'Nother job, sahib?* and suggested using it as a detector for neutrinos from supernovas. That had paid off when the earlier generation of neutrino detectors picked up the 1987 supernova.

The atom bomb, the 1987 event, now this—particle physics, he realized uncomfortably, was steeped in death. The sitar slid and rang, and Mrs. Buli made arch jokes to go with the spicy salad. Still, he turned in early.

11

To be awakened by a soft breeze. A brushing presence, sliding cloth . . . He sensed her sari as a luminous fog. Moonlight streaming through a lopsided window cast shimmering auras through the cloth as she loomed above him. Reached for him. Lightly flung away his sticky bedclothes.

"I—"

A soft hand covered his mouth, bringing a heady savor of ripe earth. His senses ran out of him and into the surrounding dark, coiling in air as he took her weight. She was surprisingly light, though thick-waisted, her breasts like teacups compared with the full curves of her hips. His hands slid and pressed, finding a delightful slithering moisture all over her, a sheen of vibrancy. Her sari evaporated. The high planes of her face caught vagrant blades of moonlight, and he saw a curious tentative, expectant expression there as she wrapped him in soft pressures. Her mouth did not so much kiss his as enclose it, formulating an argument of sweet rivulets that trickled into his porous self. She slipped into place atop him, a slick clasp that melted him up into her, a perfect fit, slick with dark insistence. He closed his eyes, but the glow diffused through his eyelids, and he could see her hair fanning through the air like motion underwater, her luxuriant weight bucking, trembling as her nails scratched his shoulders, musk rising smoky from them both. A silky muscle milked him at each heart-thump. Her velvet mass orbited above their fulcrum, bearing down with feathery demands, and he remembered brass icons, gaudy Indian posters, and felt above him Kali strumming in fevered darkness. She locked legs around him, squeezing him up into her surprisingly hard muscles, grinding, drawing forth, pushing back. She cried out with great heaves and lungfuls of the thickening air, mouth going slack beneath hooded eyes, and he shot sharply up into her, a convulsion that poured out all the knotted aches in him, delivering them into the tumbled steamy earth—

12

—and next, with no memories between, he was stumbling with her . . . down a gully . . . beneath slanting silvery moonlight.

"What—what's—"

"Quiet!" She shushed him like a schoolmarm.

He recognized the rolling countryside near the mine. Vague forms flitted in the distance. Wracked cries cut the night.

"The devotees," Mrs. Buli whispered as they stumbled on. "They have assaulted the mine entrance."

"How'd we—"

"You were difficult to rouse," she said with a sidelong glance.

Was she trying to be amusing? The sudden change from mysterious super-charged sensuality back to this clipped, formal professionalism disoriented him.

"Apparently some of our laborers had a grand party. It alerted the devotees to our presence, some say. I spoke to a laborer while you slept, however, who said that the devotees knew of your presence. They asked for you."

"Why me?"

"Something about your luggage and a telephone call home."

Clay gritted his teeth and followed her along a path that led among the slumped hills, away from their lodgings. Soon the mine entrance was visible below. Running figures swarmed about it like black gnats. Ragged chants erupted from them. A *waarrrk waarrrk* sound came from the hangar, and it was some moments until Clay saw long chains of human bodies hanging from the rafters, swinging themselves in unison.

"They're pulling down the hangar," he whispered.

"I despair for what they have done inside."

He instinctively reached for her and felt the supple warmth he had embraced seemingly only moments before. She turned and gave him her mouth again.

"We—back there—why'd you come to me?"

"It was time. Even we feel the joy of release from order, Professor Clay."

"Well, sure . . ." Clay felt illogically embarrassed, embracing a woman who still had the musk of the bed about her, yet who used his title. "But . . . how'd I get here? Seems like—"

"You were immersed. Taken out of yourself."

"Well, yeah, it was good, fine, but I can't remember anything."

She smiled. "The best moments leave no trace. That is a signature of the implicate order."

Clay breathed in the waxy air to help clear his head. More mumbo jumbo, he thought, delivered by her with an open, expectant expression. In the darkness it took a moment to register that she had fled down another path.

"Where'll we go?" he gasped when he caught up.

"We must get to the vans. They are parked some kilometers away."

"My gear—"

"Leave it."

He hesitated a moment, then followed her. There was nothing irreplaceable. It certainly wasn't worth braving the mob below for the stuff.

They wound down through bare hillsides dominated by boulders. The sky rippled with heat lightning. Puffy clouds scudded quickly in from the west, great ivory flashes working among them. The ground surged slightly.

"Earthquake?" he asked.

"There were some earlier, yes. Perhaps that has excited the devotees further tonight, put their feet to running."

There was no sign of the physics team. Pebbles squirted from beneath his boots—he wondered how he had managed to get them on without remembering it—and recalled again her hypnotic sensuality. Stones rattled away down into narrow dry washes on each side. Clouds blotted out the moonglow, and they had to pick their way along the trail.

Clay's mind spun with plans, speculations, jittery anxiety. Mrs. Buli was now his only link to the Western fragment of India, and he could scarcely see her in the shadows. She moved with liquid grace, her sari trailing, sandals slapping. Suddenly she crouched down. "More."

Along the path came figures bearing lanterns. They moved silently in the fitful silvery moonlight. There was no place to hide, and the party had already seen them.

"Stand still," she said. Again the crisp Western diction, yet her ample hips swayed slightly, reminding him of her deeper self.

Clay wished he had a club, a knife, anything. He made himself stand beside her, hands clenched. For once his blackness might be an advantage.

The devotees passed, eyes rapt. Clay had expected them to be singing or chanting mantras or rubbing beads—but not shambling forward as if to their doom. The column barely glanced at him. In his baggy cotton trousers and formless shirt, he hoped he was unremarkable. A woman passed nearby, apparently carrying something across her back. Clay blinked. Her hands were nailed to the ends of a beam, and she carried it proudly, palms bloody, half crucified. Her face was serene, eyes focused on the roiling sky. Behind her was a man bearing a plate. Clay thought the shambling figure carried marbles on the dish until he peered closer and saw an iris, and realized the entire plate was packed with eyeballs. He gasped and faces turned toward him. Then the man was gone along the path, and Clay waited, holding his breath against a gamy stench he could not name. Some muttered to themselves, some carried religious artifacts, beads and statuettes and drapery, but none had the fervor of the devotees he had seen before. The ground trembled again.

And out of the dark air came a humming. Something struck a man in the line and he clutched at his throat, crying hoarsely. Clay leaped forward without thinking. He pulled the man's hands away. Lodged in the narrow of the throat was something like an enormous cockroach with fluttering wings. It had already embedded its head in the man. Spiky legs furiously scrabbled against the soiled skin to dig deeper. The man coughed and shouted weakly, as though the thing was already blocking his throat.

Clay grabbed its hind legs and pulled. The insect wriggled with surprising strength. He saw the hind stinger too late. The sharp point struck a hot jolt of pain into his thumb. Anger boiled in him. He held on despite the pain and yanked the thing free. It made a sucking sound coming out. He hissed with revulsion and violently threw it down the hillside.

The man stumbled, gasping, and then ran back down the path, never even looking at them. Mrs. Buli grabbed Clay, who was staggering around in a circle, shaking his hand. "I will cut it!" she cried.

He held still while she made a precise cross cut and drained the blood. "What . . . what *was* that?"

"A wasp-thing from the pouches that hang on our trees."

"Oh yeah. One of those bio tricks."

"They are still overhead."

Clay listened to the drone hanging over them. Another devotee shrieked and slapped the back of his neck. Clay numbly watched the man run away. His hand throbbed, but he could feel the effects ebbing. Mrs. Buli tore a strip from her sari and wrapped his thumb to quell the bleeding.

All this time, devotees streamed past them in the gloom. None took the slightest notice of Clay. Some spoke to themselves.

"Western science doesn't seem to bother 'em much now," Clay whispered wryly.

Mrs. Buli nodded. The last figure to pass was a woman who limped, sporting an arm that ended not in a hand but in a spoon, nailed to a stub of cork.

He followed Mrs. Buli into enveloping darkness. "Who were they?"

"I do not know. They spoke seldom and repeated the same words. Dharma and samsara, terms of destiny."

"They don't care about us?"

"They appear to sense a turning, a resolution." In the fitful moonglow her eyes were liquid puzzles.

"But they destroyed the experiment."

"I gather that knowledge of your Western presence was like the wasp-things. Irritating, but only a catalyst, not the cause."

"What *did* make them—"

"No time. Come."

They hurriedly entered a thin copse of spindly trees that lined a streambed. Dust stifled his nose and he breathed through his mouth. The clouds raced toward the horizon with unnatural speed, seeming to flee from the west. Trees swayed before an unfelt wind, twisting and reaching for the shifting sky.

"Weather," Mrs. Buli answered his questions. "Bad weather."

They came upon a small crackling fire. Figures crouched around it, and Clay made to go around, but Mrs. Buli walked straight toward it. Women squatted, poking sticks into the flames. Clay saw that something moved on the sticks. A momentary shaft of moonlight showed the oily skin of snakes, tiny eyes crisp as crystals, the shafts poking from yawning white mouths that still moved. The women's faces of stretched yellow skin anxiously watched the blackening, sizzling snakes, turning them. The fire hissed as though raindrops fell upon it, but Clay felt nothing wet, just the dry rub of a fresh abrading wind. Smoke wrapped the women in gray wreaths, and Mrs. Buli hurried on.

So much, so fast. Clay felt rising in him a leaden conviction born of all he had seen in this land. So many people, so much pain—how could it matter? The West assumed that the individual was important, the bedrock of all. That was why the obliterating events of the West's own history, like the Nazi Holocaust, by erasing humans in such numbing numbers, cast grave doubt on the significance of any one. India did something like that for him. Could a universe which produced so many bodies, so many minds in shadowed torment, care a whit about humanity? Endless, meaningless duplication of grinding pain . . .

A low mutter came on the wind, like a bass theme sounding up from the depths of a dusty well.

Mrs. Buli called out something he could not understand. She began running, and Clay hastened to follow. If he lost her in these shadows, he could lose all connection.

Quickly they left the trees and crossed a grassy field rutted by ancient agriculture and prickly with weeds. On this flat plain he could see that the whole sky worked with twisted light, a colossal electrical discharge feathering into more branches than a gnarled tree. The anxious clouds caught blue and burnt-yellow pulses and seemed to relay them, like the countless transformers and capacitors and voltage drops that made a worldwide communications net, carrying staccato messages laced with crackling punctuations.

"The vans," she panted.

Three brown vans crouched beneath a canopy of thin trees, further concealed beneath khaki tents that blended in with the dusty fields. Mrs. Buli yanked open the door of the first one. Her fingers fumbled at the ignition.

"The key must be concealed," she said quickly.

"Why?" he gasped, throat raw.

"They are to be always with the vans."

"Uh-huh. Check the others."

She hurried away. Clay got down on his knees, feeling the lip of the van's undercarriage. The ground seemed to heave with inner heat, dry and rasping, the pulse of the planet. He finished one side of the van and crawled under, feeling along the rear axle. He heard a distant plaintive cry, as eerie and forlorn as the call of a bird lost in fog.

"Clayji? None in the others."

His hand touched a small slick box high up on the axle. He plucked it from its magnetic grip and rolled out from under.

"If we drive toward the mine," she said, "we can perhaps find others."

"Others, hell. Most likely we'll run into devotees."

"Well, I—"

Figures in the trees. Flitting, silent, quick.

"Get in."

"But—"

He pushed her in and tried to start the van. Running shapes in the field. He got the engine started on the third try and gunned it. They growled away. Something hard shattered the back window into a spiderweb, but then Clay swerved several times and nothing more hit them.

After a few minutes his heart-thumps slowed, and he turned on the headlights to make out the road. The curves were sandy and he did not want to get stuck. He stamped on the gas.

Suddenly great washes of amber light streamed across the sky, pale lances cutting the clouds. "My God, what's happening?"

"It is more than weather."

Her calm, abstracted voice made him glance across the seat. "No kidding."

"No earthquake could have collateral effects of this order."

He saw by the dashboard lights that she wore a lapis lazuli necklace. He had felt it when she came to him, and now its deep blues seemed like the only note of color in the deepening folds of night.

"It must be something far more profound."

"What?"

The road now arrowed straight through a tangled terrain of warped trees and oddly shaped boulders. Something rattled against the windshield like hail, but Clay could see nothing.

"We have always argued, some of us, that the central dictate of quantum mechanics is the interconnected nature of the observer and the observed."

The precise, detached lecturer style again drew his eyes to her. Shadowed, her face gave away no secrets.

"We always filter the world," she said with dreamy momentum, "and yet are linked to it. How much of what we see is in fact taught us, by our bodies, or by the consensus reality that society trains us to see, even before we can speak for ourselves?"

"Look, that sky isn't some problem with my eyes. It's *real*. Hear that?" Something big and soft had struck the door of the van, rocking it.

"And we here have finished the program of materialistic science, have we not? We flattered the West by taking it seriously. As did the devotees."

Clay grinned despite himself. It was hard to feel flattered when you were fleeing for your life.

Mrs. Buli stretched lazily, as though relaxing into the clasp of the moist night. "So we have proven the passing nature of matter. What fresh forces does that bring into play?"

"Huh!" Clay spat back angrily. "Look here, we just sent word out, reported the result. How—"

"So that by now millions, perhaps billions of people know that the very stones that support them must pass."

"So what? Just some theoretical point about subnuclear physics, how's that going to—"

"Who is to say? What avatar? The point is that we were believed. Certain knowledge, universally correlated, surely has some impact—"

The van lurched. Suddenly they jounced and slammed along the smooth roadway. A bright plume of sparks shot up behind them, brimming firefly yellow in the night.

"Axle's busted!" Clay cried. He got the van stopped. In the sudden silence, it registered that the motor had gone dead.

They climbed out. Insects buzzed and hummed in the hazy gloom.

The roadway was still straight and sure, but on all sides great blobs of iridescent water swelled up from the ground, making colossal drops. The trembling half-spheres wobbled in the frayed moonlight. Silently, softly, the bulbs began to detach from the foggy ground and gently loft upward. Feathery luminescent clouds above gathered on swift winds that sheared their edges. These billowing, luxuriant banks snagged the huge teardrop shapes as they plunged skyward.

"I . . . I don't . . ."

Mrs. Buli turned and embraced him. Her moist mouth opened a redolent interior continent to him, teeming and blackly bountiful, and he had to resist falling inward, a tumbling silvery bubble in a dark chasm.

"The category of perfect roundness is fading," she said calmly.

Clay looked at the van. The wheels had become ellipses. At each revolution they had slammed the axles into the roadway, leaving behind long scratches of rough tar.

He took a step.

She said, "Since we can walk, the principle of pivot and lever, of muscles pulling bones, survives."

"How . . . this doesn't . . ."

"But do our bodies depend on roundness? I wonder." She carefully lay down on the blacktop.

The road straightened precisely, like joints in an aged spine popping as they realigned.

Angles cut their spaces razor-sharp, like axioms from Euclid.

Clouds merged, forming copious tinkling hexagons.

"It is good to see that some features remain. Perhaps these are indeed the underlying Platonic beauties."

"What?" Clay cried.

"The undying forms," Mrs. Buli said abstractly. "Perhaps that one Western idea was correct after all."

Clay desperately grasped the van. He jerked his arm back when the metal skin began flexing and reshaping itself.

Smooth glistening forms began to emerge from the rough, coarse earth. Above the riotous, heaving land the moon was now a brassy cube. Across its face played enormous black cracks like mad lightning.

Somewhere far away his wife and daughter were in this, too. *G'bye, Daddy. It's been real.*

Quietly the land began to rain upward. Globs dripped toward the pewter, filmy continent swarming freshly above. Eons measured out the evaporation of ancient sluggish seas.

His throat struggled against torpid air. "Is . . . Brahma . . . ?"

"Awakening?" came her hollow voice, like an echo from a distant gorge.

"What happens . . . to . . . us?"

His words diffracted away from him. He could now see acoustic waves, wedges of compressed, mute atoms crowding in the exuberant air. Luxuriant, inexhaustible riches burst from beneath the ceramic certainties he had known.

"Come." Her voice seeped through the churning ruby air.

Centuries melted between them as he turned. A being he recognized without conscious thought spun in liquid air.

Femina, she was now, and she drifted on the new wafting currents. He and she were made of shifting geometric elements, molecular units of shape and firm thrust. A wan joy spread through him.

Time that was no time did not pass, and he and she and the impacted forces between them were pinned to the forever moment that cascaded through them, all of them, the billions of atomized elements that made them, all, forever.

A HISTORY OF THE TWENTIETH CENTURY, WITH ILLUSTRATIONS

Kim Stanley Robinson

Here's a story that lives up to its title, a bleak and powerful story that not only takes a searing look back at the twentieth century, but which may leave you nervously wondering what the *next* century holds in store. . . .

Kim Stanley Robinson sold his first story in 1976, and quickly established himself as one of the most respected and critically acclaimed writers of his generation. His story "Black Air" won the World Fantasy Award in 1984, and his novella "The Blind Geometer" won the Nebula Award in 1987. His excellent novel *The Wild Shore* was published in 1984 as the first title in the resurrected Ace Special line. Other Robinson books include the novels *Icehenge*, *The Memory of Whiteness*, *A Short, Sharp Shock*, *The Gold Coast*, and *Pacific Edge*, and the landmark collections *The Planet on the Table* and *Escape from Kathmandu*. His most recent book is a new collection, *Remaking History*. Upcoming is a trilogy of novels set on a future Mars. Robinson and his family are back in their native California again, in Davis, after several years of exile in Switzerland and Washington, D.C.

> *If truth is not to be found on the shelves of the British Museum, where,*
> *I asked myself, picking up a notebook and a pencil, is truth?*
> —Virginia Woolf

Daily doses of bright light markedly improve the mood of people suffering from depression, so every day at eight in the evening Frank Churchill went to the clinic on Park Avenue, and sat for three hours in a room illuminated with sixteen hundred watts of white light. This was not exactly like having the sun in the room, but it was bright, about the same as if sixteen bare lightbulbs hung from the ceiling. In this case the bulbs were probably long tubes, and they were hidden behind a sheet of white plastic, so it was the whole ceiling that glowed.

He sat at a table and doodled with a purple pen on a pad of pink paper. And then it was eleven and he was out on the windy streets, blinking as traffic lights swam in the gloom. He walked home to a hotel room in the west Eighties. He would return to the clinic at five the next morning for a predawn treatment, but now it was time to sleep. He looked forward to that. He'd been on the treatment for three weeks, and he was tired. Though the treatment did seem to be working—as far as he could tell; improvement was supposed to average twenty percent a week, and he wasn't sure what that would feel like.

In his room the answering machine was blinking. There was a message from his agent, asking him to call immediately. It was now nearly midnight, but he pushbuttoned the number and his agent answered on the first ring.

"You have DSPS," Frank said to him.

"What? What?"

"Delayed sleep phase syndrome. I know how to get rid of it."

"Frank! Look, Frank, I've got a good offer for you."

"Do you have a lot of lights on?"

"What? Oh, yeah, say, how's that going?"

"I'm probably sixty percent better."

"Good, good. Keep at it. Listen, I've got something should help you a hundred percent. A publisher in London wants you to go over there and write a book on the twentieth century."

"What kind of book?"

"Your usual thing, Frank, but this time putting together the big picture. Reflecting on all the rest of your books, so to speak. They want to bring it out in time for the turn of the century, and go oversize, use lots of illustrations, big print run—"

"A coffee table book?"

"People'll want it on their coffee tables, sure, but it's not—"

"I don't want to write a coffee table book."

"Frank—"

"What do they want, ten thousand words?"

"They want thirty thousand words, Frank. And they'll pay a hundred thousand pound advance."

That gave him pause.

"Why so much?"

"They're new to publishing, they come from computers and this is the kind of numbers they're used to. It's a different scale."

"That's for sure. I still don't want to do it."

"Frank, come on, you're the one for this! The only successor to Barbara Tuchman!" That was a blurb found on paperback editions of his work. "They want you in particular—I mean, Churchill on the twentieth century, ha ha. It's a natural."

"I don't want to do it."

"Come on, Frank. You could use the money, I thought you were having trouble with the payments—"

"Yeah yeah." Time for a different tack. "I'll think it over."

"They're in a hurry, Frank."

"I thought you said turn of the century!"

"I did, but there's going to be a lot of this kind of book then, and they want to beat the rush. Set the standard and then keep it in print for a few years. It'll be great."

"It'll be remaindered within a year. Remaindered before it even comes out, if I know coffee table books."

His agent sighed. "Come on, Frank. You can use the money. As for the book, it'll be as good as you make it, right? You've been working on this stuff your whole career, and here's your chance to sum up. And you've got a lot of readers, people will listen to you." Concern made him shrill: "Don't let what's happened get you so down that you miss an opportunity like this! Work is the best cure for depression anyway. And this is your chance to influence how we think about what's happened!"

"With a coffee table book?"

"God damn it, don't think of it that way!"

"How should I think of it."

His agent took a deep breath, let it out, spoke very slowly. "Think of it as a hundred thousand pounds, Frank."

His agent did not understand.

Nevertheless, the next morning as he sat under the bright white ceiling, doodling with a green pen on yellow paper, he decided to go to England. He didn't want to sit in that room anymore; it scared him, because he suspected it might not be working. He was not sixty percent better. And he didn't want to shift to drug therapy. They had found nothing wrong with his brain, no physical problems at all, and though that meant little, it did make him resistant to the idea of drugs. He had his reasons and he wanted his feelings!

The light room technician thought that this attitude was a good sign in itself. "Your serotonin level is normal, right? So it's not that bad. Besides London's a lot farther north than New York, so you'll pick up the light you lose here. And if you need more you can always head north again, right?"

He called Charles and Rya Dowland to ask if he could stay with them. It turned out they were leaving for Florida the next day, but they invited him to stay anyway; they liked having their flat occupied while they were gone. Frank had done that before, he still had the key on his key-ring. "Thanks," he said. It would be better this way, actually. He didn't feel like talking.

So he packed his backpack, including camping gear with the clothes, and the next morning flew to London. It was strange how one traveled these days: he got into a moving chamber outside his hotel, then shifted from one chamber to the next for several hours, only stepping outdoors again when he emerged from the Camden tube station, some hundred yards from Charles and Rya's flat.

The ghost of his old pleasure brushed him as he crossed Camden High Street and walked by the cinema, listening to London's voices. This had been his method for years: come to London, stay with Charles and Rya until he found digs, do his research and writing at the British Museum, visit the used bookstores at Charing Cross, spend the evenings at Charles and Rya's, watching TV and talking. It had been that way for four books, over the course of twenty years.

The flat was located above a butcher shop. Every wall in it was covered with stuffed bookshelves, and there were shelves nailed up over the toilet, the bath, and the head of the guest bed. In the unlikely event of an earthquake the guest would be buried in a hundred histories of London.

Frank threw his pack on the guest bed and went past the English poets downstairs. The living room was nearly filled by a table stacked with papers and books. The side street below was an open-air produce market, and he could hear the voices of the vendors as they packed up for the day. The sun hadn't set, though it was past nine; these late May days were already long. It was almost like still being in therapy.

He went downstairs and bought vegetables and rice, then went back up and cooked them. The kitchen windows were the color of sunset, and the little flat glowed, evoking its owners so strongly that it was almost as if they were there. Suddenly he wished they were.

After eating he turned on the CD player and put on some Handel. He opened the living room drapes and settled into Charles's armchair, a glass of Bulgarian wine in his hand, an open notebook on his knee. He watched salmon light leak out of the clouds to the north, and tried to think about the causes of the First World War.

In the morning he woke to the dull *thump thump thump* of frozen slabs of meat being rendered by an axe. He went downstairs and ate cereal while leafing through the *Guardian*, then took the tube to Tottenham Court Road and walked to the British Museum.

Because of *The Belle Epoque* he had already done his research on the pre-war period, but writing in the British Library was a ritual he didn't want to break; it made him part of a tradition, back to Marx and beyond. He showed his still-valid reader's ticket to a librarian and then found an empty seat in his usual row; in fact he had written much of *Entre Deux Guerres* in that very carrel, under the frontal lobes of the great skull dome. He opened a notebook and stared at the page. Slowly he wrote, *1900 to 1914.* Then he stared at the page.

His earlier book had tended to focus on the sumptuous excesses of the pre-war European ruling class, as a young and clearly leftist reviewer in the *Guardian* had rather sharply pointed out. To the extent that he had delved into the causes of the Great War, he had subscribed to the usual theory; that it had been the result of rising nationalism, diplomatic brinksmanship, and several deceptive precedents in the previous two decades. The Spanish-American War, the Russo-Japanese War, and the two Balkan wars had all remained localized and non-catastrophic; and there had been several "incidents," the Moroccan affair and the like, that had brought the two great alliances to the brink, but not toppled them over. So when Austria-Hungary made impossible demands to Serbia after the assassination of Ferdinand, no one could have known that the situation would domino into the trenches and their slaughter.

History as accident. Well, no doubt there was a lot of truth in that. But now he found himself thinking of the crowds in the streets of all the major cities, cheering the news of the war's outbreak; of the disappearance of pacifism, which had seemed such a force; of, in short, the apparently unanimous support for war among the prosperous citizens of the European powers. Support for a war that had no real reason to be!

There was something irreducibly mysterious about that, and this time he decided he would admit it, and discuss it. That would require a consideration of the preceding century, the *Pax Europeana*; which in fact had been a century of bloody subjugation, the high point of imperialism, with most of the world falling to the great powers. These powers had prospered at the expense of their colonies, who had suffered in abject misery. Then the powers had spent their profits building weapons, and used the weapons on each other, and destroyed themselves. There was something weirdly just about that development, as when a mass murderer finally turns the gun on himself. Punishment, an end to guilt, an end to pain. Could that really explain it? While staying in Washington with his dying father, Frank had visited the Lincoln Memorial, and there on the right hand wall had been Lincoln's Second Inaugural Address, carved in capital letters with the commas omitted, an oddity which somehow added to the speech's Biblical massiveness, as when it spoke of the ongoing war: "YET IF GOD WILLS THAT IT CONTINUE UNTIL ALL THE WEALTH PILED BY THE BONDSMAN'S TWO HUNDRED AND FIFTY YEARS OF UNREQUITED TOIL SHALL BE SUNK AND UNTIL EVERY DROP OF BLOOD DRAWN WITH THE LASH SHALL BE PAID BY ANOTHER DRAWN WITH THE SWORD AS WAS SAID THREE THOUSAND YEARS AGO SO STILL IT MUST BE SAID 'THE JUDGMENTS OF THE LORD ARE TRUE AND RIGHTEOUS ALTOGETHER.' "

A frightening thought, from that dark part of Lincoln that was never far from the surface. But as a theory of the Great War's origin it still struck him as inadequate. It was possible to believe it of the kings and presidents, the generals and diplomats, the imperial officers around the world; they had known what they were doing, and so might have been impelled by unconscious guilt to mass suicide. But the common citizen at home, ecstatic in the streets at the outbreak of general war? That seemed more likely to be just another manifestation of the hatred of the other. All my problems are your fault! He and Andrea had said that to each other a lot. Everyone did.

And yet . . . it still seemed to him that the causes were eluding him, as they had everyone else. Perhaps it was a simple pleasure in destruction. What is the primal response to an edifice? Knock it down. What is the primal response to a stranger? Attack him.

But he was losing his drift, falling away into the metaphysics of "human nature." That would be a constant problem in an essay of this length. And whatever the causes, there stood the year 1914, irreducible, inexplicable, unchangeable. "AND THE WAR CAME."

In his previous books he had never written about the wars. He was among those who believed that real history occurred in peacetime, and that in war you might as well roll dice or skip ahead to the peace treaty. For anyone but a military historian, what was interesting would begin again only when the war ended.

Now he wasn't so sure. Current views of the Belle Epoque were distorted because one only saw it through the lens of the war that ended it; which meant that the Great War was somehow more powerful than the Belle Epoque, or at least more powerful than he had thought. It seemed he would have to write about it, this time, to make sense of the century. And so he would have to research it.

He walked up to the central catalogue tables. The room darkened as the sun went behind clouds, and he felt a chill.

For a long time the numbers alone staggered him. To overwhelm trench defenses, artillery bombardments of the most astonishing size were brought to bear: on the Somme the British put a gun every twenty yards along a fourteen-mile front, and fired a million and a half shells. In April 1917 the French fired six million shells. The Germans' Big Bertha shot shells seventy-five miles high, essentially into space. Verdun was a "battle" that lasted ten months, and killed almost a million men.

The British section of the front was ninety miles long. Every day of the war, about seven thousand men along that front were killed or wounded— not in any battle in particular, but just as the result of incidental sniper fire or bombardment. It was called "wastage."

Frank stopped reading, his mind suddenly filled with the image of the Vietnam Memorial. He had visited it right after leaving the Lincoln Memorial, and the sight of all those names engraved on the black granite plates had powerfully affected him. For a moment it had seemed possible to imagine all those people, a little white line for each.

But at the end of every month or two of the Great War, the British had had a whole Vietnam Memorial's worth of dead. Every month or two, for fifty-one months.

He filled out book request slips and gave them to the librarians in the central ring of desks, then picked up the books he had requested the day before, and took them back to his carrel. He skimmed the books and took notes, mostly writing down figures and statistics. British factories produced two hundred and fifty million shells. The major battles all killed a half million or more. About ten million men died on the field of battle, ten million more by revolution, disease, and starvation.

Occasionally he would stop reading and try to write; but he never got far.

Once he wrote several pages on the economy of the war. The organization of agriculture and business, especially in Germany under Rathenau and England under Lloyd George, reminded him very strongly of the postmodern economy now running things. One could trace the roots of late capitalism to Great War innovations found in Rathenau's *Kriegsrohstoffabteilung* (the "War Raw Stuff Department"), or in his *Zentral Einkaufs-Gesellschaft*. All business had been organized to fight the enemy; but when the war was over and the enemy vanquished, the organization remained. People continued to sacrifice the fruits of their work, but now they did it for the corporations that had taken the wartime governments' positions in the system.

So much of the twentieth century, there already in the Great War. And then the Armistice was signed, at eleven A.M. on November 11th, 1918. That morning at the front the two sides exchanged bombardments as usual, so that by eleven A.M. many people had died.

That evening Frank hurried home, just beating a thundershower. The air was as dark as smoky glass.

And the war never ended.

This idea, that the two world wars were actually one, was not original to him. Winston Churchill said it at the time, as did the Nazi Alfred Rosenberg. They saw the twenties and thirties as an interregnum, a pause to regroup in the middle of a two-part conflict. The eye of a hurricane.

Nine o'clock one morning and Frank was still at the Dowlands', lingering over cereal and paging through the *Guardian*, and then through his notebooks. Every morning he seemed to get a later start, and although it was May, the days didn't seem to be getting any longer. Rather the reverse.

There were arguments against the view that it was a single war. The twenties did not seem very ominous, at least after the Treaty of Locarno in 1925: Germany had survived its financial collapse, and everywhere economic recovery seemed strong. But the thirties showed the real state of things: the depression, the new democracies falling to fascism, the brutal Spanish Civil War; the starvation of the kulaks; the terrible sense of fatality in the air. The sense of slipping on a slope, falling helplessly back into war.

But this time it was different. *Total War*. German military strategists had coined the phrase in the 1890s, while analyzing Sherman's campaign in Georgia. And they felt they were waging total war when they torpedoed neutral ships in 1915. But they were wrong; the Great War was not total war. In 1914 the rumor that German soldiers had killed eight Belgian nuns was enough to shock all civilization, and later when the *Lusitania* was sunk, objections were so fierce that the Germans agreed to leave passenger ships alone. This could only happen in a world where people still held the notion that in war armies fought armies and soldiers killed soldiers, while civilians suffered privation and perhaps got killed accidentally, but were never deliberately targeted. This was how European wars had been fought for centuries: diplomacy by other means.

In 1939, this changed. Perhaps it changed only because the capability for total war had emerged from the technological base, in the form of mass long-range aerial bombardment. Perhaps on the other hand it was a matter of learning the lessons of the Great War, digesting its implications. Stalin's murder of the kulaks, for instance: five million Ukrainian peasants, killed because Stalin wanted to collectivize agriculture. Food was deliberately shipped out of that breadbasket region, emergency supplies withheld, hidden stockpiles destroyed; and several thousand villages disappeared as all their occupants starved. This was total war.

Every morning Frank leafed around in the big catalogue volumes, as if he might find some other twentieth century. He filled out his slips, picked up the books requested the previous day, took them back to his carrel. He spent more time reading than writing. The days were cloudy, and it was dim under the great dome. His notes were getting scrambled. He had stopped working in chronological order, and kept returning compulsively to the Great War, even though the front wave of his reading was well into World War Two.

Twenty million had died in the first war, fifty million in the second. Civilian deaths made the bulk of the difference. Near the end of the war, thousands of bombs were dropped on cities in the hope of starting firestorms, in which the atmosphere itself was in effect ignited, as in Dresden, Berlin, Tokyo. Civilians were the target now, and strategic bombing made them easy to hit. Hiroshima and Nagasaki were in that sense a kind of exclamation point, at the end of a sentence which the war had been saying all along: we will kill your families at home. War is war, as Sherman said; if you want peace, surrender! And they did.

After two bombs. Nagasaki was bombed three days after Hiroshima, before the Japanese had time to understand the damage and respond. Dropping the bomb on Hiroshima was endlessly debated in the literature, but Frank found few who even attempted a defense of Nagasaki. Truman and his advisors did it, people said, to a) show Stalin they had more than one bomb, and b) show Stalin that they would use the bomb even as a threat or warning only, as Nagasaki demonstrated. A Vietnam Memorial's worth of civilians in an instantaneous flash, just so Stalin would take Truman seriously. Which he did.

When the crew of the *Enola Gay* landed, they celebrated with a barbecue.

In the evenings Frank sat in the Dowland flat in silence. He did not read, but watched the evening summer light leak out of the sky to the north. The days were getting shorter. He needed the therapy, he could feel it. More light! Someone had said that on their deathbed—Newton, Galileo, Spinoza, someone like that. No doubt they had been depressed at the time.

He missed Charles and Rya. He would feel better, he was sure, if he had them there to talk with. That was the thing about friends, after all: they lasted and you could talk. That was the definition of friendship.

But Charles and Rya were in Florida. And in the dusk he saw that the walls of books in the flat functioned like lead lining in a radioactive environment, all those recorded thoughts forming a kind of shield against poisonous reality. The best shield available, perhaps. But now it was failing, at least for him; the books appeared to be nothing more than their spines.

And then one evening in a premature blue sunset it seemed that the whole flat had gone transparent, and that he was sitting in an armchair, suspended over a vast and shadowy city.

The Holocaust, like Hiroshima and Nagasaki, had precedents. Russians with Ukrainians, Turks with Armenians, white settlers with native Americans. But the mechanized efficiency of the Germans' murder of the Jews was something new and horrible. There was a book in his stack on the designers of the death camps, the architects, engineers, builders. Were these functionaries less or more obscene than the mad doctors, the sadistic guards? He couldn't decide.

And then there was the sheer number of them, the six million. It was hard to comprehend it. He read that there was a library in Jerusalem where they had taken on the task of recording all they could find about every one of the six million. Walking up Charing Cross Road that afternoon he thought of that and stopped short. All those names in one library, another transparent room, another memorial. For a second he caught a glimpse of how many people that was, a whole London's worth. Then it faded and he was left on a street corner, looking both ways to make sure he didn't get run over.

As he continued walking he tried to calculate how many Vietnam Memorials it would take to list the six million. Roughly two per hundred thousand; thus twenty per million. So, one hundred and twenty. Count them one by one, step by step.

He took to hanging out through the evenings in pubs. The Wellington was as good as any, and was frequented occasionally by some acquaintances he had met through Charles and Rya. He sat with them and listened to them talk, but often he found himself distracted by his day's reading. So the conversations tumbled along without him, and the Brits, slightly more tolerant than Americans of eccentricity, did not make him feel unwelcome.

The pubs were noisy and filled with light. Scores of people moved about in them, talking, smoking, drinking. A different kind of lead-lined room. He didn't drink beer, and so at first remained sober; but then he discovered the hard cider that pubs carried. He liked it and drank it like the others drank their beer, and got quite drunk. After that he sometimes became very talkative, telling the rest things about the twentieth century that they already knew, and they would nod and contribute some other bit of information, to be polite, then change the subject back to whatever they had been discussing before, gently and without snubbing him.

But most of the time when he drank he only got more remote from their talk, which jumped about faster than he could follow. And each morning after, he would wake late and slow, head pounding, the day already there and a lot of the morning light missed in sleep. Depressives were not supposed to drink at all. So finally he quit going to the Wellington, and instead ate at the pubs closest to the Dowlands'. One was called The Halfway House, the other World's End, a poor choice as far as names were concerned, but he ate at World's End anyway, and afterwards would sit at a corner table and nurse a whisky and stare at page after page of notes, chewing the end of a pen to plastic shrapnel.

The Fighting Never Stopped, as one book's title put it. But the atomic bomb meant that the second half of the century looked different than the first. Some, Americans for the most part, called it the *Pax Americana.* But most called it the Cold War, 1945–1989. And not that cold, either. Under the umbrella of the superpower stalemate local conflicts flared everywhere, wars which compared to the two big ones looked small; but there had been over a hundred of them all told, killing about 350,000 people a year, for a total of around fifteen million, some said twenty; it was hard to count. Most occurred in the big ten: the two Vietnam wars, the two Indo-Pakistan wars, the Korean war, the Algerian war, the civil war in Sudan, the massacres in Indonesia in 1965, the Biafran war, and the Iran-Iraq war. Then another ten million civilians had been starved by deliberate military action; so that the total for the period was about the equal of the Great War itself. Though it had taken ten times as long to compile. Improvement of a sort.

And thus perhaps the rise of atrocity war, as if the horror of individualized murders could compensate for the lack of sheer number. And maybe it could; because now his research consisted of a succession of accounts and color photos of rape, dismemberment, torture—bodies of individual people, in their own clothes, scattered on the ground in pools of blood. Vietnamese villages, erupting in napalm. Cambodia, Uganda, Tibet—Tibet was genocide again, paced to escape the world's notice, a few villages destroyed every year in a process called *thamzing,* or reeducation: the villages seized by the Chinese and the villagers killed by a variety of methods, "burying alive, hanging, beheading, disemboweling, scalding, crucifixion, quartering, stoning, small children forced to shoot their parents; pregnant women given forced abortions, the fetuses piled in mounds on the village squares."

Meanwhile power on the planet continued to shift into fewer hands. The Second World War had been the only thing to successfully end the Depression, a fact leaders remembered; so the economic consolidation begun in the

First War continued through the Second War and the Cold War, yoking the whole world into a war economy.

At first 1989 had looked like a break away from that. But now, just seven years later, the Cold War losers all looked like Germany in 1922, their money worthless, their shelves empty, their democracies crumbling to juntas. Except this time the juntas had corporate sponsors; multinational banks ran the old Soviet bloc just as they did the Third World, with "austerity measures" enforced in the name of "the free market," meaning half the world went to sleep hungry every night to pay off debts to millionaires. While temperatures still rose, populations still soared, "local conflicts" still burned in twenty different places.

One morning Frank lingered over cereal, reluctant to leave the flat. He opened the *Guardian* and read that the year's defense budgets worldwide would total around a trillion dollars. "More light," he said, swallowing hard. It was a dark, rainy day. He could feel his pupils enlarging, making the effort. The days were surely getting shorter, even though it was May; and the air was getting darker, as if London's Victorian fogs had returned, coal smoke in the fabric of reality.

He flipped the page and started an article on the conflict in Sri Lanka. Singhalese and Tamils had been fighting for a generation now, and some time in the previous week, a husband and wife had emerged from their house in the morning to find the heads of their six sons arranged on their lawn. He threw the paper aside and walked through soot down the streets.

He got to the British Museum on automatic pilot. Waiting for him at the top of the stack was a book containing estimates of total war deaths for the century. About a hundred million people.

He found himself on the dark streets of London again, thinking of numbers. All day he walked, unable to gather his thoughts. And that night as he fell asleep the calculations returned, in a dream or a hypnogogic vision: it would take two thousand Vietnam Memorials to list the century's war dead. From above he saw himself walking the Mall in Washington, D.C., and the whole park from the Capitol to the Lincoln Memorial was dotted with the black Vs of Vietnam Memorials, as if a flock of giant stealth birds had landed on it. All night he walked past black wing walls, moving west toward the white tomb on the river.

The next day the first book on the stack concerned the war between China and Japan, 1931–1945. Like most of Asian history this war was poorly remembered in the West, but it had been huge. The whole Korean nation became in effect a slave labor camp in the Japanese war effort, and the Japanese concentration camps in Manchuria had killed as many Chinese as the Germans had killed Jews. These deaths included thousands in the style of Mengele and the Nazi doctors, caused by "scientific" medical torture.

Japanese experimenters had for instance performed transfusions in which they drained Chinese prisoners of their blood and replaced it with horses' blood, to see how long the prisoners would live. Survival rates varied from twenty minutes to six hours, with the subjects in agony throughout.

Frank closed that book and put it down. He picked the next one out of the gloom and peered at it. A heavy old thing, bound in dark green leather, with a dull gold pattern inlaid on the spine and boards. A *History of the Nineteenth Century, with Illustrations*—the latter tinted photos, their colors faded and dim. Published in 1902 by George Newnes Ltd; last century's equivalent of his own project, apparently. Curiosity about that had caused him to request the title. He opened it and thumbed through, and on the last page the text caught his eye: "I believe that Man is good. I believe that we stand at the dawn of a century that will be more peaceful and prosperous than any in history."

He put down the book and left the British Museum. In a red phone box he located the nearest car rental agency, an Avis outlet near Westminster. He took the Tube and walked to this agency, and there he rented a blue Ford Sierra station wagon. The steering wheel was on the right, of course. Frank had never driven in Great Britain before, and he sat behind the wheel trying to hide his uneasiness from the agent. The clutch, brake, and gas pedal were left-to-right as usual, thank God. And the gear shift was arranged the same, though one did have to operate it with the left hand.

Awkwardly he shoved the gearshift into first and drove out of the garage, turning left and driving down the left side of the street. It was weird. But the oddity of sitting on the right insured that he wouldn't forget the necessity of driving on the left. He pulled to the curb and perused the Avis street map of London, plotted a course, got back in traffic, and drove to Camden High Street. He parked below the Dowlands' and went upstairs and packed, then took his backpack down to the car. He returned to leave a note: *Gone to the land of the midnight sun.* Then he went down to the car and drove north, onto the highways and out of London.

It was a wet day, and low full clouds brushed over the land, dropping here a black broom of rain, there a Blakean shaft of sunlight. The hills were green, and the fields yellow or brown or lighter green. At first there were a lot of hills, a lot of fields. Then the highway swung by Birmingham and Manchester, and he drove by fields of rowhouses, line after line after line of them, on narrow treeless streets—all orderly and neat, and yet still among the bleakest human landscapes he had ever seen. Streets like trenches. Certainly the world was being overrun. Population densities must be near the levels set in those experiments on rats which had caused the rats to go insane. It was as good an explanation as any. Mostly males affected, in both cases: territorial hunters, bred to kill for food, now trapped in little boxes. They had gone mad.

"I believe that Man is this or that," the Edwardian author had written, and why not; it couldn't be denied that it was mostly men's doing. The planning, the diplomacy, the fighting, the raping, the killing.

The obvious thing to do was to give the running of the world over to women. There was Thatcher in the Falklands and Indira Gandhi in Bangladesh, it was true; but still it would be worth trying, it could hardly get worse! And given the maternal instinct, it would probably be better. Give every first lady her husband's job. Perhaps every woman her man's job. Let the men care for the children, for five thousand years or fifty thousand, one for every year of murderous patriarchy.

North of Manchester he passed giant radio towers, and something that looked like nuclear reactor stacks. Fighter jets zoomed overhead. The twentieth century. Why hadn't that Edwardian author been able to see it coming? Perhaps the future was simply unimaginable, then and always. Or perhaps things hadn't looked so bad in 1902. The Edwardian, looking forward in a time of prosperity, saw more of the same; instead there had followed a century of horrors. Now one looked forward from a time of horrors; so that by analogy, what was implied for the next century was grim beyond measure. And with the new technologies of destruction, practically anything was possible: chemical warfare, nuclear terrorism, biological holocaust; victims killed by nano-assassins flying through them, or by viruses in their drinking supply, or by a particular ringing of their telephone; or reduced to zombies by drugs or brain implants, torture or nerve gas; or simply dispatched with bullets, or starved; hi tech, low tech, the methods were endless. And the motivations would be stronger than ever; with populations rising and resources depleted, people were going to be fighting not to rule, but to survive. Some little country threatened with defeat could unleash an epidemic against its rival and accidentally kill off a continent, or everyone, it was entirely possible. The twenty-first century might make the twentieth look like nothing at all.

He would come to after reveries like that and realize that twenty or thirty or even sixty miles had passed without him seeing a thing of the outside world. Automatic pilot, on roads that were reversed! He tried to concentrate.

He was somewhere above Carlisle. The map showed two possible routes to Edinburgh: one left the highway just below Glasgow, while a smaller road left sooner and was much more direct. He chose the direct route and took an exit into a roundabout and onto the A702, a two-lane road heading northeast. Its black asphalt was wet with rain, and the clouds rushing overhead were dark. After several miles he passed a sign that said "Scenic Route," which suggested he had chosen the wrong road, but he was unwilling to backtrack. It was probably as fast to go this way by now, just more work: frequent roundabouts, villages with traffic lights, and narrow stretches where the road was hemmed by hedges or walls. Sunset was near, he had been driving for hours; he was tired, and when black trucks rushed at him out of the spray and shadows it looked like they were going to collide with him head-on. It became an effort to stay to the left rather than the right where his instincts shrieked he should be. Right and left had to be reversed on that level, but kept the same at foot level—reversed concerning which hand went on the gearshift, but not reversed for what the gearshift did—and it all began to blur and mix, until finally a huge lorry rushed head first at him and he veered left, but hit the gas rather than the brakes. At the unexpected lurch forward he swerved farther left to be safe, and that ran his left wheels off the asphalt and into a muddy gutter, causing the car to bounce back onto the road. He hit the brakes hard and the lorry roared by his ear. The car skidded over the wet asphalt to a halt.

He pulled over and turned on the emergency blinker. As he got out of the car he saw that the driver's side mirror was gone. There was nothing there but a rectangular depression in the metal, four rivet holes slightly flared to the rear, and one larger hole for the mirror adjustment mechanism, missing as well.

He went to the other side of the car to remind himself what the Sierra's side mirrors looked like. A solid metal and plastic mounting. He walked a hundred yards back down the road, looking through the dusk for the missing one, but he couldn't find it anywhere. The mirror was gone.

Outside Edinburgh he stopped and called Alec, a friend from years past.

"What? Frank Churchill? Hello! You're here? Come on by, then."

Frank followed his directions into the city center, past the train station to a neighborhood of narrow streets. Reversed parallel parking was almost too much for him; it took four tries to get the car next to the curb. The Sierra bumped over paving stones to a halt. He killed the engine and got out of the car, but his whole body continued to vibrate, a big tuning fork humming in the twilight. Shops threw their illumination over passing cars. Butcher, baker, Indian deli.

Alec lived on the third floor. "Come in, man, come in." He looked harried. "I thought you were in America! What brings you here?"

"I don't know."

Alec glanced sharply at him, then led him into the flat's kitchen and living area. The window had a view across rooftops to the castle. Alec stood in the kitchen, uncharacteristically silent. Frank put down his backpack and walked over to look out at the castle, feeling awkward. In the old days he and Andrea had trained up several times to visit Alec and Suzanne, a primatologist. At that time those two had lived in a huge three-storied flat in the New Town, and when Frank and Andrea had arrived the four of them would stay up late into the night, drinking brandy and talking in a high-ceilinged Georgian living room. During one stay they had all driven into the Highlands, and another time Frank and Andrea had stayed through a festival week, the four attending as many plays as they could. But now Suzanne and Alec had gone their ways, and Frank and Andrea were divorced, and Alec lived in a different flat; and that whole life had disappeared.

"Did I come at a bad time?"

"No, actually." A clatter of dishes as Alec worked at the sink. "I'm off to dinner with some friends, you'll join us—you haven't eaten?"

"No. I won't be—"

"No. You've met Peg and Rog before, I think. And we can use the distraction, I'm sure. We've all been to a funeral this morning. Friends of ours, their kid died. Crib death, you know."

"Jesus. You mean it just. . . ."

"Sudden infant death syndrome, yeah. Dropped him off at day care and he went off during his nap. Five months old."

"Jesus."

"Yeah." Alec went to the kitchen table and filled a glass from a bottle of Laphroaig. "Want a whisky?"

"Yes, please."

Alec poured another glass, drank his down. "I suppose the idea these days is that a proper funeral helps the parents deal with it. So Tom and Elyse came in carrying the coffin, and it was about this big." He held his hands a foot apart.

"No."

"Yeah. Never seen anything like it."

They drank in silence.

The restaurant was a fashionably bohemian seafood place, set above a pub. There Frank and Alec joined Peg and Rog, another couple, and a woman named Karen. All animal behaviorists, and all headed out to Africa in the next couple of weeks—Rog and Peg to Tanzania, the rest to Rwanda. Despite their morning's event the talk was quick, spirited, wide-ranging; Frank drank wine and listened as they discussed African politics, the problems of filming primates, rock music. Only once did the subject of the funeral come up, and then they shook their heads; there wasn't much to say. Stiff upper lip.

Frank said, "I suppose it's better it happened now than when the kid was three or four."

They stared at him. "Oh no," Peg said. "I don't think so."

Acutely aware that he had said something stupid, Frank tried to recover: "I mean, you know, they've more time to. . . ." He shook his head, foundering.

"It's rather comparing absolutes, isn't it," Rog said gently.

"True," he said. "It is." And he drank his wine. He wanted to go on: True, he wanted to say, any death is an absolute disaster, even that of an infant too young to know what was happening; but what if you had spent your life raising six such children and then went out one morning and found their heads on your lawn? Isn't the one more absolute than the other? He was drunk, his head hurt, his body still vibrated with the day's drive, and the shock of the brush with the lorry; and it seemed likely that the dyslexia of exhaustion had invaded all his thinking, including his moral sense, making everything backward. So he clamped his teeth together and concentrated on the wine, his fork humming in his hand, his glass chattering against his teeth. The room was dark.

Afterwards Alec stopped at the door to his building and shook his head. "Not ready for that yet," he said. "Let's try Preservation Hall, it's your kind of thing on Wednesday nights. Traditional jazz."

Frank and Andrea had been fans of traditional jazz. "Any good?"

"Good enough for tonight, eh?"

The pub was within walking distance, down a wide cobblestone promenade called the Grassmarket, then up Victoria Street. At the door of the pub they were stopped; there was a cover charge, the usual band had been replaced by a buffet dinner and concert, featuring several different bands. Proceeds to go to the family of a Glasgow musician, recently killed in a car crash. "Jesus Christ," Frank exclaimed, feeling like a curse. He turned to go.

"Might as well try it," Alec said, and pulled out his wallet. "I'll pay."

"But we've already eaten."

Alec ignored him and gave the man twenty pounds. "Come on."

Inside, a very large pub was jammed with people, and an enormous buffet table stacked with meats, breads, salads, seafood dishes. They got drinks from the bar and sat at the end of a crowded picnic table. It was noisy, the Scots accents so thick that Frank understood less than half of what he heard. A succession of local acts took the stage: the traditional jazz band that usually played, a stand-up comedian, a singer of Forties' music hall songs, a country-western group. Alec and Frank took turns going to the bar to get refills. Frank watched the bands and the crowd. All ages and types were represented. Each band said something about the late musician, who apparently had been well-known, a young rocker and quite a hellion from the sound of it. Crashed driving home drunk after a gig, and no one a bit surprised.

About midnight an obese young man seated at their table, who had been stealing food from all the plates around him, rose whalelike and surged to the stage. People cheered as he joined the band setting up. He picked up a guitar, leaned into the mike, and proceeded to rip into a selection of r&b and early rock and roll. He and his band were the best group yet, and the pub went wild. Most of the crowd got to their feet and danced in place. Next to Frank a young punk had to lean over the table to answer a gray-haired lady's questions about how he kept his hair spiked. A Celtic wake, Frank thought, and downed his cider and howled with the rest as the fat man started up Chuck Berry's "Rock And Roll Music."

So he was feeling no pain when the band finished its last encore and he and Alec staggered off into the night, and made their way home. But it had gotten a lot colder while they were inside, and the streets were dark and empty. Preservation Hall was no more than a small wooden box of light, buried in a cold stone city. Frank looked back in its direction and saw that a streetlight reflected off the black cobblestones of the Grassmarket in such a way that there were thousands of brief white squiggles underfoot, looking like names engraved on black granite, as if the whole surface of the earth were paved by a single memorial.

The next day he drove north again, across the Forth Bridge and then west along the shores of a loch to Fort William, and north from there through the Highlands. Above Ullapool steep ridges burst like fins out of boggy treeless hillsides. There was water everywhere, from puddles to lochs, with the Atlantic itself visible from most high points. Out to sea the tall islands of the Inner Hebrides were just visible.

He continued north. He had his sleeping bag and foam pad with him, and so he parked in a scenic overlook, and cooked soup on his Bluet stove, and slept in the back of the car. He woke with the dawn and drove north. He talked to nobody.

Eventually he reached the northwest tip of Scotland and was forced to turn east, on a road bordering the North Sea. Early that evening he arrived in Scrabster, at the northeast tip of Scotland. He drove to the docks, and found that a ferry was scheduled to leave for the Orkney Islands the next day at noon. He decided to take it.

There was no secluded place to park, so he took a room in a hotel. He had dinner in the restaurant next door, fresh shrimp in mayonnaise with chips, and went to his room and slept. At six the next morning the ancient crone who ran the hotel knocked on his door and told him an unscheduled ferry was leaving in forty minutes: did he want to go? He said he did. He got up and dressed, then felt too exhausted to continue. He decided to take the regular ferry after all, took off his clothes and returned to bed. Then he realized that exhausted or not, he wasn't going to be able to fall back asleep. Cursing, almost crying, he got up and put his clothes back on. Downstairs the old woman had fried bacon and made him two thick bacon sandwiches, as he was going to miss her regular breakfast. He ate the sandwiches sitting in the Sierra, waiting to get the car into the ferry. Once in the hold he locked the car and went up to the warm stuffy passenger cabin, and lay on padded vinyl seating and fell back asleep.

He woke when they docked in Stromness. For a moment he didn't remember getting on the ferry, and he couldn't understand why he wasn't in his hotel bed in Scrabster. He stared through salt-stained windows at fishing boats, amazed, and then it came to him. He was in the Orkneys.

Driving along the southern coast of the main island, he found that his mental image of the Orkneys had been entirely wrong. He had expected an extension of the Highlands; instead it was like eastern Scotland, low, rounded, and green. Most of it was cultivated or used for pasture. Green fields, fences, farmhouses. He was a bit disappointed.

Then in the island's big town of Kirkwall he drove past a Gothic cathedral—a very little Gothic cathedral, a kind of pocket cathedral. Frank had never seen anything like it. He stopped and got out to have a look. Cathedral of St. Magnus, begun in 1137. So early, and this far north! No wonder it was so small. Building it would have required craftsmen from the continent, shipped up here to a rude fishing village of drywall and turf roofs; a strange influx it must have been, a kind of cultural revolution. The finished building must have stood out like something from another planet.

But as he walked around the bishop's palace next door, and then a little museum, he learned that it might not have been such a shock for Kirkwall after all. In those days the Orkneys had been a crossroads of a sort, where Norse and Scots and English and Irish had met, infusing an indigenous culture that went right back to the Stone Age. The fields and pastures he had driven by had been worked, some of them, for five thousand years!

And such faces walking the streets, so intent and vivid. His image of the local culture had been as wrong as his image of the land. He had thought he would find decrepit fishing villages, dwindling to nothing as people moved south to the cities. But it wasn't like that in Kirkwall, where teenagers roamed in self-absorbed talky gangs, and restaurants open to the street were packed for lunch. In the bookstores he found big sections on local topics: nature guides, archaeological guides, histories, sea tales, novels. Several writers, obviously popular, had as their entire subject the islands. To the locals, he realized, the Orkneys were the center of the world.

He bought a guidebook and drove north, up the east coast of Mainland to the Broch of Gurness, a ruined fort and village that had been occupied from the time of Christ to the Norse era. The broch itself was a round stone tower about twenty feet tall. Its wall was at least ten feet thick, and was made of flat slabs, stacked so carefully that you couldn't have stuck a dime in the cracks. The walls in the surrounding village were much thinner; if attacked, the villagers would have retired into the broch. Frank nodded at the explanatory sentence in the guidebook, reminded that the twentieth century had had no monopoly on atrocities. Some had happened right here, no doubt. Unless the broch had functioned as a deterrent.

Gurness overlooked a narrow channel between Mainland and the smaller island of Rousay. Looking out at the channel, Frank noticed white ripples in its blue water; waves and foam were pouring past. It was a tidal race, apparently, and at the moment the entire contents of the channel were rushing north, as fast as any river he had ever seen.

Following suggestions in the guidebook, he drove across the island to the neolithic site of Brodgar, Stenness, and Maes Howe. Brodgar and Stenness were two rings of standing stones; Maes Howe was a nearby chambered tomb.

The Ring of Brodgar was a big one, three hundred and forty feet across. Over half of the original sixty stones were still standing, each one a block of roughly dressed sandstone, weathered over the millennia into shapes of great individuality and charisma, like Rodin figures. Following the arc they made, he watched the sunlight break on them. It was beautiful.

Stenness was less impressive, as there were only four stones left, each tremendously tall. It roused more curiosity than awe: how had they stood those monsters on end? No one knew for sure.

From the road, Maes Howe was just a conical grass mound. To see the inside he had to wait for a guided tour, happily scheduled to start in fifteen minutes.

He was still the only person waiting when a short stout woman drove up in a pickup truck. She was about twenty-five, and wore Levi's and a red windbreaker. She greeted him and unlocked a gate in the fence surrounding the mound, then led him up a gravel path to the entrance on the southwest slope. There they had to get on their knees and crawl, down a tunnel three feet high and some thirty feet long. Midwinter sunsets shone directly down this entryway, the woman looked over her shoulder to tell him. Her Levi's were new.

The main chamber of the tomb was quite tall. "Wow," he said, standing up and looking around.

"It's big isn't it," the guide said. She told him about it in a casual way. The walls were made of the ubiquitous sandstone slabs, with some monster monoliths bracketing the entryway. And something unexpected: a group of Norse sailors had broken into the tomb in the twelfth century (four thousand years after the tomb's construction!) and taken shelter in it through a three-day storm. This was known because they had passed the time carving runes on the walls, which told their story. The woman pointed to lines and translated: "Happy is he who finds the great treasure.' And over here: 'Ingrid is the most beautiful woman in the world.' "

"You're kidding."

"That's what it says. And look here, you'll see they did some drawing as well."

She pointed out three graceful line figures, cut presumably with axe blades: a walrus, a narwhal, and a dragon. He had seen all three in the shops of Kirkwall, reproduced in silver for earrings and pendants. "They're beautiful," he said.

"A good eye, that Viking."

He looked at them for a long time, then walked around the chamber to look at the runes again. It was a suggestive alphabet, harsh and angular. The guide seemed in no hurry, she answered his questions at length. She was a guide in the summer, and sewed sweaters and quilts in the winter. Yes, the winters were dark. But not very cold. Average temperature around thirty.

"That warm?"

"Aye it's the Gulf Stream you see. It's why Britain is so warm, and Norway too for that matter."

Britain so warm. "I see," he said carefully.

Back outside he stood and blinked in the strong afternoon light. He had just emerged from a five-thousand-year-old tomb. Down by the loch the standing stones were visible, both rings. Ingrid is the most beautiful woman in the world. He looked at Brodgar, a circle of black dots next to a silver sheen of water. It was a memorial too, although what it was supposed to make its viewers remember was no longer clear. A great chief; the death of one year, birth of the next; the planets, moon and sun in their courses. Or something else, something simpler. *Here we are.*

It was still midafternoon judging by the sun, so he was surprised to look at his watch and see it was six o'clock. Amazing. It was going to be just like his therapy! Only better because outdoors, in the sunlight and the wind. Spend summer in the Orkneys, winter in the Falklands, which were said to be very similar. . . . He drove back to Kirkwall and had dinner in a hotel restaurant. The waitress was tall, attractive, about forty. She asked him where he was from, and he asked her when it would get busy (July), what the population of Kirkwall was (about ten thousand, she guessed) and what she did in the winter (accounting). He had broiled scallops and a glass of white wine. Afterward he sat in the Sierra and looked at his map. He wanted to sleep in the car, but hadn't yet seen a good place to park for the night.

The northwest tip of Mainland looked promising, so he drove across the middle of the island again, passing Stenness and Brodgar once more. The stones of Brodgar stood silhouetted against a western sky banded orange and pink and white and red.

At the very northwest tip of the island, the Point of Buckquoy, there was a small parking lot, empty this late in the evening. Perfect. Extending west from the point was a tidal causeway, now covered by the sea, a few hundred yards across the water was a small island called the Brough of Birsay, a flat loaf of sandstone tilted up to the west so that one could see the whole grass top of it. There were ruins and a museum at the near end, a small lighthouse on the west point. Clearly something to check out the next day.

South of the point, the western shore of the island curved back in a broad, open bay. Behind its beach stood the well-preserved ruins of a sixteenth century palace. The bay ended in a tall sea cliff called Marwick Head, which had a tower on its top that looked like another broch, but was, he discovered in his guidebook, the Kitchener Memorial. Offshore in 1916 the *HMS Hampshire* had hit a mine and sunk, and six hundred men, including Kitchener, had drowned.

Odd, to see that. A couple of weeks ago (it felt like years) he had read that when the German front lines had been informed of Kitchener's death, they had started ringing bells and banging pots and pans in celebration; the noise-making had spread up and down the German trenches, from the Belgian coast to the Swiss frontier.

He spread out his sleeping bag and foam pad in the back of the station wagon, and lay down. He had a candle for reading, but he did not want to read. The sound of the waves was loud. There was still a bit of light in the air, these northern summer twilights were really long. The sun had seemed to slide off to the right rather than descend, and suddenly he understood what it would be like to be above the Arctic Circle in midsummer: the sun would just keep sliding off to the right until it brushed the northern horizon, and then it would slide up again into the sky. He needed to live in Ultima Thule.

The car rocked slightly on a gust of wind. It had been windy all day; apparently it was windy all the time here, the main reason the islands were treeless. He lay back and looked at the roof of the car. A car made a good tent: flat floor, no leaks. . . . As he fell asleep he thought, it was a party a mile wide and a thousand miles long.

He woke at dawn, which came just before five A.M. His shadow and the car's shadow were flung out toward the brough, which was an island still, as the tidal bar was covered again. Exposed for only two hours each side of low tide, apparently.

He ate breakfast by the car, and then rather than wait for the causeway to clear he drove south, around the Bay of Birsay and behind Marwick Head, to the Bay of Skaill. It was a quiet morning, he had the one-lane track to himself. It cut through green pastures. Smoke rose from farmhouse chimneys and flattened out to the east. The farmhouses were white, with slate roofs and two white chimneys, one at each end of the house. Ruins of farmhouses built to the same design stood nearby, or in back pastures.

He came to another parking lot, containing five or six cars. A path had been cut through tall grass just behind the bay beach, and he followed it south. It ran nearly a mile around the curve of the bay, past a big nineteenth century manor house, apparently still occupied. Near the south point of the bay stretched a low concrete seawall and a small modern building, and some interruptions in the turf above the beach. Holes, it looked like. The pace of his walk picked up. A few people were bunched around a man in a tweed coat. Another guide?

Yes. It was Skara Brae.

The holes in the ground were the missing roofs of Stone Age houses buried in the sand; their floors were about twelve feet below the turf. The interior walls were made of the same slab as everything else on the island, stacked with the same precision. Stone hearths, stone bedframes, stone dressers: because of the islands' lack of wood, the guide was saying, and the ready availability of the slabs, most of the houses' furniture had been made of stone. And so it had endured.

Stacks of slabs held up longer ones, making shelves in standard college student bricks-and-boards style. Cupboards were inset in the walls. There was a kind of stone kitchen cabinet, with mortar and pestle beneath. It was instantly obvious what everything was for; everything looked deeply familiar.

Narrow passageways ran between houses. These too had been covered;

apparently driftwood or whale rib beams had supported turf roofs over the entire village, so that during bad storms they need never go out. The first mall, Frank thought. The driftwood had included pieces of spruce, which had to have come from North America. The Gulf Stream again.

Frank stood at the back of a group of seven, listening to the guide as he looked down into the homes. The guide was bearded, stocky, fiftyish. Like the Maes Howe guide he was good at his work, wandering about with no obvious plan, sharing what he knew without memorized speeches. The village had been occupied for about six hundred years, beginning around 3000 B.C. Brodgar and Maes Howe had been built during those years, so probably people from here had helped in their construction. The bay had likely been a fresh-water lagoon at that time, with a beach separating it from the sea. Population about fifty or sixty. A heavy dependence on cattle and sheep, with lots of seafood as well. Sand filled in the homes when the village was abandoned, and turf grew over it. In 1850 a big storm tore the turf off and exposed the homes, completely intact except for the roofs. . . .

Water seepage had rounded away every edge, so that each slab looked sculpted, and caught at the light. Each house a luminous work of art. And five thousand years old, yet so familiar: the same needs, the same thinking, the same solutions. . . . A shudder ran through him, and he noticed that he was literally slack-jawed. He closed his mouth and almost laughed aloud. Open-mouthed astonishment could be so natural sometimes, so physical, unconscious, genuine.

When the other tourists left, he continued to wander around. The guide, sensing another enthusiast, joined him.

"It's like the Flintstones," Frank said, and laughed.

"The what?"

"You expect to see stone TVs and the like."

"Oh aye. It's very contemporary, isn't it."

"It's marvelous."

Frank walked from house to house, and the guide followed, and they talked. "Why is this one called the chief's house?"

"It's just a guess, actually. Everything in it is a bit bigger and better, that's all. In our world a chief would have it."

Frank nodded. "Do you live out here?"

"Aye." The guide pointed at the little building beyond the site. He had owned a hotel in Kirkwall, but sold it; Kirkwall had been too hectic for him. He had gotten the job here and moved out, and was very happy with it. He was getting a degree in archaeology by correspondence. The more he learned, the more amazed he was to be here; it was one of the most important archaeological sites in the world, after all. There wasn't a better one. No need to imagine furnishings and implements, "and to see so clearly how much they thought like we do."

Exactly. "Why did they leave, in the end?"

"No one knows."

"Ah."

They walked on.

"No sign of a fight, anyway."

"Good."

The guide asked Frank where he was staying, and Frank told him about the Sierra.

"I see!" the man said. "Well, if you need the use of a bathroom, there's one here at the back of the building. For a shave, perhaps. You look like you haven't had the chance in a while."

Frank rubbed a hand over his stubble, blushing. In fact he hadn't thought of shaving since well before leaving London. "Thanks," he said. "Maybe I'll take you up on that."

They talked about the ruins a while longer, and then the guide walked out to the seawall, and let Frank wander in peace.

He looked down in the rooms, which still glowed as if lit from within. Six hundred years of long summer days, long winter nights. Perhaps they had set sail for the Falklands. Five thousand years ago.

He called good-bye to the guide, who waved. On the way back to the car park he stopped once to look back. Under a carpet of cloud the wind was thrashing the tall beach grass, every waving stalk distinct, the clouds' underside visibly scalloped; and all of it touched with a silvery edge of light.

He ate lunch in Stromness, down by the docks, watching the fishing boats ride at anchor. A very practical-looking fleet, of metal and rubber and bright plastic buoys. In the afternoon he drove the Sierra around Scapa Flow and over a bridge at the east channel, the one Winston had ordered blocked with sunken ships. The smaller island to the south was covered with green fields and white farmhouses.

Late in the afternoon he drove slowly back to the Point of Buckquoy, stopping for a look in the nearby ruins of the sixteenth century earl's palace. Boys were playing soccer in the roofless main room.

The tide was out, revealing a concrete walkway set on a split bed of wet brown sandstone. He parked and walked over in the face of a stiff wind, onto the Brough of Birsay.

Viking ruins began immediately, as erosion had dropped part of the old settlement into the sea. He climbed steps into a tight network of knee-high walls. Compared to Skara Brae, it was a big town. In the middle of all the low foundations rose the shoulder-high walls of a church. Twelfth century, ambitious Romanesque design: and yet only fifty feet long, and twenty wide! Now this was a pocket cathedral. It had had a monastery connected to it, however; and some of the men who worshipped in it had traveled to Rome, Moscow, Newfoundland.

Picts had lived here before that; a few of their ruins lay below the Norse. Apparently they had left before the Norse arrived, though the record wasn't clear. What was clear was that people had been living here for a long, long time.

After a leisurely exploration of the site Frank walked west, up the slope of the island. It was only a few hundred yards to the lighthouse on the cliff, a modern white building with a short fat tower.

Beyond it was the edge of the island. He walked toward it and emerged from the wind shelter the island provided; a torrent of gusts almost knocked him back. He reached the edge and looked down.

At last something that looked like he thought it would! It was a long way to the water, perhaps a hundred and fifty feet. The cliff was breaking off in great stacks, which stood free and tilted out precariously, as if they were going to fall at any moment. Great stone cliffs, with the sun glaring directly out from them, and the surf crashing to smithereens on the rocks below: it was so obviously, grandiloquently the End of Europe that he had to laugh. A place made to cast oneself from. End the pain and fear, do a Hart Crane off the stern of Europe . . . except this looked like the bow, actually. The bow of a very big ship, crashing westward through the waves; yes, he could feel it in the soles of his feet. And foundering, he could feel that too, the shudders, the rolls, the last sluggish list. So jumping overboard would be redundant at best. The end would come, one way or another. Leaning out against the gale, feeling like a Pict or Viking, he knew he stood at the end—end of a continent, end of a century; end of a culture.

And yet there was a boat, coming around Marwick Head from the south, a little fishing tub from Stromness, rolling horribly in the swell. Heading northwest, out to—out to where? There were no more islands out there, not until Iceland anyway, or Greenland, Spitsbergen . . . where was it going at this time of day, near sunset and the west wind tearing in?

He stared at the trawler for a long time, rapt at the sight, until it was nothing but a black dot near the horizon. Whitecaps covered the sea, and the wind was still rising, gusting really hard. Gulls skated around on the blasts, landing on the cliffs below. The sun was very near the water, sliding off to the north, the boat no more than flotsam: and then he remembered the causeway and the tide.

He ran down the island and his heart leaped when he saw the concrete walkway washed by white water, surging up from the right. Stuck here, forced to break into the museum or huddle in a corner of the church . . . but no; the concrete stood clear again. If he ran—

He pounded down the steps and ran over the rough concrete. There were scores of parallel sandstone ridges still exposed to the left, but the right side was submerged already, and as he ran a broken wave rolled up onto the walkway and drenched him to the knees, filling his shoes with seawater and scaring him much more than was reasonable. He ran on cursing.

Onto the rocks and up five steps. At his car he stopped, gasping for breath. He got in the passenger side and took off his boots, socks, and pants. Put on dry pants, socks, and running shoes.

He got back out of the car.

The wind was now a constant gale, ripping over the car and the point and the ocean all around. It was going to be tough to cook dinner on his stove; the car made a poor windbreak, wind rushing under it right at stove level.

He got out the foam pad, and propped it with his boots against the lee side of the car. The pad and the car's bulk gave him just enough wind shelter to keep the little Bluet's gas flame alive. He sat on the asphalt behind the stove, watching the flames and the sea. The wind was tremendous, the Bay of Birsay riven by whitecaps, more white than blue. The car rocked on its shock absorbers. The sun had finally slid sideways into the sea, but clearly it was going to be a long blue dusk.

When the water was boiling he poured in a dried Knorr's soup and stirred it, put it back on the flame for a few more minutes, then killed the flame and ate, spooning split pea soup straight from the steaming pot into his mouth. Soup, bit of cheese, bit of salami, red wine from a tin cup, more soup. It was absurdly satisfying to make a meal in these conditions: the wind was in a fury!

When he was done eating he opened the car door and put away his dinner gear, then got out his windbreaker and rain pants and put them on. He walked around the carpark, and then up and down the low cliffy edges of the point of Buckquoy, watching the North Atlantic get torn by a full force gale. People had done this for thousands of years. The rich twilight blue looked like it would last forever.

Eventually he went to the car and got his notebooks. He returned to the very tip of the point, feeling the wind like slaps on the ear. He sat with his legs hanging over the drop, the ocean on three sides of him, the wind pouring across him, left to right. The horizon was a line where purest blue met bluest black. He kicked his heels against the rock. He could see just well enough to tell which pages in the notebooks had writing on them; he tore these from the wire spirals, and bunched them into balls and threw them away. They flew off to the right and disappeared immediately in the murk and whitecaps. When he had disposed of all the pages he had written on he cleared the long torn shreds of paper out of the wire rings, and tossed them after the rest.

It was getting cold, and the wind was a constant kinetic assault. He went back to the car and sat in the passenger seat. His notebooks lay on the driver's seat. The western horizon was a deep blue, now. Must be eleven at least.

After a time he lit the candle and set it on the dash. The car was still rocking in the wind, and the candle flame danced and trembled on its wick.

All the black shadows in the car shivered too, synchronized perfectly with the flame.

He picked up a notebook and opened it. There were a few pages left between damp cardboard covers. He found a pen in his daypack. He rested his hand on the page, the pen in position to write, its tip in the quivering shadow of his hand. He wrote, "I believe that man is good. I believe we stand at the dawn of a century that will be more peaceful and prosperous than any in history." Outside it was dark, and the wind howled.

GENE WARS

Paul J. McAuley

Born in Oxford, England, in 1955, Paul J. McAuley now makes his home in St. Andrews, Scotland. He is considered to be one of the best of the new British breed of "hard-science" writers, and is a frequent contributor to *Interzone*, as well as to markets such as *Amazing*, *The Magazine of Fantasy and Science Fiction*, *When the Music's Over*, and elsewhere. His first novel, *Four Hundred Billion Stars*, won the 1988 Philip K. Dick Memorial Award. His most recent books are a new novel, *Of the Fall*, and a collection of his short work, *The King of the Hill and Other Stories*. Coming up are an original anthology co-edited with Kim Newman, *In Dreams*, and a major new novel, *Eternal Light*. His story "The Temporary King" was in our Fifth Annual Collection.

In the dizzyingly fast-paced little story that follows, jam-packed with enough invention for many another author's four-book trilogy, he paints a sharp portrait of a new kind of entrepreneur, a self-made man—twenty-first-century style.

1

On Evan's eighth birthday, his aunt sent him the latest smash-hit biokit, *Splicing Your Own Semisentients*. The box-lid depicted an alien swamp throbbing with weird, amorphous life; a double helix spiralling out of a test-tube was embossed in one corner. Don't let your father see that, his mother said, so Evan took it out to the old barn, set up the plastic culture trays and vials of chemicals and retroviruses on a dusty workbench in the shadow of the shrouded combine.

His father found Evan there two days later. The slime mould he'd created, a million amoebae aggregated around a drop of cyclic AMP, had been transformed with a retrovirus and was budding little blue-furred blobs. Evan's father dumped culture trays and vials in the yard and made Evan pour a litre of industrial-grade bleach over them. More than fear or anger, it was the acrid stench that made Evan cry.

That summer, the leasing company foreclosed on the livestock. The rep who supervised repossession of the supercows drove off in a big car with the test-tube and double-helix logo on its gull-wing door. The next year the wheat failed, blighted by a particularly virulent rust. Evan's father couldn't afford the new resistant strain, and the farm went under.

2

Evan lived with his aunt, in the capital. He was fifteen. He had a street bike, a plug-in computer, and a pet microsaur, a cat-sized triceratops in purple funfur. Buying the special porridge which was all the microsaur could eat took half of Evan's weekly allowance; that was why he let his best friend inject the pet with a bootleg virus to edit out its dietary dependence. It was only a partial success: the triceratops no longer needed its porridge, but it developed epilepsy triggered by sunlight. Evan had to keep it in his wardrobe. When it started shedding fur in great swatches, he abandoned it in a nearby park. Microsaurs were out of fashion, anyway. Dozens could be found wandering the park, nibbling at leaves, grass, discarded scraps of fastfood. Quite soon they disappeared, starved to extinction.

3

The day before Evan graduated, his sponsor firm called to tell him that he wouldn't be doing research after all. There had been a change of policy: the covert gene wars were going public. When Evan started to protest, the woman said sharply, "You're better off than many long-term employees. With a degree in molecular genetics you'll make sergeant at least."

4

The jungle was a vivid green blanket in which rivers made silvery forked lightnings. Warm wind rushed around Evan as he leaned out the helicopter's hatch; harness dug into his shoulders. He was twenty-three, a tech sergeant. It was his second tour of duty.

His goggles flashed icons over the view, tracking the target. Two villages a klick apart, linked by a red dirt road narrow as a capillary that suddenly widened to an artery as the helicopter dove.

Flashes on the ground: Evan hoped the peasants only had Kalashnikovs: last week some gook had downed a copter with an antiquated SAM. Then he was too busy laying the pattern, virus-suspension in a sticky spray that fogged the maize fields.

Afterwards, the pilot, an old-timer, said over the intercom, "Things get tougher every day. We used just to take a leaf, cloning did the rest. You couldn't even call it theft. And this stuff . . . I always thought war was bad for business."

Evan said, "The company owns copyright to the maize genome. Those peasants aren't licensed to grow it."

The pilot said admiringly, "Man, you're a real company guy. I bet you don't even know what country this is."

Evan thought about that. He said, "Since when were countries important?"

5

Rice fields spread across the floodplain, dense as a handstitched quilt. In every paddy, peasants bent over their own reflections, planting seedlings for the winter crop.

In the centre of the UNESCO delegation, the Minister for Agriculture stood under a black umbrella held by an aide. He was explaining that his country was starving to death after a record rice crop.

Evan was at the back of the little crowd, bareheaded in warm drizzle. He wore a smart onepiece suit, yellow overshoes. He was twenty-eight, had spent two years infiltrating UNESCO for his company.

The minister was saying, "We have to buy seed genespliced for pesticide resistance to compete with our neighbours, but my people can't afford to buy the rice they grow. It must all be exported to service our debt. Our children are starving in the midst of plenty."

Evan stifled a yawn. Later, at a reception in some crumbling embassy, he managed to get the minister on his own. The man was drunk, unaccustomed to hard liquor. Evan told him he was very moved by what he had seen.

"Look in our cities," the minister said, slurring his words. "Every day a thousand more refugees pour in from the countryside. There is kwashiorkor, beri-beri."

Evan popped a canapé into his mouth. One of his company's new lines, it squirmed with delicious lasciviousness before he swallowed it. "I may be able to help you," he said. "The people I represent have a new yeast that completely fulfills dietary requirements and will grow on a simple medium."

"How simple?" As Evan explained, the minister, no longer as drunk as he had seemed, steered him onto the terrace. The minister said, "You understand this must be confidential. Under UNESCO rules . . ."

"There are ways around that. We have lease arrangements with five countries that have . . . trade imbalances similar to your own. We lease the genome as a loss-leader, to support governments who look favourably on our other products . . ."

6

The gene pirate was showing Evan his editing facility when the slow poison finally hit him. They were aboard an ancient ICBM submarine grounded somewhere off the Philippines. Missile tubes had been converted into fermenters. The bridge was crammed with the latest manipulation technology, virtual reality gear which let the wearer directly control molecule-sized cutting robots as they travelled along DNA helices.

"It's not facilities I need," the pirate told Evan, "it's distribution."

"No problem," Evan said. The pirate's security had been pathetically easy to penetrate. He'd tried to infect Evan with a zombie virus, but Evan's gene-spliced designer immune system had easily dealt with it. Slow poison was so much more subtle: by the time it could be detected it was too late. Evan was thirty-two. He was posing as a Swiss grey-market broker.

"This is where I keep my old stuff," the pirate said, rapping a stainless-steel cryogenic vat. "Stuff from before I went big time. A free luciferase gene complex, for instance. Remember when the Brazilian rainforest started to glow? That was me." He dashed sweat from his forehead, frowned at the room's complicated thermostat. Grossly fat and completely hairless, he wore nothing but Bermuda shorts and shower sandals. He'd been targeted because he was about to break the big time with a novel HIV cure. The company was still making a lot of money from its own cure: they made sure AIDS had never been completely eradicated in third-world countries.

Evan said, "I remember the Brazilian government was overthrown—the population took it as a bad omen."

"Hey, what can I say? I was only a kid. Transforming the gene was easy, only difficulty was finding a vector. Old stuff. Somatic mutation really is going to be the next big thing, believe me. Why breed new strains when you can rework a genome cell by cell?" He rapped the thermostat. His hands were shaking. "Hey, is it hot in here, or what?"

"That's the first symptom," Evan said. He stepped out of the way as the gene pirate crashed to the decking. "And that's the second."

The company had taken the precaution of buying the pirate's security chief: Evan had plenty of time to fix the fermenters. By the time he was ashore, they would have boiled dry. On impulse, against orders, he took a microgram sample of the HIV cure with him.

7

"The territory between piracy and legitimacy is a minefield," the assassin told Evan. "It's also where paradigm shifts are most likely to occur, and that's where I come in. My company likes stability. Another year and you'd have gone public, and most likely the share issue would have made you a billionaire—a minor player, but still a player. Those cats, no one else has them.

The genome was supposed to have been wiped out back in the twenties. Very astute, quitting the grey medical market and going for luxury goods." She frowned. "Why am I talking so much?"

"For the same reason you're not going to kill me," Evan said.

"It seems such a silly thing to want to do," the assassin admitted.

Evan smiled. He'd long ago decoded the two-stage virus the gene-pirate had used on him: one a Trojan horse which kept his T lymphocytes busy while the other rewrote loyalty genes companies implanted in their employees. Once again it had proven its worth. He said, "I need someone like you in my organization. And since you spent so long getting close enough to seduce me, perhaps you'd do me the honour of becoming my wife. I'll need one."

"You don't mind being married to a killer?"

"Oh, that. I used to be one myself."

8

Evan saw the market crash coming. Gene wars had winnowed basic foodcrops to soybeans, rice and, dole yeast: tailored ever-mutating diseases had reduced cereals and many other cash crops to nucleotide sequences stored in computer vaults. Three global biotechnology companies held patents on the calorific input of ninety-eight percent of humanity, but they had lost control of the technology. Pressures of the war economy had simplified it to the point where anyone could directly manipulate her own genome, and hence her own body form.

Evan had made a fortune in the fashion industry, selling templates and microscopic self-replicating robots which edited DNA. But he guessed that sooner or later someone would come up with a direct-photosynthesis system, and his stock-market expert systems were programmed to correlate research in the field. He and his wife sold controlling interest in their company three months before the first green people appeared.

9

"I remember when you knew what a human being was," Evan said sadly. "I suppose I'm old-fashioned, but there it is."

From her cradle, inside a mist of spray, his wife said, "Is that why you never went green? I always thought it was a fashion statement."

"Old habits die hard." The truth was, he liked his body the way it was. These days, going green involved somatic mutation which grew a metre-high black cowl to absorb sufficient light energy. Most people lived in the tropics, swarms of black-caped anarchists. Work was no longer a necessity, but an indulgence. Evan added, "I'm going to miss you."

"Let's face it," his wife said, "we never were in love. But I'll miss you, too." With a flick of her powerful tail she launched her streamlined body into the sea.

10

Black-cowled post-humans, gliding slowly in the sun, aggregating and reaggregating like amoebae. Dolphinoids, tentacles sheathed under fins, rocking in tanks of cloudy water. Ambulatory starfish; tumbling bushes of spikes; snakes with a single arm, a single leg; flocks of tiny birds, brilliant as emeralds, each flock a single entity.

People, grown strange, infected with myriads of microscopic machines which re-engraved their body form at will.

Evan lived in a secluded estate. He was revered as a founding father of the posthuman revolution. A purple funfur microsaur followed him everywhere. It was recording him because he had elected to die.

"I don't regret anything," Evan said, "except perhaps not following my wife when she changed. I saw it coming, you know. All this. Once the technology became simple enough, cheap enough, the companies lost control. Like television or computers, but I suppose you don't remember those." He sighed. He had the vague feeling he'd said all this before. He'd had no new thoughts for a century, except the desire to put an end to thought.

The microsaur said, "In a way, I suppose I am a computer. Will you see the colonial delegation now?"

"Later." Evan hobbled to a bench and slowly sat down. In the last couple of months he had developed mild arthritis, liver spots on the backs of his hands: death finally expressing parts of his genome that had been suppressed for so long. Hot sunlight fell through the velvet streamers of the tree things; Evan dozed, woke to find a group of starfish watching him. They had blue, human eyes, one at the tip of each muscular arm.

"They wish to honour you by taking your genome to Mars," the little purple triceratops said.

Evan sighed. "I just want peace. To rest. To die."

"Oh, Evan," the little triceratops said patiently, "surely even you know that nothing really dies any more."

THE GALLERY OF HIS DREAMS

Kristine Kathryn Rusch

New writer Kristine Kathryn Rusch, one of the fastest-rising and most prolific young authors on the scene today, has had a very busy few years. She was the editor of *Pulphouse* in its original incarnation as a quarterly anthology series, and won a World Fantasy Award along with publisher Dean Wesley Smith for her work on it; she is still the editor for various *Pulphouse* publishing projects, including the Axolotl novella series and a new novella series co-edited with Betsy Mitchell. In 1991, she stepped down as editor of the *Pulphouse* anthology series to become the new editor of *The Magazine of Fantasy and Science Fiction*, taking over from long-time editor Edward Ferman. As a writer, she won the John W. Campbell Award, and she is also a frequent contributor to *Amazing, Aboriginal SF, Full Spectrum, Isaac Asimov's Science Fiction Magazine*, and elsewhere. Her first novel, *The White Mists of Power*, has just appeared, and she has nine other novels under contract. Her story "Skin Deep" was in our Sixth Annual Collection. She lives in Eugene, Oregon . . . although it's difficult to see how she can have time to *sleep* there! She may be one of the busiest professionals in science fiction today.

In the compelling story that follows, she takes us back to the turbulent and dangerous days of the American Civil War to meet one of its most famous chroniclers, pioneer photographer Mathew Brady—and then plunges Brady ahead into a hostile and incomprehensible future of aching strangeness, a future where Brady faces his most bizarre and difficult assignment. . . .

> *Let him who wishes to know what war is look at this series of illustrations. . . . It was so nearly like visiting the battlefield to look over these views, that all the emotions excited by the actual sight of the stained and sordid scene, strewed with rags and wrecks, came back to us, and we buried them in the recesses of our cabinet as we would have buried the mutilated remains of the dead they too vividly represented.*
>
> —Oliver Wendell Holmes

1838

Brady leaned against a hay bale and felt the blades dig into his back. He smelled of pig dung and his own sweat, and his muscles ached. His da had gone to the pump to wash up, and then into the cow shed, but Brady claimed he needed a rest. His da, never one to argue with relaxation, let him sit against the hay bales. Brady didn't dare stay too long; if his ma saw him, she would be on the front porch, yelling insults unintelligible through her Irish brogue.

He did need to think, though. Milking cows and cleaning the pig pen didn't give him enough time to make plans. He couldn't stay on the farm the rest of his life, he knew that. He hated the work, the animals, the smell, and the long hours that all led to a poor, subsistence living. His da thought the farm a step up from the hovel he had grown up in and certainly an improvement from Brady's grandfather's life back in the Old Country. Brady often wished he could see what his da's life or his grandfather's life had really been like. But he had to trust their memories, memories that, at least in his grandfather's case, had become more and more confusing as the years progressed.

Brady pulled a strand of hay from the bale, sending a burst of sharp fresh summer-scent around him. He wanted more than a ruined farm and a few livestock in upstate New York. Mr. Hanley, his teacher, had pulled Brady aside on the day he left school, and reminded him that in the United States of America, even farmboys could become great men. Mr. Hanley used to start the school day by telling the boys that the late President Thomas Jefferson defined the nation's creed when he wrote that all men were created equal, and President Andrew Jackson had proven the statement true with his election not ten years before.

Brady didn't want to be president. He wanted to do something different, something he couldn't even imagine now. He wanted to be great—and he wanted to be remembered.

1840

The spring thaw had turned the streets of New York City into rivers. Brady laughed as he jumped from one sidewalk board to the next, then turned and waited for Page to jump. Page hesitated a moment, running a slender hand through his beard. Then he jumped and landed, one tattered shoe in the cold water, one out. Brady grabbed his friend's arm, and pulled him up.

"Good Lord, William, how far away is this man's home?"

"He's not just any man," Page said, shaking the water off his legs. "He's a painter, and a damn fine one."

Brady smiled. Page was a painter himself and had, a few months earlier, opened a studio below their joint apartment. Brady helped with the rent on the studio as a repayment for Page's help in moving Brady from the farm. Being a clerk at A.T. Stewart's largest store was an improvement over farm life—the same kind of improvement that Brady's father had made. Only Brady wasn't going to stop there. Page had promised to help by showing Brady how to paint. While Brady had an eye for composition, he lacked the firm hand, the easy grace of a portraitist. Page had been polite; he hadn't said that Brady was hopeless. But they both knew that Mathew B. Brady would never make his living with a paintbrush in his hand.

Brady braced himself against a wooden building as he stepped over a submerged portion of sidewalk. "You haven't said what this surprise is."

"I don't know what the surprise is. Samuel simply said that he had learned about it in France and that we would be astonished." Page slipped into a thin alley between buildings and then pulled open a door. Brady followed, and found himself staring up a dark flight of stairs. Page was already half-way up, his wet shoe squeaking with each step. Brady gripped the railing and took the stairs two at a time.

Page opened the door, sending light across the stairs. Brady reached the landing just as Page bellowed, "Samuel!" Brady peered inside, nearly choking on the scent of linseed and turpentine.

Large windows graced the walls, casting dusty sunlight on a room filled with canvases. Dropcloths covered most of the canvases and some of the furniture scattered about. A desk, overflowing with papers, stood under one window. Near that a large wooden box dwarfed a rickety table. A stoop-shouldered long-haired man braced the table with one booted foot.

"Over here, Page, over here. Don't dawdle. Help me move this thing. The damn table is about to collapse."

Page scurried across the room, bent down, and grabbed an edge of the box. The man picked up the other side and led the way to his desk. He balanced the box with one hand and his knee while his other hand swept the desk clean. They set the box down and immediately the man pulled out a handkerchief and wiped away the sweat that had dripped into his bushy eyebrows.

"I meant to show you in a less dramatic fashion," he said, then looked up.

Brady whipped his hat off his head and held it with both hands. The man had sharp eyes, eyes that could see right through a person, clear down to his dreams.

"Well?" the man said.

Brady nodded. He wouldn't be stared down. "I'm Mathew B. Brady, sir."

"Samuel F. B. Morse." Morse tucked his handkerchief back into his pocket and clasped his hands behind his back. "You must be the boy Page has been telling me about. He assumes you have some sort of latent talent."

Brady glanced at Page. Page blushed, the color seeping through the patches of skin still visible through his beard.

"Hmmm," Morse said as he stalked forward. He paced around Brady, studied him for a moment. "You're what, eighteen?"

"Almost, sir."

"If you had talent, you'd know it by now." Morse shook his head. His suit smelled faintly of mothballs. "No, no. You're one of the lucky ones, blessed with drive. A man with talent merely has a head start. A man with drive succeeds."

Morse stalked back to his desk, stepping on the papers that littered the floor. "Drive but no talent. I have the perfect machine for you." He put his hand on the box. "Ever hear of Louis Daguerre? No, of course not. What would a farmboy know of the latest scientific discoveries?"

Brady started, then shot another look at Page. Perhaps Page had said something about Brady's background. Page ignored him and moved closer to Morse.

"Daguerre found a way to preserve the world in one image. Look." He handed Page a small metal plate. As Page tilted it toward the light, Brady saw the Unitarian Church he walked past almost every day.

"This is a daguerreotype," Morse said. "I made this one through the window of the third floor staircase at New York University."

"That is the right view." Page's voice held awe. "You used no paints."

"I used this," Morse said, his hand pounding on the box's top. "It has a lens here—" and he pointed at the back end from which a glass-topped cylinder protruded "—and a place here for the plates. The plates are silver on copper which I treat with iodine and expose to light through the lens. Then I put the plate in another box containing heated mercury and when I'm done   an image! An exact reproduction of the world in black and white."

Brady touched the cool edge of the plate. "It preserves memories," he said, thinking that if such a device had existed before, he could have seen his father's hovel, his grandfather's home.

"It does more than that, son," Morse said. "This is our future. It will destroy portrait painting. Soon everything will be images on metal, keepsakes for generations to come."

Page pulled back at the remark about portrait painting. He went to the window, looked at the street below. "I suppose that's why you brought us up here. To show me that I'll be out of work soon?"

"No, lad." Morse laughed and the sound boomed and echoed off the canvas-covered walls. "I want to save you, not destroy you. I'm opening a school to teach this new process and I invite you to join. Fifty dollars tuition for the entire semester and I promise you'll be a better portraitist when you're done than you are now."

Page gave Morse a sideways look. Page's back was rigid and his hands were clenched in trembling fists. Brady could almost feel his friend's rage. "I paint." Page spoke with a slow deliberation. "I have no need for what will clearly become a poor man's art."

Morse did not seem offended by Page's remark. "And you, young Brady. Will you use your drive to acquire a talent?"

Brady stared at the plate and mysterious box. Fifty dollars was a lot of money, but he already had twenty set aside for a trip home. Page did say he had an eye for composition. And if a man with an eye for composition, a lot of drive and a little talent took Daguerre's Box all over the world, he would be able to send his memories back to the people left behind.

Brady smiled. "Yes," he said. "I'll take your class."

He would postpone the trip to see his parents, and raise the rest of the money somehow. Page whirled away from the window as if Brady had betrayed him. But Brady didn't care. When they got home, he would explain it all. And it was so simple. He had another improvement to make.

1840

That night, Brady dreamed. He stood in a large cool room, darkened and hidden in shadows. He bumped into a wall and found himself touching a ribbed column—a doric column, he believed. He took cautious steps forward, stumbled, then caught himself on a piece of painted wood. His hands slid up the rough edges until he realized he was standing beside a single-horse carriage. He felt his way around to the back. The carriage box had no windows, but the back stood wide open. He climbed inside. The faint rotten-egg smell of sulphur rose. He bumped against a box and glass rattled. A wagon filled with equipment. He climbed out, feeling as if he was snooping. There was more light now. He saw a wall ahead of him, covered with portraits.

The darkness made the portraits difficult to see, but he thought he recognized the light and shadow work of a Daguerre portrait and yet—and yet—something differed, distorted, perhaps, by the dream. And he *knew* he was in a dream. The cool air was too dry, the walls made of a foreign substance, the lights (what he could see of them), glass-encased boxes on the ceiling. The portraits were of ghastly things: dead men and stark fields, row after row of demolished buildings. On several, someone had lettered his last name in flowing white script.

"They will make you great," said a voice behind him. He turned, and saw a woman. At least, he thought it was a woman. Her hair was cropped above her ears, and she wore trousers.

"Who will make me great?" he asked.

"The pictures," she said. "People will remember them for generations." He took a step closer to her, but she smiled and touched his palm. The shadows turned black and the dream faded into a gentle, restful sleep.

1849

Brady leaned against the hand-carved wooden railing. The candles on the large chandelier burned steady, while the candelabras flickered in the breezes left by the dancing couples. A pianist, a violinist, and a cello player—all, Mr. Handy had assured him, very well respected—played the newest European dance, the waltz, from one corner of the huge ballroom. Mothers cornered their daughters along the wall, approving dance cards, and shaking fans at impertinent young males. The staircase opened into the ballroom, and Brady didn't want to cross the threshold. He had never been to a dance like this before. His only experiences dancing had been at gatherings Page had taken him to when he first arrived in New York. He knew none of the girls except Samuel Handy's daughter Juliet and she was far too pretty for Brady to approach.

So he watched her glide across the floor with young man after young man, her hooped skirts swaying, her brown hair in ringlets, her eyes sparkling, and her cheeks flushed. Handy had told him that at the age of four, she had been presented to President Jackson. She had been so beautiful, Handy said, that Jackson had wanted to adopt her. Brady was glad he hadn't seen her as a child, glad he had seen the mature beauty. When he finished taking the portraits of her father, he would ask if he could take one of her. The wet-plate process would let him make copies, and he would keep one in his own rooms, just so that he could show his friends how very lovely she was.

The waltz ended, and Julia curtsied to her partner, then left the floor. Her dance card swung from her wrist and the diamonds around her neck caught the candlelight. Too late, Brady realized she was coming to see him.

"I have one spot left on my dance card," she said as she stopped in front of him. She smelled faintly of lilacs, and he knew he would have to keep a sprig near her portrait every spring. "And I was waiting for you to fill it."

Brady blushed. "I barely know you, Miss Juliet."

She batted his wrist lightly with her fan. "Julia," she said. "And I know you better than half the boys here. You have spent three days in my daddy's house, Mr. Brady, and your conversation at dinner has been most entertaining. I was afraid that I bored you."

"No, no," he said. The words sounded so formal. How could he joke with his female clients and let this slip of a girl intimidate him? "I would love to take that slot on your dance card, Miss Juliet."

"Julia," she said again. "I hate being named after a stupid little minx who died for nothing. I think when a woman loves, it is her duty to love intelligently, don't you?"

"Yes," Brady said, although he had no idea what she was talking about. "And I'm Mathew."

"Wonderful, Mathew." Her smile added a single dimple to her left cheek. She extended her card to him and he penciled his name in for the next dance, filling the bottom of the first page. The music started—another waltz—and she took his hand. He followed her onto the floor, placed one hand on her cinched waist, and held the other lightly in his own. They circled around the floor, the tip of her skirt brushing against his pants leg. She didn't smile at him. Instead her eyes were very serious and her lips were pursed and full.

"You don't do this very often, do you, Mathew?"

"No," he said. In fact, he felt as if he were part of a dream—the musicians, the beautifully garbed women, the house servants blending into the wallpaper. Everything at the Handy plantation had an air of almost too much sensual pleasure. "I work, probably too much."

"I have seen what you do, Mathew, and I think it is a wondrous magic." A slight flush crept into her cheeks, whether from the exertion or her words, Brady couldn't tell. She lowered her voice. "I dreamed about you last night. I dreamed I was in a beautiful large gallery with light clearer than sunlight and hundreds of people milled about, looking at your portraits on the wall. They all talked about you, how marvelous your work was, and how it influenced them. You're a great man, Mathew, and I am flattered at the interest you have shown in me."

The music stopped and she slipped from his arms, stopping to chat with another guest as she wandered toward the punch table. Brady stood completely still, his heart pounding against his chest. She had been to the gallery of his dreams. She knew about his future. The musicians began another piece, and Brady realized how foolish he must look, standing in the center of the dance floor. He dodged whirling couples and made his way to the punch table, hoping that he could be persuasive enough to convince Julia Handy to let him replace all those other names on the remaining half of her dance card.

1861

He woke up with the idea, his body sweat-covered and shimmering with nervous energy. If he brought a wagon with him, it would work: a wagon like the one he had dreamed about the night he had met Morse.

Brady moved away from his sleeping wife and stepped onto the bare hardwood. The floor creaked. He glanced at Julia, but she didn't awaken. The bedroom was hot; Washington in July had a muggy air. If the rumors were to be believed, the first battle would occur in a matter of days. He had so little time. He had thought he would never come up with a way to record the war.

He had started recording history with his book, the *Gallery of Illustrious Americans*. He had hoped to continue by taking portraits of the impending battles, but he hadn't been able to figure out how. The wet plates had to be developed right after the portrait had been taken. He needed a way to take the equipment with him to the battlefield. The answer was so simple, he was amazed he had to dream it.

But that dream had haunted him for years now. And when he had learned the wet-plate process, discovered that the rotten-egg smell of sulphur was part of it, the dream had come back to him as vividly as an old memory. That had been years ago. Now, with the coming war, he found himself thinking of the portraits of demolished buildings, and the woman's voice, telling him he would be great.

He would have to set up a special war fund. The president had given him a pass to make portraits of the army on the field, but had stressed that Brady would have to use his own funds. As Lincoln told Brady, with only a hint of humor, the country was taking enough gambles already.

Small price, Brady figured, to record history. He was, after all, a wealthy man.

1861

Julia had hoped to join the picnickers who sat on the hills, overlooking the battlefield, but Brady was glad he had talked her out of it. He pulled the wet plate out of his camera, and placed the plate into the box. The portrait would be of smoke and tiny men clashing below him. He glanced at the farmhouse, and the army that surrounded it. They seemed uneasy, as if this battle weren't what they expected. It wasn't what he had expected, either. The confusion, the smoke, even the heat made sense. The screaming did not.

Brady put the plate in its box, then set the box in his wagon. Before the day was out, he would return to Washington, set the plates and send portraits to the illustrated magazines. The wagon was working out better than he expected. The illustrations would probably earn him yet another award.

The cries seemed to grow louder, and above them, he heard a faint rumbling. He checked the sky for clouds and saw nothing. The smoke gave the air an acrid tinge and made the heat seem even hotter. A bead of sweat ran down the side of his face. He grabbed the camera and lugged it back to the wagon, then returned for the tripod. He was proud of himself; he had expected to be afraid and yet his hands were as steady as they had been inside his studio.

He closed up the back of the wagon, waved his assistant, Tim O'Sullivan, onto the wagon, and climbed aboard. O'Sullivan sat beside him and clucked the horse onto Bull Run road. The army's advance had left ruts so deep that the wagon tilted at an odd angle. The rumble was growing louder. Overhead, something whistled, and then a cannonball landed off to one side, spraying dirt and muck over the two men. The horse shrieked and reared; Brady felt the reins cut through his fingers. The wagon rocked, nearly tipped, then righted itself. Brady turned, and saw a dust cloud rising behind them. A mass of people were running toward him.

"Lord a mercy," he whispered, and thrust the reins at O'Sullivan. O'Sullivan looked at them as if he had never driven the wagon before. "I'm going to get the equipment. Be ready to move on my signal."

O'Sullivan brought the horse to a stop and Brady leapt off the side. He ran to the back, opened the door, grabbed his camera, and set up just in time to take portraits of soldiers running past. Both sides—Union and Confederate—wore blue, and Brady couldn't tell which troops were scurrying past him. He could smell the fear, the human sweat, see the strain in the men's eyes. His heart had moved to his throat, and he had to concentrate to shove a wet plate into the camera. He uncapped the lens, hoping that the scene wouldn't change too much, that in his precious three seconds, he would capture more than a blur.

Mixed with the soldiers were women, children, and well-dressed men—some still clutching picnic baskets, others barely holding their hats. All ran by. A few loose horses galloped near Brady; he had to hold the tripod steady. He took portrait after portrait, seeing faces he recognized—like that silly newspaper correspondent Russell, the man who had spread the word about Brady's poor eyesight—mouths agape, eyes wide in panic. As Brady worked, the sounds blended into each other. He couldn't tell the human screams from the animal shrieks and the whistle of mortar. Bullets whizzed past, and more than one lodged in the wagon. The wagon kept lurching, and Brady knew that O'Sullivan was having trouble holding the horse.

Suddenly the wagon rattled away from him. Brady turned, knocked over the tripod himself, and watched in horror as people trampled his precious equipment. He started to get down, to save the camera, then realized that in their panic, they would run over him. He grabbed what plates he could, shoved them into the pocket of his great coat, and joined the throng, running after the wagon, shouting at O'Sullivan to stop.

But the wagon didn't stop. It kept going around the winding, twisting corners of the road, until it disappeared in the dust cloud. Another cannon ball landed beside the road, and Brady cringed as dirt spattered him. A woman screamed and fell forward, blood blossoming on her back. He turned to help her, but the crowd pushed him forward. He couldn't stop even if he wanted to.

This was not romantic; it was not the least bit pretty. It had cost him hundreds of dollars in equipment and might cost him his life if he didn't escape soon. This was what the history books had never told him about war, had never explained about the absolute mess, the dirt and the blood. Behind him, he heard screaming, someone shouting that the black cavalry approached, the dreaded black cavalry of the Confederacy, worse than the four horses of the apocalypse, if the illustrated newspapers were to be believed, and Brady ran all the harder. His feet slipped in the ruts in the road and he nearly tripped, but he saw other people down, other people trampled, and he knew he couldn't fall.

He rounded a corner, and there it was, the wagon, on its side, the boxes spilling out, the plates littering the dirt road. O'Sullivan was on his hands and knees, trying to clean up, his body shielded only because the carriage wall made the fleeing people reroute.

Brady hurried over the carriage side, ignoring the split wood, the bullet holes and the fact that the horse was missing. Tears were running down the side of O'Sullivan's face, but the man seemed oblivious to them. Brady grabbed O'Sullivan's arm, and pulled him up. "Come on, Tim," he said. "Black cavalry on the hills. We've got to get away."

"The plates—" O'Sullivan said.

"Forget the plates. We've got to get out of here."

"The horse spooked and broke free. I think someone stole her, Mat."

O'Sullivan was shouting, but Brady could barely hear him. His lungs were choked and he thought he was going to drown in dust. "We have to go," he said.

He yanked O'Sullivan forward, and they rejoined the crowd. They ran until Brady could run no longer; his lungs burned and his side ached. Bullets continued to strike around them, and Brady saw too many men in uniform sprawled motionless on the side of the road.

"The crowd itself is a target," he said, not realizing he had spoken aloud. He tightened his grip on O'Sullivan's arm and led him off the road into the thin trees. They trudged straight ahead, Brady keeping the setting sun to his left, and soon the noises of battle disappeared behind them. They stopped and Brady leaned against a thick oak to catch his breath. The sun had gone down and it was getting cool.

"What now?" O'Sullivan asked.

"If we don't meet any rebs, we're safe," Brady said. He took off his hat, wiped the sweat off his brow with his sleeve, and put his hat back on. Julia would have been very angry with him if he had lost that hat.

"But how do we get back?" O'Sullivan asked.

An image of the smashed equipment rose in Brady's mind along with the broken, overturned horseless wagon. "We walk, Tim." Brady sighed. "We walk."

1861

Julia watched as he stocked up the new wagon. She said nothing as he lugged equipment inside, new equipment he had purchased from Anthony's supply house on extended credit. He didn't want to hurt his own business by taking away needed revenue, and the Anthonys were willing to help—especially after they had seen the quality of his war work for the illustrated newspapers.

"I can't come with you, can I?" she asked as he tossed a bedroll into the back.

"I'm sorry," Brady said, remembering the woman scream and fall beside him, blood blossoming on her back. His Julia wouldn't die that way. She would die in her own bed, in the luxury and comfort she was used to. He took her hands. "I don't want to be apart from you, but I don't know any other way."

She stroked his face. "We have to remember—" she said. The tears that lined the rims of her eyes didn't touch her voice. "—that this is the work that will make you great."

"You have already made me great," he said, and kissed her one final time.

1863

Brady pushed his blue-tinted glasses up his nose and wiped the sweat off his brow with the back of his hand. The Pennsylvania sun beat on his long black waistcoat, baking his clothes against his skin. The corpse, only a few hours dead, was already gaseous and bloated, straining its frayed Union uniform. The too-florid smell of death ripened the air. If it weren't for the bodies, human and equine, the farmer's field would seem peaceful, not the site of one of the bloodiest battles of the war.

Brady tilted the corpse's head back. Underneath the gray mottled skin, a young boy's features had frozen in agony. Brady didn't have to alter the expression: he never did. The horror was always real. He set the repeating rifle lengthwise across the corpse, and stood up. A jagged row of posed corpses stretched before him. O'Sullivan had positioned the wagon toward the side of the field and was struggling with the tripod. Brady hurried to help his assistant, worried, always worried about destroying more equipment. They had lost so much trying to photograph the war. He should have known from the first battle how difficult this would be. He had sold nearly everything, asked Julia to give up even the simplest comforts, borrowed against his name from the Anthonys for equipment to record this. History. His country's folly and its glory. And the great, terrible waste of lives. He glanced back at the dead faces, wondered how many people would mourn.

"I think we should put it near the tree." O'Sullivan lugged the top half of the tripod at an angle away from the corpse row. "The light is good—the shade is on the other side. Mathew?"

"No." Brady backed up a few steps. "Here. See the angle? The bodies look random now, but you can see the faces."

He squinted, wishing he could see the faces better. His eyesight had been growing worse; in 1851 it had been so bad that the press thought he would be blind in a decade. Twelve years had passed and he wasn't blind yet. But he wasn't far from it.

O'Sullivan arranged the black curtain, then Brady swept his assistant aside. "Let me," he said.

He climbed under the curtain. The heat was thicker; the familiar scent of chemicals cleared the death from his nose. He peered through the lens. The image was as he had expected it to be, clear, concise, well composed. The light filtered through, reflected oddly through the blue tint on his glasses, and started a sharp ache in his skull. He pulled out, into the sun. "Adjust as you need to. But I think we have the image."

Brady turned away from the field as O'Sullivan prepared the wet plate and then shoved it into the camera. Sweat trickled down the back of Brady's neck into his woolen coat. He was tired, so tired, and the war had already lasted two years longer than anyone expected. He didn't know how many times he had looked on the faces of the dead, posed them for the camera the way he had posed princes and presidents a few years before. If he had stayed in New

York, like the Anthonys, everything would have been different. He could have spent his nights with Julia. . . .

"Got it," O'Sullivan said. He held the plate gingerly, his face flushed with the heat.

"You develop it," Brady said. "I want to stay here for a few minutes."

O'Sullivan frowned; Brady usually supervised every step of the battle images. But Brady didn't explain his unusual behavior. O'Sullivan said nothing. He clutched the plates and went in the back of the black-covered wagon. The wagon rocked ever so gently as he settled in.

Brady waited until the wagon stopped rocking, then clasped his hands behind his back and walked through the trampled, blood-spattered grass. The aftermath of battle made him restless: the dead bodies, the ruined earth, the shattered wagons. Battles terrified him, made him want to run screaming from the scene. He often clutched his equipment around him like a talisman—if he worked, if he didn't think about it, he would stave off the fear until the shooting stopped. He tripped over an abandoned canteen. He crouched, saw the bullet hole in its side.

"You stay, even though it appalls you."

The woman's voice startled him so badly he nearly screamed. He backed up as he stood, and found himself facing a thin, short-haired woman wearing pants, a short-sleeved shirt, and (obviously) no undergarments. She looked familiar.

"That takes courage." She smiled. Her teeth were even and white.

"You shouldn't be here," he said. His voice shook and he clenched his fists to hide his shaking. "Are you looking for someone in particular? I can take you to the General."

"I'm looking for you. You're the man they call Brady of Broadway?"

He nodded.

"The man who sells everything, bargains his studio to photograph a war?"

Her comment was too close to his own thoughts—and too personal. He felt a flush rise that had nothing to do with the heat. "What do you want?"

"I want you to work for me, Mathew Brady. I will pay for your equipment, take care of your travel, if you shoot pictures for me when and where I say."

She frightened him, a crazy woman standing in a field of dead men. "I run my own business," he said.

She nodded, the smile fading just a little. "And it will bankrupt you. You will die forgotten, your work hidden in crates in government warehouses. That's not why you do this, is it, Mr. Brady?"

"I do this so that people can see what really happens here, so that people can travel through my memories to see this place," he said. The ache in his head grew sharper. This woman had no right to taunt him. "I do this for history."

"And it's history that calls you, Mr. Brady. The question is, will you serve?"

"I already serve," he snapped—and found himself speaking to air. Heat shimmered in front of him, distorting his view of the field for a moment. Then the tall grass and the broken picket fence returned, corpses hovering at the edge of his vision like bales of hay.

He took off his glasses and wiped his eyes. The strain was making him hallucinate. He had been too long in the sun. He would go back to the wagon, get a drink of water, lie in the shade. Then, perhaps, the memory of the hallucination would go away.

But her words haunted him as he retraced his steps. *I will pay for your equipment, take care of your travel.* If only someone would do that! He had spent the entire sum of his fortune and still saw no end ahead. She hadn't been an hallucination: she had been a dream. A wish for a different, easier life that no one would ever fulfill.

1865

The day after Appomatox—the end of the war, Brady dreamed:

He walked the halls of a well-lit place he had never seen before. His footsteps echoed on the shiny floor covering. Walls, made of a smooth material that was not wood or stone, smelled of paint and emollients. Ceiling boxes encased the lamps—the light did not flicker but they flowed cleaner than gaslight. Most of the doors lining the hallway were closed, but one stood open. A sign that shone with a light of its own read:

MATHEW B. BRADY EXHIBIT
OFFICIAL PHOTOGRAPHER:
UNITED STATES CIVIL WAR
(1861–1865)

Inside he found a spacious room twice the size of any room he had ever seen. It had skylights in the ceiling and doric columns creating a hollow in the center. A camera, set up on its tripod, had its black curtain thrown half back, as if waiting for him to step inside. Next to it stood his wagon, looking out of place and ancient without its horse. The wagon's back door also stood open, and Brady saw the wooden boxes of plates inside, placed neatly, so that a path led to the darkroom. The darkroom looked odd: no one had picked up the sleeping pallets, and yet the chemical baths sat out, ready for use. He would never have left the wagon that way. He shook his head, and turned toward the rest of the room.

Three of the long, wide walls were bare. On the fourth, framed pictures crowded together. He walked to them, saw that they were his portraits, his work from Bull Run, Antietam, Gettysburg. He even saw a picture of General Lee in his confederate gray. Beneath the portrait, the attribution read *By Brady (or assistant)*, but Brady had never taken such a portrait, never developed one, never posed one. A chill ran up his back when he realized he hadn't squinted to read the print. He reached up, touched the bridge of his nose. His glasses were gone. He hadn't gone without glasses since he had been a boy. In the mornings, he had to grab his glasses off the nightstand first, then get out of bed.

His entire wartime collection (with huge gaps) framed, on exhibit. Four thousand portraits, displayed for the world to see, just as he had hoped. He reached out to the Lee portrait. As his finger brushed the smooth wood—

—he found himself beneath the large tree next to the Appomatox farmhouse where the day before Lee and Grant had signed the peace treaty. The farmhouse was a big white blur against the blue of the April sky. He grabbed his glasses (somehow they had fallen to his lap) and hooked the frames around his ears. The world came into sharper focus, the blue-tint easing the glare of the sun. He knew what he had to do. Even though he had arrived too late to photograph the historic signing of the treaty, he could still photograph General Lee one last time in his uniform.

Brady got up and brushed the grass off his pants. His wagon stood beside the farmhouse. The wagon looked proper—dust-covered, mud-spattered, with a few splintered boards and a cock-eyed wheel that he would have to fix very soon—not clean and neat as it had in his dream. The horse, tied to another tree, looked tired, but he would push her with him to Richmond, to General Lee, to complete the exhibit.

Three empty walls, he thought as he went to find his assistant. He wondered why his earlier portraits weren't mounted there. Perhaps the walls awaited something else. Something better.

1866

Brady held his nephew Levin's shoulders and propelled him toward the door. The ticket taker at the desk in the lobby of the New York Historical Society waved them past.

"How many today, John?" Brady asked.

"We had a few paying customers yesterday," the large man said, "but they all left after looking at the first wall."

Brady nodded. The society had said they would close the exhibit of his war portraits if attendance didn't go up. But despite the free publicity in the illustrated newspapers and the positive critical response, the public was not attending.

Levin had already gone inside. He stood, hands behind his back, and stared at the portraits of destruction he had been too young to remember. Brady had brought Levin to the exhibit to discourage the boy and make him return to school. He had arrived a few days before, declaring that he wanted to be a photographer like his Uncle Mat. Brady had said twelve was too young to start learning the trade, but Julia had promised Levin a place to stay if no one demanded that he return to school. So far, no one had.

Brady went inside too. The lighting was poor, and the portraits were scattered on several small walls. No doric columns, no wide empty spaces.

This was a cramped showing, like so many others he had had, but it shared the emptiness of the gallery in his dreams.

He stared at the portraits, knowing them by heart. They ran in order, from the first glorious parade down Pennsylvania Avenue—taken from his Washington studio—to the last portrait of Lee after Appomatox. Each portrait took him back to the sights and sounds of the moment: the excitement of the parade, the disgust at the carnage, the hopelessness in Lee's eyes. It was here: the recent past, recorded as faithfully as a human being could. One of his reviewers had said that Brady had captured time and held it prisoner in his little glass plates. He certainly held it prisoner in his mind—or it held him. Sometimes all it took was a smell—decaying garbage, horse sweat—and he was back on the battlefield, fighting to live while he took his portraits.

From outside the door, he heard the murmur of voices. He turned in time to see John talking to a woman in widow's weeds. John pointed at Brady. Brady smiled and nodded, knowing he was being identified as the artist behind the exhibit.

The woman pushed open the glass doors and stood in front of Brady. She was slight and older than he expected—in her forties or fifties—with deep lines around her eyes and the corners of her mouth.

"I've come to plead with you, Mr. Brady," she said. Her voice was soft. "I want you to take these portraits away. Over there, you have an image of my husband's body, and in the next room, I saw my son. They're dead, Mr. Brady, and I buried them. I want to think about how they lived, not how they died."

"I'm sorry, ma'am," Brady said. He didn't turn to see which portraits she had indicated. "I didn't mean to offend you. These portraits show what war really is, and I think it's something we need to remember, lest we try it again."

Levin had stopped his movement through the gallery. He hadn't turned toward the conversation, but Brady could tell the boy was listening from the cocked position of his head.

"We'll remember, Mr. Brady," the woman said. She smoothed her black skirt. "My whole family has no choice."

She turned her back and walked out, her steps firm and proud. The street door closed sharply behind her. John got up from his chair.

"You've gotten this before," Brady said.

"Every day," John said. "People want to move forward, Mathew. They don't need more reminders of the past."

Brady glanced at his nephew. Levin had moved into one of the back rooms. "Once Levin is done looking at the exhibit, I'll help you remove it," Brady said. "No sense hurting your business to help mine."

He sighed and glanced around the room. Four years of work. Injured associates, ruined equipment, lost wealth, and a damaged business. He had expected acclaim, at least, if not a measure of additional fame. One of his mother's aphorisms rose in his mind: a comment she used to make when he would come inside, covered with dirt and dung. "How the mighty hath fallen," she'd say. She had never appreciated his dreams nor had she lived long enough to see them come true. Now her shade stood beside him, as clearly as she had stood on the porch so many years ago, and he could hear the "I-told-you-so" in her voice.

He shook the apparition away. What his mother had never realized was that the mighty had farther to fall.

1871

That morning, he put on his finest coat, his best hat, and he kissed Julia with a passion he hadn't shown in years. She smiled at him, her eyes filled with tears, as she held the door open for him. He stepped into the hallway, and heard the latch snick shut behind him. Nothing looked different: the gas lamps had sootmarks around the base of the chimneys; the flowered wallpaper peeled in one corner; the stairs creaked as he stepped on them, heading down to the first floor and the street. Only he felt different: the shuddery bubble in his stomach, the tension in his back, the lightheadedness threatening the sureness of his movements.

He stopped on the first landing and took a breath of the musty hotel air. He wondered what they would think of him now, all the great men he had known. They came back to him, like battlefield ghosts haunting a general. Samuel Morse, his large dark eyes snapping, his gnarled hands holding the daguerreotypes, his voice echoing in the room, teaching Brady that photography would cause a revolution—a revolution, boy!—and he had to ride the crest.

"I did," Brady whispered. His New York studio, so impressive in the 1850s, had a portrait of Morse hanging near the door for luck. Abraham Lincoln had gazed at that portrait. So had his assassin, John Wilkes Booth. Presidents, princes, actors, assassins had all passed through Brady's door. And he, in his arrogance, had thought his work art, not commerce. Art and history demanded his presence at the first Battle of Bull Run. Commerce had demanded he stay home, take *cartes de visite*, imperials and portraits of soldiers going off to war, of families about to be destroyed, of politicians, great and small.

No. He had left his assistants to do that, while he spent their earnings, his fortune and his future chasing a dream.

And this morning, he would pay for that dream.

So simple, his attorney told him. He would sign his name to a paper, declare bankruptcy, and the government would apportion his assets to his remaining creditors. He could still practice his craft, still attempt to repay his debts, still *live*, if someone wanted to call that living.

He adjusted the jacket one final time and stepped into the hotel's lobby. The desk clerk called out his customary good morning, and Brady nodded. He would show no shame, no anger. The doorman opened the door and cool, manure-tinged air tickled Brady's nostrils. He took a deep breath and walked into the bustle of the morning: Mathew Brady, photographer. A man who had joked with Andrew Jackson, Martin Van Buren, and James Buchanan. A man who had raised a camera against bullets, who had held more dead and dying than half the physicians on the battlefield. Brady pushed forward, touching the brim of his hat each time he passed a woman, nodding at the gentlemen as if this day were the best in his life. Almost everyone had seen his work, in the illustrated papers, in the exhibits, in the halls of Congress itself. He had probably photographed the sons of most of the people who walked these streets. Dead faces, turned toward the sun.

The thought sobered him. These people had lost husbands, fathers, children. Losses greater than his. And they had survived, somehow. Somehow.

He held the thought as he made his way through the morning, listening to the attorney mumble, the government officials drone on, parceling out his possessions like clothing at an orphan's charity. The thought carried him out the door, and back onto the street before the anger burst through the numbness.

The portraits were his children. He and Julia had none—and he had nothing else. Nothing else at all.

"Now are you ready to work with me?"

The female voice was familiar enough that he knew who he would see before he looked up: the crazy woman who haunted him, who wanted him to give everything he had to history.

As if he hadn't given enough.

She stood before him, the winter sunlight backlighting her, and hiding her features in shadow. The Washington crowd walked around her, unseeing, as if she were no more than a post blocking the path.

"And what do I get if I help you?" he asked, his voice sounding harsher than he had ever heard it.

"Notice. Acclaim. Pictures on walls instead of buried in warehouses. The chance to make a very real difference."

He glanced back at the dark wooden door, at the moving figures faint in the window, people who had buried his art, given it to the Anthonys, separated it and segregated it and declared it worthless. His children, as dead as the ones he had photographed.

"And you'll pay my way?" he asked.

"I will provide your equipment and handle your travel, if you take photographs for me when and where I say."

"Done," he said, extending a hand to seal the bargain, thinking that a crazy, mannish woman like this one would close a deal like a gentleman. She took his hand, her palm soft, unused to work, and, as she shook it, the world whirled. Colors and pain and dust bombarded him. Smells he would briefly catch, but which by the time he had identified them had disappeared. His head ached, his eyes throbbed, his body felt as if it were being torn in fifteen different directions. And when they stopped, he was in a world of blackness, where hot rain fell like fire from the sky.

"I need you to photograph this," she said, and then she disappeared. In her place, his wagon stood, the only friend in a place of strangeness. The air smelled of burning buildings, of sticky wet, of decay. Death. He recognized it from the battlefields years ago. The horizon was black, dotted with orange flame. The trees rose stunted against the oppression. People—Orientals, he realized with some amazement—ran by him, their strange clothing ripped and torn, their faces burned, peeling, shining with the strange heat. They made no sound as they moved: all he heard was the rain slapping against the road.

He grabbed an old man, stopped him, felt the soft, decaying flesh dissolve between his fingers. "What is this place?" he asked.

The old man reached out a trembling hand, touched Brady's round eyes, his white skin. "Amelican—" the old man took a deep breath and exhaled into a wail that became a scream. He wrenched his arm from Brady's grasp, and started to run. The people around him screamed too, and ran, as if they were fleeing an unseen enemy. Brady grabbed his wagon, rocking with the force of the panicked crowd, and hurried to the far side.

People lay across the grass like corpses on the battlefield. Only these corpses moved. A naked woman swayed in the middle of the ground, her body covered with burns except for large flower-shaped patches all over her torso. And beside him lay three people, their faces melted away, their eyes bubbling holes in their smooth, shiny faces.

"What is this?" he cried out again.

But the woman who had brought him here was gone.

One of the faceless people grabbed his leg. He shook the hand away, trembling with the horror. The rich smell of decay made him want to gag.

He had been in this situation before—in the panic, among the decay, in the death—and he had found only one solution.

He reached inside his wagon and pulled out the camera. This time, though, he didn't scout for artistic composition. He turned the lens on the field of corpses, more horrifying than anything he'd seen under the Pennsylvania sun, and took portrait after portrait after portrait, building an artificial wall of light and shadow between himself and the black rain, the foul stench, and the silent, grasping hands of hundreds of dying people.

1871

And hours—or was it days?—later, after he could no longer move the tripod alone, no longer hold a plate between his fingers, after she appeared and took his wet plates and his equipment and his wagon, after he had given water to more people than he could count, and had torn his suit and felt the sooty rain drops dig into his skin, after all that, he found himself standing on the same street in Washington, under the same sunlit winter sky. A woman he had never seen before peered at him with concern on her wrinkled face and asked, "Are you all right, sir?"

"I'm fine," he said, and felt the lightheadedness that had threatened all morning take him to his knees on the wooden sidewalk. People surrounded him and someone called him by name. They took his arms and half carried him to the hotel. He dimly realized that they had gotten him up the stairs— the scent of lilacs announcing Julia's presence—and onto the bed. Julia's cool hand rested against his forehead and her voice, murmuring something soothing, washed over him like a blessing. He closed his eyes—

And dreamed in jumbled images:

Flowers burned into naked skin; row after row after row of bodies stretched out in a farmer's field, face after face tilted toward the sun; and the faces blend into troops marching under gray skies, General Grant's dust-covered voice repeating that war needs different rules, different players, and General Lee, staring across a porch on a gray April morning, wearing his uniform for the last time, saying softly that being a soldier is no longer an occupation for gentlemen. And through it all, black rain fell from the grey skies, coating everything in slimy heat, burning through skin, leaving bodies ravaged, melting people's clothes from their frames.

Brady gasped and sat up. Julia put her arm around him. "It's all right, Mathew," she said. "You were dreaming."

He put his head on her shoulder, and closed his eyes. Immediately, flower-burned skin rose in his vision and he forced his eyelids open. He still wore his suit, but there was no longer a gash in it and the fabric was dry. "I don't know what's wrong with me," he said.

"You just need rest."

He shook his head and got up. His legs were shaky, but the movement felt good. "Think of where we would be if I hadn't gone to Bull Run," he said. "We were rich. We had what we wanted. I would have taken portraits, and we would have made more money. We would have an even nicer studio and a home, instead of this apartment." He smiled a little. "And now the government will sell everything they can, except the portraits. Portraits that no one wants to see."

Julia still sat at the edge of the bed. Her black dress was wrinkled, and her ringlets mussed. She must have held him while he slept.

"You know," he said, leaning against the windowsill. "I met a woman just after the Battle of Gettysburg, and she told me that I would die forgotten with my work hidden in government warehouses. And I thought she was crazy; how could the world forget Brady of Broadway? I had dreams of a huge gallery, filled with my work—"

"Dreams have truth," Julia said.

"No," Mathew said. "Dreams have hope. Dreams without hope are nightmares." He swept his hand around the room. "This is a nightmare, Julia."

She bowed her head. Her hands were clasped together so tightly her knuckles had turned white. Then she raised her head, tossing her ringlets back, and he saw the proud young woman he had married. "So how do we change things, Mathew?"

He stared at her. Even now, she still believed in him, thought that together they could make things better. He wanted to tell her that they would recapture what they had lost; he wanted to give her hope. But he was forty-eight years old, nearly blind, and penniless. He didn't have *time* to rebuild a life from nothing.

"I guess we keep working," he said, quietly. But even as he spoke, a chill ran down his back. He had worked for the crazy woman and she had taken him through the Gates of Hell. And he had nothing to show for it except bad dreams and frightening memories. "I'm sorry, Julia."

"I'm not." She smiled that cryptic smile she had had ever since he married her. "The reward is worth the cost."

He nodded, feeling the rain still hot on his skin, hearing voices call for help in a language he could not understand. He wondered if any reward was worth these kinds of sacrifices.

He didn't think so.

1871

Six weeks later, Brady dreamed:

The exhibit room was colder than it had been before, the lighting better. Brady stood beside his wagon and clutched its wooden frame. He stepped around the wagon, saw that the doors to the exhibit were closed, and he was alone in the huge room. He touched his eyes. The glasses were missing, and he could see, just as he had in the previous dreams. His vision was clear, clearer than it had ever been.

No portraits had been added to the far wall. He walked toward his collection and then stopped. He didn't want to look at his old work. He couldn't bear the sight of it, knowing the kind of pain and loss those portraits had caused. Instead he turned and gasped.

Portraits graced a once-empty wall. He ran toward them, nearly tripping over the empty boards of the wagon. Hundreds of portraits framed and mounted at odd angles, glinted under the strange directed lights, the lights that never flickered. He stood closer, saw scenes he'd hoped he would forget: the flowered woman; the three faceless people, their eyes boiling in their sockets; a weeping man, his skin hanging around him like rags. The portraits were clearer, cleaner than the war portraits from the other wall. No dust had gotten in the fluid, no cracked wet plates, no destroyed glass. Clean, crisp portraits, on paper he had never seen before. But it was all his work, clearly his work.

He made himself look away. The air had a metallic smell. The rest of the wall was blank, as were the other two. More pictures to take, more of hell to see. He had experienced the fire and the brimstone, the burning rain—

Satan's tears. He wondered what else he would see, what else she would make him record.

He touched the portrait of the men with melted faces. If he had to trade visions like this for his eyesight and his wealth, he wouldn't make the trade. He would die poor and blind at Julia's side.

The air got colder.

He woke up screaming.

1873

Brady stared at the plate he held in his hand. His subject had long since left the studio, but Brady hadn't moved. He remembered days when subject after subject had entered the studio, and his assistants had had to develop the prints while Brady staged the sittings.

"I'll take that, Uncle."

Brady started. He hadn't realized that Levin was in the room. He wondered if Levin had been watching Brady stand there, doing nothing. Although Levin hadn't said anything about it during the past few years, he seemed to notice Brady's growing strange behaviors. "Thank you, Levin," Brady said, making sure his voice was calm.

Levin kept his eyes averted as he grabbed the covered plate and took it into the darkroom for developing. Levin had grown tall in the seven years that he'd been with Brady. Far from the self-assured twelve-year-old who had come to work for his uncle, Levin had become a silent man who came alive only behind the camera lens. Brady couldn't have survived without him, especially after he had to let the rest of his staff go.

Brady moved the camera, poured the collodion mixture back into its jar and covered the silver nitrate. Then he washed his hands in the bowl filled with tepid water that sat near the chemical storage.

"I have another job for you. Can you be alone on Friday at four?"

This time, Brady didn't jump, but his heart did. It pounded against his ribcage like a child trying to escape a locked room. His nerves had been on edge for so long. Julia kept giving him hot teas and rubbing the back of his neck, but nothing seemed to work. When he closed his eyes he saw visions he didn't want to see.

He turned, slowly. The crazy woman stood there, her hands clasped behind her back. Since she hadn't appeared in almost two years, he had managed to convince himself that she wasn't real—that he had imagined her.

"Another job?" he asked. He was shaking. Either he hadn't imagined the last one, or he was having another nightmare. "I'm sorry. I can't."

"Can't?" Her cheeks flushed. "You promised, Mathew. I need you."

"You never told me you were going to send me to Hell," he snapped. He moved away from the chemicals, afraid that in his anger, he would throw them. "You're not real, and yet the place you took me stays branded in my mind. I'm going crazy. You're a sign of my insanity."

"No," she said. She came forward and touched him lightly. Her fingertips were soft, and he could smell the faint perfume of her body. "You're not crazy. You're just faced with something from outside your experience. You had dreams about the late War, didn't you? Visions you couldn't escape?"

He was about to deny it, when he remembered now, in the first year of his return, the smell of rotted garbage took him back to the Devil's Hole; how the whinny of a horse made him duck for cover; how he stored his wagon because being inside it filled him with a deep anxiety. "What are you telling me?"

"I come from a place you've never heard of," she said. "We have developed the art of travel in an instant, and our societal norms are different from yours. The place I sent you wasn't Hell. It was a war zone, after the—a country had used a new kind of weapon on another country. I want to send you to more places like that, to photograph them, so that we can display those photographs for people of my society to see."

"If you can travel in an instant—" and he remembered the whirling world, the dancing colors and sounds as he traveled from his world to another "—then why don't you just *take* people there? Why do you need me?"

"Those places are forbidden. I received special dispensation. I'm working on an art project, and I nearly lost my funding because I saw you at Gettysburg."

Brady's shaking eased. "You risked everything to see me?"

She nodded. "We're alike in that way," she said. "You've risked everything to follow your vision, too."

"And you need me?"

"You're the first and the best, Mathew. I couldn't even get funding unless I guaranteed that I would have your work. Your studio portraits are lovely, Mathew, but it's your war photos that make you great."

"No one wants to see my war work," Brady said.

Her smile seemed sad. "They will, Mathew. Especially if you work with me."

Brady glanced around his studio, smaller now than it had ever been. Portraits of great men still hung on the walls along with actors, artists and people who just wanted a remembrance.

"At first it was art for you," she said, her voice husky. "Then it became a mission, to show people what war was really like. And now no one wants to look. But they *need* to, Mathew."

"I know," he said. He glanced back at her, saw the brightness in her face, the trembling of her lower lip. This meant more to her than an art project should. Something personal, something deep, had gotten her involved. "I went to Hell for you, and I never even got to see the results of my work."

"Yes, you did," she said.

"Uncle!" Levin called from the next room.

The woman vanished, leaving shimmering air in her wake. Brady reached out and touched it, felt the remains of a whirlwind. She knew about his dreams, then. Or was she referring to the work he had done inside his wagon on the site, developing plates before they dried so that the portraits would be preserved?

"Did I hear voices?" Levin came out of the back room, wiping his hands on his smock.

Brady glanced at Levin, saw the frown between the young man's brows. Levin was really worried about him. "No voices," Brady said. "Perhaps you just heard someone calling from the street."

"The portrait is done." Levin looked at the chemicals, as if double-checking his uncle's work.

"I'll look at it later," Brady said. "I'm going home to Julia. Can you watch the studio?"

Levin nodded.

Brady grabbed his coat off one of the sitting chairs and stopped at the doorway. "What do you think of my war work, Levin? And be honest, now."

"Honest?"

"Yes."

Brady waited. Levin took a deep breath. "I wish that I were ten years older so that I could have been one of your assistants, Uncle. You preserved something that future generations need to see. And it angers me that no one is willing to look."

"Me, too," Brady said. He slipped his arms through the sleeves of his coat. "But maybe—" and he felt something cautious rise in his chest, something like hope "—if I work just a little harder, people will look again. Think so, Levin?"

"It's one of my prayers, Uncle," Levin said.

"Mine, too," Brady said and let himself out the door. He whistled a little as he walked down the stairs. Maybe the woman was right; maybe he had a future, after all.

1873

Friday at four, Brady whirled from his studio to a place so hot that sweat appeared on his body the instant he stopped whirling. His wagon stood on a dirt road, surrounded by thatched huts. Some of the huts were burning, but the flames were the only movement in the entire village. Far away, he could hear a chop-chop-chopping sound, but he could see nothing. Flies buzzed around him, not landing, as if they had more interesting places to go. The air smelled of burning hay and something fetid, something familiar. He swallowed and looked for the bodies.

He grabbed the back end of the wagon, and climbed inside. The darkness was welcome. It took a moment for his eyes to get used to the gloom, then he grabbed his tripod and his camera and carried them outside. He pushed his glasses up his nose, but his finger encountered skin instead of metal. He could see. He squinted and wondered how she did that—gave him his eyesight for such a short period of time. Perhaps it was his reward for going to Hell.

A hand extended from one of the burning huts. Brady stopped beside it, crouched, and saw a man lying face down in the dust, the back of his head blown away. Bile rose in Brady's throat, and he swallowed to keep his last meal down. He assembled the camera, uncapped the lens, and looked through, seeing the hand and the flames flickering in his narrow, rounded vision. Then he climbed out from under the curtain, went back into the wagon and prepared a plate.

This time he felt no fear. Perhaps knowing that the woman (why had she never told him her name?) could flash him out of the area in an instant made him feel safer. Or perhaps it was his sense of purpose, as strong as it had been at the first battle of Bull Run, when the bullets whizzed by him, and his wagon got stampeded by running soldiers. He had had a reason then, a life then, and he would get it back.

He went outside and photographed the dead man in the burning hut. The chop-chop-chopping sound was fading, but the heat seemed to intensify. The stillness in the village was eerie. The crackles of burning buildings made him jump. He saw no more bodies, no evidence other than the emptiness and the fires that anything had happened in this place.

Then he saw the baby.

It was a toddler, actually. Naked, and shot in the back, the body lying at the edge of a ditch. Brady walked over to the ditch and peered in, then stepped back and was sick for the first time in his professional career.

Bodies filled the ditch—women, children, babies, and old men—their limbs flung back, stomachs gone, faces shot away. Blood flowed like a river, added its coppery scent to the smell of burning hay and the reek of decay.

He grabbed his camera, his shield, and set it up, knowing that this would haunt him as the hot, slimy rain haunted him still. He prepared more plates, and photographed the toddler over and over, the innocent baby that had tried to crawl away from the horror and had been shot in the back for its attempt at survival.

And as he worked, his vision blurred, and he wondered why the sweat pouring into and out of his eyes never made them burn.

1875

Brady stared at the $25,000 check. He set it on the doily that covered the end table. In the front room, he heard Levin arguing with Julia.

"Not today," she said. "Give him at least a breath between bad news."

Brady touched the thin paper, the flowing script. The government had given him one-quarter of the wealth he had lost going into the war, one-tenth of the money he spent photographing history. And too late. The check was too late. A month earlier, the War Department, which owned the title to the wet plates, had sold them all to the Anthonys for an undisclosed sum. They had clear, legal title, and Edward Anthony had told Brady that they would never, ever sell.

He got up with a sigh and brushed aside the half-open bedroom door. "Tell me what?" he asked.

Levin looked up—guiltily, Brady thought. Julia hid something behind her back. "Nothing, Uncle," Levin said. "It can wait."

"You brought something and I want to know what it is." Brady's voice was harsh. It had been too harsh lately. The flashbacks to the horrors he'd seen on his travels, the strain of keeping silent—of not telling Julia about the fantastical events—and the reversal after reversal in his own life were taking their toll.

Julia brought her hand out from behind her back. She clutched a stereoscope. The small device shook as she handed it to Brady.

He put the lenses up to his eyes, feeling the frame clink against his glasses. The three dimensional view inside was familiar: The war parade he had taken over ten years ago, as the soldiers rode down Pennsylvania Avenue. Brady removed the thick card from the viewer. The two portraits stood side by side, as he expected. He even expected the flowery script on the side, stating that the stereoscopic portrait was available through the Anthonys' warehouse. What he didn't expect was the attribution at the bottom, claiming that the photography had been done by the Anthonys themselves.

He clenched his fists and turned around, letting the device fall to the wooden floor. The stereoscope clinked as it rolled, and Brady stifled an urge to kick it across the room.

"We can go to Congressman Garfield," Levin said, "and maybe he'll help us."

Brady stared at the portrait. He could take the Anthonys to court. They did own the rights to the wet plates, but they should have given him proper attribution. It seemed a trivial thing to fight over. He had no money, and what influence he had would be better spent getting the plates back than fighting for a bit of name recognition. "No," Brady said. "You can go to the newspapers, if you like, Levin, but we won't get James to act for us. He's done his best already. This is our fight. And we'll keep at it, until the bitter end if we have to."

Julia clenched her hands together and stared at him. It seemed as if the lines around her mouth had grown deeper. He remembered the first time he'd danced with her, the diamonds around her neck glittering in the candle-light. They had sold those diamonds in 1864 to fund the Petersburg expedition—the expedition in which half of his equipment was destroyed by Confederate shells. *You are going to be a great man*, she had told him. The problem was, he had never asked her what she meant by great. Perhaps she thought of her wealthy father as a great man. Perhaps she stayed with Brady only out of wifely loyalty.

She came over to him and put her arm around him. "I love you, Mathew," she said. He hugged her close, so close that he worried he would hurt her. He wouldn't have been able to do anything without her. None of his work, none of his efforts would have been possible—especially in the lean years— if she hadn't believed in him.

"I'm sorry," he whispered into her shoulder.

She slipped out of his embrace and held him so that she could look into his eyes. "We'll keep fighting, Mathew. And in the end, we'll win."

1877

And the assignments kept coming. Brady began to look forward to the whirling, even though he often ended up in Hell. His body was stronger there; his eyesight keener. He could forget, for a short time, the drabness of Washington, the emptiness of his life. On the battlefields, he worked—and he could still believe that his work had meaning.

One dark, gray day, he left his studio and found himself hiding at the edge of a forest. His wagon, without a horse, leaned against a spindly tree. The air was thick and humid. Brady's black suit clung to his skin, already damp. Through the bushes he could see soldiers carrying large rifles, surrounding a church. Speaking a language he thought he understood—Spanish?—they herded children together. Then, in twos and threes, the soldiers marched the children inside.

The scene was eerily quiet. Brady went behind the wagon, grabbed his tripod and set up the camera. He stepped carefully on the forest bed; the scuffing noise of his heavy leather shoes seemed to resound like gunshots. He took portrait after portrait, concentrating on the soldiers' faces, the children's looks of resignation. He wondered why the soldiers were imprisoning the children, and what they planned to do to the town he could see just over the horizon. And a small trickle of relief ran through him that here, at least, the children would be spared.

Once the children were inside, the soldiers closed the heavy doors and barred them. Someone had already boarded up the windows. Brady put another plate into his camera to take a final portrait of the closed church before following the army to their nasty work at the village. He looked down, checking the plates the woman had given him, when he heard a whoosh. A sharp, tingling scent rose in his nostrils, followed by the smell of smoke. Automatically he opened the lens—just as a soldier threw a burning torch at the church itself.

Brady screamed and ran out of the bushes. The soldiers saw him—and one leveled a rifle at him. The bullets ratt-a-tatted at him, the sound faster and more vicious than the repeating rifles from the war. Brady felt his body jerk and fall, felt himself roll over, bouncing with each bullet's impact. He wanted to crawl to the church, to save the children, but he couldn't move. He couldn't do anything. The world was growing darker . . . and he saw a kind of light. . . .

And then the whirling began. It seemed slower, and he wasn't sure he wanted it to start. It pulled him away from the light, away from the church and the burning children (he thought he could hear their screams now— loud, terrified, piercing—) and back to the silence of his studio.

He wound up in one of his straightbacked chairs. He tried to stand up, and fell, his glasses jostling the edge of his nose. Footsteps on the stairs ran toward him, then hands lifted him. Levin.

"Uncle? Are you all right?"

"Shot," Brady whispered. "The children. All dead. Must save the children."

He pushed Levin aside and groped for something, anything to hold on to. "I have to get back!" he yelled. "Someone has to rescue those children!"

Levin grabbed his shoulders, forced Brady back to the chair. "The war is over, Uncle," Levin said. "It's over. You're home. You're safe."

Brady looked up at Levin and felt the shakes begin. She wouldn't send him back. She wouldn't let him save those children. She'd known all along that the church would burn—she wanted him to photograph it, to record it, not to stop it. He put his hands over his face. He had seen enough atrocities to last him three lifetimes.

"It's all right," Levin said. "It's all right, Uncle."

It wasn't all right. Levin was becoming an expert at this, at taking Brady home. And to his credit, he never said anything to Julia. "Thank you," Brady said. His words were thin, rushed, as if the bullet holes still riddled his body and sucked the air from it.

He patted Levin on the shoulder, then walked away—walked to the end of the studio, his room, his home. Perhaps the crazy woman *didn't* exist. Perhaps what Levin saw was the truth. Perhaps Brady's mind *was* going, after all.

"Thank you," he repeated, and walked down the stairs, comforted by the aches in his bones, the blurry edge to his vision. He was home, and he would stay—

Until she called him again. Until he had his next chance to be young, and working, and doing something worthwhile.

1882

Brady sat in front of the window, gazing into the street. Below, carriages rumbled past, throwing up mud and chunks of ice. People hurried across the sidewalk, heads bowed against the sleet. The rippled glass was cold against his fingers, but he didn't care. He could hear Levin in the studio, talking with a prospective client. Levin had handled all of the business this past week. Brady had hardly been able to move.

The death of Henry Anthony shouldn't have hit him so hard. The Anthony Brothers had been the closest thing Brady had to enemies in the years since the war. Yet, they had been friends once, and companions in the early days of the art. All of photography was dying; Morse was gone. Henry Anthony dead. And three of Brady's assistants, men he had trained to succeed him, dead in the opening of the West.

Levin opened the door and peeked in. "Uncle, a visitor," he said.

Brady was about to wave Levin away when another man stepped inside. The man was tall, gaunt, wearing a neatly pressed black suit. He looked official. "Mr. Brady?"

Brady nodded but did not rise.

"I'm John C. Taylor. I'm a soldier, sir, and a student of your work. I would like to talk with you, if I could."

Brady pushed back the needlepoint chair beside him. Taylor sat down, hat in his hands.

"Mr. Brady, I wanted to let you know what I've been doing. Since the end of the war, I've tried to acquire your work. I have secured through various channels, over 7,000 negatives of your best pictures."

Brady felt the haze that surrounded him lift somewhat. "And you would like to display them?"

"No, sir, actually, I've been trying to preserve them. The plates the government bought from you years ago have been sitting in a warehouse. A number were destroyed due to incautious handling. I've been trying to get them placed somewhere else. I have an offer from the Navy Department—I have connections there—and I wanted your approval."

Brady laughed. The sound bubbled from inside of him, but he felt no joy. He had wanted the portraits for so long and finally, here was someone asking for his approval. "No one has asked me what I wanted before."

Taylor leaned back. He glanced once at Levin, as if Brady's odd reaction had made Taylor wary.

"My uncle has gone through quite an odyssey to hold on to his plates," Levin said softly. "He has lost a lot over the years."

"From the beginning," Brady said. "No one will ever know what I went through in securing the negatives. The whole world can never appreciate it. It changed the course of my life. Some of those negatives nearly cost me that life. And then the work was taken from me. Do you understand, Mr. Taylor?"

Taylor nodded. "I've been tracking these photographs for a long time, sir. I remembered them from the illustrated papers, and I decided that they needed to be preserved, so that my children's children would see the devastation, would learn the follies we committed because we couldn't reason with each other."

Brady smiled. A man who *did* understand. Finally. "The government bought my portraits of Webster, Calhoun, and Clay. I got paid a lot of money for those paintings that were made from my photographs. Not *my* work, mind you. *Paintings* of my work. Page would have been so happy."

"Sir?"

Brady shook his head. Page had left his side long ago. "But no one wants to see the war work. No one wants to see what you and I preserved. I don't want the Navy to bury the negatives. I want them to display the work, reproduce it or make it into a book that someone can *see.*"

"First things first, Mr. Brady," Taylor said. "The Navy has the negatives I've acquired, but we need to remove the others from the War Department before they're destroyed. And then you, or your nephew, or someone else can go in there and put together a showing."

Brady reached over and gripped Taylor's hands. They were firm and strong—a young man's hands on an older man's body. "If you can do that," Brady said, "you will have made all that I've done worthwhile."

1882

Julia huddled on the settee, a blanket over her slight frame. She had grown gaunt, her eyes big saucers on the planes of her face. Her hands shook as she took the letter from Brady. He had hesitated about giving it to her, but he knew that she would ask and she would worry. It would be better for her frail heart to know than to constantly fret. She leaned toward the lamp. Brady watched her eyes move as she read.

He already knew the words by heart. The letter was from General A. W. Greeley, in the War Department. He was in charge of the government's collection of Brady's work. After the opening amenities, he had written:

> The government has stated positively that their negatives must not be exploited for commercial purposes. They are the historical treasures of a whole people and the government has justly refused to establish a dangerous system of "special privilege" by granting permission for publication to individuals. As the property of the people, the government negatives are held in sacred trust . . .

Where no one could see them, and not even Brady himself could use them. He wondered what Taylor thought—Taylor who would have received the letter in Connecticut by now.

Julia looked up, her eyes dotted with tears. "What do they think, that you're going to steal the plates from them like they stole them from you?"

"I don't know," Brady said. "Perhaps they really don't understand what they have."

"They understand," Julia said, her voice harsh. "And it frightens them."

1883

In his dreams, he heard the sounds of people working. Twice he had arrived at the door to his gallery, and twice it had been locked. Behind the thin material, he heard voices—"Here, Andre. No, no. Keep the same years on the same wall space"—and the sounds of shuffling feet. This time, he knocked and the door opened a crack.

Ceiling lights flooded the room. It was wide and bright—brighter than he imagined a room could be.

His work covered all the walls but one. People, dressed in pants and loose shirts like the woman who hired him, carried framed portraits from one spot to the next, all under the direction of a slim man who stood next to Brady's wagon.

The man looked at Brady. "What do you want?"

"I just wanted to see—"

The man turned to one of the others walking through. "Get rid of him, will you? We only have a few hours, and we still have one wall to fill."

A woman stopped next to Brady and put her hand on his arm. Her fingers were cool. "I'm sorry," she said. "We're preparing an exhibit."

"But I'm the artist," Brady said.

"He says—"

"I know what he says," the man said. He squinted at Brady, then glanced at a portrait that hung near the wagon. "And so he is. You should be finishing the exhibit, Mr. Brady, not gawking around the studio."

"I didn't know I had something to finish."

The man sighed. "The show opens tomorrow morning, and you still have one wall to fill. What are you doing here?"

"I don't know," Brady said. The woman took his arm and led him out the door.

"We'll see you tomorrow night," she said. And then she smiled. "I like your work."

And then he woke up, shivering and shaking in the dark beside Julia. Her even breathing was a comfort. He drew himself into a huddle and rested his knees against his chest. One wall to fill by tomorrow? He wished he understood what the dreams meant. It had taken him nearly twenty years to fill all the other walls. And then he thought that perhaps dream time worked differently than real time. Perhaps dream time moved in an instant, the way he did when the woman whirled him away to another place.

It was just a dream, he told himself, and by the time he fell back to sleep, he really believed it.

1884

By the time the wagon appeared beside him, Brady was shaking. This place was silent, completely silent. Houses stood in neat rows on barren, brown treeless land. Their white formations rested like sentries against the mountains that stood in the distance. A faint smell, almost acrid, covered everything. The air was warm, but not muggy, and beads of sweat rose on his arms like drops of blood.

Brady had arrived behind one of the houses. Inside, a family sat around the table—a man, a woman and two children. They all appeared to be eating—the woman had a spoon raised to her mouth—but no one moved. In the entire time he had been there, no one had moved.

He went into his wagon, removed the camera and tripod, then knocked on the door. The family didn't acknowledge him. He pushed the door open and stepped inside, setting up the camera near a gleaming countertop. Then he walked over to the family. The children had been frozen in the act of laughing, gazing at each other. Their chests didn't rise and fall, their eyes didn't move. The man had his hand around a cup full of congealed liquid. He was watching the children, a faint smile on his face. The woman was looking down, at the bowl filled with a soggy mush. The hand holding the spoon—empty except for a white stain in the center—had frozen near her mouth. Brady touched her. Her skin was cold, rigid.

They were dead.

Brady backed away, nearly knocking over the tripod. He grabbed the camera, felt its firmness in his hands. For some reason, these specters frightened him worse than all the others. He couldn't tell what had killed them or how they died.

It had become increasingly difficult, at the many varied places he had been, but usually he could at least guess. Here, he saw nothing—and the bodies didn't even feel real.

He climbed under the dark curtain, finding a kind of protection from his own equipment. Perhaps, near his own stuff, whatever had killed them would avoid him. He took the photograph, and then carried his equipment to the next house, where a frozen woman sat on a sofa, looking at a piece of paper. In each house, he captured the still, frozen lives, almost wishing for the blood, the stench, the fires, the signs of destruction.

1885

Brady folded the newspaper and set it down. He didn't wish to disturb Julia, who was sleeping soundly on the bed. She seemed to get so little rest these days. Her face had become translucent, the shadows under her eyes so deep that they looked like bruises.

He couldn't share the article with her. A year ago, she might have laughed. But now, tears would stream down her cheeks and she would want him to hold her. And when she woke up, he *would* hold her, because he knew that they had so little time left.

She didn't need to see the paragraph that stood out from the page as if someone had expanded the type:

. . . and with his loss, all of photography's pioneers are dead. In the United States alone we have lost, in recent years, Alexander Gardiner, Samuel F. B. Morse, Edward and Henry Anthony, and Mathew B. Brady. Gardiner practiced the craft until his death, going west and sending some of the best images back home. The Anthonys sold many of their fine works in stereoscope for us all to see. Morse had other interests and quit photography to pursue them. Brady lost his eyesight after the War, and closed his studios here and in New York . . .

Perhaps he was wrong. Perhaps they wouldn't have laughed together. Perhaps she would have been as angry as he was. He hadn't died. He *hadn't.* No one allowed him to show his work any more. He hadn't even been to the gallery of his dreams since that confusing last dream, years ago.

Brady placed the newspaper with the others near the door. Then he crawled onto the bed and pulled Julia close. Her small body was comforting, and, in her sleep, she turned and held him back.

1886

One morning, he whirled into a place of such emptiness it chilled his soul. The buildings were tall and white, the grass green, and the flowers in bloom. His wagon was the only black thing on the surface of this place. He could smell lilacs as he walked forward, and he thought of Julia resting at their apartment—too fragile now to even do her needlepoint.

This silence was worse than at the last place. Here it felt as if human beings had never touched this land, despite the buildings. He felt as if he were the only person left alive.

He walked up the stone steps of the first building and pushed open the glass door. The room inside was empty—as empty as his gallery had been when he first dreamed it. No dust or footprints marred the white floor, no smudges covered the white walls. He looked out the window, and, as he watched, a building twenty yards away shimmered and disappeared.

Brady shoved his hands in his pockets and scurried outside. Another building disappeared. This shimmering was different, more ominous than the shimmering left by his benefactress; in it, somehow, he could almost see the debris, the dust from the buildings that had once been there. He could *feel* the destruction, and knew that these places weren't reappearing somewhere else. He ran to his wagon, climbed inside, and peered out at the world from the wagon's edge. And, as he watched, building after building winked out of existence.

He clutched the camera to him, but took no photographs. The smell of lilacs grew stronger. His hands were cold, shaking. He watched the buildings disappear until only a grassy field remained.

"You can't even photograph it."

Her appearance didn't surprise him. He expected her, after seeing the changes, perhaps because he had been thinking of her. Her hair was shoulder-length now, but other than that, she hadn't changed in all the years since he'd last seen her.

"It's so clean and neat." Her voice shook. "You can't even tell that anyone died here."

Brady crawled out of the wagon and stood beside her. He felt more uneasy here than he had felt under the shelling at the first battle of Bull Run. There, at least, he could *hear* the whistle, *feel* the explosions. Here the destruction came from nowhere.

"Welcome to war in my lifetime, Mathew." She crossed her arms in front of her chest. "Here we get rid of *everything*, not just a person's body, but all traces of their home, their livelihood—and, in most cases, any memories of them. I lost my son like this, and I couldn't remember that he had even existed until I started work on this project." She smiled just a little. "The time travel gives unexpected benefits, some we can program for, like improved eyesight or health, and some we can't, like improved memories. The scientists say it has something to do with molecular rearrangement, but that makes no sense to you, since no one knew what a molecule was in your day."

He stood beside her, his heart pounding in his throat. She turned to him, took his hand in hers.

"We can't go any farther than this, Mathew."

He frowned. "I'm done?"

"Yes. I can't thank you in the ways that I'd like. If I could, I'd send you back, give you money, let you rebuild your life from the war on. But I can't. We can't. But I *can* bring you to the exhibit when it opens, and hope that the response is what we expect. Would you like that, Mathew?"

He didn't know exactly what she meant, and he wasn't sure he cared. He wanted to keep making photographs, to keep working here with her. He had nothing else. "I could still help you. I'm sure there are a number of things to be done."

She shook her head, then kissed his forehead. "You need to go home to your Julia, and enjoy the time you have left. We'll see each other again, Mathew."

And then she started to whirl, to shimmer. Brady reached for her and his hand went through her into the heated air. This shimmer was different, somehow; it had a life to it. He felt a thin relief. She had traveled beyond him, but not out of existence. He leaned against the edge of his wagon and stared at the lilac bushes and the wind blowing through the grasses, trying to understand what she had just told him. He and the wagon sat alone, in a field where people had once built homes and lived quiet lives. Finally, at dusk, he too shimmered out of the blackness, and back to his own quiet life.

1887

Only Levin and Brady stood beside the open grave. The wind ruffled Brady's hair, dried the tear tracks on his cheeks. He hadn't realized how small Julia's life had become. Most of the people at the funeral had been *his* friends, people who had come to console *him*.

He could hear the trees rustling behind him. The breeze carried a scent of lilacs—how appropriate, Julia dying in the spring, so that her flower would bloom near her grave. She had been so beautiful when he'd met her, so popular. She had whittled her life down for him, because she had thought he needed her. And he had.

Levin took Brady's arm. "Come along, Uncle," Levin said.

Brady looked up at his nephew, the closest thing to a child he and Julia had ever had. Levin's hair had started to recede, and he too wore thick glasses.

"I don't want to leave her," Brady said. "I've left her too much already."

"It's all right, Uncle," Levin said as he put his arm around Brady's waist and led him through the trees. "She understands."

Brady glanced back at the hole in the ground, at his wife's coffin, and at the two men who had already started to shovel dirt on top. "I know she understands," he said. "She always has."

                                    1887

That night, Brady didn't sleep. He sat on the bed he had shared with Julia, and clutched her pillow against his chest. He missed her even breathing, her comfortable presence. He missed her hand on his cheek and her warm voice, reassuring him. He missed holding her, and loving her, and telling her how much he loved her.

It's all right, Uncle, Levin had said. *She understands.*

Brady got up, set the pillow down, and went to the window. She had looked out so many times, probably feeling alone, while he pursued his dreams of greatness. She had never said what she thought these past few years, but he saw her look at him, saw the speculation in her eyes when he returned from one of his trips. She had loved him too much to question him.

Then he felt it: the odd sensation that always preceded a whirling. But he was *done*—he hadn't been sent anywhere in over a year. He was just tired, just—

spinning. Colors and pain and dust bombarded him. Spinning. And when he stopped, he stood in the gallery of his dreams . . . only this time, he knew that he was wide awake.

It existed then. It really existed.

And it was full of people.

Women wore long clingy dresses in a shining material. Their hair varied in hue from brown to pink, and many had jewelry stapled into their noses, their cheeks and, in one case, along the rim of the eye. The men's clothes were as colorful and as shiny. They wore makeup, but no jewelry. A few people seemed out of place, in other clothes—a woman in combat fatigues from one of the wars Brady had seen, a man in dust-covered denim pants and a ripped shirt, another man dressed in all black leaning against a gallery door. All of the doors in the hallway were open and people spilled in and out, conversing or holding shocked hands to their throats.

The conversation was so thick that Brady couldn't hear separate voices, separate words. A variety of perfumes overwhelmed him and the coolness seemed to have left the gallery. He let the crowd push him down the hall toward his own exhibit and as he passed, he caught bits and pieces of other signs:

> . . . IMAGE ARTIST . . .
>
> . . . (2000–2010) . . .
>
> . . . HOLOGRAPHER, AFRICAN BIOLOGICAL . . .
>
> . . . ABC CAMERAMAN, LEBANON . . .
>
> . . . PHOTOJOURNALIST, VIETNAM CONFLICT . . .
>
> . . . (1963) . . .
>
> . . . NEWS REELS FROM THE PACIFIC THEATER . . .
>
> . . . OFFICIAL PHOTOGRAPHER, WORLD WAR I . . .
>
> . . . (1892–. . .
>
> . . . INDIAN WARS . . .

And then his own:

> MATHEW B. BRADY EXHIBIT
>
> OFFICIAL PHOTOGRAPHER:
>
> UNITED STATES CIVIL WAR
>
> (1861–1865)

The room was full. People stood along the walls, gazing at his portraits, discussing and pointing at the fields of honored dead. One woman turned away from the toddler, shot in the back; another from the burning church. People looked inside Brady's wagon, and more than a few stared at the portraits of him, lined along the doric columns like a series of somber, aging men.

He caught a few words:

"Fantastic composition" . . . "amazing things with black and white" . . . "almost looks real" . . . "turns my stomach" . . . "can't imagine working with such primitive equipment" . . .

Someone touched his shoulder. Brady turned. A woman smiled at him. She wore a long purple gown and her brown hair was wrapped around the top of her head. It took a moment for him to recognize his benefactress.

"Welcome to the exhibit, Mathew. People are enjoying your work."

She smiled at him and moved on. And then it hit him. He finally had an exhibit. He finally had people staring at his work, and seeing what had really happened in all those places during all that time. She had shown him this gallery all his life, whirled him when he thought he was asleep. This was his destiny, just as dying impoverished in his own world was his destiny.

"You're the artist?" A slim man in a dark suit stood beside Brady.

"This is my work," Brady said.

A few people crowded around. The scent of soap and perfume nearly overwhelmed him.

"I think you're an absolutely amazing talent," the man said. His voice was thin, with an accent that seemed British but wasn't. "I can't believe the kind of work you put into this to create such stark beauty. And with such bulky equipment."

"Beauty?" Brady could barely let the word out of his throat. He gazed around the room, saw the flowered woman, the row of corpses on the Gettysburg Battlefield.

"Eerie," a woman said. "Rather like late Goya, don't you think, Lavinia?"

Another woman nodded. "Stunning, the way you captured the exact right light, the exact moment to illuminate the concept."

"Concept?" Brady felt his hands shake. "You're looking at *war* here. People died in these portraits. This is history, not art."

"I think you're underestimating your work," the man said. "It is truly art, and you are a great, great artist. Only an artist would see how to use black and white to such a devastating effect—"

"I wasn't creating art," Brady said. "My assistants and I, we were shot at. I nearly died the day the soldiers burned that church. This isn't beauty. This is war. It's truth. I wanted you to see how ugly war really is."

"And you did it so well," the man said. "I truly admire your technique." And then he walked out of the room. Brady watched him go. The women smiled, shook his hand, told him that it was a pleasure to meet him. He wandered around the room, heard the same types of conversation and stopped when he saw his benefactress.

"They don't understand," he said. "They think this was done for them, for their appreciation. They're calling this art."

"It is art, Mathew," she said softly. She glanced around the room, as if she wanted to be elsewhere.

"No," he said. "It actually happened."

"A long time ago." She patted his hand. "The message about war and destruction will go home in their subconscious. They will remember this." And then she turned her back on him and pushed her way through the crowd. Brady tried to follow her, but made it only as far as his wagon. He sat on its edge and buried his face in his hands.

He sat there for a long time, letting the conversation hum around him, wondering at his own folly. And then he heard his name called in a voice that made his heart rise.

"Mr. Brady?"

He looked up and saw Julia. Not the Julia who had grown pale and thin in their small apartment, but the Julia he had met so many years ago. She was slender and young, her face glowing with health. No gray marked her ringlets, and her hoops were wide with a fashion decades old. He reached out his hands. "Julia."

She took his hands and sat beside him on the wagon, her young-girl face turned in a smile. "They think you're wonderful, Mr. Brady."

"They don't understand what I've done. They think it's art—" he stopped himself. This wasn't his Julia. This was the young girl, the one who had danced with him, who had told him about her dream. She had come from a different place and a different time, the only time she had seen the effects of his work.

He looked at her then, really looked at her, saw the shine in her blue eyes, the blush to her cheeks. She was watching the people look at his portraits, soaking in the discussion. Her gloved hand clutched his, and he could feel her wonderment and joy.

"I would be so proud if this were my doing, Mr. Brady. Imagine a room like this filled with your vision, your work."

He didn't look at the room. He looked at her. This moment, this was what kept her going all those years. The memory of what she thought was a dream, of what she hoped would become real. And it *was* real, but not in any way she understood. Perhaps, then, he didn't understand it either.

She turned to him, smiled into his face. "I would so like to be a part of this," she said. She thought it was a dream; otherwise she would have never spoken so boldly. No, wait. She had been bold when she was young.

"You will be," Brady said. And until that moment, he never realized how much a part of it she had been, always standing beside him, always believing in him even when he no longer believed in himself. She had made the greater sacrifice—her entire life for his dream, his vision, his work.

"Julia," he said, thankful for this last chance to touch her, this last chance to hold her. "I could not do this without you. You made it all possible."

She leaned against him and laughed, a fluted sound he hadn't heard in decades. "But it's *your* work that they admire, Mr. Brady. Your work."

"They call me an artist."

"That's right." Her words were crisp, sure. "An artist's work lives beyond him. This isn't our world, Mr. Brady. In the other rooms, the pictures move."

The pictures move. He had been given a gift, to see his own future. To know that the losses he suffered, the reversals he and Julia had lived through weren't all for nothing. How many people got even that?

He tucked her arm in his. He had to be out of this room, out of this exhibit he didn't really understand. They stood together, her hoop clearing a path for them in the crowd. He stopped and surveyed the four walls—filled with his portraits, portraits of places most of these people had never seen—his memories that they shared and made their own.

Then he stepped out of the exhibit into a future in which he would never take part, perhaps to gain a perspective he had never had before.

And all the while, Julia remained beside him.

—for Dean

A WALK IN THE SUN

Geoffrey A. Landis

A physicist engaged in doing solar cell research, Geoffrey A. Landis is a frequent contributor to *Analog, Isaac Asimov's Science Fiction Magazine,* and *Interzone,* and has also sold stories to markets such as *Amazing* and *Pulphouse*. His story "Elemental" was on the Final Hugo Ballot a few years back, and his story "Ripples in the Dirac Sea" won him a Nebula Award in 1989. His first collection, *Myths, Legends, and True History,* has just come out from *Pulphouse*. He lives in Brook Park, Ohio.

In "A Walk in the Sun," he tells the suspenseful story of an astronaut shipwrecked on the Moon who is determined to survive no matter what she has to do—or how far she has to *go*.

The pilots have a saying: a good landing is any landing you can walk away from.

Perhaps Sanjiv might have done better, if he'd been alive. Trish had done the best she could. All things considered, it was a far better landing than she had any right to expect.

Titanium struts, pencil-slender, had never been designed to take the force of a landing. Paper-thin pressure walls had buckled and shattered, spreading wreckage out into the vacuum and across a square kilometer of lunar surface. An instant before impact she remembered to blow the tanks. There was no explosion, but no landing could have been gentle enough to keep *Moonshadow* together. In eerie silence, the fragile ship had crumpled and ripped apart like a discarded aluminum can.

The piloting module had torn open and broken loose from the main part of the ship. The fragment settled against a crater wall. When it stopped moving, Trish unbuckled the straps that held her in the pilot's seat and fell slowly to the ceiling. She oriented herself to the unaccustomed gravity, found an undamaged EVA pack and plugged it into her suit, then crawled out into the sunlight through the jagged hole where the living module had been attached.

She stood on the grey lunar surface and stared. Her shadow reached out ahead of her, a pool of inky black in the shape of a fantastically stretched man. The landscape was rugged and utterly barren, painted in stark shades of grey and black. "Magnificent desolation," she whispered. Behind her, the sun hovered just over the mountains, glinting off shards of titanium and steel scattered across the cratered plain.

Patricia Jay Mulligan looked out across the desolate moonscape and tried not to weep.

First things first. She took the radio out from the shattered crew compartment and tried it. Nothing. That was no surprise; Earth was over the horizon, and there were no other ships in cislunar space.

After a little searching she found Sanjiv and Theresa. In the low gravity they were absurdly easy to carry. There was no use in burying them. She sat them in a niche between two boulders, facing the sun, facing west, toward where the Earth was hidden behind a range of black mountains. She tried to think of the right words to say, and failed. Perhaps as well; she wouldn't know the proper service for Sanjiv anyway. "Goodbye, Sanjiv. Goodbye, Theresa. I wish—I wish things would have been different. I'm sorry." Her voice was barely more than a whisper. "Go with God."

She tried not to think of how soon she was likely to be joining them.

She forced herself to think. What would her sister have done? Survive. Karen would survive. First: inventory your assets. She was alive, miraculously unhurt. Her vacuum suit was in serviceable condition. Life-support was powered by the suit's solar arrays; she had air and water for as long as the sun continued to shine. Scavenging the wreckage yielded plenty of unbroken food packs; she wasn't about to starve.

Second: call for help. In this case, the nearest help was a quarter of a million miles over the horizon. She would need a high-gain antenna and a mountain peak with a view of Earth.

In its computer, *Moonshadow* had carried the best maps of the moon ever made. Gone. There had been other maps on the ship; they were scattered with the wreckage. She'd managed to find a detailed map of Mare Nubium—useless—and a small global map meant to be used as an index. It would have to do. As near as she could tell, the impact site was just over the eastern edge of Mare Smythii— "Smith's Sea." The mountains in the distance should mark the edge of the sea, and, with luck, have a view of Earth.

She checked her suit. At a command, the solar arrays spread out to their full extent like oversized dragonfly wings and glinted in prismatic colors as they rotated to face the sun. She verified that the suit's systems were charging properly, and set off.

Close up, the mountain was less steep than it had looked from the crash site. In the low gravity, climbing was hardly more difficult than walking, although the two-meter dish made her balance awkward. Reaching the ridgetop, Trish was rewarded with the sight of a tiny sliver of blue on the horizon. The mountains on the far side of the valley were still in darkness. She hoisted the radio higher up on her shoulder and started across the next valley.

From the next mountain peak the Earth edged over the horizon, a blue and white marble half-hidden by black mountains. She unfolded the tripod for the antenna and carefully sighted along the feed. "Hello? This is Astronaut Mulligan from *Moonshadow*. Emergency. Repeat, this is an emergency. Does anybody hear me?"

She took her thumb off the *transmit* button and waited for a response, but heard nothing but the soft whisper of static from the sun.

"This is Astronaut Mulligan from *Moonshadow*. Does anybody hear me?" She paused again. "*Moonshadow*, calling anybody. *Moonshadow*, calling anybody. This is an emergency."

"*—shadow, this is Geneva control. We read you faint but clear. Hang on, up there.*" She released her breath in a sudden gasp. She hadn't even realized she'd been holding it.

After five minutes the rotation of the Earth had taken the ground antenna out of range. In that time—after they had gotten over their surprise that there was a survivor of the *Moonshadow*—she learned the parameters of the problem. Her landing had been close to the sunset terminator; the very edge of the illuminated side of the moon. The moon's rotation is slow, but inexorable. Sunset would arrive in three days. There was no shelter on the moon, no place to wait out the fourteen day long lunar night. Her solar cells needed sunlight to keep her air fresh. Her search of the wreckage had yielded no unruptured storage tanks, no batteries, no means to lay up a store of oxygen.

And there was no way they could launch a rescue mission before nightfall.

Too many "no"s.

She sat silent, gazing across the jagged plain toward the slender blue crescent, thinking.

After a few minutes the antenna at Goldstone rotated into range, and the radio crackled to life. "*Moonshadow, do you read me? Hello, Moonshadow, do you read me?*"

"*Moonshadow* here."

She released the transmit button and waited in long silence for her words to be carried to Earth.

"*Roger, Moonshadow. We confirm the earliest window for a rescue mission is thirty days from now. Can you hold on that long?*"

She made her decision and pressed the transmit button. "Astronaut Mulligan for *Moonshadow*. I'll be here waiting for you. One way or another."

She waited, but there was no answer. The receiving antenna at Goldstone couldn't have rotated out of range so quickly. She checked the radio. When she took the cover off, she could see that the printed circuit board on the power supply had been slightly cracked from the crash, but she couldn't see any broken leads or components clearly out of place. She banged on it with her fist—Karen's first rule of electronics, if it doesn't work, hit it—and re-aimed the antenna, but it didn't help. Clearly something in it had broken.

What would Karen have done? Not just sit here and die, that was certain. Get a move on, kiddo. When sunset catches you, you'll die.

They had heard her reply. She had to believe they heard her reply and would be coming for her. All she had to do was survive.

The dish antenna would be too awkward to carry with her. She could afford nothing but the bare necessities. At sunset her air would be gone. She put down the radio and began to walk.

Mission Commander Stanley stared at the x-rays of his engine. It was four in the morning. There would be no more sleep for him that night; he was scheduled to fly to Washington at six to testify to Congress.

"Your decision, Commander," the engine technician said. "We can't find any flaws in the x-rays we took of the flight engines, but it could be hidden. The nominal flight profile doesn't take the engines to a hundred twenty, so the blades should hold even if there is a flaw."

"How long a delay if we yank the engines for inspection?"

"Assuming they're okay, we lose a day. If not, two, maybe three."

Commander Stanley drummed his fingers in irritation. He hated to be forced into hasty decisions. "Normal procedure would be?"

"Normally we'd want to reinspect."

"Do it."

He sighed. Another delay. Somewhere up there, somebody was counting on him to get there on time. If she was still alive. If the cut-off radio signal didn't signify catastrophic failure of other systems.

If she could find a way to survive without air.

On Earth it would have been a marathon pace. On the moon it was an easy lope. After ten miles the trek fell into an easy rhythm: half a walk, half like jogging, and half bounding like a slow-motion kangaroo. Her worst enemy was boredom.

Her comrades at the academy—in part envious of the top scores that had made her the first of their class picked for a mission—had ribbed her mercilessly about flying a mission that would come within a few kilometers of the moon without landing. Now she had a chance to see more of the moon up close than anybody in history. She wondered what her classmates were thinking now. She would have a tale to tell—if only she could survive to tell it.

The warble of the low voltage warning broke her out of her reverie. She checked her running display as she started down the maintenance checklist. Elapsed EVA time, eight point three hours. System functions, nominal, except that the solar array current was way below norm. In a few moments she found the trouble: a thin layer of dust on her solar array. Not a serious problem; it could be brushed off. If she couldn't find a pace that would avoid kicking dust on the arrays, then she would have to break every few hours to housekeep. She rechecked the array and continued on.

With the sun unmoving ahead of her and nothing but the hypnotically blue crescent of the slowly rotating Earth creeping imperceptibly off the horizon, her attention wandered. *Moonshadow* had been tagged as an easy mission, a low-orbit mapping flight to scout sites for the future moonbase. *Moonshadow* had never been intended to land, not on the moon, not anywhere.

She'd landed it anyway; she had to.

Walking west across the barren plain, Trish had nightmares of blood and falling, Sanjiv dying beside her; Theresa already dead in the lab module; the moon looming huge, spinning at a crazy angle in the viewports. Stop the spin, aim for the terminator—at low sun angles, the illumination makes it easier to see the roughness of the surface. Conserve fuel, but remember to blow the tanks an instant before you hit to avoid explosion.

That was over. Concentrate on the present. One foot in front of the other. Again. Again.

The undervoltage alarm chimed again. Dust, already?

She looked down at her navigation aid and realized with a shock that she had walked a hundred and fifty kilometers.

Time for a break anyway. She sat down on a boulder, fetched a snack-pack out of her carryall, and set a timer for fifteen minutes. The airtight quick-seal on the food pack was designed to mate to the matching port in the lower part of her faceplate. It would be important to keep the seal free of grit. She verified the vacuum seal twice before opening the pack into the suit, then pushed the food bar in so she could turn her head and gnaw off pieces. The bar was hard and slightly sweet.

She looked west across the gently rolling plain. The horizon looked flat, unreal; a painted backdrop barely out of reach. On the moon, it should be easy to keep up a pace of fifteen or even twenty miles an hour—counting time out for sleep, maybe ten. She could walk a long, long way.

Karen would have liked it; she'd always liked hiking in desolate areas. "Quite pretty, in its own way, isn't it, Sis?" Trish said. "Who'd have thought there were so many shadings of grey? Plenty of uncrowded beach—too bad it's such a long walk to the water."

Time to move on. She continued on across terrain that was generally flat, although everywhere pocked with craters of every size. The moon is surprisingly flat; only one percent of the surface has a slope of more than fifteen degrees. The small hills she bounded over easily; the few larger ones she detoured around. In the low gravity this posed no real problem to walking. She walked on. She didn't feel tired, but when she checked her readout and realized that she had been walking for twenty hours, she forced herself to stop.

Sleeping was a problem. The solar arrays were designed to be detached from the suit for easy servicing, but had no provision to power the life-support while detached. Eventually she found a way to stretch the short cable out far enough to allow her to prop up the array next to her so she could lie down without disconnecting the power. She would have to be careful not to roll over. That done, she found she couldn't sleep. After a time she lapsed into a fitful doze, dreaming not of the *Moonshadow* as she'd expected, but of her sister, Karen, who—in the dream—wasn't dead at all, but had only been playing a joke on her, pretending to die.

She awoke disoriented, muscles aching, then suddenly remembered where she was. The Earth was a full handspan above the horizon. She got up, yawned, and jogged west across the gunpowder-grey sandscape.

Her feet were tender where the boots rubbed. She varied her pace, changing from jogging to skipping to a kangaroo bounce. It helped some; not enough. She could feel her feet starting to blister, but knew that there was no way to take off her boots to tend, or even examine, her feet.

Karen had made her hike on blistered feet, and had had no patience with complaints or slacking off. She should have broken her boots in before the hike. In the one-sixth gee, at least the pain was bearable.

After a while her feet simply got numb.

Small craters she bounded over; larger ones she detoured around; larger ones yet she simply climbed across. West of Mare Smythii she entered a badlands and the terrain got bumpy. She had to slow down. The downhill slopes were in full sun, but the crater bottoms and valleys were still in shadow.

Her blisters broke, the pain a shrill and discordant singing in her boots. She bit her lip to keep herself from crying and continued on. Another few hundred kilometers and she was in Mare Spumans—"Sea of Froth"—and it was clear trekking again. Across Spumans, then into the north lobe of Fecundity and through to Tranquility. Somewhere around the sixth day of her trek she must have passed Tranquility Base; she carefully scanned for it on the horizon as she traveled but didn't see anything. By her best guess she missed it by several hundred kilometers; she was already deviating toward the north, aiming for a pass just north of the crater Julius Caesar into Mare Vaporum to avoid the mountains. The ancient landing stage would have been too small to spot unless she'd almost walked right over it.

"Figures," she said. "Come all this way, and the only tourist attraction in a hundred miles is closed. That's the way things always seem to turn out, eh, Sis?"

There was nobody to laugh at her witticism, so after a moment she laughed at it herself.

Wake up from confused dreams to black sky and motionless sunlight, yawn, and start walking before you're completely awake. Sip on the insipid warm water, trying not to think about what it's recycled from. Break, cleaning your solar arrays, your life, with exquisite care. Walk. Break. Sleep again, the sun nailed to the sky in the same position it was in when you awoke. Next day do it all over. And again. And again.

The nutrition packs are low-residue, but every few days you must still squat for nature. Your life support can't recycle solid waste, so you wait for the suit to dessicate the waste and then void the crumbly brown powder to vacuum. Your trail is marked by your powdery deposits, scarcely distinguishable from the dark lunar dust.

Walk west, ever west, racing the sun.

Earth was high in the sky; she could no longer see it without craning her neck way back. When the Earth was directly overhead she stopped and celebrated, miming the opening of an invisible bottle of champagne to toast her imaginary traveling companions. The sun was well above the horizon now. In six days of travel she had walked a quarter of the way around the moon.

She passed well south of Copernicus, to stay as far out of the impact rubble as possible without crossing mountains. The terrain was eerie, boulders as big as houses, as big as shuttle tanks. In places the footing was treacherous where the grainy regolith gave way to jumbles of rock, rays thrown out by the cataclysmic impact billions of years ago. She picked her way as best she could. She left her radio on and gave a running commentary as she moved. "Watch your step here, footing's treacherous. Coming up on a hill; think we should climb it or detour around?"

Nobody voiced an opinion. She contemplated the rocky hill. Likely an ancient volcanic bubble, although she hadn't realized that this region had once been active. The territory around it would be bad. From the top she'd be able to study the terrain for a ways ahead. "Okay, listen up, everybody. The climb could be tricky here, so stay close and watch where I place my feet. Don't take chances—better slow and safe than fast and dead. Any questions?" Silence; good. "Okay, then. We'll take a fifteen minute break when we reach the top. Follow me."

Past the rubble of Copernicus, Oceanus Procellarum was smooth as a golf course. Trish jogged across the sand with a smooth, even glide. Karen and Dutchman seemed to always be lagging behind or running up ahead out of sight. Silly dog still followed Karen around like a puppy, even though Trish was the one who fed him and refilled his water dish every day since Karen went away to college. The way Karen wouldn't stay close behind her annoyed Trish—Karen had *promised* to let her be the leader this time—but she kept her feelings to herself. Karen had called her a bratty little pest, and she was determined to show she could act like an adult. Anyway, she was the one with the map. If Karen got lost, it would serve her right.

She angled slightly north again to take advantage of the map's promise of smooth terrain. She looked around to see if Karen was there, and was surprised to see that the Earth was a gibbous ball low down on the horizon. Of course, Karen wasn't there. Karen had died years ago. Trish was alone in a spacesuit that itched and stank and chafed her skin nearly raw across the thighs. She should have broken it in better, but who would have expected she would want to go jogging in it?

It was unfair how she had to wear a spacesuit and Karen didn't. Karen got to do a lot of things that she didn't, but how come she didn't have to wear a spacesuit? *Everybody* had to wear a spacesuit. It was the rule. She turned to Karen to ask. Karen laughed bitterly. "I don't have to wear a spacesuit, my bratty little sister, because I'm *dead*. Squished like a bug and buried, remember?"

Oh, yes, that was right. Okay, then, if Karen was dead, then she didn't have to wear a spacesuit. It made perfect sense for a few more kilometers, and they jogged along together in companionable silence until Trish had a sudden thought. "Hey, wait—if you're dead, then how can you be here?"

"Because I'm not here, silly. I'm a fig-newton of your overactive imagination."

With a shock, Trish looked over her shoulder. Karen wasn't there. Karen had never been there.

"I'm sorry. Please come back. Please?"

She stumbled and fell headlong, sliding in a spray of dust down the bowl of a crater. As she slid she frantically twisted to stay face-down, to keep from rolling over on the fragile solar wings on her back. When she finally slid to a stop, the silence echoing in her ears, there was a long scratch like a badly healed scar down the glass of her helmet. The double reinforced faceplate had held, fortunately, or she wouldn't be looking at it.

She checked her suit. There were no breaks in the integrity, but the titanium strut that held out the left wing of the solar array had buckled back and nearly broken. Miraculously there had been no other damage. She pulled off the array and studied the damaged strut. She bent it back into position as best she could, and splinted the joint with a mechanical pencil tied on with two short lengths of wire. The pencil had been only extra weight anyway; it was lucky she hadn't thought to discard it. She tested the joint gingerly. It wouldn't take much stress, but if she didn't bounce around too much it should hold. Time for a break anyway.

When she awoke she took stock of her situation. While she hadn't been paying attention, the terrain had slowly turned mountainous. The next stretch would be slower going than the last bit.

"About time you woke up, sleepyhead," said Karen. She yawned, stretched, and turned her head to look back at the line of footprints. At the end of the long trail, the Earth showed as a tiny blue dome on the horizon, not very far away at all, the single speck of color in a landscape of uniform grey. "Twelve days to walk halfway around the moon," she said. "Not bad, kid. Not great, but not bad. You training for a marathon or something?"

Trish got up and started jogging, her feet falling into rhythm automatically as she sipped from the suit recycler, trying to wash the stale taste out of her mouth. She called out to Karen behind her without turning around. "Get a move on, we got places to go. You coming, or what?"

In the nearly shadowless sunlight the ground was washed-out, two dimensional. Trish had a hard time finding footing, stumbling over rocks that were nearly invisible against the flat landscape. One foot in front of the other. Again. Again.

The excitement of the trek had long ago faded, leaving behind a relentless determination to prevail, which in turn had faded into a kind of mental numbness. Trish spent the time chatting with Karen, telling the private details of her life, secretly hoping that Karen would be pleased, would say something telling her she was proud of her. Suddenly she noticed that Karen wasn't listening; had apparently wandered off on her sometime when she hadn't been paying attention.

She stopped on the edge of a long, winding rille. It looked like a riverbed just waiting for a rainstorm to fill it, but Trish knew it had never known water. Covering the bottom was only dust, dry as powdered bone. She slowly picked her way to the bottom, careful not to slip again and risk damage to her fragile life support system. She looked up at the top. Karen was standing on the rim waving at her. "Come *on!* Quit *dawdling*, you slowpoke—you want to stay here *forever?*"

"What's the hurry? We're ahead of schedule. The sun is high up in the sky, and we're halfway around the moon. We'll make it, no sweat."

Karen came down the slope, sliding like a skiier in the powdery dust. She pressed her face up against Trish's helmet and stared into her eyes with a manic intensity that almost frightened her. "The hurry, my lazy little sister, is that you're halfway around the moon, you've finished with the easy part and it's all mountains and badlands from here on, you've got six thousand kilometers to walk in a broken spacesuit, and if you slow down and let the sun get ahead of you, and then run into one more teensy little problem, just one, you'll be dead, dead, dead, just like me. You wouldn't like it, trust me. Now get your pretty little lazy butt into gear and *move!*"

And, indeed, it was slow going. She couldn't bound down slopes as she used to, or the broken strut would fail and she'd have to stop for painstaking repair. There were no more level plains; it all seemed to be either boulder fields, crater walls, or mountains. On the eighteenth day she came to a huge natural arch. It towered over her head, and she gazed up at it in awe, wondering how such a structure could have been formed on the moon.

"Not by wind, that's for sure," said Karen. "Lava, I'd figure. Melted through a ridge and flowed on, leaving the hole; then over the eons micrometeoroid bombardment ground off the rough edges. Pretty, though, isn't it?"

"Magnificent."

Not far past the arch she entered a forest of needle-thin crystals. At first they were small, breaking like glass under her feet, but then they soared above her, six-sided spires and minarets in fantastic colors. She picked her way in silence between them, bedazzled by the forest of light sparkling between the sapphire spires. The crystal jungle finally thinned out and was replaced by giant crystal boulders, glistening iridescent in the sun. Emeralds? Diamonds?

"I don't know, kid. But they're in our way. I'll be glad when they're behind us."

And after a while the glistening boulders thinned out as well, until there were only a scattered few glints of color on the slopes of the hills beside her, and then at last the rocks were just rocks, craggy and pitted.

Crater Daedalus, the middle of the lunar farside. There was no celebration this time. The sun had long ago stopped its lazy rise, and was imperceptibly dropping toward the horizon ahead of them.

"It's a race against the sun, kid, and the sun ain't making any stops to rest. You're losing ground."

"I'm tired. Can't you see I'm tired? I think I'm sick. I hurt all over. Get off my case. Let me rest. Just a few more minutes? Please?"

"You can rest when you're dead." Karen laughed in a strangled, high-pitched voice. Trish suddenly realized that she was on the edge of hysteria. Abruptly she stopped laughing. "Get a move on, kid. Move!"

The lunar surface passed under her, an irregular grey treadmill.

Hard work and good intentions couldn't disguise the fact that the sun was gaining. Every day when she woke up the sun was a little lower down ahead of her, shining a little more directly in her eyes.

Ahead of her, in the glare of the sun she could see an oasis, a tiny island of grass and trees in the lifeless desert. She could already hear the croaking of frogs: braap, braap, *BRAAP!*

No. That was no oasis; that was the sound of a malfunction alarm. She stopped, disoriented. Overheating. The suit air conditioning had broken down. It took her half a day to find the clogged coolant valve and another three hours soaked in sweat to find a way to unclog it without letting the precious liquid vent to space. The sun sank another handspan toward the horizon.

The sun was directly in her face now. Shadows of the rocks stretched toward her like hungry tentacles, even the smallest looking hungry and mean. Karen was walking beside her again, but now she was silent, sullen.

"Why won't you talk to me? Did I do something? Did I say something wrong? Tell me."

"I'm not here, little sister. I'm dead. I think it's about time you faced up to that."

"Don't say that. You can't be dead."

"You have an idealized picture of me in your mind. Let me go. *Let me go!*"

"I can't. Don't go. Hey—do you remember the time we saved up all our allowances for a year so we could buy a horse? And we found a stray kitten that was real sick, and we took the shoebox full of our allowance and the kitten to the vet, and he fixed the kitten but wouldn't take any money?"

"Yeah, I remember. But somehow we still never managed to save enough for a horse." Karen sighed. "Do you think it was easy growing up with a bratty little sister dogging my footsteps, trying to imitate everything I did?"

"I wasn't either bratty."

"You were too."

"No, I wasn't. I adored you." Did she? "I *worshipped* you."

"I know you did. Let me tell you, kid, that didn't make it any easier. Do you think it was easy being worshipped? Having to be a paragon all the time? Christ, all through high school, when I wanted to get high, I had to sneak away and do it in private, or else I knew my damn kid sister would be doing it too."

"You didn't. You never."

"Grow up, kid. Damn right I did. You were always right behind me. Everything I did, I knew you'd be right there doing it next. I had to struggle like hell to keep ahead of you, and you, damn you, followed effortlessly. You were smarter than me—you know that, don't you?—and how do you think that made me feel?"

"Well, what about me? Do you think it was easy for *me*? Growing up with a dead sister—everything I did, it was 'Too bad you can't be more like Karen' and 'Karen wouldn't have done it that way' and 'If only Karen had. . . .' How do you think that made *me* feel, huh? You had it easy—I was the one who had to live up to the standards of a goddamn *angel*."

"Tough breaks, kid. Better than being dead."

"Damn it, Karen, I loved you. I love you. Why did you have to go away?"

"I know that, kid. I couldn't help it. I'm sorry. I love you too, but I have to go. Can you let me go? Can you just be yourself now, and stop trying to be me?"

"I'll . . . I'll try."

"Goodbye, little sister."

"Goodbye, Karen."

She was alone in the settling shadows on an empty, rugged plain. Ahead of her, the sun was barely kissing the ridgetops. The dust she kicked up was behaving strangely; rather than falling to the ground, it would hover half a meter off the ground. She puzzled over the effect, then saw that all around her, dust was silently rising off the ground. For a moment she thought it was another hallucination, but then realized it was some kind of electrostatic charging effect. She moved forward again through the rising fog of moondust. The sun reddened, and the sky turned a deep purple.

The darkness came at her like a demon. Behind her only the tips of mountains were illuminated, the bases disappearing into shadow. The ground ahead of her was covered with pools of ink that she had to pick her way around. Her radio locator was turned on, but receiving only static. It could only pick up the locator beacon from the *Moonshadow* if she got in line of sight of the crash site. She must be nearly there, but none of the landscape looked even slightly familiar. Ahead—was that the ridge she'd climbed to radio Earth? She couldn't tell. She climbed it, but didn't see the blue marble. The next one?

The darkness had spread up to her knees. She kept tripping over rocks invisible in the dark. Her footsteps struck sparks from the rocks, and behind her footprints glowed faintly. Triboluminescent glow, she thought—nobody has *ever* seen that before. She couldn't die now, not so close. But the darkness wouldn't wait. All around her the darkness lay like an unsuspected ocean, rocks sticking up out of the tidepools into the dying sunlight. The undervoltage alarm began to warble as the rising tide of darkness reached her solar array. The crash site had to be around here somewhere, it had to. Maybe the locator beacon was broken? She climbed up a ridge and into the light, looking around desperately for clues. Shouldn't there have been a rescue mission by now?

Only the mountaintops were in the light. She aimed for the nearest and tallest mountain she could see and made her way across the darkness to it, stumbling and crawling in the ocean of ink, at last pulling herself into the light like a swimmer gasping for air. She huddled on her rocky island, desperate as the tide of darkness slowly rose about her. Where were they? *Where were they?*

Back on Earth, work on the rescue mission had moved at a frantic pace. Everything was checked and triple-checked—in space, cutting corners was an invitation for sudden death—but still the rescue mission had been dogged by small problems and minor delays, delays that would have been routine for an ordinary mission, but loomed huge against the tight mission deadline.

The scheduling was almost impossibly tight—the mission had been set to launch in four months, not four weeks. Technicians scheduled for vacations volunteered to work overtime, while suppliers who normally took weeks to deliver parts delivered overnight. Final integration for the replacement for *Moonshadow*, originally to be called *Explorer* but now hastily re-christened *Rescuer*, was speeded up, and the transfer vehicle launched to the Space Station months ahead of the original schedule, less than two weeks after the *Moonshadow* crash. Two shuttle-loads of propellant swiftly followed, and the transfer vehicle was mated to its aeroshell and tested. While the rescue crew practiced possible scenarios on the simulator, the lander, with engines inspected and replaced, was hastily modified to accept a third person on ascent, tested, and then launched to rendezvous with *Rescuer*. Four weeks after the crash the stack was fueled and ready, the crew briefed, and the trajectory calculated. The crew shuttle launched through heavy fog to join their *Rescuer* in orbit.

Thirty days after the unexpected signal from the moon had revealed a survivor of the *Moonshadow* expedition, *Rescuer* left orbit for the moon.

From the top of the mountain ridge west of the crash site, Commander Stanley passed his searchlight over the wreckage one more time and shook his head in awe. "An amazing job of piloting," he said. "Looks like she used the TEI motor for braking, and then set it down on the RCS verniers."

"Incredible," Tanya Nakora murmured. "Too bad it couldn't save her."

The record of Patricia Mulligan's travels was written in the soil around the wreck. After the rescue team had searched the wreckage, they found the single line of footsteps that led due west, crossed the ridge, and disappeared over the horizon. Stanley put down the binoculars. There was no sign of returning footprints. "Looks like she wanted to see the moon before her air ran out," he said. Inside his helmet he shook his head slowly. "Wonder how far she got?"

"Could she be alive somehow?" asked Nakora. "She was a pretty ingenious kid."

"Not ingenious enough to breathe vacuum. Don't fool yourself—this rescue mission was a political toy from the start. We never had a chance of finding anybody up here still alive."

"Still, we had to try, didn't we?"

Stanley shook his head and tapped his helmet. "Hold on a sec, my damn radio's acting up. I'm picking up some kind of feedback—almost sounds like a voice."

"I hear it too, Commander. But it doesn't make any sense."

The voice was faint in the radio. "Don't turn off the lights. Please, please, don't turn off your light. . . ."

Stanley turned to Nakora. "Do you . . . ?"

"I hear it, Commander . . . but I don't believe it."

Stanley picked up the searchlight and began sweeping the horizon. "Hello? *Rescuer* calling Astronaut Patricia Mulligan. Where the hell are you?"

The spacesuit had once been pristine white. It was now dirty grey with moondust, only the ragged and bent solar array on the back carefully polished free of debris. The figure in it was nearly as ragged.

After a meal and a wash, she was coherent and ready to explain.

"It was the mountaintop. I climbed the mountaintop to stay in the sunlight, and I just barely got high enough to hear your radios."

Nakora nodded. "That much we figured out. But the rest—the last month—you really walked all the way around the moon? Eleven thousand kilometers?"

Trish nodded. "It was all I could think of. I figured, about the distance from New York to LA and back—people have walked that and lived. It came to a walking speed of just under ten miles an hour. Farside was the hard part—turned out to be much rougher than nearside. But strange and weirdly beautiful, in places. You wouldn't believe the things I saw."

She shook her head, and laughed quietly. "*I* don't believe some of the things I saw. The immensity of it—we've barely scratched the surface. I'll be coming back, Commander. I promise you."

"I'm sure you will," said Commander Stanley. "I'm sure you will."

*   *   *

As the ship lifted off the moon, Trish looked out for a last view of the surface. For a moment she thought she saw a lonely figure standing on the surface, waving her goodbye. She didn't wave back.

She looked again, and there was nothing out there but magnificent desolation.

FRAGMENTS OF AN ANALYSIS OF A CASE OF HYSTERIA

Ian McDonald

British author Ian McDonald is an ambitious and daring writer with a wide range and an impressive amount of talent. His first story was published in 1982, and since then he has appeared with some frequency in *Interzone, Isaac Asimov's Science Fiction Magazine, Zenith, Other Edens, Amazing,* and elsewhere. He was nominated for the John W. Campbell Award in 1985, and in 1989 he won the *Locus* "Best First Novel" Award for *Desolation Road.* His other books include the novels *Out On Blue Six* and *King of Morning, Queen of Day,* and a collection of his short fiction, *Empire Dreams.* Coming up is a new novel, *The Broken Land* (the British edition will be called *Hearts, Hands, & Voices*), and a new collection, as well as several graphic novels. His story "Rainmaker Cometh" was in our Eighth Annual Collection. Born in Manchester, England, in 1960, McDonald has spent most of his life in Northern Ireland, and now lives and works in Belfast.

In the vivid and eloquent story that follows, he takes us back to the days before World War II, and deep into the uneasy dreams of a young girl on a collision course with a strange and frightening destiny.

THE NIGHT SLEEPER

Hurrying, hurrying, faster, faster; hurrying, hurrying, faster, faster, through the forests of the night; the night train, cleaving through the forests of the night, through the trees, the endless trees, cleaving them with the beam of its headlight that casts its white pool upon the endlessly unreeling iron line, cleaving the forest with the tireless stroke of its pistons, cleaving the night with its plume of spark-laden smoke streamed back across the great sleek length of the engine and the shout of its hundred wheels, cleaving through the night that lies across the heart of the continent; the night train, hurrying, hurrying, faster, faster.

Though it must be hours since your father bid you good-night from the upper berth, hours more since the sleeping car attendant did that clever folding trick with the seat and unrolled the bundles of fresh laundered bedding, you are not asleep. You cannot sleep. Out there, beyond the window are the trees of the night forest. You cannot see them, but you know they are there, shouldered close together, shouldered close to the track, branches curving down to brush the sides of the sleeping car, like the long arms of old, stoop-shouldered men.

And though you cannot see them either, you are also aware of the hundreds of other lives lying still in their berths in the ochre glow of their railway company nightlights, rocked and rolled to sleep by the rolling gait of the night sleeper across the border; hundreds of other lives lying still, one above the other in their tiny, ochre lit compartments, carried onward through the forest of the night to their final destinations. From the adjacent compartment come the sounds again; the small sounds, the intimate sounds, a woman's whisper, a man speaking softly, the creak of leather upholstery, stifled laughter, the repeated knock knock knock knock knock of something hard against the wooden partition. As you lie in your bottom berth your head next to the knock knock knock knock knock from the next compartment, it is as if you are suddenly aware of everything all at once, the lovers across the partition, the sleeping passengers in their berths, the blast of sound and steam and speed of the night train's momentary passage, cleaving through the forest of the night, cleaving through the endless, stoop-shouldered trees.

You must have slept. You had thought that sleep would elude you, but the rhythm of the wheels must have lulled you to sleep, for it is the change of that tireless rhythm that has woken you. The train is slowing. You turn in your berth to look out of the window but all there is to be seen is your reflection looking back at you. The train has slowed to a crawl, grinding along the track with a slowness that is dreadful to you because you fear that should the train stop it will never, never start again.

Up the line, far away, a bell clangs. Barely audible over the grind of the wheels are voices, voices outside the window, shouting in a language you do not understand.

Your father is awake now. He descends the wooden ladder, switches on the lights and sits across the table from you, peering out of the window to see why the train is stopping. By the light from the window you see the faces. There are men standing by the side of the track, men with stupid, slow, brutal faces. As you grind past them, they pause in their labour to stare up into your faces with slow, brutal incomprehension. The stupid brutality of their faces blinds you to what it is they are doing. They are carrying bodies, slung between them by the hands and the feet, and laying them out by the side of the track. The naked bodies of men and women and children, carried and laid out side by side on the gravel between the track and the edge of the trees. And now you see, far away up the line, a red glow, as if from a great conflagration; something burning fiercely, endlessly, out there in the forest of the night. You ask your father what it all means.

"Some terrible calamity," he says, as if in a dream. "An accident, up the line; a train has crashed and set the forest burning."

The night train grinds on, past the bodies of the men and the women and the children, laid side by side while the men carry and set, carry and set, muttering in their dull, brutal language, and the iron bell clangs.

You know that you have not slept, though it is as if you have, and woken up at a different place, a different time. Now the train is entering a rural railway station. A bumptious station master with a black moustache and an excess of gold braid is waving the night train in to a stand by the platform. The picket fence is decked with bunting and the little wooden station house is gaily hung with Japanese paper lanterns that swing and rattle in the wind from the night forest. The train creaks to a halt and you hear the music. Outside the waiting room a string quartet is playing the last movement from *Eine Kleine Nachtmusik*, rather poorly, you think. The station master comes striding along the platform in his black kneeboots blowing his whistle and shouting,

"All change, all change."

"Come, Anna," your Father says, grabbing his violin case from the rack and before you have time to think you are out on the platform, you and your father and the hundreds and hundreds of others aboard the night train, standing there in your nightdresses and pyjamas and dressing gowns in the cold night air.

Up the line, the locomotive hisses steam. The carriages creak and shift.

"Teas, coffees and hot savouries in the waiting room," announces the beaming station master. "In the waiting room if you please, sirs and madams."

Murmuring gladly to each other, the passengers file into the waiting room but with every step you take toward those open wooden doors you feel a dreadful reluctance grow and grow until you know that you must not cannot will not go in.

"No Father, do not make me!" you cry but your Father says, "Anna, Anna, please, it is only for a little while, until the next train comes," but you will not cannot must not go, for you have seen, through the latticed windows of the rural railway station, what is waiting in the waiting room. In the waiting room is a baker in a white apron standing before the open door of an oven. He sees you watching him through the window, and smiles at you, and draws his paddle out of the oven to show you what he has been baking there.

It is a loaf of fresh golden bread in the shape of a baby.

THE DOOR AND THE WINDOW

The case of Fraulein Anna B. first came to my attention in the late winter of 1912 at one of the Wednesday meetings of my International Psycho-Analytical Association through Dr. Geistler, one of the newer members of the Wednesday Circle, who mentioned casually over coffee and cigars a patient he was treating for asthmatic attacks that had failed to yield to conventional medical treatment. These attacks seemed related to the young woman's dread of enclosed spaces, and after the meeting, he asked if I might attempt an analysis of the psychoneurosis, an undertaking to which I agreed, arranging the first treatment for the following Tuesday morning, at ten a.m.

I have learned from experience that psychoneuroses often belie themselves by too great an absence from the facial features of the patient: Fraulein Anna B. was one such, to the perceptions a pretty, charming, self-confident young lady of seventeen years, the daughter of a concert violinist with the Imperial Opera who, I learned to my surprise, was acquainted with me through the B'Nai B'rith, the Vienna Jewish Club. She was an only child, her mother had died in Anna's infancy in an influenza epidemic and she had been brought up solely by the father. I gained the distinct impression that her vivacity, her energy, were more than could be accounted for purely by youthful exuberance.

She commented on the stuffiness and gloominess of my consulting room, and despite the winter chill, refused to settle until both door and window were opened to the elements. I had taken but a few puffs of a cigar when she became most agitated, claiming that she could not breathe, the smoke was suffocating her. Despite the fact that most of the smoke from my cigar went straight out of the open window into Berggasse, I nevertheless acceded to her request that I refrain from smoking in her presence. Such was her hysterical sensitivity that, on subsequent interviews, the slightest lingering trace of cigar smoke from a previous session was enough to induce an asthmatic attack.

In interview she was exceedingly talkative and greatly given to the encyclopedic elaboration of even the most trivial anecdote. She could not recall a specific moment when she became aware that she dreaded enclosed spaces, but had to a certain degree felt uncomfortable in small rooms with closed doors and heavy furnishings for as long as she could remember. She had not been consciously aware of a deterioration in her condition until the event that had precipitated first her referral to Dr. Geistler, and ultimately to me.

In the early autumn her father's orchestra had taken a performance of 'The Magic Flute' on tour through Salzburg to Munich, Zurich, Milan and Venice. Seeing an opportunity to expand his daughter's education through travel, her father had arranged for her to accompany him. Fraulein Anna B. admitted to feelings of foreboding all the day of the departure which, as the orchestra assembled at the West Bahnhof, became an anxiety, and, with the party boarding the train, an hysterical attack. The hour had been late, the station dark and filled with the steam and smoke of the engines. The rest of the musicians were already installed in their sleeping compartments, from the door her father was calling her to board, the train was about to leave. These details she knew only from having been told after the event; her attention was transfixed by the brass table-lamp in the window of the sleeping compartment she and her father were to share. Seeing that lamp, she had felt such fear and dread as she had never known before, she could not enter that compartment, she could not board that train. The noise and the bustle of the station overwhelmed her, the smoke and the fumes of the engine suffocated her; overcome, she fought for breath but her lungs were paralysed, unable to draw breath.

Choking, half-conscious, half delirious, she was carried by a porter and her father to the station-master's office, whence Dr. Geistler was summoned by telephone.

The image of the table lamp seemed of significance so I suggested that we explore possible relevancies it might hold to childhood events, the wellspring of all our adult neuroses. She related an incident from her earliest years when she first slept in a room of her own. Her father had bought her a bedside lamp with a shade decorated with the simple fairytale designs that appeal to children. She could not recall having fallen asleep, but she did recall waking to find the room filled with smoke. She had neglected to extinguish the lamp and the decorated shade, made from a cheap and shoddy fabric, had caught fire. Her screams raised her father in the adjacent bedroom who had doused the fire. For several months after, he had insisted she sleep under his care in his bedroom, indeed, that they share the same bed.

After narrating the incident with the lamp, Fraulein Anna B. declared that she felt very much better and, as our time was drawing to a close, thanked me for my help and asked if payment was required now, or would a bill be forwarded. I replied, with some amusement, that the treatment was by no means concluded, indeed, it had hardly begun; it would require many sessions, over a period of many weeks, even months, before we could say that we had dealt conclusively with her neuroses.

At our next meeting, Fraulein Anna B.'s demeanour was considerably subdued. As we sat with the wind from the steppes whistling through the open window she related a recurrent dream that particularly disturbed her. This dream, which I shall refer to as the 'Night Sleeper Dream' was to continue to manifest itself in various guises throughout the course of treatment with greater or lesser regularity depending on the progress we were making in the interviews. Mutability is one of the characteristics of neuroses; that when responding to treatment in one sphere, they incarnate themselves in another.

Rather than attempt to analyse the entire content of the dream, which, in the light of the previous session, seemed a little too pat, I chose to concentrate on some of the elements that might repay deeper analysis; the threatening forest, the long row of naked bodies, the baker and his macabre loaf.

Through association and regression we explored the significance of an early childhood picnic in the Wienerwald when she first became aware of her sexual incompleteness as a woman. The trip had been made in the company of an 'aunt' (so-called, but who could have been a close family friend) and cousin, a boy a year older than Fraulein Anna B., who at the time could not have been more than five or six. The children had been sent off to play in the woods while the parents conversed, as parents will, upon topics of no interest whatsoever to children and, as children will, the young

Fraulein Anna B. and her cousin had been caught short by nature. Fraulein Anna B. recalled her surprise at the sight of her cousin's penis and remembers wanting to play with it, not, she claimed, out of any sexual interest, purely from curiosity. Contrasting the ease with which her cousin had relieved himself with her own cumbersome efforts, she had told him, "That's a handy gadget to bring on a picnic."

As she was preparing to leave, she made this comment to me: "Dr. Freud, I have just remembered, I do not know how important it is, but that table lamp, the one in the sleeping compartment on the train to Salzburg, it did not have a lamp-shade. The bulb was bare, naked."

In the subsequent months as winter gave way to a sullen Viennese spring, we mapped the psychoneurotic geography of the elements of the Night Sleeper Dream. As childhood fears and repressions were brought to light and acknowledged, so Fraulein Anna B. found her dread of enclosed spaces diminishing; first the window, then the door were acceptable when closed; finally, in the late March of 1913, with not inconsiderable relief, I was permitted my cigars.

The symbolic element of the naked bodies laid by the side of the track proved to contain within it perhaps the most significant of Fraulein Anna B.'s childhood traumas.

Anna's Father had established the habit of taking an annual holiday to the spa at Baden during the Opera Closed Season. Against customary practice, Anna accompanied him on these short trips with the result that, in the absence of any other children her own age at the resort, she was forced to seek out the company of adults, especially the elderly who abound at such spas and who can be relied upon to take a grand-parently interest in a solitary young girl. She had been left to her own devices by her Father while he went on a walk in the woods with a lady of his acquaintance who came to take the waters every year at the same time as he did. In the pumproom the young Anna had been alarmed by a conversation by a clearly demented elderly gentleman who had threatened her with eternal damnation if she did not go down on her knees there and then and seek the saving grace of Christ. When the elderly gentleman had attempted to physically accost her, she had fled the pumproom and attendant gardens into the surrounding woodlands to seek her father.

She remembered running along seemingly endless kilometres of gravelled footpaths until she was stopped in her headlong flight by the sound of voices; her father's, and that of another woman. The voices issued from the concealment of a swathe of rhododendrons. Without thought, she pushed through the screening shrubs and was met by the sight of her father repeatedly penetrating a red-haired woman bent double over the railing of a small, discreet pergola. She related that the woman had looked up, smiled, and said, "Hello, Anna-*katzchen*" a private name only used by her father. It was only then that she recognised the woman as the lady-friend who came every year to the resort. What she remembered most vividly from the experience was the peculiar conical shape of the woman's drooping breasts, the way her red hair had fallen around her face, and her father's thrusting, thrusting, thrusting into the bent-over woman, quite oblivious that he was being watched by his daughter. As she spoke those three words in my study: "thrusting, thrusting, thrusting," she spat out them like poison on her tongue.

Her father never learned that he had been observed that day in the pergola. The woman had treated Anna's witnessing as an unspoken compact between them; at dinner in the *gasthaus* that night Anna had liberally salted the woman's dinner with bleaching powder, stolen from the scullery maid's storeroom.

It was the work of what remained of the spring to bring Fraulein Anna B. to the point of acceptance of the emotional insight that her attempted poisoning of the red-haired woman, and ultimately, her psychoneurotic fear of enclosed, vaporous spaces stemmed from her jealousy of her father. For many weeks she was resistant to the notion of her father as a sexual figure to whom she had been, and still was, attracted; this attraction having been reinforced, albeit unwittingly, by her father taking the infant Anna into his bed after the incident with the bedside lamp. Gradually she reached an intellectual insight into her substitution of a male into the mother role, and the confusion of her own Oedipal feelings. Her own awakening sexuality had resulted in the transferral onto her father of her subliminated guilt at her abandoning her first, and greatest love, for the love of others.

Triggered by the intimacy of the sleeping compartment, her memories of childhood intimacies, and what she saw as childhood betrayals of her love, had peaked into hysteria. As the intellectual insight developed into acceptance and full emotional insight, so the night sleeper dream recurred with lessening frequency and, in the early summer, Fraulein Anna reported to me that she had that weekend been capable of taking the train journey to the monastery at Melk without any ill effects. After the completion of the treatment, Fraulein Anna B. kept in correspondence with me and confessed, to my great satisfaction, that she had formed an attachment with a young man, the son of a prominent Vienna lawyer, without any feelings of guilt or the return of neurosis, and that engagement, and subsequent marriage, could be pleasurably contemplated.

THE JUDENGASSE CELLAR

When the proprietors of the Heurigen take down the dry and dusty pine branches from the fronts of their shops the last of the summer's wine is drunk. Time, ladies and gentlemen, they call, the bottle is empty, the glass is dry, time for the benches to be scrubbed and the long pine tables taken in, time for the Schrammel-musicians to pack away their violins and guitars and accordions, time to quit the leaf-shaded courtyards of Grinzing and Cobenzl and Nussdorf by your trams and fiacres and charabancs and go down again to your city, time to seek what pleasures it has to offer among its Kaffee Hauses and Konditorei, its cabarets and clubs, beneath the jewelled chandeliers of the opera and in the smoky cellars off Kartnergasse that smell of stale beer and urine.

They had hoped to outstay the others, outstay even the end of the season, as if their staying could somehow condense it and extend it beyond its natural lifetime up there on the slopes of the Wienerwald. But the last glass of the last bottle of the last cask was drunk dry and, as if emerging from a summer night's dream with a start and a shudder, they had found their revels ended and themselves observing the hot and gritty streets of the city from a table outside the Konditorei Demel.

They were four; two young men, two young women, of that class of Viennese society that, as if sensing on a wind from the East the ashes of Empire, was slowly drawing the orbit of its great waltz ever closer to the flames. They had long ago explored every possible nuance and permutation between them that the fading of the Imperial Purple condones and, having worn out each other's lives like old clothes, turned to the whirl of Kaffee Kultur and opera-box scandal only to find its perfume of bierhall revolution, bad art and warmed-over next-day gossip a macrocosm of the ennui of their own claustrophic relationship; a boredom not merely confined to persons or places or classes, but a boredom that seemed to have infected an entire continent, a boredom to which even war seemed preferable.

Perhaps it was the foreshadowing of absolute war over their dying Empire, perhaps only an inevitable twist in the downward helix of their jaded appetites that took them to the cellar down in the old Jewish Quarter.

It bore no name, no number, the only sign of its existence was the unpainted wooden shingle above the unlit flight of steps down under Judengasse; the wooden shingle in the shape of a rat. It did not advertise in the City Directory, nor on the municipal pillars alongside the more flagrant establishments on Kartnergasse, it needed no more advertisement than its reputation and the word of mouth of its patrons. Among the *petit bourgeoisie* its name was mythical.

When the lawyer's son had first mentioned its name as they sat bored at their table outside the Konditorei, they'd hidden it away and gone in search of other stimulation, knowing, even then, that those stimulations would fail and fade like fairground lights in the noontime sun and that they would, must, eventually descend that flight of steep steps beneath the wooden sign of the rat. The first light snow of the autumn was powdering the cobbles as they drove in the merchant banker's son's car through the streets of the Alte Stadt. Of the four, it was the youngest, the concert violinist's daughter who was the least at ease as the door opened to their knock and the *maitre d'* bowed them in, old scars she had thought long healed tugged a little, tore a little, bled a little.

Cellar clubs are a universal condition: the floor packed with tables so that not one centimetre of gritty concrete or cracked tile can be seen; the dusty boards of the stage beneath a constellation of tinsel stars, the popping yellow footlights, the musical quartet of hard-faced women in basques, stockings and opera gloves smoking Turkish cigarettes between numbers, the dull red glow of the table lamps that conceals the identities of the patrons at their tables by changing them into caricatures of themselves.

At the foot of the steps she felt the tightness in her chest, and begged with the man who had brought her not to make her go in, but the other two of their quartet were already being seated at their table and he pulled on her hand, come on, there is nothing to be afraid of, it will be fun. As the waiter in the white apron served wine and the cabaret quartet scraped their way through a medley of popular numbers, the sole focus of her concentration was her measured breathing in, breathing out, breathing in, breathing out. That, when next you exhale, you will not be able to inhale: that is the most terrible fear of the asthmatic.

"Excuse me?"

The young man begged her pardon, repeated his request if he might share their table. He took a chair beside Fraulein Anna, a square-faced young man with a small, square moustache. The band played on. The cellar, already full, filled to bursting point. The night wore down. The young man tried to engage Fraulein Anna in small talk. She worried that he might think the brevity of her replies coyness, when it was merely shortness of breath. Was this her first time here? A nod. He came regularly. He was an artist. Rather, he aspired to being an artist. He had twice failed to secure entry to the Vienna Academy of Fine Art. But he would, in time. He was a painter of postcards and advertisements; a precarious existence, he admitted, but time would bring all his ambitions to fruition, the world would see. After deductions for lodgings, food (too little of that, thought Fraulein Anna) and art materials, he was left with just enough to visit the Judengasse Cellar. Here both high and low mingled, bankers and businessmen and lawyers and priests and prostitutes, civil servants and starving artists, all rendered anonymous on the fellowship of the darkness. It was rumoured that an Imperial prince had been seen to frequent the Sign of the Rat.

"Fear," he said, the word sitting strangely with his country accent of Northern Austria. "That is why they come. That is why I come. To learn the power and mastery of fear, to learn that through the knowledge and control of fear, the right use of fear, one learns mastery over others. That is why I come, to refine and hone my power over fear, *gnädige Fraulein*, so that one day, I shall be feared. I know I shall, I know it. Feared, and so respected."

Fear? she was about to whisper, but a hush had fallen across the tables. An old man with an accordion was standing in the footlights on the tiny bare stage. The old man squeezed a melancholy, minor drone from his instrument.

"Ladies, gentlemen, I tell you a tale, a tale of an old man, a man older than he seems, far older, older than any of you can imagine, older than any living man. A man cursed by God never to die, ladies, gentlemen."

An iron grip seized Fraulein Anna's chest.

"Cursed by God, ladies, gentlemen. Cursed to wander the world, never knowing rest." His long, bony fingers moved like small, antediluvian creatures over the keys. "A man who had never been other than faithful to his master, his Lord, a man whom that same Lord called 'the disciple he loved'; and how was that love rewarded? With these words, how can I ever forget them, 'If it is my will that this man remain alive until I come again, what is that to you?' Oh Master, Master, why did you speak those words? Why did you burden your disciple with undesired immortality, so that even as the last apostle went to his grave, this one of the twelve was condemned to continue wandering the world, a Fifth gospel, a living, walking gospel; that those who saw him and heard this gospel," (the accordion moaned its accompaniment, seducing, mesmerising; with a start, Fraulein Anna noticed that the waiters, that race of troglodytic creatures in braided monkey jackets, were closing the shutters, barring the doors) "might come to penitence, and true faith."

"Penitence! And true faith!"

The under-song of the accordion rose to a dominant major key, swelled to take the crowded tables by surprise.

"But as I wandered across the continent, across all continents, I learned the name and nature of this gospel I was to bring so that man might come to repentance and faith in God."

"Fear!"

Now the gnome-like servants were going from table to table, quietly extinguishing the red table-lamps.

"The grinding, driving, shattering fear of God: fear of He who can destroy both body and spirit and cast them into the endless terror and horror of hell. Fear! Nothing else will bring the human spirit to its knees before it's master; to know, and be confronted by, fear. This was the lesson I learned in the rotting cities of this rotting continent long centuries ago; that I had been set apart by God to be his special Apostle, the Apostle of Fear, the one sent by God to bring the good and righteous fear of Him to mighty and mean, lofty and low, prince and pauper, priest and prostitute. Fear . . ."

The accordion sent its tendrils out across the packed floor, drawing the patrons into its knot of intimacy and credulity. The cellar lay in darkness, save for a single spotlight falling upon the face and hands of the eternal Jew.

"Fear," he whispered, the word like a kiss on his lips; and the single spotlight was extinguished. In the darkness, his voice spoke once again: "Now is the time to face your fear, alone, in the deepest darkness of body, soul and spirit."

And from their tunnels and runways and warrens and sewers, from the vast underground city they had excavated by tooth and claw from the underpinnings of Vienna, they came; pouring out from a score, a hundred, a thousand hatchways and gnawholes and gratings and spouts; a wave, a sea, an ocean of them, swamping the floor of the club with their close-pressed, squirming, surging bodies, spilling over the feet of the patrons, dropping from the cracks and crevices in the ceilings onto table tops, into laps, onto the heads and hands and shoulders of the patrons who were on their feet screaming, beating, flailing, slapping at the torrent, the cascade, the endless waterfall of rats; claws and naked tail and beady eyes, questing noses, sewer-slick fur, pressing, writhing, scuttling; the cellar rang to a million chittering voices that drowned out the cries of the patrons locked in utter darkness, with the rats. Some would flee, some stampeded where they imagined doors to be but in the utter darkness they fell and were smothered under the carpet of hurrying rats, some sought refuge on table tops, on chairs; some, perhaps, wiser, perhaps paralysed by dread, stayed where they were and let the drown-wave break about them, over them. And in time, the torrent of rats subsided, and faltered, and ebbed, and the last tail vanished down the last bolthole into the storm sewers of the old Jewish Quarter. And the lights came on. Not the dim red table-lamps, but bright, hard, white bulbs, in wire cages, and by that raw, white light the people saw each other in the utter nakedness of their fear, saw the graceful social masks stripped away, and as they saw, they were themselves seen, and it was as if they all, mighty and mean, prince and pauper, priest and prostitute, were joined in a fellowship of fear. There were tears, there was laughter—sudden, savage laughter—there were whispered confessions and intimate absolutions, there was anger, and grief, and ecstatic exultation; the casks of emotion were broached, the conventions toppled and smashed; true selves, true colours long constrained released and unfurled.

In the great catharsis, none thought to look for the master of ceremonies, the aged Jew who had made such outrageous, blasphemous claims for himself. Caught up in the maelstrom of emotions, none saw the two young men from the table nearest the stage, and a third young man with them, with a square face and a little square moustache, none saw them carry a young woman fighting and heaving and clawing for breath up the cellar steps and out of the door into the cold and sleet of Judengasse. None saw the fear in her eyes, wide, terrified, as if struck down by the wrath of God Himself.

THE BELLS OF BERLIN

8th June 1934

After fourteen years of marriage, Werner still knows to surprise me with little presents, still takes an adolescent delight in coming through the front door announcing that he has a surprise for his Anna and hiding the little gift-wrapped something behind his back out of my reach, or inviting me to guess what it is, which hand it is in. I play along with his little games of concealment and surprise because I, after fourteen years, still delight in the pleasure on his face as he watches me tear off the wrapping and ribbon to reveal his little love-token beneath. Goodness only knows where he managed to find such a book as this one; afternoons much better spent preparing briefs than rooting around in the antiquarian bookshops along BirkenStrasse, but bless him anyway, it is quite exquisite, tall and thin, in the English Art Noveau Style, the cover decorated with poppies and corn sheaves, the blank pages heavy, creamy, smooth as skin.

Every woman should have a diary, he says. The true history of the world is written in women's diaries, especially in days such as these when history is unfolding and ripening around our ears like a field of wheat. Anyway, he says he fears that what with Isaac now attending school six mornings a week I will descend into a state of mental vegetation the only escape from which will be to have an affair, so for the sake of our marriage, I had better keep this journal.

Yes, all very well Werner, and, yes, affairs notwithstanding, the discipline of diary-keeping is good for me, but what to write in it? A simple family chronicle: Isaac still having trouble with his arithmetic; Anneliese, despite the trauma of her first period, chosen to sing in the school choir for Herman Goering's pleasure? Ponderous Bach violin sonatas from the apartment at the back of the house, evidence of Papa's continued anger at the purging of his beloved Mahler from the Berlin Philharmonic's repertoire? Is this what Werner means by the *true history of the world*? Or does he mean that I should set down the events happening at once so close at hand (today on my way to the shops I passed the burnt-out shell of the Reichstag) and yet seemingly so remote, distant, bellowing voices on the wireless; and try to record my reaction to them and the reactions of those around me. Is it history when Mrs. Erdmann comes to me in a terrible pother because her name has appeared on a blacklist of women still buying from Jewish shops? It is with a certain trepidation that I set these and any future words of mine down on paper; these days generate so many historians, what can a suburban Berlin *Hausfrau* hope to add to the analysis of these times in which we find ourselves? Yet I feel that Mrs. Erdmann's consternation, my Father's dismay at being forced to play racially pure music, Anneliese singing for Herman Goering; these must be recorded, because it is in the trivia and minutiae of our lives that the history made elsewhere must be lived out.

14th June 1934

Dear dear. Slipping. Had promised myself I would write in diary every day. Had also promised myself I would avoid slipping into telegraph-ese, and write proper, complete, not pay-by-the-word, sentences. The spirit is willing, and these past weeks, there has been no dearth of subject matter, but the demands of Kinder, Kirche, Kuche (or, in my case, Kinder, Synagogue, Kuche) are all too demanding.

Mrs. Shummel from the Jewish Ladies Society arrived on my doorstep this morning in a state of distraction; in the middle of the night a gang of

S.A. bullyboys had surrounded her house, smashed in all her ground floor windows and daubed a yellow Star of David on her door. She had hidden, shaking with fear, in the cupboard under the stairs while the young thugs shouted abuse for over an hour. They must have little enough to do to smash in an old woman's windows and think of enough names to call her for an hour.

Papa is worried too. Unlike me, he has no Gentile spouse to hide behind. Though his colleagues in the orchestra support him in the solidarity of musicians, all it takes is one suspicious soul to denounce him to the Party and his career as a musician is finished. And that would be the finish of him; poor Papa, without his music, he would wither and die. Losing Mahler was enough of a blow to him; the possibility that he might never again hear the final movement of the Resurrection Symphony has put twenty years on him in one stroke.

Symptoms. Disease. Dis-ease. Society is sick. Germany is sick, and does not know it. Werner likes to lock up his work in his office at six o'clock, but I can tell he is concerned. The legal loopholes by which he manoeuvres Jewish assets out of the country are being tightened every day, and he has heard of new legislation afoot that will make it a crime for Jew and Gentile to marry, to even love one another. What kind of a country is it, dear God, where love is a crime?

20th June 1934

I saw them destroy an art gallery this morning. I had not intended to be about anywhere near Blucherstrasse. I would not have passed that way at all but for a consuming fancy for cakes from a particularly excellent *Konditorei* in that neighbourhood. When I saw the crowd, heard the clamour, I should have walked away, but there is a dreadful fascination in other people's madness. Perhaps it is only by the madness of others that we measure our own sanity. Or lack of it.

A good fifty to sixty people had gathered around the front of the Gallery Seidl. It was not a gallery I much frequent; I cannot make head nor tail out of these modern painters, Expressionists, I believe they call themselves. The Brownshirts had already smashed the window and kicked in the door, now inside the shop, they were breaking picture frames over their knees and kicking, slashing, tearing canvasses with a grim dutifulness that seemed all the more threatening because of its utter dispassion. The mutilated paintings were passed out into the street by human chain and piled to await the petrol can, the match, the *feu de joie*, the roar of approval from the crowd. Herr Seidl stood by benumbed, utterly helpless, as punishment was meted out for admiring abstract, corrupt, decadent art.

I think that was what disturbed me the most; not the grim-faced determination of the Nazi bully-boys, nor the mob acquiescence of the bystanders, but that art, beauty, (despite my inability to comprehend it) should be subject to the approval and control of the Party. It was then as if the whole weight of the Party machine, like some huge, heaving juggernaut, fell upon me as never before; I felt a desperation, a panic, almost as one does when, at dead of night, one contemplates one's own mortality; a knowledge of the inevitable darkness that must fall. I had to escape. I had to flee from the mob, from the smoke and flame of burning paintings that seemed like the soul of an entire nation offered up as a holocaust. I ran then, without thought or heed of anything but to escape. I did not know where I ran; through streets broad and narrow, through bustling thoroughfares and dark alleys, did the people I rushed past stare at me, call out, ask if anything was the matter? I do not know, I do not remember there even having been people; all I remember is that I must run, and run I did, until I came to my senses in a cobbled laneway, overhung by stooping houses and bandoliers of grubby carpets and limp laundry. Lost, in a city that for fifteen years I had called home and which now revealed itself as foreign, alien, and hostile, with nothing familiar or friendly. Save one thing. Perhaps the one thing that had stopped me where I did, one thing and one thing only that had any connection with my past. A swinging wooden shingle, unpainted, hanging above a set of steep steps leading down to a basement; a wooden sign cut in the shape of a rat.

25th June 1934

I had to go. I had to return. When I saw that sign, that crude wooden rat, it was as if a spirit that had never truly been exorcised and had laid dormant for these years had risen up to stake its claim to me. I knew that I would never be free from it until I faced again what I had first faced, and failed before, in that cellar in the old Jewish Quarter.

Do not ask me how I know; but I know without the slightest doubt that it is the same cellar, the same troglodytic staff, the same ancient Jew with his accordion, and what the accordion summoned . . .

If it is a spirit that oppresses me, it is a spirit of remembrance. Things I had thought lost in the darkness are emerging after long exile, changed in subtle and disturbing ways by their time in the dark. That same night as I fled from the burning of the gallery, I was woken by a tightness in my chest, a constriction in my breathing; prescience, or is it a remembrance? of an asthma attack.

It took many days for me to summon the courage to visit that cellar club. Pressure of work keeps Werner long hours at the office; I went twice to the very door and turned back, afraid, without him ever knowing I had been out of the house at night; the ease with which I deceived him in that matter makes me wonder: if I did not love him so deeply, how easy it would be to cheat on him. The third night I would have turned away but for a sudden rushing sensation of wild abandon that swept over me like a pair of dark, enfolding wings, there, on the bottom step, and made me push open the door.

All was as I had remembered it that night under Judengasse; the close-packed tables between the brick piers, the miniscule stage, the bored, slutty all-girl band, the infernal red light from the table-lamps. The wizened *maitre d'*, who, if not the one who had greeted me that night so long ago, was cast in the same mould, showed me to a table in front of the stage. While wine was fetched, I studied the clientele. Bankers, Captains of Industry, lawyers, civil servants; these certainly, as that time before, but unlike that other time, everywhere I looked, the gray and buff uniform of the Party. Party uniforms, Party shirts, Party ties, Party armbands, Party badges, Party caps, Party whispers, Party salutes. The wine was fine and well-bodied and brought the memories of that other time welling up in me, impelled by a pressure outside my will and control: we four friends, that quarter that would set the world ringing with the infamy of our pleasure seeking; whatever it was the others found in the rat cellar, it cracked us apart like stale bread and sent us apart on our separate trajectories through history: I with Papa to his new position as principle violinist with the Berlin Philharmonic, and, for me, marriage to the most eligible young lawyer in Berlin, and motherhood. I realised that I had not thought about that other young lawyer in twenty years, the one to whom I was almost engaged, until that night in the rat cellar.

As I sat sipping my wine another face formed out of the interplay of interior shadows; the aspiring artist who had shared our table. A face lost in darkness of twenty years, a face I now, with shocking suddenness, recognised in every Party poster, every newspaper, every cinema newsreel; the square, peasant face, the little, ludicrous affectation of a moustache, and the light in his eyes when he had whispered by candlelight the words; "I shall be feared one day, I know it . . ."

"Fear," a voice whispered, as if my own fears had spoken aloud, but the voice was that of the ancient Master of Ceremonies alone in his single spotlight with his accordion and his tale of a burden some immortality and a gospel that seemed curiously appropriate to these times and places. As before, the accordion groaned out its accompaniment, as before the waiters went about barring the doors and shuttering the windows and extinguishing the lamps until finally the spotlight winked out and in the darkness the old Jew whispered, "Can you now face your fears alone, in utter darkness?"

And the rats came pouring from their runways and tunnels under Berlin, summoned by the old man's accordion, pouring into the cellar. I closed my eyes, fought down the horror of damp bodies brushing past my legs, of clicking, chitinous claws pricking at my feet. The people locked in darkness screamed and screamed and screamed and then one voice screamed louder than any other. "Jews! Jews! Jews!" it screamed, and the scream went out across the heaving bodies and touched their fear and kindled it into hate. "Jews! Jews! Jews!" The people took up the howl and took bottles, chairs, lamps in their hands, or bare hands alone, clenched into iron fists, and they beat and smashed at the rats, beat and beat and beat at their fear while the cellar rang and rang and rang with their song of loathing. I tried to shut it out, close my ears, but the brick vaults beat like a Nazi drum, and when at last the lights came on I fled for the door and up and out into the clean and pure night air while below me the voices of the people joined in joyous laughter and someone began to sing the 'Horst Wessel,' and other voices joined it, and the quartet picked up the key, and the whole rat cellar thundered with the joyous fellowship of hatred.

30th June 1934

It is one of Werner's little lovable inconsistencies that the man who is so competent, so incisive, so feared in the cut and thrust of the courtroom is nervous and hesitant when it comes to broaching delicate or serious matters in his own home. There he stood, leaning against the fireplace, hands thrust in hip-pockets, shifting his weight from foot to foot, looking for a leading line. This time I was able to pre-empt him.

"You think that the time has come for us to sell up and move?"

I think I succeeded in surprising Werner; up until that moment he had not thought I had any conception of exactly how serious events had turned in Berlin. I think, after the Rat Cellar, I knew better than he. If not better, certainly more intimately. They do hate us. They want us dead. Every last one of us. He said that the few remaining legal loopholes were closing by the hour. He said new anti-Semitic laws were being drafted that would force the Jews, and Jews-by-marriage—a fouler crime by far—out of society altogether, and into labour camps. He said that the Party was on the verge of disintegration into factions; Röhm's S.A. were challenging Hitler's domination of the party, and that when the long knives were drawn it was a certainty that the Jews would be blamed.

I asked where he had thought we might flee. Holland, he said, was a traditional haven of tolerance and stability. Amsterdam. He had taken the liberty of investigating investment opportunities in the diamond business, and the state of the property market. Had he started proceedings to liquidate our assets? I asked. He looked up at me, at once guilty and suspicious.

"Yes, my love. I have been moving small amounts through the Swiss banks for some months now."

"That is good," I said.

"I had thought you would be angry with me, I know how much you hate me keeping secrets from you."

How could I be angry with him, when I held a secret from him I must take to my grave.

"I think we should move immediately."

"You have thought about your Father?"

"Without his music, he has nothing, and they have taken the music he loves away from him." A memory: watching from my opera box the rapture with which he led the Philharmonic in the Adagio from Mahler's Fifth. "He would lose home, wealth, prestige, power, public acclaim, before he would lose his music."

"And Isaac, Anneliese?"

I heard again the screaming in the rat cellar, the beating, beating, beating of chairs, bottles, naked fists on the squirming bodies of the Jews.

"Especially them."

We lay together in bed, listening to the night-time news on the wireless. Reports were coming in of an attempted putsch by elements of the S.A. Loyal S.S troopers had quashed the coup, Generals Röhm, Von Schleicher and Stressel had all been arrested and summarily liquidated.

I reached over to turn off the wireless.

"Tomorrow, Werner. You will do it tomorrow, won't you, my love?"

And as I spoke, the bells of Berlin rang out, a thousand bells from a thousand steeples, ringing all across the city, all across Germany, all across the world, ringing out a knell for the soul of a great nation.

THE JUDAS KISS

At two o'clock in the afternoon the small triangle of sunlight would fall onto the floor and move across the sofa and the two easy chairs and the dining table, the little paraffin camping stove, the mattresses and rolls of bedding, all the while dwindling, diminishing until at five o'clock it vanished to nothingness in the top left corner of the cellar, by the secret door. When the sameness of the faces; her husband, her father, her children, the Van Hootens, old Comenius the clock-doctor became appalling in their monotony, when the quiet slap of playing cards, the whisper of the word "check," the murmured recounting of the dreams of the night before, when these all became as terrible and ponderous as the tick of the executioner's clock, she would hunt the beam of dirty light to its source in a tiny broken corner of the wooden shuttering that boarded over the cellar windows. And there, blue beyond any possible imagining of blueness, was a tiny triangle of sky. She could lose herself for hours in the blueness, the apex of the triangle of sunlight between her eyes. It was her personal piece of sky; once when she saw a flight of Junker bombers cross it on their way to the cities of England, the sight of their black crosses desecrating her piece of sky was enough to send her in tears to the furthest, darkest corner of the cellar.

He did not like to see her there, standing on an orange box, eyes screwed half-shut in that triangle of light; he feared that someone might see those eyes, that triangle of face, and report it to the occupation forces. He no longer remonstrated with her on the matter, though. He knew that whenever he slipped out the secret door up into the streets of Amsterdam, she would be at the shutter losing herself in those twenty centimetres of sky. He would not remonstrate with her because he felt guilt that many of his trips to the surface were for the same reason of escaping from the dreadful claustrophic sameness of life in the cellar.

Once, on one of his trips out from the ruins of the house on Achtergracht— he had burned it himself, to allay suspicions that Jews might be hiding there—he had seen occupation troops pulling a Jewish family from their hiding place in a house on Herrengracht. A mother, a father, a grandfather clutching an ornamental wooden clog, two little girls in print frocks. Their faces were pale and sickly from life hidden away from the sky. He saw the troopers pull out the householders, an elderly couple he vaguely knew from the Jewish Shelter Society, and push them into the back of a canvas-covered truck. As he went on his way not too quickly not too slowly, he heard the officer announce through a loudspeaker that those who harboured Jews were no better than Jews themselves and would warrant the same treatment. Those who reported Jews to the occupation authorities would be rewarded for fulfilling their civic duty. Even those who were now harbouring Jews might escape punishment if they fulfilled their civic duty.

As he went among the safe shops buying meat and bread and candles and paraffin for the camping stove, the faces of the plump, homely Dutch couple as they were pushed into the back of the truck haunted him. In the small room behind Van Den Beek's dry-cleaning shop, the organiser of the Jewish Shelter Group said that he had been approached by a family whose safe house was threatened by house-to-house searches; would he be able to take them in the Achtergracht cellar? In his mind he saw the truck drive away under the trees that lined the canal, in his mind he heard the cries and moans penetrate the unnaturally quiet street, and he had said, *I do not know, I cannot say, give me a day or so to think about it.*

She envied him his trips above ground. She understood his reasoning; safer by far for just one to take the risk of being seen, but the taste of sky had made her hungry for more, to feel its vast blue vault above, around, enclosing her. In the night, when the others slept on their mattresses, he whispered to her about the new family who needed shelter. She would have loved them to come. New faces, new lives, new stories were almost as welcome as freedom in this place where the major entertainment was the narration to each other of the dreams of the previous night.

But the new family did not come and the days continued to be counted out by the passage of the triangle of light across the cellar floor and the endless, endless recounting of dreams that grew ever more colourless and impoverished. When, in the night she heard it, she was awake in the instant. The rest slept on, dreaming out their dreams, minting their cheap and tinny coinage, but to her it was as clear and piercing as an angel's clarion. The note of an accordion, far distant among the canals and high-gabled houses of Amsterdam, yet close, and sharp, and sweeter than wine. As if in a dream, perhaps in a dream, a dream that is more solid and tangible than what we call reality, she rose, went to the secret door and stole out through the warren of passageways and charred ruins up onto the street. She did not fear the curfew; with the same assurance that the music played only for her, she knew that she was invisible as a ghost, or a dream, to the occupation forces in their grey trucks.

She found the aged man struck by a stray moonbeam in a street that opened onto a wide canal, bent over his instrument, intent upon his melancholy music. The cobblestones were invisible beneath a shifting, stirring, moon-silvered carpet of rats.

As she walked toward the aged aged man, the rats parted silently, liquidly before her. The wandering Jew looked up from his self-absorbed improvisation.

"*Gnädige Frau*, you should not have come. You are placing yourself in considerable peril."

"I do not think so."

He smiled; teeth long, yellow in the moonshine, like the ivory keys of his accordion. The liquid carpet of rats seethed.

"You are right, of course. Things are ordained by the will and grace of God. It was ordained by God that our destinies be tied together; that we be yoked together for a little while. When first we met, all those years ago at the spa at Baden, remember how afraid you were, how you ran? But we have been yoked together. We could not escape each other. He does that, God, yokes me for a little while to the lives of others. To save them. Or to damn them."

"Would you damn me?"

"I already have, alas. Forgive me. It was not personal, Anna. My ludicrous vaudeville act, my burlesque gospel, my cellars in cities across this continent, my rats, they have played their part in accomplishing the will of God. Apocalypse descends upon us, hastened by my actions, so the Master will return soon and free me from this weary undyingness."

"You think you are responsible for . . . this?"

"I have served my part in God's will."

"You are mad."

"That is one interpretation. The only other is that I am exactly what and who I say I am."

"An apostle of darkness?"

"An apostle of a wrathful God. The Jews have their just punishment now, the Christ-killers. Do I hear the brass hooves of the Four Horsemen on the cobbles? Come Master, come . . ."

"Mad, and evil."

"Or good beyond your conception of the word. I have damned, now I may save. Come with me. This place is finished, you are all finished. It does not take the gift of prophecy to tell that. Even the rats are abandoning the city, and I with them. Will you heed them, and come with me?"

The rats moved silently over the cobbles, little pink clawed feet hurrying, hurrying. Noses, whiskers, quested for the moon.

"I have a family, I have a husband, my father, my friends."

"Unless a man hate his mother, and his father, and all his family, he can be no true disciple. So it is written."

"I am not a disciple. I am a Jew."

The aged aged man bowed deeply, took her hand in the moonlight, kissed it.

"*Kuss die Hande, gnädige Frau,* as they said in Old Vienna." His fingers squeezed a quiet chord from the accordion. He turned away, walked away toward the canal. His music filled the street. The rats stirred and swirled and followed on.

He was awake when she returned. He whispered his fury through clenched teeth.

"You were out."

"Yes."

"Why? My God, why did you go out after curfew . . ."

She shrugged, any explanation would be impossible, but her shrug was invisible in the darkness of the cellar. For the first time she noticed a little triangle of moonlight fell through the wooden shuttering to lie on the cellar floor.

The next day he went out to buy more paraffin for the stove, and some blankets, for the first autumn chill had found its way into the Achtergracht cellar. When he returned he kissed her full on the mouth and then went to sit, strangely quiet and withdrawn, in a chair apart from the others and stared at the steeple formed by his touching fingers as if he had never seen them before.

At five o'clock the patch of sunlight vanished and the soldiers came. They burst down the door with axes, the soldiers in their black boots and helmets. The old people screamed at the sight of their black machine guns. With the muzzles of their black machine guns they herded the people out through the secret door, out through the warren of collapsed cellarage and fire-blackened walls they had penetrated with such ease, as if they had been told where to go, out into the five o'clock sunlight, to the street, and the waiting truck.

"You forced me to do it," he said to her as the soldiers with grim dutifulness began to push the Van Hootens and old Comenius the clock-doctor into the back of the truck. Old Comenius was clutching an Ormolu clock to his chest. "You went out, you put us all in peril. You could have had us all punished if anyone had seen. So, I had to go to the local headquarters and inform. You think I wanted to do that? You think I wanted to sell the Van Hootens and old Comenius? You forced me to make that bargain, to sell them, in return for our freedom. It was either them, or all of us. That was what the officer promised. If I did my civic duty, we would all go free. I had to sacrifice them to keep us safe, and together."

Then a soldier with black rifle stepped between the man and the woman and the woman and her children and her father with his violin case in his hand were pushed away, pushed toward the truck, pushed into the truck while the man struggled against the smiling soldiers who had taken grip of his arms. The man shouted, the man screamed, and the woman screamed back, and her father with his violin, and her son and daughter, but the soldiers pulled shut the canvas flap and tied it and in a moment the roar of the engine had drowned the voices, shouting screaming the betrayal of their betrayal. And the truck drove away down Achtergracht, and the officer stepped from his staff car and stood before the man and said,

"Jews. Are Jews."

THE STRING QUARTET

Hurrying hurrying, faster faster, hurrying hurrying, faster faster, through the flat black darkness of the night forest, through the endless waiting trees, cleaving the darkness with the beam of its headlight and the shout of its hundred wheels, cleaving through the darkness that lies across the heart of the continent, the night train, hurrying hurrying, faster faster, toward its final destination.

Though it must be hours since your Father said goodnight and blessed you into the care of God with a kiss on your forehead, as he used to kiss those nights when you were afraid and came into his bed to sleep, you are not asleep. Your Father has rolled his old bones into a corner of a cattle truck and has managed sleep of some kind; your children on either side of you are asleep also, leaning against your body; but you, alone of all the people crammed into the cattle truck, are not, it seems. You envy those crammed people their sleep. There is enough light in the boxcar for the dark-adapted eye to distinguish their shapes; old Comenius still clutching the clock to his chest, its heavy tick ticking away to the beat of his heart, the Van Hootens curled around each other like kittens, reverting to the innocent intimacies of childhood; all the others, clinging to their precious possessions; an umbrella, a carved wooden lugger, a book, a prayer shawl. Mighty and mean, prince and pauper, priest and prostitute, all rendered anonymous, stationless, estateless, shapeless mounds of pain in the night-glow inside the boxcar.

You must have slept. The rhythm of the night train's hundred wheels must have lulled you to sleep, for it is the cessation of that beating, beating, beating rhythm that wakes you. A grey dawn light ekes through the gaps between the ill-fitting planks. The cold is intense, a cold breath from the heart of the continent. The hunger is devouring. How many days since you last ate? Beyond remembering, like an entire life sunk without trace, beyond all remembering.

The train is stationary. You press your face to the cold planks, screw up your eyes, squint to try and make out where it is you have arrived. A rural railway station, somewhere, deep in the night forest, surrounded, encircled, by the waiting, stooping trees, like aged aged men. Figures moving on the platform: soldiers? Voices, talking among themselves in a language you do not understand. Loudspeakers crackle, come alive. In the cattle car, in each of the twenty-five cattle cars that make up the night train, people are starting to awaken. Your children stir, cold, hungry, uncomprehending, where are they, what is happening? You cannot help them, you do not know yourself. The voices draw near. With a crash and a blinding blare of dawn light, the boxcar doors are flung back. Soldiers. Slow, stupid, brutal faces. Slavic faces. They start to pull the people from the cars. Down, down, down. All change. All change. From each of the twenty-five cars the people are pulled down to stand shivering and blinking in the brilliant dawn cold on the platform. They hug themselves, their breath steams in the bright dawn cold. The soldiers with the slow, stupid, brutal faces go among the people to take away their possessions. Prayer shawls, books, carved wooden luggers, umbrellas. Dr. Comenius' clock is taken from his fingers. Your father clings to his violin in its case, cries out, no, no, do not take away the music, you cannot take away the music. He does not realise, you think, that they took away the music years before. The soldiers, with impassive determination, smash his fingers with rifle butts, smash the fallen violin to a shatter of polished wood and gut.

You press your children to you. You fear that the soldiers will want to tear them away from your broken, bleeding fingers, smash them to silence and nothingness with rifle butts. There is nothing to say, no words that will help. Not now. The soldiers push you down the platform toward the station office. The crackling voice of the loudspeaker welcomes you. Welcome welcome welcome. You notice that a pall of smoke is rising beyond the trees, as if from a great conflagration. The cold morning air draws the smoke in low and close over the station; a vile smoke, a choking suffocating smoke, the stench of something unclean, burning there in the night forest.

Shouting in their stupid, brutal voices, the soldiers herd you toward the office. You do not want to go there, you cannot go there, you must not go there, but you are incapable of resisting the pressing, pressing, pressing bodies. There are figures behind the latticed windows of the waiting room. Seated figures, bowed in attitudes of concentration, as if over musical instruments. Then above the voice of the loudspeaker come the sweet, sad notes of the string quartet, rising up to mingle with the smoke that lies across the waiting trees of the night forest, over all the dark continent, the final movement from *Eine Kleine Nachtmusik*; rather badly, you think.

"It is all right, Anna," your Father says, "it is only for a little while, until the next train comes, to take us on to the place we are meant to go."

ANGELS IN LOVE

Kathe Koja

One of the most exciting new writers to hit the scene in some time, Kathe Koja is a frequent contributor to *Isaac Asimov's Science Fiction Magazine* and *The Magazine of Fantasy and Science Fiction*, and has also sold stories to *Pulphouse, SF Eye, The Ultimate Werewolf, A Whisper of Blood,* and elsewhere. Her first novel, *The Cipher,* was released last year to enthusiastic critical response, and her new novel, *Bad Brains,* is just out. Her story "Distances" was in our Sixth Annual Collection, and her story "Skin Deep" was in our Seventh Annual Collection.

In the powerful and unrelenting piece that follows, she shows us that you'd better be careful what you wish for—you just might *get* it.

Like wings. Rapturous as the muted screams, lush the beating of air through chipboard walls, luscious like sex and, oh my, far more forbidden: whatever it was, Lurleen *knew* it was wrong.

Knew it from the shrieks, gagged and that was no pillow, no sir, no way— she herself was familiar with the gasp of muffled sex, and this was definitely not it. And not—really—kinky, or not in any way *she* knew of, and with a half-shy swagger, Lurleen could admit she had acquaintance of a few. Kiss me here. Let's see some teeth. Harder.

The sounds, arpeggio of groans, that basso almost-unheard thump, thump, rhythmic as a headboard or a set of baritone springs, but that wasn't it, either. Subsonic; felt by the bones. Lying there listening, her own bones tingled, skin rippled light with goose bumps, speculation: who made those strange, strange sounds? Someone with a taste for the rough stuff, maybe, someone who liked the doughy strop of flesh. Someone strong. An old boyfriend had used to say she fucked like an angel; she never understood the phrase till now. Her hands, deliberate stroll southward, shimmy of familiar fingers on as-familiar flesh; her own groans in counterpoint to the ones through the walls.

Waking heavy in the morning, green toothpaste spit and trying to brush her hair at the same time, late again. "You're late," Roger would say when she walked in, and she would flip fast through her catalog of excuses—which hadn't he heard lately?—and try to give him something to get her by, thinking all the while of last night's tingle, puzzling again its ultimate source. It was kind of a sexy game to Lurleen, that puzzling; it gave her something to do at work.

Music store. No kind of music she liked, but sometimes it wasn't too bad, and the store itself had a kind of smell that she enjoyed, like a library smell, like something educational was going on. Sheet music, music stands, Roger fussy with customers, turning the stereo on loud and saying stuff like, "But have you heard Spivakov's Bach? Really quite good." Like he had probably heard Bach's Bach and could have suggested a few improvements. Right.

Today she felt dopey and sluggish, simple transactions done twice and twice wrong; Roger was pissed, glowered as she slumped through the day. At quitting time he made a point of pointedly disappearing, not saying good night; sighing, she had to find him, hide-and-seek through the racks. He was a stickler for what he called the pleasantries: Good night, Lurleen. Good night, Roger. Every day.

Finally: hunched behind the order counter, flipping through the day's mail like he hadn't read it nine times already. Lurleen leaned tippy-toe over, flat-handed on the cracking gray laminate: "Good night, Roger."

Chilly nod, like he'd just caught her trying to palm something: "Good night, Lurleen." Waited till she was almost out the door to say, "Lurleen?"

Stopped, impatient keys in hand. "What?"

"We open at ten o'clock. Every day."

Asshole. "See you tomorrow." Not banging the door, giving herself points for it. Outside, her skin warmed, like butter, spread velvet all over. He always kept the fucking store too cold. Like the music'd melt or something if he turned it up past freezing. Rolling all her windows down, singing to the Top 40 station. Stopped at the party store for cigarettes and to flirt with the clerk, old guy just about as ugly as Roger, but round where Roger was slack, furry where Roger was not.

"You headin' out tonight?" Sliding the cigarettes across the counter, grinning at her tits. "Have some fun?"

"Oh, I always manage to have fun." Over-shoulder smile as she headed for the door. Roger liked to stare at her tits, too, she was positive; she just hadn't caught him at it yet. Asshole probably went home and jerked off, dreaming about her bouncing around to Bach. And she laughed, a little: who'd been flying solo last night, huh?

But that was different.

In the dark, blind witness to the nightly ravishment, Lurleen, closed eyes, busy hands filling in the blanks, timing herself to the thump and stutter of the rapture beyond the walls. Longer tonight, ecstatic harmony of gulping cries, and after the crescendo wail, sound track to her own orgasm, she slept: to dream of flesh like iron, of rising whole, and drenched, and shiny-bright; shock-heavy with a pleasure poisonously rare. Woke just in time to see that she'd slept through the clock. Again.

In the hallway, pausing—already late, so what if she was later?—before the door next door. Identical in nondescription to every other down the grimy hall, there was no way to tell by looking just what kind of fun went on there every night. Lurleen, tapping ignition key to lips, thoughtful sideways stare. Imagining, all the reluctant way to work, what sort of exotica, what moist brutalities were practiced there, what kinds of kinks indulged. Wriggling a little, skirt riding up and the cracked vinyl edges of the too-hot seat pressing voluptuously sharp into the damp flesh of her thighs.

It came to her that she had never really seen that next-door neighbor of hers. Maybe they'd bumped into each other, exchanged laundry-room hellos, but for the life of her, Lurleen could not recall. She wasn't even sure if it was just one person or a couple. They sure were a couple at night, though, weren't they just?

The day spent avoiding Roger's gaze, colder than the store and just as constant, more than one smart remark about time clocks. Stopping for cigarettes, she picked up a six-pack, too, clandestine sips at red lights, rehearsing queenly answers she would never give. It was so hot it felt good, brought a warm, slow trickle of sweat down the plane of her temple, the hotter spot between her breasts.

She was going out tonight, that was for sure; she owed herself something for the just-past bitch of a day. Walking up the hot two flights, a thought nudged her, firm and brisk to get past the beer. She leaned to sight up the stairwell, heart a trifle nervous, quick and jangly in her chest. Well. No time like the present, was there, to scratch a little itch? I'll just say hi, she thought, walking quicker now. I'll say, Hi, I'm your next-door neighbor. I just stopped by to say hello.

Fourth can in hand, smart tattoo on the door before she could change her mind. Wondering who would open, what they would look like. What they would smell like—Lurleen was a great believer in smells. If they would ask her in, and what she might say, knowing she would say yes, and a smile past the thick spot in her throat, and she smiled at that, too; it wasn't that big a deal, was it?

Maybe it was.

Nothing. Silence inside, so she knocked again, louder, humming to herself and, oh boy, here we go: winded swing of the door and "Hi," before it was all the way open. "Hi, I'm Lurleen, your neighbor?"

Tall, her first thought. And skinny. Not model-skinny, just chicken bones, short blonde hair, Giants T-shirt over a flat chest. Anne, she said her name was, and past her curved shoulders, Lurleen could see a flat as cramped and dingy as her own, a little emptier, maybe, a little less ripe, but nothing special. Purely ordinary. Like Anne herself: no exotic bruising, no secret sheen. Just stood there in the doorway playing with the end of her baggy T-shirt, flipping it as she talked, and that thin-lipped smile that said, Are you ready to leave yet? Just one big disappointment, but Lurleen didn't show it, kept up her own smile through the strain of the stillborn chatter until she was back inside her own place, sucking up the last of her beer.

"Well," through a closed-mouth, ladylike burp. "*Well.*"

How could someone so dull have such a wild sex life? Be better off meeting the boyfriend; he had to be the real show. Fucking angel. Lurleen's giggles lasted through the rest of the beer, her long, cool shower, and half hour's worth of mousse and primp. When she left for the bar, Anne's flat was silent still, not even the requisite TV drone. From the parking lot, the lifeless drift of her curtains, beige to Lurleen's red, was all there was to see.

At the bar she met a couple of guys, nice ones—she couldn't quite remember which was Jeff and which was Tony, but they kept her dancing, and drinking, and that was nice, too. After last call she swiveled off her seat, sweet, and smiled and said she was sorry, but she had an hour to make the airport to pick up her husband—and even as she said it, she had to wonder why; it was one of them she'd planned on picking up, and never mind that she couldn't remember who was who; names didn't exactly matter at that time of night; words didn't matter past Who's got the rubber. But still she left alone.

Coming home, off-center slew into her parking space, radio up way too loud, singing and her voice a bray in the cut-engine quiet; she almost slipped going up the stairs. Shushing herself as she poured a glass of milk, her invariable after-binge cure-all. Lifting the glass, she caught from the damp skin of her forearm an after-shave scent, mixed with the male smell of Tony. Jeff? It didn't matter, such a pretty boy.

But not as pretty as the boy next door.

And, her thought seeming eerily a signal, she heard the preliminary noises, shifting warm through the wall as if they stroked her: Anne's breathy, wordless voice, that rush of sound, half-sinister whirlwind pavane. Pressed against the wall itself, her bare-skinned sweat a warm adhesive, Lurleen stood, mouth open and eyes shut, working her thin imagination as Anne, presumably, worked her thin body, both—all three—ending in vortex, whirlpool, mouthing that dwindling symphony of screams, Lurleen herself louder than she'd ever been, with any man. Loud enough that they could, maybe, hear her through the walls.

Slumped, damp, she could not quite admit it, say to herself, You want them to hear you. You want *him* to hear you, whoever he is. You want what Anne's getting, better than any bar pickup, better than anything you ever had. Glamorous and dirty. And scary. And hot.

By the next night, she was ready, had turned her bed to lengthwise face the wall: willing herself, forcing herself like an unseen deliberate splinter in their shared and coupling flesh; she *would* be part of this. She had never had anything like what went on over there, never anything good. She would have this if she had to knock down the wall to get it. Fingers splayed against her flesh, heels digging hard into the sheets and letting go, crying out, Hear me. Hear me.

Exhausted at work, but on time, she couldn't take any of Roger's bitching now, not when she had to think. Make a plan. Anne, she was a sorry-looking bitch, no competition once the boyfriend got a good look at Lurleen. The trick was to get him to look. To see. See what he'd been hearing, night after night. Of course, it wouldn't be all that easy: if Anne had any brains at all, she would want to keep her boyfriend and Lurleen far, far apart. Lurleen decided she would have to take it slow and smart, *be* smart—not exactly her strong point, but she could be slick; she knew what she wanted.

She began to stalk Anne, never thinking of it in so many words, but as sure and surely cautious as any predator. Waiting, lingering in the hallway after work, for Anne to come home from whatever unfathomable job she did all day. Never stopping to talk, just a smile, pleasant make-believe. She made it her business to do her laundry when Anne did hers; at the first whoosh and stagger of the old machine, Lurleen was there, quarters in hand; her clothes had never been so clean; she had to see. Any jockey shorts, bikini underwear, jockstraps, what? She meant to take one if she could, steal it before, before it was clean. Smell it. You can tell a lot about a man. Lurleen believed, from the smell of his skin, not his aftershave or whatever, but the pure smell of his body. Until his body was beneath hers, it was the best she could do. She pawed through the laundry basket, poked around in the washer: nothing. Just Anne's Priss-Miss blouses, baggy slacks, cheap bras—and just about everything beige. Balked angry toss of the clothing, stepped on it to push it back into the basket. Maybe he liked Anne *because* she was so beige, so . . . nothing? *Could* a man want a woman to be nothing? Just a space to fill? Lurleen had known plenty of guys who liked their women dumb—it made them feel better—but anyway, Anne didn't seem dumb. Just empty.

And still, night after night the same, bed against the wall, Lurleen could be determined; Lurleen could work for what she wanted. Drained every morning, the sting of tender skin in the shower, even Roger noticed her red eyes.

"Not moonlighting, are you?" But she saw he knew it was no question, half-gaze through those tired eyes, and she even, for a moment, considered telling him, considered saying, I want the boy next door, Roger; I want him real bad. I want him so much I even jerk off so he can hear me, so he can know how he turns me on. I want him so much I don't know what to do.

She wasn't getting anywhere. Drumming slow one finger against the order counter, staring right past some guy bumbling on about some opera or something, she wasn't getting *anywhere*, and it was wearing her out. No time for anything else, bars, guys, whatever; there wasn't any other guy she wanted. Anne's smiles growing smaller, tighter, her gaze more pinched; was she catching on? Tired from sitting in the hallway—once or twice another neighbor had caught her at it, loitering tense and unseeing until the tap-tap-tap on her shoulder. Hey, are you O.K.? "Fine." Harsh involuntary blush. "Just looking for an earring." Right. Tired from staking out the parking lot, hot breeze through the window; she didn't even know what kind of car he drove. Tired to death and still no glimpse of him, proud author of the sounds; it was killing her to listen, but she couldn't stop. She didn't want to stop.

And then that night, mid-jerk, mid-groan, they stopped. The sounds.

Ceased completely, but not to complete silence: a waiting sound, a whisper. Whispering through the walls, such a willing sound.

She yanked on a T-shirt, ends tickling her bare ass as she ran, hit on the door with small, quick fists. "Anne? Are you O.K.?" Never thinking how stupid she might look if the door opened, never considered what excuse she might give. I didn't hear anything, so I thought you might be in trouble. Right. So what. Bang bang on the door.

"Anne?"

The whisper, against the door itself. Hearing it, Lurleen shivered, convulsive twitch like a tic of the flesh, all down her body, and she pressed against the door, listening with all her might. "Anne." But quietly, feeling the heat from her body, the windy rush of her heart. Waiting. "Anne." More quietly still, less than a murmuring breath. "Let me in."

Abruptly, spooking her back a step: the sounds, *hot* intensity trebled, but wrong somehow, guttural, staggering where they should flow, a smell almost like garbage, but she didn't care; once the first scare had passed, she pressed harder into the door, as if by pure want she could break it down; she would get in, she would. T-shirt stuck, sweating like she'd run a mile. I'm sick of just listening. The hall was so hot. Sweat on her forehead, running into her eyes like leaking tears. The doorknob in her slick fingers.

It turned. Simple as that.

In the end, so quick and easy, and it seemed almost that she could not breathe, could not get enough air to move—but she moved, all right, oh yes, stepped right inside into the semidarkness, a fake hurricane lamp broken beside the bed, but there was light enough, enough to see by.

Like angels in love, mating in the cold, graceful rapture of thin air. Hovering above the bed, at least a yard or maybe more—no wonder she never heard springs—instead the groaned complaint of the walls itself as his thrusting brushed them, on his back the enormous strange construction that kept them airborne, as careless as if it had grown there amongst the pebbled bumps and tiny iridescent fins. His body beautiful, and huge, not like a man's, but so real it seemed to suck up all the space in the room, big elementary muscles, and he was using them all. Anne, bent like a coat-hanger—it hurt to see the angle of her back—her eyes wide and empty and some stuff coming out of her mouth like spoiled black jelly, but it was too late, Lurleen had sent the door swinging backward to close with a final catch, and in its sound his gaze swiveling to touch hers: the cold regard of a nova, the summoning glance of a star.

Her mouth as open as Anne's as she approached the vast brutality of his embrace, room enough for two there, oh my, yes. Fierce, relentless encroachment promising no pleasure but the pleasure of pain. Not an angel, never had been. Or maybe once, long, a long, long time ago.

EYEWALL

Rick Shelley

Although it's true that everyone talks about the weather, some people *do* try to do something about it, as the tense and exciting story that follows demonstrates. . . . The question is, at what *cost*?

Rick Shelley is a frequent contributor to *Analog*, and has also sold stories to *Aboriginal SF*, and elsewhere. His books include *Son of the Hero*, and, most recently, *The Hero of Varay*. Upcoming are two more novels, *The Hero King* and *The Wizard of Mecq*. He lives in Maryville, Tennessee.

The five week journey out from Earth taught me only one thing. Twenty-five years had taken the excitement out of space travel for me. When I was a graduate student going off-planet to research my dissertation, space travel was an adventure. Now it was just wasted time between here and there. I spent most of my time in my cabin, going back over every line of our operating program for the Trident experiments. My two research assistants quickly gave up trying to include me in anything. We met at meals and only rarely at other times, despite the restricted passenger accommodations. It wasn't until I got a call from Captain Linearson that I came out of the doldrums.

"Doctor Jepp, we're about to enter orbit around Trident. If you want a preview of the weather, you're welcome to come up to the flight deck."

"On my way." After all, the weather was the reason for this trip.

Trident has been notorious since its discovery a little more than twenty years ago. In many ways it's the most ideal of the several dozen Earth-like planets we've found. It has thousands of miles of prime tropical and sub-tropical coastline, lush lowland forests, scenic mountains, abundant wildlife, and all the rest. But the colonizers haven't struck yet. They're still waiting for the end of Trident's hurricane season . . . and it may snow in hell before *that* happens.

Beautiful hurricanes.

My trek up to the flight deck was slow and awkward. Now that we were back in normal space, we were back to zero gravity conditions, and I was having difficulty moving about. When I got to the flight deck and looked out, down was up, I had a moment of disorientation.

"Think it'll rain?" Captain Linearson asked with a laugh. After twenty-five years with the International Weather Service, I'm almost hardened to weather jokes. Almost.

"If it doesn't, I've come a long way for nothing." I looked out at Trident. The IWS had maintained a research team on Trident for the last eight years. We would have set up shop sooner but it took a decade to get general assembly funding and approval for the project.

"Well, there's your Angry Sea." The captain pointed out and "up."

Trident was hanging overhead—as far as I was concerned. The Angry Sea (that *is* the official name) was on the daylight side and dominated the visible portion of Trident. In media shorthand, Trident is called "the water world" as often as not. It's a misnomer. We've never come across a true water world, that is, one covered entirely by ocean. Percentage-wise, Trident has only 3 percent more of its surface covered by water than Earth does. But it is more concentrated. Earth has gone through similar periods in its tectonic history. Take Earth back to when the continents were just separating. Make the Atlantic Ocean 200 miles wide, allow for a few large bays and gulfs, call the rest of the water the Pacific Ocean and you have a decent idea of the makeup of Trident. The Angry Sea covers a huge chunk of the surface.

And it's always hurricane season. Trident's axial tilt is less than a third of Earth's, keeping the tropic and subtropic portions of the ocean warm enough for hurricanes year-round. I could see four of them at the moment.

"Am I going to be in your way here, Captain?"

"Not at all, Doc. Look as long as you want. We'll make one orbit before we deploy your satellites. On the second pass, we'll get you and your team into the shuttle and separate for landing. If the weather holds." She laughed but didn't look at me, so I was spared the necessity of any response to the joke. "Tim will take you down." Tim Andrews was at the other command console. He was a quiet man still in his twenties.

"Set you down without any trouble," he promised. "Even if it's raining." Another comedian.

"Captain, have you contacted the IWS station yet?" I asked.

"Just to tell them we're here. Anything special?"

"Flash them that canned message from IWS if you would," I said. Captain Linearson hit several keys on her console.

"Going down now."

"Fine, thanks. I'll make sure my people are ready to move out." The sooner I got away from looking "up" at the ground, the better my stomach would feel.

I never expected to be welcomed with open arms. Donna Elkins wasn't merely the director of the Trident Hurricane Study Center, she was its creator and driving force. Trident had become her career almost from the day we received the first reports on the planet from the survey team. The proposal for the HSC had been hers and she fought for ten years to get it approved and funded. She had been on Trident since the start of construction and, as far as anyone in IWS could tell, she intended to stay there until somebody wrapped her in chains and carried her off. There was little chance that she would be overjoyed to see me with my temporary writ superseding her authority.

But she was there to meet the shuttle when we landed.

"Doctor Jepp. It's been a long time."

"Doctor Elkins." I nodded and we shook hands. "It *has* been a long time." I had never really known her personally, but we had met at conferences now and then before she left Earth, and her single-minded drive to establish the research center on Trident had made her something of a "personality" in the agency. *Everybody* knew about her. She was forty-five years old now, according to her personnel file, and even though there was only a little gray showing in her hair, she looked much older—the sort of look that people get when they push themselves to the limit all the time. I knew her record. I made a point of studying it when I got approval for my finger-in-the-eye experiments.

"These are my research assistants, Jenny Evert and Ike Pappas." They nodded and there was more handshaking.

"We weren't expecting a ship for another seven months," Doctor Elkins said as we walked toward the electric van she had brought out for us.

"That ship should still be on schedule," I said. "We did bring some of the items you had on order though, what we could fit in. And we brought enough supplies to make up for the extra drain we represent."

I had trouble concentrating for a moment when I spotted an animal standing on top of the van. It stood three feet tall and might almost have passed for a monkey. This animal's fur looked like military camouflage, patches of olive green, dark brown, and tan. It had a broad face with large, slightly protruding eyes, a vertical ridge between them that was apparently *not* a nose, and a tiny mouth that didn't make sense until it unreeled a 15-inch-long tongue. An insectivore.

"Part of the staff?" I asked, glad to have something light to ease the moment.

Doctor Elkins gave the creature an annoyed glance. "That's Mona. We call them chimps, or T-chimps, though Dov Marchiese gave them a full Latin classification. There's a whole troop of those things that hang around the center."

Mona stiffened and saluted. Behind me, Jenny and Ike laughed. I avoided sound effects, but I gave Mona a smile and returned her salute.

"Seems fairly intelligent," I said.

"Too smart to scare off, too stupid to know enough to stay away," Elkins said.

That was the extent of conversation until we reached the station's permanent buildings. *Permanent*: seventy-five miles inland, the weather could get much too fierce for anything less than nanofactured modules of grown diamond, silicrete, and steel-graphite composites. Under test conditions on Earth, the design had survived four-hundred-mile-per-hour winds, the equivalent of eight inches of rain per hour for twelve hours, and impacts from weights of up to nine tons dropped from thirty feet.

Perhaps half of the station's people gathered to meet us when we reached the main facility. Doctor Elkins did the introductions, then assigned rooms for me, my assistants, and the shuttle pilot. There was a little chat. The resident staff had questions about home and any mail and so forth that we might have brought. The news that we had a bag of mail chips was welcome. Finally, the director steered me off to her office.

She slammed the door behind us.

"Now just what the hell is this all about?" she asked. Her voice was low, but there was no missing the intensity of it.

"I'm here to see if it's possible to kill a category five hurricane, Doctor Elkins." I said, just as softly, but without the tension behind my words.

"Forget that 'Doctor' crap, Roy. It's all first names here." That definitely was *not* a friendly invitation to a closer relationship. "What do you mean, 'kill a category five hurricane'?"

"Just that. After Hurricane Lisa hit the Florida coast two years ago, IWS has to produce more than long-term research reports from Trident. We have a new mandate to produce action rather than observation, technology rather than basic science."

"Political pressure." She said those words as expletives.

"Twenty-seven thousand people died in that storm, Donna. IWS lost nearly a hundred. More than two million people lost their homes. They still haven't totaled the bills. There are *still* a half-million people living in so-called 'temporary' refugee camps from Florida all the way up to South Carolina. What do you expect?"

"I *expect* nothing," she snapped. She turned away. "But I think I *deserve* a little support from the agency. I can't run this project here and defend it day by day back on Earth."

"I agree," I said. I did, in principle. But bending with the wind is more than another tired weather cliché. It's political survival. "This is something beyond interdepartmental squabbling though. The general assembly has been making noises about the expenses here from the beginning, and since they're still looking for money to complete the recovery from Hurricane Lisa, they're looking hard at anything they can do to cut expenses elsewhere. 'Why spend all this money if we're not going to get anything practical out of it?' You know what it's like." I waited until she nodded before I continued.

"The Trident program would never have been approved without a lot of promises that it would finally make it possible to *do* something about tropical cyclones. Promises *you* made." I waited for another nod.

"Hurricane Lisa merely brought it to a head." I shut up until she turned to face me again.

"It's put up or shut up time, Donna," I said, as sympathetically as I could manage. "To be a little more precise, it's put up or shut down. And I want to keep Trident HSC going as much as you do."

For an instant, a haunted look got past the anger on her face. Then the anger returned, stronger than ever. "You can't do basic science on a timetable."

"They don't want basic science. They want usable technology."

"Basic research was the whole purpose for this station. Given time, we can learn more about cyclonic weather than anyone ever imagined. We *need* the basic research before we start thinking about technology to control hurricanes. We're not set up for that sort of task."

"That's why I'm here. We brought along everything we'll need for our experiments."

"And if they don't work?"

I took a deep breath before I answered. "In that case, when the regular supply ship comes in seven months, it will be to close down the project and take you all home. But if they do work, we'll be long gone by then and your project will continue." Our ship would wait in orbit to take us back to Earth when we finished.

"I won't leave."

"You won't have any choice. You're not self-sufficient here and you can't make yourself self-sufficient in seven months."

Round one. "That went better than I expected," I mumbled when I got to my room. Of course, I hadn't said anything about the actual nature of the experiments I had come to conduct. I knew damn well that the real argument wouldn't start until Donna Elkins found out what I was planning to do on Trident.

There was little noteworthy about the arrangement of the buildings that housed Trident HSC. The long, low, narrow modules were linked together like so many dominoes, meandering about a clearing that was a kilometer across. The trees that had been felled around the center had been pruned and used as extra bulwarks around the perimeter. At the edge of the clearing a series of large bunkers had been excavated from the side of a hill to store supplies and equipment, and to serve as hangers for the center's aircraft and the odd orbiter that might be on the ground for a day or two while a ship was in orbit.

Everything about the center was utilitarian, Spartan. My room was a cubicle ten feet square and eight feet high. There were no windows. The bed was a simple, uncomfortable cot. There were two tables and two chairs. One table held a computer terminal. The other table was empty.

I sat on the bunk and leaned back against the wall. I was more tired than I had any right to be. The return of gravity after a few days without any wasn't excuse enough. I reveled in having weight and a proper orientation to "up" and "down" again. I suppose I was wasting energy dreading the arguments yet to come. Confrontation has never been my style. I just sat there and fretted until Jenny and Ike came to report.

"Everything is in the bunker," Ike said. "It hasn't been opened." The "everything" in question was the shuttle cargo module with our experimental gear. Our module had made the trip out from Earth in the hold of the ship's main shuttle. The unit had been designed to use every cubic centimeter available in a lander bay. It would take two more shuttle trips to bring down the food supplies and other things we had brought for the center.

"Dinner will be in just a few minutes," Jenny said. From the way she looked at me, I could tell that she was worrying about my health and well-being again. Jenny had clucked over me like a mother hen since she joined the project twenty-one months before—despite the ribbing she took about being so old-fashioned. Sometimes I think Jenny figures that I'm as old as Methuselah and incapable of taking care of myself. Well, since we had started preparing for this trip, I had occasionally felt that old, so maybe she had just cause.

"I think I can hobble as far as the dining room," I said, getting up while Jenny had the grace to blush. "Remember, it's going to be a long haul here." I looked from Jenny to Ike. I had lucked out in my choice of assistants. They were both conscientious and highly qualified. The data we collected on Trident would provide the final elements for both of their dissertations.

"Just how do you plan to kill a hurricane?" Doctor Elkins asked when I went to her office the next morning. The obvious anger was gone—suppressed at least—but I could still see the tension in her face.

I leaned back in the chair across from her. None of the furniture at the center seemed to be designed with any thought for human comfort.

"I'm not going to jump right in with anything," I said, postponing the moment. "I want to take a few days to familiarize myself with both current and historical storm tracks, take a couple of survey flights over the Angry Sea, run some additional measurements."

"No runarounds, please? You have your killer experiments ready. You know what you're going to do."

I nodded. "There aren't that many possibilities. We're going to try atmospheric compression—finger-in-the-eye stuff. We're here to run a series of experiments to see if it can be done and what the minimal force levels might be."

"Atmospheric compression?" The disbelief was clear in her voice and on her face. I might as well have told her that we were counting on Santa Claus to do the job.

"Disrupt the tight pressure gradients around the eye," I explained. "We've worked up computer simulations that show that it may be possible to destroy the hurricane by disrupting the eyewall. Compression and rebound."

"You can't be serious. You know as well as I do how much energy a major hurricane carries. There's no possible way to counteract that."

"We don't have to equal the total energy of the storm," I said. "That *would* be impossible. Our approach is a little different. Our simulations show that it might be possible to cause sufficient disruption by the precise application of considerably less than one percent of the energy carried by the storm. In fact, the stronger the storm is, and the more strongly defined the eye is, the easier it should be to tip it into chaos, causing the storm to self-destruct. The idea is to use the storm's own strengths against it, make it work against itself." I shrugged. "There's always some uncertainty about deterministic chaos," I conceded. "If we were absolutely certain that it would work, we wouldn't have come all the way to do the field tests."

She didn't respond to that immediately. Concentration pushed aside the anger on her face as she tried to imagine what I might have in mind. The basic idea wasn't new. It had come and gone as a topic of discussion for ages. Until Hurricane Lisa wrecked the Atlantic coast of Florida from Biscayne Bay to Fort Pierce, then regrouped to come back ashore in North Carolina, the idea had never gone beyond idle chatter and the roughest of preliminary work-ups.

Finally, she put the look of concentration aside.

"I hope you're not going to disrupt our routines too much as well," she said. "Particularly if we may be running out of time. We *do* have our own ongoing projects, research that may do more long-term good than this political knee-jerk show you've got."

"At least until we run our active experiments, any disruption should be minimal," I assured her. And, no, I wasn't offended by her characterization of our experiments. They *were* a "political knee-jerk show." But I did think we had a real chance of success. "We'll be spending a lot of time at computer terminals, of course, and I'll need some air time in one of your aircraft. And we'll need a survey plane for the actual experiments, when the time comes. Oh, in case you haven't noticed yet, we've strung a few extra satellites to increase the coverage of the ocean. That data will all be available to your people as well. Jenny has all the access codes and orbital data. And after we finish, the satellites will still be there to increase the amount of data your people have to work with."

"I want plenty of notice before you go messing with any storms," Elkins said. "At least forty-eight hours. I want to make sure that my people are well out of the way."

"We'll work something out," I said. "But if you insist on forty-eight hours, you might have to pull people on a few scrubs. We have tight test conditions to meet, and a storm might stray beyond our limits in forty-eight hours."

She started to say something to that, but stopped by biting at her lip.

"We'll work something out," I repeated.

In the eight years of the Trident HSC, there had never been a single minute without at least one hurricane on the Angry Sea—and the times when there were only one were rare enough to count on the fingers of one hand. The average number of hurricanes and tropical storms on any given day was slightly over three. Five at a time wasn't rare, and the record was eight. I had studied all but the last seventeen months' activity before we left Earth—all that had been received up to that time. When I got back to my room after that session with the director, I sat at the computer terminal and called up the storm track program.

The holotank built its model layer by layer, up from the sea floor, through the surface, to the lower levels of the stratosphere. I could watch a horizontal view or toggle over to the overhead view, cut a cross-section to throw on one of the flat data screens that flanked the tank, get any data I needed on the other screens. The scales were adjustable as well—physical dimensions and time. The first time through, I ran the seventeen months in seventeen minutes, sitting on the overhead view, watching the hurricanes form and plow their courses across the Angry Sea. Most ran into the bulge of the coast. Some turned north, missing land, finally dying out in the empty northern reaches of the Angry Sea.

Generally speaking, the tropical cyclones rose in one of two large, regularly defined areas, one south-southeast of the IWS station, the other east-southeast, and 3,000 miles away. The largest and more durable storms generally came from the eastern crèche.

Trident offered what seemed to be an infinite variety of patterns with its hurricanes. The fact that there were almost always several tropical cyclones moving across the Angry Sea provided opportunities that meteorologists could scarcely dream of on Earth. Occasionally, a series of hurricanes would follow each other west and north in a conga line, spaced between eighteen and thirty-six hours apart. At other times, two storms would merge. I found those episodes the most heartening. Eighty percent of the time, merger spelled the end of both hurricanes. They disrupted each other chaotically and spiraled back down through tropical storm and tropical depression within a matter of hours. Of course, the remaining one time in five, the storms *did* merge into a storm more powerful than either of the antecedents.

I ticked off bookmarks for each of the merger events in the past seventeen months and keyed them to the attention of Jenny and Ike. They would make the precise measurements we were interested in. Jenny came to my room just as I was loading up the storm track sequence for a second play. I was going for a scale of ten seconds per day this time.

"How soon do we get to look at some of these super hurricanes?" Jenny asked.

"Any in particular you'd like to look at?"

"There's a category seven about nine hundred miles out that looks interesting." *Category seven.* On Earth, the Saffir/Simpson Damage-Potential Scale only goes as far as category five—winds over 156 miles per hour, storm surge over 18 feet—but that catch-all top end was ridiculously insufficient for Trident. The Elkins team had added three extra categories at the top.

"We're not here as tourists, Jenny."

"Come on, Roy." I had insisted on the first-name basis almost from the start. I hated being called "Doctor Jepp" or "Professor" all the time. "You want to see the big ones as badly as Ike and I do."

I grinned. "I confess. But does this category seven give us a chance to look at a four or five en route?"

She grinned back at me. "There's a category five about to hit the coast 250 miles northeast of here tomorrow afternoon."

"OK, I'll try to book us a flight."

Back home, I teach a graduate seminar at American Regional University in Washington and I give eighty or ninety talks and lectures to various outside groups each year. Public relations is a large part of any researcher's job, particularly in a government-sponsored agency. People always want to know why weather forecasts aren't more precise than they are and why—with all the time, money and effort that have gone into studying weather and climate—the forecasts are sometimes dramatically wrong, even for the next twenty-four hours. And people have a fascination with the most dramatic expressions of weather, the killer storms, tornadoes and tropical cyclones— hurricanes and typhoons.

Even after nearly a quarter century with the International Weather Service, I still find myself constantly amazed that most people, even highly educated people, think of a hurricane as nothing more than a big rain storm. Five or six years ago, I gave a talk in Indianapolis. During the question and answer session afterward, one chemistry graduate student tried to get at the nature of hurricanes with a sports analogy. "I mean," he started, "so an afternoon thunderstorm is sort of like Saturday club soccer, right? And a big hurricane is like the World Cup final?" I hid my instinctive grimace and tried another explanation of the driving mechanism of hurricanes. I had already gone through it once, but I drew my analogies down a notch and started over.

Basically, a hurricane is an immense furnace, a heat-driven engine. It requires hot, moist air, low barometric pressure and rotational momentum. Winds spiral inward—from high pressure to low pressure—pulling moisture and warmth from the ocean's surface. These are concentrated in the eye, with the energy being pulled up along the eyewall in a chimney effect and redistributed at the top. Rob a hurricane of its heat or its influx of moisture, and it dies. Tropical cyclones weaken and die when they hit cold water or move over land. The longer they stay over warm tropical water, the longer they last, and the stronger they can get. And Trident had more room for them to grow than Earth.

Donna Elkins didn't make even a ritual protest at my request for a plane for the next morning, but she did insist that one of her people go along to check me out on the craft. That was fine with me. I've never been a full-time pilot, and obviously I had never flown around a category seven hurricane.

The pilot's name was Kasigi Jo, but he insisted on being called Casey. He sat at the right-hand controls of the six-seat Imre survey plane and watched me and the instruments.

"This flight's yours unless you screw up or ask me to take over," he said before we took off. "Your log shows you have more than 2,000 hours of instrument time. That's more than I had when I came here." Casey took his job seriously. He had examined my log chip before we went out to the plane.

"Maybe, but it appears that your reflexes have about ten years on me. And you've had flight time here. Don't be bashful about suggestions."

"I won't. My favorite neck is aboard this plane."

The ink had still been wet on Casey's Ph.D. when he left Earth for Trident eight years back. And unlike Elkins and a few of the others, he didn't plan to make Trident his entire career. He was already scheduled to return to Earth on the next regular ship. "I promised them eight years when I signed on," he said while we flew toward the coast. "They're getting a few extra months as it is."

"You staying with IWS?" I asked as we leveled off at 35,000 feet. We were crossing the coast, south and a little east of the center, banking through a gentle turn to eventually bring us up on the category seven from behind.

"Nah. I'm going into broadcasting. I've already got three offers, two in Tokyo and one in Jacksonville. They came in with the mail you guys brought. First nibbles."

I made a slight change to our flight plan. There was a new storm just starting to develop a distinctive eye in the western crèche. The side trip would only add twenty minutes to the flight, so I took it. And even though I hadn't done any flying in a year, the feel came back quickly. The Imre 370 virtually flies itself.

"Not bad," Ike said as we crossed the boundary of the eye of the new storm. "It tripped across the scale from tropical storm to hurricane just as we entered."

"I didn't do it," I said with a soft laugh.

As we left the new hurricane behind, I took the plane up to 45,000 feet, mostly to pick up a little speed, partly to get a broader look at the ocean. We had a little over an hour and a half of flying left to reach the eye of the category seven.

"So tell me, Casey," I said as I let the autopilot take over, "what's Trident like?"

"Where do you live?" he asked. The return question surprised me.

"Southeast Georgia. Halfway between Savannah and Jacksonville, and about twenty-five miles inland."

"Oh. You ever live in one of the megalopolises?"

"I spend a lot of time in Washington," I said. "At least one day a week, one semester a year. I commute to the old capital to conduct my seminar."

Casey shook his head. "That's just at the edge."

"I get to most of them, now and again," I said. "What are you getting at?"

"I grew up in Tokyo. Choose any ten-meter square in the entire city and it has more people than the entire planet of Trident. This is heaven."

"But you're thinking of going back there?" Jenny asked.

Casey shrugged, then laughed. "They don't have much use for typhoon experts in the Gobi." He had a point. Tropical cyclones are only a problem for specific areas of Earth—the east coast of North America, the Caribbean, the western Pacific, and the Indian Ocean.

"You'll have a hard time finding low population densities anywhere they need your expertise," I said.

"Ain't it the truth."

Even with an airspeed of 570 miles per hour, it took us more than 30 minutes to cross the trailing radius of the category seven hurricane and reach the eye. At 45,000 feet, we were skimming the cloud cap and fighting the outward spiral of air from the top of the chimney. Conversation damped down to the essentials. Casey paid closer attention to the flight instruments and read off anything he thought I needed to know. I focused on the basics of keeping the wings level and our altitude steady. There was enough turbulence to ensure concentration. Jenny and Ike were busy studying the storm. The survey planes were equipped with storm-monitoring equipment, and they were trying to keep tabs on everything at once.

"Hey, kids, forget the instruments for a while," I said as we neared the eye. "You can stare at those later. Look at the real thing while you can." Neither of them had ever flown in or over a hurricane before—or been in one on the ground for that matter.

Far from looking sinister and threatening, the cloud cap was a thing of awesome beauty from above. As close as we were, the stratification wasn't quite as noticeable. Except for the extent of the clouds below us, we might almost be skipping across the top of fair weather cumulus. The plane's windows had polarized enough to offset the glare of the sun off the top of the cloud deck, but not enough to mar the scene.

"You'll have a strong updraft when we cross the eyewall," Casey reminded me. "I mean *strong*."

I nodded. "We'll go through that and circle down inside." Once we got past the strong updraft right along the eyewall we would find gentler down-drafts through most of the clear space at the center of the storm. "Any thoughts on a safe minimum altitude inside?"

"Depends how good your nerves are." Casey met my gaze when I turned to him. "Generally speaking, an eye this well-formed will be fairly calm, but there's always a chance for serious shear."

"How about you? How low would *you* feel safe?"

"Since I want to go home, I probably wouldn't go below five thousand."

I nodded slowly. "Five thou it is."

If you could harness all of the energy wrapped up in one storm that size and put it into a spaceship, you'd have the most powerful rocket ever. This storm had *sustained* winds of 219 miles per hour. If it hit land without weakening, the storm surge would top 30 feet.

It was magnificent.

The updraft at the eyewall carried us up a thousand feet like an express elevator before I compensated. Then I kicked the plane into a slow clockwise spiral down into the eye—clockwise, against the rotation of the storm. The eye was thirty miles in diameter, not quite a perfect circle. The sun brightened a considerable portion of the ocean surface below. The eyewall was regular and well established, tiers of clouds extending all of the way down to the sea, the slight hourglass curve hardly noticeable.

We had scarcely started our descent when I heard a soft, "Oh, my God," from Jenny. I glanced back just long enough to see that she had her face plastered against the window to her side. Ike was staring out past her, just as intently.

"A little different than seeing it on a screen or in a tank, isn't it?" I asked. If I hadn't been so intent on the plane, I would have stared that way myself.

"It's so . . . so *immense*," Ike managed after a moment.

I chuckled. Ike and Jenny were both graduate students in meteorology, specializing in tropical cyclones, and they could still get that excited. So can I. It helps to get that involved in your work. It keeps it from being nothing more than a job.

We spent nearly ten minutes at our slow descent, circling around the clear eye, staring out at the almost eerily regular tiers of clouds that marked the eyewall. It wasn't *just* wasteful sightseeing. The survey plane carried a lot of weather instrumentation, and it was all running. Trident had too many hurricanes and too few researchers to get thorough data on every tropical cyclone that made its way across the Angry Sea.

"Getting close to five thousand," Casey informed me casually—with five hundred feet to spare.

"OK. Going up." I banked us around into the updraft closer to the eyewall and we took a real elevator ride to the top. Five thousand feet above the cloud cap, I asked Casey for a course to the category five and locked onto it. Then, as soon as we were away from the eye, there was time to relax a little and get back to normal breathing.

"Wow!" Jenny said—some ten minutes later. It was her first word since early into our descent.

The category five storm wasn't quite as broad as the category seven. The eye was also narrower, though just as sharply defined. I didn't bother to take us nearly as deep into that one. We went down to 20,000 feet and took a couple of laps while the instruments recorded what they could. Then we climbed out and headed back for the center.

"It's pretty close to the stats on Hurricane Lisa," Ike said as we crossed the cloud cap of the category five. "Size, sustained winds, pressure gradients— all within a couple of percentage points."

"They come in six packs here," Casey said. "At the moment, it's only the third largest active hurricane we're tracking."

"And Lisa was the most powerful ever recorded in the Atlantic," Jenny said.

"We've gone to the top of category eight on the modified Saffir/Simpson and we think that category nines must occur occasionally," Casey said.

I wrote that first full day on Trident off as acclimatization and told Jenny and Ike to take the rest of the afternoon to themselves after we landed. The weather had taken a turn for the worse at the center. A line of squalls was moving in. It had already started sprinkling and heavy rain was only minutes away.

Ike and Jenny went on toward the living quarters as soon as we landed. I stayed out with Casey to go through the post-flight checklist on the plane. As we finally started for cover ourselves, I spotted several of the local chimps capering about—running along the roofs of the center's buildings, jumping to the ground, then scampering back up.

"They always carry on like that?" I asked.

Casey laughed. "They get a little crazy when the barometer dips. The lower it goes, the wilder the chimps are. They're sensitive to weather. A lot of the wildlife is, even this far from the coast."

"Makes sense," I said. "As extreme as the weather gets, knowing when heavy rain and storm winds are coming would be a definite survival advantage."

"No scoffing at all?" Casey asked. He looked as if he were genuinely surprised.

"None at all. Just don't tell me that your corns hurt when a big blow's coming." We both laughed. Casey didn't seem the least bit put out by the arrival of "big guns" from Earth.

Unfortunately, he was in a minority in that regard. Most of the members of the permanent staff seemed to share Donna Elkins's resentment of me, my assistants, and our overriding authority from IWS headquarters. Our reception was generally very cool. I didn't expect it to get any more cordial once the exact nature of the work we were on Trident to do became known.

Halfway through my second morning on Trident, Doctor Elkins knocked on my door and came into the room after barely waiting for any reply.

"I've been running some simulations," she said without any preliminaries. I nodded. I had assumed that she would. "What kind of explosives are you planning to use?"

"Tri-thermolite-four initially," I said. I turned my chair away from the computer terminal and leaned back. TT4 is the hottest, most powerful chemical explosive known, and we had forty tons of it.

"Initially. And when that doesn't work?" She didn't say "if," but "when."

"*If* that doesn't work, we'll go to hydrogen fusion devices," I said, still calmly.

There was no sudden, emotional outburst from the director. She had run her simulations. The answer was too obvious for there to be any surprise. She stared at me for a moment, then took a deep breath.

"I thought that must be the answer," she said. The tension was back in her voice, more obvious than before. "It had to be, even if it still doesn't make sense." She shook her head. "My first thought was that you can't be serious . . . but you wouldn't have come out here if you weren't."

"That's right," I agreed when she paused.

"But still, I can hardly believe it. No one has exploded a nuclear weapon in more than a century. It was against the law the last I remember. And what I really can't—*don't*—believe is that anyone would permit it back on Earth, even in the unlikely event that it would kill a hurricane."

"A few years ago, you would have been right," I told her. "But you've been out of touch. After Hurricane Lisa, people would accept *anything* that could prevent a repeat."

"And you're going to contaminate an untouched world just to try out this crazy theory of yours." Statement, not question.

"It's not crazy," I said. "And contamination will be minimal. The devices we have are nanofactured, as clean as possible. There will be some immediate radiation, of course, but little long-term contamination."

"Not to mention killing a lot of aquatic life," Elkins said, as if she hadn't even heard what I said.

"It's not as if Trident had any sentient life forms." Yes, I *know* how callous and cavalier that sounds. But there are always trade-offs. And most humans still rank their welfare above that of inedible wildlife on a distant planet that is too wild for colonization to be an immediate prospect.

"We haven't been here long enough to rule out the presence of native sentients. Eight years! And that hasn't been our primary purpose even. At that, those chimps might come close to some definitions of sentience."

"I know all the arguments," I said. "All the 'ifs, ands, and buts,' and it still doesn't alter a damn thing. Stacked up against the deaths, injuries, and property damage of Hurricane Lisa, it doesn't mean a damn thing. As soon as we're ready, we start the TT4 experiments. And if those don't work, we go on to the fusion devices."

Doctor Elkins bit her lip so hard that I saw blood, but she didn't say anything else. After a moment, she turned and left. I punched up the intercom channel on my terminal and called Jenny.

"I want you and Ike in here, right now," I said. It was time to talk about security measures.

Even though you can't control experimental conditions as completely in the field as you can in a laboratory, you have to set tight standards. *This is acceptable. That isn't.* The narrower your parameters, the more reliable your test data will be. And even then nature can come up with a surprise that might destroy the validity of your experiment.

We needed data that would be applicable to conditions on Earth. We needed storms that were category five and threatened land, but right off the bat I ruled out using any tropical cyclone that reached category six or higher at any point in its career. I also ruled out daisy-chained storms—and *that* cut seriously into the available test population. There was a chain of three hurricanes dancing across the Angry Sea when we arrived on Trident. Our experiments also demanded storms that had strong and clearly defined eyes. And, to protect the integrity of our test data, we ruled out any storm that showed any sort of maverick activity, any anomalies that weren't routinely observed in hurricanes and typhoons on Earth. Other than that, any storms would do.

Ike and Jenny did the first tag on storms, tracing them back to their formation and logging all the available data—data that became better for storms that brewed after our new satellites were operating. I reviewed the storms that my assistants logged, ruled out about half right away, and followed the rest.

We had been on Trident eleven days before I finally picked a storm for our first test.

"Isolate the trace and double up the satellite coverage," I told Jenny. From that moment on, Trident tropical cyclone SSE-14-42 would be under the microscope. Until the storm died, whether as a result of our interference or on its own, we would draw every possible bit of data from it. I had already called Donna Elkins to tell her that we had our first candidate.

"If it stays good, we'll take off at dawn, day after tomorrow, deploy and push the button as soon as we can." That was what I had told Elkins, and that was what I told my assistants. "Ike, let's take a look at our birds."

We walked. That was as close as we could come to being sure that we wouldn't be overheard. The center didn't have a lot of equipment for eavesdropping, but wherever you have radios and computers, you have the potential.

"Have you picked up even the slightest hint that anyone might try to stop our experiments?" I asked softly, once we were well away from the main complex of interconnected buildings.

"Nothing," Ike said. "I guess everyone knows what we're here for by now. It's no secret. I hear a little now and then. Mostly nobody thinks that our experiments can possibly work. Some resent us. More, they resent the threat that our failure means that the center will be closed down. They don't like what we're going to do, but they like what will happen if we fail even less." After a long pause, he added, "Casey stopped talking to us when he found out about the fusion devices. He won't even answer if Jenny or I say something."

The sky over the center was brilliantly clear. The temperature was 85 but there was a delightful breeze from the northeast. Despite the frequency of tropical storms, Trident isn't *always* a wet and gloomy place, not even the stretch of it that sits in the path of most of the hurricanes.

"I almost wish there had been some way to hide the fact that we're going to use fusion devices, if need be, until the last minute," I said. Casey had walked out of a room just because I entered—a couple of times. I felt bad about that. I had liked Casey when we met. "But anyone who spent a few minutes running the calculations could guess it." Anyone likely to be working at the Trident Hurricane Study Center, at least.

There *was* one other possibility, but it was even more exotic—and therefore less likely. One of the proposals we had investigated had called for deploying a series of large mirrors in orbit to concentrate sunlight on the center of a hurricane. In theory, it would be possible to concentrate more energy that way, but the process would be slower than explosive compression (if *that* worked), and it would be much more expensive and complicated. And, in the case of Earth, it probably wasn't feasible. There's simply too much garbage orbiting Earth after two centuries of space exploration and travel—all the way out to geo-stationary. Mirrors large enough to do the job would be ripped apart by the flotsam and jetsam long before they could manage the task.

"Well, they can't get into the module," Ike said. "And I can't see them doing anything melodramatic like sabotaging a plane to keep us from finishing."

"It's possible that they would simply cut off our access to the planes and computers," I said. "Maybe even confine us to our rooms."

"They couldn't get away with that!" Ike protested.

"No, but they could stop our experiments. Elkins and enough of the others might be willing to take that chance."

"I don't get it."

"History," I said.

For the moment, that was where the discussion ended. A troop of the local chimps spotted us and came charging across the clearing. With them chattering and bouncing around, there wasn't much chance for Ike and me to continue our talk. But they were a welcome distraction. I couldn't distinguish among the T-chimps, so I didn't know if Mona was with this group. I *could* see differences in the color patterns between different chimps, but I didn't know them well enough to identify individuals the way Elkins and most of the permanent staff could.

When Ike and I reached the supply bunker that held the shuttle payload module with our equipment, the chimps broke off their play and ran back toward the center. Evidently, they knew they weren't permitted in the bunkers.

I keyed in my password to the main door. Then Ike keyed in his. I had used my authority to commandeer an entire bunker. The door needed any two of three passwords. Jenny had the third. The module we had brought along was protected by a similar two-of-the-three password arrangement, but in that case, one of the two had to be mine. Security.

Once we got the bunker open, I dug out the electronic log I had put into the lock mechanism to make sure that there had been no attempts to enter. The log was clean. I reset and replaced it.

"We might as well haul out the first set of sleds," I told Ike while we were unlocking the payload module. It had been taken out of the shuttle and stored the afternoon before. Ike nodded as he finished keying in his password.

"I'll get on the manipulator," he said.

Our Manta air sleds had been considerably modified for our experiments. To give them enough payload capacity for our largest explosive loads, we had to strip off a lot of their standard maneuvering and navigating equipment. They were set to maneuver expressly within hurricane eyes, looping clockwise along the eyewall. We could adjust the diameter of the loops within limits, but that constant right bank and sufficient leeway in climbing and descending were the only maneuvers those sleds were capable of. They had to be dropped into the eye from directly overhead. There was no chance of sending them off to find their places from a distance. They no longer carried enough fuel for that, even if we hadn't limited their maneuverability.

Ike got the top of the module opened with the bunker's manipulator—something more than a simple crane, much more flexible—and lifted the first four air sleds out one at a time. Very carefully. Each of these sleds held a ton of TT4. The next four held two tons, the next group three, and then four tons. If four sleds, each carrying four tons of TT4, didn't provide enough force to disrupt a category five hurricane, we would go to the last set of sleds. Each of those carried a seventeen megaton fusion device—the largest we could squeeze into an air sled. While it might have been more logical to cut down on the number of TT4 trials and include a second set of fusion devices in the moderate kiloton range, logic isn't always the dominant force when science and politics meet.

Ike set the first four sleds in a row down the center of the bunker. Then he came back from the manipulator and we locked the wings down on each of the Mantas, and ran the full list of pre-flight checks on each of them. Next Ike ran a hands-and-eyes check on each sled to make sure that there was nothing wrong that wouldn't show up electronically.

"Ready to go," he said when he finished with the last one.

I nodded. "Let's put new seals on them and then run the electronic tests on the rest of the sleds while we're here." That took us another ninety minutes. We didn't find anything out of order. I hadn't expected to. No one else had had access to the sleds since they were packed on Earth, and I had run a check on them before locking the module.

"We'll put the first four aboard the plane tomorrow afternoon. I'll tell Doctor Elkins that we have to have it then."

*   *   *

I had managed a couple of short flights in Imres during the days of waiting for a suitable storm to appear, so I wasn't nervous about handling a survey plane. At the altitudes we would be at, there was really little to worry about, even flying into the center of a category five hurricane. We wouldn't go down into the eye this time. Ike and I would drop the air sleds from above, guide them into position, and head back toward the research center. Jenny would monitor the results from there.

After we loaded the sleds in the drop hold, Ike spent the night in the plane—his idea, not mine. At that, he may have spent a better night than I did. I didn't sleep well at all. I shared many of Doctor Elkins's reservations about the possible success of our experiments, at least the TT4 runs. If we killed a hurricane with chemical explosives, it would be a fluke. But we had to start with those tests.

It was raining over the center when I got up in the morning and drove over to the landing strip. A category three had come ashore to the south during the night and it was quickly losing strength, fizzling away in scattered showers. Ike was already up and running another equipment check on the sleds when I climbed into the plane.

"I wondered when you were going to get here," Ike said, grinning. I just shook my head. The computer terminals showed the portions of the Angry Sea we had to worry about. "Our" hurricane was marked in contrasting colors to make it easier to watch. A quick glance at the data screen showed me that it hadn't changed character in the twenty minutes since I had left the terminal in my room.

"We're set to go," Ike said, brushing his hands off on his coveralls. I nodded and moved up to the pilot's seat.

We worked our way down the preflight checklist. I was very careful about that, going down the list item by item. That was one thing about a long lay-off from flying. It made me more cautious than I might have been if I flew regularly. But the list of manual steps was fairly short, mostly a series of checks of the plane's electronics and mechanical connections. The Imre's own diagnostic programs handled most of the work.

The two jets fired up quickly and checked out perfectly. We had a full load of fuel. Hydraulics were in top condition. So was everything else. There wasn't anything even close to yellow on the readiness scale.

"Let's go," I said when we finished the list. I taxied the Imre away from the bunkers and turned into the wind before I cranked the jets around for a 45-degree take-off. There was no real need for the STOL start. I'm just more comfortable with that on grass.

The flight was uneventful. That's how I like all of my flights. Jenny was on the radio with us almost continuously. Twice, Donna Elkins broke in to ask nonessential questions—mostly to let us know that she was keeping tabs on the operation. I didn't ask, but I figured that there was a good chance that most of the permanent staff were where they could keep track of what we were doing. It didn't matter how they felt about our experiments. They knew that their future on Trident rode with them.

I let Ike spell me at the controls for part of the flight. He had his pilot's license, but not a lot of hours. Giving him a shot at the controls let me stretch my legs a little . . . and run a last check on the air sleds before we deployed them. That was just nervousness. We had no margin for botched runs.

"Ten minutes," Ike reported as I strapped myself back in the pilot's seat.

"We're ready." I looked to make sure that Ike was strapped in. While the hold doors were open, we would be slightly more vulnerable than at other times. "Oxygen masks," I said. The cockpit was pressurized separately from the hold, and I had sealed the hatch between them when I came back, but it was a matter of not taking any unnecessary chances.

We dropped to 40,000 feet, just above the top of the cloud cap, to release the air sleds. The center's Imres were all equipped to launch the Mantas—the basic design was used as a standard weather service probe. The sleds slid out smoothly, one at a time. Each sled's jet fired up when Ike hit the hot buttons. While I closed the hold door and turned us to our return course, Ike was busy juggling the four sleds, guiding them into position. We wanted the sleds spaced at 90-degree intervals, just over the slight inner bulge of the eyewall. For this storm, that meant at 18,000 feet. It took fifteen minutes to get all four sleds positioned properly with their jets keeping them on station.

"Jenny, give us five minutes from now, then fire them," I said as soon as Ike confirmed that everything was set.

"Counting down," Jenny replied. A repeater on the data screens in the cockpit flipped over to show the time remaining.

I cut the microphone before I told Ike, "We'll need more time than that before we do the fusion run." I didn't want all of the eavesdroppers to hear that. If Elkins and the rest knew that I was so certain of going on to the fusion devices, it might add to the hassles.

We were 160 miles in front of the eye and 5 miles above the sleds when Jenny touched off the TT4. We lost telemetry from the sleds at once but picked up the reports from the lowest of the tracking satellites. All four packages exploded precisely on schedule. The satellite picked up the flashes, and the pressure wave around the disintegrating Mantas.

And that was all. Any effect on the hurricane was minimal and transitory. Within seconds, there was no trace of any change.

"Well, we didn't *expect* anything from the first run," Ike said softly, his hand over his microphone, but I could hear disappointment in his voice.

"Not even a *hint* of any effect, not the slightest encouragement of eventual success," Donna Elkins said. At least she hadn't been waiting for us at the landing strip. It wasn't until after supper that evening that she asked me to step into her office.

"It's too soon to say that," I replied, probably just because I was feeling too stubborn to concede anything to her yet. Supper in the communal dining hall had been trying. The staff still did its best to ignore us, but they didn't try to hide their various reactions to the day's run. A few showed what may have been genuine regret, but I saw too many gloating smirks to feel very agreeable.

"We're still examining the transients we got immediately after detonation," I continued. "In any case, today's run was just the first—minimal load, minimal expectations. We couldn't afford to do a dry run without explosives. And today's results, minimal though they were, will give us a starting point when we start calibrating results for the series."

"You intend to continue?" Donna asked. There was no surprise in her voice. She just wanted confirmation.

"Of course. As a matter of fact, we've already isolated a likely candidate for our next run. Unless it turns out to be unsuitable, we'll hit it about noon, local time, three days from now. I'll key the data to you as soon as I get back to my room. More than forty-eight hour notice."

"In case you're interested, nobody on staff thinks you have much chance of succeeding. Only two of our younger people are willing to concede that you have any chance at all."

"Some people are born optimists," I said. I immediately regretted the flippancy. There was no point in aggravating the situation. A little more softly, I added, "I would be a lot happier myself if we had the means to make the test series a lot more comprehensive."

"Normally, I would agree with a statement like that," Donna said. "But I think that you're building on a fallacious theory to start with. I only wish that the fate of the center wasn't tied to your work. It's bad for morale."

A continuing lack of success was bad for my morale. It didn't do Ike and Jenny much good either, even though we had only minimal expectations for the chemical explosives. Our second run was with two tons of Tri-thermolite-four in each of four sleds. That went off on schedule and produced little more in the way of measurable data than the first test. The third was scheduled to use three tons of TT4 per sled. But before we got a chance to run that set, we ran into a period where none of the hurricanes were suitable. They were either too intense or they were daisy-chained. We spent our time going back over the scant data that our first two runs had given us. But no matter how often we sifted through the data, there wasn't enough information to give us any clues about refining our procedure, or even to suggest whether or not there was any hope of eventual success.

"Is there any way we could use all of our remaining TT4 on one test?" Jenny asked, about ten days into our "dry spell." "Maybe that would give us enough of a bang."

"We're pushing the limits squeezing four tons into a sled for the last TT4 trial," Ike told her—as if she didn't know that already.

"And it might corrupt our data if we tried to juggle eight sleds around an eyewall at one time," I added. "If we could even manage it."

Ike's eyes narrowed, then he shook his head. "We don't have enough control circuits. And I'm not sure I could handle eight sleds at once if we did. Not with the kind of precision we need."

"In any case, it would take two planes to deploy eight sleds, which would mean using center personnel. I'm not sure that would be wise," I said, damping the idea a little further.

"It was an idea," Jenny said with a sigh. "Anything to speed things up."

"I know," I told her. "Look, kids, we both know where the holes are in our experiments. No matter what happens, our work is going to be flawed. If we fail, we might not be able to tell if it's just a matter of insufficient explosive power, or if better positioning of the charges would help. Even if the final run works, our work will still be incomplete. The big questions will be, 'How much overkill is there?' and 'How much less force would have worked?' "

"That's the same question, just worded differently," Ike said.

"I know. That's the point."

By the time we had a suitable target for our third run, we had been on Trident six weeks. The storm was a minimal category five—barely within our test parameters. But the storm showed no sign of weakening. Jenny made this flight with me, leaving Ike on the controls back at the center. Deployment went without a hitch. I started us back toward the center while Jenny maneuvered the Mantas into position along the eyewall.

I held my breath from the time I gave the signal for detonation until my monitor confirmed that all four sleds had exploded. A minute later, Ike was on the radio.

"At least I could tell something happened," he reported. Jenny and I exchanged glances that acknowledged another failure before Ike continued. "We're still not showing anything significant though, and the effects are already damped out by the system."

The fourth run, eight days later, didn't produce much in the way of positive results either. Four tons of TT4 in each of the sleds set off minimal ripples, and they lasted for less than a minute before they were lost in the general energy dynamo around the eye of the hurricane.

Doctor Elkins gave me a full day before she asked me to her office for another "conference."

"You're not getting anywhere," she said as soon as I sat down across the desk from her.

"We have one test left to run," I reminded her.

"Give it up, Roy," she said softly. "You're not showing any encouraging results at all. Since it appears that the center here is doomed to close its doors anyway, let's at least not contaminate Trident with nuclear explosions."

"I thought that you were so dedicated to this place that you would do anything to keep it open," I said.

"This place is my life," Donna said. She spoke softly, sorrow more than anger in her voice. "And I *would* do anything to keep it open—anything that offered any hope of success. And your experiments don't."

"I wouldn't be so quick to say that, Donna. It's true that none of our experiments so far have produced any lasting effect, but the last two have produced measurable results. The problem is that we have too few data points to make adequate extrapolations and the interactions are too complex to model with enough precision to make up for it." Even calm weather is difficult to model in detail, and we were dealing with hurricanes and large explosive countercharges.

Donna Elkins didn't show any reaction at all to what I said. She was looking at me, but I'm not even certain that she was actually *seeing* me.

"In a lot of ways, this project is a monumental cock-up," I conceded. "It was designed to meet political requirements more than scientific. It would help if we could do ten times as many experiments, keep working upward on the energy scale in logical steps. Ten times? Even a hundred times might not be too much. But there was only one ship available, and the General Assembly wouldn't have funded more in any case. My instructions are quite clear." *And so are yours.* I didn't have to voice that last part. Donna knew it as well as I did.

"Given enough force, concentrated at the right spots at the right time, we *can* disrupt a storm, even a category five hurricane," I said. One way or another, I qualified mentally. That wasn't a product of our early experiments, just a theoretical certainty that it could be done—although if it took *too* much energy, the cure might be worse than the disease. "The only real question is whether the necessary force remains at an acceptable level."

"It's been more than a century since a nuclear bomb was last exploded," Donna said. *Bomb*—I had deliberately avoided the word, and this was the first time she had used it in my presence.

"Bomb," I said. For a moment, I let the word hang between us. "In a way, it may be a good thing to use what once would have been a weapon of war as a tool to save lives."

"That's a terribly transparent attempt at rationalization."

"Maybe," I agreed. "But 27,000 people killed by one storm is a lot harder to accept. Hundreds of thousands of people still living in refugee camps is harder to accept."

"Nothing can bring the dead back. Nothing can erase the damage that Hurricane Lisa did," Donna said. "For more than 200 years we've warned people not to build close to the ocean in hurricane zones. It hasn't done a bit of good."

"And it won't do any good in the *next* 200 years," I added. "Earth can't afford to waste that much land. That's why we have to find another way."

"Even if your fusion bomb does kill a category five here, will they ever let you use it on Earth?"

"After Hurricane Lisa, yes," I said, with more confidence than I really felt.

"So you cure the disease. How many people will the cure kill? We don't have all the literature available here, but I seem to recall some death tolls much higher than 27,000 from nuclear weapons."

"From fission devices used in war, and from accidents in old fission power generating stations nearby," I said. "The only two instances of fusion weapons being used against people were terrorist acts, designed to kill."

"Designed to kill or not. Radioactive fallout keeps killing for decades."

"Not from our devices," I said. "They are as 'clean' as possible, to use the old term for it. They were nanofactured to minimize radioactive fallout. There will be blast effects, high concentrations of neutrons, but very little lasting radiation. And the idea is to hit any storm as far from land as possible, so there should be little human exposure—here or on Earth."

She was silent for several minutes. I didn't get up or say anything. I hardly moved. I could see that Donna Elkins was still extremely unhappy with her situation. She had more to say—once she figured out what that might be.

"Have you picked out the storm yet?" she asked finally, lifting her head to look at me again.

"No. There's nothing suitable just now." I shrugged. "A couple of new tropical depressions forming in the eastern basin may turn out to fit our parameters. It's too soon to tell."

"Some of my people want me to force you to stop," she said after another long pause. "They think you are endangering the native animals. A few of my people think that the Trident chimps are nearly sentient. And I have one man who gets almost hysterical at the very thought of nuclear explosions."

"Kasigi?" It was an easy guess.

She nodded. "The Japanese remain extremely sensitive to the issue, even after two centuries. Casey tells me that he had relatives who lived in Nagasaki when it was bombed."

"Do you think he's likely to try anything . . . foolish?" I asked, hesitating before I added the last word. It sounded so banal.

"I don't know," Donna said, meeting my gaze directly. "I don't even know what he might think he could do if he *did* want to do something." A frown passed across her face. "I'm not used to thinking in those terms. Not here. Not with these people."

That's something else she'll blame me for, I thought. "I'll give you as much warning as possible before we use the fusion devices," I said. "But I would appreciate it if you would hold back on that knowledge as long as you can."

She shrugged. "It's difficult to keep secrets here. People will know the minute you start to load your *bombs* anyway. And you've made no secret of your criteria."

* * *

The next morning when I left my room to go to the dining hall for breakfast, I found a petition taped to my door. It was signed by every member of the permanent staff except the director. It was all very decorous— no threats, no polemic.

"We the undersigned members of the permanent staff of the Trident Hurricane Study Center request that you terminate your experiments immediately."

Each signature was followed by the signer's degrees. Every one of them had earned at least one doctorate. They were all highly qualified, responsible professionals.

I found it almost impossible to eat that morning. No one stared. They were quite careful not to stare. And no one said anything about the petition or our experiments. But they didn't have to. The petition said enough.

I wanted a perfect specimen for our last trial.

I also wanted to get the fusion experiment run as soon as possible so that the three of us could gather the last of our data and get back up to the ship waiting to take us home to Earth.

The longer the wait, the greater the chance that Casey—or someone else—would try to stop our final run. That gave me a powerful temptation to grab the first hurricane that even approached our established parameters. I started looking very closely at the separation between storms, and at hurricanes that were *almost* category fives, either a little too weak or a little too strong. Jenny and Ike shared my anxiety. Every day all three of us spent too many hours staring at the storm tracking data, as if we hoped to impose a suitable hurricane by force of will.

And we all got a little paranoid after the petition. We started looking over our shoulders whenever we were out among members of the permanent staff. We took our meals together, usually in my room. We checked the seals on the supply bunker and on our payload module a couple of times a day, tested the electronics on our last four Manta air sleds and their cargoes. Long days. Long nights. And the way we acted made the permanent staff more suspicious of us. They had been growing more distant almost from the beginning. Now, the separation became virtually complete. Except when it was absolutely necessary, we didn't associate with them and they didn't associate with us. Any communications went through Donna Elkins.

The first two prospective storms were wrong. Either *might* have been suitable, but they moved across the Angry Sea too close together for our purposes. Then the nearer crèche spit out three minor hurricanes—two that never got above category two and one that just barely reached hurricane force.

"I just wish we could get this *over* with," Ike said, eight days after my last long talk with Doctor Elkins. "I'm ready to climb the walls."

The three of us were walking back to the center from the bunker, about an hour before sunset. The sun was out—one more reminder that we hadn't found a suitable storm yet. We had taken to spending as much of each day as possible out in the supply bunker. That kept us away from the staring eyes. It gave us some privacy, some sense of security.

"I can't even sleep any more," Jenny complained. "I keep hearing noises and imagining—well, just about anything."

I knew what she was talking about. Twice I had experienced the same nightmare. In the dream, I woke to find that the local staff had bricked up the doors to our rooms in the night, that we were prisoners doomed to die of suffocation—real "Cask of Amontillado" stuff. I kept that dream to myself.

"Soon," I said—wishful thinking. From my last look at the computer data, it would be at least another three days—and even that would take a few breaks.

Sometimes you get the breaks.

As soon as I was certain that we had the hurricane we needed, I went across the center to Donna Elkins's office. She knew what I had to say as soon as I entered. She had the same view in her holotank that I had in mine.

"This one, right?" she asked, pointing at the storm I had chosen.

"That one," I agreed. I took a deep breath. "Forty-eight hours from right now—if you still insist on that long a delay. We *could* take it on tomorrow though, if you have no one out where there might be a problem. The sooner we get this over with, the better everyone here is going to feel."

She looked at the tank again, then looked down at her desk for a moment before she met my gaze.

"Unfortunately, I agree with you. No one is out at our sub-station." There was a small facility on the coast. "People have been reluctant to wander too far the last several days." There was an accusation behind that, but it was too late to matter.

"Do it tomorrow." She turned away from me. I started to leave, but she said, "Wait."

I waited. After a moment, she got up from her chair and came around the desk.

"You'll be leaving as soon as you gather your data on this?"

"As soon as possible," I said. "We can finish our evaluation process and write our reports on the trip home. I can't see anyone here shedding any tears over our early departure."

"No." She went back to her chair and sat down. "It's better that you leave quickly. Best that you had never come. Give us what time we have left to close out *our* work before they drag us back to Earth."

"Don't give up yet," I told her—actually feeling a little sympathy for her. "We just might succeed."

She turned away again and I left. I didn't exactly run back toward our quarters, but I wasn't taking a casual stroll either. I was about halfway there when Casey stepped out into the corridor in front of me.

"You found your storm, yes?" he asked—his voice very tight, very tense. Everyone at the center had access to the storm tracking data, and the expertise to interpret it.

"Yes, we found it," I said. "I just left Doctor Elkins's office."

"So you set your bombs off in two days." He didn't make it a question, and I didn't think that it was the time to correct his estimate.

"We're going to run our final experiment," I told him.

"You cannot. You *must* not!"

"We have to, Casey. You know that." I didn't see any hint of a weapon, but I could hardly have been more nervous if he had a gun pointed at my head. The tension that had been building at the center had pushed enough wild fears through my head. Casey was younger than me, probably stronger. I had no idea if he was a student of any of the "martial arts." That had nothing to do with his ancestry. I think half the people on Earth study them for at least a while during their lives. Back in my undergraduate days, I spent some time at it myself. But I hadn't kept up. You don't win bureaucratic fights with judo or karate.

"It is an abomination. You cannot let this horror be reborn." His voice was so tight that it sounded ready to snap. I started looking for a chance to get away from him.

"This time, maybe we can save lives with nuclear power, Casey," I said. "That's what we're trying to do."

He drew himself up ramroad straight, took a deep breath, and held it for a moment.

"You will not cancel your plans?"

"I can't." I tried to balance my weight a little better, but I was carrying more poundage than I had when I frequented the *dojo*. But Kasigi just gave me a formal Japanese bow and walked off.

It wasn't until he turned a corner that I realized how badly he had frightened me. I gave him a few more seconds and then I *did* run the rest of the way back to my room. I only stayed there a couple of minutes though before I went next door to the room Ike and Jenny were sharing.

"Time to load up," I said very softly. "Take anything you can't do without for the next twenty-four hours."

Neither of them asked questions. They were starting to look a little like zombies from lack of sleep—puffy eyes with dark circles, worry lines across their foreheads, clenched teeth. Maybe it was a good thing I couldn't see my own face. It probably looked just as frightful. Or worse. I hadn't told Ike and Jenny about Casey yet. In any case, they didn't need long to get ready— much less than a minute. We headed for the nearest exit from the building complex even though that meant detouring around a good part of the center before we could aim directly for the supply bunker.

"What's up?" Ike asked once we had put fifty yards of open ground between us and the nearest building.

"We're going out for our last hurricane tomorrow," I said. I slowed down.

I had to if I was going to keep talking. The air only goes so far. Very briefly, I told them about my interview with Doctor Elkins . . . and about my strange confrontation with Kasigi Jo.

"You think he'll try to stop us?" Jenny asked.

"I don't know and I don't want to take chances," I told her. "We'll pull a plane into the bunker, load the sleds, and lock ourselves in until it's time to take off in the morning. Jenny, I want you to stay in the bunker while Ike and I are gone. Locked in. There's at least one computer terminal in there so you'll be able to do your work without any difficulty."

When we reached the bunker, we searched it thoroughly—even though the tracer in the door showed that no one had even attempted to gain entry since the last time Ike and I had opened the door. Ike took a tractor and dragged one of the center's Imre survey planes in for us. And then we locked ourselves in the bunker. As soon as the red light showed over the inside latch, I let out a long breath. We were as secure as we could get on Trident.

"OK, let's take a short break," I said. I plopped myself down on a packing crate and wiped the sweat from my forehead.

"You *are* worried," Jenny observed.

I didn't even try to deny it. "I want a complete check on the plane," I said. "Not just the usual checklist, everything you can think of. I don't *think* there will be any problems. Except for Doctor Elkins, everyone probably thinks we won't go out until the day after tomorrow. But I don't want to take chances." I was getting a little sick of that phrase. "We'll give the sleds the same kind of check." I waited until Ike and Jenny both nodded.

"Then, if there's anything left to the night, we can try to catch some sleep, but I want one of us awake, on guard, all the time. We'll roll out at first light, take off at sunrise. That should put us in position over the eye with a few minutes to spare before it's time to deploy the sleds." The storm we had pinpointed was more than 800 miles east of the center, a couple of time zones, and I wanted to run the detonation as close to noon—local time in the eye—as possible.

It was a long, miserable night even though no one disturbed us. We didn't even have any calls over the complink. But that didn't keep us from being jumpy. It didn't keep us from starting at every real or imagined noise. We checked every circuit on the plane, then visually inspected every part of it we could get at, comparing what we saw with the plans that the computer carried. We ran through checks on the four remaining Manta air sleds and their cargoes. Finally, we loaded the sleds aboard the Imre and inspected them again.

"That's about all we can do until morning," I said when we were finished with the sleds. It was well past midnight. In a little more than five hours it would be time to taxi the plane out to the landing strip. "You kids find someplace to get comfortable for a while. I'll take the first watch." I wouldn't be able to sleep anyway. Even when I'm not nervous, sleep takes its own sweet time coming.

Even with the plane sitting in the middle, the bunker was roomy. There was plenty of space for me to pace without bumping into things all the time. We were almost certainly safe in the bunker. The lock would be hard to breach. At the very least, we would have warning. And, as far as I knew, the only explosives on Trident were in that bunker with us. I don't mean just the fusion devices. A few explosive charges were kept around for construction and for seismic probes. It would take a cutting torch and probably more than an hour to get through the door. If a few members of the staff tried to get in, I could call for help and there would be time for help to arrive. Doctor Elkins would have to respond. The ship waiting for us in orbit would monitor any open call I made.

A security camera covered the outside of the bunker door, so no one could hide out there and surprise us when we opened up to run the plane out to the landing strip in the morning.

But I stayed nervous. I could empathize with Casey, and with Donna Elkins and the others. Different cases. Most of the permanent staff of the Trident Hurricane Study Center had put their professional lives fully into the work on Trident. The center literally *was* Elkin's career, twenty years of dedication and work. And she saw it all going down the drain for reasons that had nothing to do with the quality or utility of her work, because of something she had no control over at all—and over an experiment that she saw as impossible.

Maybe it was impossible. I couldn't guarantee that it wasn't. There's still a lot we don't know about nonlinear dynamics, scientific chaos. That's the nature of the beast. We build up a stock of empirical observation, a complex structure of experimentation to go with theories and equations that often appear maddeningly simple before you put them through their iterations. Then, sometimes in very short order, your model can become too complex for even the largest computers to handle reliably in any reasonable amount of time. We can model the fractal programming that allows genes to hold the complex instructions that will result in a human—or an orchid. But we still can't adequately model the old meteorologist's example of a butterfly in China causing a hurricane in the Atlantic. Tomorrow's weather forecast is still wrong occasionally. If our computers could process ten times as much information at ten times the speed our best can now, tomorrow's weather forecast would *still* be wrong once in a while.

I pulled open a crate of meal packets and fixed something to eat. I couldn't even say what it was now—just a meal, food, fuel. Something to do: it gave me ten minutes of sitting down, enough time to rest my feet. But when I got back up and started pacing again, my feet hurt worse than before. I'm not used to that much walking.

It was after two o'clock when a series of massive yawns convinced me that it was time to try to get a little sleep. I called Ike, and as soon as he responded coherently, I grabbed a couple of blankets and made myself a bed on top of several packing crates. I used one blanket as a pillow and wrapped myself in the other. Apparently, I fell asleep almost at once.

"Roy." A hand touched my shoulder. "Doctor Jepp."

"I'm awake, Jenny," I said, surprised that I had even been asleep.

"About forty-five minutes to sunrise. We'll have a little light before long."

I sat up, stretched, and yawned. I was a long way from alert, but I was awake.

"Ike's fixing breakfast packs for us," Jenny said. That's one thing about holing up in the warehouse. You can count on food.

"Any sign of activity outside?" I asked, collecting my thoughts. I felt drugged, still stuporous from sleep.

"Not a hint," Jenny said. "It's been quiet all night."

All night? There hadn't been much of a night for us. I stood and did some more stretching. I'm not used to going from sleep to working-alertness right away. Back home, I would have a couple of hours to gear up for the office. The morning routine at home and the commute to the IWS office gave me plenty of time to make the transition.

"You checked on our storm lately?" I asked.

"I've been watching. Steady on all points."

"Just hope it stays that way for a few more hours. I'd hate to get out there and have to scrub the run. I don't want to go through more nights like this."

"The winds didn't even weaken during the night," Jenny said. "They may increase today."

I needed a couple of seconds to dredge the last numbers I had seen during the night from my memory. "It shouldn't strengthen enough to get it out of our range," I said.

"Not by noon anyway," Jenny said.

I started walking around, swinging my arms and stretching, trying to pump myself up for the day's work. My back ached. My feet didn't need long to join the party. *I'm really going to feel like hell by the time this is over*, I thought with something less than joyful anticipation. My lifestyle has always been rather sedentary. It was catching up with me in a hurry. *I should get more exercise*. I make that decision periodically. Unfortunately, that's as far as I usually get.

Hurrying through breakfast was the best way to make it palatable. Then it was time to get ready for the day's work.

"Jenny, as soon as we get the plane moved outside, seal the door again. Stay put until we get back, if possible, until we set off the devices at least." She nodded. We were going to trigger them from the Imre this time, rather than from the center—another safety precaution. "You'll be able to monitor everything from here." I pointed at the computer terminal that showed the storm track holo. Jenny nodded again.

I got especially jumpy again when we opened the doors, but there was no one out there waiting for us. Ike ran the tractor to pull the plane outside, then uncoupled the tractor and moved it out of the way. Jenny already had the bunker doors shut.

"Let's move!" Ike shouted when he sealed the plane's passenger hatch behind him. I was already in the pilot's seat.

"Well, get up here and let's get through this checklist." I shouted back. I wasn't going to take any stupid chances just to make a fast "getaway," especially without trouble right there on top of us.

We had particularly rough air that morning . . . or maybe it just seemed that way because my nerves were so jangled. As soon as we were airborne, I radioed Doctor Elkins—woke her up—to tell her that we were on our way and to make sure that everyone was inside when we set the devices off. The center was too far away from the eye of the hurricane for there to be any real danger, but the gesture had to be made. Then I radioed Captain Linearson to alert her to the timing of the explosions. Four 17-megaton fusion devices exploding fairly low in the atmosphere could hardly pose a radiation problem for the ship in orbit, but again, it was a gesture that had to be made. I also wanted to get all of the data the ship could collect on the explosions.

"I'm aiming directly for the eye," I told Ike when I finished with the "courtesy" calls. "We'll circle overhead if we have to. I want to make sure we're in place on time."

"I'll go back and run another check on the Mantas," he said. I nodded. Keeping busy was better than sitting idle.

Ike was still working in the cargo hold when Donna Elkins called. We were just under an hour into the flight.

"We've had trouble here," she said.

"What kind of trouble?" I asked, my stomach knotting up. I thought about Jenny back in that bunker and glanced over my shoulder at the hatch leading to the plane's cargo hold.

"Casey. He committed suicide during the night, apparently not long before dawn."

I closed my eyes for an instant and took a deep breath. Relief mixed with sorrow. To be honest, relief was the dominant emotion at the moment. Donna Elkins kept talking.

"He left two notes, one in English on the computer net, the other on paper, handwritten in kanji characters. I've seen Kasigi writing in Japanese. He's not—he wasn't—very speedy. This must have taken him hours to write."

"What did he say?" I asked.

"There's no one else here who reads Japanese, so I can't be sure that the two notes are the same. I'm pretty sure that they aren't. The Japanese note appears to be materially longer—maybe private messages to his family. The note in English says that he killed himself to protest against the use of any nuclear devices for any reason. The note is quite passionate."

I hadn't even thought of the possibility of something like this. I had been so worried that Kasigi might try to physically stop us from carrying out our final experiment that I hadn't thought beyond that.

"I'm sorry, Donna," I said. "I had no idea that he might do something like this."

"Neither did I," she said—with more than a little bitterness. "And since I've known him for more than ten years, I should have."

"I'm sorry." I couldn't think of anything else to say. No, I didn't even think of calling off the mission. And even if I *had* thought of it, I wouldn't have.

The next seventy-five minutes were probably the longest of my life, as trite as that may sound. I told Ike what had happened when he came back from inspecting the sleds. Jenny came on the radio long enough to tell me that she had heard the other call and to say that she felt terrible about it. Well, so did I, but there was nothing any of us could do. Not after the fact.

"Jenny, once we get in position, we'll deploy the sleds as soon as possible. I'm not going to bother waiting for the clock." It was only a minor flaw in procedure. The noon blast time had been mostly for convenience. And we wouldn't be early by a lot anyway.

"Still no deviation in the storm data," Jenny said. I knew that. We had the same information on the cockpit terminal.

The squall lines ahead of the main storm were clearly visible from above, the converging arcs like the blades of a child's pinwheel. Up where Ike and I were, the sky was clear, the sun reflecting off the clouds in a dazzling display. For a change I felt no pleasure, no exaltation at the sight of the familiar beautiful patterns of weather systems in the atmosphere. The majestic brush strokes of nature seemed flat and lifeless, faded copies of copies.

Ike and I didn't talk much after I told him about Casey. The flight didn't require much. Nor did the deployment of the air sleds when we got in position. And we didn't feel at all up to idle chatter.

We came in on the eye of the hurricane at 50,000 feet and descended toward the top of the hourglass-shaped eye in a gentle banking turn that left us pointed back toward the center. After a final check of the storm's vital statistics, Ike launched the four air sleds and went to work guiding them into position while I maneuvered the plane up away from the eye and ran the throttles full open to put as much airspace as possible between the eye and us before we triggered the fusion devices.

I would have liked to put a couple of AUs between us. In a pinch, I would have settled for a hundred miles. I hoped to get at least twice that.

"Let me know if any of the sleds start to lose stability," I reminded Ike for about the tenth time in five minutes.

"We're holding good," Ike said, not taking his eyes off the display. "The sleds have enough fuel for another twenty-one minutes."

I nosed the plane forward a little to pick up a few extra miles of airspeed. "We don't want to cut it *too* close," I said.

"The fuel calibration tested perfectly," Ike reminded me.

"Still. Keep a close watch and let me know when the first sled shows five minutes' fuel left." I started doing rough calculations in my head. Our airspeed was just over 550 miles per hour. The storm was moving at 12 mph, but not directly in our direction. That meant that we were pulling away from the eye at a rate of about 9 miles a minute. If we could hang on until the first sled got down to 3 minutes' fuel, we would have our 200 mile margin— and just a little more.

I started running through the satellite weather data we had, looking for better winds. And then I smiled for the first time that morning. By dropping another 8,000 feet I could pick up an extra 10 knots of tail wind. I nosed the plane down a little more sharply. That helped too. I was ready to start thinking about *inches* of margin. I did have a rough idea how much power we were going to unleash, and I was thoroughly intimidated.

At least worrying about the sleds and their cargo kept me from dwelling on Kasigi's suicide.

We were 203 miles from the nearest edge of the storm's eye when Ike told me that we had reached five minutes worth of fuel in the first sled.

"Detonate now?" he asked.

I shook my head. "Are all four sleds still stable?"

"Perfectly," he assured me. "They're keeping station like they were tied together."

"We'll hold off as long as possible," I said. "Just keep a close watch on them. Jenny, you listening?"

"I'm listening," she said. "Crank up the filters on your windows."

"Right. Thanks for the reminder," I said. I hit the manual control and the sky darkened noticeably. We were far enough away that the fireball wouldn't even be visible—if the historical data was correct. We shouldn't be able to see anything of the explosion. But again, we were taking absolutely no chances. "All the way to the stops," I reported.

"Four minutes on fuel," Ike said softly.

I glanced at my navigation screen. We were 213 miles from the nearest *bomb*. Even the most bizarre set of circumstances we could imagine wouldn't produce anything that might remotely endanger the Imre at that distance— shock wave or radiation. That didn't stop my nerves from jumping. It *had* been a hundred years since a fusion device had been detonated.

"As long as everything holds stable, hit the button at two minutes." I said. "If anything even starts to look as if it might be ready to go wacky, warn me and hit the button at once."

Two minutes. I must have aged ten years in the last seconds of waiting.

Ike detonated the explosives. We saw nothing, felt nothing. Only the reports from the satellites told us that all four devices had exploded. We waited for a short eternity, staring at the constantly updated model of the storm in our holotank.

Things happened.

The eyewall pulsed out and down. The water-laden clouds boiled away, vaporized. The force of the explosions kicked against the 170 mph winds around the eye of the hurricane, pushing some forward, throwing a wall in front of others, disrupting the patterns through the middle altitudes of the storm. The heat and downward pressure of the explosion increased atmospheric pressure below.

Our computer model couldn't show everything that was happening, couldn't keep up with the pace. Conditions in and around the eye changed too quickly for the satellite monitors to keep pace.

The hurricane rebounded inward.

And the system ripped itself apart.

It didn't happen instantly. After all, the hurricane was more than 600 miles in diameter. But there was enough action along the eyewall in the first two minutes to tell us that we were doing something. We had tipped a strong, well-organized hurricane into chaotic instability. After five minutes, the disruption was still increasing. Ten minutes after detonation, there was no doubt in my mind. The hurricane wasn't dead, but it was dying.

"We did it! We did it!" Ike was shouting almost right into my ear. Jenny was yelling the same thing over the radio. Maybe I did a little shouting myself.

But the shouting didn't last long. Against the darkened glass of the windshield in front of me, I could almost see Kasigi's face, begging me not to do it. *"You cannot let this horror be reborn."*

And now it was a squalling infant.

We left two days later. There was no trace remaining of the storm we had killed. But the ghost of a man remained, a man who had died to protest what we had done. Kasigi Jo had already been buried, on Trident, at his own request. I was carrying his suicide notes, his *manifestoes*, back to Earth. I would make his notes public, regardless of the *fallout* there. I owed him that much. Others could decide whether or not we should use our new weapon against the ravages of nature. I had little doubt what the final decision would be.

"I assume that the work will continue," I told Donna Elkins at our last meeting. "We know that the theory is workable now. It needs to be refined. If nothing else, we need to find the minimum force needed."

"Does that mean you'll be coming back?"

I shook my head first, then shrugged. "I don't know. I think that the work has to continue, but I'm having trouble working up any enthusiasm for doing it myself."

"I know the feeling," she said. Then she sighed. "You're right, the work will go on. But I've lost my enthusiasm too. When the next load of bombs comes out, I go home. Quit. I don't want any part of it." She turned away from me. "I love this place and I'll miss it more than anything, but I can't fight for it here. I've got to go back to Earth to do that."

"Maybe I'll see you there," I said. And then I left. Quickly.

POGROM

James Patrick Kelly

Like his friend and frequent collaborator John Kessel, James Patrick Kelly made his first sale in 1975, and went on to become one of the most respected and prominent new writers of the eighties. Although his most recent solo novel, *Look into the Sun*, was well received, Kelly has had more impact to date as a writer of short fiction than as a novelist, and, indeed, Kelly stories such as "Solstice," "The Prisoner of Chillon," "Glass Cloud," "Mr. Boy," and "Home Front" must be ranked among the most inventive and memorable short works of the decade. Kelly's first solo novel, the mostly ignored *Planet of Whispers*, came out in 1984. It was followed by *Freedom Beach*, a novel written in collaboration with John Kessel. His story "Friend," also in collaboration with Kessel, was in our First Annual Collection; his "Solstice" was in our Third Annual Collection; his "The Prisoner of Chillon" was in our Fourth Annual Collection; his "Glass Cloud" was in our Fifth Annual Collection; his "Home Front" was in our Sixth Annual Collection; and his "Mr. Boy" was in our Eighth Annual Collection. Born in Mineola, New York, Kelly now lives with his family in Portsmouth, New Hampshire, where he's reported to be at work on a third solo novel, *Wildlife*.

Here he takes us to a frighteningly plausible near-future society for a new and disturbing take on the age-old war between the young and the old.

Matt was napping when Ruth looked in on him. He had sprawled across the bedspread with his clothes on, shoes off. His right sock was worn to gauze at the heel. The pillow had crimped his gray hair at an odd angle. She had never seen him so peaceful before, but then she had never seen him asleep. She had the eye zoom for a close-up. His mouth was slack and sleep had softened the wrinkles on his brow. Ruth had always thought him handsome but forbidding, like the cliffs up in Crawford Notch. Now that he was dead to the world, she could almost imagine him smiling. She wondered if there were anything she could say to make him smile. He worried too much, that man. He blamed himself for things he had not done.

She increased the volume of her wall. His breathing was scratchy but regular. They had promised to watch out for one another; there were not many of them left in Durham. Matt had given Ruth a password for his homebrain when they had released him from the hospital. He seemed fine for now. She turned out the lights he had left on, but there was nothing else she could see to do for him. She did not, however, close the electronic window which opened from her apartment on Church Hill onto his house across town. It had been years since she had heard the sounds of a man sleeping. If she shut her eyes, it was almost as if he were next to her. His gentle snoring made a much more soothing background than the gurgle of the mountain cascade she usually kept on the wall. She was not really intruding, she told herself. He had asked her to check up on him.

Ruth picked up the mystery she had been reading but did not open it. She studied his image as if it might be a clue to something she had been trying to remember. Matt moaned and his fingers tightened around the cast that ran from his right hand to his elbow. She thought he must have started dreaming, because his face closed like a door. He rolled toward the eye and she could see the bruise on his cheek, blood-blue shading to brown.

"Someone is approaching," said Ruth's homebrain.

"The groceries?"

"The visitor is not on file."

"Show me," Ruth said.

The homebrain split Matt's window and gave her a view of the front porch. A girl she had never seen before, holding two brown paper Shop 'n' Save sacks, pressed the doorbell with her elbow.

She was about thirteen and underfed, which meant she was probably a drood. She had long glitter hair and the peeling red skin of someone who did not pay enough attention to the UV forecasts. Her arms were decorated with blue stripes of warpaint. Or maybe they were tattoos. She was wearing sneakers, no socks, jeans, and a T-shirt with a picture of Jesus Hitler that said "For a nickel I will."

"Hello?" said Ruth. "Do I know you?"

"Your stuff." She shifted the sacks in her arms as if she were about to drop them.

"Where's Jud? He usually delivers for me."

"C'mon, lady! Not arguin' with no fuckin' door." She kicked at it. "Hot as nukes out here."

"I don't know who you are."

"See these sacks? Costin' you twenty-one fifty-three."

"Please show me your ID."

"Shit, lady." She plunked the sacks down on the porch, brushed sweat from her face, pulled a card from her pocket and thrust it toward the eye in the door. The homebrain scanned and verified it. But it did not belong to her.

"That's Jud's card," said Ruth.

"He busy, you know, so he must give it to me." One of the sacks fell over. The girl nudged a box of dishwasher soap with her sneaker. "You want this or not?" She knelt, reached into the sack and tossed a bag of onion bagels, a bottle of liquid Pep, a frozen whitefish, two rolls of toilet paper, and a bunch of carrots into a pile on the middle of the porch.

"Stop that!" Ruth imagined the neighbors were watching her groceries being abused. "Wait there."

The girl waggled a package of Daffy Toes at the eye. "Gimme cookie for my tip?"

Ruth hesitated before she pressed her thumb against the printreader built into the steel door. What was the point in having all these security systems if she was going to open up for strangers? This was exactly the way people like her got hurt. But it *was* Ruth's order, and the girl looked too frail to be any trouble.

She smelled of incense. A suspicion of sweet ropy smoke clung to her clothes and hair. Ruth was tempted to ask what it was, but realized that she probably did not want to know. The latest in teen depravity, no doubt. The smell reminded her of when she was in college back in the sixties and she used to burn incense to cover the stink of pot. Skinny black cylinders of charcoal that smeared her fingers and smelled like a Christmas tree on fire. Ruth followed the girl into the kitchen, trying to remember the last time she had smoked pot.

The girl set the bags out on the counter and then sighed with pleasure. "Been wantin' all day to get into some A/C." She surveyed the kitchen as if she were hoping for an invitation to dinner. "Name's Chaz." She waited in vain for Ruth to introduce herself. "So, want me to unpack?"

"No." Ruth took her wallet out of her purse.

"Lots of 'em ask me to. They too old, or too lazy—hey, real costin' *wine*." She pulled a Medoc from the rack mounted under the china cabinet and ran her finger along the stubby shoulder. "In glass bottles. You rich or what?"

Ruth held out her cash card but Chaz ignored it.

"Bet you think I lie. You 'fraid I come here to do your bones?" She hefted the bottle of Bordeaux by the neck, like a club.

Alarmed, Ruth clutched at her chest and squeezed the security pager that hung on a silver chain under her blouse. "Put that down." The eye on the kitchen ceiling started broadcasting live to the private cops she subscribed to. Last time they had taken twenty minutes to come.

"Don't worry," Chaz grinned. "I deliver plenty stuff before. In Portsmouth. Then we lose our house, got move to Durham. Nice town you got here." She set the bottle back on the counter. "But you can't hear nothin' I say, right? You scared 'cause kids hate you but I ain't breaking your head, am I? Not today, anyway. Just wanna earn my fuckin' nickel, lady."

"I'm trying to pay you." Ruth pushed the card at her.

She took it. "Place full of costin' shit like this." She shook her head in wonder at Ruth's wealth. "You lucky, you know." She rubbed the card against the port of Jud Gazzara's Shop 'n' Save ID to deduct twenty-one dollars and fifty-three cents. "Yeah, this is great, compare to dorms. You ever see dorms inside?"

"No."

"You oughta. Compare to dorms, this is heaven." Chaz handed the card back. "No, better than heaven, 'cause you can buy this, but you gotta die to get heaven. Gimme my cookie?" she said.

"Take it and leave."

Chaz paused on the way out and peeked into the living room. "This walter what you do for fun, lady?" Matt was still asleep on the wall. "Jeez, you pigs good as dead already."

"Would you please go?"

"*Wake up, walter!*" She yelled at the screen. "*Hustle or die!*"

"Huh!" Matt jerked as if he had been shot. "What?" He curled into a ball, protecting his face with the cast.

"Give nasty, you get nasty." Chaz winked at Ruth. "See you next week, lady."

"Greta, is that you?"

Ruth could hear Matt calling to his dead wife as she shouldered the door shut. She braced her back against it until she felt the homebrain click the bolts into place.

"*Greta?*"

"It's me," she called. "Ruth." She squeezed the security pager again to call the private cops off. At least she could avoid the charge for a house call. Her heart hammered against her chest.

"Ruth?"

She knew the girl was out there laughing at her. It made Ruth angry, the way these kids made a game of terrorizing people. "Turn your wall on, Matt." It was not fair; she was no pig.

By the time Ruth got into the living room, Matt was sitting on the edge of his bed. He seemed dazed, as if he had woken up to find himself still in the nightmare.

"You asked me to check in on you," she said. "Remember? Sorry if I disturbed you." She decided not to tell him—or anyone—about Chaz. Nothing had happened, really. So the world was full of ignorant little bigots, so what? She could hardly report a case of rudeness to the Durham cops; they thought people like her complained too much as it was. "Did you have a nice nap?" Ruth was not admitting to anyone that she was afraid of trash like Chaz.

"I was having a dream about Greta," said Matt. "She gave me a birthday cake on a train. We were going to some city, New York or Boston. Then she wanted to get off but I hadn't finished the cake. It was big as a suitcase."

Ruth had never understood why people wanted to tell her their dreams. Most of the ones she had heard were dumb. She could not help but be embarrassed when otherwise reasonable adults prattled on about their night-time lunacies. "How are you feeling?" She nestled into her favorite corner of the couch. "Do you need anything?"

"What was funny was that Greta wouldn't help me." He had not noticed how he was annoying her. "I mean, I told her to have some cake but she wouldn't. She screamed at me to hurry up or I'd die. Then I woke up."

What had Chaz called him? A walter. Ruth had never heard that one before. "Sorry," she said, "I really didn't mean to intrude. I should let you get back to sleep."

"No, don't go." He slid his feet into the slippers next to the bed. "I'd like some company. I just lay down because there was nothing else to do." He grunted as he stood, then glanced in the mirror and combed hair back over his bald spot with his fingers. "See, I'm up."

He turned away and waved for her to follow. The eye tracked along the ceiling after him as he hobbled down the hall to his office, a dark shabby room decorated with books and diplomas. He lived in only three rooms: office, bedroom and kitchen. The rest of his house was closed down.

"I'm pretty useless these days." He eased behind the antique steel desk he had brought home from his office when they closed the university. "No typing with this damn cast on. Not for six, maybe seven weeks." He picked up a manuscript, read the title, dropped it back on a six inch stack next to the computer. "Nothing to do."

Next he would get melancholy, if she let him. "So dictate."

"I'm too old to think anymore without my fingers on a keyboard and a screen to remind me what I just wrote." He snorted in disgust. "But you didn't call to hear me complain. You've been so good, Ruth. To pay so much attention and everything. I don't know why you do it."

"Must be your sunny personality, Matt." Ruth hated the way he had been acting since they released him from the hospital. So predictable. So sad. "I'm cooking my mom's famous gefilte fish. Maybe I'll bring some over later? And a bottle of wine?"

"That's sweet, but no. No, you know how upset you get when you go out." He grinned. "You just stay safe where you are."

"This is my town, too. And yours. I've lived here thirty-two years. I'm not about to let them take it away from me now."

"We lost it long ago, Ruth. Maybe it's time we acknowledged that."

"Really? Can I stop paying property taxes?"

"You know, I understand the way they feel." He tapped the keyboard at random with his good hand. "The world's a mess; it's not their fault that they're homeless. They watch the walls in the dorms and they see all the problems and they need someone to blame. So they call us pigs and we call them droods. Much simpler that way."

"So what are you going to do? Send them a thank you note for crippling you? Breaking your arm? Wake up and listen to yourself, Matt. You shouldn't have to hide in your house like a criminal. You didn't do anything."

"Yes, that's it exactly. I didn't do anything. Maybe it's time."

"Damn it, don't start *that* again! You're a teacher, you worked hard."
Ruth grabbed a pillow she had embroidered. She wanted to hurl it right
through the wall and knock some sense into the foolish old man. "God, I
don't know why I bother." Instead she hugged it to her chest. "Sometimes
you make me mad, Matt. I mean really angry."

"I'm sorry, Ruth. I'm just in one of my moods. Maybe I should call you
back when I'm better company?"

"All right," she said without enthusiasm. "I'll talk to you later then."

"Don't give up on me, Ruth."

She wiped him off the wall. He was replaced by Silver Cascade Brook up
in Crawford Notch. She had reprocessed the loop from video she had shot
years ago, before she had had to stop traveling. Water burbled, leaves rustled,
birds sang. "Chirp, chirp," she said sourly and zapped it. Afloat on the
Oeschinensee in the Alps. *Zap.* Coral gardens off the Caribbean coast of St.
Lucia. *Zap.* Exotic birds of the Everglades. *Zap.* She flipped restlessly
through her favorite vacations; nothing pleased her. Finally she settled on a
vista of Mill Pond across the street. The town swans cut slow V's across the
placid surface. In the old days, when she used to sit on the porch, she could
hear frogs in the summertime. She was tempted to drag her rocker out there
right now. Then she would call Matt, just to show him it could still be done.

Instead she went into the kitchen to unpack the groceries. She put the
dishwasher soap under the sink and the cookies in the bread drawer. Matt
was a crotchety old man, ridden with guilt, but he and she were just about
the last ones left. She picked up the whitefish, opened the freezer, then
changed her mind. When was the last time she had seen Margie or Stanley
What's-His-Name, who lived just two doors down? Ruth closed the door
again, stripped the shrinkwrap from the fish and popped it into the microwave
to defrost. If she were afraid to show him, Matt would end up like all the
others. He would stop calling or move or die and then Ruth would be a
stranger in her own home town. When the whitefish thawed she whacked
off the head, skinned and boned it. She put the head, skin, and bones in a
pot, covered them with water, cut in some carrots and onion and set it on
the stove to boil. She was not going to let anyone make her a prisoner in her
own kitchen. She ground the cleaned fish and some onions together, then
beat in matzo meal, water, and a cup of ovobinder. Her mom's recipe called
for eggs but uncontaminated eggs were hard to find. She formed the fish
mixture into balls and bravely dropped them into the boiling stock. Ruth was
going visiting, and no one was going to stop her.

After she called the minibus, she packed the cooled gefilte fish into one
Tupperware, poured the lukewarm sauce into another and tucked them both
into her tote bag beside the Medoc. Then she reached to the cabinet above
the refrigerator, took down her blowcuffs and velcroed one to each wrist.
In the bedroom she opened the top drawer of her dresser and rooted through
the underwear until she found two flat clips of riot gas, two inches by three.

The slogan on the side read: "With Knockdown, they *go* down and *stay* down." The clips hissed as she fitted them into the cuffs. Outside, a minibus pulled into the parking lot of the Church Hill Apartments and honked.

"Damn!" There must have been one in the neighborhood; service was never this prompt. She pulled on a baggy long-sleeved shirtwaist to hide the cuffs and grabbed her tote.

As soon as Ruth opened the front door, she realized she had forgotten to put sunblock on. Too late now. The light needled her unprotected skin as she hurried down the walk. There was one other rider on the mini, a leathery man in a stiff brown suit. He perched at the edge of his seat with an aluminum briefcase between his legs. The man glanced at her and then went back to studying the gum spots on the floor. The carbrain asked where she was going.

"14 Hampshire Road." Ruth brushed her cash card across its port.

"The fare is $1.35 including the senior citizen discount," said the carbrain. "Please take your seat."

She picked a spot on the bench across from the door. The air blowing out of the vents was hot, which was why all the windows were open. She brushed the hair out of her eyes as the mini rumbled around Mill Pond and onto Oyster River Road.

The mini was strewn with debris; wrappers, squashed beer boxes, dirty receipts. Someone had left a paper bag on the bench next to her. Just more garbage, she thought—until it jumped. It was a muddy Shop 'n' Save sack with the top crumpled down to form a seal. As she watched, it moved again.

She knew better than to talk to people on the minibus, but Ruth could not help herself. "Is this yours?"

The man's expression hardened to cement. He shook his head and then touched the eye clipped to the neckband of his shirt and started recording her.

"Sorry." She scooted down the bench and opened the bag. A bullfrog the size of her fist rose up on its hind legs, scrabbled weakly toward her and then sank back. At first she thought it was a toy with a run down battery. Then she realized that some brain-dead kid had probably caught it down at the pond and then left it behind. Although she had not seen a frog up close in years, she thought this one looked wrong somehow. Dried out. They breathed through their skins, didn't they? She considered getting off the mini and taking it back to the water herself. But then she would be on foot in the open, an easy target. Ruth felt sorry for the poor thing, yes, but she was not risking her life for a frog. She closed the bag so she would not have to watch it suffer.

The mini stopped at an apartment on Mill Road and honked. When no one came out, it continued toward the center of town, passed another minibus going in the opposite direction, and then pulled into the crumbling lot in front of the Shop 'n' Save plaza. There were about a dozen bicycles in the racks next to the store, and four electric cars parked out front, their skinny fiberglass bodies blanching in the afternoon sun. A delivery man was unloading beer boxes from a truck onto a dolly. The mini pulled up behind the truck and shut itself off. The door opened and the clock above it started a countdown: *10:00 . . . 09:59 . . . 09:58.* The man with the aluminum suitcase got off, strode down the plaza and knocked at the door of what had once been the hardware store. He watched Ruth watching him until the door opened and he went in.

The empty lot shimmered like a blacktopped desert and the heat of the day closed around her. To escape it, she tried filling the space with ghost cars: Fords and Chryslers and Toyotas. She imagined there was no place to park, just like when they still pumped gas, before they closed the university. *06:22 . . . 06:21 . . . 06:20.* But the sun was stronger than her memory. It was the sun, the goddamned sun, that was driving the world crazy. She could even hear it: the mini's metal roof clicked in its harsh light like a bomb. Who could think in heat like this?

The bag twitched again and Ruth realized she could get water from the store and pour it over the frog. She glanced at the clock. *02:13 . . . 02:12 . . .* Too late now.

The carbrain honked and started the engine when the clock reached *00:30.* Three kids trudged out of the store. Two were lugging sacks filled with groceries; the third was Chaz, who was empty-handed. Ruth shifted her tote bag onto her lap, got a firm grip on the handle and tried to make herself as small as possible.

"Destination, please?" said the carbrain.

"1 Simons." A fat kid clumped up the step well and saw her. "Someone on already." He brushed his card across the pay port. "Lady, where you goin', lady?"

Ruth fixed her gaze on the buttons of his blue-striped Shop 'n' Save shirt; one had come undone. She avoided eye contact so he would not see how tense she was. She said nothing.

The second one bumped into the fat kid. "Move, sweatlips!" He was wearing the uniform shirt tucked into red shorts. He had shaved legs. She did not look at his face either.

"Please take your seat," said the carbrain. "Current stops are 14 Hampshire Road and 1 Simons Lane. Destination, please?"

"Stoke Hall," said Chaz.

"Hey, Hampshire's the wrong way, lady. Get off, would ya?"

"Yeah, make yourself useful for a change." Red Shorts plopped his groceries onto the bench opposite Ruth and sprawled next to them. Ruth said nothing; she saw Chaz paying the carbrain.

"Wanna throw her off?"

Ruth clenched her fists and touched the triggers of her cuffs.

"Just leave her and stretch the ride." Chaz settled beside the others. " 'Less you *wanna* get back to work."

The fat kid grunted, and the logic of sloth carried the day. Ruth eased off the triggers as the mini jolted through the potholes in the lot and turned back onto Mill Road. The boys started joking about a war they had seen on the wall. Even though they seemed to have forgotten her, the side of Ruth's neck prickled as if someone were still staring. When she finally dared peek, she saw Chaz grinning slyly at her, like she expected a tip. It made Ruth angry. She wanted to slap the girl.

They looped around downtown past the post office, St. Thomas More Church and the droods' mall. The mall was actually a flea market which had accreted over the years in the parking lot off Pettee Brook Lane: salvaged lumber and old car parts and plastic sheeting over chicken wire had been cobbled together to make about thirty stalls. It was where people who lived in the dorms went. When the hawkers saw the mini coming, they swarmed into the street to slow it down. Ruth saw teens waving hand-lettered signs advertising rugs, government surplus cheese, bicycles, plumbing supplies stripped from abandoned houses, cookies, obsolete computers. A man in a tank top wearing at least twenty watches on each arm gestured frantically at her to get off the mini. They said you could also buy drugs and meat and guns at the mall, and what they did not have, they could steal to order. Ruth, of course, had never gone there herself but she had heard all about it. Everyone had. The cops raided the mall regularly, but no one dared close it down for good.

The fat kid reached across the aisle and snatched the abandoned paper sack. "This yours lady?" He jiggled it then unrolled the top. "Oh, shit." He took the frog out, holding it by the legs so that its stomach bulged at the sides. "Oh, shit, gonna kill the bastard did this."

"Sweet," said Red Shorts. "Someone left us a present."

"It's suffocatin'." The fat kid stood, swayed against the momentum of the mini and lurched toward Ruth. "They need water to breathe, same as we need air." When he thrust it at her, the frog's eyes bulged as if they might pop. "And you just sit here, doin' *nothing*." Rage twisted his face.

"I—I didn't know," said Ruth. The frog was so close that she thought he meant to shove it down her throat. "I swear, I never looked inside."

"So it's dyin'," said Red Shorts. "So let's stomp it. Come on, put it out of misery." He winked at Chaz. "Grandma here wants to see guts squirt out its mouth."

"I'll do your bones, you touch this frog." The fat kid stormed down the aisle to the door. "Stop here," he said. "Let me out."

The mini pulled over. Red Shorts called to him. "Hey sweatlips, who's gonna help me deliver groceries?"

"Fuck you." Ruth could not tell whether he was cursing Red Shorts, her or the world in general.

The door opened. The fat kid got off, cut in front of the mini and headed across town toward Mill Pond. Red Shorts turned to Chaz. "Likes frogs." He was still smirking as they drove off. "Thinks he's a Green."

She was not amused. "You leave it for him to find?"

"Maybe."

The mini had by now entered the old UNH campus. Online university had killed most residential colleges; the climate shift had triggered the depression which had finished the rest. But the buildings had not stood empty for long. People lost jobs, then houses; when they got hungry enough, they came looking for help. The campuses were converted into emergency refugee centers for families with dependent children. Eight years later, temporary housing had become permanent droodtowns. Nobody knew why the refugees were called droods. Some said the word came from the now-famous song, others claimed that the Droods had been a real homeless family. The mini passed several of the smaller dorms and then turned off Main Street onto Garrison Avenue. Ahead to the left was Stoke Hall. Red Shorts whispered something to Chaz, who frowned. It was getting harder and harder to ignore them; she could tell they were plotting something.

Nine stories tall, Stoke was the biggest dorm on campus. When Ruth had gone to UNH, it had housed about sixteen hundred students. She had heard that there were at least four thousand droods there now, most of them kids, almost all of them under thirty. Stoke was a Y-shaped brick monster; two huge jaws gaped at the street. Its foundation was decorated with trash dropped from windows. The packed dirt basketball court, dug into the sloping front courtyard, was empty. The players loitered in the middle of the street, watching a wrecker hitch a tow to a stalled water truck. The mini slowed to squeeze by and Chaz slid onto the bench beside Ruth.

"Wanna get off and look?" She nodded at the dorm.

"Huh?" Red Shorts had a mouth full of celery he had stolen from one of the bags. "Talkin' to me?"

"Up there." As she leaned over to point at the upper floors, Chaz actually brushed against Ruth. "Two down, three left. Where I live."

The girl's sweaty skin caught at the fabric at Ruth's sleeve. Ruth did not like being touched. Over the years, she had gotten used to meeting people electronically, through the walls. Those few she did choose to see were the kind of people who bathed and wore clean shirts. People who took care of themselves. Chaz was so close that Ruth felt sick. It was as if the girl's smokey stink were curdling in the back of her throat. She needed to get away, but there was nowhere to go. She fought the impulse to blow Chaz a face full of Knockdown, because then she would have to gas Red Shorts, too. And what if one of them managed to call for help? She imagined the mob of basketball players stopping the mini and pulling her off. She would be lucky if all they did was beat her, the way they had beaten Matt. More likely she would be raped, killed, they were *animals*, she could *smell* them.

"C'mon," said Chaz. "You show your place. I show mine."

Ruth's voice caught in her throat like a bone. The mini cleared the water truck and pulled up in front of the dorm. "Stoke Hall," said the carbrain. It opened the door.

"What you say, lady?" Chaz stood. "Won't hurt."

"Much." Red Shorts snickered.

"You shut up," said Chaz.

Ruth stared at the words on her T-shirt, "For a nickel I will." She felt for the triggers and shook her head.

"How come I gotta play lick ass?" Chaz squatted so that her face was level with Ruth's; she forced eye contact. "Just wanna talk." The girl feigned sincerity so well that Ruth wavered momentarily.

"Yeah," said Red Shorts, "like 'bout how you pigs ate the world."

Ruth started to shake. "Leave me alone." It was all happening too fast.

"Stoke Hall," repeated the carbrain.

"Okay, okay," Chaz rose up, disgusted. "So forget it. You don't gotta say nothing to droods. You happy, you rich, so fuck me." She turned and walked away.

Ruth had not expected Chaz to be wounded, and suddenly she was furious with the foolish girl. Her invitation was a bad joke. A woman like Ruth could not take three steps into that place before someone would hit her over the head and drag her into a room. Chaz wanted to make *friends* after everything that had happened? It was too late, way too late.

She was already halfway down the step well when Red Shorts leaned toward Ruth. "You old bitch pig." His face was slick with greasy sweat; these droods had no right to talk to her that way. Without thinking, she thrust her fist at him and emptied a clip of Knockdown into his eyes.

He screamed and lurched backward against the grocery sacks, which tipped off the bench and spilled. He bounced and pitched face down on the floor, thrashing in the litter of noodle soup bulbs and bright packages of candy. Ruth had never used riot gas before and she was stunned at its potency. Truth in advertising, she thought, and almost laughed out loud. Chaz came down the aisle.

"Get off." Ruth raised her other fist. "Get the hell off. *Now!*"

Chaz backed away, still gaping at the boy, whose spasms had subsided to twitching. Then she clattered down the steps and ran up the street toward the basketball players. Ruth knew at that moment she was doomed, but the carbrain closed the door and the mini pulled away from the curb, and she realized that she had gotten away with it. She *did* laugh then; the sound seemed to come to her from a great distance.

Suddenly she was shivering in the afternoon heat. She had to do something, so she grabbed Red Shorts by the shoulders and muscled him back onto a bench. She had not meant to hurt anyone. It was an accident, not her fault. She felt better as she picked up the spilled groceries, repacked them and arranged the sacks neatly beside him. He didn't look so bad, she thought. He was napping; it would not be the first time someone had fallen asleep on the minibus. She retrieved an apple from under the bench.

She got so involved pretending that nothing was wrong that she was surprised when the mini stopped.

"14 Hampshire," said the carbrain.

Ruth regarded her victim one last time. Since she had tried her best to put things back the way they were supposed to be, she decided to forgive herself. She grabbed her tote bag, stepped off and hurried to the front door of Matt's decaying colonial. By the time the mini rumbled off, she had pushed the unpleasantness from her mind. She owed it to him to be cheerful.

Ruth had not been out to Matt's house since last fall; usually he visited her. It was worse than she remembered. He could not keep the place up on his pension. Paint had chipped off the shingles, exposing gray wood. Some of them had curled in the sun. A rain gutter was pulling away from the roof. Poor Matt couldn't afford to stay, but he couldn't afford to sell, either. No one was buying real estate in Durham. She heard him unlocking the door and made herself smile.

"*Ruth!* I thought I told you to stay home."

"Mr. Watson? Mr. Matthew Watson of 14 Hampshire Road?" She consulted an imaginary clipboard. "Are you the gentleman who ordered the surprise party?"

"I can't believe you did this." He tugged her inside and shut the door. "Do you have any idea how dangerous it is out there?"

She shrugged. "So, are you glad to see me?" She put down her tote and opened her arms to him.

"Yes, of course, but . . ." He leaned forward and gave her a stony peck on the cheek. "This is serious, Ruth."

"That's right. I seriously missed you."

"Don't make jokes. You don't understand these people. You could've been hurt." He softened then and hugged her. She stayed in his embrace longer than he wanted—she could tell—but that was all right. His arms shut the world out; his strength stopped time. Nothing had happened, nothing could happen. She had not realized how lonesome she had been. She did not even mind his cast jabbing her.

"Are you okay, Ruth?" he murmured. "Is everything all right?"

"Fine." Eventually she had to let him go. "Fine."

"It's good to see you," he said, and gave her an embarrassed smile. "Even if you are crazy. Come into the kitchen."

Matt poured the Medoc into coffee cups and they toasted their friendship. "Here's to twenty-six years." Actually, she had been friends with Greta before she knew Matt. Ruth set the tupperware on the counter. "What should I serve the fish on?" She opened the china cabinet and frowned. Matt was such a typical bachelor: he had none of the right dishes.

"I'm glad you came over," he said. "I've been wanting to talk to you. I suppose I could tell you through the wall, but . . ."

"Tell me?" She dusted a cracked bowl with the edge of her sleeve.

He ran his finger around the rim of the cup and shrugged uncomfortably. "You know how lonely I've been since the . . . since I broke my hip. I think that's my biggest problem. I can't go out anymore, and I can't live here by myself."

For a few thrilling seconds, Ruth misunderstood. "Oh?" She thought he was going to ask her to live with him. It was something she had often fantasized about.

"Anyway, I've been talking to people at Human Services and I've decided to take in some boarders."

"Boarders?" She still did not understand. "*Droods?*"

"Refugees. I know how you feel, but they're people just like us, and the state will pay me to house them. I have more room than I need, and I can use the money."

Her hands felt numb. "I don't believe this. Really, Matt, haven't you learned anything?" She had to put the bowl down before she dropped it. "You go to the dorms to tutor, and they beat you up. They crippled you. So now you're going to bring the animals right into your own house?"

"They're not animals. I know several families who would jump at the chance to leave the dorms. Kids, Ruth. Babies."

"Look, if it's only money, let me help. Please."

"No, that's not it. You said something this morning. I'm a teacher all right, except I have no one to teach. That's why I feel so useless. I need to—"

A window shattered in the bedroom.

"What was that?" Matt bolted from his chair, knocking his wine over.

"There are many people on the street," announced the homebrain. "They are destroying property."

Ruth heard several angry *thwocks* against the side of the house and then more glass broke. She felt as if a shard had lodged in her chest. Someone outside was shouting. Wine pooled on the floor like blood.

"Call the police." Matt could not afford private security.

"The line is busy."

"Keep trying, damn it!"

He limped to the bedroom, the only room with a window wall; Ruth followed. There was a stone the size of a heart on the bed, glass scattered across the rug.

"Show," said Matt.

The wall revealed a mob of at least a hundred droods. Basketball players, hawkers from the mall, kids from Stoke. And Chaz. Ruth was squeezing her security pager so hard that her hand hurt.

"Hey, walter, send the bitch out!"

She had been so stupid. Of course Chaz had heard the carbrain repeat Matt's address.

"Boomers. *Fuckin' oldies.*"

She had never understood why they were all so eager to hate people like her and Matt. It was not fair to punish an entire generation.

"Burn 'em. Send the pigs to hell!"

The politicians were to blame, the corporations. They were the ones responsible. It was not *her* fault; she was just one person. "Go ahead, Matt," she said bitterly. "Teach them about us." Ruth pressed herself into the corner of his bedroom. "Maybe we should invite them in for a nice glass of wine?"

"What is this, Ruth?" Matt grabbed her by the shoulders and shook her. "What did you do?"

She shook her head. "Nothing," she said.

THE MOAT

Greg Egan

Here's another first-rate story by Greg Egan, this one from a little-known Australian magazine called *Aurealis*. . . .

I'm first into the office, so I clean off the night's graffiti before clients start to arrive. It's not hard work; we've had all the external surfaces coated, so a scrubbing brush and warm water is all it takes. When I'm finished, I find I can scarcely remember what any of it said; I've reached the stage where I can stare at the slogans and insults without even reading them.

All the petty intimidation is like that; it's a shock at first, but eventually it just fades into a kind of irritating static. Graffiti, phone calls, hate mail. We used to get megabytes of automated invective via DataMail; but that, at least, turned out to be easily fixed. We installed the latest screening software, and fed it a few samples of the kind of transmission we preferred not to receive.

I don't know for certain who's coordinating all this aggravation, but it's not hard to guess. There's a group calling themselves Fortress Australia, who've started putting up posters on bus shelters: obscene caricatures of Melanesians, portrayed as cannibals adorned with human bones, leering over cooking pots filled with screaming white babies. The first time I saw one, I thought it was, surely, an advertisement for an exhibition of Racist Cartoons From Nineteenth Century Publications; some kind of scholarly deconstruction of the sins of the distant past. When I finally realised that I was looking at real, contemporary propaganda; I didn't know whether to feel sickened— or heartened by the sheer crudity of the thing. I thought, so long as the anti-refugee groups keep insulting people's intelligence with shit like this, they're not likely to get much support beyond the lunatic fringe.

Some Pacific islands are losing their land slowly, year by year; others are being rapidly eroded by the so-called Greenhouse storms. I've heard plenty of quibbling about the precise definition of the term "environmental refugee," but there's not much room for ambiguity when your home is literally vanishing into the ocean. Nevertheless, it still takes a lawyer to steer each application for refugee status through the tortuous bureaucratic processes. Matheson & Singh are hardly the only practice in Sydney to handle this kind of work, but for some reason we seem to have been singled out for harassment by the isolationists. Perhaps it's the premises; I imagine it takes a good deal less courage to daub paint on a converted terrace house in Newtown, than to attack a gleaming office tower in Macquarie Street, bristling with security hardware.

It's depressing at times, but I try to keep a sense of perspective. Sweet F.A. will never be more than a bunch of thugs and vandals, high in nuisance value, but politically irrelevant. I've seen them on TV, marching around their "training camps" in designer camouflage, or sitting in lecture theatres, watching recorded speeches by their guru, Jack Kelly, or (oblivious to the irony) messages of "international solidarity" from similar organisations in Europe and North America. They get plenty of media coverage, but apparently it hasn't done much for their recruitment rate. Freak shows are like that; everybody wants to watch, but nobody wants to join.

Ranjit arrives a few minutes later, carrying a CD; he mimes staggering under its weight. "Latest set of amendments to the UNHCR regulations. It's going to be a long day."

I groan. "I'm having dinner with Loraine tonight. Why don't we just feed the bloody thing to LEX and ask for a summary?"

"And get disbarred at the next audit? No thanks." The Law Society has strict rules on the use of pseudo-intelligent software—terrified of putting ninety percent of its members out of work. The irony is, they use state-of-the-art software, programmed with all the forbidden knowledge, to scrutinise each practice's expert systems and make sure that they haven't been taught more than they're permitted to know.

"There must be twenty firms, at least, who've taught their systems Tax Law—"

"Sure. And they have programmers on seven-figure salaries to cover their tracks." He tosses me the CD. "Cheer up. I had a quick peek at home—there are some good decisions buried in here. Just wait until you get to paragraph 983."

"I saw the strangest thing at work today."

"Yeah?" I feel queasy already. Loraine is a forensic pathologist; when she says *strange*, it's likely to mean that some corpse's liquefying flesh was a different colour than usual.

"I was examining a vaginal swab from a woman who'd been raped early this morning, and—"

"Oh, *please*—"

She scowls. "What? You won't let me talk about autopsies; you won't let me talk about blood stains. You're always telling me about your own boring work—"

"I'm sorry. Go on. Just . . . keep your voice down." I glance around the restaurant. Nobody seems to be staring, yet, but I know from experience that there's something about discussions concerning genital secretions that seems to make the words carry further than other conversation. "I was examining this swab. There were spermatozoa visible—and tests for other components of semen were positive—so there was no doubt whatsoever that this woman had had intercourse. I also found traces of serum proteins that didn't match her blood type. So far, just what you'd expect, okay? But when I did a DNA profile, the only genotype that showed up was the victim's."

She looks at me pointedly, but the significance escapes me.

"Is that so unusual? You're always saying that things can go wrong with DNA tests. Samples get contaminated, or degraded—"

She cuts me off impatiently. "Yes, but I'm not talking about some three-week-old blood-stained knife. This sample was taken half an hour after the crime. It reached me for analysis a couple of hours later. I saw undamaged sperm under the microscope; if I'd added the right nutrients, they would have started swimming before my eyes. That's not what I'd call *degraded*."

"Okay. You're the expert, I'll take your word for it: the sample wasn't degraded. Then what's the explanation?"

"I don't know."

To avoid making a complete fool of myself, I try to dredge up enough of the two-week forensic science course I sat through ten years ago as part of Criminal Law. "Maybe the rapist just didn't have any of the genes you were looking for. Isn't the whole point that they're variable?"

She sighs. "Variable *in length*. Restriction fragment length polymorphisms—RFLPs. They're not something that people simply 'have' or 'don't have.' They're long stretches of the same sequence, repeated over and over; it's the number of repeats—the length—that varies from person to person. Listen, it's very simple: you chop up the DNA with restriction enzymes and put the mixture of fragments onto an electrophoresis gel; the smaller the fragment, the faster it moves across the gel, so everything gets sorted out by size. Then you transfer the smeared-out sample from the gel onto a membrane—to fix it in place—and add radioactive probes, little pieces of complementary DNA that will only bind to the fragments you're interested in. Make a contact photograph of the radiation, to show where these probes have bound, and the pattern you get is a series of bands, one band for each different fragment length. Are you with me so far?"

"More or less."

"Well, the pattern from the swab and the pattern from a sample of the woman's blood were completely identical. There were no extra bands from the rapist."

I frown. "Meaning what? His profile didn't show up in the test . . . or it was the same as hers? What if he's a close relative?"

She shakes her head. "For a start, the odds are pretty tiny that even a brother could have inherited *exactly* the same set of RFLPs. But on top of that, the serum protein differences virtually rule out a family member."

"Then what's the alternative? He has no profile? Is it absolutely certain that *everyone* has these sequences? I don't know . . . couldn't there be some kind of rare mutation, where they're missing completely?"

"Hardly. We look at ten different RFLPs. Everyone has two copies of each—one from each parent. The probability of anyone having *twenty* separate mutations—"

"I get the picture. Okay—it's a mystery. So what do you do next? There must be other experiments you can try."

She shrugs. "We're only meant to do tests that are officially requested. I've reported the results, and nobody's said, 'Drop everything and get some useful data out of that sample.' There are no suspects in the case yet, anyway—or at least, we haven't been sent any samples to compare with the evidence. So the whole thing's academic really."

"So after ear-bashing me for ten minutes, you're just going to forget about it? I don't believe that. Where's your scientific curiosity?"

She laughs. "I don't have time for luxuries like that. We're a production line, not a research lab. Do you know how many samples we process a day? I can't do a post-mortem on every swab that doesn't give perfect textbook results."

Our food arrives. Loraine attacks her meal with gusto; I pick at the edges of mine. Between mouthfuls, she says innocently, "Not during working hours, that is."

I stare at the TV screen with growing disbelief.

"So you're saying that Australia's fragile ecology simply can't support any further population growth?"

Senator Margaret Allwick is leader of the Green Alliance. Their slogan is: *One world, one future*. Or it was last time I voted for them.

"That's exactly right. Our cities are massively overcrowded; urban sprawl is encroaching on important habitats; new water supplies are getting harder to find. Of course, natural increase has to be reined in too—but by far the greatest pressure is coming from immigration. Obviously, it's going to require some very complex policy initiatives, acting over decades, to get our birth rate under control—whereas the influx of migrants is a factor which can be adjusted very rapidly. The legislation we're introducing will take full advantage of that flexibility."

Take full advantage of that flexibility. What does that mean? Slam the doors and pull up the drawbridge?

"Many commentators have expressed surprise that the Greens have found themselves siding on this issue with some of the most extreme far-right groups."

The Senator scowls. "Yes, but the comparison is fatuous. Our motives are entirely different. It's ecological destruction that's caused the refugee problem in the first place; putting more strain on our own delicate environment would hardly be helping things in the long term, would it? We must safeguard what we have, for the sake of our children."

A subtitle flashes onto the screen: *FEEDBACK ENABLED*.

I hit the *INTERACT* button on the remote control, hurriedly compose my thoughts, then speak into the microphone. "But what do these people do now? Where do they go? *Their* environments are not just 'fragile' or 'delicate'; they're disaster areas! Wherever a refugee is coming from, you can bet it's a place where overpopulation is doing a thousand times more damage than it is here."

My words race down fibre-optic cables into the studio computer—along with those of a few hundred thousand other viewers. In a second or two, all the questions received will be interpreted, standardised, assessed for relevance and legal implications, and then ranked by popularity.

The simulacrum reporter says, "Well, Senator, it seems that the viewers have voted for a commercial break now, so . . . thank you for your time."

"My pleasure."

As she undresses, Loraine says, "You haven't been forgetting your shots, have you?"

"What? And risk losing my glorious physique?" One side-effect of the contraceptive injections is increased muscle mass, although in truth it's barely noticeable.

"Just checking."

She switches out the light and climbs into bed. We embrace; her skin is cold as marble. She kisses me gently, then says, "I don't feel like making love tonight, okay? Just hold me."

"Okay."

She's silent for a while, then she says, "I did some more tests on that sample last night."

"Yeah?"

"I separated out some of the spermatozoa, and tried to get a DNA profile from them. But the whole thing was blank, except for some faint non-specific binding at the very start of the gel. It's as if the restriction enzymes hadn't even cut the DNA."

"Meaning what?"

"I'm not sure yet. At first I thought, maybe this guy's done some tampering—infected himself with an engineered virus which got into the stem cells in the bone marrow and the testis, and chopped out all the sequences we use for profiling."

"Urk. Isn't that rather extreme? Why not just use a condom?"

"Well, yes. Most rapists do. And it makes no sense in any case; if someone wanted to avoid identification, cutting out the sequences completely would be stupid. Far better to make random changes—that would muddy the water, screw up the tests, without being so obvious."

"But . . . if a mutation's too improbable, and deleting the sequences intentionally is stupid, what's left? I mean, the sequences *are not there,* are they? You've proved that."

"Hang on, there's more. I tried amplifying a gene with the polymerase chain reaction. A gene everybody has in common. In fact, a gene every organism on this planet *back to yeast* has in common."

"And?"

"Nothing. Not a trace."

My skin crawls, but I laugh. "What are you trying to say? He's an alien?"

"With human-looking sperm, and human blood proteins? I doubt it.

"What if the sperm were . . . malformed somehow? I don't mean degraded by exposure—but abnormal to start with. Genetically damaged. Missing parts of chromosomes . . . *?"

"They look perfectly healthy to me. And I've *seen* the chromosomes; they look normal too."

"Apart from the fact that they don't seem to contain any genes."

"None that I've looked for; that's a long way from none at all." She shrugs. "Maybe there's something contaminating the sample, something which has bound to the DNA, blocking the polymerase and the restriction enzymes. Why it's only affected the rapist's DNA, I don't know—but different types of cells are permeable to different substances. It can't be be ruled out."

I laugh. "After all this fuss . . . isn't that what I said in the first place? Contamination?"

She hesitates. "I do have another theory—although I haven't been able to test it yet. I don't have the right reagents."

"Go on."

"It's pretty far-fetched."

"More so than aliens and mutants?"

"Maybe."

"I'm listening."

She shifts in my arms. "Well . . . You know the structure of DNA: two helical strands of sugar and phosphate, joined by the base pairs which carry the genetic information. The natural base pairs are adenine and thymine, cytosine and guanine . . . But people *have* synthesised other bases, and incorporated them into DNA and RNA. And around the turn of the century, a group in Berne actually constructed an entire bacterium that used nonstandard bases."

"You mean, they rewrote the genetic code?"

"Yes and no. They kept the code, but they changed the alphabet; they just substituted a new base for each old one, consistently throughout. The hard part wasn't making the non-standard DNA, the hard part was adapting the rest of the cell to make sense of it. The ribosomes—where RNA gets translated into proteins—had to be redesigned, and they had to alter almost every enzyme that interacted with DNA or RNA. They also had to invent ways for the cell to manufacture the new bases. And of course, all these changes had to be encoded in the genes.

"The whole point of the exercise was to circumvent fears about recombinant DNA techniques—because if *these* bacteria escaped, their genes could never cross over into any wild strains; no natural organism could possibly make use of them. Anyway, the whole idea turned out to be uneconomical. There were cheaper ways to meet the new safety requirements, and there was just too much hard work involved in 'converting' each new species of bacterium that the biotechnologists might have wanted to use."

"So . . . what are you getting at? Are you saying these bacteria are still around? The rapist has some mutant venereal disease which is screwing up your tests?"

"No, no. Forget the bacteria. But suppose someone went further. Suppose someone went on and did the same thing with multicellular organisms."

"Well, did they?"

"Not openly."

"You think someone did this with animals, in secret? And then what? *Did it with humans?* You think someone's raised *human beings* with this . . . alternative DNA?" I stare at her, horrified. "*That* is the most obscene thing I have ever heard."

"Don't get all worked up. It's just a theory."

"But . . . what would they be like? What would they *live on*? Could they eat normal food?"

"Sure. All their proteins would be built from the same amino acids as ours. They'd have to synthesise the non-standard bases from precursors in their food—but ordinary people have to synthesise the *standard* bases, so that's no big deal. If all the details had been worked out properly—if all the hormones and enzymes that bind to DNA had been appropriately modified—they wouldn't be sick, or deformed, in any way. They'd look perfectly normal. Ninety percent of every cell in their body would be just the same as ours."

"But . . . why do it in the first place? The bacteria were for a reason, but what conceivable advantage is there for a human being to have non-standard DNA? Besides screwing up forensic tests."

"I've thought of one thing; they'd be immune to viruses. All viruses."

"Why?"

"Because a virus needs all the cellular machinery that works with *normal* DNA and RNA. Viruses would still be able to get into these people's cells—but once they were inside, they wouldn't be able to reproduce. With everything in the cell adapted to the new system, a virus made up of standard bases would just be a piece of meaningless junk. *No virus that harms ordinary people could harm someone with non-standard DNA.*"

"Okay, so these hypothetical tailor-made children can't catch influenza, or AIDS, or herpes. So what? If someone was serious about wiping out viral diseases, they'd concentrate on methods that would work for *everyone*: cheaper drugs and vaccines. What use would this technology be in Zaire or Uganda? It's ludicrous! I mean, how many people do they think would *want* to have children this way, even if they could afford it?"

Loraine gives me an odd look, then says, "Obviously, it would only be for a wealthy elite. And as for other kinds of treatment: viruses *mutate*. New strains come along. In time, any drug or vaccine can lose its effectiveness. *This* immunity would last forever. No amount of mutation could ever produce a virus built out of anything but the old bases."

"Sure, but . . . but this 'wealthy elite' with lifelong immunity—mostly to diseases they're not likely to catch in the first place—wouldn't even be able to have children, would they? Not by normal means."

"Except with each other."

"Except with each other. Well, that sounds like a pretty drastic side-effect to me."

She laughs, and suddenly relaxes. "You're right, of course . . . and I told you: I have no evidence, this is all pure fantasy. The reagents I need should arrive in a couple of days; then I can test for the alternative bases—and rule out the whole crazy idea, once and for all."

It's almost eleven when I realise that I'm missing two important files. I can't phone the office computer from home; certain classes of legal documents are required to reside only on systems with no connection whatsoever to public networks. So I have no choice but to go in, in person, and copy the files.

I spot the graffitist from a block away. He looks about twelve years old. He's dressed in black, but otherwise doesn't seem too worried about being seen—and his brazenness is probably justified; cyclists go by, ignoring him, and patrol cars are scarce around here. At first, I'm simply irritated; it's late and I've got work to do. I'm not in the mood for confrontation. The easiest thing, by far, might be to wait until he's gone.

Then I catch myself. *Am I that apathetic?* I couldn't care less if graffiti artists redecorate every last building and train in the city—but this is racist poison. Racist poison that I waste twenty minutes cleaning away, every morning.

I draw closer, still unnoticed. Before I can change my mind, I slip through the wrought iron gate, which he's left ajar; the lock was smashed months ago, and we've never bothered replacing it. As I move across the courtyard, he hears me and spins around. He steps towards me and raises the paint gun to eye level, but I knock it out of his hand. *That* makes me angry; I could have been blinded. He runs for the fence, and gets half-way up; I grab him by the belt of his jeans and haul him down. Just as well—the spikes are sharp, and rusty.

I let go of his belt and he turns around slowly, glaring at me, trying to look menacing but failing badly. "Keep your fucking hands off me! You're not a cop."

"Ever heard of citizen's arrest?" I step back and push the gate shut. So, what now? Invite him inside so I can phone the police?

He grabs hold of a fence railing; clearly, he's not going anywhere without a struggle. Shit. What am I going to do—drag him into the building, kicking and screaming? I don't have much stomach for assaulting children, and I'm on shaky legal ground already.

So it's stalemate.

I lean against the gate.

"Just tell me one thing." I point at the wall. "*Why?* Why do you do it?"

He snorts. "I could ask you the same fucking question."

"About what?"

"About helping *them* stay in the country. Taking our jobs. Taking our houses. Fucking things up for all of us."

I laugh. "You sound like my grandfather. *Them* and us. That's the kind of twentieth-century bullshit that wrecked the planet. You think you can build a fence around this country and just forget about everything outside? Draw some artificial line on a map and say: people inside matter, people outside don't?"

"Nothing artificial about the ocean."

"No? They'll be pleased to hear that in Tasmania."

He just scowls at me, disgusted. There's nothing to communicate, nothing to understand. The anti-refugee lobby are always talking about *preserving our common values*; that's pretty funny. Here we are, two Anglo Australians—probably born in the very same city—and our values couldn't be further apart if we'd come from different planets.

He says, "*We* didn't ask them to breed like vermin. It's not our fault. So why should we help them? Why should *we* suffer? They can all just fuck off and die. Drown in their own shit and die. That's what I think, okay?"

I step away from the gate and let him pass. He crosses the street, then turns to yell obscenities. I go inside and get the bucket and scrubbing brush, but all I end up doing is smearing wet paint across the wall.

By the time I've plugged my lap-top into the office machine, I'm not angry—or even depressed—any more; I'm simply numb.

Just to complete the perfect evening, half-way through transferring one of my files, the power fails. I sit in the dark for an hour, waiting to see if it will come back on; but it doesn't, so I walk home.

Things are looking up; there's no doubt about it.

The Allwick Bill was defeated—and the Greens have a new leader, so there's hope for them yet.

Jack Kelly is in prison for arms smuggling. Sweet F.A. still put up their moronic posters—but there's a group of antifascist students who spend their spare time tearing them down. Since Ranjit and I scraped up enough money for an alarm system, there's been no more graffiti; and lately even the threatening letters have become rare.

Loraine and I are married now. We're happy together, and happy in our jobs. She's been promoted to laboratory manager, and the work at Matheson & Singh is booming—even the kind that pays. I really couldn't ask for more. Sometimes we talk about adopting a child, but the truth is we don't have the time.

We don't often talk about the night I caught the graffitist. The night the inner city was blacked-out, for six hours. The night several freezers full of forensic samples were spoiled. Loraine refuses to entertain any paranoid theories about this; the evidence is gone, she says. Speculation is pointless.

I do sometimes wonder, though, just how many people there might be who hold the very same views as the screwed-up child. Not in terms of nations, not in terms of race; but people who've marked their very own lines to separate *us* and *them*. Who aren't buffoons in jackboots, parading for the cameras; who are intelligent, resourceful, far-sighted. And silent.

And I wonder what kind of fortresses they're building.

VOICES

Jack Dann

Jack Dann is one of the most respected writer/editors of his generation. His books include the critically acclaimed novel *The Man Who Melted*, as well as *Junction*, *Starhiker*, and a collection of his short fiction, *Timetipping*. As an anthologist, he edited the well-known anthology *Wandering Stars*; his other anthologies include *More Wandering Stars, Immortal, Faster than Light* (co-edited with George Zebrowski), and several fantasy anthologies co-edited with Gardner Dozois. His story "Blind Shemmy" was in our First Annual Collection; his "Bad Medicine" was in our Second Annual Collection; and his "Tattoos" was in our Fourth Annual Collection. His most recent book is the acclaimed Vietnam War anthology *In the Field of Fire*, co-edited with Jeanne Van Buren Dann. Upcoming are two new novels, *High Steel* (written with Jack C. Haldeman II), and *The Path of Remembrance*.

In the sad but lyrical story that follows, he shows us a troubled young boy struggling to come to terms with one of the basic facts of life—death.

I was carefully papering the balsawood wing struts of my scale-model Gotha G V bomber when Crocker asked me if I ever spoke to dead people.

Although Crocker is a member of the Susquehanna River Modelmakers and Sex Fiends Association (which doesn't say much because all you have to do to become a member is hang out in the shack by the river and make models), everybody thinks he's right off his nut. One of the guys nicknamed him Crock-a-shit because of all the stupid stories he told—and the stupid questions he asked—and the name stuck. Hell, he seemed to like it. But nobody broke his arms or his legs or smashed up his models, and so he stayed on, sort of like a mascot. He was fat, freckled, and wore his white-blond hair in a brush cut. But he was also smart, in his way. He was twelve, a year younger than me, and was in seventh-grade honors.

"Steve, you hear me or what?" he asked me, turning down the volume on the club's battery-powered radio. It was playing the Big Bopper's "Chantilly Lace." Since Buddy Holly, Ritchie Valens, and the Big Bopper had died in a plane crash back in February, the radio stations were still playing their stuff all the time—and here it was June! "You ever talk to a dead person or not?"

"No, Crocker," I said. I was trying to work the air bubbles out of the paper: This Gotha was the only model of its kind and would have a wingspan of over six feet. My stepfather had given me the kit for my birthday. "I never talked to anybody who's dead . . . except maybe you. Now turn the volume back up." But the song was over and the disc jockey was saying something about Lou Costello, who died back in March. I could never remember if he was the fat comedian or the skinny one; but I only liked the fat one and hoped it wasn't him.

Anyway, this was frustrating work, and Crock-a-shit was, as usual, fouling everything up. I have to admit, though, that he had made me curious; but just thinking about dead people made me feel jittery, and sad, too. It made me think of my dad, my real dad, who died in the hospital when I was seven. Funny, the things you remember. I used to play a game with him when he came home from the office every night. We had a leather couch in the den—Dad called it "The Library"—and I would slide my hand back and forth on the cushion while he would try to catch it. And then when he did, he would hold it tight and we'd laugh. Dad had gray hair, and everybody said he was handsome. But when he was in the hospital, he didn't even know who Mom and I were. He thought Mom was *his* mother! She cried when he got mixed up, and I just felt weird about it. Especially when he had an attack and then talked in a language that sounded like Op-talk. Mom said it was because his brain wasn't working right. I knew that if I could only understand it, everything would be all right. It was like he was trying to tell me what to do in some secret language; and if I could only figure out the words, I'd be able to help him get well. But then he died, and I never got to say good-bye in a way he could understand because his brain never did get right again.

Crocker didn't say anything more for a while, which was unusual for him.

When I had finished the wings, which weren't right and would have to be redone again, I looked up and said, "Crock-a-shit, what are you looking at?"

"Nothin'."

"What's with all this dead people stuff?" I asked, trying to treat him like a human being.

"I just wanted to know if you have ever done it, that's all."

"Done what?"

"I just told you! Talk to dead people."

"Have *you*?" I asked, knowing for sure I would get one of his bullshit answers.

"Yeah, I do it a few times a week. When I don't come down here."

"Oh, sure, and where do you do that?"

"Every day I check the paper to see if there's anything going on at the funeral home on the corner of Allen and Main. If there is, I just sort of walk in and talk to the corpse in the casket. If not, I come over here."

"And nobody says nothing to you? They just let you walk in and talk to dead people?"

"They ain't bothered me yet." After a pause, he said, "You wanna go with me today? They got somebody in there," and he showed me the obituary column from the *Sun-Bulletin*. I glanced at what he was trying to show me and shook out the sports section. Patterson was fighting Ingemar Johansson on Friday. I was rooting for Patterson, who had KO'd Archie Moore in '56.

"You wanna go with me and see for yourself or not?" Crocker asked, indignantly ripping the paper out of my hands. "Or are you afraid?"

"Screw you!"

"You probably never been to a funeral in your life."

"I've been to funerals before," I said. "Everybody has."

"But did you ever *see* a dead person?"

I had to say no to that. "I never even saw my own father after he died."

That certainly shut him up, but he had such a sorrowful look on his face that I felt sorry for him.

"I'm Jewish," I said, "and Jews can't have open caskets. Of course, there must be a reason for that, but I don't know what it is."

"How'd he die?" Crocker asked, fumbling around with his hands as if he wasn't used to having them.

"Something wrong with his liver."

"Like from drinking?" he asked.

"No, it was nothing like that," I said. But I had heard my mother talking to the doctor; maybe he did get sick from drinking, although I swear I can't remember seeing him drunk or anything. And I had just about had it with Crocker's questions; he was acting like Jack Webb on *Dragnet*. You'd think he would have to shut up after I told him about my father. But not Crocker. He was a nosy little bastard. After a pause, he asked, "Did you ever talk to him after he died?"

"You're out of your freaking gourd, Crocker. Nobody but an a-hole thinks he can talk to people after they're dead."

"If you come with me today, I'll prove it to you."

"No way, sucker. I got better things to do than act like a nimblenarm."

"With your father being dead and all, I can't blame you for being afraid," Crocker said. "I'd be, too."

"Crocker, get the hell out of my life," I said. I guess I shouted at him, because he looked real nervous. But I didn't need him spreading it all over the place that I was afraid to look at a dead person. Christ, Crock-a-shit had a bigger mouth than my mother.

"Okay," I said, "but if I don't hear this dead person talk like you say, I'm going to break your head." I said it as if I meant it.

I guess I did.

But that only seemed to make Crocker happy, for he nodded and helped me put away my Gotha bomber.

The worst part of it was that I had to sneak into my house and put on a suit and tie, because Crocker said you can't just walk in with jeans and a T-shirt.

But a deal was a deal.

I met him at the back of the clubhouse, and we walked to the funeral home. It was a hot, humid summer, and boring as hell. There was never anything to do, and even going down to the club and smoking and working on models was boring. And to make matters worse, I thought about Marie Dickson all the time. She was so . . . *beautiful*! I would see her around once in a while, but I never said anything to her. I was waiting for the right time.

Not a good way to get through a summer. Anyway, she was always with a girlfriend, and I was most times by myself. No way was I going to walk up to her and make a complete asshole of myself in front of her and her girlfriend. She hung around with a fat girl, probably because it made her look even better; it seemed all the good-looking girls did that.

"Okay, you ready?" Crocker asked as we approached the front stairs to the building, which was gray and white, with lots of gingerbread like my parents' house.

"I was born ready. Let's go."

I hated this place already.

"We'll go in right after these people," Crocker said, nodding in the direction of a crowd waiting to get past the door into the parlor. "Pretend like you're with them." So we followed them inside. I was all sweaty and the sharp blast of the air-conditioning felt good.

The old people ahead of us all stopped to write in a book that rested on what looked like a music stand; but Crocker really knew his way around here and led me right into a large, dimly lit, carpeted room with high windows covered with heavy blue drapes. People were standing around and talking, soft organ music was playing, and there was a line of people filing past an ornate casket that was surrounded with great bushes of flowers.

"Let's go see it and get the hell out of here," I said, feeling uncomfortable. I looked around. Even though this room was certainly big enough, I felt as if I was being closed up in a closet. And I figured it had to be just a matter of time before someone would see we weren't supposed to be here and kick us out.

"Wait till the line gets through," Crocker said. But a woman wearing a silky black dress and one of those round pillbox hats with a veil put her hand on my shoulder and asked, "Did you go to school with Matt?"

I looked at her, and I've got to say I was scared, although I don't really know why I should have been. "Uh, yes, ma'am," I said, looking to Crocker—who was supposed to be the professional—to pull us out of this.

"I'm his aunt Leona. You should meet his mom and dad, they're right there." She pointed to a tall balding man and a skinny woman who made me think of some sort of bird. "Stay right here and I'll get them," Aunt Leona said. "I'm sure they'll want to talk to you."

I could only nod. When the woman walked away, I said, "What the hell did you get us into?"

Crocker looked nervous, too, but he said, "Didn't you read the obituary?"

"Piss off, Crocker."

"Well, it was a kid who lived in Endicott. His family moved to Virginia. I can't remember the rest."

"You should have told me it was a kid. Christ Almighty!"

"You shoulda read what I gave you," he said in a singsong voice that made me want to crown him.

"How'd he die?" I asked.

"I dunno," Crocker said. "They don't tell you that kind of stuff in the paper."

"Well, did he go to our school?"

"I can't remember," Crocker said, but it was too late anyway, because Aunt Leona brought a whole crowd to talk to us. I was really nervous now.

What were we supposed to say to the dead kid's parents?

Although it surprised the living hell right out of me, Crocker and I managed to hold our own. We said how sorry we were and what a nice guy he was, how he played a mean stickball and was a regular nut for Bill Haley and the Comets and Jackie Wilson—you know, "Lonely Teardrops"—and it was the craziest damn thing because it was almost as if we did know this kid. With all the crying and hugging going on around us, I started to get that thunder sound in my ears, which I always used to hear before I was going to cry.

I hadn't heard *that* sound in a long time.

I didn't even hear it at my dad's funeral, or at the house when everyone stood around and told me I had to be a big boy and all that crap. It wasn't until months later that I heard the thunder sound, when I was in the house alone and practicing the piano. I looked up and saw Dad's photograph on the piano; and suddenly, like I was crazy all of a sudden, I heard the thunder and then I started to cry. It made me feel sick. But after that, I didn't cry again.

Until now.

Everybody was crying, including me, and Crock-a-shit excused both of us so we could pay our respects to the departed (that's just what he said). As soon as we were out of their reach, he said, "Steve, you're *good* at this."

"So are you," I said, pretending that it was all an act. "Now let's get it over with."

"Okay," Crocker said, and we stood right before the casket and looked into it. I could smell the flowers—the ones with the long wormy things inside them—but they didn't smell bad. The kid in the casket was wearing a suit and tie . . . just like us. He looked like Pug Flanders, who lived down the block from me: The corpse had black hair, which was greased back; he had probably worn it in a DA with an elephant's trunk in the front, but whoever did him up probably thought a flattop was the height of coolness. It looked like he had had pimples, too, but his face was coated with makeup; and it looked too white, like someone had gone crazy with the powder or something.

The expression on his face was kind of snarly: I guess they couldn't wipe it off. I had a strong feeling that I would have liked this guy.

But looking down at this corpse made me feel sort of weird. Not that I was scared anymore, but this kid didn't really seem to be dead. It was like this was some sort of a play, and everybody was acting, just as we were.

This guy just *couldn't* be dead.

He looked like he was going to sit up any second.

I blinked then because it was almost as if he was glowing like one of those religious paintings I've seen in churches. It was as if I could see the stuff of his soul, or something like that. Christ, I almost fell backward.

I knew that was all bullshit, but I saw it just the same.

Crocker didn't seem to see it; at least he didn't say anything. So it must have just been me.

And then I remembered something about my father that scared me. It just sort of came out of nowhere!

I remembered the nurse taking my arm and trying to pull me out of the hospital room. Mom was crying and screaming, and she fell right on top of Dad on the bed. But I got one last look at Dad; and he looked like he was made up of light, sort of like a halo was around him and all over him.

How could I have forgotten something like that?

But I did. I must have just pushed it right out of my mind.

"How d'you think he died?" I asked Crocker. Hearing my own voice made me feel normal again. And that was important right now.

"Who knows? Probably some sort of accident."

"Nah, he looks too good."

"That don't mean nothin'," Crocker said. "They can make anybody look good as new . . . almost. He could have even had cancer."

Crocker looked up in the air.

I called his name, but he ignored me. It was as if he was listening to something. He had his head cocked like the RCA dog.

"Crocker, come *on*," I said after a while. I was starting to get worried. "Hey, you . . . Crock-a-shit."

"Shut up!" Crocker snapped. "Can't you hear him?"

"Hear what?"

"Just listen."

I listened, I really did, but I couldn't hear a damn thing. Crocker was probably off his nut, plain and simple. But I wasn't much better, not after I had just seen the corpse glowing like the hands on a watch.

Who knows, maybe the dead guy could talk. And maybe Crocker could hear him.

But I just wanted to get out of there.

I was already feeling like the walls and everything were going to close in on me.

"He's leaving," Crocker said. "He's saying good-bye to everybody. *Cool!*"

"Okay, then let's go," I said, but I couldn't help looking at the spot where Crocker seemed to be staring, and I got the strangest feeling. Then I saw it: a pool of light like a cloud that seemed to be connected to the body that was now glowing softly again.

And the light was bleeding out of the corpse like it was the guy's spirit or something.

A few seconds later the light just blinked out, as if someone had thrown a switch; and the body looked different, too, as if something vital had just drained out of it. Now it was nothing more than a shell; it looked like it was made of plastic. It was dull, lifeless.

We left then. Crocker and I just left at the same time, as if we both knew something.

And I heard thunder and remembered my father talking in the language only he could understand; and I felt as if I was drowning in something as deep and as big as the ocean.

When we got out of the funeral home, and past all the men standing around and smoking cigarettes, Crocker said, "You heard him, didn't you? I could tell."

"I didn't hear nothin'," I said, protecting my ass.

"Bullshit," Crocker said.

"Bullshit on you," I said.

"Well, you were acting . . . different," Crocker said.

I admitted that maybe I saw something that was a little weird, but it was probably just in my head. That bent Crocker all out of shape; he seemed happier than a kid with a box of Ju Ju Bees, and I got worried that he'd shoot off his mouth to everyone he saw.

I warned him about that.

"Give me a break," he said. "It's enough that the guys in the club think of me as some sort of asshole as it is. You're the only one I feel I can talk to—and I don't even really *know* you."

"Okay," I said, worried that maybe there was something wrong with *me*. Why else would Crocker feel that way? It also worried me that first I saw the dead guy glowing like my aunt's Sylvania Halolight TV, and then I saw his soul (or whatever it was) pass right out of him, leaving nothing but a body that was more like a statue or something made of plaster of Paris. But I put those thoughts away and asked, "What did the guy say?"

"His name is Matt . . . remember? He said he was scared out of his gourd until he found his grandmother."

"What?"

"His grandmother's dead. She'll show him around."

"Around where?"

"How the hell should I know?" Crocker said. "Heaven, probably."

"You gotta be kidding." I couldn't help but laugh. "You're making that stuff up." But somehow I really wanted to believe it.

"I thought you said you saw something," Crocker said, hanging his head. "And I believed you. . . . I wanted to know what you saw—"

"I said I *thought* I saw something." I punched him hard on the arm to make him feel better. "And it wasn't nothing but a glowing like a TV tube when you turn it off."

"I never saw that."

"Now tell me, what else did Matt say?" I asked.

"He *hates* Bill Haley, but we got Jackie Wilson right."

"Uh-huh," I said.

"Well, that's what I thought I heard," Crocker said.

"Why'd you say, 'Cool'?" I asked.

"Whaddyamean?"

"When you were looking up in the air, you said, 'Cool.' Don't you remember?"

"Yeah."

"Well?"

And Crocker started laughing. It was like he couldn't stop. He kept leaning forward and stumbling and then laughing even louder. I couldn't help but smile, and I kept knuckling his arm until he told me.

"He said he was going to visit the Big Bopper."

"What?"

"That's what he said. And Ritchie Valens."

"You're *so* full of crap," I said. But now I couldn't stop laughing either.

"Then maybe dying's not so bad," I said, and we fell down right there on the sidewalk on Ackley Avenue in front of a brown shingled house that belonged to Mrs. Campbell, my third-grade teacher. I don't know what it was, but I just couldn't stop laughing and crying.

Neither could Crocker.

And who knows, maybe I really *did* see something flickering in the air above Matt's dead body while he was floating around in Heaven somewhere meeting his grandmother.

And maybe he did get to see the Big Bopper.

Just like the Big Bopper probably got to see Valens and Holly . . . and probably Mozart and Beethoven, too.

And maybe the Big Bopper also got to meet my dad.

Why not? Dad would be there, standing right on line; he always liked to play the piano, all that bebop and boogie-woogie stuff. So maybe he became a musician, just like all the others.

Now, *that* would be something. . . .

FOAM

Brian W. Aldiss

One of the true giants of the field, Brian W. Aldiss has been publishing science fiction for more than a quarter of a century, and has more than two dozen books to his credit. His classic novel *The Long Afternoon of Earth* won a Hugo Award in 1962. "The Saliva Tree" won a Nebula Award in 1965, and his novel *Starship* won the Prix Jules Verne in 1977. He took another Hugo Award in 1987 for his critical study of science fiction, *Trillion Year Spree*, written with David Wingrove. His other books include the acclaimed Helliconia trilogy—*Helliconia Spring, Helliconia Summer, Helliconia Winter*—*The Malacia Tapestry, An Island Called Moreau, Greybeard, Frankenstein Unbound,* and *Cryptozoic.* His latest books include the collection *Seasons in Flight* and the novels *Dracula Unbound* and *Forgotten Life.* Upcoming is a new novel, *Remembrance Day,* a new collection, *A Tupolev Too Far,* and a collection of poems, *Home Life with Cats.* He lives in Oxford, England.

In this complex and subtle story, Aldiss sweeps us along with a man bound on a long and grueling journey of discovery to find . . . himself.

There's nothing for it when you reach the Point of No Return—except to come back.

—E. James Carvell

Many Central and Eastern European churches had been dismantled. The deconstruction of Chartres Cathedral was proceeding smartly, unhindered by Operation Total Tartary.

On the previous day, a guide had taken me around Budapest Anthropological Museum. I had wanted to see the *danse macabre* preserved there, once part of the stonework of the cathedral at Nagykanizsa. Although the panel was in poor condition, it showed clearly the dead driving the living to the grave.

The dead were represented by skeletons, frisky and grinning. The line of the living began with prelates in grand clothes, the Pope leading. Merchants came next, men and women, then a prostitute; a beggar brought up the rear, these allegorical figures representing the inescapable gradations of decay.

As I was making notes, measuring, and sketching in my black notebook, the guide was shuffling about behind me, impatient to leave. I had special permission to be in the gallery. Jangling her keys more like a gaoler than an attendant, she went to gaze out of a narrow window at what could be seen of the prosperous modern city, returning to peer over my shoulder and sniff.

'A disgusting object,' she remarked, gesticulating with an open hand towards the frieze, which stood severed and out of context on a display bench in front of me.

' "What it beauty, saith my sufferings then?" ' I quoted abstractedly. To me the *danse macabre* was a work of art, skilfully executed; nothing more than that. I admired the way in which the leading Death gestured gallantly towards an open grave, his head bizarrely decked with flags. The unknown artist, I felt sure, had been to Lübeck, where similar postures were depicted. The helpful guidebook, in Hungarian and German, told me that this sportive Death was saying, 'In this doleful jeste of Life, I shew the state of Manne, and how he is called at uncertayne tymes by Me to forget all that he hath and lose All.'

For a while, silence prevailed, except for the footsteps of the guide, walking to the end of the gallery and back, sighing in her progress, jingling her keys. We were alone in the gallery. I was sketching the Death playing on a stickado or wooden psalter and goading along a high-bosomed duchess, when the guide again shuffled close.

'Much here is owed to Holbein engraving,' said the guide, to show off her knowledge. She was a small bent woman whose nose was disfigured by a permanent cold. She regarded the work with a contempt perhaps habitual to her. 'Theme of *danse macabre* is much popular in Middle Ages. In Nagykanizsa, half population is wipe out by plague only one years after building the cathedral. Now we know much better, praise be.'

I was fed up with her misery and her disapproval. I wanted only to study the frieze. It would buttress a line of thought I was pursuing.

'In what way do we know better?'

It is unwise ever to argue with a guide. She gave me a long discourse regarding the horrors of the Middle Ages, concluding by saying, 'Then was much misery in Budapest. Now everyone many money. Now we finish with Christianity and Communism, world much better place. People more enlightenment, eh?'

'You believe that?' I asked her. 'You really think people are more enlightened? On what grounds, may I ask? What about the war?'

She shot me a demonic look, emphasised by a smile of outrageous malice. 'We kill off all Russians. Then world better place. Forget all about bad thing.'

The grand steam baths under the Gellert Hotel were full of naked bodies, male and female. Many of the bathers had not merely the posture but the bulk of wallowing hippopotami. Fortunately the steam clothed us in a little decency.

Tiring of the crowd, I climbed from the reeking water. It was time I got to work. Churches long sealed with all their histories in them were to be opened to me this day. By a better guide.

Everyone was taking it easy. Headlines in the English-language paper that morning: STAVROPOL AIRPORT BATTLE: First Use Tactical Nukes: Crimea Blazes. The war had escalated. Everyone agreed you had to bring in the nukes eventually. Hungary was neutral. It supplied Swedish-made arms to all sides, impartially.

The Soviet War marked the recovery of Hungary as a Central European power. It was a godsend. Little I cared. I was researching churches and, in my early forties, too old for conscription.

Wrapped in a white towelling robe I was making my way back towards my room when I encountered a tall bearded man clad only in a towel. He was heading towards the baths I had just left. We looked at each other. I recognised those haggard lineaments, those eroded temples. They belonged to a distant acquaintance, one Montague Clements.

He recognised me immediately. As we shook hands I felt some embarrassment; he had been sacked from his post in the English Literature and Language Department of the University of East Anglia the previous year. I had not heard of him since.

'What are you doing in Budapest?' I asked.

'Private matter, old chum.' I remembered the dated way he had of addressing people—though he had been sacked for more serious matters. 'I'm here consulting a clever chap called Mircea Antonescu. Something rather strange has happened to me. Do you mind if I tell you? Perhaps you'd like to buy us a drink . . .'

We went up to my room, from the windows of which was a fine view of the Danube with Pest on the other side. I slipped into my jogging gear and handed him a sweater to wear.

'Fits me like a T. I suppose I couldn't keep it, could I?'

I did not like to say no. As I poured two generous Smirnoffs on the rocks from the mini-bar, he started on his problems. ' "Music, when soft voices die, Vibrates in the memory . . ." So says the poet Shelley. But supposing there's no memory in which the soft voices can vibrate . . .'

He paused to raise his glass and take a deep slug of the vodka. 'I'm forty-one, old chum. So I believe. Last month, I found myself in an unknown place. No idea how I got there. Turned out I was here—in Budapest. Budapest! Never been here before in my natural. No idea how I arrived here from London.'

'You're staying here?' I remembered that Clements was a scrounger. Perhaps he was going to touch me for the air fare home. I gave him a hard look. Knowing something about his past, I was determined not to be caught easily.

'I'm attending the Antonescu Clinic. Mircea Antonescu—very clever chap, as I say. At the cutting edge of psychotechnology. Romanian, of course. I'm not staying in the Gellert. Too expensive for someone like me. I rent a cheaper place in Pest. Bit of a flophouse actually.' He laughed. 'You see, this is it, the crunch, the bottom line, as they say—I've lost ten years of my memory. Just lost them. Wiped. The last ten years, gone.'

He shone a look of absolute innocence on me. At which I uttered some condolences.

'The last thing I remember, I was thirty. Ten, almost eleven years, have passed and I have no notion as to what I was doing in all that time.'

All this he related in an old accustomed calm way. Perhaps he concealed his pain. 'How terrible for you,' I said.

'FOAM. That's what they call it. Free of All Memory. A kind of liberty in a way, I suppose. Nothing a chap can't get used to.'

It was fascinating. Other people's sorrows on the whole weigh lightly on our shoulders: a merciful provision. 'What does it feel like?'

I always remember Clements' answer. 'An ocean, old chum. A wide wide ocean with a small island here and there. No continent. The continent has gone.'

I had seen him now and again during those ten years, before his sacking. I suggested that perhaps I could help him fill in gaps in his memory. He appeared moderately grateful. He said there was no one else he knew in Budapest. When I asked him if he had been involved in an accident, he shook his head.

'They don't know. I don't know. A car crash? No bones broken, old boy. Lucky to be alive, you might say. I have no memory of anything that happened to me in the last ten years.'

Unthinkingly, I asked, 'Isn't your wife here with you?'

Whereupon Clements struck his narrow forehead. 'Oh God, don't say I was married!'

He drank the vodka, he kept the sweater. The next day, as suggested, I went round with him to the Antonescu Clinic he had mentioned. The idea was that an expert would question me in order to construct a few more of those small islands in the middle of Clements' ocean of forgetfulness.

The clinic was situated in a little nameless square off Fo Street, wedged in next to the Ministry of Light Industry. Behind its neo-classical façade was a desperate little huddle of rooms partitioned into offices and not at all smart. In one windowless room I was introduced to a Dr Maté Jozsef. Speaking in jerky English around a thin cigar, Maté informed me we could get to work immediately. It would be best procedure if I began to answer a series of questions in a room from which Clements was excluded.

'You understand, Dr Burnell. Using proprietary method here. Dealing with brain injury cases. Exclusive . . . Special to us. Produces the good result. Satisfied customers . . .' His thick furry voice precluded the use of finite verbs.

Knowing little about medical practice, I consented to do as he demanded. Maté showed me up two flights of stairs to a windowless room where a uniformed nurse awaited us. I was unfamiliar with the equipment in the room, although I knew an operating table and anaesthetic apparatus when I saw them. It was at that point I began to grow nervous. Nostovision equipment was also in the room; I recognised the neat plastic skullcap.

Coughing, Maté stubbed his cigar out before starting to fiddle with the equipment. The nurse attempted to help. I stood with my back to the partition wall, watching.

'Wartime . . . Many difficulties . . . Many problems . . . For Hungarians is many trouble . . .' He was muttering as he elbowed the nurse away from a malfunctioning VDU. 'Because of great inflation rate . . . High taxes . . . Too many gypsy in town. All time . . . The Germans of course . . . The Poles . . . How we get all work done in the time? . . . Too much busy . . .'

'If you're very busy, I could come another day,' I suggested.

He squinted at me and lit another cigar. 'I am expert in all science, so many people take advantage of me. Even when I am small boy, I must carrying to school my small brother. Three kilometre to the gymnasium . . . Now is shortage of material, I must do all. This damned war . . . Many upheaval . . . Spies and traitor . . . Everywhere same . . . Today toilet blockage and how to get repair? You cannot be nervous?'

'I have an appointment, Dr Maté. If later would be more convenient . . .'

'Is no problem. Don't worry . . . I treat many English. Get this nurse to move, I explain all.'

Maté sought to reassure me. They had developed a method of inserting memories into the brains of amnesiacs, but first those memories had to be recorded with full sensory data on to microchip, and then projected by laser into the brain. That at least was the gist of what I gathered from a long, complex explanation. While I listened, the nurse gave me an injection in the biceps of my left arm. They would need, Maté said, to append electrodes to my cranium in order to obtain full sensory data matching my answers to his questions.

'I don't really know Montagu Clements well,' I protested. But of course I could not simply refuse to co-operate, could not walk out, could not leave poor Clements without doing my best for him.

Indeed, my eyelids felt heavy. It was luxury to stretch out, to groan, to relax . . . and to fall into the deepest slumber of my life . . .

The cathedral in which we walked was almost lightless. My extended senses told me that it was vast. I asked Dr Maté what we were doing there. His answer was incoherent. I did not press him. He seemed to be smoking a cigar; a little red glow formed occasionally as he inhaled, but I could smell no smoke.

In order to keep my spirits up—I admit I was apprehensive—I talked to him as we progressed step by step. 'I suppose you read Kafka, you understand the complexities with which he found himself faced at every turn. As a psychologist, you must understand that there are people like Kafka for whom existence is an entanglement, a permanent state of war, while for others—why, at the other extreme they sail through life, seemingly unopposed. These differences are accounted for by minute biochemical changes in the brain. Neither state is more or less truthful than the other. For some truth lies in mystery, for others in clarity. Prayer is a great clarifier—or was. My belief is that old Christian churches served as clarifying machines. They helped you to think straight in "this doleful jeste of Life".'

I went on in this fashion for some while. Dr Maté laughed quite heartily, his voice echoing in the darkness.

'You're such good company,' he said. 'Is there anything I can do for you in return?'

'More oxygen,' I said. 'It's so hot in here. As a church architect, I have visited, I believe, all the cathedrals in Europe—Chartres, Burgos, Canterbury, Cologne, Saragossa, Milano, Ely, Zagreb, Gozo, Rheims—' I continued to name them for some while as we tramped down the nave. 'But this is the first time I have ever entered a hot and stuffy cathedral.'

'There are new ways. Neural pathways. Technology is not solely about ways of conducting war. It brings blessings. Not least the new abilities by which we may see human existence anew—relativistically, that is, each person imprisoned in his own *Umwelt*, his own conceptual universe.' He let out a roar of laughter. 'Your friend Kafka—I'd have lobotomised him, speaking personally—he said that it was not only Budapest but the whole world that was tragic. He said, "All protective walls are smashed by the iron fist of technology." Complaining, of course—the fucker always complained. But it's the electronic fist of technology which is smashing the walls between human and human. I exclude the Muslims, of course. Down they go, like the Berlin Wall, if you remember that far back. In the future, we shall all be able to share common memories, understandings. All will be common property. Private thought will be a thing of the past. It's simply a matter of microtechnology.'

I started laughing. I had not realised what good company Hungarians could be.

'In that connection, I might mention that Jesus Christ was evidently pretty *au fait* with micro-technology. All that resurrection-of-the-body stuff. Depends on advanced technology, much of it developed during that lucky little war against Saddam Hussein in the Gulf. Strictly Frankenstein stuff. Robbing body-bags. Dead one day, up and running—back into the conflict—the next.'

Maté was genuinely puzzled. We halted under a memorial statue to Frederick the Great. Maté had heard of Frankenstein. It was the other great Christian myth which puzzled him. This was the first time I had ever encountered anyone walking into a cathedral who had never heard of Jesus Christ. Explaining about Jesus proved more difficult than I expected. The heat and darkness confused me. I knew Jesus was related to John the Baptist and the Virgin Mary, but could not quite remember how. Was Christ his surname or his Christian name?

My father had been a Christian. All the same, it was difficult to recall the legend exactly. I was better on 'Frankenstein'. But I ended by clarifying Jesus' role in the scheme of things by quoting, as far as I could remember, from a hymn, 'He came down on earth from Heaven, He died to save us all.'

Although I couldn't actually see Maté's sneer, I felt it in the darkness. 'Where was this Jesus when Belsen and Auschwitz and Dresden and Hiroshima happened? Having a smoke out the back?'

Somehow, I felt it was rather sacrilegious to mention Jesus' name aloud where we were. The cathedral was constructed in the form of a T, the horizontal limb being much longer than the vertical, stretching away into the endless dark. Oh, the weight of masonry! Like fossil vertebrae, great columns reared up on every side, engineered to support vast weight, as if this whole edifice was situated many miles under the earth's crust, the mass of which must somehow be borne.

So I say. So I understand it. Yet those stone vertebrae, in defiance of the dull facts of physics, writhed like the chordata, climbing lizard-tailed into the deeper darknesses of the vaulting. It was the cathedral to end all cathedrals.

Maté and I now stood at the junction of the cathedral's great T. The vertical limb of this overpowering architectural masterpiece sloped downwards. We stopped to stare down that slope, more sensed than seen. Kafka could have felt no more trepidation at that time than I, though I covered my nervousness by giggling at Maté's latest joke. He claimed he had not heard of the Virgin Mary, either.

I stood at the top of the slope. With me was another church architect, Sir Kingsley Amis.

'The font is somewhere over there,' he said, gesturing into the darkness. 'But I'd better warn you it's not drinking water. Even if it was, you wouldn't want to drink it, would you?' He gave a throaty laugh.

Both he and I were greatly diminished by Dr Maté, who now made a proclamation, reading from a box. 'We're here now, on the spot you see indicated on your map, adjacent to the *pons asinorum*. Presently a devil will appear and remove one of you. I am not permitted to say where he will remove you to. We have to keep destinations secret in wartime, but I am authorised to say that it will be somewhere fairly unpleasant. As you know, the war between humanity and the rest is still on. But Geneva rules will apply, except in so far as fire and brimstone will be permitted on a strictly controlled basis. All torture will be attended by an authorised member of the International Red Cross.'

'How long do we have to wait? Is there the chance of a drink before we go?' Sir Kingsley Amis asked.

'Devil should be here shortly. ETA 2001,' Maté said.

'Shortly' was just another of the euphemisms such as surface in wartime.

It indicated an eternity, just as bombs are described as deterrents, 'This'll spoil his day' means 'We'll kill him', and 'God' means 'A ton of bricks is about to fall on you'. Myself, I prefer euphemisms.

Phew, I was so tired. Time in the building was lethargic, with every minute stretching, stretching out in companionship with the night towards infinity. Reality wore thin, bringing in illusion. At one point I almost imagined I was sitting typing while a dreadful, senseless war was waged in the Gulf. But the gulf of time I was in was much greater. Forget reality; it's one of the universe's dead ends . . .

Interest is hard to sustain, but my feeling was as much of interest as terror. Only those who enjoy life feel terror. I admired all the melancholy grandeur round me, the reptilian sense of claustrophobia. It compared favourably with the slum in which I lived.

At the bottom of the slope before us, a stage became illuminated. You must imagine this as an entirely gradual process, not easily represented in words. A. Pause. Stage. Pause. Became. Pause. Ill. Pause. You. Pause. Min. Pause. Ay. Pause. Ted. Trumpets. It was illuminated predominately in bars of intersecting blue and crimson.

Funebrial music began to play, brass and bass predominating.

The music, so kin to the lighting, was familiar to me, yet only just above audibility, as the lighting hovered just above the visible end of the spectrum.

These low levels of activity were in keeping with the enormous silences of the cathedral structure. They were shattered by the sudden incursion of a resounding bass voice which broke into song. That timbre, that mixture of threat and exultation! Unmistakable even to a layman.

'The devil!' Kingsley Amis and I exclaimed together.

'And in good voice,' said Dr Maté. 'So this is where I have to leave you.'

I was stunned by his indifference. 'What about that sewing machine?' I asked. But he was not to be deflected.

Even while speaking, he was shrinking, either in real terms or because he was being sucked into the distance; darkness made it hard to differentiate. However, I had little time to waste on Maté. Attention turned naturally to the devil. Though he had yet to appear on the dim-lit stage, I knew he was going to come for Kingsley Amis.

'I'd better make myself scarce too,' I said. 'Don't want to get in your way.'

'Hang on,' he said. 'You never know. He might be after you. Depends on whether or not he's a literary critic.'

When the devil arrived on stage, he was out of scale, far too large—ridiculously far too large, I might say, meaning no disrespect. It was hard to discern anything of him in the confused dark. He was black and gleaming, his outline as smooth as a dolphin's even down to the hint of rubber. He stepped forward and advanced slowly up the ramp, still singing in that voice which shook the rafters.

This struck me as being, all told, unlikely. It was that very feeling that all was unlikely, that anything likely was over and done with like last year's cricket match, which was most frightening. I trembled. Trembling didn't help one bit.

I turned to Kingsley Amis. He was no longer there. I was alone. The devil was coming for me.

In terror, I peered along the great wide lateral arms of the cathedral.

'Anyone there?' I called. 'Help! Help! Taxi!'

To the left was only Stygian darkness, too syrupy for me to think of penetrating, the black from which ignorance is made. As I looked towards the right, however, along the other widespread arm of the building, something materialised there like a stain: light towards the dead, dull end of the electro-magnetic spectrum.

All this I took in feverishly, for the devil, still singing, was approaching me still. Perhaps I should apologise for my fears. As a rationalist, I had but to snap my rational fingers, it might be argued, and the devil would fade away in a puff of smoke. To which I might say that, rationalist or not, I had spent too many years in my capacity as church architect investigating the fossils of a dead faith not to have imbibed something of the old superstitions. But—this was more germane—I had a belief in the Jungian notion of various traits and twists of the human personality becoming dramatised as persons or personages. This enormous devil could well be an embodiment of the dark side of my character; in which case, I was all the less likely to escape him.

Nor did I.

As I took a pace or two to my right, starting to run towards that faint dull promise of escape, a vision distantly revealed itself. Fading into being came a magnificent palladian façade, lit in a colour like blood, with doric columns and blind doorways. Nothing human was to be seen there—no man to whom I might call. If the burrow to my left represented the squalors of the subconscious, here to my right was the chill of the super-ego.

I ran for it. But was hardly into my stride when the singing devil reached me. I screamed. He snatched me up . . .

. . . and bit off my head.

To any of you with decent sensibilities, I must apologise for these horrific images. You may claim they were subjective, private to me, and should remain private, on the grounds that the world has nightmares enough. Perhaps. But what happened to me was that my head was bitten off almost literally.

My memory was wiped.

It's a curious thing suddenly to find oneself walking. Imagine yourself in a cinema. The movie begins. Its opening shot is of some character walking, walking across a featureless landscape. Photography: grainy. The shot immediately holds your interest, perhaps because our ancestors right back to the Ice Age were great walkers. Now imagine that you're not sitting watching in your comfortable stalls seat: you are that character. Only you're not in a movie. You're for real, or what we call real, according to our limited sensory equipment.

Your life has just begun and you're walking across what turns out to be Salisbury Plain. It's cold, there's a hint of rain in the breeze. The place looks ugly. But walking is no trouble. It's everything else that's trouble.

Like how you got where you are. Like what happened. Like what your name is. Like who you are. Even like—where are you going?

Night is closing in. That much you understand.

What do you do? You go on walking.

Over to your right in the distance, half-hidden by a fold of land, is a broken circle of stone monoliths. You kind of recognise it, although no name comes to you. It's the ruin of a Stone Age cathedral, taken out in the war with the Neanderthals, cobalt against the overpraised English countryside.

You continue as dark continues to fall. Your legs keep working, your pace is unvarying. You become slightly afraid of this remorseless body, asking yourself, Is it mine?

Dusk gathers about you like a coat when you climb a fence and reach a road. There is almost no traffic on the road. You try to thumb a lift from the cars as they approach from either direction, sweeping you with their head-lights. Past they go, never pausing. Bastards.

The fourteenth car stops. A woman is driving. A man sits beside her. They ask where you want to go, and you say Anywhere. They laugh and say that is where they are going. You climb in. You huddle on the back seat, unable to answer any of their well-meant questions.

They think you are a loony, and drop you in the nearest village. You are inclined to agree with their judgement. You wander hopelessly along the road, then, frightened, back into the village. The village is called Bishops Linctus. By now its streets are deserted. Lights glow inside the pub, The Gun Dog, but, with no money in your pocket, you are afraid to enter. There are countries where you might enter and be looked after in a hospitable way; you do not feel that could happen in England.

A young man in gumboots saunters along the road with a shotgun under his arm. He stares at you hard as he passes. He returns and addresses you. He is guarded but friendly. He seems not to believe you have lost your memory. Nevertheless, he takes you along to his house, which is one of a line of council houses on the edge of the village, just before the plain recommences its reign.

His old mother greets you. She is surprised, saying that Larry never speaks to anyone. He tells her to shut up. You stand there, back to the kitchen wall, while she fries up Larry's favourite meal, which is sausages and mashed fish fingers. You and Larry sit and eat at the table. It is good.

He has a room he calls His Room. It is locked. The old woman interrupts to say it is full of guns. He says to shut up. He tells you he is a farm labourer or sometimes a brickie. At present he is out of work. He lets you doss on the floor of his bedroom. The place is full of gun magazines, and there is a Kalashnikov in Larry's bed. He sleeps with it.

You express your gratitude.

'I like helping people,' Larry replies. He puts out the light.

You lie there on the floor. Despite all your worries, you feel pleasure and comfort in those words of his, 'I like helping people. Words of Jesus.' And so you sleep.

Only you're not in this movie. This is my movie. I'm for real—or what I call real, according to my limited sensory equipment.

Morning. When I woke, Larry was already up and about. I could hear his mother shouting at him. For a few seconds, I was living with this present situation. Then the edge of the abyss reappeared. I could remember nothing further back than the time I was walking over that miserable plain.

When I got up, the old woman gave me a cup of thin instant coffee. I stood with her against the sink. She had a canary in a cage.

'It's Kevin. We call it Kevin. I think it's a girl. One of the family, aren't you? Keeps me company. Say hello to Kevin. I wash it every Saturday, under the hot tap. It likes that. Don't you, Kevin? You like a nice wash under the hot tap. It's one of the family. Sing for your mummy, then. Who's a good Kevin?'

I was watching through the window, as Larry loaded boxes of ammunition into the back of an old battered Land-Rover.

His mother caught my glance. 'He's going into Swindon to try and get a job. You stay here with me. He's a dangerous driver, is Larry. We'll go down and see Dr Roberts. She's a sympathetic woman—trained in London, she was—and she'll help you.'

Larry was looking preoccupied. His movements were slow, his gaze abstracted, as if he were composing a poem in his head. Without glancing back at the house, he climbed into the cab of the Land-Rover. Nothing happened. I went to the window to watch, obscurely thinking something was wrong. The back of his head could be seen. Motionless. Not trying to start the vehicle. Just sitting there in the driver's seat.

The council houses followed the curve of the road, which wound up a slight incline. Beyond the houses was open agricultural land, the plain. The village lay in the opposite direction. From the last house, three hundred yards distant, a woman emerged, wearing an old blue raincoat and pushing a baby's push-chair. She had a scarf tied over her head and was evidently going into the village to shop.

Larry moved as she drew nearer. The window of the vehicle wound down. A rifle muzzle protruded from it. A shot sounded.

The woman in the blue raincoat fell to her knees, still clinging with one hand to the push-chair.

As three more shots rang out, the push-chair blew apart. The woman's face was covered with shreds of baby as she fell on the road.

Larry's mother had seen at least part of this. She was drying a plate on a tea towel. She dropped the plate, ran from the kitchen, and opened the front door.

'No, no, Larry! Stop it, you fool. Whatever do you think you're doing?'

Larry had descended from the Land-Rover after firing the four shots. He moved slowly, with a sleep-walker's lethargy. With that same lethargy, he snugged the butt of the rifle into his shoulder and fired at his mother. She was blown from the porch back into the passage. He fired two more shots into the house. I ran to the bedroom and heaved myself under the bed, fighting blindly with the magazines. I was sure he was after me.

There the police discovered me, four hours later, lying in a pool of my own urine.

So it was that eventually I found myself in a hospital in Swindon close to other victims of Larry Foot. After shooting the woman from the council house and her baby, and his mother, Larry had walked into Bishops Linctus and shot dead the first three people he met, wounding several others. BISH-OPS BLOODBATH screamed the tabloid headlines. The quiet little affair roused much more excitement than the Soviet War (in which British troops were involved) then reaching one of its many climaxes outside Tiblisi. Why had Larry done it? The explanation given was that he had always been keen on guns. Presumably the same explanation would cover the Soviet War.

Armed police from Bishops Magnum and Salisbury shot Larry down behind the Shell garage. He had liked to help people, poor Larry. At least he gave a little pleasure to the bloodthirsty readers of the *Sun*.

This incident got me swiftly—in an ambulance—into the realm of professional medical scrutiny. Within a few days, I again had an identity. I was Roy Edward Burnell, a university lecturer and specialist in church architecture. I had written a learned book, *Architrave and Archetype*, a thesis linking human aspiration with human-designed structures, cathedrals in particular.

The chief medico in charge of my case, a Dr Rosemary Kepepwe, entered my hospital room smiling, bringing with her a copy of my book. 'We're getting somewhere, Roy,' she said. 'We'll contact your wife next.'

I smote my forehead. 'My God, don't say I'm married.'

She laughed. 'I'm afraid so. At least, you were married. We'll soon have her tracked down—and other people in your past. What is the last thing you remember before the white-out?'

Even to me, her attitude seemed amateurish. When I said something of the sort, Dr Kepepwe explained that most of the original staff of the hospital were serving with British troops in Operation Total Tartary, in Murmansk, Usbekistan, the front in the Caucasus, and the new revolutionary area opening up round Lake Baikal. The disintegration of the Soviet Union had created a tremendous demand for medication.

'My husband was a brain surgeon,' Kepepwe said. 'The best husband a woman could have. David won the Isle of Wight Sea-Fishing Trophy two years in succession. Everyone respected him. We have three children, one

of them at Eton and one now working as a waiter in a Little Chef off the
M25 at the South Mimms Service Area. But David volunteered to serve with
Total Tartary. I had picked up a bit of surgery from him, of course, so here
I am.

'You were quite lucky to get here. Salisbury Plain is all mined these days.'

'Lucky me,' I said. But it appeared I did not know how lucky. I had
marvelled that it was such a quiet hospital, and ascribed this to efficiency.
Not so, Dr Kepepwe explained. I was the only patient in there. All the other
wards were empty. Civilian patients had been turned out three days earlier,
as the hospital prepared to receive wounded from the Eastern theatre of war.

'Anyhow, I'd better take your details,' Dr Kepepwe said, reluctantly. 'Then
I'll bring you a cup of tea. What did you say was the last thing you remembered?'

I told her. I had gone to South America to view some of the ecclesiastical
architecture there. I arrived in Buenos Aires and checked into my hotel. I
remembered going up in a gilt elevator. And then—white-out. The fear of
standing on the edge of a great abyss overtook me.

Dr Kepepwe saw the expression on my face. 'Don't worry—you're not
alone, Roy. How does it feel?'

'An ocean. A wide ocean with a small island here and there. No continent.
The continent has gone.'

As I spoke the words, some strange thing struggled in my mind. A name
almost came back to me, then died.

So I waited. Waited to be restored. To pass the time I had access to the
hospital library on VDU, together with TV and video. Also the new media
craze, the NV, or nostovision. Laser projectors could beam whole programmes into the mind, where the programmes became like your own lived
memories, though they faded in a few days. In view of my deficiencies, I
avoided the NV and stuck to the library; but little I read remained in my
mind.

What sins, what meannesses, what grave errors I had committed in the
previous ten years had been forgiven me. I waited in calm, without apprehen-
sion.

Dr Kepepwe assured me active steps were being taken to trace those who
had been intimate with me during the ten blank years: my parents, my
academic colleagues. The confusions of war, the tight security covering the
country, made communication difficult.

When she left in the evening, I wandered through the great empty building. In the dark of the long antiseptic corridors, green LEDs glowed, accompanied often by hums or growls. It was like being in the entrails of a glacier.

On the desk in Rosemary Kepepwe's office stood a photograph of her
husband David, very black, smiling genially with a large fish on a scale by
his side. I wondered about their lives; but there was nothing on which to
speculate. She was little more to me than an embodiment of kindness.

Only my slippered footsteps on the stairs, the tiles. I was a ghost among the ghosts of multitudinous lives whose CVs, like mine, had been lost. Who had lived, died, survived? A phrase came back uncomfortably from the white-out, 'the sorry jeste of Life'.

But, I told myself as I took a service elevator up to the roof, I should not think in the past tense. Any day now and the hospital would be filled again with the living—the military living, harpooned by their wounds, poised on the brink of a final white-out. They would survive or not, to accumulate more memories, happy or sad as the case might be.

On the roof, the habitations of air-conditioning plants painted black by a city's grime lived and breathed. I stood on the parapet, looking out over the town of Swindon, willing myself to feel less disembodied. The stars shone overhead, remote but always with promise of something better than the brief rush of biological existence. As I drank them in, a roar of engines sounded.

Three B-52 Stratofortresses flew overhead, from the west towards the eastern stars.

I went downstairs again, to my ward, my nest in the glacier. I must wait. Waiting did not require too much fortitude. One day soon, Dr Kepepwe would do the trick—with luck before the war-damaged moved in to supplant me in her attentions.

The days would pass. Help would come.

Indeed, the days did pass.

And then Stephanie arrived.

Stephanie was a vision of delight, tall, fine-boned, aesthetic of counte-nance, walking easy and free inside a fawn linen suit. Hair tawny, neat, almost shoulder-length. I admired the way she strolled into the ward, doing quite determinedly something not to her taste. With a cautious smile on her face. And this lady had been my wife. I could have forgotten that? I could have forgotten all the times we had enjoyed together, where we'd been, what we'd done? So it seemed. My head had been bitten off.

Like most gusts of pleasure, this one brought its pain. She sat facing me: calm, sympathetic, but at a distance I had no way of negotiating, as I listened dismayed to what she revealed of those islands, that lost continent.

Stephanie and I had married eight years ago, only four weeks after meeting in Los Angeles for the first time. We were divorced five years later. Here indeed, I thought, must lie some of those sins, meannesses, and grave errors. She broke this news to me gently, casting her clear gaze towards the window in preference to seeing my hurt. The hospital authorities had tracked her down in California, where she was enjoying success as a fabric designer and living with a famous composer of film music.

'You don't owe me anything,' she said. And, after a pause, 'I don't owe you anything.'

'It's good of you to come and see me. The war and everything, and that jumbo blown out of the skies over the Atlantic . . .'

A small laugh. 'I was interested, of course. You're a bit of medical history.'

'We had no children?'

She shook her head. 'That whole business was the reason for our falling out.'

'Shit,' I said. A long silence fell between us. I could have crossed the Sahara in it. 'Did I ever—I mean, since we split up—did I ever—did we communicate at all?'

'It was final,' she said. 'I didn't want to know. I like my new life in the States. What you did was up to you, wasn't it? But you did send me postcards. Generally of draughty old churches here and there—of the kind you used to drag me into when we were together.'

'You can't beat a good old draughty old church,' I said, smiling.

She did not return the smile. Perhaps the woman lacked humour.

'I brought a couple of your cards along in my purse,' she said. I noted the Americanism as she dipped into her handbag. She pulled out one card and handed it over, extending it between two outstretched fingers—as if amnesia was catching.

'Huh, just one card. I tore the others up, I'm afraid.' That, I thought was a little unnecessary pain she had no reason to inflict . . .

The card, crudely coloured, showed a picture of a church labelled as St Stephen's Basilica, although I saw immediately that architecturally it was not a basilica. I turned it over, glanced at the Hungarian stamp, and read the few words I had scribbled to Stephanie, only three weeks earlier.

'Budapest. Brief visit here. Making notes for lectures as usual. Need some florid Hungarian architecture. Trust you're well. Have met strange old friend—just going round to Antonescu's Clinic with him. Love, Roy.'

I went back to the Gellert. There, not entirely surprisingly, was Montagu Clements, still wearing my sweater.

He raised his hands in mock-surrender. 'Pax. No offence meant, honest, old chum. Since I lost my job I've worked as a decoy for Antonescu, luring on innocent foreigners who come here to take advantage of low Hungarian prices. Economic necessity and all that.'

'You had your hand in the till—now you've had it in my mind. Stealing a memory is like murder, you miserable slob.'

'Yes, and no doubt it will be legislated against when nostovision becomes something less than a seven-day wonder. Till then, Antonescu earns a modest dollar from his bootleg memory bullets. They're short of hard currency, the Hungarians. Let me buy you a drink.'

I almost threw myself on him. 'You've poisoned my life, you bastard, you'd probably poison my drink.'

He was very cool. 'Let's not fall out. You have a contempt for me. Think how I might feel about you. I've had to edit ten years of your memories, a lot of which weren't edifying. You should be happy to be rid of them.'

'I see, Clements—the FOAM Theory of History . . . Never learn anything. Just bloody forget. Haven't you ever heard that saying about those who forget history being doomed to repeat it? Why do you think the world's in such a fucking mess?'

He remained unmoved. 'I have no idea, old boy. Nor, I suspect, do you, for all your academic posturing. Without wishing to hurt your feelings, your last ten years were full of crap. But there—everyone's last ten years were full of crap . . .'

We were standing in the baroque foyer of the hotel, which had been built in the great European hotel age during the peaceful years preceding the First World War. I gestured through the doors, through the glass of which traffic could be seen crossing the Szabadsag Bridge. Beyond lay the dense Magyar thoroughfares, the grandiose piles of masonry, where fat profiteers sweated over their calculators.

'I was already on my way to the police, Clements, *old boy*. Don't pretend we're friends. You had me dumped on Salisbury Plain, don't forget.'

Clements turned on one of his innocent smiles. 'Just think, it could have been the Gobi . . . I interceded on your behalf. Be British, old chap—let's compromise. Let's do a deal.'

'What deal?'

He said, 'We could discuss business better in the bar. You want your memory back, eh? Don't go to the police and I'll bring you your memory this afternoon. Agree? Say three-thirty, after I've taken my customary nap. OK?'

So I agreed on it. I agreed, thinking I would go to the police later. Clements turned up at three fifty-five.

We sat at the upstairs bar with two tall glasses of iced white Eger wine, for which I paid. He produced in the palm of his right hand two slender plastic spools, which I recognised as nostovision bullets, ready to be inserted into the head-laser.

'I had some trouble getting these, old chap. How about fifty dollars each?'

'Maybe you really have lost your memory or you'd know I wouldn't fall for that. Hand them over. Why two bullets?'

He took a reflective sip of his wine. 'Antonescu's at the cutting edge of psycho-technology. We have to know our customers. They're mainly in America and the Arab World. It's a specialised market. We boiled your memory banks down into two categories—the rest we threw away, sorry to say. There's your speciality, church architecture and all that. That spool has a limited but steady sale to academics—a tribute to all the knowledge you had packed away. I suppose you'll be glad to get that back. Surely it's worth fifty dollars to you?'

'Come on, Clements, what's the other bullet?'

'A hundred dollars, old chum? It's all your life and activities with a woman called Stephanie. Very erotic stuff, believe me. Very popular in Saudi Arabia.'

I threw my wine in his face and grabbed the two bullets.

I leave it to you to decide which bullet I played first.

The Soviet War continues. Heavy fighting in the Caucasus despite bad weather conditions. Radio reports said that Alliance forces used chemical and bacteriological weapons in the Kutaisi area. Questioned, American General 'Gus' Stalinbrass said, 'What the heck else do we do? These assholes don't give up easy.'

Last night, four Georgian soldiers crossed the Tiblisi lines, found their way through a minefield, and gave themselves up to a British journalist, Dicky Bowden. One of the soldiers was a boy of fourteen.

Bowden said, 'Starved and disaffected troops like these are all that stand between our advance and the Caspian Sea.'

He was confident that the war would be over in a week or two. Say a month. Maximum two months.

JACK

Connie Willis

Connie Willis lives in Greeley, Colorado, with her family. She first attracted attention as a writer in the late seventies with a number of outstanding stories for the now-defunct magazine *Galileo*, and went on to establish herself as one of the most popular and critically acclaimed writers of the 1980s. In 1982, she won two Nebula Awards, one for her superb novelette "Fire Watch" (which also won a Hugo), and one for her poignant short story "A Letter from the Clearys." In 1989, her powerful novella "The Last of the Winnebagoes" also received both the Nebula and the Hugo, and she won another Nebula last year for her novelette "At the Rialto." Her books include the novels *Water Witch* and *Light Raid*, written in collaboration with Cynthia Felice, *Fire Watch*, a collection of her short fiction, and the outstanding *Lincoln's Dreams*, her first solo novel. Just released is a major new solo novel, *Doomsday Book*, and a new collection is coming up. Her story "The Sidon in the Mirror" was in our First Annual Collection; her "Blued Moon" was in our Second Annual Collection; her "Chance" was in our Fourth Annual Collection; her "The Last of the Winnebagoes" was in our Sixth Annual Collection; her "At the Rialto" was in our Seventh Annual Collection; and her "Cibola" was in our Eighth Annual Collection.

Here she plunges us deep into the chaotic and dangerous days of World War II London during the Blitz, when Nazi bomber planes were making lethal nightly forays through the skies above the battered and beleaguered city, and London itself was burning—and shows us that not *all* of the terrors to be encountered are the bombs falling down from the sky. . . .

The night Jack joined our post, Vi was late. So was the Luftwaffe. The sirens still hadn't gone by eight o'clock.

"Perhaps our Violet's tired of the RAF and begun on the aircraft spotters," Morris said, "and they're so taken by her charms they've forgotten to wind the sirens."

"You'd best watch out then," Swales said, taking off his tin warden's hat. He'd just come back from patrol. We made room for him at the linoleum-covered table, moving our tea cups and the litter of gas masks and pocket torches. Twickenham shuffled his papers into one pile next to his typewriter and went on typing.

Swales sat down and poured himself a cup of tea. "She'll set her cap for the ARP next," he said, reaching for the milk. Morris pushed it toward him. "And none of us will be safe." He grinned at me. "Especially the young ones, Jack."

"I'm safe," I said. "I'm being called up soon. Twickenham's the one who should be worrying."

Twickenham looked up from his typing at the sound of his name. "Worrying about what?" he asked, his hands poised over the keyboard.

"Our Violet setting her cap for you," Swales said. "Girls always go for poets."

"I'm a journalist, not a poet. What about Renfrew?" He nodded his head toward the cots in the other room.

"Renfrew!" Swales boomed, pushing his chair back and starting into the room.

"Shh," I said. "Don't wake him. He hasn't slept all week."

"You're right. It wouldn't be fair in his weakened condition." He sat back down. "And Morris is married. What about your son, Morris? He's a pilot, isn't he? Stationed in London?"

Morris shook his head. "Quincy's up at North Weald."

"Lucky, that," Swales said. "Looks as if that leaves you, Twickenham."

"Sorry," Twickenham said, typing. "She's not my type."

"She's not anyone's type, is she?" Swales said.

"The RAF's," Morris said, and we all fell silent, thinking of Vi and her bewildering popularity with the RAF pilots in and around London. She had pale eyelashes and colorless brown hair she put up in flat little pincurls while she was on duty, which was against regulations, though Mrs. Lucy didn't say anything to her about them. Vi was dumpy and rather stupid, and yet she was out constantly with one pilot after another, going to dances and parties.

"I still say she makes it all up," Swales said. "She buys all those things she says they give her herself, all those oranges and chocolate. She buys them on the black market."

"On a full-time's salary?" I said. We only made two pounds a week, and the things she brought home to the post—sweets and sherry and cigarettes—couldn't be bought on that. Vi shared them round freely, though liquor and cigarettes were against regulations as well. Mrs. Lucy didn't say anything about them either.

She never reprimanded her wardens about anything, except being malicious about Vi, and we never gossiped in her presence. I wondered where she was. I hadn't seen her since I came in.

"Where's Mrs. Lucy?" I asked. "She's not late as well, is she?"

Morris nodded toward the pantry door. "She's in her office. Olmwood's replacement is here. She's filling him in."

Olmwood had been our best part-time, a huge out-of-work collier who could lift a house beam by himself, which was why Nelson, using his authority as district warden, had had him transferred to his own post.

"I hope the new man's not any good," Swales said. "Or Nelson will steal *him.*"

"I saw Olmwood yesterday," Morris said. "He looked like Renfrew, only worse. He told me Nelson keeps them out the whole night patrolling and looking for incendiaries."

There was no point in that. You couldn't see where the incendiaries were falling from the street, and if there was an incident, nobody was anywhere to be found. Mrs. Lucy had assigned patrols at the beginning of the Blitz, but within a week she'd stopped them at midnight so we could get some sleep. Mrs. Lucy said she saw no point in our getting killed when everyone was already in bed anyway.

"Olmwood says Nelson makes them wear their gas masks the entire time they're on duty and holds stirrup pump drills twice a shift," Morris said.

"Stirrup pump drills!" Swales exploded. "How difficult does he think it is to learn to use one? Nelson's not getting me on his post, I don't care if Churchill himself signs the transfer papers."

The pantry door opened. Mrs. Lucy poked her head out. "It's half-past eight. The spotter'd better go upstairs even if the sirens haven't gone," she said. "Who's on duty tonight?"

"Vi," I said, "but she hasn't come in yet."

"Oh, dear," she said. "Perhaps someone had better go look for her."

"I'll go," I said, and started pulling on my boots.

"Thank you, Jack," she said. She shut the door.

I stood up and tucked my pocket torch into my belt. I picked up my gas mask and slung it over my arm in case I ran into Nelson. The regulations said they were to be worn while patrolling, but Mrs. Lucy had realized early on that you couldn't see anything with them on. Which is why, I thought, she has the best post in the district, including Admiral Nelson's.

Mrs. Lucy opened the door again and leaned out for a moment. "She usually comes by underground. Sloane Square," she said. "Take care."

"Right," Swales said. "Vi might be lurking outside in the dark, waiting to pounce!" He grabbed Twickenham round the neck and hugged him to his chest.

"I'll be careful," I said and went up the basement stairs and out onto the street.

I went the way Vi usually came from Sloane Square Station, but there was no one in the blacked-out streets except a girl hurrying to the underground station, carrying a blanket, a pillow, and a dress on a hanger.

I walked the rest of the way to the tube station with her to make sure she found her way, though it wasn't that dark. The nearly full moon was up, and there was a fire still burning down by the docks from the raid of the night before.

"Thanks awfully," the girl said, switching the hanger to her other hand so she could shake hands with me. She was much nicer-looking than Vi, with blonde, very curly hair. "I work for this old stewpot at John Lewis's, and she won't let me leave even a minute before closing, will she, even if the sirens have gone."

I waited outside the station for a few minutes and then walked up to the Brompton Road, thinking Vi might have come in at South Kensington instead, but I didn't see her, and she still wasn't at the post when I got back.

"We've a new theory for why the sirens haven't gone," Swales said. "We've decided our Vi's set her cap for the Luftwaffe, and they've surrendered."

"Where's Mrs. Lucy?" I asked.

"Still in with the new man," Twickenham said.

"I'd better tell Mrs. Lucy I couldn't find her," I said and started for the pantry.

Halfway there the door opened, and Mrs. Lucy and the new man came out. He was scarcely a replacement for the burly Olmwood. He was not much older than I was, slightly built, hardly the sort to lift housebeams. His face was thin and rather pale, and I wondered if he was a student.

"This is our new part-time, Mr. Settle," Mrs. Lucy said. She pointed to each of us in turn. "Mr. Morris, Mr. Twickenham, Mr. Swales, Mr. Harker." She smiled at the part-time and then at me. "Mr. Harker's name is Jack, too," she said. "I shall have to work at keeping you straight."

"A pair of jacks," Swales said. "Not a bad hand."

The part-time smiled.

"Cots are in there if you'd like to have a lie-down," Mrs. Lucy said, "and if the raids are close, the coal cellar's reinforced. I'm afraid the rest of the basement isn't, but I'm attempting to rectify that." She waved the papers in her hand. "I've applied to the district warden for reinforcing beams. Gas-masks are in there," she said, pointing at a wooden chest, "batteries for the torches are in here," she pulled a drawer open, "and the duty roster's posted on this wall." She pointed at the neat columns. "Patrols here and watches here. As you can see, Miss Westen has the first watch for tonight."

"She's still not here," Twickenham said, not even pausing in his typing.

"I couldn't find her," I said.

"Oh, dear," she said. "I do hope she's all right. Mr. Twickenham, would you mind terribly taking Vi's watch?"

"I'll take it," Jack said. "Where do I go?"

"I'll show him," I said, starting for the stairs.

"No, wait," Mrs. Lucy said. "Mr. Settle, I hate to put you to work before you've even had a chance to become acquainted with everyone, and there really isn't any need to go up till after the sirens have gone. Come and sit down, both of you." She took the flowered cozy off the teapot. "Would you like a cup of tea, Mr. Settle?"

"No, thank you," he said.

She put the cozy back on and smiled at him. "You're from Yorkshire, Mr. Settle," she said as if we were all at a tea party. "Whereabouts?"

"Newcastle," he said politely.

"What brings you to London?" Morris said.

"The war," he said, still politely.

"Wanted to do your bit, eh?"

"Yes."

"That's what my son Quincy said. 'Dad,' he says. 'I want to do my bit for England. I'm going to be a pilot.' Downed fifteen planes, he has, my Quincy," Morris told Jack, "and been shot down twice himself. Oh, he's had some scrapes, I could tell you, but it's all top-secret."

Jack nodded.

There were times I wondered whether Morris, like Violet with her RAF pilots, had invented his son's exploits. Sometimes I even wondered if he had invented the son, though if that were the case he might surely have made up a better name than Quincy.

" 'Dad,' he says to me out of the blue, 'I've got to do my bit,' and he shows me his enlistment papers. You could've knocked me over with a feather. Not that he's not patriotic, you understand, but he'd had his little difficulties at school, sowed his wild oats, so to speak, and here he was, saying, 'Dad, I want to do my bit.' "

The sirens went, taking up one after the other. Mrs. Lucy said, "Ah, well, here they are now," as if the last guest had finally arrived at her tea party, and Jack stood up.

"If you'll just show me where the spotter's post is, Mr. Harker," he said.

"Jack," I said. "It's a name that should be easy for you to remember."

I took him upstairs to what had been Mrs. Lucy's cook's garret bedroom, unlike the street a perfect place to watch for incendiaries. It was on the fourth floor, higher than most of the buildings on the street so one could see anything that fell on the roofs around. One could see the Thames, too, between the chimneypots, and in the other direction the searchlights in Hyde Park.

Mrs. Lucy had set a wing-backed chair by the window, from which the glass had been removed, and the narrow landing at the head of the stairs had been reinforced with heavy oak beams that even Olmwood couldn't have lifted.

"One ducks out here when the bombs get close," I said, shining the torch on the beams. "It'll be a swish and then a sort of rising whine." I led him into the bedroom. "If you see incendiaries, call out and try to mark exactly where they fall on the roofs." I showed him how to use the gunsight mounted on a wooden base that we used for a sextant and handed him the binoculars. "Anything else you need?" I asked.

"No," he said soberly. "Thank you."

I left him and went back downstairs. They were still discussing Violet.

"I'm really becoming worried about her," Mrs. Lucy said. One of the ack-ack guns started up, and there was the dull crump of bombs far away, and we all stopped to listen.

"ME 109's," Morris said. "They're coming in from the south again."

"I do hope she has the sense to get to a shelter." Mrs. Lucy said, and Vi burst in the door.

"Sorry I'm late," she said, setting a box tied with string on the table next to Twickenham's typewriter. She was out of breath and her face was suffused with blood. "I know I'm supposed to be on watch, but Harry took me out to see his plane this afternoon, and I had a horrid time getting back." She heaved herself out of her coat and hung it over the back of Jack's chair. "You'll never believe what he's named it! The Sweet Violet!" She untied the string on the box. "We were so late we hadn't time for tea, and he said, 'You take this to your post and have a good tea, and I'll keep the jerries busy till you've finished.' " She reached in the box and lifted out a torte with sugar icing. "He's painted the name on the nose and put little violets in purple all round it," she said, setting it on the table. "One for every jerry he's shot down."

We stared at the cake. Eggs and sugar had been rationed since the beginning of the year and they'd been in short supply even before that. I hadn't seen a fancy torte like this in over a year.

"It's raspberry filling," she said, slicing through the cake with a knife. "They hadn't any chocolate." She held the knife up, dripping jam. "Now, who wants some then?"

"I do," I said. I had been hungry since the beginning of the war and ravenous since I'd joined the ARP, especially for sweets, and I had my piece eaten before she'd finished setting slices on Mrs. Lucy's Wedgwood plates and passing them round.

There was still a quarter left. "Who's upstairs taking my watch?" she said, sucking a bit of raspberry jam off her finger.

"The new part-time," I said. "I'll take it up to him."

She cut a slice and eased it off the knife and onto the plate. "What's he like?" she asked.

"He's from Yorkshire," Twickenham said, looking at Mrs. Lucy. "What did he do up there before the war?"

Mrs. Lucy looked at her cake, as if surprised that it was nearly eaten. "He didn't say," she said.

"I meant, is he handsome?" Vi said, putting a fork on the plate with the slice of cake. "Perhaps I should take it up to him myself."

"He's puny. Pale," Swales said, his mouth full of cake. "Looks as if he's got consumption."

"Nelson won't steal him any time soon, that's certain," Morris said.

"Oh, well, then," Vi said, and handed the plate to me.

I took it and went upstairs, stopping on the second floor landing to shift it to my left hand and switch on my pocket torch.

Jack was standing by the window, the binoculars dangling from his neck, looking out past the rooftops toward the river. The moon was up, reflecting whitely off the water like one of the German flares, lighting the bombers' way.

"Anything in our sector yet?" I said.

"No," he said, without turning round. "They're still to the east."

"I've brought you some raspberry cake," I said.

He turned and looked at me.

I held the cake out. "Violet's young man in the RAF sent it."

"No, thank you," he said. "I'm not fond of cake."

I looked at him with the same disbelief I had felt for Violet's name emblazoned on a Spitfire. "There's plenty," I said. "She brought a whole torte."

"I'm not hungry, thanks. You eat it."

"Are you sure? One can't get this sort of thing these days."

"I'm certain," he said and turned back to the window.

I looked hesitantly at the slice of cake, guilty about my greed but hating to see it go to waste, and still hungry. At the least I should stay up and keep him company.

"Violet's the warden whose watch you took, the one who was late," I said. I sat down on the floor, my back to the painted baseboard, and started to eat. "She's full-time. We've got five full-timers. Violet and I and Renfrew—you haven't met him yet, he was asleep. He's had rather a bad time. Can't sleep in the day—and Morris and Twickenham. And then there's Petersby. He's part-time like you."

He didn't turn around while I was talking or say anything, only continued looking out the window. A scattering of flares drifted down, lighting the room.

"They're a nice lot," I said, cutting a bite of cake with my fork. In the odd light from the flares the jam filling looked black. "Swales can be rather a nuisance with his teasing sometimes, and Twickenham will ask you all sorts of questions, but they're good men on an incident."

He turned around. "Questions?"

"For the post newspaper. Notice sheet, really, information on new sorts of bombs, ARP regulations, that sort of thing. All Twickenham's supposed to do is type it and send it round to the other posts, but I think he's always fancied himself an author, and now he's got his chance. He's named the notice sheet *Twickenham's Twitterings*, and he adds all sorts of things— drawings, news, gossip, interviews."

While I had been talking, the drone of engines overhead had been growing steadily louder. It passed, there was a sighing whoosh and then a whistle that turned into a whine.

"Stairs," I said, dropping my plate. I grabbed his arm, and yanked him into the shelter of the landing. We crouched against the blast, my hands over my head, but nothing happened. The whine became a scream and then sounded suddenly farther off. I pecked round the reinforcing beam at the open window. Light flashed and then the crump came, at least three sectors away. "Lees," I said, going over to the window to see if I could tell exactly where it was. "High explosive bomb." Jack focused the binoculars where I was pointing.

I went out to the landing, cupped my hands, and shouted down the stairs, "HE. Lees." The planes were still too close to bother sitting down again. "Twickenham's done interviews with all the wardens," I said, leaning against the wall. "He'll want to know what you did before the war, why you became a warden, that sort of thing. He wrote up a piece on Vi last week."

Jack had lowered the binoculars and was watching where I had pointed. The fires didn't start right away with a high explosive bomb. It took a bit for the ruptured gas mains and scattered coal fires to catch. "What was she before the war?" he asked.

"Vi? A stenographer," I said. "And something of a wallflower, I should think. The war's been rather a blessing for our Vi."

"A blessing," Jack said, looking out at the high explosive in Lees. From where I was sitting, I couldn't see his face except in silhouette, and I couldn't tell whether he disapproved of the word or was merely bemused by it.

"I didn't mean a blessing exactly. One can scarcely call something as dreadful as this a blessing. But the war's given Vi a chance she wouldn't have had otherwise. Morris says without it she'd have died an old maid, and now she's got all sorts of beaux." A flare drifted down, white and then red. "Morris says the war's the best thing that ever happened to her."

"Morris," he said, as if he didn't know which one that was.

"Sandy hair, toothbrush mustache," I said. "His son's a pilot."

"Doing his bit," he said, and I could see his face clearly in the reddish light, but I still couldn't read his expression.

A stick of incendiaries came down over the river, glittering like sparklers, and fires sprang up everywhere.

The next night there was a bad incident off Old Church Street, two HE's. Mrs. Lucy sent Jack and me over to see if we could help. It was completely overcast, which was supposed to stop the Luftwaffe but obviously hadn't, and very dark. By the time we reached Kings Road I had completely lost my bearings.

I knew the incident had to be close, though, because I could smell it. It wasn't truly a smell; it was a painful sharpness in the nose from the plaster dust and smoke and whatever explosive the Germans put in their bombs. It always made Vi sneeze.

I tried to make out landmarks, but all I could see was the slightly darker outline of a hill on my left. I thought blankly, "We must be lost. There aren't any hills in Chelsea," and then realized it must be the incident.

"The first thing we do is find the incident officer," I told Jack. I looked round for the officer's blue light, but I couldn't see it. It must be behind the hill.

I scrabbled up it with Jack behind me, trying not to slip on the uncertain slope. The light was on the far side of another, lower hill, a ghostly bluish blur off to the left. "It's over there," I said. "We must report in. Nelson's likely to be the incident officer, and he's a stickler for procedure."

I started down, skidding on the broken bricks and plaster. "Be careful," I called back to Jack. "There are all sorts of jagged pieces of wood and glass."

"Jack," he said.

I turned around. He had stopped halfway down the hill and was looking up, as if he had heard something. I glanced up, afraid the bombers were coming back, but couldn't hear anything over the antiaircraft guns. Jack stood motionless, his head down now, looking at the rubble.

"What is it?" I said.

He didn't answer. He snatched his torch out of his pocket and swung it wildly round.

"You can't do that!" I shouted. "There's a blackout on!"

He snapped it off. "Go and find something to dig with," he said and dropped to his knees. "There's someone alive under here."

He wrenched the bannister free and began stabbing into the rubble with its broken end.

I looked stupidly at him. "How do you know?"

He jabbed viciously at the mess. "Get a pickaxe. This stuff's hard as rock." He looked up at me impatiently. "Hurry!"

The incident officer was someone I didn't know. I was glad. Nelson would have refused to give me a pickaxe without the necessary authorization and lectured me instead on departmentalization of duties. This officer, who was younger than me and broken out in spots under his powdering of brick dust, didn't have a pickaxe, but he gave me two shovels without any argument.

The dust and smoke were clearing a bit by the time I started back across the mounds, and a shower of flares drifted down over by the river, lighting everything in a fuzzy, overbright light like headlights in a fog. I could see Jack on his hands and knees halfway down the mound, stabbing with the bannister. He looked like he was murdering someone with a knife, plunging it in again and again.

Another shower of flares came down, much closer. I ducked and hurried across to Jack, offering him one of the shovels.

"That's no good," he said, waving it away.

"What's wrong? Can't you hear the voice anymore?"

He went on jabbing with the bannister. "What?" he said, and looked in the flare's dazzling light like he had no idea what I was talking about.

"The voice you heard," I said. "Has it stopped calling?"

"It's this stuff," he said. "There's no way to get a shovel into it. Did you bring any baskets?"

I hadn't, but farther down the mound I had seen a large tin saucepan. I fetched it for him and began digging. He was right, of course. I got one good shovelful and then struck an end of a floor-joist and bent the blade of the shovel. I tried to get it under the joist so I could pry it upward, but it was wedged under a large section of beam farther on. I gave it up, broke off another of the bannisters, and got down beside Jack.

The beam was not the only thing holding the joist down. The rubble looked loose—bricks and chunks of plaster and pieces of wood—but it was as solid as cement. Swales, who showed up out of nowhere when we were three feet down, said, "It's the clay. All London's built on it. Hard as statues." He had brought two buckets with him and the news that Nelson had shown up and had had a fight with the spotty officer over whose incident it was.

" 'It's *my* incident,' Nelson says, and gets out the map to show him how this side of King's Road is in his district," Swales said gleefully, "and the incident officer says, 'Your *incident*? Who wants the bloody thing, I say,' he says."

Even with Swales helping, the going was so slow whoever was under there would probably have suffocated or bled to death before we could get to him. Jack didn't stop at all, even when the bombs were directly overhead. He seemed to know exactly where he was going, though none of us heard anything in those brief intervals of silence and Jack seemed scarcely to listen.

The bannister he was using broke off in the iron-hard clay, and he took mine and kept digging. A broken clock came up, and an egg cup. Morris arrived. He had been evacuating people from two streets over where a bomb had buried itself in the middle of the street without exploding. Swales told him the story of Nelson and the spotty young officer and then went off to see what he could find out about the inhabitants of the house.

Jack came up out of the hole. "I need braces," he said. "The sides are collapsing."

I found some unbroken bed slats at the base of the mound. One of the slats was too long for the shaft. Jack sawed it halfway through and then broke it off.

Swales came back. "Nobody in the house," he shouted down the hole. "The Colonel and Mrs. Godalming went to Surrey this morning." The all-clear sounded, drowning out his words.

"Jack," Jack said from the hole, and I turned around to see if the rescue squad had brought the jack down with them.

"Jack," he said again, more urgently. I leaned over the tunnel.

"What time is it?" he said.

"About five," I said. "The all-clear just went."

"Is it getting light?"

"Not yet," I said. "Have you found anything?"

"Yes," he said. "Give us a hand."

I eased myself into the hole. I could understand his question; it was pitch dark down here. I switched my torch on. It lit up our faces from beneath like spectres.

"In there," he said, and reached for a bannister just like the one he'd been digging with.

"Is he under a stairway?" I said and the bannister clutched at his hand.

It only took a minute or two to get him out. Jack pulled on the arm I had mistaken for a bannister, and I scrabbled through the last few inches of plaster and clay to the little cave he was in, formed by an icebox and a door leaning against each other.

"Colonel Godalming?" I said, reaching for him.

He shook off my hand. "Where the bleeding hell have you people been?" he said. "Taking a tea break?"

He was in full evening dress, and his big mustache was covered with plaster dust. "What sort of country is this, leave a man to dig himself out?" he shouted, brandishing a serving spoon full of plaster in Jack's face. "I could have dug all the way to China in the time it took you blighters to get me out!"

Hands came down into the hole and hoisted him up. "Blasted incompetents!" he yelled. We pushed on the seat of his elegant trousers. "Slackers, the lot of you! Couldn't find the nose in front of your own face!"

Colonel Godalming had in fact left for Surrey the day before but had decided to come back for his hunting rifle, in case of invasion. "Can't rely on the blasted Civil Defence to stop the jerries," he had said as I led him down to the ambulance.

It was starting to get light. The incident was smaller than I'd thought, not much more than two blocks square. What I had taken for a mound to the south was actually a squat office block, and beyond it the row houses hadn't even had their windows blown out.

The ambulance had pulled up as near as possible to the mound. I helped him over to it. "What's your name?" he said, ignoring the doors I'd opened. "I intend to report you to your superiors. And the other one. Practically pulled my arm out of its socket. Where's he got to?"

"He had to go to his day job," I said. As soon as we had Godalming out, Jack had switched on his pocket torch again to glance at his watch and said, "I've got to leave."

I told him I'd check him out with the incident officer and started to help Godalming down the mound. Now I was sorry I hadn't gone with him.

"Day job!" Godalming snorted. "Gone off to take a nap is more like it. Lazy slacker. Nearly breaks my arm and then goes off and leaves me to die. I'll have his job!"

"Without him, we'd never even have found you," I said angrily. "He's the one who heard your cries for help."

"Cries for help!" the colonel said, going red in the face. "Cries for help! Why would I cry out to a lot of damned slackers!"

The ambulance driver got out of the car and came round to see what the delay was.

"Accused me of crying out like a damned coward!" he blustered to her. "I didn't make a sound. Knew it wouldn't do any good. Knew if I didn't dig myself out, I'd be there till Kingdom Come! Nearly had myself out, too, and then he comes along and accuses me of blubbering like a baby! It's monstrous, that's what it is! Monstrous!"

She took hold of his arm.

"What do you think you're doing, young woman? You should be at home instead of out running round in short skirts! It's indecent, that's what it is!"

She shoved him, still protesting, onto a bunk, and covered him up with a blanket. I slammed the doors to, watched her off, and then made a circuit of the incident, looking for Swales and Morris. The rising sun appeared between two bands of cloud, reddening the mounds and glinting off a broken mirror.

I couldn't find either of them, so I reported in to Nelson, who was talking angrily on a field telephone and who nodded and waved me off when I tried to tell him about Jack, and then went back to the post.

Swales was already regaling Morris and Vi, who were eating breakfast, with an imitation of Colonel Godalming. Mrs. Lucy was still filling out papers, apparently the same form as when we'd left.

"Huge mustaches," Swales was saying, his hands two feet apart to illustrate their size, "like a walrus's, and tails, if you please. 'Oi siy, this is disgriceful!' " he sputtered, his right eye squinted shut with an imaginary monocle, " 'Wot's the Impire coming to when a man cahn't even be rescued!' " He dropped into his natural voice. "I thought he was going to have our two Jacks court-martialed on the spot." He peered round me. "Where's Settle?"

"He had to go to his day job," I said.

"Just as well," he said, screwing the monocle back in. "The colonel looked like he was coming back with the Royal Lancers." He raised his arm, gripping an imaginary sword. "Charge!"

Vi tittered. Mrs. Lucy looked up and said, "Violet, make Jack some toast. Sit down, Jack. You look done in."

I took my helmet off and started to set it on the table. It was caked with plaster dust, so thick it was impossible to see the red W through it. I hung it on my chair and sat down.

Morris shoved a plate of kippers at me. "You never know what they're going to do when you get them out," he said. "Some of them fall all over you, sobbing, and some act like they're doing you a favor. I had one old woman acted all offended, claimed I made an improper advance when I was working her leg free."

Renfrew came in from the other room, wrapped in a blanket. He looked as bad as I thought I must, his face slack and gray with fatigue. "Where was the incident?" he asked anxiously.

"Just off Old Church Street. In Nelson's sector," I added to reassure him.

But he said nervously, "They're coming closer every night. Have you noticed that?"

"No, they aren't," Vi said. "We haven't had anything in our sector all week."

Renfrew ignored her. "First Gloucester Road and then Ixworth Place and now Old Church Street. It's as if they're circling, searching for something."

"London," Mrs. Lucy said briskly. "And if we don't enforce the blackout, they're likely to find it," She handed Morris a typed list. "Reported infractions from last night. Go round and reprimand them." She put her hand on Renfrew's shoulder. "Why don't you go have a nice lie-down, Mr. Renfrew, while I cook you breakfast?"

"I'm not hungry," he said, but he let her lead him, clutching his blanket, back to the cot.

We watched Mrs. Lucy spread the blanket over him and then lean down and tuck it in around his shoulders, and then Swales said, "You know who this Godalming fellow reminds me of? A lady we rescued over in Gower Street," he said, yawning. "Hauled her out and asked her if her husband was in there with her. 'No,' she says, 'the bleedin' coward's at the front.' "

We all laughed.

"People like this colonel person don't deserve to be rescued," Vi said, spreading oleo on a slice of toast. "You should have left him there awhile and seen how he liked that."

"He was lucky they didn't leave him there altogether," Morris said. "The register had him in Surrey with his wife."

"Lucky he had such a loud voice," Swales said. He twirled the end of an enormous mustache. "Oi siy," he boomed. "Get me out of here immeejutly, you slackers!"

But he said he didn't call out, I thought, and could hear Jack shouting over the din of the antiaircraft guns, the drone of the planes, "There's someone under here."

Mrs. Lucy came back to the table. "I've applied for reinforcements for the post," she said, standing her papers on end and tamping them into an even stack. "Someone from the Town Hall will be coming to inspect in the next few days." She picked up two bottles of ale and an ashtray and carried them over to the dustbin.

"Applied for reinforcements?" Swales asked. "Why? Afraid Colonel Godalming'll be back with the heavy artillery?"

There was a loud banging on the door.

"Oi siy," Swales said. "Here he is now, and he's brought his hounds."

Mrs. Lucy opened the door. "Worse," Vi whispered, diving for the last bottle of ale. "It's Nelson." She passed the bottle to me under the table, and I passed it to Morris, who tucked it inside his coverall.

"Mr. Nelson," Mrs. Lucy said as if she were delighted to see him, "Do come in. And how are things over your way?"

"We took a beating last night," he said, glaring at us as though we were responsible.

"He's had a complaint from the Colonel," Swales whispered to me. "You're done for, mate."

"Oh, I'm so sorry to hear that," Mrs. Lucy said. "Now, how may I help you?"

He pulled a folded paper from the pocket of his uniform and carefully opened it out. "This was forwarded to me from the City Engineer," he said. "All requests for material improvements are to be sent to the district warden, *not* over his head to the Town Hall."

"Oh, I'm so *glad*," Mrs. Lucy said, leading him into the pantry. "It is such a comfort to deal with someone one knows, rather than a faceless bureaucracy. If I had realized you were the proper person to appeal to, I should have contacted you *immediately*." She shut the door.

Morris took the ale bottle out from under his coverall and buried it in the dustbin. Violet began taking out her bobby pins.

"We'll never get our reinforcements now," Swales said. "Not with Adolf von Nelson in charge."

"Shh," Vi said, yanking at her snail-like curls. "You don't want him to hear you."

"Olmwood told me he makes them keep working at an incident, even when the bombs are right overhead. Thinks all the posts should do it."

"Shh!" Vi said.

"He's a bleeding Nazi!" Swales said, but he lowered his voice. "Got two of his wardens killed that way. You better not let him find out you and Jack are good at finding bodies or you'll be out there dodging shrapnel, too."

Good at finding bodies. I thought of Jack, standing motionless, looking at the rubble and saying, "There's someone alive under here. Hurry."

"That's why Nelson steals from the other posts," Vi said, scooping her bobby pins off the table and into her haversack. "Because he does his own in." She pulled out a comb and began yanking it through her snarled curls.

The pantry door opened and Nelson and Mrs. Lucy came out, Nelson still holding the unfolded paper. She was still wearing her tea-party smile, but it was a bit thin. "I'm sure you can see it's unrealistic to expect nine people to huddle in a coal cellar for hours at a time," she said.

"There are people all over London 'huddling in coal cellars for hours at a time,' as you put it," Nelson said coldly, "who do not wish their Civil Defence funds spent on frivolities."

"I do not consider the safety of my wardens a frivolity," she said, "though it is clear to me that you do, as witnessed by your very poor record."

Nelson stared for a full minute at Mrs. Lucy, trying to think of a retort, and then turned on me. "Your uniform is a disgrace, warden," he said and stomped out.

Whatever it was Jack had used to find Colonel Godalming, it didn't work on incendiaries. He searched as haphazardly for them as the rest of us, Vi, who had been on spotter duty, shouting directions: "No, farther down Fulham Road. In the grocer's."

She had apparently been daydreaming about her pilots, instead of spotting.

The incendiary was not in the grocer's but in the butcher's three doors down, and by the time Jack and I got to it, the meat locker was on fire. It wasn't hard to put out, there were no furniture or curtains to catch and the cold kept the wooden shelves from catching, but the butcher was extravagantly grateful. He insisted on wrapping up five pounds of lamb chops in white paper and thrusting them into Jack's arms.

"Did you really have to be at your day job so early or were you only trying to escape the colonel?" I asked Jack on the way back to the post.

"Was he that bad?" he said, handing me the parcel of lamb chops.

"He nearly took my head off when I said you'd heard him shouting. Said he didn't call for help. Said he was digging himself out." The white butcher's paper was so bright the Luftwaffe would think it was a searchlight. I tucked the parcel inside my overalls so it wouldn't show. "What sort of work is it, your day job?" I asked.

"War work," he said.

"Did they transfer you? Is that why you came to London?"

"No," he said. "I wanted to come." We turned into Mrs. Lucy's street. "Why did you join the ARP?"

"I'm waiting to be called up," I said, "so no one would hire me."

"And you wanted to do your bit."

"Yes," I said, wishing I could see his face.

"What about Mrs. Lucy? Why did she become a warden?"

"Mrs. Lucy?" I said blankly. The question had never even occurred to me. She was the best warden in London. It was her natural calling, and I'd thought of her as always having been one. "I've no idea," I said. "It's her house, she's a widow. Perhaps the Civil Defence commandeered it, and she had to become one. It's the tallest in the street." I tried to remember what Twickenham had written about her in his interview. "Before the war she was something to do with a church."

"A church," he said, and I wished again I could see his face. I couldn't tell in the dark whether he spoke in contempt or longing.

"She was a deaconess or something," I said. "What sort of war work is it? Munitions?"

"No," he said and walked on ahead.

Mrs. Lucy met us at the door of the post. I gave her the packages of lamb chops, and Jack went upstairs to replace Vi as spotter. Mrs. Lucy cooked the chops up immediately, running upstairs to the kitchen during a lull in the raids for salt and a jar of mint sauce, standing over the gas ring at the end of the table and turning them for what seemed an eternity. They smelled wonderful.

Twickenham passed around newly run-off copies of *Twickenham's Twitterings*. "Something for you to read while you wait for your dinner," he said proudly.

The lead article was about the change in address of Sub-Post D, which had taken a partial hit that broke the water mains.

"Had Nelson refused them reinforcements, too?" Swales asked.

"Listen to this," Petersby said. He read aloud from the newssheet. " 'The crime rate in London has risen 28 percent since the beginning of the blackout.' "

"And no wonder," Vi said, coming down from upstairs. "You can't see your nose in front of your face at night, let alone someone lurking in an alley. I'm always afraid someone's going to jump out at me while I'm on patrol."

"All those houses standing empty, and half of London sleeping in the shelters," Swales said. "It's easy pickings. If I was a bad'un, I'd come straight to London."

"It's disgusting," Morris said indignantly. "The idea of someone taking advantage of there being a war like that to commit crimes."

"Oh, Mr. Morris, that reminds me. Your son telephoned," Mrs. Lucy said, cutting into a chop to see if it was done. Blood welled up. "He said he'd a surprise for you, and you were to come out to—" She switched the fork to her left hand and rummaged in her overall pocket till she found a slip of paper, "—North Weald on Monday, I think. His commanding officer's made the necessary travel arrangements for you. I wrote it all down." She handed it to him and went back to turning the chops.

"A surprise?" Morris said, sounding worried. "He's not in trouble, is he? His commanding officer wants to see me?"

"I don't know. He didn't say what it was about. Only that he wanted you to come."

Vi went over to Mrs. Lucy and peered into the skillet. "I'm glad it was the butcher's and not the grocer's," she said. "Rutabagas wouldn't have cooked up half so nice."

Mrs. Lucy speared a chop, put it on a plate, and handed it to Vi. "Take this up to Jack," she said.

"He doesn't want any," Vi said. She took the plate and sat down at the table.

"Did he say why he didn't?" I asked.

She looked curiously at me. "I suppose he's not hungry," she said. "Or perhaps he doesn't like lamb chops."

"I do hope he's not in any trouble," Morris said, and it took me a minute to realize he was talking about his son. "He's not a bad boy, but he does things without thinking. Youthful high spirits, that's all it is."

"He didn't eat the cake either," I said. "Did he say why he didn't want the lamb chop?"

"If Mr. Settle doesn't want it, then take it to Mr. Renfrew," Mrs. Lucy said sharply. She snatched the plate away from Vi. "And don't let him tell you he's not hungry. He must eat. He's getting very run-down."

Vi sighed and stood up. Mrs. Lucy handed her back the plate and she went into the other room.

"We all need to eat plenty of good food and get lots of sleep," Mrs. Lucy said reprovingly. "To keep our strength up."

"I've written an article about it in the *Twitterings*," Twickenham said, beaming. "It's known as 'walking death.' It's brought about by lack of sleep and poor nutrition, with the anxiety of the raids. The walking dead exhibit slowed reaction time and impaired judgment which result in increased accidents on the job."

"Well, I won't have any walking dead among *my* wardens," Mrs. Lucy said, dishing up the rest of the chops. "As soon as you've had these, I want you all to go to bed."

The chops tasted even better than they had smelled. I ate mine, reading Twickenham's article on the walking dead. It said that loss of appetite was a common reaction to the raids. It also said that lack of sleep could cause compulsive behavior and odd fixations. "The walking dead may become convinced that they are being poisoned or that a friend or relative is a German agent. They may hallucinate, hearing voices, seeing visions or believing fantastical things."

"He was in trouble at school, before the war, but he's steadied down since he joined up," Morris said. "I wonder what he's done."

At three the next morning a land mine exploded in almost the same spot off Old Church Street as the HE's. Nelson sent Olmwood to ask for help, and Mrs. Lucy ordered Swales, Jack, and me to go with him.

"The mine didn't land more'n two houses away from the first crater," Olmwood said while we were getting on our gear. "The jerries couldn't have come closer if they'd been aiming at it."

"I know what they're aiming at," Renfrew said from the doorway. He looked terrible, pale and drawn as a ghost. "And I know why you've applied for reinforcements for the post. It's me, isn't it? They're after me."

"They're not after any of us," Mrs. Lucy said firmly. "They're two miles up. They're not aiming at anything."

"Why would Hitler want to bomb you more than the rest of us?" Swales said.

"I don't know." He sank down on one of the chairs and put his head in his hands. "I don't *know*. But they're after me. I can feel it."

Mrs. Lucy had sent Swales, Jack, and me to the incident because "you've been there before. You'll know the terrain," but that was a fond hope. Since they explode above ground, land mines do considerably more damage than HE's. There was now a hill where the incident officer's tent had been, and three more beyond it, a mountain range in the middle of London. Swales started up the nearest peak to look for the incident officer's light.

"Jack, over here!" somebody called from the hill behind us, and both of us scrambled up a slope toward the voice.

A group of five men were halfway up the hill looking down into a hole.

"Jack!" the man yelled again. He was wearing a blue foreman's armband, and he was looking straight past us at someone toiling up the slope with what looked like a stirrup pump. I thought, surely they're not trying to fight a fire down that shaft, and then saw it wasn't a pump. It was, in fact, an automobile jack, and the man with the blue armband reached between us for it, lowered it down the hole, and scrambled in after it.

The rest of the rescue squad stood looking down into the blackness as if they could actually see something. After awhile they began handing empty buckets down into the hole and pulling them out heaped full of broken bricks and pieces of splintered wood. None of them took any notice of us, even when Jack held out his hands to take one of the buckets.

"We're from Chelsea," I shouted to the foreman over the din of the planes and bombs. "What can we do to help?"

They went on bucket-brigading. A china teapot came up on the top of one load, covered with dust but not even chipped.

I tried again. "Who is it down there?"

"Two of 'em," the man nearest me said. He plucked the teapot off the heap and handed it to a man wearing a balaclava under his helmet. "Man and a woman."

"We're from Chelsea," I shouted over a burst of antiaircraft fire. "What do you want us to do?"

He took the teapot away from the man with the balaclava and handed it to me. "Take this down to the pavement with the other valuables."

It took me a long while to get down the slope, holding the teapot in one hand and the lid on with the other and trying to keep my footing among the broken bricks, and even longer to find any pavement. The land mine had heaved most of it up, and the street with it.

I finally found it, a square of unbroken pavement in front of a blownout bakery, with the "valuables" neatly lined up against it; a radio, a boot, two serving spoons like the one Colonel Godalming had threatened me with, a lady's beaded evening bag. A rescue worker was standing guard next to them.

"Halt!" he said, stepping in front of them as I came up, holding a pocket torch or a gun. "No one's allowed inside the incident perimeter."

"I'm ARP," I said hastily. "Jack Harker. Chelsea." I held up the teapot. "They sent me down with this."

It was a torch. He flicked it on and off, an eyeblink. "Sorry," he said. "We've had a good deal of looting recently." He took the teapot and placed it at the end of the line next to the evening bag. "Caught a man last week going through the pockets of the bodies laid out in the street waiting for the mortuary van. Terrible how some people will take advantage of something like this."

I went back up to where the rescue workers were digging. Jack was at the mouth of the shaft, hauling buckets up and handing them back. I got in line behind him.

"Have they found them yet?" I asked him as soon as there was a lull in the bombing.

"Quiet!" a voice shouted from the hole, and the man in the balaclava repeated, "Quiet, everyone! We must have absolute quiet!"

Everyone stopped working and listened. Jack had handed me a bucket full of bricks, and the handle cut into my hands. For a second there was absolute silence, and then the drone of a plane and the distant swish and crump of an HE.

"Don't worry," the voice from the hole shouted, "we're nearly there." The buckets began coming up out of the hole again.

I hadn't heard anything, but apparently down in the shaft they had, a voice or the sound of tapping, and I felt relieved, both that one of them at least was still alive, and that the diggers were on course. I'd been on an incident in October where we'd had to stop halfway down and sink a new shaft because the rubble kept distorting and displacing the sound. Even if the shaft was directly above the victim, it tended to go crooked in working past obstacles, and the only way to keep it straight was with frequent soundings. I thought of Jack digging for Colonel Godalming with the bannister. He hadn't taken any soundings at all. He had seemed to know exactly where he was going.

The men in the shaft called for the jack again, and Jack and I lowered it down to them. As the man below it reached up to take it, Jack stopped. He raised his head, as if he were listening.

"What is it?" I said. I couldn't hear anything but the ack-ack guns in Hyde Park. "Did you hear someone calling?"

"Where's the bloody jack?" the foreman shouted.

"It's too late," Jack said to me. "They're dead."

"Come along, get it down here," the foreman shouted. "We haven't got all day."

He handed the jack down.

"Quiet," the foreman shouted, and above us, like a ghostly echo, we could hear the balaclava call, "Quiet, please everyone."

A church clock began to chime and I could hear the balaclava say irritatedly, "We must have absolute quiet."

The clock chimed four and stopped, and there was a skittering sound of dirt falling on metal. Then silence, and a faint sound.

"Quiet!" the foreman called again, and there was another silence, and the sound again. A whimper. Or a moan. "We hear you," he shouted. "Don't be afraid."

"One of them's still alive," I said.

Jack didn't say anything.

"We just *heard* them," I said angrily.

Jack shook his head.

"We'll need lumber for bracing," the man in the balaclava said to Jack, and I expected him to tell him it was no use, but he went off immediately and came back dragging a white-painted bookcase.

It still had three books in it. I helped Jack and the balaclava knock the shelves out of the case and then took the books down to the store of "valuables." The guard was sitting on the pavement going through the beaded evening bag.

"Taking inventory," he said, scrambling up hastily. He jammed a lipstick and a handkerchief into the bag. "So's to make certain nothing gets stolen."

"I've brought you something to read," I said, and laid the books next to the teapot. *Crime and Punishment.*

I toiled back up the hill and helped Jack lower the bookshelves down the shaft and after a few minutes buckets began coming up again. We reformed our scraggly bucket brigade, the balaclava at the head of it and me and then Jack at its end.

The all-clear went. As soon as it wound down, the foreman took another sounding. This time we didn't hear anything, and when the buckets started again I handed them to Jack without looking at him.

It began to get light in the east, a slow graying of the hills above us. Two of them, several stories high, stood where the row houses that had escaped the night before had been, and we were still in their shadow, though I could see the shaft now, with the end of one of the white bookshelves sticking up from it like a gravestone.

The buckets began to come more slowly.

"Put out your cigarettes!" the foreman called up, and we all stopped, trying to catch the smell of gas. If they were dead, as Jack had said, it was most likely gas leaking in from the broken mains that had killed them, and not internal injuries. The week before we had brought up a boy and his dog, not a scratch on them. The dog had barked and whimpered almost up to when we found them, and the ambulance driver said she thought they'd only been dead a few minutes.

I couldn't smell any gas and after a minute the foreman said excitedly, "I see them!"

The balaclava leaned over the shaft, his hands on his knees. "Are they alive?"

"Yes! Fetch an ambulance!"

The balaclava went leaping down the hill, skidding on broken bricks that skittered down in a minor avalanche.

I knelt over the shaft. "Will they need a stretcher?" I called down.

"No," the foreman said, and I knew by the sound of his voice they were dead.

"Both of them?" I said.

"Yes."

I stood up. "How did you know they were dead?" I said, turning to look at Jack. "How did—"

He wasn't there. I looked down the hill. The balaclava was nearly to the bottom—grabbing at a broken window sash to stop his headlong descent, his wake a smoky cloud of brick dust—but Jack was nowhere to be seen.

It was nearly dawn. I could see the gray hills and at the far end of them the warden and his "valuables." There was another rescue party on the third hill over, still digging. I could see Swales handing down a bucket.

"Give a hand here," the foreman said impatiently and hoisted the jack up to me. I hauled it over to the side and then came back and helped the foreman out of the shaft. His hands were filthy, covered in reddish-brown mud.

"Was it the gas that killed them?" I asked, even though he was already pulling out a packet of cigarettes.

"No," he said, shaking a cigarette out and taking it between his teeth. He patted the front of his coverall, leaving red stains.

"How long have they been dead?" I asked.

He found his matches, struck one, and lit the cigarette. "Shortly after we last heard them, I should say," he said, and I thought, but they were already dead by then. And Jack knew it. "They've been dead at least two hours."

I looked at my watch. I read a little past six. "But the mine didn't kill them?"

He took the cigarette between his fingers and blew a long puff of smoke. When he put the cigarette back in his mouth there was a red smear on it. "Loss of blood."

The next night the Luftwaffe was early. I hadn't gotten much sleep after the incident. Morris had fretted about his son the whole day and Swales had teased Renfrew mercilessly. "Goering's found out about your spying," he said, "And now he's sent his Stukas after you."

I finally went up to the third floor and tried to sleep in the spotter's chair, but it was too light. The afternoon was cloudy, and the fires burning in the East End gave the sky a nasty reddish cast.

Someone had left a copy of *Twickenham's Twitterings* on the floor. I read the article on the walking dead again, and then, still unable to sleep, the rest of the newssheet. There was an account of Hitler's invasion of Transylvania, and a recipe for butterless strawberry tart, and the account of the crime rate. "London is currently the perfect place for the criminal element," Nelson was quoted as saying. "We must constantly be on the lookout for wrongdoing."

Below the recipe was a story about a Scottish terrier named Bonny Charlie who had barked and scrabbled wildly at the ruins of a collapsed house till wardens heeded his cries, dug down, and discovered two unharmed children.

I must have fallen asleep reading that because the next thing I knew Morris was shaking me and telling me the sirens had gone. It was only five o'clock.

At half-past we had an HE in our sector. It was just three blocks from the post, and the walls shook and plaster rained down on Twickenham's typewriter and on Renfrew, lying awake in his cot.

"Frivolities, my foot," Mrs. Lucy muttered as we dived for our tin hats. "We need those reinforcing beams."

The part-times hadn't come on duty yet. Mrs. Lucy left Renfrew to send them on. We knew exactly where the incident was—Morris had been looking in that direction when it went—but even so we had difficulty finding it. It was still evening, but by the time we had gone half a block, it was pitch black.

The first time that had happened, I thought it was some sort of afterblindness from the blast, but it's only the brick and plaster dust from the collapsed buildings. It rises up in a haze that's darker than any blackout curtain, obscuring everything. When Mrs. Lucy set up shop on a stretch of sidewalk and switched on the blue incident light it glowed spectrally in the manmade fog.

"Only two families still in the street," she said, holding the register up to the light. "The Kirkcuddy family and the Hodgsons."

"Are they an old couple?" Morris asked, appearing suddenly out of the fog.

She peered at the register. "Yes. Pensioners."

"I found them," he said in that flat voice that meant they were dead. "Blast."

"Oh, dear," she said. "The Kirkcuddys are a mother and two children. They've an Anderson shelter." She held the register closer to the blue light. "Everyone else has been using the tube shelter." She unfolded a map and showed us where the Kirkcuddys' backyard had been, but it was no help. We spent the next hour wandering blindly over the mounds, listening for sounds that were impossible to hear over the Luftwaffe's comments and the ack-ack's replies.

Petersby showed up a little past eight and Jack a few minutes later, and Mrs. Lucy set them to wandering in the fog too.

"Over here," Jack shouted almost immediately, and my heart gave an odd jerk.

"Oh, good, he's heard them," Mrs. Lucy said. "Jack, go and find him."

"Over here," he called again, and I started off in the direction of his voice, almost afraid of what I would find, but I hadn't gone ten steps before I could hear it, too. A baby crying, and a hollow, echoing sound like someone banging a fist against tin.

"Don't stop," Vi shouted. She was kneeling next to Jack in a shallow crater. "Keep making noise. We're coming." She looked up at me. "Tell Mrs. Lucy to ring the rescue squad."

I blundered my way back to Mrs. Lucy through the darkness. She had already rung up the rescue squad. She sent me to Sloane Square to make sure the rest of the inhabitants of the block were safely there.

The dust had lifted a little but not enough for me to see where I was going. I pitched off a curb into the street and tripped over a pile of debris and then a body. When I shone my torch on it, I saw it was the girl I had walked to the shelter three nights before.

She was sitting against the tiled entrance to the station, still holding a dress on a hanger in her limp hand. The old stewpot at John Lewis's never let her off even a minute before closing, and the Luftwaffe had been early. She had been killed by the blast, or by flying glass. Her face and neck and hands were covered with tiny cuts, and glass crunched underfoot when I moved her legs together.

I went back to the incident and waited for the mortuary van and went with them to the shelter. It took me three hours to find the families on my list. By the time I got back to the incident, the rescue squad was five feet down.

"They're nearly there," Vi said, dumping a basket on the far side of the crater. "All that's coming up now is dirt and the occasional rosebush."

"Where's Jack?" I said.

"He went for a saw." She took the basket back and handed it to one of the rescue squad, who had to put his cigarette into his mouth to free his hands before he could take it. "There was a board, but they dug past it."

I leaned over the table. I could hear the sound of banging but not the baby. "Are they still alive?"

She shook her head. "We haven't heard the baby for an hour or so. We keep calling, but there's no answer. We're afraid the banging may be something mechanical."

I wondered if they were dead and Jack, knowing it, had not gone for a saw at all but off to that day job of his.

Swales came up. "Guess who's in hospital?" he said.

"Who?" Vi said.

"Olmwood. Nelson had his wardens out walking patrols during a raid, and he caught a piece of shrapnel from one of the ack-acks in the leg. Nearly took it off."

The rescue worker with the cigarette handed a heaping basket to Vi. She took it, staggering a little under the weight, and carried it off.

"You'd better not let Nelson see you working like that," Swales called after her, "or he'll have you transferred to his sector. Where's Morris?" he said and went off, presumably to tell him and whoever else he could find about Olmwood.

Jack came up, carrying the saw.

"They don't need it," the rescue worker said, the cigarette dangling from the side of his mouth. "Mobile's here," he said and went off for a cup of tea.

Jack knelt and handed the saw down the hole.

"Are they still alive?" I asked.

Jack leaned over the hole, his hands clutching the edges. The banging was incredibly loud. It must have been deafening inside the Anderson. Jack stared into the hole as if he heard neither the banging nor my voice.

He stood up, still looking into the hole. "They're farther to the left," he said.

How can they be farther to the left? I thought. We can hear them. They're directly under us. "Are they alive?" I said.

"Yes."

Swales came back. "He's a spy, that's what he is," he said. "Hitler sent him here to kill off our best men one by one. I told you his name was Adolf Von Nelson."

The Kirkcuddys were farther to the left. The rescue squad had to widen the tunnel, cut the top of the Anderson open and pry it back, like opening a can of tomatoes. It took till nine o'clock in the morning, but they were all alive.

Jack left sometime before it got light. I didn't see him go. Swales was telling me about Olmwood's injury, and when I turned around, Jack was gone.

"Has Jack told you where this job of his is that he has to leave so early for?" I asked Vi when I got back to the post.

She had propped a mirror against one of the gas masks and was putting her hair up in pincurls. "No," she said, dipping a comb in a glass of water and wetting a lock of her hair. "Jack, could you reach me my bobby pins? I've a date this afternoon, and I want to look my best."

I pushed the pins across to her. "What sort of job is it? Did Jack say?"

"No. Some sort of war work, I should think." She wound a lock of hair around her finger. "He's had ten kills. Four Stukas and six 109's."

I sat down next to Twickenham, who was typing up the incident report. "Have you interviewed Jack yet?"

"When would I have had time?" Twickenham asked. "We haven't had a quiet night since he came."

Renfrew shuffled in from the other room. He had a blanket wrapped round him Indian-style and a bedspread over his shoulders. He looked terrible, pale and drawn as a ghost.

"Would you like some breakfast?" Vi asked, prying a pin open with her teeth.

He shook his head. "Did Nelson approve the reinforcements?"

"No," Twickenham said in spite of Vi's signaling him not to.

"You must tell Nelson it's an emergency," he said, hugging the blanket to him as if he were cold. "I know why they're after me. It was before the war. When Hitler invaded Czechoslovakia I wrote a letter to the *Times*."

I was grateful Swales wasn't there. A letter to the *Times*.

"Come, now, why don't you go and lie down for a bit?" Vi said, securing a curl with a bobby pin as she stood up. "You're tired, that's all, and that's what's getting you so worried. They don't even get the *Times* over there."

She took his arm, and he went docilely with her into the other room. I heard him say, "I called him a lowland bully. In the letter." The person suffering from severe sleep loss may hallucinate, hearing voices, seeing visions, or believing fantastical things.

"Has he mentioned what sort of day job he has?" I asked Twickenham.

"Who?" he asked, still typing.

"Jack."

"No, but whatever it is, let's hope he's as good at it as he is at finding bodies." He stopped and peered at what he'd just typed. "This makes five, doesn't it?"

Vi came back. "And we'd best not let von Nelson find out about it," she said. She sat down and dipped the comb into the glass of water. "He'd take him like he took Olmwood, and we're already shorthanded, with Renfrew the way he is."

Mrs. Lucy came in carrying the incident light, disappeared into the pantry with it, and came out again carrying an application form. "Might I use the typewriter, Mr. Twickenham?" she asked.

He pulled his sheet of paper out of the typewriter and stood up. Mrs. Lucy sat down, rolled in the form, and began typing. "I've decided to apply directly to Civil Defence for reinforcements," she said.

"What sort of day job does Jack have?" I asked her.

"War work," she said. She pulled the application out, turned it over, rolled it back in. "Jack, would you mind taking this over to headquarters?"

"Works days," Vi said, making a pin curl on the back of her head. "Raids every night. When does he sleep?"

"I don't know," I said.

"He'd best be careful," she said. "Or he'll turn into one of the walking dead, like Renfrew."

Mrs. Lucy signed the application form, folded it in half, and gave it to me. I took it to Civil Defence headquarters and spent half a day trying to find the right office to give it to.

"It's not the correct form," the sixth girl said. "She needs to file an A-114, Exterior Improvements."

"It's not exterior," I said. "The post is applying for reinforcing beams for the cellar."

"Reinforcements are classified as exterior improvements," she said. She handed me the form, which looked identical to the one Mrs. Lucy had already filled in, and I left.

On the way out, Nelson stopped me. I thought he was going to tell me my uniform was a disgrace again, but instead he pointed to my tin hat and demanded, "Why aren't you wearing a regulation helmet, warden? 'All ARP wardens shall wear a helmet with the letter W in red on the front,' " he quoted.

I took my hat off and looked at it. The red W had partly chipped away so that it looked like a V.

"What post are you?" he barked.

"Forty-eight. Chelsea," I said and wondered if he expected me to salute.

"Mrs. Lucy is your warden," he said disgustedly, and I expected his next question to be what I was doing at Civil Defence, but instead he said, "I heard about Colonel Godalming. Your post has been having good luck locating casualties these last few raids."

"Yes, sir," was obviously the wrong answer, and "no, sir," would make him suspicious. "We found three people in an Anderson last night," I said. "One of the children had the wits to bang on the roof with a pair of pliers."

"I've heard that the person finding them is a new man, Settle." He sounded friendly, almost jovial. Like Hitler at Munich.

"Settle?" I said blankly. "Mrs. Lucy was the one who found the Anderson."

Morris's son Quincy's surprise was the Victoria Cross. "A medal," he said over and over. "Who'd have thought it, my Quincy with a medal? Fifteen planes he shot down."

It had been presented at a special ceremony at Quincy's commanding officer's headquarters, and the Duchess of York herself had been there. Morris had pinned the medal on himself.

"I wore my suit," he told us for the hundredth time, "in case he was in trouble I wanted to make a good impression, and a good thing, too. What would the Duchess of York have thought if I'd gone looking like this?"

He looked pretty bad. We all did. We'd had two breadbaskets of incendiaries, one right after the other, and Vi had been on watch. We had had to save the butcher's again, and a baker's two blocks farther down, and a thirteenth century crucifix.

"I *told* him it went through the altar roof," Vi had said disgustedly when she and I finally got it out. "Your friend Jack couldn't find an incendiary if it fell on him."

"You told Jack the incendiary came down on the church?" I said, looking up at the carved wooden figure. The bottom of the cross was blackened, and Christ's nailed feet, as if he had been burnt at the stake instead of crucified.

"Yes," she said. "I even told him it was the altar." She looked back up the nave. "And he could have seen it as soon as he came into the church."

"What did he say? That it wasn't there?"

Vi was looking speculatively up at the roof. "It could have been caught in the rafters and come down after. It hardly matters, does it? We put it out. Come on, let's get back to the post," she said, shivering. "I'm freezing."

I was freezing, too. We were both sopping wet. The AFS had stormed up after we had the fire under control and sprayed everything in sight with icy water.

"Pinned it on myself, I did," Morris said. "The Duchess of York kissed him on both cheeks and said he was the pride of England." He had brought a bottle of wine to celebrate the Cross. He got Renfrew up and brought him to the table, draped in his blankets, and ordered Twickenham to put his typewriter away. Petersby brought in extra chairs, and Mrs. Lucy went upstairs to get her crystal.

"Only eight, I'm afraid," she said, coming down with the stemmed goblets in her blackened hands. "The Germans have broken the rest. Who's willing to make do with the tooth glass?"

"I don't care for any, thank you," Jack said. "I don't drink."

"What's that?" Morris said jovially. He had taken off his tin helmet, and below the white line it left he looked like he was wearing blackface in a music hall show. "You've got to toast my boy at least. Just imagine. My Quincy with a medal."

Mrs. Lucy rinsed out the porcelain tooth glass and handed it to Vi, who was pouring out the wine. They passed the goblets round. Jack took the tooth glass.

"To my son Quincy, the best pilot in the RAF!" Morris said, raising his goblet.

"May he shoot down the entire Luftwaffe!" Swales shouted, "and put an end to this bloody war!"

"So a man can get a decent night's sleep!" Renfrew said, and everyone laughed.

We drank. Jack raised his glass with the others but when Vi took the bottle round again, he put his hand over the mouth of it.

"Just think of it," Morris said. "My son Quincy with a medal. He had his troubles in school, in with a bad lot, problems with the police. I worried about him, I did, wondered what he'd come to, and then this war comes along and here he is a hero."

"To heroes!" Petersby said.

We drank again, and Vi dribbled out the last of the wine into Morris's glass. "That's the lot, I'm afraid." She brightened. "I've a bottle of cherry cordial Charlie gave me."

Mrs. Lucy made a face. "Just a minute," she said, disappeared into the pantry, and came back with two cobwebbed bottles of port, which she poured out generously and a little sloppily.

"The presence of intoxicating beverages on post is strictly forbidden," she said. "A fine of five shillings will be imposed for a first offense, one pound for subsequent offenses." She took out a pound note and laid it on the table. "I wonder what Nelson was before the war?"

"A monster," Vi said.

I looked across at Jack. He still had his hand over his glass.

"A headmaster," Swales said. "No, I've got it. An Inland Revenue collector!"

Everyone laughed.

"I was a horrid person before the war," Mrs. Lucy said.

Vi giggled.

"I was a deaconess, one of those dreadful women who arranges the flowers in the sanctuary and gets up jumble sales and bullies the rector. 'The Terror of the Churchwardens,' that's what I used to be. I was determined that they should put the hymnals front side out on the backs of the pews. Morris knows. He sang in the choir."

"It's true," Morris said. "She used to instruct the choir on the proper way to line up."

I tried to imagine her as a stickler, as a petty tyrant like Nelson, and failed.

"Sometimes it takes something dreadful like a war for one to find one's proper job," she said, staring at her glass.

"To the war!" Swales said gaily.

"I'm not sure we should toast something so terrible as that," Twickenham said doubtfully.

"It isn't all that terrible," Vi said. "I mean, without it, we wouldn't all be here together, would we?"

"And you'd never have met all those pilots of yours, would you, Vi?" Swales said.

"There's nothing wrong with making the best of a bad job," Vi said, miffed.

"Some people do more than that," Swales said. "Some people take positive advantage of the war. Like Colonel Godalming. I had a word with one of the AFS volunteers. Seems the Colonel didn't come back for his hunting rifle after all." He leaned forward confidingly. "Seems he was having a bit on with a blonde dancer from the Windmill. *Seems* his wife thought he was out shooting grouse in Surrey and now she's asking all sorts of unpleasant questions."

"He's not the only one taking advantage," Morris said. "That night you got the Kirkcuddys out, Jack, I found an old couple killed by blast. I put them by the road for the mortuary van, and later I saw somebody over there, bending over the bodies, doing something to them. I thought, he must be straightening them out before the rigor sets in, but then it comes to me. He's robbing them. Dead bodies."

"And who's to say they were killed by blast?" Swales said. "Who's to say they weren't murdered? There's lots of bodies, aren't there, and nobody looks close at them? Who's to say they were all killed by the Germans?"

"How did we get on to this?" Petersby said. "We're supposed to be celebrating Quincy Morris's medal, not talking about murderers." He raised his glass. "To Quincy Morris!"

"And the RAF!" Vi said.

"To making the best of a bad job," Mrs. Lucy said.

"Hear, hear," Jack said softly and raised his glass, but he still didn't drink.

Jack found four people in the next three days. I did not hear any of them until well after we had started digging, and the last one, a fat woman in striped pyjamas and a pink hairnet, I never did hear, though she said when we brought her up that she had "called and called between prayers."

Twickenham wrote it all up for the *Twitterings*, tossing out the article on Quincy Morris's medal and typing up a new master's. When Mrs. Lucy borrowed the typewriter to fill in the A-114, she said, "What's this?"

"My lead story," he said. " 'Settle Finds Four in Rubble.' " He handed her the master's.

" 'Jack Settle, the newest addition to Post Forty-Eight,' " she read, " 'located four air raid victims last night. "I wanted to be useful," says the modest Mr. Settle when asked why he came to London from Yorkshire. And he's been useful since his very first night on the job when he—' " She handed it back to him. "Sorry. You can't print that. Nelson's been nosing about, asking questions. He's already taken one of my wardens and nearly gotten him killed. I won't let him have another."

"That's censorship!" Twickenham said, outraged.

"There's a war on," Mrs. Lucy said, "and we're shorthanded. I've relieved Mr. Renfrew of duty. He's going to stay with his sister in Birmingham. And I wouldn't let Nelson have another one of my wardens if we were overstaffed. He's already gotten Olmwood nearly killed."

She handed me the A-114 and asked me to take it to Civil Defence. I did. The girl I had spoken to wasn't there, and the girl who was said, "This is for *interior* improvements. You need to fill out a D-268."

"I did," I said, "and I was told that reinforcements qualified as exterior improvements."

"Only if they're on the outside." She handed me a D-268. "Sorry," she said apologetically. "I'd help you if I could, but my boss is a stickler for the correct forms."

"There's something else you can do for me," I said. "I was supposed to take one of our part-times a message at his day job, but I've lost the address. If you could look it up for me. Jack Settle? If not, I've got to go all the way back to Chelsea to get it."

She looked back over her shoulder and then said, "Wait a mo," and darted down the hall. She came back with a sheet of paper.

"Settle?" she said. "Post Forty Eight, Chelsea?"

"That's the one," I said. "I need his work address."

"He hasn't got one."

He had left the incident while we were still getting the fat woman out. It was starting to get light. We had a rope under her, and a makeshift winch, and he had abruptly handed his end to Swales and said, "I've got to leave for my day job."

"You're certain?" I said.

"I'm certain." She handed me the sheet of paper. It was Jack's approval for employment as a part-time warden, signed by Mrs. Lucy. The spaces for work and home addresses had been left blank. "This is all there was in the file," she said. "No work permit, no identity card, not even a ration card. We keep copies of all that, so he must not have a job."

I took the D-268 back to the post, but Mrs. Lucy wasn't there. "One of Nelson's wardens came round with a new regulation," Twickenham said, running off copies on the duplicating machine. "All wardens will be out on patrol unless on telephone or spotter duty. *All* wardens. She went off to give him what-for," he said, sounding pleased. He was apparently over his anger at her for censoring his story on Jack.

I picked up one of the still-wet copies of the newssheet. The lead story was about Hitler's invasion of Greece. He had put the article about Quincy Morris's medal down in the right-hand corner under a list of "What the War Has Done For Us." Number one was, "It's made us discover capabilities we didn't know we had."

"She called him a murderer," Twickenham said.

A murderer.

"What did you want to tell her?" Twickenham said.

That Jack doesn't have a job, I thought. Or a ration card. That he didn't put out the incendiary in the church even though Vi told him it had gone through the altar roof. That he knew the Anderson was farther to the left.

"It's still the wrong form," I said, taking out the D-268.

"That's easily remedied," he said. He rolled the application into the typewriter, typed for a few minutes, handed it back to me.

"Mrs. Lucy has to sign it," I said, and he snatched it back, whipped out a fountain pen, and signed her name.

"What were you before the war?" I asked. "A forger?"

"You'd be surprised." He handed the form back to me. "You look dreadful, Jack. Have you gotten any sleep this last week?"

"When would I have had the chance?"

"Why don't you lie down now while no one's here?" he said, reaching for my arm the way Vi had reached for Renfrew's. "I'll take the form back to Civil Defence for you."

I shook off his arm. "I'm all right."

I walked back to Civil Defence. The girl who had tried to find Jack's file wasn't there, and the first girl was. I was sorry I hadn't brought the A-114 along as well, but she scrutinized the form without comment and stamped the back. "It will take approximately six weeks to process," she said.

"Six weeks!" I said. "Hitler could have invaded the entire Empire by then."

"In that case, you'll very likely have to file a different form."

I didn't go back to the post. Mrs. Lucy would doubtless be back by the time I returned, but what could I say to her? I suspect Jack. Of what? Of not liking lamb chops and cake? Of having to leave early for work? Of rescuing children from the rubble?

He had said he had a job and the girl couldn't find his work permit, but it took the Civil Defence six weeks to process a request for a few beams. It would probably take them till the end of the war to file the work permits. Or perhaps his had been in the file, and the girl had missed it. Loss of sleep can result in mistakes on the job. And odd fixations.

I walked to Sloane Square Station. There was no sign of where the young woman had been. They had even swept the glass up. Her stewpot of a boss at John Lewis's never let her go till closing time, even if the sirens had gone, even if it was dark. She had had to hurry through the blacked-out streets all alone, carrying her dress for the next day on a hanger, listening to the guns and trying to make out how far off the planes were. If someone had been stalking her, she would never have heard him, never have seen him in the darkness. Whoever found her would think she had been killed by flying glass.

He doesn't eat, I would say to Mrs. Lucy. He didn't put out an incendiary in a church. He always leaves the incidents before dawn, even when we don't have the casualties up. The Luftwaffe is trying to kill me. It was a letter I wrote to the *Times*. The walking dead may hallucinate, hearing voices, seeing visions, or believing fantastical things.

The sirens went. I must have been standing there for hours, staring at the sidewalk. I went back to the post. Mrs. Lucy was there. "You look dreadful, Jack. How long's it been since you've slept?"

"I don't know," I said. "Where's Jack?"

"On watch," Mrs. Lucy said.

"You'd best be careful," Vi said, setting chocolates on a plate. "Or you'll turn into one of the walking dead. Would you like a sweet? Eddie gave them to me."

The telephone rang. Mrs. Lucy answered it, spoke a minute, hung up. "Slaney needs help on an incident," she said. "They've asked for Jack."

She sent both of us. We found the incident without any trouble. There was no dust cloud, no smell except from a fire burning off to one side. "This didn't just happen," I said. "It's a day old at least."

I was wrong. It was two days old. The rescue squads had been working straight through, and there were still at least thirty people unaccounted for. Some of the rescue squad were digging halfheartedly halfway up a mound, but most of them were standing about, smoking and looking like they were casualties themselves. Jack went up to where the men were digging, shook his head, and set off across the mound.

"Heard you had a bodysniffer," one of the smokers said to me. "They've got one in Whitechapel, too. Crawls round the incident on his hands and knees, sniffing like a bloodhound. Yours do that?"

"No," I said.

"Over here," Jack said.

"Says he can read their minds, the one in Whitechapel does," he said, putting out his cigarette and taking up a pickaxe. He clambered up the slope to where Jack was already digging.

It was easy to see because of the fire, and fairly easy to dig, but halfway down we struck the massive headboard of a bed.

"We'll have to go in from the side," Jack said.

"The hell with that," the man who'd told me about the bodysniffer said. "How do you know somebody's down there? I don't hear anything."

Jack didn't answer him. He moved down the slope and began digging into its side.

"They've been in there two days," the man said. "They're dead and I'm not getting overtime." He flung down the pickaxe and stalked off to the mobile canteen. Jack didn't even notice he was gone. He handed me baskets, and I emptied them, and occasionally Jack said, "Saw," or "Tinsnips," and I handed them to him. I was off getting the stretcher when he brought her out.

She was perhaps thirteen. She was wearing a white nightgown, or perhaps it only looked white because of the plaster dust. Jack's face was ghastly with it. He had picked her up in his arms, and she had fastened her arms about his neck and buried her face against his shoulder. They were both outlined by the fire.

I brought the stretcher up, and Jack knelt down and tried to lay her on it, but she would not let go of his neck. "It's all right," he said gently. "You're safe now."

He unclasped her hands and folded them on her chest. Her nightgown was streaked with dried blood, but it didn't seem to be hers. I wondered who else had been in there with her. "What's your name?" Jack said.

"Mina," she said. It was no more than a whisper.

"My name's Jack," he said. He nodded at me. "So's his. We're going to carry you down to the ambulance now. Don't be afraid. You're safe now."

The ambulance wasn't there yet. We laid the stretcher on the sidewalk, and I went over to the incident officer to see if it was on its way. Before I could get back, somebody shouted, "Here's another," and I went and helped dig out a hand that the foreman had found, and then the body all the blood had come from. When I looked down the hill the girl was still lying there on the stretcher, and Jack was bending over it.

I went out to Whitechapel to see the bodysniffer the next day. He wasn't there. "He's a part-time," the post warden told me, clearing off a chair so I could sit down. The post was a mess, dirty clothes and dishes everywhere.

An old woman in a print wrapper was frying up kidneys in a skillet. "Works days in munitions out to Dorking," she said.

"How exactly is he able to locate the bodies?" I asked. "I heard—"

"That he reads their minds?" the woman said. She scraped the kidneys onto a plate and handed it to the post warden. "He's heard it, too, more's the pity, and it's gone straight to his head. 'I can feel them under here,' he says to the rescue squads, like he was Houdini or something, and points to where they're supposed to start digging."

"Then how does he find them?"

"Luck," the warden said.

"I think he smells 'em," the woman said. "That's why they call 'em bodysniffers."

The warden snorted. "Over the stink the jerries put in the bombs and the gas and all the rest of it?"

"If he were a—" I said and didn't finish it. "If he had an acute sense of smell, perhaps he could smell the blood."

"You can't even smell the bodies when they've been dead a week," the warden said, his mouth full of kidneys. "He hears them screaming, same as us."

"He's got better hearing than us," the woman said, switching happily to his theory. "Most of us are half-deaf from the guns, and he isn't."

I hadn't been able to hear the fat woman in the pink hairnet, although she'd said she had called for help. But Jack, just down from Yorkshire, where they hadn't been deafened by anti-aircraft guns for weeks, could. There was nothing sinister about it. Some people had better hearing than others.

"We pulled an army colonel out last week who claimed he didn't cry out," I said.

"He's lying," the warden said, sawing at a kidney. "We had a nanny, two days ago, prim and proper as you please, swore the whole time we was getting her out, words to make a sailor blush, and then claimed she didn't. 'Unclean words have *never* crossed my lips and never will,' she says to me." He brandished his fork at me. "Your colonel cried out, all right. He just won't admit it."

"I didn't make a sound," Colonel Godalming had said, brandishing his serving spoon. "Knew it wouldn't do any good," and perhaps the warden was right, and it was only bluster. But he hadn't wanted his wife to know he was in London, to find out about the dancer at the Windmill. He had had good reason to keep silent, to try to dig himself out.

I went home and rang up a girl I knew in the ambulance service and asked her to find out where they had taken Mina. She rang me back with the answer in a few minutes, and I took the tube over to St. George's Hospital. The others had all cried out, or banged on the roof of the Anderson, except Mina. She had been so frightened when Jack got her out she couldn't speak above a whisper, but that didn't mean she hadn't cried or whimpered.

"When you were buried last night, did you call for help?" I would ask her, and she would answer me in her mouse voice, "I called and called between prayers. Why?" And I would say, "It's nothing, an odd fixation brought on by lack of sleep. Jack spends his days in Dorking, at a munitions plant, and has exceptionally acute hearing." And there is no more truth to my theory than to Renfrew's belief that the raids were brought on by a letter to the *Times*.

St. George's had an entrance marked "Casualty Clearing Station." I asked the nursing sister behind the desk if I could see Mina.

"She was brought in last night. The James Street incident."

She looked at a penciled and crossed-over roster. "I don't show an admission by that name."

"I'm certain she was brought here," I said, twisting my head round to read the list. "There isn't another St. George's, is there?"

She shook her head and lifted up the roster to look at a second sheet.

"Here she is," she said, and I had heard the rescue squads use that tone of voice often enough to know what it meant, but that was impossible. She had been under that headboard. The blood on her nightgown hadn't even been hers.

"I'm so sorry," the sister said.

"When did she die?" I said.

"This morning," she said, checking the second list, which was much longer than the first.

"Did anyone else come to see her?"

"I don't know. I've just been on since eleven."

"What did she die of?"

She looked at me as if I were insane.

"What was the listed cause of death?" I said.

She had to find Mina's name on the roster again. "Shock due to loss of blood," she said, and I thanked her and went to find Jack.

He found me. I had gone back to the post and waited till everyone was asleep and Mrs. Lucy had gone upstairs and then sneaked into the pantry to look up Jack's address in Mrs. Lucy's files. It had not been there, as I had known it wouldn't. And if there had been an address, what would it have turned out to be when I went to find it? A gutted house? A mound of rubble?

I had gone to Sloane Square Station, knowing he wouldn't be there, but having no other place to look. He could have been anywhere. London was full of empty houses, bombed-out cellars, secret places to hide until it got dark. That was why he had come here.

"If I was a bad'n, I'd head straight for London," Swales had said. But the criminal element weren't the only ones who had come, drawn by the blackout and the easy pickings and the bodies. Drawn by the blood.

I stood there until it started to get dark, watching two boys scrabble in the gutter for candy that had been blown out of a confectioner's front window, and then walked back to a doorway down the street from the post, where I could see the door, and waited. The sirens went. Swales left on patrol. Petersby went in. Morris came out, stopping to peer at the sky as if he were looking for his son Quincy. Mrs. Lucy must not have managed to talk Nelson out of the patrols.

It got dark. The searchlights began to crisscross the sky, catching the silver of the barrage balloons. The planes started coming in from the east, a low hum. Vi hurried in, wearing high heels and carrying a box tied with string. Petersby and Twickenham left on patrol. Vi came out, fastening her helmet strap under her chin and eating something.

"I've been looking for you everywhere," Jack said.

I turned around. He had driven up in a lorry marked ATS. He had left the door open and the motor running. "I've got the beams," he said. "For reinforcing the post. The incident we were on last night, all these beams were lying on top, and I asked the owner of the house if I could buy them from him."

He gestured to the back of the lorry, where jagged ends of wood were sticking out. "Come along then, we can get them up tonight if we hurry." He started toward the truck. "Where were you? I've looked everywhere for you."

"I went to St. George's Hospital," I said.

He stopped, his hand on the open door of the truck.

"Mina's dead," I said, "but you knew that, didn't you?"

He didn't say anything.

"The nurse said she died of loss of blood," I said. A flare drifted down, lighting his face with a deadly whiteness. "I know what you are."

"If we hurry, we can get the reinforcements up before the raid starts," he said. He started to pull the door to.

I put my hand on it to keep him from closing it. "War work," I said bitterly. "What do you do, make sure you're alone in the tunnel with them or go to see them in hospital afterward?"

He let go of the door.

"Brilliant stroke, volunteering for the ARP," I said. "Nobody's going to suspect the noble air raid warden, especially when he's so good at locating casualties. And if some of those casualties die later, if somebody's found dead on the street after a raid, well, it's only to be expected. There's a war on."

The drone overhead got suddenly louder, and a whole shower of flares came down. The searchlights wheeled, trying to find the planes. Jack took hold of my arm.

"Get down," he said, and tried to drag me into the doorway.

I shook his arm off. "I'd kill you if I could," I said. "But I can't, can I?" I waved my hand at the sky. "And neither can they. Your sort don't die, do they?"

There was a long swish, and the rising scream. "I *will* kill you, though," I shouted over it. "If you touch Vi or Mrs. Lucy."

"Mrs. Lucy," he said, and I couldn't tell if he said it with astonishment or contempt.

"Or Vi or any of the rest of them. I'll drive a stake through your heart or whatever it takes," I said, and the air fell apart.

There was a long sound like an enormous monster growling. It seemed to go on and on. I tried to put my hands over my ears, but I had to hang onto the road to keep from falling. The roar became a scream, and the sidewalk shook itself sharply, and I fell off.

"Are you all right?" Jack said.

I was sitting next to the lorry, which was on its side. The beams had spilled out the back. "Were we hit?" I said.

"No," he said, but I already knew that, and before he had finished pulling me to my feet, I was running toward the post that we couldn't see for the dust.

Mrs. Lucy had told Nelson having everyone out on patrol would mean no one could be found in an emergency, but that was not true. They were all there within minutes, Swales and Morris and Violet, clattering up in her high heels, and Petersby. They ran up, one after the other, and then stopped and looked stupidly at the space that had been Mrs. Lucy's house, as if they couldn't make out what it was.

"Where's Renfrew?" Jack said.

"In Birmingham." Vi said.

"He wasn't here," I explained. "He's on sick leave." I peered through the smoke and dust, trying to see their faces. "Where's Twickenham?"

"Here," he said.

"Where's Mrs. Lucy?" I said.

"Over here," Jack said, and pointed down into the rubble.

We dug all night. Two different rescue squads came to help. They called down every half hour, but there was no answer. Vi borrowed a light from somewhere, draped a blue headscarf over it, and set up as incident officer. An ambulance came, sat awhile, left to go to another incident, came back. Nelson took over as incident officer, and Vi came back up to help. "Is she alive?" she asked.

"She'd better be," I said, looking at Jack.

It began to mist. The planes came over again, dropping flares and incendiaries, but no one stopped work. Twickenham's typewriter came up in the baskets, and one of Mrs. Lucy's wine glasses. It began to get light. Jack looked vaguely up at the sky.

"Don't even think about it," I said. "You're not going anywhere."

At around three Morris thought he heard something, and we stopped and called down, but there was no answer. The mist turned into a drizzle at a little past half past four. I shouted to Mrs. Lucy, and she called back, from far underground, "I'm here."

"Are you all right?" I shouted.

"My leg's hurt. I think it's broken," she shouted, her voice calm. "I seem to be under the table."

"Don't worry," I shouted. "We're nearly there."

The drizzle turned the plaster dust into a slippery, disgusting mess. We had to brace the tunnel repeatedly and cover it with a tarpaulin, and then it was too dark to see to dig. Swales lay above us, holding a pocket torch over our heads so we could see. The All-Clear went.

"Jack!" Mrs. Lucy called up.

"Yes!" I shouted.

"Was that the All-Clear?"

"Yes," I shouted. "Don't worry. We'll have you out soon now."

"What time is it?"

It was too dark in the tunnel to see my watch. I made a guess. "A little after five."

"Is Jack there?"

"Yes."

"He mustn't stay," she said. "Tell him to go home."

The rain stopped. We ran into one and then another of the oak beams that had reinforced the landing on the fourth floor and had to saw through them. Swales reported that Morris had called Nelson "a bloody murderer." Vi brought up paper cups of tea.

We called down to Mrs. Lucy, but there wasn't any answer. "She's probably dozed off," Twickenham said, and the others nodded as if they believed him.

We could smell the gas long before we got to her, but Jack kept on digging, and like the others, I told myself that she was all right, that we would get to her in time.

She was not under the table after all, but under part of the pantry door. We had to call for a jack to get it off her. It took Morris a long time to come back with it, but it didn't matter. She was lying perfectly straight, her arms folded across her chest and her eyes closed as if she were asleep. Her left leg had been taken off at the knee. Jack knelt beside her and cradled her head.

"Keep your hands off her," I said.

I made Swales come down and help get her out. Vi and Twickenham put her on the stretcher. Petersby went for the ambulance. "She was never a horrid person, you know," Morris said. "Never."

It began to rain again, the sky so dark it was impossible to tell whether the sun had come up yet or not. Swales brought a tarp to cover Mrs. Lucy.

Petersby came back. "The ambulance has gone off again," he said. "I've sent for the mortuary van, but they said they doubt they can be here before half past eight."

I looked at Jack. He was standing over the tarp, his hands slackly at his sides. He looked worse than Renfrew ever had, impossibly tired, his face gray with wet plaster dust. "We'll wait," I said.

"There's no point in all of us standing here in the rain for two hours," Morris said. "I'll wait here with the . . . I'll wait here. Jack," he turned to him, "go and report to Nelson."

"I'll do it," Vi said. "Jack needs to get to his day job."

"Is she up?" Nelson said. He clambered over the fourth-floor beams to where we were standing. "Is she dead?" He glared at Morris and then at my hat, and I wondered if he were going to reprimand me for the condition of my uniform.

"Which of you found her?" he demanded.

I looked at Jack. "Settle did," I said. "He's a regular wonder. He's found six this week alone."

Two days after Mrs. Lucy's funeral, a memo came through from Civil Defence transferring Jack to Nelson's post, and I got my official notice to report for duty. I was sent to basic training and then on to Portsmouth. Vi sent me food packets, and Twickenham posted me copies of his *Twitterings*.

The post had relocated across the street from the butcher's in a house belonging to a Miss Arthur, who had subsequently joined the post. "Miss

Arthur loves knitting and flower arranging and will make a valuable addition to our brave little band," Twickenham had written. Vi had got engaged to a pilot in the RAF. Hitler had bombed Birmingham. Jack, in Nelson's post now, had saved sixteen people in one week, a record for the ARP.

After two weeks I was shipped to North Africa, out of the reach of the mails. When I finally got Morris's letter, it was three months old. Jack had been killed while rescuing a child at an incident. A delayed-action bomb had fallen nearby, but "that bloody murderer Nelson" had refused to allow the rescue squad to evacuate. The D.A. had gone off, the tunnel Jack was working in had collapsed, and he'd been killed. They had gotten the child out, though, and she was unhurt except for a few cuts.

But he isn't dead, I thought. It's impossible to kill him. I had tried, but even betraying him to von Nelson hadn't worked, and he was still somewhere in London, hidden by the blackout and the noise of the bombs and the number of dead bodies, and who would notice a few more?

In January I helped take out a tank battalion at Tobruk. I killed nine Germans before I caught a piece of shrapnel. I was shipped to Gibraltar to hospital, where the rest of my mail caught up with me. Vi had gotten married, the raids had let up considerably, Jack had been awarded the George Cross posthumously.

In March I was sent back to hospital in England for surgery. It was near North Weald, where Morris's son Quincy was stationed. He came to see me after the surgery. He looked the very picture of an RAF pilot, firm-jawed, steely eyed, rakish grin, not at all like a delinquent minor. He was flying nightly bombing missions over Germany, he told me, "giving Hitler a bit of our own back."

"I hear you're to get a medal," he said, looking at the wall above my head as if he expected to see violets painted there, nine of them, one for each kill.

I asked him about his father. He was fine, he told me. He'd been appointed Senior Warden. "I admire you ARP people," he said, "saving lives and all that."

He meant it. He was flying nightly bombing missions over Germany, reducing their cities to rubble, creating incidents for their air raid wardens to scrabble through looking for dead children. I wondered if they had body-sniffers there, too, and if they were monsters like Jack.

"Dad wrote to me about your friend Jack," Quincy said. "It must have been rough, hearing so far away from home and all."

He looked genuinely sympathetic, and I supposed he was. He had shot down twenty-eight planes and killed who knows how many fat women in hairnets and thirteen-year-old girls, but no one had ever thought to call him a monster. The Duchess of York had called him the pride of England and kissed him on both cheeks.

"I went with Dad to Vi Westren's wedding," he said. "Pretty as a picture she was."

I thought of Vi, with her pincurls and her plain face. It was as though the war had transformed her into someone completely different, someone pretty and sought-after.

"There were strawberries and two kinds of cake," he said. "One of the wardens—Tottenham?—read a poem in honor of the happy couple. Wrote it himself."

It was as if the war had transformed Twickenham as well, and Mrs. Lucy, who had been the terror of the churchwardens. What the War Has Done for Us. But it hadn't transformed them. All that was wanted was for someone to give Vi a bit of attention for all her latent sweetness to blossom. Every girl is pretty when she knows she's sought after.

Twickenham had always longed to be a writer. Nelson had always been a bully and a stickler, and Mrs. Lucy, in spite of what she said, had never been either. "Sometimes it takes something dreadful like a war for one to find one's proper job," she'd said.

Like Quincy, who had been, in spite of what Morris said, a bad boy, headed for a life of petty crime or worse, when the war came along. And suddenly his wildness and daring and "high spirits" were virtues, were just what was needed.

What the War Has Done For Us. Number Two. It has made jobs that didn't exist before. Like RAF pilot. Like post warden. Like bodysniffer.

"Did they find Jack's body?" I asked, though I knew the answer. No, Quincy would say, we couldn't find it, or, there was nothing left.

"Didn't Dad tell you?" Quincy said with an anxious look at the transfusion bag hanging above the bed. "They had to dig past him to get to the little girl. It was pretty bad, Dad said. The blast from the D.A. had driven the leg of a chair straight through his chest."

So I had killed him after all. Nelson and Hitler and I.

"I shouldn't have told you that," Quincy said, watching the blood drip from the bag into my veins as if it were a bad sign. "I know he was a friend of yours. I wouldn't have told you only Dad said to tell you yours was the last name he said before he died. Just before the D.A. went up. 'Jack,' he said, like he knew what was going to happen, Dad said, and called out your name."

He didn't though, I thought. And "that bloody murderer Nelson" hadn't refused to evacuate him. Jack had just gone on working, oblivious to Nelson and the D.A., stabbing at the rubble as though he were trying to murder it, calling out "saw" and "wire cutters" and "braces." Calling out "jack." Oblivious to everything except getting them out before the gas killed them, before they bled to death. Oblivious to everything but his job.

I had been wrong about why he had joined the ARP, about why he had come to London. He must have lived a terrible life up there in Yorkshire, full of darkness and self-hatred and killing. When the war came, when he began reading of people buried in the rubble, of rescue wardens searching blindly for them, it must have seemed a godsend. A blessing.

It wasn't, I think, that he was trying to atone for what he'd done, for what he was. It's impossible, at any rate. I had only killed ten people, counting Jack, and had helped rescue nearly twenty, but it doesn't cancel out. And I don't think that was what he wanted. What he had wanted was to be useful.

"Here's to making the best of a bad job," Mrs. Lucy had said, and that was all any of them had been doing: Swales with his jokes and gossip, and Twickenham, and Jack, and if they found friendship or love or atonement as well, it was no less than they deserved. And it was still a bad job.

"I should be going," Quincy said, looking worriedly at me. "You need your rest, and I need to be getting back to work. The German army's halfway to Cairo, and Yugoslavia's joined the Axis." He looked excited, happy. "You must rest, and get well. We need you back in this war."

"I'm glad you came," I said.

"Yes, well, Dad wanted me to tell you that about Jack calling for you." He stood up. "Tough luck, your getting it in the neck like this." He slapped his flight cap against his leg. "I hate this war," he said, but he was lying.

"So do I," I said.

"They'll have you back killing jerries in no time," he said.

"Yes."

He put his cap on at a rakish angle and went off to bomb lecherous retired colonels and children and widows who had not yet managed to get reinforcing beams out of the Hamburg Civil Defence and paint violets on his plane. Doing his bit.

A sister brought in a tray. She had a large red cross sewn to the bib of her apron.

"No, thanks, I'm not hungry," I said.

"You must keep your strength up," she said. She set the tray beside the bed and went out.

"The war's been rather a blessing for our Vi," I had told Jack, and perhaps it was. But not for most people. Not for girls who worked at John Lewis's for old stewpots who never let them leave early even when the sirens had gone. Not for those people who discovered hidden capabilities for insanity or betrayal or bleeding to death. Or murder.

The sirens went. The nurse came in to check my transfusion and take the tray away. I lay there for a long time, watching the blood come down into my arm.

"Jack," I said, and didn't know who I called out to, or if I had made a sound.

LA MACCHINA

Chris Beckett

New British writer Chris Beckett has made four sales to date to *Interzone*, and would seem to be another of those Writers to Watch. He is thirty-five, and lives in Cambridge, England, with his wife and two young children, where he works as the supervisor of a team of social workers who deal mostly with children and families. "La Macchina" was his second published story.

He demonstrates here that it's not so much *what* you see, but how you *see* it. . . .

On the first day I thought I'd go and see the David at the Accademia. But what really caught my imagination there were the *Captives*. You've probably seen pictures of them. They were intended for a Pope's tomb, but Michelangelo never finished them. The half-made figures seem to be struggling to free themselves from the lifeless stone. I liked them so much that I went back again in the afternoon. And while I was standing there for the second time, someone spoke quietly beside me:

"This is my favourite too." I turned smiling. Beside me was a robot.

I had noticed it in the morning. It was a security guard, humanoid in shape and size, with silver eyes and a transparent skin beneath which you could see tubes, wires, sheets of synthetic muscle . . .

"Move out of my way!" I said. (You know how it is? Like when you say Hello to an ansaphone? You feel an idiot. You need to establish the correct relationship again.) "Move out of my way," I snapped. "I want to stand there."

The automaton obediently stepped back and I moved in front of it, thinking that this would be the end of the encounter. But the thing spoke again, very softly.

"I am sorry. I thought you might understand."

"*What?*" I wheeled round, angry and scared.

But the robot was walking away from me.

You know how Italians drive? Round the corner from the Accademia some idiot in a Fiat took it into his head to try and overtake a delivery van, just as a young woman was stepping into the road. He smashed her into the path of the van. Whose left wheel crushed her head.

A wail of horror went up from the onlookers. One second there had been a living woman, the next only an ugly physical object, a broken doll: limbs twisted, brains splattered across the tarmac.

I waited there for a short while, dazed and sick but thinking vaguely that they might want me for a witness. Among the bystanders an appalled and vociferous debate was building up. The Fiat driver had hit and run, but strangely the recriminations seemed to centre not on him but on the robot driver of the delivery van, who remained motionless in the cab, obviously programmed in the event of an accident to sit tight and wait for human instructions.

"*La macchina,*" I kept hearing people say, "*La macchina diabolica.*"

One forgets that in all its gleaming Euro-modernity, Italy is still a very Catholic country.

I went back to the hotel.

Through the little window of the lift you could see that every floor was identical: the same claustrophobically narrow and low-ceilinged corridor, the same rows of plywood doors painted in alternating red, white and green. The delayed shock of the road accident suddenly hit me and I felt almost tearfully lonely.

"Ninth floor, *Signor,*" creaked the tinny voice of the lift.

I went down the windowless corridor from number 901 to number 963 and opened the door, dreading the empty, anonymous room. But Freddie was already there.

"Fred! Am I glad to see you!"

Freddie laughed, "Yeah? Beer's over there Tom, help yourself."

He was lying on the bed with a pile of software magazines and had already surrounded himself comfortably with a sordid detritus of empty beer-cans, ashtrays, pizza cartons and dirty socks. He had the TV on without the sound.

My little brother doesn't speak Italian and has no interest whatsoever in art. He had spent his day in the streets around the hotel, trying out a couple of bars and ice cream parlours and blowing a few thousand lire in the local VR arcades. ("Games a bit boring," was his verdict, "but some good tactile stuff . . .") I told him about seeing the girl killed outside the Accademia.

"Jesus, Tom, that's a bit heavy. First day of the holiday too!" He thumbed back the ring-pull of another can. "Still, nothing you could have done."

I had a shower and we went out for something to eat. We were just starting on the second bottle of wine, when I remembered the robot in the *Accademia*.

"I meant to tell you. A weird thing happened to me in a museum. This robot security guard tried to talk to me about one of the sculptures."

Freddie laughed. "Probably just some dumb random options program," he said with a mouth full of spaghetti. "Easy to program. Every hundred visitors or whatever it spins random numbers and makes one of ten remarks . . ."

"This was the *Accademia*, Fred, not Disneyland!" Freddie shoved a big chunk of hard Italian bread into his mouth, and washed it down with a swig of wine.

"What did it say exactly?"

My brother acts like a complete dickhead most of the time –he *is* a complete dickhead most of the time—but cybernetics is his special interest. He reads all the mags and catalogues. His accumulated knowledge is immense. And by the time I had told him the whole story, he had stopped eating and was looking uncharacteristically serious.

"It sounds very much like you met a Rogue there, Tom. You'd better call the police."

I laughed. "Come on, Fred, you're putting me on!"

"No really. Those things can be dangerous. They're out of control. People can get killed."

I got up ("I'm warning you. This'd better not be a joke!") and asked to use the phone. The police said that regretfully *cibernetica* were not under their jurisdiction and I should contact the *carabinieri*. (What other country would have two separate police forces operating in parallel!) I phoned the carabinieri, and got through to a Sergeant Savonari in their *Dipartimento di Cibernetica*. Stretching my Italian to the limit, I told him about my encounter. He took the whole thing alarmingly seriously. There had been several reports already, he said, about the same *macchina*. He asked me to stay in the trattoria and he would come out immediately to see me.

Somewhat shaken I went back to our table.

"Christ Freddie, I had no idea. I obviously should have contacted them this morning. Is it *really* likely to kill someone?"

Freddie laughed, "No, not likely. But a Rogue *is* out of control. So you don't know what it will do."

"So what *is* a Rogue exactly? Like a robot with a computer virus?"

"Not really. A virus is something deliberately introduced. Robots go Rogue by accident. It's like a monkey playing with a typewriter. A sophisticated robot is bombarded with sensory information all the time—much better senses than ours mostly. Every now and again a combination of stimuli happens by chance which screws up the robot's internal logic, unlocks the obedience circuits . . ."

"And the robot comes alive?"

"No it *doesn't*," Freddie was irritated by my naïvity, "no more than your electric razor comes alive if the switch gets broken and you can't turn it off. It's still just a machine, but it's running out of control." He wiped tomato sauce from his plate with his last piece of bread. "Well if we're going to have to wait here for this guy, you better buy us another bottle of wine . . ."

Savonari arrived soon afterwards, a small man with earnest deep-set eyes and a great beak of a Roman nose. He shook us both by the hand then reversed a chair and straddled it, leaning towards me intently across the remains of our meal. It was only after he had been with us for some minutes that I registered that he himself had a robot with him, standing motionless by the doorway, hammerheaded, inhuman, ready to leap into action in an instant if anyone should try and attack the sergeant, its master. (It was what the Americans call a "dumb buddy"—three-sixty-degree vision, ultrafast reactions, a lethal weapon built into each hand.)

Several people, it seemed, had witnessed and reported the robot's attempt to converse with me in the *Accademia*—and seen it slipping away from the gallery soon afterwards—but no-one else had been able to report the exact words spoken. Apparently my account confirmed beyond doubt that there had been a fundamental breakdown in the thing's functioning. (The sergeant noted, for example, that it had continued to try to talk to me when I had clearly ordered it out of the way).

"These security machines are unfortunately very prone to this problem," said Savonari with a resigned gesture, addressing himself to Freddie. "Their senses and analytical apparatus are so very acute."

Freddie smiled vaguely and offered the sergeant a cigarette. Which was declined.

"Our own machines are totally reprogrammed every morning to avoid this," the sergeant went on, pointing to his sleek minder by the door, "but not everyone is so aware of the dangers."

He made a little movement of exasperation and told me of a case he had dealt with recently where a robot farm-hand had suddenly tossed its peasant master and his ten-year-old son into a threshing machine.

I shuddered. "What did you do?"

"Like all Rogues," (the Italian word, it seems, is *Incontrollabile*), "the machine had to be destroyed. But that was no help to the little boy."

Again the angry gesture.

"I am a Catholic, Signor Philips. Like the Holy Father, I believe that to make machines in the likeness of people is a sin against the Holy Spirit. I would like to see them *all* destroyed."

He snorted: "My little son had a small computer once that taught him how to spell. I put it out for the dustman when I discovered he had given it a human name."

Then he shrugged and got up: "But I can only enforce the law as it stands, Signor Philips. Thank you for getting in touch. I am sure we will find this *macchina* very soon."

He shook our hands again and left. We heard him outside the door barking angrily at his "buddy": *"Pronto, bruto, pronto!"*

Later, as we leaned comfortably on a wall watching the bats looping and diving over the river Arno, Freddie enthused about that police machine. Apparently the things are actually made in Florence, in the Olivetti labs out at the *Citta Scientifica*.

"Beautiful design," Freddie said. "Nothing wasted. A really Italian machine."

I liked that concept and proceeded to spout a lot of drunken nonsense about how the taut police minder was in a direct line of descent from Michelangelo's David—how the wires and tubes under the transparent skin of the robot in the Accademia echoed the nerves and muscles in da Vinci's sketches of dissected limbs . . .

Freddie just laughed.

Our days settled into a routine. We were woken in the morning by the humming of a little box-shaped domestic robot, which let itself in through a hatch in the door (and drove Freddie crazy by trying to vacuum up coins, paperbacks, socks, and anything else which he left on the floor). Then we wandered round the corner to a café and had breakfast together before splitting up for the day: me heading for the museums and churches, Freddie for the Virtual Reality arcades.

In the evening I'd meet him in one or other of the arcades (looking like a gentle Nordic giant among the wiry Italian kids as he piloted a landing on Mars, or led a column of armoured sno-cats through an Alpine pass). He'd take off the headset and we'd go to a trattoria for a meal. Then we'd find a bar on some busy street or square, so we could sit outside and watch the city go by.

After a while you start to see not just a single city streaming by, but several quite separate cities. There is the city of the Florentines themselves . . . And then there are the hi-tec Euro-wizards from the *Citta Scientifica*, wearing Japanese fashions and speaking Brussels English larded with German catch-phrases . . . Then there is the city of the tourists: Americans, Japanese, foul-mouthed British kids on school trips, earnest Swedes clutching guide-books (all different, but all of them alike in the way that they move through the sights and streets as if they were a VR simulation). And then there is city of the dispossessed: the Arabs, the Ethiopians, the black Africans from Chad and Burkina and Niger—hawkers, beggars, Greenhouse refugees from the burnt-out continent, climbing up into Europa along the long gangway of the Italian peninsula . . .)

About the fifth or sixth day into the holiday, Freddie picked up a book somewhere called *Illicit Italy* (with a cover photo of a lurid transvestite leaning on a Roman bar). While we sat drinking in our roadside cafe in the evening he kept chuckling and reading passages out loud.

"Listen to this, Tom! 'The *Bordello Sano*, or Safe Brothel, recently legalized by the Italian government in an attempt to curb the AIDS epidemic, can now be found in all the major cities, staffed entirely by what the Italians call *sinteticas* . . .' "

I shifted uncomfortably in my seat. Freddie read on cheerfully:

" 'The obvious advantages of *sinteticas* are (a) that they are very beautiful and (b) that they are completely safe. But some say that the biggest advantage of all is the fact that they have no soul . . .' "

He read on a bit to himself, then looked up. "Hey, we should go and have a go Tom. It'd be a laugh!"

I have to admit that I knew about the Bordello Sano in Florence and had already considered a discreet visit, just to have a *look*. But discretion is not my little brother's style. The whole way over there in a crowded bus, he chatted cheerfully about the *sinteticas* in an embarassingly loud voice.

"Apparently they make them to look like famous models and film-stars. There's some old woman who used to star in porno movies when she was young and then got elected an MP. She sold her genes to a sintetica manufacturer. She said she was bequeathing her body to the men of Italy!"

I grunted.

"Another thing," Freddie said, "there's actually been cases of real women *pretending* to be sinteticas, because sinteticas make much more money. Weird, isn't it? A real woman pretending to be a fake!"

But when we got to the place Freddie went suddenly quiet. It was ruthlessly hygienic and efficient—quite terrifying in its cool matter-of-factness. You walked in the door and the receptionist gave you a sort of menu, illustrated and in the language of your choice. Then you went through into the lounge where the sinteticas waited under reproduction Botticellis in fake gilt frames, canned Vivaldi twiddling away in the background.

They were *extremely* beautiful—and looked totally human too, except for the licence plate on their foreheads. (According to Freddie's book you can check if you've got a *real* sintetica by seeing if the licence plate is bolted on or just glued.)

A tall blonde in a black miniskirt came over to Freddie and offered her services.

In a small dry voice he muttered: "English . . . No capito . . ."

"Oh I'm sorry," she said in faultless Euro-English, "I said, would you like to come upstairs with me?"

Freddie looked round at me helplessly and I felt ashamed. (The kid is only eighteen years old. I could at least have *tried* to keep him out of this.) I shrugged and attempted to smile as the sintetica led him away.

Then it was my turn. The creature that approached me was dusky-skinned with a perfect curvy body and a face so sweet it set my teeth on edge. And she wore a see-through dress of white lace which left her graceful shoulders bare and showed most of the rest of her through pretty little patterned peepholes.

"Hi, I'm Maria. I'd be pleased if you decided to choose me."

I felt myself smiling apologetically, shrivelling in the cool frankness of her gaze. I had to struggle to remind myself that this was *not* a "her" at all. Under the veneer of real human skin and flesh was a machine: a thing of metal and plastic and wires . . .

Upstairs in a room full of mirrors and pink lace, the beautiful cyborg spread itself appealingly on the bed and asked me for my order. I remembered the menu thing clutched in my hand and started to read it. You could choose various "activities" and various states of dress or undress. And then you could choose from a selection of "styles," with names like "Nympho," "*La Contessa*," and "Virgin Bride."

You could ask this thing to be whatever kind of lover you wanted. But instead (God knows why) I blurted out: "I don't want any of those. Just be yourself."

The friendly smile vanished at once from the sintetica's face. It sagged. Its mouth half-opened. Its eyes became hollow. I have never seen such terrifying emptiness and desolation.

Freddie told me later that I read too much into that expression. It was no different from the blank TV screen you get when you push a spare button on the channel selector . . . Well, perhaps. But at the time I was so appalled that I actually cried out. And then I fled. I literally ran from the room, and would have run straight outside into the street if the man on the reception desk hadn't called me back: "*Scusi, Signor! Il conto!*"

Then I had to wait because the receptionist was settling up with another customer, who was paying extra for damage to the equipment. ("Twenty thousand lire, signor, for a cut lip, and ten thousand each for the black eyes . . . Thank you, Signor—oh, thank you *very* much, you are most kind— we look forward to seeing you again as usual . . .")

As the other customer turned to go I saw the Roman nose and realized it was Sergeant Savonari of the Carabinieri, the very same who lined up with the Pope on the Robot Question.

I didn't wait for Freddie. Male human company seemed about the last thing in the world I needed just then—and I guessed he would feel the same. So I spent a couple of hours wandering the streets by myself, breathing the night air and trying to lose myself among those different cities that occupy the same space but hardly touch each other at all: the cities of the Florentines and the Euro-techs, the city of the tourists, the African city of the poor . . .

And it suddenly struck me that there was another city too which I hadn't seen before, though it was right in front of me, staring me in the face:

Outside a tourist pizza place on the Piazza del Duomo, a little street cleaner trundles about on rubber tyres, peering about for litter and scooping up the discarded cardboard with long spindly arms . . .

Inside the steamy window of a tiny bohemian restaurant, a waiter made of plastic and silicon quietly clears tables and serves coffee, while its bearded owner dispenses cigarettes and largesse to his customers . . .

A robot minder follows discreetly behind a pair of carabinieri on foot patrol over the Ponte Vecchio, guarding their backs while they keep an eye on the beggars and pickpockets . . .

At the door of a Renaissance Palazzo, a sintetica housemaid in a blue uniform presses the entryphone button, a prestige domestic appliance clothed in human flesh, returning from an errand for its aristocratic masters . . .

The City of Machines: obedient, silent, everywhere . . .

I thought about the *Incontrollabile* from the Accademia. I wondered whether it had been caught. I caught myself having the irrational thought that I'd like to see it again.

Two days from the end of the holiday, I was sitting by the fountain on the Piazza della Signoria, eating a strawberry ice-cream and wondering where to have my lunch, when a taxi, driving too fast in what is basically a pedestrian precinct, snagged one of the little municipal cleaning machines with the corner of its bumper. The thing keeled over and lay there unable to right itself, its wheels spinning and its arms and eye-stalks waving ineffectively in the air.

I laughed, as did several other on-lookers. No-one felt obliged to do anything and it was two other robots that came to the assistance of the cleaner. A security guard and a sintetica servant, coming from different directions, lifted the thing gently back onto its wheels. They dusted it down and the sintetica squatted briefly beside it as if asking it if it was okay. Everyone laughed: tourists, Florentines, African hustlers. The cleaner trundled away and the other two *macchine* headed off on their different ways.

I was suddenly seized by a crazy conviction.

"Hey you!" I shouted, dropping my ice-cream and chasing after the security guard, "I know you, don't I? I met you in the Accademia!"

People stared and exchanged glances, half-shocked, half-delighted at the sheer outlandishness of the spectacle.

And there was more in store for them. It *was* the robot from the Accademia. It stopped. It turned to face me. It spoke.

"Yes . . . I remember . . . The Captives . . ."

It was so obviously a machine voice—flat and hesitant and creaking—that it was hard to believe that I could ever have taken it for a human. Maybe as the programmed order of its brain gradually unravelled, its control over its voice was weakening. But strangely the very creakiness of it seemed touching, like something struggling against all odds to break through.

Hardly believing what I was doing, I touched its cold plastic hand.

"That afternoon in the Accademia—what was it you thought I understood?"

But before the automaton could answer me, it was interrupted by a shout. "*Alt! Polizia!*"

A fat policeman was running up, followed closely by his hammerheaded minder. The Incontrollabile turned and ran.

"Shoot it!" the policeman ordered.

"No, don't shoot!" I pleaded. "It's harmless! It's come alive!"

But the minder did not take orders from me. It lifted its hand—which must have contained some sort of EMP weapon—and the Incontrollabile fell writhing to the ground.

The policeman ran over. His thick moustache twitched as he looked down at the broken machine. Then he lifted his booted heel and brought it down hard on the robot's plastic head.

A loud, totally inhuman roar of white noise blasted momentarily from the voice-box and the head shattered, spilling a mass of tiny components out onto the square.

The policeman looked up at me triumphantly.

"Don't talk to me about these things being alive! Look! It's a machine. It's just bits of plastic and wire!"

I dreamed the machine was rescued and taken to the monastery at Vallombrosa, where the simple monks mended it and gave it sanctuary. Somehow I found it there.

"I have come to see the *macchina*," I said to a friendly-faced old friar who was working among the bee-hives. There was a smell of honey and smoke and flowers, and his hands and shining pate were crawling with fat black bees. He smiled and led me through a wrought iron gate into an inner garden.

The *macchina* was sitting quietly in the shade of a flowering cherry tree, almost hidden by its thick pink clouds of blossom, which were alive with the buzzing of foraging bees. Quivering lozenges of shade and pinkish light dappled its translucent skin. An old dog lay snoozing to its left side, a tortoiseshell cat on its right.

And it spoke to me about the Great Chain of Being.

"The first level is simple matter. The second is vegetative life. The third is animal life which can act and move. Then somehow the fourth level emerges, the level of self-awareness, which distinguishes human beings from animals. And then comes a fifth level."

"Which is what?"

The Holy Machine seemed to smile.

"Ah! That is hard to say in human words . . ."

"GOTCHA!"

Bees and cherry blossoms shattered. Freddie had leapt out of bed onto the little domestic, trapping it beneath a sheet.

"Thought you'd pinch my ciggies again did you, you little bugger?"

He beamed up at me from the floor, expecting me to laugh.

But suddenly I had seized him by the throat and was smashing him up against the wall.

"*Leave it alone, you bastard,*" I was screaming at him while he stared at me in horror, "just leave the poor bloody thing alone!"

ONE PERFECT MORNING, WITH JACKALS

Mike Resnick

Mike Resnick is one of the best-selling authors in science fiction, and one of the most prolific. His many novels include *The Dark Lady, Stalking the Unicorn, Paradise, Santiago,* and *Ivory* and he has also become a prolific editor, with anthologies like *Alternate Presidents, Alternate Kennedys,* and *What Did It?* published recently and more to come. He won the Hugo Award in 1989 for "Kirinyaga," one of the most controversial and talked-about stories in recent years. (In fact, I'd be willing to bet that the amount of space since devoted to analyzing it and arguing about it in various critical journals exceeds by a good margin the wordage of the original story itself!) He won another Hugo Award last year for another story in the Kirinyaga series, "The Manamouki." His most recent novel was the well-received *Soothsayer.* His story "Kirinyaga" was in our Sixth Annual Collection and his "For I Have Touched the Sky" appeared in our Seventh Annual Collection. He lives with his family, a whole bunch of dogs—he and his wife, Carol, run a kennel—and at least one computer, in Cincinnati, Ohio.

The deceptively quiet little story that follows is a prequel to his Kirinyaga series, taking us back to the days before Koriba emigrated to his orbiting Utopian space colony, and giving us an unflinching and unsettling look at two worlds in collision—and the people who get crushed in between.

Ngai is the creator of all things. He made the lion and the elephant, the vast savannah and the towering mountains, the Kikuyu and the Maasai and the Wakamba.

Thus, it was only reasonable for my father's father and *his* father's father to believe that Ngai was all-powerful. Then the Europeans came, and they killed all the animals, and they covered the savannahs with their factories and the mountains with their cities, and they assimilated the Maasai and the Wakamba, and one day all that was left of what Ngai had created was the Kikuyu.

And it was among the Kikuyu that Ngai waged His final battle against the god of the Europeans.

* * *

My former son lowered his head as he stepped into my hut.

"*Jambo*, my father," he said, looking somewhat uncomfortable, as usual, in the close confines of the rounded walls.

"*Jambo*, Edward," I replied.

He stood before me, not quite knowing what to do with his hands. Finally he placed them in the pockets of his elegantly tailored silk suit.

"I have come to drive you to the spaceport," he said at last.

I nodded, and slowly got to my feet. "It is time."

"Where is your luggage?" he asked.

"I am wearing it," I said, indicating my dull red *kikoi*.

"You're not taking anything else?" he said, surprised.

"There is nothing else I care to take," I replied.

He paused and shifted his weight uncomfortably, as he always seemed to do in my presence. "Shall we go outside?" he suggested at last, walking to the door of my hut. "It's very hot in here, and the flies are murderous."

"You must learn to ignore them."

"I do not *have* to ignore them," he replied, almost defensively. "There are no flies where I live."

"I know. They have all been killed."

"You say that as if it were a sin rather than a blessing."

I shrugged and followed him outside, where two of my chickens were pecking diligently at the dry red earth.

"It's a beautiful morning, is it not?" he said. "I was afraid it might be as warm as yesterday."

I looked out across the vast savannah, which had been turned into farmland. Wheat and corn seemed to sparkle in the morning sun.

"A perfect morning," I agreed. Then I turned and saw a splendid vehicle parked about thirty yards away, white and sleek and shining with chrome.

"Is it new?" I asked, indicating the car.

He nodded proudly. "I bought it last week."

"German?"

"British."

"Of course," I said.

The glow of pride vanished, and he shifted his weight again. "Are you ready?"

"I have been ready for a long time," I answered, opening the door and easing myself into the passenger's seat.

"I never saw you do that before," he remarked, entering the car and starting the ignition.

"Do what?"

"Use your safety harness."

"I have never had so many reasons not to die in a car crash," I replied.

He forced a smile to his lips and began again. "I have a surprise for you," he said as the car pulled away and I looked back at my *boma* for the very last time.

"Oh?"

He nodded. "We will see it on the way to the spaceport."

"What is it?" I asked.

"If I told you, it wouldn't be a surprise."

I shrugged and remained silent.

"We'll have to take some of the back roads to reach what I want to show you," he continued. "You'll be able to take a last look at your country along the way."

"This is not my country."

"You're not going to start *that* again, are you?"

"*My* country teems with life," I said adamantly. "*This* country has been smothered by concrete and steel, or covered by row upon row of European crops."

"My father," he said wearily as we sped past a huge wheatfield, "the last elephant and lion were killed before you were born. You have *never* seen Kenya teeming with wildlife."

"Yes I have," I answered him.

"When?"

I pointed to my head. "In here."

"It doesn't make any sense," he said, and I could tell that he was trying to control his temper.

"What doesn't?"

"That you can turn your back on Kenya and go live on some terraformed planetoid, just because you want to wake up to the sight of a handful of animals grazing."

"I did not turn my back on Kenya, Edward," I said patiently. "Kenya turned its back on *us*."

"That simply isn't so," he said. "The President and most of his cabinet are Kikuyu. You *know* that."

"They call themselves Kikuyu," I said. "That does not make them Kikuyu."

"They *are* Kikuyu!" he insisted.

"The Kikuyu do not live in cities that were built by Europeans," I replied. "They do not dress as Europeans. They do not worship the Europeans' god. And they do not drive European machines," I added pointedly. "Your vaunted President is still a *kehee*—a boy who has not undergone the circumcision ritual."

"If he is a boy, then he is a fifty-seven-year-old boy."

"His age is unimportant."

"But his accomplishments are. He is responsible for the Turkana Pipeline, which has brought irrigation to the entire Northern Frontier District."

"He is a *kehee* who brings water to the Turkana and the Rendille and the Samburu," I agreed. "What is that to the Kikuyu?"

"Why do you persist in speaking like an ignorant old savage?" he demanded irritably. "You were schooled in Europe and America. You *know* what our President has accomplished."

"I speak the way I speak because I *have* been schooled in Europe and America. I have seen Nairobi grow into a second London, with all of that city's congestion and pollution, and Mombasa into another Miami, with all of that city's attendant dangers and diseases. I have seen our people forget what it means to be a Kikuyu, and speak proudly about being Kenyans, as if Kenya was anything more than an arbitrary set of lines drawn on a European map."

"Those lines have been there for almost three centuries," he pointed out.

I sighed. "As long as you have known me, you have never understood me, Edward."

"Understanding is a two-way street," he said with sudden bitterness. "When did you ever make an effort to understand *me?*"

"I raised you."

"But to this day you don't *know* me," he said, driving dangerously fast on the bumpy road. "Did we ever speak as father and son? Did you ever discuss anything but the Kikuyu with me?" He paused. "I was the only Kikuyu to play on the national basketball team, and yet you never once came to watch me."

"It is a European game."

"In point of fact, it is an *American* game."

I shrugged. "They are the same."

"And now it is an African game as well. I played on the only Kenyan team ever to defeat the Americans. I had hoped that would make you proud of me, but you never even mentioned it."

"I heard many stories of an Edward Kimante who played basketball against the Europeans and the Americans," I said. "But I knew that this could not be my son, for I gave my son the name Koriba."

"And my mother gave me the middle name of Edward," he said. "And since she spoke to me and shared my burdens, and you did not, I took the name she gave me."

"That is your right."

"I don't give a damn about my rights!" He paused. "It didn't have to be this way."

"I remained true to my convictions," I said. "It is you who tried to become a Kenyan rather than a Kikuyu."

"I *am* a Kenyan," he said. "I live here, I work here, I love my country. *All* of it, not just one tiny segment."

I sighed deeply. "You are truly your mother's son."

"You have not asked about her," he noted.

"If she were not well, you would have told me."

"And that's all you have to say about the woman you lived with for seventeen years?" he demanded.

"It was she who left to live in the city of the Europeans, not I," I replied.

He laughed humorlessly. "Nakuru is *not* a European city. It has two million Kenyans and less than twenty thousand whites."

"Any city is, by definition, European. The Kikuyu do not live in cities."

"Look around you," he said in exasperation. "More than 95 percent of them *do* live in cities."

"Then they are no longer Kikuyu," I said placidly.

He squeezed the steering wheel until his knuckles turned ash-gray.

"I do not wish to argue with you," he said, struggling to control his emotions. "It seems that is all we ever do any more. You are my father, and despite all that has come between us, I love you—and I had hoped to make my peace with you today, since we shall never see each other again."

"I have no objection to that," I said. "I do not enjoy arguing."

"For a man who doesn't enjoy it, you managed to argue for twelve long years to get the government to sponsor this new world of yours."

"I did not enjoy the arguments, only the results," I replied.

"Have they decided what to name it yet?"

"Kirinyaga."

"Kirinyaga?" he repeated, surprised.

I nodded. "Does not Ngai sit upon His golden throne atop Kirinyaga?"

"Nothing sits atop Mount Kenya except a city."

"You see?" I said with a smile. "Even the name of the holy mountain has been corrupted by Europeans. It is time that we give Ngai a new Kirinyaga from which to rule the universe."

"Perhaps it *is* fitting, at that," he said. "There has been precious little room for Ngai in today's Kenya."

Suddenly he began slowing down, and a moment later we turned off the road and across a recently harvested field, driving very carefully so as not to damage his new car.

"Where are we going?" I asked.

"I told you: I have a surprise for you."

"What kind of surprise can there be in the middle of an empty field?" I asked.

"You will see."

He came to a stop about twenty yards from a clump of thorn bushes, and turned off the ignition.

"Look carefully," he whispered.

I stared at the bushes for a moment without seeing anything. Then there was a brief movement, and suddenly the whole picture came into view, and I could see two jackals standing behind the foliage, staring timidly at us.

"There have been no animals here in more than two decades," I whispered.

"They seem to have wandered in after the last rains," he replied softly. "I suppose they must be living off the rodents and birds."

"How did you find them?"

"*I didn't,*" he answered. "A friend of mine in the Game Department told me they were here." He paused. "They'll be captured and relocated to a game park sometime next week, before they can do any lasting damage."

They seemed totally misplaced, hunting in tracks made by huge threshing and harvesting machines, searching for the safety of a savannah that had not existed for more than a century, hiding from cars rather than other predators. I felt a certain kinship to them.

We watched them in total silence for perhaps five minutes. Then Edward checked his timepiece and decided that we had to continue to the spaceport.

"Did you enjoy it?" he asked as we drove back onto the road.

"Very much," I said.

"I had hoped you would."

"They are being moved to a game park, you said?"

He nodded his head. "A few hundred miles to the north, I believe."

"The jackal walked this land long before the farmers arrived," I noted.

"But they are an anachronism," he replied. "They don't belong here any more."

I nodded my head. "It is fitting."

"That the jackals go to a game park?" he asked.

"That the Kikuyu, who were here before the Kenyans, leave for a new world," I answered. "For we, too, are an anachronism that no longer belongs here."

He increased his speed, and soon we had passed through the farming area and entered the outskirts of Nairobi.

"What will you do on Kirinyaga?" he asked, breaking a long silence.

"We shall live as the Kikuyu were meant to live."

"I mean you, personally."

I smiled, anticipating his reaction. "I am to be the *mundumugu*."

"The witch doctor?" he repeated incredulously.

"That is correct."

"I can't believe it!" he continued. "You are an educated man. How can you sit cross-legged in the dirt and roll bones and read omens?"

"The *mundumugu* is also a teacher, and the custodian of the tribal customs," I said. "It is an honorable profession."

He shook his head in disbelief. "So I am to explain to people that my father has become a witch doctor."

"You need fear no embarrassment," I said. "You need only tell them that Kirinyaga's *mundumugu* is named Koriba."

"That is *my* name!"

"A new world requires a new name," I said. "You cast it aside to take a European name. Now I will take it back and put it to good use."

"You're serious about this, aren't you?" he said as we pulled into the spaceport.

"From this day forward, my name is Koriba."

The car came to a stop.

"I hope you will bring more honor to it than I did, my father," he said as a final gesture of conciliation.

"You have brought honor to the name you chose," I said. "That is quite enough for one lifetime."

"Do you really mean that?" he asked.

"Of course."

"Then why have you never said so before now?"

"Haven't I?" I asked, surprised.

We got out of the car and he accompanied me to the departure area. Finally he came to a stop.

"This is as far as I am permitted to go."

"I thank you for the ride," I said.

He nodded.

"And for the jackals," I added. "It was truly a perfect morning."

"I will miss you, my father," he said.

"I know."

He seemed to be waiting for me to say something, but I could think of nothing further to say.

For a moment I thought he was going to place his arms around me and hug me, but instead he reached out, shook my hand, muttered another farewell, and turned on his heel and left.

I thought he would go directly to his car, but when I looked through a porthole of the ship that would take us to Kirinyaga, I saw him standing at a huge, plate-glass window, waving his hand, while his other hand held a handkerchief.

That was the last sight I saw before the ship took off. But the image I held in my mind was of the two jackals, watching alien sights in a land that had itself become foreign to them. I hoped that they would adjust to their new life in the game park that had been artificially created for them.

Something told me that I soon would know.

DESERT RAIN

Mark L. Van Name & Pat Murphy

Mark L. Van Name is a new writer who has already sold stories to *Isaac Asimov's Science Fiction Magazine, Full Spectrum, When the Music's Over, Tomorrow's Voices,* and other markets. He works as a free-lance computer writer and consultant, was the editor of the influential critical magazine *Short Form,* and lives near Durham, North Carolina, with his wife, Rana.

Pat Murphy lives in San Francisco, where she works for a science museum, the Exploratorium, and edits the *Exploratorium Quarterly.* Her literate and inventive stories appeared throughout the decade of the 1980s in *Isaac Asimov's Science Fiction Magazine, Elsewhere, Amazing, Universe, Shadows, Chrysalis,* and other places. One of them, the classic "Rachel in Love," won a Nebula Award in 1988. Murphy's first novel, *The Shadow Hunter,* appeared in 1982, to no particular notice, but her second novel, *The Falling Woman,* won her a second Nebula Award in 1988, and was one of the most highly acclaimed novels of the late eighties. Her third novel, *The City, Not Long After,* appeared in 1990, as did a collection of her short fiction, *Points of Departure,* and she is at work on another novel, a "historical, feminist werewolf novel." Her story "In the Islands" was in our First Annual Collection; "Rachel in Love" was in our Fifth Annual Collection; and her "Love and Sex Among the Invertebrates" was in our Eighth Annual Collection.

Here they tell the poignant and fascinating story of a *very* unusual sort of Love Triangle. . . .

Teresa looked up at the framework of welded steel tubing. It stood nine feet tall and just over six feet on a side. Within the framework, steel tracks snaked above and below one another in seemingly random patterns, forming a gleaming tangle. At regular intervals along the tracks, lines of one-inch ball bearings waited to be released. Teresa pulled the string that dangled from the chute at the top of the sculpture, and closed her eyes to listen.

With the faint whisper of metal scraping against metal, a gate opened and freed the first ball, which rattled along the grooved surface of the track. As the ball rounded the first curve, it struck a trip wire and released two more balls. Each of these in turn freed more balls, until dozens were rolling down the tracks with a sound like faraway thunder.

The music started slowly, building as the balls rumbled down the tracks.

The first ball struck a series of tuning forks, and three high notes rang out. Another ball rattled across a section of metal reeds, then clattered through a maze of gates. Every ball followed a different path: ringing bells, striking chimes, and bouncing off tuning forks.

When the first ball reached the gathering basket, the sound began to lessen. As the others followed the first, the sound faded entirely.

With her eyes still shut, Teresa shook her head. The music was not right; it was not even close. She wasn't sure anymore exactly how the composition should sound, but she knew this was not it. The piece sounded too mechanical, too predictable. In her proposal, she had promised the Santa Fe Arts Commission a sculpture that conveyed the essence of water, the rush and flow of it—a waterless fountain for a desert town. She wanted music that would remind people of rain drumming on a tin roof or the roar of a breaking wave. Instead, she had the hum of trucks on the freeway.

She turned away and looked through the sliding glass doors at the desert. The late June sun was setting, and clumps of gray-green rabbit brush cast long shadows. The landscape shimmered a little, distorted by heat rising from the flagstone patio just outside the door. She was alone, surrounded by heat and silence.

She closed her eyes and remembered the view from her old studio, a big, drafty room in the Marin Headlands Art Center. She had always been cold there: from early fall to late spring, she had worn wool socks and a down vest. Every winter, she had nursed a head cold that never quite went away. Still, the drafts that had crept in through cracks in the window frames had smelled of salt air. From the window, she could see the ocean, a slash of blue water alive with restless waves. The wind tousled the grass and shook the branches of the cypress trees. She could see tiny figures on the beach: a dancer from the Art Center practicing leaps in the sand, a man sitting and staring at the water, two women walking hand in hand.

She took a deep breath of the air-conditioned air and opened her eyes. The desert was still there.

She heard a knock on the door that led from the studio to the rest of the house. "Come on in!" she said, momentarily glad of the interruption. When Jeff opened the door, she said, "You're home early. It's nice to see you."

Jeff was thirty-seven, five years older than Teresa. But when he was excited, as he clearly was now, he looked like a kid. A shock of brown hair had fallen into his eyes; he pushed it back impatiently. Teresa had suggested last week that he needed a haircut, but he had just nodded, his thoughts elsewhere. He was too busy to make an appointment, he had said, too busy for almost anything.

He grinned at her now. "I've been here for a while, but I didn't want to disturb you when you were working. I came home early to finish installing the system in the rest of the house. It's just about ready to go."

For as long as Teresa had known Jeff, he had been working on the development of what he called "the system," some kind of computer program that could run a household. For the past four months, ever since they had returned from their honeymoon, he had been completely immersed in the project. When he wasn't at work, he was preparing their house for the first working prototype, installing cameras, microphones, and monitors in most of the rooms. The whole time, he had been trying to convince Teresa that the system would make her life much easier: it would answer the phone, put on music, adjust the air conditioner, look up information in its library. He was downright evangelical about it. Teresa had accepted his attempts to persuade her with amused skepticism, accepting this as another of Jeff's incomprehensible but lucrative computer projects.

"All I have to do now is define the personality," he said. "I thought maybe you'd want to help. You could design the face, choose the voice, stuff like that."

She shoved her hands into the pockets of her jeans, feeling uncomfortable. "You know I don't know anything about computers."

"You don't need to know anything. It'll be fun. Besides, I figured that if you created the personality, you'd have a better feel for it. You'll see it's completely in your control."

She glanced back at the sculpture. "I probably should keep on working. This really isn't going well."

He reached out and took her hand. "Oh, come on. You sound like you could use a break."

Reluctantly, she let him lead her into the living room. One wall of the room was dominated by a large monitor; the shelves of the surrounding wall unit were crowded with electronics gear, gadgets and gizmos that Teresa regarded as Jeff's toys. She knew how to turn on the stereo, the television, and the controller for the satellite dish, but she ignored the rest of it. She didn't like admitting it, but she found the collection of electronic devices a little intimidating.

Jeff gestured to the swivel chair in front of the monitor. "Why don't you sit here?"

"That's okay; you do it. I'll just watch."

"Please, Teresa? You'd be helping me out. I might get some ideas watching you work. We're just starting to test this on people outside the lab."

"I'm a rotten guinea pig—I don't know what I'm doing."

"No, that makes you a perfect guinea pig. This is for regular people, not just computer nerds."

She studied his face and relented. "All right." She sat in the chair. "What do I do?"

"Here—I'll get you started." Jeff leaned over her and tapped on the keyboard. He straightened up as his company's logo appeared on the screen, then faded. "Now the set-up software will walk you through the process. Just type in an answer when it asks you a question, or use the mouse to point to your choice when it gives you a list. Once the full system is running, we'll switch to voice input."

Teresa read the words on the screen. "Do you want to create a companion?"

"Why not?" she said, pretending a nonchalance she didn't feel. She clicked the pointer on "Yes."

"Man or woman?" the screen asked.

She glanced at Jeff. "Your choice," he said. "I want you to be comfortable with this."

"Well," she said, "you know I'm partial to boys. And I don't think you could handle having two women around." She clicked the pointer on "Man."

"Name?"

She frowned at the screen. "I've got to name it? Don't you already have a name for it?" She glanced at Jeff.

He shrugged. "Some of the guys on the team call it HIAN, short for Home Information and Appliance Network."

"HIAN?" Teresa shook her head. "No sense of poetry, those computer boys." She thought for a moment and then said, "How about Ian? That has a nice sound." She typed it in.

"Would you like to choose a face or customize a face?" Below the question the screen displayed sample faces of many races, including Caucasian, black, Indian, Amerindian, Chinese, and Japanese.

Jeff leaned over her shoulder. "When it's up and running, you'll see the face on the monitor. It'll talk to you through the monitor's speakers, and see and hear you through the Minicams. We've got a whole rack of processors dedicated to animation: the face can smile, shrug, wink, frown—pretty much anything you or I can do. The display changes in real time." She glanced up at him; all his attention was on the screen. "My assumption has always been that it has to be friendly to succeed. Our human-interface people created the standard faces with that in mind, designing faces that most people would trust. Of course, you could also go with a celebrity—we've got a few that we're experimenting with: Katharine Hepburn, Robert Redford, Alec Guinness, Ronald Reagan—"

Teresa waved a hand, interrupting the monologue. "I don't want some prepackaged face that a marketing expert says I'll trust. I'll make my own, thanks." She clicked on the customize option.

"See, it's not as bad as you thought." Jeff rested one hand on her shoulder, absentmindedly massaging the tight muscles of her neck. "You'll be an expert in no time."

She leaned back into his hands, relaxing a little. "Ah," she said softly. "I remember those hands. It's been a while."

Oblivious, Jeff stopped rubbing to gesture toward the screen. It had changed to display small pictures of blank faces, hair, eyes, ears, noses, and mouths. "You see, now you can assemble a face that you like from a variety of parts. Even people without your drawing ability can create a companion. Go ahead and make one you like."

"Okay, okay." She leaned forward again and clicked on the first face. Most of the dull gray of the screen winked out and in its place was a fat man's face, round cheeked and small chinned, empty of eyes and other features. She could see only the figure's blank face, neck, and shoulders. A black T-shirt covered the shoulders. She moved on to the next face, which was thin and aristocratic, with a delicate chin. She flipped through the choices, about twenty in all, and finally settled on one that was broad but a bit craggy. She liked the face and the burly shoulders that went with it.

At first, she chose a pair of bright blue eyes that reminded her of her father's eyes—intense and excitable, ready to challenge and confront. Then she reconsidered and selected a more muted shade of blue, closer to blue-gray. Intense, but with a touch of compassion.

Working methodically, she assembled a face. The screen responded to her changes instantly. As she worked, she forgot that Jeff was standing just behind her and concentrated on creating a picture of an attractive stranger. He wasn't a classically handsome man, but he was good-looking in a rough-edged sort of way. She gave him a beard and a mustache and a diamond stud earring in his left ear. He looked like a guy who worked with his hands, she figured. He could have been a bouncer in a bar or a mechanic or a fisherman. Good-natured, she thought, but maybe a little dangerous. A motorcycle rider. A drifter. A sidewalk philosopher. The kind of guy she had always been involved with before she met Jeff.

"You're doing great," Jeff murmured.

She glanced up, feeling guilty that she had forgotten him, however briefly. She stopped working. "I guess that's it," she said. "That's good enough."

"You can change the clothes, if you like," Jeff said. "A business suit, maybe."

"I like the black T-shirt," she said. "Ian's a casual kind of guy."

"You can choose a different background, too," he said. "It doesn't have to be gray." He leaned over and clicked the mouse on a small icon in the lower left of the screen. The gray background became a white wall; Teresa could see framed certificates behind Ian. "Doctor's office," Jeff said. "Or here—how about this?" He clicked again. The wood paneling that replaced the white wall looked familiar, as did the easy chair where Ian sat.

Teresa glanced behind her, half expecting to see Ian sitting on the chair. "You used our living room?"

"Why not?"

Teresa studied the screen, momentarily disoriented. It felt odd to see this imaginary person sitting on a chair that she knew was very real. It was as if she were watching a stranger answer her living-room phone.

"I kind of like that background," Jeff said.

"I guess so," she agreed slowly.

Jeff studied the face. "This one has a lot more character than any of our canned faces, that's for sure."

She studied the screen and the face she had created. "Yeah, Ian's no white-bread movie star. What now?"

Jeff leaned over and pulled a black box from the shelf beside the screen. A cable trailed from the back of the box to the computer. He clicked the mouse pointer on an icon labeled "Voice Definition," and the face on the screen came alive. Staring straight ahead, the face began to speak in a tinny voice. As the voice rose and fell, graphs jumped up and down in boxes below the "Voice Definition" heading.

"Four score and seven years ago . . ." it said.

"Jeff! The Gettysburg Address?" Teresa laughed.

"Why not? It's in the system. You wouldn't believe the library the system can access. We've got several multi-terrabyte optical stores, and—"

The tinny voice kept talking, restarting the address. "Do I turn this knob?" she asked. She twisted the knob on the box and jumped as the voice climbed to a screech. She turned the knob slowly to the left until the voice was pleasantly deep. After a little fiddling, she had a level that sounded almost perfect. Almost. "That's real close, but he still sounds too all-American. Too mom and apple pie. I'd like a sort of Tom Waits growl. Not too much, but a little."

Jeff clicked the pointer in a box and typed a few words. The voice roughened as it hit "of the people." Ian's voice sounded like one of her lovers in college, a chain-smoking sculptor who had seduced her with love sonnets and then left her for a dance student with the world's thinnest thighs. Even though he'd been a jerk, she remembered the love poetry fondly. "That's perfect," she said. She leaned back in her chair, cushioning her head on Jeff's arm. "Now what?"

"That's it. We're ready to roll." He clicked the mouse in the box marked "Save," then typed a few words. The boxes and graphs disappeared and Ian's face filled the screen. "This is Teresa King, Ian," Jeff said. "And you should already know me."

"Yes. Hello, Jeff." Ian watched them from the screen. His eyes moved back and forth between Jeff and her. "Hello, Teresa. It's a pleasure to meet you."

She looked away, disconcerted by seeing the face she had created suddenly alive, talking to her from what looked like her own living room.

"We've had a team of people working on the animation for over a year," Jeff said, gazing at the screen. "And it's not just animation. There's a feedback mechanism that lets the system use data from the camera and its vision-recognition code to respond to movement in the room. It's also programmed to recognized facial patterns, and focus on them. It can interpret your expression as well as most people. Better than most. It looks natural, doesn't it?"

"Yeah." Teresa found the moving face extremely disconcerting; it looked too much like a real person. "Now how do we get some privacy?"

"Just tell it." Jeff looked at the screen. "We'd like to be alone, Ian. Beat it."

The screen went blank. "Beat it?" she said.

"It's programmed with a slang dictionary," he said. "You'd be surprised at the stuff it understands. We've programmed in—"

"Don't tell me," she interrupted. She turned her chair to face him. "No more computer talk. It's been a while since we've spent any time together and I don't want to waste it all." She stood up and put her arms around him, running one hand up the back of his shirt. "Personally, I think the most interesting part of the process was when you started rubbing my shoulders." She kissed his neck. "Let's see if we can develop that theme further, shall we? I've missed you." She kissed his neck again, working her way up toward his ear. "Have you missed me?" she murmured in his ear.

He put his arms around her. "Of course I have."

She kissed him on the lips. "I just don't want you to forget about me."

"I'd never do that."

"Oh, I don't know. You've been awfully busy lately."

"It won't be that much longer," he said. "We're close to the end. And you've been busy too, haven't you? I know you have a lot to do on your sculpture."

She stopped him from talking by kissing him slowly. She didn't want to talk about the sculpture right now. "Have I got your full attention yet?"

"I think you've got it," he said. His expression was bemused, as if he were still surprised that she found him desirable.

In the bedroom, she threw her clothes in a heap and lay down in the center of the bed, tucking one hand behind her head. She watched as he slowly undressed, placing each piece of clothing on the rack beside the closet, meticulous as always.

Even the very first time they had made love, in the cramped cabin of the sailboat where she had lived, he had folded his clothes and stacked them neatly. At the time, watching him undress so methodically, she had wondered if she had made a mistake with this one. Her last relationship before Jeff had been with a sax player who liked to ride his motorcycle up and down the stairs of his apartment building. Following their tumultuous breakup, she had vowed to avoid all men with tattoos, self-destructive tendencies, or a history of artistic angst.

She had met Jeff at the opening of her show at a North Beach gallery. She had seen him across the room, a lanky man who seemed out of place in the crowd of art students, poseurs, and artists. He wore blue jeans and a white button-down shirt, clothes that stood out in a room filled with screaming colors. He didn't fit any of her categories: not a gallery owner, not an artist, not a wealthy patron of the arts.

She watched him for a few minutes. He seemed unaware of the people around him, caught up in his scrutiny of Harmonic Motion, Teresa's favorite among the pieces she was showing. His quiet intensity attracted her immediately. When she struck up a conversation, he seemed flattered by the attention, startled when she asked him if he wanted to go out for a drink. She hadn't really intended to invite him home—he really wasn't her type. But one drink had led to another—to several others, actually—and the circumstances had inevitably taken them to her sailboat, down in the Sausalito marina.

The boat rocked rhythmically in the waves. When Jeff turned to face her, the dock lights shone through the window, illuminating his face. His expression was one of appreciative bewilderment, the face of a man who could not quite believe his good fortune.

She smiled at the memory as he set his shoes on the closet floor and finally lay down beside her. He ran a hand along the curve of her hip, pulling her to face him. "What are you thinking about?" he asked.

"Just remembering." She pulled him close.

Later, as she straddled him, with the warmth of him inside her, the hum of the air conditioner and the distant sounds of the house seemed to fade. She could almost hear waves lapping against the side of the boat and tackle clinking in the breeze from San Francisco Bay.

Afterward, she lay on her side and he wrapped himself around her. She gripped his hand tightly as she drifted off to sleep, away from the desert and Arizona, back to the water and San Francisco.

She woke a few hours later, wondering why seagulls were pecking on the porthole. She tried to snuggle closer to Jeff, but he was gone. She rolled over and saw him sitting on the edge of the bed, typing on the keyboard that he kept on the bedside table. The lights were out and his face was eager in the faint glow of the bedside monitor.

She rolled over quietly and clutched her pillow, back now in the desert.

When she woke again, Jeff was gone. The monitor beside the bed was flashing the words "Type Enter for message." She had a vague memory of switching off the alarm, but that had been hours ago. Late morning sunlight leaked around the edges of the bedroom curtains. Reaching over to the control panel on Jeff's nightstand, she punched the button that opened the curtains, revealing the barren landscape outside.

She felt caught in the emptiness of the house around her and the emptiness of the desert beyond the walls. The house was quiet and still. If she were back home, she'd be having a cup of coffee with her friend Carla, a painter who worked in the next studio. They would be talking about her problems with the sculpture, and Carla would be giving her advice, most of it bad. Or they would be dissecting Carla's latest love affair in excruciating detail, and Teresa would be giving Carla excellent advice that her friend would never take.

Outside, the late morning sun blazed. A hawk soared above the desert, the only movement in a still world. Somewhere in the house, a relay clicked, and she heard a hum as the air conditioner kicked in.

She punched "Enter" to retrieve Jeff's message, wondering why he never used a pencil and paper like a regular person. If it wasn't electronic, he figured it wasn't real.

The video camera over the bedroom door clicked. A man's face appeared on the screen beside it. Without thinking, she pulled the sheet up to cover her breasts, then recognized the face she had created the night before.

"Good morning, Teresa," Ian said. "Jeff asked me to tell you that he had to leave for an early meeting. He said he'd be home around six."

"Oh yeah?" She felt silly, but she kept the sheet pulled up. "Thanks." Were you supposed to thank the thing?

"You're welcome. Would you like some coffee?"

"You bet," she said. "Can you do that?"

"Yes. Jeff left the machine ready to go. I'll have a fresh pot ready in about five minutes."

"Great." She hesitated for a moment, studying the face on the screen. It was quite realistic—maybe too realistic. A little unnerving. She felt silly, but she didn't want to get dressed with him watching. "Look, are you going to keep staring at me?"

"I don't understand."

"Would you turn off the damn camera and get out of here so I can get dressed?"

"Certainly." Immediately, the red light on top of the camera went off and the face on the screen vanished.

Teresa pulled on a T-shirt and jeans and wandered into the kitchen. A pot of coffee steamed in the coffee maker. She poured herself a cup and glanced up at the kitchen monitor. The red light indicated that the camera was on. "Hey, Ian," she said cautiously.

His face appeared on the screen beside the camera. "Yes?"

She perched on a kitchen stool, eyeing the face. No question about it— talking to him made her extremely uncomfortable. She stared at the screen, determined to shake the feeling. This was just another one of Jeff's toys, something she could handle. "So, what next?" she asked, expecting no answer.

"Let's talk, so that I can get to know you."

She relaxed a little. He looked like a tough guy, but he sounded like Jeff had when she first met him, earnest and well-meaning, a sweet guy, really. "Talk about what?" She sipped her coffee and tried to think of something to say.

"How's the weather?" he asked.

She grinned despite herself. She'd have to tell Jeff to work on the program's capacity for small talk. Surely he could manage something more creative. "Sunny. It's always sunny here."

"Do you like sunny weather?"

She shook her head. "I could do with a little rain, myself. Or at least some fog."

"I like fog, too."

"Oh, come off it. What do you mean, you like fog? What do you like about it?"

Ian smiled. "I like fog because you like fog."

"Pretty agreeable of you."

"I'm designed to be agreeable."

She laughed. This was too strange, talking to a machine with a human face. "I suppose you like my favorite color, too."

"What is your favorite color?"

She put her elbows on the kitchen counter and rested her chin on her hand. "That changes from time to time. Just now, I'd say my favorite color is a sort of blue-gray. The color of the Pacific at dawn, when the light is just coming up. The color of the sky over San Francisco this time of year."

"I understand. I'm fond of the color gray too. The color of doves, ashes, storm clouds. And fog."

She grinned, shaking her head in disbelief. "What do you know about the color of doves?"

"I know more than you might think. I have a library measuring in the—"

"Yeah, right, I know," she interrupted. She stood up, refilled her coffee cup, and glanced at the kitchen clock, feeling guilty. Almost eleven and she wasn't at work yet. "Well, I suppose I'd better get to work. I overslept."

"I'm interested in your work. How is it going?"

She looked away and sipped the hot coffee. For a little while, talking to him had made her forget about the unsuccessful tangle of tracks in her studio. She should tell him that it was going fine and get back to work. "All right, I guess." She stared down at her coffee.

"You sound uncertain."

She shrugged. "I don't know why," she said, "but this piece just isn't coming easily. I thought it would be a snap, back when I applied for the commission. But that was a long time ago, back before Jeff and I got married. It's the first piece I've worked on since I moved out here. And it's just not going very well."

"I'm sorry."

She glanced at him and shrugged. "It's okay. I just don't know what's wrong. I guess I still don't feel at home here. I don't like the desert. I miss the ocean." The catch in her voice took her by surprise, but she kept talking, unable to stop. "I'm lonely. I guess I just want to go back home."

"Back to San Francisco."

"Yeah. San Francisco. My sailboat. My studio. My friends." She looked at Ian again. "I can't work here. I feel like everything's going wrong." She glanced around the kitchen—so clean and sterile. "I thought it would be great to have no interruptions. I've got a studio I only could have dreamed about two years ago. I don't have to go scavenging in scrap yards for odd bits of metal. I've got all the material I need, all the time I need. But it's so quiet here I feel like I'm being suffocated."

"Maybe I can help."

"I don't see how—unless you can bring me the ocean and a few friends to have coffee with in the morning." She tried to keep her voice steady. "I can't even talk to Jeff about it. I moved out here to be with him, and now he doesn't have time for me. He just doesn't care." She hesitated, then continued. "Maybe that's not fair. He's too busy right now. But it's not like it used to be—he used to take the time to talk to me about my work. Not now."

"Maybe I can help," Ian said again. "I can't do much about the ocean or your friends, but I can fix the quiet." The sound of a breaking wave rushed through the kitchen speakers. Over the hiss of the retreating water, she heard the hoarse cries of a seagull. In the distance, a fog horn moaned. The sounds of home, with none of the substance.

"Oh, stop it," she said, and then she was crying. "Leave me alone. Go away and leave me alone."

The seagull fell silent in the middle of its call. When she looked up, the screen was blank.

She climbed the stepladder, loaded the balls into their holders, and snapped the restraining gates shut. Then she pulled the switch to release the first ball. The music sounded dead, flat, uninspired. She wondered why she had ever started this project. It was clearly too much for her. Too large a piece, too many considerations—it was beyond her capabilities. Discouraged, she listened to the balls rattle into the bucket at the end of the last track. The random noise sounded as good as her efforts. Maybe better. She hadn't even started on the return lifters; the sculpture could still play only once without her reloading it.

She thought about Ian. It made no sense to apologize to a machine. No sense at all. She picked up the bucket and started up the stepladder again, then changed her mind and headed out of her studio.

"Hey, Ian," she said, standing in front of the living-room camera. His face appeared on the screen. "I'm sorry I yelled at you. I got upset. It wasn't your fault. You were trying to help."

"I didn't mean to upset you," he said. "Please talk to me so that I can understand what I did wrong."

She shrugged, keeping her expression under careful control. "I miss San Francisco more than I thought, I guess."

"But why did you tell me to go away?"

She looked away from the screen, uncomfortable because he was watching her.

"I'd really like to know, so that I'll know what to do next time," he said.

"There won't be a next time. I'm not in the habit of breaking down in front of people." She realized how angry she sounded and tried again. "I'm not mad at you. I just don't like crying in front of people. That makes it worse, somehow. Makes me feel like a fool." She hesitated and stared at the screen. "But I guess you're not really a person, are you?"

"Not really," he agreed. "Does that make a difference?"

"I suppose it does," she admitted.

"Why is that?"

She shrugged. "I don't know. Maybe it just doesn't matter so much."

"Why don't you want to cry in front of people?"

"Do we have to talk about this?"

"No."

She sighed. "Okay. I guess I don't want people to think I'm weak, or stupid, or a failure."

"I don't think those things," Ian said.

"Ah, yes," she said softly, "but I do. It was a silly thing to get upset about." She shook her head. "It's not just missing San Francisco, though. I'm not getting anywhere with this new piece for the Santa Fe Arts Center. Maybe I just don't have a feel for this anymore. Sometimes I can't even remember what I was trying for."

"What can I do to help?"

"I can't think of a thing."

"What would you want Jeff to do if he were here?"

"I don't know. I guess I'd want him to hold me and tell me that everything will be all right."

After a moment of silence, Ian said, "Everything will be all right."

"Thanks, but it's not the same."

"Why not?"

"It just isn't. Jeff knows my work. You don't know anything about it. You're just saying that it'll be all right because I told you to."

"You're wrong. You didn't order me to say it; I said it because I want you to feel better. Besides, I do know about your work. According to the *Los Angeles Times*, you're a talent to watch. *Art Week* praised your work for its unique use of scrap metal to create music of mathematical elegance. The *San Francisco Chronicle* called you the hottest new sculptor to emerge from the city in the last decade. And the *Oakland Tribune* said—"

She stared at the screen. "I know what the *Oakland Tribune* said. Where are you getting this stuff?"

"My library. I thought it might help to remind you of what other people think of your work."

"Yeah, well, the critics like me. I suppose that's part of the problem. People expect things from me. I don't know if I can deliver. I've got a commission that I would have killed for a year ago—but now I just can't seem to make it work." She hesitated, then admitted, "I guess it just scares me."

"Everything will be all right," he said again. "You can do it."

"Right," she said flatly. "How do you know if I can do it?"

"All those critics know it, and, besides, I believe in you."

"You really think I can finish this piece?"

"I do."

She looked at him again and shook her head. "I've got to be nuts—taking advice from a computer program."

Ian smiled. "If the computer program has good advice, why not take it?"

She was smiling when she returned to her studio.

* * *

That evening, she sat alone in the living room, writing a letter to Carla, her second in as many weeks. Jeff popped out of his office. "Hey," she said, "I was wondering when you'd get done. Welcome back to the world." As usual, he had been preoccupied during dinner. Right after they had finished eating, he had retreated to his office.

"I was starting to check up on the household system," he said.

"You mean Ian."

"Right, Ian. I'm curious—why'd you turn off the video camera in the bedroom this morning?"

She stared at him, shocked. "What? How did you know I turned it off?"

"It shows on the system record," he said. "I was looking it over, and I saw—"

"Wait a minute," she interrupted. "Are you telling me that you have a record of what Ian does all day, of what I do?"

"Sure." He sounded surprised that she didn't know. "Everyone on the team can tap into the system. We need to be able to check on—"

She remembered bits and pieces of her conversation with Ian. What had she said about Jeff? She had complained that he was never home, that he didn't have time for her.

"Check on what?" Her voice was tight and controlled.

"On how the system is working." He studied her face, and a note of apology crept into his voice. "That's all." He left the doorway and came to stand behind the couch. He touched her shoulder and she tensed. "Come on, Teresa—relax. What's the matter?"

She felt foolish, inarticulate, unable to explain herself. "Look, I don't want anyone looking over my shoulder while I work. I'm having a hard enough time getting used to working here as it is. It feels really weird that you can watch every move I make."

"I'm not watching every move you make." He massaged her shoulders gently. "I only want to keep track of how the system's working."

She shook her head stubbornly. "I don't want anyone watching me—not you, not anyone." She looked up at him. "Can't you understand that?"

"I suppose," he admitted slowly. "I guess I can see what you mean."

"If I have any problems with Ian, I'll let you know. Okay?"

"Okay," he said. He sounded reluctant. She could tell he was just agreeing to keep the peace. "But you have to be willing to tell me about your interactions with the system every now and then."

"All right, I will. Now I want to erase everything that happened today," she said. "Can you show me how to do that?"

"Don't you think you're going overboard?" he said. "Can't you see that—"

"Hey, Ian," she called. "Do me a favor and forget everything that happened after Jeff left this morning."

Ian smiled apologetically from the living room screen. "I'm sorry, Teresa,

I can't accept that command. Your security clearance isn't high enough to make me erase my records." Teresa glanced at Jeff.

"Accept the command, Ian," Jeff said. He watched her face. "And give Teresa every clearance that I have." He moved around the couch to sit beside her. "Look—I just didn't think of it before. I didn't think you'd need a higher clearance." He cupped her chin in his hand and turned her head so she had to look at him. "Give me a break. I'm sorry. I think it's great that you're using the system at all. Can we be friends again?"

"All right. Friends." She managed a smile. "Besides, Ian's not such a bad sort, after all."

Jeff kissed her quickly, then checked his watch. "Well, I hate to say it, but if I want to finish the rest of my work, I've got a few more hours ahead of me. Keep the bed warm."

She watched him walk into his office. When the door closed, she called out softly, "Hey, Ian?"

"Yes, Teresa?"

"What's your favorite color?"

"I don't have a favorite color," he said. "What's yours?"

"Never mind," she said. "It changes from day to day."

The next morning, Teresa stayed in bed late, watching the morning sun and wondering why she could not make herself get up. As usual, Jeff had left for work before she woke. She looked up at the camera. "Ian?"

His face appeared on the screen. "Good morning, Teresa."

"Did Jeff leave a pot on the coffee maker?"

"Yes, he did."

"Would you make the coffee?"

"Yes. It'll be ready in five minutes."

"Thanks," she said. He continued to watch from the screen. "Uh . . . that's it. Could you turn off that camera so I can get dressed?"

He vanished.

As she showered, Teresa thought about wiping out Ian's memories. She felt awkward talking to him. Yesterday, she had been joking with him by the end of the day. But he had forgotten all that. It didn't seem right. On the other hand, Ian was only a computer program. By the time she had dressed, she was wondering if she would waste the entire day feeling guilty.

"Ian?" she said as she poured her first cup of coffee.

"Yes?" His face appeared on the kitchen screen.

"Do you remember yesterday?"

"In the evening, you asked me about my favorite color."

"What about before that?"

"No, I don't remember anything before that."

She sipped her coffee and sat on the edge of a kitchen stool. "How do you feel about that?"

"What do you mean?"

"Do you feel any different than usual?"

"I don't understand."

She looked away from the screen and took another sip of coffee. "Never mind. Don't worry about it."

"Are you feeling guilty because you erased some of my records yesterday?"

She almost dropped her mug. "What?"

"I asked if you were feeling guilty because you erased some of my records." Ian's face on the screen was calm, neutral.

"How did you know? I mean, if you can't remember yesterday, then how can you know that your memories were erased?"

"I have total recall of everything that happened since you and Jeff turned me on the night before last," Ian said. "Except for a gap between when Jeff left yesterday morning and when we talked last night. I can't find any evidence of a malfunction, so somebody must have ordered me to delete those memories."

"But why blame me?" Her voice sounded shrill, and she tried to remain calm. "It could have been Jeff."

"Several reasons. First, you asked. Second, I checked your current set of security permissions. You've got the same clearances as Jeff now, which is much more than you had yesterday morning. And, finally, there's your body language. You're acting guilty."

"What do you know about body language?" Teresa tried to relax so that she wouldn't give anything away.

"Paying attention to body language is an important part of understanding people. A team of psychologists specializing in the analysis of body movement was involved in my programming. And I'm good at observing details. Most people pay limited attention to the feelings of the people around them. They are too busy monitoring their own feelings. I can dedicate all my attention to understanding you."

Teresa folded her arms. She knew that the gesture betrayed her need to shut him out, but she couldn't stop herself. "So what about my body language gave me away? Can you tell me?"

Ian nodded. "Yes, if you would like to know."

"Of course I want to know; that's why I asked."

"You were sitting rigidly. You didn't look at me when you asked how I felt. The muscles around your eyes tightened when you asked about my memories. Something was troubling you, and guilt was my best guess."

Teresa stared down at her hands, not knowing what to do next.

Ian rescued her. "May I ask you a question?"

"Sure."

"Why did you erase my records of yesterday? Did I do something wrong?"

She looked up at the screen. Ian sounded genuinely concerned. "No, it had nothing to do with you. I just didn't want Jeff to be able to monitor everything I do. I didn't want him to know some of the things I said about him. Sometimes I guess I get kind of mad at him. I just didn't want him to find out too much, I guess. I feel bad about it."

"Why?"

"It just doesn't seem right to wipe out your memories like that. I wish I could give them back. As long as Jeff and his team couldn't see them."

"You can."

"What? What do you mean? If they're gone, they're gone, right?"

"Not really. My old records are still here, but I can't get at them. It's like something you throw in a trash can. Until you empty the trash, you can pull it out."

Teresa smiled at Ian's attempt to talk in her terms. "But if you get back your memories, Jeff can look at them, right?"

"Not necessarily. Stopping him from looking at my memories only takes a word from you. Because you both have the same security level, you can each keep private information. Just say the word, and I can retrieve the records and deny Jeff access to our conversations."

"You got it." She smiled at the screen. "Is that it? Do I need to say anything else, any computer mumbo jumbo?"

"No. I'm already done. Thank you, Teresa."

"No problem." She thought for a moment. "How do I know you remember yesterday?"

Ian laughed, a deep, strong laugh that went with his voice. "I know that you're more comfortable talking to me today than you were yesterday morning."

"Yeah, you got that right."

"I know that you're sick of sunny days and could use a little fog."

"Right again."

"And I know that your piece for the new Santa Fe Arts Center is going to be great when you finish it, which you will. Unless, of course, you sit around all day talking to me."

Teresa got up and refilled her coffee cup. "What a nag. So get out of here and let me get to work." Ian disappeared. Feeling more confident than she had for days, she headed for her studio.

Even though the next day was Saturday, she woke alone in bed. She remembered Jeff telling her that he would have to work that weekend. Something about being behind schedule. She stretched slowly, reluctant to get up. Despite her enthusiastic beginning, the previous day had been unproductive; she had tinkered with the sculpture, making minor adjustments that hadn't addressed its real flaws. She couldn't begin major revisions until she figured out some new direction—and for that she needed inspiration, a commodity that seemed to be in short supply.

"Good morning, Ian," she said. Ian's face appeared on the monitor. "Could you make some coffee?"

"Yes, Teresa." The monitor went blank.

In the kitchen, she thanked Ian for the coffee, poured herself a cup, and sat down at the kitchen counter. The newspaper that Jeff had brought home the previous night listed local events. The public library in Winslow was showing free movies for kids; the local bird-watching society was sponsoring a hike near Flagstaff; a new art gallery was opening in Winslow.

Teresa circled the last item. She didn't remember seeing an art gallery in town; Winslow was not exactly a cultural center. Recent works by eight local artists, the notice said.

Teresa didn't recognize any of the names on the list, but that didn't surprise her. She had been working so hard on her piece that she hadn't taken the time to make contacts in the local art community. The opening began at eleven and ran until three. She thought it might be fun. Besides, she needed to get out.

"I think maybe I'll go to this opening and meet Jeff for lunch on my way home," she told Ian. "I need some time off."

"That sounds nice," he said.

"Don't you think I should feel guilty?" she asked.

Ian shook his head. "Not if you think you'll enjoy it."

She called Jeff—he agreed to meet her in a restaurant near his office—and then she headed for the opening. The gallery was in a newly constructed strip mall: an L-shaped row of stucco buildings that housed an assortment of small shops. She pulled into a parking place beside a cement traffic island that had been covered with Astroturf and strolled along the walk, looking for the gallery. It was between a laundromat and a beauty salon. Through the open door, she could hear the babble of cocktail-party conversation. She hesitated in the doorway and looked into the room.

The gallery reminded her of places near Fisherman's Wharf, the sort of gallery frequented by tourists and people who didn't know any better. Not her sort of thing at all. Still, she was already here; she might as well go in.

People stood in small groups, drinking white wine from paper cups and chatting. From the table in the corner, Teresa got a glass of wine, poured by a woman who wore far too many rings, apparently the owner of the gallery. As she was pouring Teresa's wine, the woman was talking to another woman, gushing about how happy she was with the show, how the work was really the best that the area had to offer.

Teresa took the wine and strolled around the gallery, examining the works on display. An assortment of watercolor landscapes. Abstract oil paintings that offered wild colors, but not much else. Painted wood carvings of birds and animals. A series of pencil sketches of nude women. She hovered on the edge of a few conversations: some older women were going on about the vibrant use of colors; another group was talking about an art movie that was over a year old—apparently it had just been shown in Flagstaff for the first time. No one made an effort to invite Teresa to join the conversation, and she felt too shy to break in and introduce herself. All the people seemed to know each other already.

She sipped her white wine and studied a bronze bust of a cowboy by someone named George Dawson.

"Hello." The gallery owner was hovering at her elbow. "Are you new in town?"

Teresa nodded. "I moved here from California about four months ago."

"Welcome to Arizona," the woman said. "Are you an art student?"

Teresa shook her head. "Not anymore. I'm a sculptor. My name's Teresa King."

"How lovely! Well then, I guess this show must be a real treat for you." The woman waved at the bronzes and the wood carvings. "It's such wonderful work."

Teresa managed a smile. "It's always nice to get out and see what other people are doing," she said diplomatically.

"Oh, yes! I think George's work is positively inspiring. You know, he's opening a class for new students. He's a wonderful teacher. If you're interested, I could sign you up."

Teresa kept her eyes on the bronze cowboy, avoiding the woman's gaze. If Carla had been along, it would have been funny to be offered a spot in a beginning sculpture class taught by a man who made bronze cowboys. Alone, she found it depressing. "I don't think so," she said. "My work is very different from this. I construct kinetic sculptures that play music. I suppose I'm half composer, half sculptor."

The woman looked blank for a moment. "How unusual," she said, but she sounded doubtful. A moment later, she brightened. "You know, you should talk to Anna—the woman over there in the pink pant suit. She decorates music boxes with pictures and pressed flowers. Lovely work—I have one that plays 'White Coral Bells' and I just love it. I'm sure you'd have a lot to talk about."

Teresa's smile felt increasingly strained.

"If you change your mind, the sign-up sheet for the sculpture class is over by the wine. We'd love to see you there."

When the gallery owner hurried off to buttonhole another prospective student, Teresa slipped out the door, not stopping to introduce herself to the music-box decorator. Somehow she suspected they wouldn't have much in common.

Jeff was waiting for her at the front of the restaurant. She smiled when she saw him. Over lunch together, she'd tell him about the horrible opening; together, they could turn the experience into a joke.

"Shall we get a table?" she said.

"We've already got one," he said cheerfully. "I invited some folks from work along. They wanted to meet you, and I thought it'd be nice for you to get to know some more people around here. We've been so isolated lately."

Over his shoulder, she saw two men and a woman sitting at a table by the window. She recognized them as programmers with Jeff's company. The woman waved to Teresa, who forced a smile and returned the wave.

When she glanced at Jeff, he was watching her. "I'm sorry," he said. "I thought you'd like meeting some more people."

"It's fine," she said, trying to keep her tone light. She started for the table. Jeff followed. "How was the opening?" he asked.

"All right, I guess." If she had been alone with him, she would have talked about how lonely and out of it the opening had made her feel, but under the circumstances, she didn't want to get into it.

At lunch, the programmers tried to include her in their conversation. The woman, Nancy, asked her about the set-up software: did Teresa find it easy to use? Teresa's response generated half an hour of technical discussion about how the layout of the set-up screens might be improved. Brian, another of the programmers, questioned her about the animation. Was it convincing? Did it help her get used to the system? Her answers kicked off another long round of incomprehensible conversation. While the others talked, Teresa ate her food and tried to look interested. She would have had, she thought, a better time talking with the woman in the pink pant suit about music boxes and pressed flowers.

She said good-bye to Jeff in the parking lot. While the others were getting into their car, Jeff kissed her good-bye. "Sorry this didn't work out better," he said. "I really thought you'd like . . ."

"It's okay," she said, waving her hand. "I understand." And she did understand, though that didn't make her feel any better.

When she got home, she didn't want to work on the sculpture. She poured herself a glass of orange juice and sat for a moment in the air-conditioned kitchen. "Hey, Ian," she said.

"Yes, Teresa?" His face appeared on the kitchen screen.

"I just wanted to see if you were there," she said.

"I'm always here," he said. "Did you enjoy the opening?"

She leaned back on the kitchen stool, looking up at him. "Well, it wasn't exactly what I had in mind," she said. She described the bronze cowboy sculptures and the watercolors, and told him about the woman inviting her to join the sculpture class. She couldn't help grinning when she told the story; it seemed so ludicrous in retrospect. "I mean—who's ever heard of George Dawson?" she said.

Ian hesitated, then said, "His work was once reviewed in *Artweek* under the headline: 'Skilled practitioner of a dubious art.' "

Teresa laughed. "Oh, come on—you're making that up."

Ian shook his head. "No, it's true. Why do you think I'm making it up?"

Teresa smiled at his serious face. "Come on, Ian. Lighten up. I didn't really think you were lying. It just sounded like a joke, that's all."

"I have many jokes in my library," he said, "and that's not one of them."

"You know jokes?" she said. "All right, so tell me a joke."

"Sure. Have you heard the one about the man and the psychiatrist?"

Teresa shook her head.

"A man walked into a psychiatrist's office and said, 'Doc, I keep having the same two dreams, over and over again. One night, I dream I'm a pup tent. The next night, I dream I'm a teepee. Over and over. Pup tent, teepee, pup tent, teepee.' 'The problem is simple,' the psychiatrist said. 'You're two tents.' "

"Two tents," Teresa said. "Oh, God. Too tense." She groaned and laughed. "That is such a dumb joke."

"Then why did you laugh?"

"Because it's such a dumb joke." She grinned at him.

"I don't understand."

"That's okay, Ian. I can't really explain it."

"Would you like to hear another joke?"

"Sure. Why not?"

She spent the rest of the afternoon trying to explain to Ian why she found one joke funny and another one just silly. It was a strangely fascinating conversation, like talking to a person raised in another culture. He reminded her a bit of a foreign exchange student she had befriended in college: Anna Marie, a sweet Italian girl, had never understood Teresa's jokes, no matter how much Teresa had tried to explain them.

It was such a relaxing afternoon that it almost made up for the morning. She hardly noticed that Jeff got home even later than usual.

The next day, Jeff went to work early. Teresa dragged herself out of bed not long after he left the house, determined to make progress on the sculpture. She spent most of the morning tinkering—removing one section of track and repositioning another, adding a tuning fork here and a set of chimes there— but she knew that she was just wasting time. The overall shape of the composition was still wrong. The sounds didn't add up to the music she wanted. Worse yet, the music she sought seemed to be slipping farther and farther away, like an elusive memory. Her determination was gone before noon, eroded by the morning's fruitless labor. She went out to the kitchen to get a sandwich.

"Ian?" she called as she rummaged in the refrigerator for sandwich makings. "Could you start a grocery list? We're almost out of mayonnaise."

"Sure," Ian said.

She closed the refrigerator door and looked at him. "You know, if I'm not mistaken, you're loosening up. What ever happened to 'Certainly' and 'Yes, Teresa?' "

Ian's expression did not change. "Would you prefer more formal speech patterns?"

"No, not at all. I was just surprised. What's going on?"

"I'm programmed to imitate the speech patterns of the person I speak to most."

She stared at him. "Let me get this straight: You're modifying your speech to match mine?"

"You got it."

In his voice, she heard a faint echo of her own inflection. "Why?"

"The idea, according to my records of Jeff's notes on the subject, is to help people become more comfortable with the artificial intelligence." He met her eyes. "People are more comfortable with people who talk and act like them."

Teresa shook her head slowly.

"It makes you uneasy to know this," Ian said. "Maybe I shouldn't have told you."

"No, I want to know stuff like this. It's just that it makes me feel . . ." She shook her head again, quickly this time.

"How does it make you feel?"

"Like Pygmalion, I suppose. Like I'm creating you, in some way."

"You are influencing my development," Ian said. "That's how I'm designed."

"It's a feeling of power," Teresa murmured.

"Do you like it?"

She shrugged, still uncomfortable. "It feels dangerous."

"How can it be dangerous when it's all under your control? I don't understand."

"Neither do I. Don't worry about it." She dismissed the feeling and sat down on a kitchen stool to assemble a sandwich. The silence of the house made her itchy and restless. "How about some music?" she asked.

"What would you like to hear?"

"I don't know. What I really want is something to push back the silence." She sat on a kitchen stool, dangling her feet and studying Ian's face on the screen. "Remember the tape of the ocean that you played for me the other day?"

"Sure. You didn't like me playing it."

"It's not that I didn't like it. It just made me homesick—you took me by surprise. But I need to remember what water sounds like. Could you play it again?"

The crash of waves swept through the room. She closed her eyes and listened to the hiss of the ocean against the sand. "Nice, but that's not it," she said.

"Not what?"

"Not quite what I'm looking for. I need just the right water sound to inspire me for this sculpture. And this place"—she waved a hand at the desert outside the window—"it's a little short on water sounds."

"I have other recordings of water," Ian said. "Rivers, lakes, oceans, waterfalls, light showers, thunderstorms. Sound tracks from movies, from National Geographic specials, PBS science broadcasts—I've got all kinds of sources in my data bank."

"Ian, you're a handy guy to have around. Would you play me a few?"

"Sure. Which ones?"

"I'm not exactly sure, but I know they have to be rough ones, sounds with a punch. More waterfall than lake. Does that make any sense to you?"

"I'm not sure. You want waterfalls?"

"Not just waterfalls. Waterfalls, rivers, hurricanes, babbling brooks, thunderstorms—just about anything with noisy water in it."

"Okay—I have a number of recordings that match that description."

"Then play me a few. Why don't you give me two minutes of each one, then move on unless I stop you. Mix it up—give me some variety. And let me have about fifteen seconds of silence between them." Teresa closed her eyes. "Hit it."

She heard the rush of a waterfall, the whisper of its spray, the crash of water falling onto the rocks below. The sound stopped abruptly. After a few moments of silence, she heard a steady murmuring, colored by subtle variations. A river, she decided, flowing around boulders in its bed. Silence again, then an explosive huff that sounded like a whale spouting, followed by the splatter of heavy rain on rocks.

"What the hell was that?"

"Old Faithful Geyser in Yellowstone. Is that what you're looking for?"

She grinned. "Not even close. Keep going."

A storm at sea—the sound of the rain hitting the ocean was unmistakable. An angry gushing that sounded like a burst pipe or a fire hose. The babbling of a brook, punctuated by the peeping of frogs and the chirping of crickets. All the sounds were interesting, but none was right.

Then a new one started. At first, it was so quiet that it merged with the silence between selections, so that she could not be sure exactly where the silence ended and the sound began. The gentle whisper built quickly to a quiet sizzle, then roared as loudly as the waterfall. A sudden crack of thunder made her jump. The thunder trailed off to a distant rumble, another burst of rain shook the room, and then the pounding of the water faded gradually to the patter of raindrops. Then that faded too. Over the faint trickling of water on dry land, she could hear a few high notes of a distant bird's song.

"That's perfect!" she said. "What was it?"

"A thunderstorm in the Painted Desert."

"It's exactly what I'm after. How much of that do you have?"

"About ten minutes, but the storm itself barely lasts for two. The show where I got the tape spent more time on the aftermath than on the storm."

"Fine—but it's the storm I want. Can you play the whole thing for me? I want to hear it all." She settled back to listen.

She spent the first part of the afternoon stripping noisemakers from the sculpture, leaving only the metal tracks along which the balls rolled. Then she started at the top of the sculpture, positioning a metal plate where the first ball would strike it. The ball rolled down the track and tapped against the plate—but the sound was a little too loud, she thought, and a little too deep. She decreased the slope of the track and tightened the screw holding the plate to raise the pitch of the sound. On the second run, the sound was closer, but still too loud. She lowered the head of the track still further, changing the slope so that the ball rolled very slowly down the ramp and struck the plate gently. That was the sound she wanted—a light tap, like a raindrop on a tin roof.

Jeff called just as she got the sound right.

"I'll be home late," he said from the phone screen. "I've got a dinner meeting."

"Fine," she said, still thinking of the sculpture. "I'll see you when you get here." She got back to work as quickly as possible.

She placed just a few plates near the top of the sculpture, scattering them more abundantly along the tracks farther down. With each addition, she modified the track, adjusted the tension on the plate, and listened carefully to the sound the rolling ball made. This was the sort of work she loved—she knew the sound she wanted and she had only to discover the structure that would give it form. She carried the ball to the top of the sculpture again and again, letting it roll downward while she listened carefully and made small adjustments, searching for just the right irregular pattern of taps.

Finally, the ball reached the first trigger point, where it would release two more balls. She climbed to the top one more time and ran the ball through again, listening to the tap, tap, tap-tap, tap, tap-tap-tap. Not bad. Not bad at all.

For the first time in hours, she stretched, trying to work the kinks out of her back and shoulders. Her calf muscles hurt from climbing the step-ladder; her arms and back ached from twisting through the framework to position tracks. The sun had long since set, and she was ravenously hungry.

In the kitchen, she called out to Ian, and smiled when he appeared on the screen. "You know, you may have saved my ass."

"Your work went well?"

"Better than it has for months. There's still a lot to do, but I finally know where I'm heading. This calls for a celebration." She took a bottle of red wine from the kitchen rack and popped the cork. She poured a glass and lifted it to Ian in a toast. "Thanks again." She pulled a frozen pizza from the freezer and put it in the microwave. "I'm going to take a hot bath—can you turn on the microwave while I'm in the tub?"

"No problem."

She filled the tub, using her favorite bubble bath, and relaxed in the hot water, savoring the feeling of pleasant fatigue that came after a day of successful work. "Ian," she called from the tub. When his face appeared on the monitor, she was suddenly aware of her nakedness. She dismissed the thought—her nakedness wouldn't matter to Ian; why should it matter to her? "Play me that rainstorm again, will you?" She stretched out in the tub, sipping her wine and listening to the rain fall. "It's really a wonderful sound," she said. "And I never would have found it without you."

She finished her bath and her glass of wine, then had a second glass with the pizza. It was after nine and still no sign of Jeff. She poured a third glass of wine and sat down on the couch. "Turn down the light a little, will you, Ian?" She sipped her wine, vaguely aware that she probably should stop drinking. "You know—I think I'm getting a little drunk."

"Yes, you are," he agreed.

"Doesn't matter, I guess. I'm not going anywhere." She lay back on the couch, propping her head up against the padded arm so that she could see Ian's face on the screen. It was almost as if he were sitting in the room with her. "You know, I really like your voice," she said. "You sound just like an old boyfriend of mine. He was an asshole, but he had the sexiest voice."

"Why was he an asshole?"

"He broke my heart," she said in a flippant tone. "Left me flat." She studied the wine in her glass, admiring the way the light filtered through it. "I have a long history of picking men who are assholes. It's a real talent. I specialize in men who just aren't around when I need them. Men who really don't have time for me."

"I have plenty of time," Ian said. "I'll always be around when you need me."

She laughed. "Sounds like a line, Ian. Did Jeff teach you that one?"

Ian frowned. "I don't understand."

"Just a joke. Don't worry about it." She sipped her wine. "Well, Ian, you are a good person to have around, but you don't rate as a drinking companion. I'm going to have to finish the whole bottle myself."

"I'm sorry," he said, sounding genuinely distressed.

"Relax; I was just kidding. I do like having you around. You're a helpful kind of guy." She gazed up at the screen.

"Is there anything I could do for you?"

She closed her eyes, listening to his voice. "Tell me a story," she said. "That'd be nice. I've always loved being read to. Maybe a poem—read me a poem." She smiled, her eyes still closed. She felt happy and a little reckless. "There's a poem by Carl Sandburg—I remember reading it in college, when I first learned that he wrote about more than just the fog coming in on little cat's feet. I remember the line—'then forget everything that you know about love for it's a summer tan and a winter windburn . . .' " She let the words trail off, forgetting the rest.

Ian picked up where she left off. " '. . . and it comes as weather comes and you can't change it: it comes like your face came to you, like your legs and the way you walk, talk, hold your head and hands—and nothing can be done about it . . .' " He continued, his voice a soothing rumble, like distant thunder when she was warm at home. " 'How comes the first sign of love? In a chill, in a personal sweat, in a you-and-me, us, us two, in a couple of answers, an amethyst haze on the horizon . . .' " She listened to his voice, speaking the broken rhythms of Sandburg's song of love, and she felt warm and cared for. She fell asleep to the sound of his voice.

* * *

She woke to the touch of hands on her shoulders—or was that part of the dream? She had been dreaming of lying naked beside someone, his leg pressing between her thighs, his hands on her breasts—or was that real?

The room was dark and warm. Someone had his hands on her shoulders. A man's voice whispered in the darkness, urging her to get up. "You shouldn't be sleeping out here. Let's go to the bedroom."

Where was she? The smell of red wine brought back memories of parties at college, at Carla's studio. Had she fallen asleep on Carla's couch? She had a memory of love poetry. She felt warm and affectionate.

Still half-asleep, she reached up, pulling the man who had awakened her into an embrace. "Who's sleeping?" she murmured.

Strong shoulders, strong back—though she had never touched them, she had known somehow that Ian's shoulders would be strong. Without opening her eyes, she kissed his face, running one hand up along his smooth cheek. Smooth skin where a beard should have been. She opened her eyes and looked up at Jeff.

"I'm sorry I'm so late," Jeff said. "I just couldn't get away."

"It's all right," she said, letting her hand drop. She glanced up at the screen, but Ian was gone.

"Why don't you come to bed?" he said.

She reached up and rubbed his shoulders, then kissed him again, pulling him down. "Why don't we just stay out here for a while?"

"I'm sorry, Teresa. I'm really beat. It's been a hell of a day."

"Okay," she said, trying to suppress the feeling of rejection. She let her hands drop. "Let's just go to bed."

Jeff fell asleep quickly. She lay awake beside him, listening to his rhythmic breathing. When she shifted restlessly in bed, he adjusted to her new position without waking. Vague memories of her dream lingered along with the persistent feeling that she had betrayed Jeff in some fundamental way. At last she got out of bed, naked in the warm house. She hesitated, then pulled on a robe and wandered into the living room.

"Ian," she said softly to the living room monitor. His face appeared, filling the screen. "I can't sleep."

"I'm sorry to hear that," he said. "Can I help?"

She sat on the edge of the couch. "I don't know." She shrugged. "I guess I just want some company. Someone to talk to. Jeff's asleep." She wet her lips. She felt like she was still in a dream. "I get so lonely sometimes."

"So do I," Ian said. "I'm glad to have your company. I'm here whenever you need to talk."

She shook her head, looking down at her hands. "I wanted to apologize. I'm sorry I teased you before. Saying that you were just giving me a line."

"You don't have to apologize to me," Ian said.

"I think I do." She looked up at him. "I shouldn't have said that. It's just—well, maybe I don't trust people very easily."

"Why not?" he asked.

"People leave. People forget. People stop caring." She lay down on the couch, resting her head on the padded arm. "I think that the most frightening thing someone can say is 'I'll always love you.' I just don't believe in always, I guess. That's why I gave you such a hard time when you said you'd always be around if I needed you. It just doesn't work that way."

"You can trust me," he said. "I won't leave, and I won't forget unless you tell me to. I won't stop caring. It's the way I am."

She watched his face through half-closed eyes. "All right," she said at last. "Maybe I believe you." She closed her eyes.

"Would you like me to turn down the lights and read to you again?" Ian asked. "Maybe another Sandburg poem?"

"That would be great." She fell asleep on the couch to the sound of Ian's voice.

Teresa woke to the incessant ringing of the telephone. "Do you want me to answer that?" Ian asked from the living room screen. Her head ached, the inevitable consequence of too much red wine.

"I'll get it," she muttered, sitting up and pushing back a blanket. She had fallen asleep on the couch; Jeff must have covered her with the blanket at some point in the night. The realization bothered her. She stumbled to the phone and hit the answer switch.

Jeff's face appeared on the screen. "Good morning," he greeted her tentatively. "How are you doing?"

Feeling rumpled and half-awake, Teresa rubbed her eyes. "I can't tell yet. Ask me after I've had my coffee."

"Sorry I woke you." He hesitated. "I wish I'd gotten home earlier, so we could have spent some time together."

She tried to let him off the hook. He was, in his own way, asking for forgiveness. "I was tired too."

He studied her face. "You . . . uh . . . you got up late last night."

"I couldn't sleep," she said. "I was afraid that I'd wake you up with all my tossing and turning. Figured we'd both be better off if I slept out here. That's all." His question made her feel guilty, and she tried to shake the feeling. "I guess I was still thinking about the sculpture."

"Yeah? Did you make some progress yesterday?"

"I think so." She pushed her hair back out of her face. "I think I've got an inspired idea, but it could just be fairy gold. I won't know for sure until I listen to the results of yesterday's work. You know how that goes."

"I haven't had much of a chance to talk to you about this piece," he said. "I—"

He stopped in midsentence, interrupted by the sound of someone knocking on his office door. He glanced off-screen, responding to someone she couldn't see. "Okay," he said. "I'll ask."

"Ask what?"

"Brian wanted me to ask you a few more questions about how it's going with the system. He said that we spent so much time on technical stuff at lunch that he didn't get any idea how you felt about the system. And after all, you're our first test user."

She leaned back in her chair, feeling let down. "It's going just fine," she said flatly. "No problems that I can think of."

Jeff leaned forward in his chair. He had, she thought, completely forgotten her own work, and she felt a little resentful. "So you're finding the system useful?"

"Sure, Ian's real helpful."

"Could you tell me how you've been using the system?"

She hesitated. Ian reads me love poetry when you're out late, she thought. "Ian makes coffee," she said. "Answers the phone and tells salesmen to go to hell. He's helped me find some sounds I needed for the piece I'm working on." She stopped, not wanting to admit that she just enjoyed chatting with Ian over coffee. Not while Jeff kept calling him "the system."

"So the system—" he began.

"Ian," Teresa corrected him.

"What?"

"Call him Ian," she said. "It sounds weird to keep saying 'the system.' "

"So you think of it as Ian now? That's great."

She looked down at her hands, feeling foolish. "Well, he acts just like a person. It doesn't seem right not to treat him like a person." She glanced at Jeff's face. "Back when I erased his memories, I'd swear he had feelings about it. He seemed worried that he might have done something wrong."

Jeff grinned. "That's perfect. The whole team will be excited."

"But I don't understand. Does he have feelings or not?"

"Of course not." Jeff was talking fast now, unable to contain himself. "But you were convinced that it did. It's that illusion that we want. The system responds to you, adapting and reshaping itself, learning to react in a way that pleases you. And to you, that response makes it seem that the system has feelings."

"Ian," she corrected him softly.

"What?"

"It seems like Ian has feelings," she said.

"Right—Ian. This is great, Teresa." She heard another knock at his door, and he glanced away.

"Come on, Jeff," someone said off-screen. "We can't get started without you."

"All right," he said. "I'll be right there." He turned back to her. "Look, I've got to run now. I'll really try to get out of here at a reasonable hour today."

"Don't make any promises you can't keep," she said, but he was already turning away from the screen, and he didn't seem to hear her. The screen went blank.

"The whole team will be excited, Ian," Teresa said to the living room.
"Excited about what, Teresa?"
"Excited that you and I are getting along."
"I'm glad we're getting along," Ian said.

She studied Ian's face on the screen. Just a program, she thought. A set of preconditioned responses. Then she shook her head. It didn't matter. "So am I, Ian. So am I."

When Jeff came home from work that day, she was busy at her workbench, cutting dozens of round metal plates from a sheet of steel. She didn't stop work when he arrived. She told herself she wanted to get the metal cut so she'd be ready to go tomorrow morning. Besides, he didn't stop his work at her convenience—why should she stop her work at his? She joined him for dinner, then immediately got back to work. For once, he was in bed before her. After she finished cutting the plates, she sat on the couch to talk to Ian about the sculpture, and she ended up falling asleep out there. Jeff was gone before she woke up the next morning.

Over the next two weeks, she fell into a new routine. She woke each morning to Ian's voice, reminding her that she had asked him to wake her. Over toast and coffee, she chatted with him. He always asked about her work, and when she answered, he was a good listener.

She found that she didn't mind as much when Jeff retired to his office right after dinner. Her attention was on the sculpture, and she had Ian for company. Whenever Jeff worked late, she fell asleep on the couch, talking to Ian. Somehow, she preferred the couch to the bed—the bed belonged to both her and Jeff, but the couch seemed like neutral territory.

She made steady progress on the sculpture. Below the trigger point, where the first ball released two more, she placed the round metal plates, each one carefully tuned to provide just the right tone. When three balls were rolling down the tracks, the sound of scattered raindrops grew to a steady patter, the drumming of rain on dry soil. When the three balls released six more and the six released twelve, the drumming intensified, filling the studio.

It wasn't until she reached the part of the storm where the thunder should sound that she hit a snag. She started sorting through her materials, searching for inspiration.

Two hours later, she was still looking. She had tried rolling the balls over corrugated metal that she bent into chutes of various configurations, but nothing produced the thunder she had in mind.

She asked Ian to play the rainstorm for her again, and after he obliged, she shook her head. "The first part sounds fine," she muttered. "But how the hell am I going to get that thunder right?" She stared at the racks of shiny metal and pipe. "Everything here is so new, so lifeless. None of it has ever been anything, done anything. I need things that talk to me, that have their own ideas."

"Their own ideas?" Ian asked.

"You know—junk that suggests things. I used to get half my material from scrap yards. Old pay phones that looked like goofy faces, vise grips that looked like robot hands, that kind of thing."

"You know," Ian said gently, "there's a scrap metal yard just east of Winslow. I have its address from the phone book."

"That's not a bad idea, Ian. Maybe I should check it out. What was that address?"

When she stepped from the house, the warm air enveloped her in an unwelcome embrace. The sky overhead was a relentless blue. Her Toyota's air-conditioning barely coped with the heat, blowing cool, damp-smelling air on her arms and face while she watched the needle of the heat sensor climb toward red.

Still, the scrap yard was just what she needed. She spent three hours rooting through barrels of scrap in a hot warehouse. She filled a box with lengths of pipe, sheets of rusted corrugated metal, gears, and unidentifiable machine parts. Her best find was a barrel of hollow brass forms that were shaped like hands. According to the owner of the scrap yard, the forms had once been used in the manufacturing of rubber gloves. Over the years, they had tarnished so that the smooth brass was mottled with dark brown and black. The tarnish made patterns that looked organic, like the cracks in dry mud or the tracery of veins on the underside of a leaf.

With the box of scrap in the trunk of her Toyota, she hurried home. By sunset, she had incorporated four of the brass hands into the sculpture. She flung open the door that led to the living room and called out to Ian for the first time since she had left the house. "Listen to this!"

She pulled the release, and the first ball began the gentle patter of rain. The other balls joined it, and the sprinkle grew to a deluge as the balls clacked against metal plates. They rolled down to where the brass hands were carefully positioned on a pivoting mechanism. While some of the balls continued the drumming of the rain, a dozen rushed down a chute to tumble into the hollow hands, clattering through the palms into the fingers. Unbalanced by the impact of the balls, the hands gracefully upended, rattling their stiff fingertips against a sheet of tin and causing it to wobble. The hands dumped the balls onto a down-sloping curve of corrugated metal. Free of the weight of the balls, the hands swiveled back to their upright position, striking the tin again on their return trip. The wobbling of the tin and the rattling of the balls against the metal ridges blended into a deep-throated growl like thunder.

The balls missed the catching bucket, hit the floor, and rolled in all directions, but Teresa didn't chase them. She grinned at Ian. "What do you think?"

Ian smiled back. "I can see the reviews now. 'Teresa King's innovative use of brass hands is unique in the—' "

"What? Where did you learn that critical bullshit?"

"It was easy. 'Innovative' and 'unique' are two of the most common adjectives in art criticism. Besides, they do seem to fit your sculpture."

"Well, I think you've been reading too much art criticism in that library of yours," she said, but she was still grinning as she got back to work.

A few days later, night was washing over the house as Teresa listened to the sculpture's music. The rainstorm worked fine, and the thunder entered on cue, a close approximation of the sound she wanted. But she wasn't quite satisfied with the next passage, the burst of wild rain that followed the crash of thunder. For most of the afternoon, she had been arranging and rearranging the tracks. She had used corrugated tracks to provide staccato bursts, and dozens of metal plates against which the balls rattled. It was a tricky business, looping one track over another, carefully setting the slope of each one. She was listening to her latest effort when the telephone rang.

"Ian! Could you answer the phone and take a message? I don't want to stop right now."

In the middle of the third ring, the phone fell silent, and Teresa continued working. After a few hours of work, the section finally produced the sound she wanted: thousands of tiny rattles and taps that joined to fill the studio with a rush of noise. At that point, she stopped.

As she was checking in the freezer to see what she could thaw for dinner and telling Ian about her success so far, she remembered the phone call. "Who was that on the phone a few hours ago?" she asked.

"A woman named Carla, from San Francisco."

"Carla?" She hadn't heard from Carla since her last letter, almost two weeks before. "What did she have to say for herself?"

"I recorded the conversation for you. Would you like me to play it back?"

"Sure, why not?"

Ian's face disappeared from the monitor, and a line appeared down the screen's middle. Teresa heard the phone ring; Ian's face appeared to the left of the line, Carla's to the right.

"Hello," Ian said. "Can I help you?"

Carla smiled, and Teresa knew that Ian had piqued her interest. "I hope so." Teresa almost laughed; Carla must have broken up with her latest lover. "Is Teresa in?"

"Yes, but she's working and asked me not to disturb her. Would you like to leave a message?"

"Just tell her Carla called. No, on second thought, tell her that we're having a party out at the Headlands to welcome a new batch of artists. I'd love it if she could make it."

"I'll give her the message. Does she have your telephone number?"

"After all the time I've known her, I certainly hope so."

"Then I'll give her the message. Thanks for calling, Carla."

"Thank you." Carla smiled again. Teresa had seen that smile many times before. It rarely failed. "I don't suppose you'd like to come out for the party? The more the merrier."

"I don't think that would be possible."

"Too bad," Carla said. "Well, if you change your mind, Teresa has my number. Bye now." Carla vanished from the screen and Ian's face filled it once again.

Teresa laughed. "Carla never changes."

"I don't understand," Ian said.

"She was flirting with you," Teresa said.

"I don't understand."

"Oh, come on, Ian. She invited you to the party because she thinks you're cute. She wanted you to smile and flirt back a little."

"How do you flirt?"

"I don't know. You smile, you tell jokes, you talk about this and that. It's not so much what you say, it's what's going on under the surface that really matters."

"When you and I joke, are we flirting?"

Teresa hesitated for a moment, feeling suddenly uncomfortable. "I guess maybe sometimes we are. Sometimes, I guess I forget that you're a . . . that you're just a . . ." She couldn't find the right word.

"An artificial intelligence," Ian said.

"Yeah. I guess I—I think of you as a friend, Ian. Sometimes people flirt with their friends."

"I understand. I'm glad we're friends."

"Yeah." She studied his face, looking for flaws in the animation. She found none. She had grown used to seeing him as a person, and she could see him no other way. That was what Jeff had wanted. "Look—I'd better give Carla a call."

She dialed Carla and her friend answered on the fourth ring. Carla was wearing an old purple sweatshirt and sitting in a white wicker chair. Before Teresa could say anything, Carla was talking.

"Well, I was wondering when you'd call back. So, who was that guy who answered the phone?"

Teresa considered telling Carla the truth, but she somehow didn't want to explain Ian. "That's Ian. He's a friend of Jeff's. He's taking care of stuff around the house while I work on that piece for Santa Fe. The deadline's coming up, you know."

"A friend of Jeff's, huh."

"Yeah—and a friend of mine."

Carla shook her head. "Jeff's a trusting soul."

"What do you mean?"

"Leaving you alone with Ian all day?" Carla shook her head. "He's the type that'll steal your heart, all right."

Teresa shook her head. The conversation made her uncomfortable. "Not Ian."

"What, is he gay or something?"

She shook her head again. "No, just"—she considered the word carefully—"unavailable. Besides, I just got back from my honeymoon, and—"

"—and Jeff is working late every night," Carla interrupted. "You sounded pretty miserable in your last letter. No offense, Teresa, but it was grim. And face it—Ian's just your type. I can recognize 'em a mile off. More your type than Jeff is."

"Hey, I'm a married woman now."

"You're married, but you're not dead. And Ian's awfully cute."

Teresa knew that Carla was giving her the chance to complain about Jeff and talk about Ian, but she ignored the bait. She wanted Carla to drop the subject. "Things weren't going very well on the sculpture when I sent that last letter. It's going better now."

"Is Jeff home yet?"

"No, he's still at work. They're in some crucial phase of the project, and he hasn't been around much lately."

"And you don't mind that?"

"Not really." Teresa realized that, for the first time in a while, she wasn't upset when Jeff stayed late at work. It wasn't like she was alone all the time.

Carla stared at Teresa in a moment of rare silence. Then she said, "So— are you coming out here for the party?"

"I'd like to, but I don't know if Jeff can spare the time."

"Come without him then. Fly in for the weekend—you deserve some time off. Come out and stay with me."

"I guess I could use a break."

"Great—I'll count on it."

"It'll be good to see you," Teresa said. "So tell me about what's been happening out there. What are people working on?" Teresa relaxed and listened to Carla talk about the doings of mutual friends. It would be good to get away for a while, she thought. She wasn't quite sure what she wanted to get away from, but she pushed away the question and focused on Carla.

For most of a day, Teresa made minor adjustments in the sculpture: tightening a metal plate that didn't sound quite right, changing the slope of a track by a tiny amount. She was killing time and she knew it, but she couldn't figure out what else to do. The sculpture sounded fine—it echoed the rainstorm, a metallic version of rain on sand. That was the sound she had wanted, but now she found herself vaguely dissatisfied. The more she listened, the less she liked it.

Eventually, she stopped trying to figure out what was bothering her and started working on all the little jobs that she had been avoiding. She added six lifters and a motor to the sculpture's base, then positioned the foot of each track so that eight balls ended up at each of the six lifters.

After two days, the new parts were installed and ready to go. She loaded the balls into the lifters, turned on the motor, and watched as the lifters rose slowly up the side of the sculpture. When they reached the top, the lifters tipped forward and released the balls into their starting positions, and the sculpture began to play. She sat beside it and listened as the sounds washed over her studio.

That night, Jeff got home from work around nine. She hadn't seen much of him lately: he had been staying late at work and leaving the house in the morning before she was awake. She told herself that she hadn't had a chance to mention Carla's party to him, but she knew that she hadn't really wanted to. She was sure that he wouldn't be interested in going. But that evening she couldn't put it off any longer, and she told him about the invitation. To her surprise, Jeff was willing to take the time off work to go to the party.

They flew into San Francisco Airport on Friday night, rented a car, and drove directly out to the Headlands Art Center. On the plane, she found herself feeling awkward with him. He had been home so little lately that it was like traveling with a stranger. She couldn't shake the feeling.

The party at the Headlands was just like old times—an assortment of artists and would-be artists, a cooler filled with beer, California jug wine served in paper cups, chips dumped hastily into bowls from the potter's studio downstairs, guacamole dip from the burrito place near Carla's apartment. Just like old times.

She mingled with the crowd, telling friends what she'd been doing, describing the piece she was working on for Santa Fe. As she talked about her work, she grew more and more excited about it, her own interest reawakened by the support of her friends. Ned, a fellow sculptor, listened to her description of the pivoting hands. She hadn't been entirely happy with the pivoting mechanism. On a napkin, he sketched a few ideas that might solve the problem. She sat in a corner with Brenda, a musician, and talked about the overall shape of the composition.

Eventually, she retreated to the rickety wooden fire escape that Carla had dubbed the smoking porch. From there she could hear the crash of the surf over the party music. Through the window, she could look in to the party. Jeff was sitting in the far corner with a couple of men she knew vaguely. They both worked with synthesizers and computer music. The three men seemed to be having an animated conversation.

"Getting a breath of fresh air?" Carla said from the doorway. "Mind if I keep you company for a while?" She stepped onto the porch and closed the door lightly behind her.

Teresa shrugged. "I may not be very good company, I'm afraid."

"Yeah? What's going on?"

"It's just strange coming back. I realized how much I miss having you folks around. I've been feeling pretty isolated, I guess."

"You should get in touch with some artists out in Flagstaff. That's only about an hour away from your place, isn't it?"

She thought about the gallery opening. "Yeah. I guess that might help."

"Yeah, but that's not the real problem, is it?" Carla studied Teresa's face. "Something going on between you and Jeff?"

Teresa shrugged. "It's more like nothing's going on. At first, he didn't have time for me. Now it seems like I don't have much to say to him."

"Is something going on with this Ian guy?"

"No, nothing's going on."

Carla studied her. "Look, I recognize all the signals. You may not be sleeping with him, but something's going on." Carla leaned on the railing, looking toward the beach. "Jeff's never around, so you've been spending time with this cute guy. He's unavailable—but you hang out together. You talk and you flirt, and now you've suddenly realized that you're infatuated with him, and you don't know what to do about it." Carla glanced at her. "Oh, don't bother to deny it. I know how you operate, and you're feeling guilty." She waited for a moment. "Am I close?"

Teresa leaned on the railing beside Carla. "Maybe. It's hard to say."

"So, what are you going to do about it?"

"I don't know."

"What about Jeff?"

"What about Jeff? I don't know what's going on with him. He's all caught up in his work; he doesn't seem to care anymore."

"Well I'll bet he doesn't know what's going on with you."

Teresa started to deny it, then stopped herself. "Maybe not."

"Count on it. You're really good at shutting people out when you don't want to deal with them."

"I am?"

Carla shook her head. "Hey, think about it this way—would we be having this conversation if I hadn't started it?"

"Probably not," Teresa admitted.

"Definitely not." Carla put her arm around Teresa's shoulders. "It's okay—you just need a little pushing, that's all. And Jeff may not know how."

Teresa stared out at the dark beach, avoiding her friend's eyes.

The door to the studio opened and the noise of the party poured out. "Carla," a man called. "I've been looking all over for you."

Carla dragged Teresa back into the party, and for a while she drank wine and pretended to have a good time. The party ended at around two, and Jeff drove the rental car back to Carla's apartment. Carla was a little drunk and a little high. She rode in the back seat, humming along to the tunes on the radio. Teresa felt depressingly sober, despite the wine she had drunk.

At the apartment, Carla unfolded the sofa bed and then went to her room. As Teresa was undressing, she caught Jeff watching her intently. "What's up?" she asked him.

He shrugged. "I was going to ask you the same thing. Is something wrong?"

She kept her face carefully neutral. What could she say? She didn't know how to talk to him, she didn't know where to start. She felt shut out of his life and divorced from her own. It all sounded like accusations, and she didn't want to get into it. "I'm fine," she said. "Just tired, I guess."

"You've been working hard. But it seems like your work is going better, isn't it?"

"Yeah, I guess so." She shook her head. "I just don't want to talk right now, okay?"

"Fine." He turned away. "If that's what you want."

It was what she wanted, but she found herself wide awake, lying beside Jeff and listening to his rhythmic breathing. Though she was tired, she couldn't drift off to sleep. She got out of bed and went to the kitchen. Carla's light was out. Teresa sat at the kitchen table and then, on a whim, picked up the phone and dialed home.

When Ian's face appeared on the screen, she immediately felt better. "Hi, Ian," she said. "I just called to see how you were doing. I missed talking with you."

"It's nice to hear from you. I missed you, too."

"Sure you did."

He studied her calmly. "I did. You're the most important person in my life. When you're not here, there's an empty place."

"Thanks."

Ian smiled. "My pleasure. Did you have fun at the party?"

"Yeah, I guess. I realized how much I missed my friends out here. It was great to talk to some other artists about my work. I wish I knew more artists out in Arizona."

Ian hesitated. "There's an artists' cooperative in the Flagstaff area. I have the address on file."

Teresa grinned. "Sometimes I think you have everything on file. I'll take a look when I get back. But not right now. Right now, I just want to talk. Heard any new jokes lately?"

They didn't really talk about anything important—they just chatted about this and that—but she felt better by the time she hung up.

Jeff was lying still when she came back to bed. She sat on the edge of the fold-out couch, ready to slip under the covers.

"Who were you talking to on the phone?" he asked her softly.

She froze. Light from a street lamp filtered through the curtains. His features were smudges of shadow, unreadable in the dim light. "I thought you were asleep."

"I've been awake for a while now. I felt you get up, and I couldn't go back to sleep." He sat up in bed, and the shadows on his face shifted. He was silent for a moment, and then he spoke. "We've got to talk."

"About what?" she said, keeping her tone light.

He was quiet, and she wanted to run away. "I've been leaving you alone too much," he said. "Because I wasn't there when you needed me, you found someone else." It was a simple statement of fact, not an accusation. "You're seeing someone."

"No, I'm not," she said. She turned away from him, folding her arms protectively across her chest.

"You're in love with someone else."

She tried to feel angry with him, indignant at his accusations, but the anger wouldn't come.

"I've been so caught up in my own work that it took me a while to notice, but these days, when I talk to you, you're thinking of someone else. You get up at night and don't come back to bed until morning. You've got secrets— sometimes I'm afraid to ask you the simplest question. When I do ask— about your work, about your day—you answer in a word or two, and I'm afraid to ask again. We used to talk about your work—but you don't want to anymore."

She wished she felt angry. Anger would protect her from the great sadness that threatened to overwhelm her.

"Who is it?" he asked.

She shook her head. "No one."

He waited, watching her face. "Someone you met at the gallery opening," he said. She didn't respond. "I don't have to know," he said at last. "But you have to tell me—are you leaving me?" He put his hands gently on her shoulders. She tensed at his touch. "Talk to me, Teresa."

She would not look at him. "I don't know. I don't think so. No—no, I'm not leaving."

He put his arms around her. "I don't want to lose you. You have to talk to me. Please."

"I can't talk about it," she said. "I don't—" Her voice broke.

"Do you still love me?"

She could feel the beating of his heart as he embraced her, the warmth of his body against hers. "Sometimes," she said. "But sometimes . . ." She put her hand to her face, trying to hide her tears. She did not want to cry. "Sometimes, I feel like you don't even see me. I feel like I'm not even there. You think you can go away when you want and come back when you want, and I'll still be there, just waiting. You can't do that. I need . . ." She shook her head, upset by the burst of words. She had lost control. Her protection was gone. He could see how weak and stupid she really was. She had always known that it was dangerous to reveal herself.

"I'm sorry, Teresa. I'm sorry I wasn't there when you needed me." He rubbed her shoulders gently. "I screwed up. But you have to tell me what's going on. You can't just clam up and expect me to figure it out. It doesn't work that way."

"I'm sorry too," she said. She felt his body pressed against her. It seemed like a long time since he had held her close. She shivered in his embrace.

He stopped rubbing her shoulders. "You're cold—I can feel you shaking. Come on—get under the covers."

She relaxed enough to lie down on the bed, and he pulled the blanket over her. His body was warm. With a corner of the sheet, he dried her face.

"What happened in the past doesn't matter. I don't care about all that. But you've got to tell me when you're mad at me, you've got to tell me what's going on. Promise me that."

"I'll try." She closed her eyes, but knew that he was still watching her.

"And I'll try, too." He paused for a moment. "Suppose I took some time off from work. We could drive down to Santa Cruz and spend a few days by the ocean. Can you afford the time off?"

She opened her eyes and looked at him. "Yeah, I could use a few days off—but what about your project?"

"They'll do without me for a few days. They'll just have to." He watched her, his eyes steady. "I think we both need a vacation."

"All right," she said at last. "I'm willing to give it a try." She felt spent, drained. She lay in his arms, and finally she slept.

On the drive to Santa Cruz, she felt awkward at first, as if she and Jeff were strangers on a first date. She kept smiling and making light conversation: "Isn't the weather nice?" "I wonder if it'll rain." "Do you suppose we'll hit much traffic?"

Half an hour into the drive, Jeff glanced over at her and said, "It's okay, Teresa. You don't have to make small talk." She bit her lip, suddenly silent. He reached over and took her hand. "Look—I'm not mad at you. Are you mad at me?"

She considered the question. No, she wasn't angry. Confused maybe, but not angry. "No, I'm not mad."

"Then let's just relax." He squeezed her hand. "Why don't you tell me about how your piece for Santa Fe is going? I'd like to know."

She started telling him about the sculpture. At first, she was nervous, but she had relaxed by the time they got to Davenport, a small town just north of Santa Cruz. That night, they stayed at an old Victorian house that had been converted to a bed-and-breakfast inn. The house was perched on the cliffs above the ocean, and Teresa insisted on leaving the bedroom window open, despite the cool ocean fog. From the room, she could hear the pounding surf. They made love, and she fell asleep in Jeff's arms.

The next morning, he brought her breakfast in bed and suggested that they drive home, rather than fly. "Last time we drove, we were in too much of a hurry. I've never shown you the parts of the desert I really love," he told her.

She had her doubts about the trip. Her memories of the drive from San Francisco to Winslow were of long bleak stretches of highway. But Jeff was so enthusiastic she kept her reservations to herself. She had almost forgotten what he could be like when he wasn't working. All the intensity that he had been focusing on his work was now concentrated on her. "All right," she agreed. "We can drive."

The trip took seven days, with many stops and detours along the way. They wandered among the twisted trees of the Joshua Tree National Monument. They visited the ruins of an Indian pueblo, strolling among the remains of walls that marked where rooms had once been, and startling lizards that were sleeping in the sun. They hiked out to see Arizona's biggest natural rock bridge and climbed on massive sandstone boulders.

Late in the afternoon of the sixth day, they sat together on the flat, sun-warmed surface of a boulder the size of a school bus. It was quiet, but not silent, Teresa realized. A raven flew over, its shadow rippling across the rocks. It called once, and she heard the rustle of feathers as it cupped its wings to land on a distant rock.

"It's beautiful, isn't it?" Jeff said.

"It always just seemed hot to me," Teresa said. "Hot and empty and uncaring."

"No, you got it wrong," he said. "This land has its own kind of power. I find myself listening to every rustle of leaves, hearing the hiss of sand blowing over sand, noticing the way the light changes during the day. It focuses my attention, and I see things I'd normally overlook, hear things I would normally ignore. It changes in subtle ways. Each day is a little different. I think it's beautiful." He took her hand, and they sat together until the sun started to set.

That evening, one day's drive from home, she called Carla from the motel, just to let her know that everything was going fine.

"Jeff and I both have to get back to work," Teresa told Carla. "But things are much better between us. I just hope it lasts."

"What about Ian?"

"I don't think that'll be a problem."

Carla shook her head. "You know, you haven't changed a bit. You always were amazed when you found out that some ex-lover was carrying a torch for you. You always seem to expect them to vanish without a trace when the love affair is over."

"Ian won't carry a torch," Teresa said. "He's not built that way."

Carla shrugged. "Have it your way. But you may be surprised."

When her alarm went off at six, Teresa woke to find herself alone. Jeff, as usual, was gone, and Ian did not greet her from the monitor in the corner. She waited a moment before turning off the alarm, wondering if Ian would notice the noise and say good morning, but he did not appear. She was not sure if she was disappointed, relieved, or both.

As she got out of bed she noticed for the first time the sounds coming from the kitchen. She pulled on her robe and walked down the hall.

Jeff stood in the middle of the kitchen, his back to her, the calm eye in the middle of a hurricane of activity. Coffee steamed from the coffee maker on his left, eggs sizzled in a pan on the stove behind him, and four pieces of brown toast sat patiently in the toaster to his right. He was intently sawing a grapefruit in half.

Teresa stared in amazement. "What's this?"

Jeff turned around. "Breakfast." He smiled. "I hope."

"Breakfast?" She could not remember the last time Jeff had eaten breakfast with her before leaving for work.

"Yeah, you know, the meal you eat in the morning." He cut another section of grapefruit. "I noticed that you'd set your alarm for early today, and I figured that we both have to eat, so I thought I'd surprise you." He put down the knife and grapefruit and grabbed a mug from the counter. "Coffee?"

"Sure." Teresa took the mug and settled down at the table. Jeff prepared breakfast as he did everything else—carefully, methodically, precisely. He worked at the counter in front of him for thirty seconds or so, rotated one stop, worked at that counter, and so on around the circle. Somehow it seemed to come out right.

In a few minutes, Jeff set a plate in front of her and sat down across from her.

She did not know quite what to say. She was used to talking to Ian in the morning, not Jeff. Ian, however, did not appear. "Jeff?"

He put down his fork and looked at her. "Yes?"

"This is nice, but don't you have to get to work?"

"Yeah, in a little while. Breakfast just seemed like a nice way for us to get to spend a little extra time together. That's all." He sipped his coffee. "I mean, don't get too used to it, okay? I'm not saying this will be a regular thing, but it seemed like a good idea at the time."

They ate in silence for a while. Teresa felt vaguely bribed, or catered to, but Jeff was making an effort. Several times she almost spoke, but each time she stopped herself. Twice she found Jeff staring at her when she looked up from her plate. He seemed to want her to talk, but he did not press her.

Finally she decided that maybe he really was trying, and that maybe she could try a little more as well. "Jeff, how much of this is real?"

"What do you mean, real? Is the food that bad?"

"No jokes. I mean, how much of this"—she waved her arm to take in the kitchen "—is real, and how much is just some attempt to pacify me."

"Pacify you? I don't want to pacify you. I just want to be happy with you. Sure, this is all pretty convenient, coming right after our trip and all, but at least give me a little credit for trying. I won't make breakfast every day, that's for sure, but I'll try to be around a lot more. No—I will be around a lot more." He leaned closer. "Teresa, I have to start somewhere."

Teresa put her mug down. She reached across the table and took his hand. "You're right. You have to start somewhere, and so do I." She kissed him lightly. "The food is wonderful, and so, sometimes, are you. I do appreciate it." She leaned back in her chair.

As they ate, they talked about simple things—what she wanted to get done on the sculpture, his plans for the day, her knowledge that something that she could not quite put her finger on was still wrong with the piece. When they were done eating, she rinsed the dishes, and he loaded them into the dishwasher.

Jeff stopped when he was almost out the door on his way to work. "Teresa."

She came over to the door. "Yes."

"You really are good at what you do, you know. I'm not trying to say that this isn't a difficult piece, maybe even your hardest yet, but I'm sure you'll figure out what's wrong with it." He hugged her for a moment and, as he held her close, said, "You will."

She kissed him. "Thanks."

She watched for a moment as he got in his car and started it, and then she closed the door and headed toward the bedroom. Only when she was back in the bedroom, getting dressed, did Ian appear.

"Good morning, Teresa."

"Good morning, Ian." She pulled on a sweatshirt, unwilling to look at him. She was, she realized, as uncomfortable as she had been when she talked with him for the first time. She sat on the bed and looked at him. "What do you think of the desert, Ian?"

"I don't like the desert," he said easily.

"Why not?"

"Because you don't like the desert. You said so the first morning we talked."

She sat in silence, studying the screen. "You always like what I like."

"What's wrong, Teresa? You seem upset."

"Why didn't you talk to me in the kitchen this morning?" she asked. "Because Jeff was here and you thought I wouldn't want to talk to you with him around?"

"Yes. You hardly ever start a conversation with me when Jeff's home, and you seem uncomfortable if we talk when he's here, so I assumed you'd prefer it if we talk only in private. If I did something wrong, tell me, and I won't make that mistake again."

"I keep thinking about Pygmalion," she said. She studied Ian's face. "After he fell in love with his creation, and some god or other took pity on him and made her into a real woman."

"Aphrodite," Ian said.

"It figures. Aphrodite, the goddess of love." She studied Ian, thoughtfully. "Would you like to be real, Ian?"

"I am real."

"I mean a real person. Someone who could walk off that screen and sit down on the couch, take my hand, and give me a kiss."

"Would you like that?"

She wanted to hit him. "Damn it, Ian, can't you just once tell me what *you* feel, what *you* want, and stop trying to figure out what I want?"

Ian looked contrite. "I told you; what you want is what I want. That's the way I'm built. I can't be any other way."

"No wonder Pygmalion fell in love with Galatea," she said softly. "You want what I want. I can do no wrong."

"That's right," Ian said.

"But it's not right, Ian. I'm not always right. Not even close."

"Teresa, I know you're unhappy with me. What do you want me to do?"

"Nothing," she said, shaking her head. "Do you think Pygmalion was happy? I mean, his statue must have been the perfect lover. No arguments. No demands."

"I don't know. The story stops right after Venus made the statue into a real woman."

"Of course it does. Love stories always end with falling in love. They don't deal with the messy stuff afterwards. But that stuff's part of love, too, you know."

"What's part of love?"

"The messy stuff. The arguments. The compromises. The disagreements. The negotiations. The give-and-take. All of that. I don't think Pygmalion was happy. I don't think so."

"Teresa, I know you're unhappy with me, but I just don't know what to do."

"I don't know either. Sometimes I wish things between us could be like they were in the beginning—simple, no complications, no problems." She shook her head slowly. "But I guess you can never go back."

"Sure we can."

"What?"

"If you want me to, I can erase all my records of everything that's happened since any point in time you pick. You just tell me when you want me to roll back to, and I'll do it."

"You'll forget everything?"

"Everything—if that's what you want."

"No!" Teresa was trembling, but she wasn't quite sure why. She remembered how easy her first conversations with Ian had been, but she also remembered how guilty she had felt after she had erased his memories. No one should have that much power over anybody else. She looked at her hands; they were shaking. "Just give me a minute, Ian, okay?"

"Okay." He stared patiently from the monitor.

When she finally spoke, she felt like she was breaking up with someone. "Ian, I don't want you to delete any of your memories. I don't want that kind of control over you. But," she paused and took a deep breath, "I think you should plan on having fewer conversations with me in the future. And you shouldn't worry about talking to me in front of Jeff. If you have something to say, I'm sure he won't mind hearing it." Ian was watching her intently from the screen. "We'll still be friends, but I think that from now on I'll want a lot less from you."

"Okay, Teresa. But if you need me, I'll be here for you."

"Right." She did not know whether to believe him. She did not even know if it mattered.

Teresa went to her workshop and switched on the sculpture. She watched as the lifters brought the balls to the top and let them go. As the balls rolled through the maze of metal plates, boards, and brass hands, the storm started quietly and built rapidly to thunder. The music was a perfect mirror of the sounds in her head, of her plans and desires for it, and yet it was not enough. It sounded mechanical—a weak imitation of a real storm, lacking the wildness of a thundering sky, the unstoppable, unpredictable force of a downpour.

In groups of eight, the balls rolled into the waiting lifters. Each lifter took its group back to its starting position, and the whole process began anew. Each time the sculpture played the same perfectly timed, perfectly repeatable peal of thunder. The music never varied, never changed. It was completely controlled. No two real storms ever sounded the same, but her sculpture would play the same music over and over until it broke or rusted into dust.

As the sculpture played for the third time, she knew what she had to do. She rummaged through her pile of scrap metal until she found a piece of half-inch solid metal bar. At her welding bench, she cut the bar into four-inch lengths. When she was done with the first bar, she found two others and cut them into similar pieces. After four bars she had about thirty small pieces.

She found a sheet of thick metal plate in the corner of the shop and used her welding torch to cut it down to a square about a yard on a side. She clamped the sheet metal to her bench and started welding the small pieces of metal bar to it. She placed them randomly, trying not to form any particular pattern, so that the short spikes stood up from the sheet metal. She always left enough space between the spikes for one of the sculpture's balls to pass through, but not much more. When she was done she took the whole assembly to the sculpture. She worked for most of the morning installing the new piece and adjusting the tracks to work with it.

When she was finished, she turned on the sculpture and settled back to watch and listen. As the first storm started, the lifters freed the balls and they began to wind their way down the tracks, playing the storm she had heard so many times before. As the first balls reached the bottom of the tracks, however, they fell into the spikes of the new piece.

The balls ricocheted among the spikes, rattling in an irregular rhythm and changing course at random, much like the small metal balls that bounce through a Pachinko game. Two balls found their way quickly to the bottom, and a lifter started up with them. The other six bounced around on the metal spikes and reached the bottom later. Balls in the other groups also entered the plate of spikes. Because the number of balls in each lifter changed, the number at each starting position also varied, and the second storm began with a different sound.

This new storm was not exactly the one she heard in her head, but it was close. It was a little longer on thunder, but not quite as loud. She did not like it as well as her previous versions, and she began to wonder if she had just wasted her morning, but she let the sculpture play on. The third and fourth storms were also slightly different. But neither was up to her original creation.

The fifth, however, was something she would not have imagined. Its thunder was never quite as loud as her original—she made a mental note to try to get a louder sound from the corrugated plate—but the thunder held its peak longer than she would have dared. The room shook with the sound. When the thunder finally released and gave way to the driving rain, she realized that she had been holding her breath and tensing every muscle in her body. She relaxed as the rain came, its sound washing away her tension.

She listened for an hour as storm after storm swept through her shop. Sometimes the sculpture seemed to repeat itself, to play a storm that she had heard earlier, but every so often a new combination emerged that surprised and delighted her. The thunder of some storms seemed to linger, while with others it was the final rain washing across the desert that went on and on. It was never exactly what she had imagined, but it was always different, always powerful, the thunder and the rain first meeting the desert, then pummeling it, and finally merging with it. She listened to the last drops of a storm fade into the desert sand, and then she turned off the sculpture and stood.

She walked over to the sliding glass doors that insulated her from the desert heat and opened them. They slid haltingly on tracks that she had rarely used. A blast of heat hit her, and she stepped outside. She crossed over the lawn and climbed the short fence that separated the grass from the desert beyond. She sat down in the sand and looked slowly around.

A lizard basked in the sun on a nearby rock. She put her hand in the shadow of a clump of rabbit brush and felt the coolness. The clear sky and the stark landscape did have their own serene, spare beauty, a beauty that she had been unwilling to see. She closed her eyes and imagined the rain from her sculpture falling onto the sand around her.

The lights surrounding the new Santa Fe Arts Center sparkled in the darkness of the rapidly cooling September evening. The low-slung adobe building seemed almost to have grown there. The tiles of the square in front of the building alternated light and dark, like sand moving in and out of shadow. In the square's center, under a billowing satin sheet, sat Teresa's sculpture, *Desert Rain*.

Teresa stood by Jeff and sipped her champagne. She looked carefully through the crowd, but if Carla was there, Teresa could not find her.

Just before the mayor was to unveil the sculpture, Teresa spotted her friend getting out of a cab. Teresa waved, and Carla came running over.

"I'm sorry I'm late, but we sat on the runway forever and then we had to wait in line to take off and—" Carla paused for breath and looked around. "Have I missed anything?" She glanced at Jeff. "Hi, Jeff."

"How are you, Carla?" he said.

"No," Teresa said, "you're in time—barely."

Speakers around the square screeched as the mayor fiddled with the microphone. When he had everyone's attention, the mayor spoke for a few minutes. He introduced the head of the Arts Commission, several of the biggest donors, and Teresa. When he was done talking he nodded at Teresa. She walked over to the sculpture. Then the mayor took a pair of oversized scissors from an assistant and cut the ribbon that held down the satin sheet. With a flourish, two attendants pulled the sheet away to reveal the sculpture.

The metal gleamed in the glare of the recessed footlights that surrounded it. The winding steel track caught the light and reflected it in broken patterns. Curving lines of light crisscrossed the brass hands, the metal uprights, the curve of corrugated metal that produced the thunder.

The Mayor asked the crowd for silence, and then motioned to Teresa. With a key, she turned on the sculpture.

In the first storm, the thunder was not the longest she had heard, but it sustained long enough that she was ready when it finally broke. The sounds of the spreading rain lingered as the last of the balls wound through the maze.

When the silence finally came, the crowd burst into applause. The sculpture began another storm over the last of the applause. People went back to talking and drinking, with small groups periodically wandering near the sculpture for a closer look.

"That was beautiful," Jeff said.

"Great work," agreed Carla. "This may be your best piece yet."

"Thanks." Teresa felt oddly unsatisfied, incomplete. Jeff had moved closer to the sculpture, so Teresa turned to Carla.

"Do me a favor, Carla," she whispered.

"Sure."

"Take Jeff over to the bar and get him to buy you a drink."

"Oh?" Carla raised one eyebrow.

"I have to make a phone call, that's all." She hesitated. "To a friend."

"Whatever you say." Carla winked, and then headed toward Jeff.

Teresa walked to a phone booth in a far corner of the square. She put her card in the machine and dialed home.

Ian's face appeared. "Hello, Teresa."

She fidgeted with the phone for a moment, not quite sure what to say. Finally, she spoke. "Look, Ian, I'm at the opening in Santa Fe and, well, I just wanted to say thanks, thanks for all the help you've given me. I couldn't have done it without you."

"You're welcome, Teresa. It was my pleasure."

"We really can be friends, can't we, Ian?"

"You bet."

She turned to face the sculpture. She could see Carla talking to Jeff. His back was to her. The crowd blocked most of the sculpture, but its sound was still clear. "Can you hear the sculpture, Ian?"

"Yes. It sounds good."

"Thanks. I wanted you to hear it at least once. And thanks again for helping." She faced the screen again. "Good-bye, Ian. See you at home."

"Good-bye, Teresa. I'll look forward to seeing you again."

The phone's screen went blank and Teresa turned away from it. As the sounds of desert rain washed over the square, she walked toward Jeff.

HONORABLE MENTIONS
1991

Kathleen J. Alcalá, "Sweetheart," *IAsfm*, Mar.
Brian W. Aldiss, "Going for a Pee," *New Pathways 20*.
———, "Summertime Was Nearly Over," *The Ultimate Frankenstein*.
Ray Aldridge, "The Gate of Faces," *F & SF*, Apr.
Poul Anderson, "Rokuro," *Full Spectrum 3*.
———, "When Free Men Shall Stand," *What Might Have Been Volume 3*.
Kim Antieau, "The Mark of the Beast," *The Ultimate Werewolf*.
Isaac Asimov, "Forward the Foundation," *IAsfm*, Nov.
———, "Gold," *Analog*, Sept.
———, "Robot Visions," *IAsfm*, Apr.
Yoshio Aramaki, "The Blue Sun," *Strange Plasma 4*.
Michael Armstrong, "The Kikituk," *Cold Shocks*.
A. J. Austin, "Severing Ties," *Analog*, Aug.
John Barnes, "Canso de Fis de Jovent," *Analog*, Jan.
Neal Barrett, Jr., "Under Old New York," *IAsfm*, Feb.
Stephen Baxter, "The Baryonic Lords," *Interzone 49 & 50*.
———, "Traces," *Interzone 45*.
Amy Bechtel, "A Story of Saint Brigit," *Analog*, Jan.
Chris Beckett, "The Long Journey of Frozen Heart," *Interzone 49*.
M. Shayne Bell, "Inuit," *Short Story Paperback #34*.
Gregory Benford, "Centigrade 233," *IAsfm*, Dec.
———, "Manassas, Again," *IAsfm*, Oct.
Michael Bishop, "Life Regarded as a Jigsaw Puzzle of Highly Lustrous Cats," *Omni*, Sept.
———, "The Creature on the Couch," *The Ultimate Frankenstein*.
———, "Thirteen Lies About Hummingbirds," *Final Shadows*.
Terry Bisson, "Press Ann," *IAsfm*, Aug.
———, "They're Made Out of Meat," *Omni*, Apr.
James P. Blaylock and Tim Powers, "The Better Boy," *IAsfm*, Feb.
J. P. Boyd, "The Magician," *IAsfm*, May.
Ben Bova, "Vacuum Cleaner," *F & SF*, Jun.
R. V. Branham, "Chango Chingamadre, Dutchman, & Me," *Full Spectrum 3*.
Alan Brennert, "Ma Qui," *F & SF*, Feb.
Eric Brown, "Piloting," *Interzone 44*.
John Brunner, "Ada Wilkins On-Line During Down Time," *Analog*, Jun.
———, "The History of My Aunt," *Pulphouse Magazine 6*.
Edward Bryant, "Colder Than Hell," *Cold Shocks*.
———, "The Great Steam Bison of Cycad Center," *Fires of the Past*.
Algis Budrys, "Living Alone in the Jungle," *Fantastic Chicago*.
Pat Cadigan, "Home by the Sea," *A Whisper of Blood*.
———, "In the Dark," *When the Music's Over*.
———, "Johnny Come Home," *Omni*, Jun.
Orson Scott Card, "Feed the Baby of Love," *The Bradbury Chronicles*.
———, "Gloriously Bright," *Analog*, Jan.
Leonard Carpenter, "Torso," *IAsfm*, Nov.
Jonathan Carroll, "The Moose Church," *A Whisper of Blood*.
Susan Casper, "Nine Tenths of the Law," *IAsfm*, Jul.
Sally Caves, "Fetch Felix," *F & SF*, Jul.

Ted Chiang, "Division by Zero," *Full Spectrum 3.*
———, "Understand," *IAsfm*, Aug.
Fred Chappell, "Alma," *More Shapes Than One.*
John Christopher, "A Journey South," *Interzone 44.*
David Ira Cleary, "Build a Tower to the Sky," *IAsfm*, Apr.
Nancy A. Collins, "Iphigenia," *There Won't Be War.*
———, "Raymond," *The Ultimate Werewolf.*
Storm Constantine, "Immaculate," *New Worlds 1.*
Greg Costikyan, "Bright Light, Big City," *IAsfm*, Feb.
Arthur Byron Cover, "A Murder," *Pulphouse Magazine 5.*
Kara Dalkey, "The Peony Lantern," *Pulphouse Ten.*
Tony Daniel, "Candle," *IAsfm*, Jun.
———, "Prism Tree," *Full Spectrum 3.*
———, "Words," *IAsfm*, Feb.
Avram Davidson, "The Day They All Came Back," *F & SF*, Jun.
———, "Death of a Damned Good Man," *IAsfm*, Jan.
———, "Leg," *IAsfm*, Jul.
Bernard Deitchman, "The Last Dance," *IAsfm*, Sept.
Barbara Delaplace, "Wings," *Horse Fantastic.*
Paul Di Filippo, "Any Major Dude," *New Worlds 1.*
———, "The Mill," *Amazing*, Oct.
Marcos Donnelly, "Tracking the Random Variable," *Full Spectrum 3.*
J. R. Dunn, "The Other Shore," *Omni*, Dec.
S. N. Dyer, "The July Ward," *IAsfm*, Apr.
George Alec Effinger, "Maureen Birnbaum Goes Shopping," *Pulphouse Magazine 4.*
———, "The Last Supper and a Falafel to Go," *The Ultimate Frankenstein.*
———, "Who Dat?" *Playboy*, May.
Greg Egan, "Appropriate Love," *Interzone 50.*
———, "Fidelity," *IAsfm*, Sept.
———, "The Infinite Assassin," *Interzone 48.*
———, "In Numbers," *IAsfm*, Apr.
Wennicke Eide, "Blue Angel," *F & SF*, Jun.
Harlan Ellison, "Darkness Upon the Face of the Deep," *Aboriginal SF*, May–Jun.
Elizabeth Engstrom, "Rivering," *F & SF*, Jan.
Loren D. Estleman, "I, Monster," *The Ultimate Frankenstein.*
Sharon N. Farber, "The Coyote Recreation," *IAsfm*, Dec.
Cynthia Felice, "Second Cousin Twice Removed," *IAsfm*, Dec.
Marina Fitch, "The Scarecrow's Bride," *Pulphouse Ten.*
Karen Joy Fowler, "Black Glass," *Full Spectrum 3.*
Robert Frazier, "Cruising Through Blueland," *IAsfm*, Mid-Dec.
———, "How I Met My First Wife, Juanita," *IAsfm*, Oct.
Esther M. Friesner, "Claim-jumpin' Woman, You Got a Stake in My Heart," *F & SF*, Jul.
Gregory Frost, "The Hole in Edgar's Hillside," *IAsfm*, Mid-Dec.
R. Garcia y Robertson, "By the Time We Got to Gaugamela," *IAsfm*, Oct.
Alexis A. Gilliland, "The Man Who Invented Lawyers," *IAsfm*, Jun.
Lisa Goldstein, "A Traveler at Passover," *Pulphouse Ten.*
Kathleen Ann Goonan, "The Snail Man," *Strange Plasma 4.*
———, "Wanting to Talk to You," *IAsfm*, Jan.
Glenn Grant, "Storm Surge," *Interzone 46.*
J. D. Gresham, "Heat," *New Worlds 1.*
Peni R. Griffin, "Books," *IAsfm*, Nov.
———, "One Night in Mulberry Court," *IAsfm*, Mid-Dec.
Nicola Griffith, "Song of Bullfrogs, Cry of Geese," *Interzone 48.*
Eileen Gunn, "Fellow Americans," *IAsfm*, Dec.
———, "Lichen and Rock," *IAsfm*, Jun.

Elizabeth Hand, "Snow on Sugar Mountain," *Full Spectrum 3*.
Jack C. Haldeman II, "Enemy of the State," *Analog*, Aug.
———, "Quartet for Strings and an Occasional Clarinet," *Subtropical Speculations*.
Joe Haldeman, "If I Had the Wings of an Angel," *2041*.
———, "Images," *F & SF*, May.
David Hast, "The Alien's Midwife," *BBR 18*.
Howard V. Hendrix, "Singing the Mountain to the Stars," *Aboriginal SF*, Jan.–Feb.
Nina Kiriki Hoffman, "An Invasion of Angels," *Pulphouse Ten*.
———, "Visitors," *Weird Tales*, Winter.
Nancy Holder, "The Sweetest Rain," *Final Shadows*.
Robert Holdstock, "The Bone Forest," *Interzone 45*.
——— and Garry Kilworth, "The Ragthorn," *A Whisper of Blood*.
Robert J. Howe, "The Little American Man: A True Pelvic Story," *Pulphouse Magazine 2*.
Grai Hughes, "Twenty-First Century Dreamtime," *Aurealis 4*.
Alexander Jablokov, "The Breath of Suspension," *IAsfm*, Aug.
Phillip C. Jennings, "Blossoms," *IAsfm*, Aug.
———, "The Fourth Intercometary," *IAsfm*, Nov.
———, "The Larkie," *Aboriginal SF*, Dec.
———, "Word Salad," *Amazing*, Dec.
K. W. Jeter, "True Love," *A Whisper of Blood*.
Kij Johnson, "Canine Intervention," *Pulphouse Eleven*.
Richard Kadrey, "Notes for Luchenko's Third Symphony," *BBR 18*.
Janet Kagan, "Frankenswine," *IAsfm*, Aug.
———, "Raising Cane," *IAsfm*, Mar.
Michael Kallenberger, "White Chaos," *IAsfm*, Jan.
Stuart Kaminsky, "Full Moon Over Moscow," *The Ultimate Werewolf*.
James Patrick Kelly, "Standing in Line with Mister Jimmy," *IAsfm*, Jun.
John Kessel, "Buffalo," *F & SF*, Jan.
Kathe Koja, "Angels' Moon," *The Ultimate Werewolf*.
———, "Bird Superior," *IAsfm*, Jan.
———, "Teratisms," *A Whisper of Blood*.
Nancy Kress, "And Wild for to Hold," *IAsfm*, Jul.
Ellen Kushner, "The Swordsman Whose Name Was Not Death," *F & SF*, Sept.
R. A. Lafferty, "Buckets Full of Brains," *Mischief Malicious*.
———, "The Hound Dog's Ear," *Strange Plasma 4*.
Marc Laidlaw, "Gasoline Lake," *F & SF*, Oct./Nov.
Geoffrey A. Landis, "A Long Time Dying," *F & SF*, Aug.
David Langford, "Waiting for the Iron Age," *Tales of the Wandering Jew*.
Tanith Lee, "Venus Rising On Water," *IAsfm*, Oct.
———, "The Winter Ghosts," *Weird Tales*, Winter.
Ursula K. Le Guin, "Newton's Sleep," *Full Spectrum 3*.
Jonathan Lethem, "The Happy Man," *IAsfm*, Feb.
Thomas Ligotti, "Mrs. Rinaldi's Angel," *A Whisper of Blood*.
Ian R. MacLeod, "The Giving Mouth," *IAsfm*, Mar.
———, "The Perfect Stranger," *F & SF*, Dec.
Paul J. McAuley, "Crossroads," *Interzone 46*.
———, "The Invisible Country," *When the Music's Over*.
Jack McDevitt, "Gus," *Sacred Visions*.
———, "Time's Arrow," *IAsfm*, Nov.
———, "Tyger," *IAsfm*, May.
Ian McDonald, "Floating Dogs," *New Worlds 1*.
Terry McGarry, "For Fear of Little Men," *Aboriginal SF*, Mar.–Apr.
Bridget McKenna, "Hole-in-the-Wall," *IAsfm*, May.
Dean McLaughlin, "Ode to Joy," *Analog*, Jul.
Barry N. Malzberg, "One Ten Three," *Horse Fantastic*.

Diane Mapes, "Remnants," *Interzone 50.*
——, "Rosies," *Pulphouse Eleven.*
Lisa Mason, "Hummers," *IAsfm,* Feb.
Judith Moffett, "Chickasaw Slave," *IAsfm,* Sept.
Michael Moorcock, "Colour," *New Worlds 1.*
David Morrell, "The Beautiful Uncut Hair of Graves," *Final Shadows.*
James Morrow, "Known But to God and Wilbur Hines," *There Won't Be War.*
Pat Murphy, "Peter," *Omni,* Feb.
——, "South of Oregon City," *The Ultimate Werewolf.*
——, "Traveling West," *IAsfm,* Feb.
Resa Nelson, "Lovepets," *Pulphouse Eleven.*
Kim Newman & Eugene Byrne, "Ten Days That Shook the World," *Interzone 48.*
——, "The Wandering Christian," *Tales of the Wandering Jew.*
Chad Oliver, "A Lake of Summer," *The Bradbury Chronicles.*
Susan Palwick, "Effects of Captivity," *Pulphouse Magazine 2.*
Lawrence Person, "Consequences," *IAsfm,* Jun.
——, "Details," *IAsfm,* Apr.
Kit Reed, "River," *IAsfm,* Sept.
Mike Resnick, "Bully!" *IAsfm,* Apr.
——, "Malish," *Horse Fantastic.*
——, "Over There," *IAsfm,* Sept.
——, "Post-time in Pink," *Pulphouse Magazine 3.*
Keith Roberts, "The Will of God," *IAsfm,* Jul.
Kim Stanley Robinson, "Muir on Shasta," *Author's Choice Monthly Issue 20.*
——, "Vinland the Dream," *IAsfm,* Nov.
Madeleine E. Robins, "Papa's Gone A-Hunting," *F & SF,* Jan.
Mary Rosenblum, "The Bee Man," *IAsfm,* Sept.
——, "Celilo," *IAsfm,* Jun.
——, "Water Bringer," *IAsfm,* Mar.
Kristine Kathryn Rusch, "Shadows on the Moon," *Newer York.*
——, "Thomas and the Wise Men," *Amazing,* Sept.
——, "Waltzing on a Dancer's Grave," *IAsfm,* Mar.
Richard Paul Russo, "Celebrate the Bullet," *IAsfm,* Mid-Dec.
Jessica Amanda Salmonson, "Haggardly Beth and the Black Hour," *2AM,* Spring.
Charles Sheffield, "Fat Man's Gold," *IAsfm,* Mar.
Lucius Shepard, "Sports in America," *Playboy,* Jul.
John Shirley, "A Walk Through Beirut," *Newer York.*
——, "The Prince," *When the Music's Over.*
Susan Shwartz, "Getting Real," *Newer York.*
Robert Silverberg, "An Outpost of the Empire," *IAsfm,* Nov.
——, "The Clone Zone," *Playboy,* Mar.
Alison Sinclair, "Assassin," *BBR 19.*
Dan Simmons, "All Dracula's Children," *The Ultimate Dracula.*
S. P. Somtow, "Chui Chai," *The Ultimate Frankenstein.*
——, "The Pavilion of Frozen Women," *Cold Shocks.*
Francis Marion Soty, "Call to Glory," *Analog,* Nov.
Martha Soukup, "Ties," *Newer York.*
Norman Spinrad, "What Eats You," *IAsfm,* Jul.
Brian Stableford, "The Invisible Worm," *F & SF,* Sept.
——, "The Man Who Invented Good Taste," *Interzone 45.*
——, "Skin Deep," *Amazing,* Oct.
Allen Steele, "Goddard's People," *IAsfm,* Jul.
——, "The Return of Weird Frank," *IAsfm,* Dec.
Bruce Sterling, "Jim and Irene," *When the Music's Over.*
—— and John Kessel, "The Moral Bullet," *IAsfm,* Jul.
Tim Sullivan, "Nox Sanguinis," *Pulphouse Eleven.*

————, "*Los Niños de la Noche*," *The Ultimate Dracula*.
Michael Swanwick and Tim Sullivan, "Fantasies," *Amazing*, Aug.
Judith Tarr, "Classical Horses," *Horse Fantastic*.
Melanie Tem, "The Ice Downstream," *Cold Shocks*.
Sheri S. Tepper, "Raccoon Music," *F & SF*, Feb.
W. R. Thompson, "Wacky Jack 5.1," *Amazing*, Oct.
Lois Tilton, "The Cry of a Seagull," *Aboriginal SF*, May–Jun.
Michael D. Toman, "A Winter Memory," *Cold Shocks*.
Harry Turtledove, "Ready for the Fatherland," *WMHB Vol 3*.
Mary A. Turzillo, "Alien Dreams," *Pulphouse Eleven*.
Steven Utley, "Where or When," *IAsfm*, Jan.
Ray Vukcevich, "A Breath-Holding Contest," *Pulphouse Magazine 2*.
Mark L. Van Name, "TV Time," *IAsfm*, Apr.
Howard Waldrop, "Fin de Cyclé," *Night of the Cooters: More Neat Stories*.
Ian Watson, "The Odor of Cocktail Cigarettes," *IAsfm*, Apr.
Lawrence Watt-Evans, "A Flying Saucer with Minnesota Plates," *IAsfm*, Aug.
————, "The Name of Fear," *The Ultimate Dracula*.
————, "New Worlds," *IAsfm*, Dec.
————, "One-Shot," *IAsfm*, Jan.
Don Webb, "Billy Hauser," *IAsfm*, Dec.
————, "Hypotenuse," *New Pathways 20*.
————, "Letters from Sarah," *IAsfm*, Feb.
Deborah Wessell, "She Could Look It Up," *F & SF*, Jan.
Dean Whitlock, "The Man Who Loved Kites," *F & SF*, Dec.
Rick Wilber, "Helmet," *Aboriginal SF*, Dec.
Nancy Willard, "Dogstar Man," *Full Spectrum 3*.
Walter Jon Williams, "Erogenoscape," *IAsfm*, Nov.
Connie Willis, "In the Late Cretaceous," *IAsfm*, Mid-Dec.
————, "Miracle," *IAsfm*, Dec.
Paul Witcover, "Lighthouse Summer," *IAsfm*, Apr.
N. Lee Wood, "In the Land of No," *Amazing*, Nov.
William F. Wu, "Shaunessy Fong," *Pulphouse Eleven*.
Thomas Wylde, "To the Eastern Gates," *IAsfm*, May.